Y0-ABP-950

BOSTON
PUBLIC
LIBRARY

T H E

MAD
MAN

A N O V E L

SAMUEL R.
DELANY

FIC
DELANY
S

The Mad Man
Copyright © 1994 Samuel R. Delany

"Risk Factors for Seroconversion to Human Immunodeficiency
Virus Among Male Homosexuals: Results from the Multicenter AIDS
Cohort Study." by Kingsley, Kaslow, Rinaldo, *et alia*. Reprinted by
permission from *The Lancet*, Saturday, February 14, 1987.

First Richard Kasak Book Edition 1994

First printing May 1994

ISBN 1-56333-193-4 (cloth)
ISBN 1-56333-194-2 (U.K. pbk.)

Manufactured in the United States of America
Published by Masquerade Books, Inc.
801 Second Avenue
New York, N.Y. 10017

T H E

MAD MAN

SAMUEL R. DELANY

A RICHARD KASAK BOOK

To
David Demchuk;
and once again
for Sam and Leonard.

THE MAD MAN

DISCLAIMER

The Mad Man is a work of fiction—and fairly imaginative fiction at that. No character, major or minor, is intended to represent any actual person, living or dead. (Correspondences are not only coincidental but preposterous.) Nor are any of its scenes laid anywhere representing actual establishments or institutions. Certain parks, commercial sites, churches, and city landmarks, mentioned as locations of minor off- or on-stage actions, do exist (or have existed). But those mentions are only to lend verisimilitude to what the reader is expected to take wholly as a pornotopic fantasy: a set of people, incidents, places, and relations among them that never happened and could not happen for any number of surely self-evident reasons.

But a second disclaimer is needed in such a work as this: *The Mad Man* is not a book about "safe sex." Rather it is specifically a book about various sexual acts whose status as vectors of HIV contagion we have no hard-edged knowledge of because the monitored studies that would give statistical portraits of the relation between such acts and Seroconversion (from HIV- to HIV+) have not been done. Reprinted as an appendix is the last large-scale such study to be made widely and publicly available, back in 1987, in the British journal, *The Lancet.* The fact that this study dates from as far back as it does, and the fact that anyone and everyone concerned with AIDS and AIDS education cannot today cite a dozen such studies, far more up-to-date, using both women and men, covering a far wider range of specific sexual activities, is appalling, horrifying, and ultimately criminal—given the 350 thousand-odd cases of the disease in this country and its continuing and growing devastation.

But the broad statistical studies with careful monitoring have not been done. And the few small ones which have are given little or no attention—while vast amounts of hearsay are collected, tabulated, and presented as knowledge and fact.

A third disclaimer: *The Mad Man* is not a book about the homeless of New York—or, indeed, of the country. No book could be which all-but-omits all scenes of winter and does not deal with—indeed, focus on—the criminally inadequate attempts by the municipality to feed, clothe, and shelter these men, women, and children. Such a novel would have to be substantially darker than this one—which, I suspect, will be found quite dark enough. Indeed, it is sobering to think that the Great American Novel to come will have so little to do with the famous "American Dream" but will have to be far nearer a contemporary *Les Misérables*.

—SRD

T H E

MAD
MAN

A   N O V E L

Black, raddled, roped with veins, it rose like a charred tallboy from snarled bronze. Below, the texture and color of overripe avocados, testicles hung like rocks. It sagged in the envelope of flesh that held it to the belly, almost as high as the navel's gnarled pit. A black cock on a hulking white man? A dog's dick on a humongous buck? Only, beyond seven feet, it wasn't a man, though yellow hair tufted the crevice beneath its thick and blocky arm. The head turned polished copper horns above the barrel chest, penny-colored nipples—silver-dollar sized—ghosted in wiry brass. The tongue slathered up to lave bright mucus from the taurine pad enveloping the nostrils, muzzle tusked nearer boar than bull. It breathed cold steam in winter-thin dawnlight. Its gut was heavy as some gone beer-hound's, though muscle-ridged. The boulder of its fist opened, nails gnawed back on fingers heavy as ax hafts and engrimed at nutty knuckles, at the crowns' rock-rough rims. Its other hand's brass claws gleamed along scapular curves, green with verdigris, where, like demonic plumbing, each erupted from beneath cracked and thickened cuticle. Clawed fingers rose to scratch the scrotum, paused on the columnar sex, brushing the thickened under-conduit twice, thrice, and twice again. Above its ever-wet tuft, crisp and curling, the thick cuff thrust out, like a dog's, a slow inch of meat.

One creviced, callused, and engrimed foot was, anyway, human.

Where it stood, ice had formed under the roc's claw, that, scaled in green was its other foot, on a leg feathered, ashen, ebon, and misshapen as a condor's. Needles of moisture had frozen, glittering over the park path's asphalt and on the rocks beside. Neither bird's nor bat's, but stretched on spines like an insect's or a fish's, letting low, mottled sun through filigrees of veins in the leather, its wings stopped their sway, to quiver—thirteen feet high.

It turned.

Hanging from the small of its back, covering the crevice between beast-broad buttocks, creased at the jointure, brown at the base but become, lower, thin as a cobra and armored with green, its tail hung to within an inch of the gray paving. The triple barb twitched twice left, once right, twice left, once right, beside its human heel's soiled pilaster. Now the tail jerked aside, to let honking gases, then drop its crumbling turd, black, grass- and bone-rich, steaming on the frost—while before its belly, urine arched, heavy, sudden, gold, to spill and splat, angrily on the macadam. Unconcerned with where it slopped, first it reached back to maul its still-delivering sphincter, then to raise the thick man hand, swung inadvertently through its stream, to its mouth, to enjoy its salts, the stench on its fingers, gnaw at the wrecked nails with taurine teeth, blinking with goat-slit eyes (black crevices rising over corner-clotted crimson), while its waters crawled under the iron rail at the path's edge, overflowed the cement, and dripped, boiling, bubbling, onto the Hudson's glass-green rush.

PART
ONE

THE
SYSTEMS OF THE WORLD

The *bios philosophicus* is the animality of being human, renewed as a challenge, practiced as an exercise—and thrown in the face of others as a scandal.

—Michel Foucault

Durch des Todes Tor, wo en mir floss,
weit un offen er mir er schloss
darin ich sonst nur träumend gewacht,
das Wonderreich der Nacht.

—*Tristan und Isolde*, II, ii.

I do not have AIDS. I am surprised that I don't. I have had sex with men weekly, sometimes daily—without condoms—since my teens, though true, it's been overwhelmingly...no, more accurately it's been—since 1980—*all* oral, not anal. My adventures with homosexuality started in the early-middle seventies, in the men's room of the terminal on the island side of the Staten Island Ferry: a guy at least thirty years older than I, clearly scared to death someone might walk in, pulled his small, uncircumcised dick out of my mouth the moment he came, stuffed himself back in his fly, leaving semen tracks on his sharkskin pants, grunted a perfunctory "...yeah, thanks," fingered through his red hair, and pushed out the door as a bored policeman walked in. "All right." He banged his club on the rusted blue jamb and blinked at me, a very tired man. "You get out of here, too."

Because my father bucked what I once thought the entire New York City Board of Education, when I excelled in elementary school, I was allowed to skip a couple of grades.

"His family," my father intoned in the drear office (we'd just heard the psychological traumas and debilitating miseries and mal-adjustments befalling the child wrenched untimely from his peer group), "will take care of his socialization. You take care of his education. But I just hope you understand the miseries and mal-adjustments from spending years among lots of people stupider than you are." Actually, it was just the Staten Island branch. A more civilized borough—Manhattan, or even Brooklyn—probably would not have allowed it; not in the sixties.

Dad's request for my acceleration granted, Mom rode hard on my homework to see that I kept up, habituating me to a certain kind of "hard work." Bless them both. (Dad is a city librarian. Mom is a supermarket manager. Neat people—though they worry too much, about me and everything else.) I entered high school at twelve, college at sixteen, and graduate school at twenty, A's, A-minuses, and attendant scholarships generally and generously trailing behind. Also, I was that terror of my fellows, "a good test taker." Still, though sometimes I liked to imagine I was, in no way was I really precocious.

Except, possibly, sexually.

Recalling that afternoon at the ferry terminal john, I note it was during my junior year of high school. I'd been on my way home from taking my SATs. (790 on the math; 710 on the English—not bad for a black kid in sneakers and jeans, not living in a major borough.) I'd heard about the ferry from at least three different sources. Stopping off in the john had been a treat I'd dared give myself as a reward for taking the test. But like so many things we dare, the doing had been a matter of real smells (musty disinfectant), real textures (metal partitions between the stained commodes, rusting through blue paint), real lights (the yellowing bulb in the ceiling's wire cage) and shadows. My response to the encounter had been simple enough: without having been blown away by it, I'd liked it. I wanted to do it some more. Walking from the terminal up the ramp to the bus, I wondered, though, if anyone at home would comment on the smudges I still couldn't brush off the knees of my denims.

Nobody did.

Given what is generally said of AIDS, I would have thought that time and exposure would have ensured my infection since then. But my last HIV test, this past June—and since 1988 I've had one once a year—says they haven't.

I'd like to think that, in certain ways, it's not that unusual a story, however infrequently it's told. But then, in certain others…depravity, murder, mystery, love…. Well—if I'm *going* to tell it, I must pick an arbitrary moment and begin.

I pick one in May '80, perhaps a week after my twenty-second birthday. It was the close of my third term T.A.-ing for Irving Mossman, toward the end of my second year at Enoch State University. Papers were marked. Grades were in. With all the good feeling that accrues to you upon a term well taught, I turned the aluminum knob and came into the comfortably cluttered office, full of papers, spring sun, and books.

"Hi," I said. "What're you doing?"

At his desk, Mossman had just taken a photographic frame, with positions across its beige satin face for three pictures, and finished bending down the metal tabs on the velveteen backing. Turning it over, he grinned up hawkishly. Lifting it, he swiveled in the office chair. The silvery plastic overlay was rumpled, as usual, across his Olympic Selectric. Scissors lay on top of slivers cut from some photograph edges.

"Hey…!" I bent closer to see.

The middle picture showed the slightly dazed, Asiatic features of Timothy Hasler—from the only photograph of him I'd yet seen: the open-shirted one from the back of *Pascal, Nietzsche, Peirce.*

Gaunt and smiling, the photo to Hasler's right was Mossman.

Full-lipped, chocolatey, broad-nosed but, I like to think, handsome for all that, the picture to Hasler's left was me.

"Professor Irving Mossman," Mossman intoned, pointing at his own image with his fore knuckle. Now he indicated the (in *that* photo) twenty-five-year-old Korean-American, who had once jotted in the margin on his seventh published article: *Does the ocean swallow every image reflected on its innumerable wavelets? Imagine suddenly giving them all back to the sky!* "The late Timothy Hasler, philosopher extraordinaire." Mossman's pale knuckle moved on: "And here we have our redoubtable graduate student, John Marr."

My first thought, looking at those three faces, was that I hadn't realized before we all wore glasses.

"Now that," Mossman said, "is Hasler studies—in a couple of years. When I wind up this biography and you finish your thesis."

I dutifully smiled. While I was looking down, I noticed the stain darkening my jeans knee.

"Looks like the secondary players in an old RKO war movie," Mossman went on. "The Jew, the Oriental, the black boy…"

It wasn't more than twenty minutes since I'd been on the cement floor in the library basement john, by the gray-painted partition, sucking on the dick of that nervous lacrosse player on his knees in the next stall; or had I just been creaming in my hand when the maintenance guy who'd settled in the stall to my left finally slid his scuffed work shoe with his frayed blue pants cuff toward my running shoe—with him, for the first five times, I'd never gotten a thing; until that once, when I heard him chuckle—but that's another story.

Mossman put the frame on his desk. Slants of sunlight crossed it from the thin blinds at the window. Staring at those photographs, I tried to assess just who the three of us were.

Myself, first: a young, bright, moderately middle-class black kid from Staten Island, who'd managed to get an undergraduate degree in philosophy—about as meaningful as an undergraduate degree ever was. But, in my senior year, two fluke seminars on Hegel—one on *The Philosophy of History*, one on *The Phenomenology of Spirit*—had pushed me on to graduate school on another coast, naively certain my thesis would be a six hundred-page tome on psychology, history, reality, and metaphysics, putting them once and for all in their grandly ordered relation. (Another way to put it, I suppose: an underweight black cocksucker—with glasses—who knew that Wittgenstein was queer, not to mention Plato; and that there was this Frenchman some of my friends in college used to talk about, Foucault…) I don't think anyone can understand the shock, the disorientation, the disillusion of that first year as a philosophy graduate, during which I learned that—today—a six hundred-page tome about everything of philosophical interest was less likely to be considered a work of serious philosophy than a self-help manual starting off: "It's important to feel really *good* about yourself.…" Mossman had been there to inform me of the fact—as gently as he could. Then he worked hard to pick up the pieces: I'll always be grateful for that. Next he took that very disoriented graduate student—me—and introduced him to the work of Timothy Hasler.

The late Timothy Hasler.

Timothy Hasler, the picture in the middle: I always wondered where Hasler got *his* sense of what philosophy—contemporary, Anglo-American philosophy—was. But then, Hasler *was* a prodigy. (Certainly he got it from reading. But, like contemporary poetry, philosophy is one of those things, especially at the beginning stages, most people would rather do than study—which is why most of what gets done is so impoverished.) The first of Hasler's sixteen published papers appeared a month after his seventeenth birthday, in May 1961 (when I was a cuddly coffee bean of three): "On the Disjunctive Force in Certain Conjunctive Coupulas." Hasler's grandfather had been a thin, bespectacled Englishman, Ethan Hasler, working as an engineer in Korea, a little man with a volcanic personality, who had married a Korean woman and come with his whole, large, close family to America at the start of the Second World War. Hasler's father, Kwok Hasler, married another Korean, Jeng Shoon, who had come to the States just before the U.S.–Korean War. A cultured and sensitive woman, apparently Shoon been shocked into madness by the turn of events in the early fifties. (Korea, Kefauver, the House Un-American Activities Committee, McCarthy...) She died in an asylum in 1954, leaving Timothy Kim Hasler (he had two younger sisters), a shy, brilliant ten-year-old, only a year away from the start—at eleven— of his three-year-tenure at Stuyvesant High School, before his early admission—at fourteen—to sprawling Stilford University.

Besides his sixteen referenced articles, Hasler was his book on the rhetoric of Blaise Pascal, Friedrich Nietzsche, and Charles Sanders Peirce, published the year of Hasler's father's death, 1969, by an alternative philosophical press, Black Phoenix, that printed its texts offset from typescript, but with thick board bindings and snazzy four-color book jackets (hence Mossman's photograph of him), a book that looked at the semiotic aspects of all three philosophers, and that could be looked at in turn as an interesting contribution to what would eventually be called "the New Nietzsche." (Hasler had apparently *read*—in German—those thousand pages of lecture notes Heidegger had left on the bad boy of German philosophy, published in four volumes at Pfullingen in 1961. And he'd done some serious searching in *The Hidden God*.) Hasler was also seven elegant review articles on two interesting and five wholly inconsequential new works of philosophy. As well, he was a fabled friendship in his third year of graduate school with Almira Adler. (The Old Poet, as first Mossman, then Mossman and I, sometimes called her.) She was sixteen years Hasler's senior. But they had spent five of his eight remaining summers together at her stone tower at Breakers' Point, California, including his last—when together they corrected galleys on "The Black Comet." Hasler was several year-plus dropouts from graduate school. During one of those, in 1966, he'd gone to Europe, mostly Italy, Greece, and Turkey. During another, in 1970, in Chicago, he'd worked as a shoe (!) salesman. And (my favorite), Hasler was six published (and, we discovered, two fragmentary and unpublished) science-fiction stories, that, against titanic intergalactic backgrounds to dwarf *Star Trek*, *Stars Wars*, and *Dune*, turned on some of the finer mathematics that informed his articles on the philosophy of natural languages. But finally, ultimately, Timothy Hasler was his own shocking death. The prodigy who had entered graduate school at eighteen was still working on his thesis eleven years later at twenty-nine. Back in New York from Breakers' Point, in the autumn of 1973, the twenty-nine-year-old Korean-American philosophy graduate was stabbed to death in—or just behind—a bar off Ninth Avenue at Fiftieth Street, in New York City, shortly after two o'clock in the morning, the night of September 23— two weeks after he should have reported back to Stilford to take up a teaching assistantship that a number of faculty had gone out on a limb to secure him: He'd officially run out of department support by several years.

Hasler's absence had already caused a disturbance in the school when news of his murder crossed the country from New York to California and—in one fellow graduate student's words—reduced the rest of the term at Stilford's philosophy department to chaos. But even as far back as two years before Hasler's death, Irving M. had told me, he had already noticed several prominent philosophers' references to "Hasler structures" and, sometimes, even "Hasler grammars." And in the half-dozen years after Hasler's death, the number of references to those structures and grammars had only increased.

For over half a dozen years now, everyone had just expected the two final chapters of Hasler's thesis to turn up—at least in early draft. But they probably had never been written.

No one even came close to getting caught for the murder.

Then there was a posthumous collection from the University of California Press of Hasler's papers and review articles: *Formal Conjunctions/Informal Disjunctions* (1976). Two years later, *Pascal, Nietzsche, Peirce* was reissued (1978)—this time in real type, with a rather intelligent introduction by someone I'd never heard of (Edwin Schaliapin—that really *was* his name), but who, after I read it, *I* certainly thought should have had a place in Mossman's rogues' gallery of important Hasler scholars. *Samizdat* Xeroxes of some three different drafts of the first five chapters of Hasler's thesis got copied and recopied till they were all but unreadable and passed to...fifty? A hundred fifty eager readers? (Hasler really *was* a lively writer.) I got a Xerox of Mossman's Xerox.

And so we reach the picture on the right: forty-seven-year-old Associate Professor Irving Mossman. A year before—when, indeed, I had been at my most distraught over the undoability of my grand Hegelian project (*The Systems of the World*; that really *was* the title I'd settled on, even before I came to Enoch—though I'd had the good sense—or the luck—not to tell too many people)—while he sat with me in a student beer hall, Mossman had explained: "You know, John, I'm going to be writing the full critical biography. It'll survey Hasler's life and work, and whatever clear and concise correspondences can be drawn between them. Nothing complicated—I intend it to be very basic. Really, what I'll be doing is fundamentally an introduction to Hasler. But, I mean, the statement's appeared in print more than ten times: if like Wittgenstein, he'd been at Cambridge, exceptions would have been made, *Pascal, Nietzsche, Peirce* would have been substituted for a thesis—and Hasler would have been a professor. John, why don't you—for *your* thesis, I mean—do an account of the *published* work? You can touch on the unpublished stuff where it's relevant, of course. But you could do a careful, concise, straightforward description of the ideas in the refereed papers and the review articles—the stories, too, if you like, and *Pascal, Nietzsche, Peirce.* You'll be doing a useful job that scholars can turn to for years! You'll have the benefit of my research—as, certainly, I'll have the benefit of yours. Both of us, of course, will be doing very different things. But I think you're up to it. It'll be eminently publishable, and the two works will compliment each other. You can even throw in an appendix on the thesis material. What do you say? Three years, we'll both be finished. I'll have my book, and you'll have your doctorate…if not your doctorate *and* a publishable book!"

The suggestion didn't garner much excitement. I was silent a long time, whereupon Mossman turned his beer stein around on its wet ring and leaned a little closer. "You're just feeling discouraged now, John. But give it some thought. The paper you wrote on Hasler's twin predicate logic for me was the best of anybody's in that whole seminar. If you can negotiate that, you can negotiate all of it. Think about it."

So I thought—mostly, I confess, sitting in a john stall in the library basement. I remember there was an Asian kid—Chinese, I think—who used to come in there, in T-shirt and baggy shorts, looking to get sucked off, whom, even though I'd seen him there half a dozen times, I'd simply never thought about doing.

Pure (as they say) prejudice.

But now, as an experiment, when I saw him pass before the vertical slit bright with the drab john's fluorescent lighting, I decided to try him. I flapped my stall door a few times. Horny little fuck, he was over and in, thumbing down the waist of those green plaid Bermudas to reveal the incomplete tick-tack-toe markings of an appendectomy scar on his tanned right loin. Of average size, he was uncut—but as soon as I started to suck him, he grabbed my head and fucked hell out of my face, his shorts sliding down farther and farther with each thrust, finally to bind around his white tube socks. At last, panting, "Oh, shit…!" he dropped—I swear— a quarter of a *cup* of cream. He rubbed my rough hair a few times. Then, with a grin, he stepped away, pulled up his shorts, and backed from the stall, nodding as the door swung in. Listening to him leave, I thought: it wasn't *that* bad…!

The year between that evening at the Beer-Bung and the afternoon at Mossman's office with the photos was a study in shifting identifications. In outline, it approximated this:

In 1807 at thirty-seven, Hegel published his *Phenomenology*.

About 175 years later, I came to graduate school, planning to have my *Systems of the World* (named, yeah, after Galileo: *Dialogo Sopra i due Massimi Sistemi del Mondo, Tolemaico, e Copernicano*. Only I considered myself quite something having gotten beyond the Late Renaissance Italian's scientific dualism) finished by the time I was twenty-three, with a year on the upper end, in case.

But *The Systems of the World* was, in terms of philosophy today, a joke—and right then, I felt, so was the dumb-ass nigger with the glasses who'd proposed to write it.

However, Timothy Hasler had been a *real* philosopher—even a brilliant one. I mean, when he was nineteen, twenty-one, twenty-five, he had published work now regularly cited in philosophy journals.

About this point, I had a date with an anorexically thin white girl over in anthropology, Sally-May Wallace, six (!) years older than I was, who insisted that everyone call her Sally-May, though she allowed a few of us to shorten this to Sam, who'd told me an ex-boyfriend of hers had been at Stilford seven years before as an undergraduate and, after news of Hasler's murder, had helped the department secretary clear Timothy's things out of the office he'd shared with two other philosophy graduates. There was a pile of old spiral notebooks in a bottom desk drawer. The boyfriend had opened one to come across this entry in Hasler's hand: "...The captured spume of space foams in our ears...." Boyfriend had been impressed enough to copy it and half a dozen others down. What *were* the others, I wanted to know. But that was the only one he'd actually told her—or at least that she remembered.

Maybe, I thought, if I studied Hasler, I might *learn* what it was to be a real philosopher...?

Thank God for the science fiction: six weeks later, I dropped into Mossman's office with twenty-seven pages of notes relating the denouement or the basic plots of Hasler's "Dawn over Rigal-VII," "The Red Star's Thunder," and "Mirror of the Mighty," to some point in one or another of the logic articles. On my last page, I also mentioned that "The Black Comet," the last published SF novella, from *Amazing*, September '73—the year of Hasler's death—seemed to relate, rather, to the second half of the ghostly Xerox of Hasler's thesis "Chapter Four."

Mossman leaned forward in his chair, elbows on his knees, reading my pages for eight, nine, ten minutes. Finally he sat back, slapped his calf, and declared, "*That's* the ticket, boy!"

Somehow from then on, he, me, and everybody else in the department just went around assuming that "boy" had said yes to the proposal our philosophical Tarzan had put forward for my thesis topic.

That's the photos' story.

Looking at them, I wondered only about one thing. After a third date with Sally-May I had decided to trust her sympathetic demeanor and told her I was gay. Three weeks later, now from a joke by a football player who was a friend of one of my housemates, now from a flyer for a gay-studies program, suddenly thrust at me with much too much grinning goodwill by the graduate resident in the hall where I taught my Philosophy Survey 121 discussion section, I realized that, somehow, now, the whole *school* knew!

When, after ten minutes of maneuvering, I finally got Sam away from her friends in the cafeteria, to speak with me alone, I demanded, "But Sam, how could you go and *tell* everybody?"

"Jesus, John, it's not a crime," she protested. "Besides, I didn't even know black guys *could* be gay....I had to talk to *someone!*"

But since Mossman ("Are you going to be at the Strawson lecture—but then, I guess, you'll probably be at that Gay Pride rally they're supposed to be holding over at the Union....") was clearly one of the people who'd been told, I wondered how it would affect *him*.

The effect was not what I'd have predicted. It didn't really manifest itself until eight months later (when I was taking an unspecified amount of time off and working in New York), when Mossman discovered—his letter practically crackled—that Timothy Hasler was *also* gay! Its half-dozen pages were full of a peevish sense of betrayal by all of Hasler's friends, just barely suppressed. How could they have kept it from him? after all, Mossman had been doing research among them in some cases for more than three years:

"Why didn't I tell you? Up till now, Irving, you never asked!"

"Frankly, Irving, I just thought you knew and weren't interested."

And the one that tickled me most, from the Old Poet: "In a word, Professor Mossman, I didn't think Tim's sexual orientation was any of your business. You're supposed to be writing the biography of a philosopher!"

Here Mossman's letter exploded: "What do they think I am, some kind of *idiot?*"

More of his letters came, asking questions of me that, frankly

("Do you think, John, as a gay man yourself, it's likely Hasler was in love with that undergraduate there was all that trouble over?" "Do you think there's a possible sexual angle—I mean, specifically, a gay one—to Hasler's move to South Rushdale in '64?" "Helga Nostrand says that New York bar on Fiftieth Street—The Pit—was a gay bar! You're from New York, John. Do you know it?" "John—this probably seems an awkward thing to ask, especially after all this time; but, before I wrote you about it, *you* didn't know Hasler was gay, did you?"), seemed about as naïve as I would have expected from Sammy Wallace. I answered them, feeling more and more distant toward the project. But when I remembered the three portrait photos, doubtless still in Mossman's office, I knew they looked quite different to him, now that they were a picture of *two* queers—with a bewildered Jewish (associate) professor off to the right.

Of course, there were other things I knew by now. I knew, for example, that Irving Mossman believed he was long overdue for promotion to full professor; but he was in a philosophy department where the idea of "publishing prematurely" was tantamount to walking down the hallowed halls with your dick hanging out of your fly.

A biography of an eccentric contemporary figure, a bit on the sensational side, like Timothy Hasler: that would have been a book, in philosophical terms, not really a book—a book proving only that you could write one, that you could give an account of ideas and events that were not really, in either case, yours.

In the publish or perish atmosphere that defines the modern university, a lot of people would have considered our philosophy department a model for heaven. Basically once you were on the faculty, you weren't expected to *do* anything—besides teach and work on your own little two inches of carved and polished ivory. But for a more ambitious sort, like Irving, such a department could be hell. If, for instance, you actually placed a seven- or nine-page article in *Modern Logic* or *Philosophy Today*, which drew a comment from Clapstone (our August Chair) as you passed him in the hall: "Very interesting piece. Very interesting. Still, one of our people, talking about it to me, was wondering whether you'd really thought through *all* the ramifications of that business with the non-abelian sets in terms of some of the less well-defined propositional attitudes...." Well, *then* you knew your career was on hold for minimum a year and probably three—since obviously you'd published prematurely.

A harsh system, true. But, as one department wit once quipped, they needed *some* basic attitudinal difference to distinguish them from mathematics. It was called "keeping the world safe for the more prudent."

Never call them lazy.

Though Mossman did, within my hearing—angrily, and on more than one occasion.

So, while you worked reticently, endlessly, silently on your "own material," such a book as Mossman's biography of Hasler was the sort of thing that *could* get you promoted—especially if you had a graduate student or six. And by now Mossman was the outside committee member on thesis committees of three students besides me working on aspects of Hasler, in two other colleges.

It was like writing murder mysteries on the side if you were a Renaissance scholar.

It was quaint, eccentric, charming…

My classwork was finished. I got a passing mark on my comps (but barely: an incredibly pumped-up, handsome, hairy, and hung Italian undergraduate named Michael Ballagio fell into bed with me the day after registration [and into the beds of some half-dozen other black guys on campus, too, I later found out]; the first time we made it, with his stellar, hazel-eyed, Styrofoam-white smile, he told me: "I only came to Enoch State for one reason, John: that's to eat out as many black assholes as I can—and do as much for Gay Liberation as I can while I'm at it. You let me suck out that black shit-crack of yours, Mr. Marr, and you can do anything to me you want—and I mean *anything*!" Mike and I actually became pretty close—until, over Thanksgiving break, he was killed in a Long Island car wreck that left an older cousin of his wheelchair-bound—and I almost had a nervous breakdown. But there was no one to talk about it with: Mike was widely known to be the official lover of another black kid in school, who was active in the Gay, Lesbian, and Bisexual Union [as Mike had been] and was getting all the sympathy; but you just couldn't say, well, the little wop was chowing down on my tailgate a couple of times a week, too, and letting me do things to him in the boiler room of Havers Hall—sometimes with, sometimes without, that maintenance man I mentioned—too perverse to name), I had moved back to New York.

To write that thesis.

"And, Irving," I finally scrawled on a postcard, "I'm actually going to *visit* that bar!"

Between a deli and a parking lot off Ninth Avenue, within the Pit's dark and mirrored depths, the owner, a huge woman named Aline, sat at the back of the counter and demanded, "How you doin', honey?" to every middle-aged patron who tried to slip anonymously past her; while, at the pool table in the back, a platoon of white, black, and Hispanic boys, with ancient cues, knocked colored balls across the baize, setting their beer on the table's green edge.

One—save that he was hairless and tattooed, instead of a muscle-bound furball—when you looked at him from the proper angle, while he leaned over to make his shot, I swear, could have been Mike, leaning over the pool table at the back of the Beer-Bung.

I bought a gin and tonic and sat at the counter, looking now at that Italian hustler in the tight red jeans and the baggy T-shirt over among the others around the green-edged table, then at the finger marks in the frost on my glass—Mike, whose existence a year ago had winked out in the driver's seat of his Camaro, somewhere beside a winter's beach near Montauk, in a moment even his cousin, quadrapelegic Vinny, couldn't remember too clearly. What if I were researching Mike Ballagio's brief, gloriously post-Stonewall life, I wondered, and not the (also pretty brief) largely pre-Stonewall life of the genius Hasler? (Those whom the gods love die...) After ten minutes in the bar, without taking more than a sip of my drink, I fled.

That autumn the Old Poet won the Pulitzer Prize—*Mountain and Tower: New and Selected Poems*, by Almira Adler. The rumor went round she'd be in the running for next year's Nobel! It galvanized Mossman. After some months' silence, three letters arrived from him in two weeks. And in the letters I wrote back, I pretended—to him, to myself—I, too, was galvanized:

Dear Irving,

Maybe what would pull my thesis together is a chapter on the relation between cantos seven through nine of Adler's

long poem "Meridian" and Hasler's two "predicate nega-
tion" papers. After all, the poem and the papers were all written in the summer of '71—when Hasler and Adler were
together at Breakers' Point. The fact is, I've already got more
than forty pages of notes and a box of index cards on the
topic. To sit down, to put it into readable shape—possibly to
show it to the Old Poet herself for comment (you say she's suddenly become amenable to us—well, to you—after all this
time) might get my part of the project on track! And it wouldn't
impinge on *your* work....

It also galvanized Almira Adler.

After more than a year of being barely civil to Mossman and letting him know in no uncertain terms that she would offer only
minimal help, and none that put her out, suddenly Adler wrote
him, wrote him again, invited him to lunch, then to dinner—this last
to tell him she'd suddenly "remembered" some of Hasler's notebooks
he'd left with her that last summer before he'd quit Breakers' Point
for New York. As well, there were even some letters she might
show Mossman from New York written within weeks of the fateful
twenty-third....

"But why," I asked her [feverish Mossman wrote me], "did
you wait so long to show me these things?" And do you know
what the old redheaded crone said, from the glittering depths
of her wheelchair, eye distorted through the glass-bound tides
of her third martini? She said: "I suppose I had to see how serious you were. When you first came to me, you'd only been
working on your project for weeks—a few months, at most. But
now you've been working on it for...well, years. In my eyes,
Professor Mossman, that makes you a very different sort of
scholar from the man who first approached me about doing
Tim's biography."

I think it's all nonsense, John. I think the Old Poet's just feeling more outgoing because people are beginning to pay attention to her—as, I suppose, she deserves. But whatever the
reason, I'm grateful. At least I think I am. She also said (to give
her *some* credit): "Timothy was very important to me, when he
was alive. I've been doing a lot of thinking recently. And I'm

beginning to realize that he was important to other people, too. And that's beginning to bring home to me a finer sense of that importance."

The paradox was—to *me*—that I'd have trusted the scholar who'd first inquired of her far more than I would have the scholar of today—and, though I could not have said so to *him*, I suspected Mossman felt the same. That scholar had had a purpose, a passion, a sense of enterprise. The scholar of today had a jumble of notes, a welter of contradictory information: in my case that was five plastic boxes full of index cards labeled "problems" and not a jot of drive to solve them—in short, what *I* had, at any rate, was the imponderable wreckage of a project, over which your current scholar sat and gazed, like a sphinx whose ineffable secret was that the years' "work" making me, in the eyes of friends and colleagues, if not of people like the Old Poet and Mossman, a "serious Hasler scholar," had also made me—in my *own* eyes—a gibbering, jerking, half-blind creature, buried under the contradictions, stalled in the gaps, paralyzed by the sheer unknowability of the fast-fading shadows that were the dense, lingering texts of Timothy Hasler.

Secretly, I couldn't believe it was much different for Mossman. With the more complex project of a biography, for him it was probably more so.

Perhaps you can understand, then, how *not* surprised I was when, a week later, I got another letter from Mossman—of a very different tone from the earlier ones. (I have it on file, with all his others, in the stack of gray and maroon plastic file boxes beside the library radiator):

...At this point, I'm unearthing material about Timothy Hasler that—finally, John, I confess—has upset me. Last night I sat in my study, looking across the recent papers from the Old Poet, my notes on our last conversation, hers and mine and I thought: this biography has now become really problematic. Between April and June of '73 (I know you don't have my most recent revision of the chronology; but at some point I will send it to you,—I will! At any rate, that's the period just before he plunged into the composition of the three brief "Parallelograms and Perspicacity" essays, ten weeks before his death, his murder, his slaughter), I now know, from Hasler's journals the Old Poet only last week broke down and let me look through (and make Xeroxes of), plus some rather muted references in two of his letters to her from that time, Hasler must have been indulging in the most degrading—and depressing—sexual "experiments": bums on the New York City streets, homeless alcoholics in Riverside Park, white, black, or Hispanic winos lounging about on the island in the middle of upper Broadway, about whom his only criterion could have been, as far as I can make out, the dirtier the better…! Really, John, I have to consider seriously whether Timothy Hasler is the man I want to be writing about.

Looking at it now, Mossman's moment of confusion, disillusion, and degradation, signaled in his letter, marks a kind of beginning for me—even as it marks an end to a pristine naïveté figured in that moment with the photographs, back in his office, two years before.

I was no longer twenty-two, but going on twenty-four. To be exact, I was six years and four months younger than Timothy Hasler in the September of his death. I'd been in my fifth-floor walk-up here at 196 West Eighty-second Street—where I still am, by the by, a decade on—about fifteen weeks, back then.

I pause, because if any serious Hasler scholars are among my readers, yes, with Holy Trinity just across Amsterdam Avenue on the other side of the street to the west and St. Volodymyr—the old Ukrainian church—just down the street to the east, that is the address Timothy Hasler lived at in New York from late '70 until his murder in '73: he was in apartment 4-S. I'm one flight up, in Apartment 5-S. And the fact that I'm here attests to my enthusiasm for the whole thing when I first got back from graduate school to the city. The story of how I came by the place would involve telling you a lot about my friend Pheldon and these two city sanitation truck drivers he was seeing fairly regularly—and with whom, yes, he finally let me spend an evening alone; I had them both, one after the other, the older redheaded white guy with the freckles (Lewey) and the younger, Spanish one (Angel), who used to laugh, I swear, at everything. But the redhead was the cousin of the landlord, Milt, and Angel was, somehow, friends with Jimmy the super—a tall blue-black man, who drank Myers's Rum and smoked cigars.

"This is a stupid idea, Phel—"

"After you suck Lewey's dick, ask him to speak to his cousin. Or at least to have Angel put in a good word with Jimmy."

"Phel, I—"

But I got down on my knees and sucked off two very friendly sanitation workers.

Two weeks later (after a bottle of Myers's as my thank-you present to Jimmy), I moved into the top-floor rent-stabilized apartment. Like Pheldon said, this is New York.

Living downstairs from me in Hasler's old apartment was a small butterball of a woman named Hilda Conkling, who at first I thought was just too young to have a teenage daughter—very shy, very serious, the week I moved in the daughter had purple hair. Hilda had more books than I did, at least at the beginning; and, yes, she knew a philosopher of interest had once lived in her apartment—named...Hulser...? Kestler...? Helsner...? The first week I was here, Hilda showed me through her entire place—the layout was identical to mine—but told me, sadly, that two other tenants had been there between Hasler and herself. No, the place had been completely cleaned out, even to the upper cabinets in the little storage room on the side and the drawer beneath the built-in wardrobe in the back. (When I'd seen them in *my* place, I thought they'd be a natural in which to find old papers and manuscripts from previous tenants.) But there was *nothing* left from Hasler's stay.

Hilda even introduced me to the old Spanish couple on the first (European style) floor, Mr. and Mrs. Espedrosa, who'd lived there for twenty years. In boxer shorts and slippers, Mr. Espedrosa sat on their collapsing blue couch with bone-white antimacassars pinned to the back and arms, looking as though he received company like this every day, while in her blue robe buttoned up to her neck Mrs. Espedrosa told me, "Oh, yes, I remember him. That very nice young Chinese man—"

"Korean—"

"Whatever. Yes." As one hairpin dangled half out of the left of her two white buns, she explained, "I didn't have my cataracts, so I did some sewing back then. He was here, oh, two, three years. I must have mended some dozen pairs of jeans for that boy—he was very nice, very...yes, frugal." The religious pictures and ancient family photos in tarnished silver frames made the apartment seem wholly different from mine, though it was in the same file, like Hilda's, and of identical layout. "But he was hard on a pair of pants. I charged him eighty cents a pair to mend, I remember. Can you believe that? To have somebody do that today for you would cost six, seven, eight dollars."

Hasler's mad Korean-born mother had been Catholic. Had that, I wondered, left any sign on his walls up at Hilda's? But no one seemed to have ever left a real description of Hasler's living quarters—so, as I trudged back up the steps to the fifth floor, I went on assuming, now that I had moved as close as I could get to them, that those walls had been more or less like mine.

Office-temp work just about covered my very reasonable rent, as well as a couple of pork shoulders for roasting, salad fixings, and a loaf of Italian bread for a dinner to which, a couple of times a month, I could invite three or four friends (almost always Pheldon; almost as many times redheaded sanitation driver Lewey); it covered, too, my dry-cleaning bill and the odd bottle of wine to take for a gift when I was invited to dinner in return. If you never wanted to go anywhere and in summer were content with window fans instead of air conditioning and used cinder blocks and boards for the bookshelves that crept, now up this wall, now up that one, it was a negotiable life. Even if it wasn't Mike, with the sweat plastering the hair to his biceps and shoulders and his face full of my dick (and more sweat beading his eyelashes), naked over the asbestos-covered ventilation conduit, while Rod—the maintenance man, gold ring bright on the thick third finger of his left hand as he grasped Mike's hirsute flanks, that ring a sign, as I understood it, for two wives and some seven kids strewn between Rome, Georgia, and Goshen Park, Maryland—his shirt flung to the floor, his blues down around his black Jamaican thighs, and his oil-darkened work shoes rasping concrete, slamming again and again into Mike's butt, while the boiler croaked and roared and Mike came off my dick long enough to whisper, "Fuck me, you goddamned black bastards—fuck the shit out of me, you fuckin' niggers!" then once more skewered his face to the larynx on my upcurved cock, so that I could again feel Rod's rhythm through Mike's chin against my balls—like the Chinese kid in the library basement, it wasn't *that* bad.

Two full feet of one of my bookshelves—at about chest level—were actually related to my Hasler work; as were three of the plastic file boxes among the seven along the baseboard in what I called the dining room, though the round oak table in the middle was always covered with papers. (At those dinner parties, we pretty much buffeted it in the living room.) The night before, Pheldon had called to ask me out for brunch, but because I was sure he expected us to go Dutch—and, other than the emergency twenty in the desk, I was on the short side that weekend—I'd declined, with the excuse that I really had to use the time to work on my fabled thesis. But now I was sitting at the paper-sloughed table, of a late Saturday morning, rereading Mossman's letter for the fifth time that week, staring at the row of original journals over on the bookshelf with Hasler's sixteen articles and seven reviews, beside the *Formal Conjunctions/Informal Disjunctions* reprint collection. And what the hell were "degrading sexual experiments" supposed to be, anyway?

In my jeans, suddenly I stood up, took my short sleeve plaid shirt from the back of the chair, put it on, took out the four singles and put them in the drawer in the bedroom, then, leaving only a five in my wallet, went out, locked the door, put the key ring back on my belt holder, and started the long, dark steps, with their endless turnings, down the five flights. On the sunny stoop, I looked around, debating whether to go toward Central Park or Riverside. Maybe you can tell me why Riverside won.

Nobody was on West End Avenue when I crossed it at Eighty-second Street.

Wandering over the Drive, I stepped to the cobbled sidewalk under the trees, strolled the hexagonally paved path down the center, to turn in at the park, bearing downtown behind the playground. The asphalt was cool and tree-shadowed. Through the playground bars, out in the sun, on the other side, someone walked a dog. But no one was on the path here—except up ahead, thirty yards: three bums were talking.

I sat on a shadow-splashed bench, my arms out across the back, from time to time glancing at the trio.

The oldest and fattest was black. One of the others was clearly Hispanic. The third—the one sitting on the bench— from here I couldn't tell *what* he was.

In an army-green tank top, the Hispanic was the most animated, stepping around, sitting a moment, getting up again and waving his hands, making some argumentative point I couldn't really hear, though his voice reached me now and again above the rushing breeze in the leaves all around.

Whatever the Hispanic's point was, the old black guy thought it was real funny. And when his laughter moved him over to the side, I saw that the other guy on the bench was barefoot.

I looked at them and tried not to look as if I were looking.

How did you do this? In the midst of his "degrading experiments," had Hasler ever sat here in the park, I wondered, looking at bums and wondering the same? If you're going to follow someone like Hasler into this, I remember thinking, it would have been nice to have had Hasler's own account, rather than Mossman's synopsis. But Mossman was the biographer. *I* was concerned only with the intellectual side....

Finally the black guy turned away from the others and started up the path. His blue T-shirt was too small, and a band of belly showed above where his jeans were held up by twine. He wore a suit jacket on top of the T-shirt, one sleeve torn off. That arm—a footlong scar wormed down the brown flesh—looked pretty strong. But his hair was kind of tufty and gray, sticking out over his ears, gnarling across his chin. He lumbered slowly toward me in his old running shoes—with the retarded and unfocused gait of someone not really coming from anywhere, not really going anywhere.

"Hey," I said as he wandered past, "you want me to suck your dick?"

He frowned over at me, still walking. "Huh...?"

"I'll suck your dick for you, if you want."

He stopped, turning to blink at me with eyes whose whites were the color of ivory. He still frowned.

I took one hand from the bench back and gestured toward his pants. "Go on—nobody's around. Take it out. I'll give you a blowjob right here."

His rough, dark hand went to his pants—but just to scratch. (I tried to make out what was hanging in there.) "Why, that's right nice of you," he said thickly. "But...well, naw. I don't think I ought to do that, just right now."

"Come on," I said. "I'll give you a good suck. You can fuck hell out of my face, drop a load. It'll make you feel good. Set you up for the weekend—come on."

Still frowning, still scratching, he shook his head. "Yeah, I know, but I don't think so. That's real nice of you, though." He turned, started away, hand still working between his legs. "Nice of you to offer. Real nice. Thank ya'. Real nice...."

I'd been ready for him to throw a punch.

His gratitude tickled me, though. He kept on walking. Once, when he paused, I thought he was going to change his mind and come back. But it was just for more scratching. Again he lumbered on. I stood and turned toward the two others still down the path from me.

When I was about fifteen feet away, I said: "Hey—either of you guys want me to suck your cock?"

Standing now, the Hispanic in the tank top turned around and blinked. Shadowed all around with black stubble, his mouth was open. His upper incisors were gone, but you could see the yellow canines on either side of the gap. "What the fuck you jus' say to me...?"

"I said I'll suck your cock if you want."

"Ah, man...what the fuck is a' matter with these fuckin' cocksuckers? Ah, shit...a goddamn fuckin' cocksucker. What the fuck you want, man?"

"To suck your dick. Or his, if he wants."

With his stringy brown hair, the one sitting, was getting a bald patch high on his forehead.

"Don't bother my friend, man!" the Hispanic guy snapped. Under the scooped neck of his tank top, his chest was sunken, though he looked pretty defined in the muscles of his arms and shoulders. Around one wrist was the plastic band they give you when you go into one of the city hospitals. "You leave my fuckin' friend alone, cocksucker!"

"I'm not bothering him. I just want to give you a blowjob—if you want one."

"Suck my fucking dick?" the guy exclaimed, stepping around on the path. For shoes, he was wearing some kind of old bedroom slippers. "Suck on my fuckin' dick? Whyn't you just eat out my fuckin' asshole? Here—" he turned, bent over, grabbed the buttocks of his filthy greens with dirty fingers (the forefinger on his left hand—the one with the hospital band on the wrist—was missing its first two joints), and tugged.

The seam down his pants seat had split some time before.

Through ripped threads, I glimpsed of his crack between scrawny buttocks. It was hairy. It wasn't very clean. And from what I could see underneath, his single ball was as small as a quail's egg. In the seconds he exposed himself, I didn't catch any dick on him at all.

"Sure," I said. "I'll lick your asshole out." I was thinking of Mike—

But he straightened, whirled, and danced away from me. "Get the fuck outta my face, you black bastard...you fuckin' cocksucker—you nigger scumbag...you got any money?" He stepped up toward me again, shaking his head. "You don't got no fuckin' money. No cocksucker who comes on like that ever got no fuckin' money." With one hand he grasped the crotch of his greens. "You wanna suck my fuckin' dick, nigger? You wanna suck my dirty, cheesy, long-skin spic dick? You wanna eat out my fuckin' ass? Then you just get some fuckin' money an' come back here tonight." He screwed up his face like someone suddenly gone nearsighted. "You gimme some money, an' I let you suck my fuckin' dick...okay?" He jabbed his finger stub at me. "But now...you fuckin' crazy cocksucker—comin' up right in the middle of the day, askin' some fuckin' question like that. You come back tonight—with some money, you hear me? You can suck my fuckin' dick!" He turned away, started off— "Fuckin', crazy, nigger cocksucker"—but whirled back. "You leave my friend alone! Don't you go botherin' my fuckin' friend, now!" He pointed to the shoeless guy with the thinning hair, still sitting on the bench. "He ain't no fuckin' faggot, doin' all that cocksucker shit, you hear me? So leave him the fuck alone!"

The guy on the bench—a white guy, not as tall as I was—had lifted one bare foot to the boards and was picking at his toes. My first thought was—goddamn!—he had to have the biggest feet I'd ever seen!

The Hispanic guy, with his raggedy-ass greens, bopped off down the path, after the black fellow. A last time he turned around, walking backwards, to call: "Don't bother my friend, now! You leave him the fuck alone—faggot!" He turned back and hurried away.

I took a breath, then sat on the bench—about three feet from the guy bent over his jackknifed knee. Watching him finger his feet, I realized it wasn't that they were so big; rather his toes, gray with dirt, looked as swollen as five new potatoes.

And his fingers—his hands, just as dirty—were equally enlarged. His nails were like helmets, big across as quarters, curved down over the ends of his weirdly wide fingers. He wasn't paying me any attention at all.

I said: "I'll suck *your* dick...."

He picked for another thirty seconds. Where his hair was going, you could see the dirt on the scalp beneath. When, at last, he looked up, though his face was soiled, he was younger than I thought: maybe in his early thirties; maybe thirty-five. Despite the dirt, he was good-looking. "You aimin' to party?" His voice was out of the South, the West; and he smiled.

His teeth had about rotted out—what I could see were broken, brown, missing, or just green stubs.

"I *like* to party." He went back to picking. "It'd be nice if we could get us some beer, though. It's better, you know, when you're a little high, doin' that stuff. For the imagination." (Just then it came back to me, an old black guy who'd lived a block away from us on Staten Island: he'd had fingers like that, and—once, I'd seen him ambling down to Fenton's Grocery in sandals—toes, too. It was kind of like a birth defect, I guess, where your toes and fingers just kept growing, till they were like clubs.) "But I love me a nigger—you know, I mean a colored fella—suckin' on my crank." He put his foot on the ground again and laid his hands on his jeans' frayed thighs. "Kinda nice to run into you."

I didn't see any shoes or sneakers around. But maybe that was because, with his enlarged toes, the front part of his foot was half again as wide as even big feet are supposed to be. Both his broad fingernails and his great toenails were picked or bitten back to the crowns. Even with ordinary-sized fingers, I realized, he'd have been a ham-handed man.

Starting to pull at something at his torn knee, he said: "You know, I think cocksuckers are about the best fuckin' thing God put on this world. I mean, I'm old enough to know it; I ain't never gonna get me no chicks. You can't get no chicks when you're poor, bald, toothless, an' ugly."

"Actually," I said, "you're not that ugly—or that bald...yet."

He grinned over at me with his bombed-out smile. Then he reached out and, with his fist loose, gave me a playful half-hit on the shoulder. "You fuckin' cocksucker!" He dropped his head to the side, kind of quizzical, then slid toward me about a foot. "Sometimes cocksuckers think that about me. I guess that's why them an' me, we get along." He lifted one great soiled hand from his lap. "Me, you see—like that Spanish feller told you I ain't no faggot. I'm straight, man. I really *like* women! 'Specially black ones—older ones. But I always had me a good imagination. So if a cocksucker don't mind me doin' a little thinkin', a little imaginin', I sure don't mind no cocksucker—especially a big-mouthed, liver-lipped nigger—" again he grinned at me—"nursin' on my fuckin' peter. I don't need me no picture magazines. No dirty movies—though, if you got 'em, I don't mind takin' a look at 'em. But I can do it all in my head." Here he tapped three fingers, wider together than all five of mine, against his forehead: "Imagination. I mean, I been a fuckin' bum since I was about seventeen years old. An' I know I ain't worth dog shit—an' I ain't never gonna *be* worth dog shit. Me an' dog shit, man, just step in us, and it takes a long time to get either one of us off your damned shoe. But that's the only side of me that's even as *good* as a dog turd. I'll tell you, man, if there's ever a contest, you take the dog shit and leave me behind—you'll come out a winner."

I laughed. "What's your name?"

"What's yours?"

"Might as well call me 'cocksucker,'" I said. "Since that's what I do. And yourself?"

"Well, I'll tell you," he said. "You call me a piece o' shit, and you'll be callin' me a lot better'n what most people done called me most of my life."

I smiled. "Okay, Piece o' Shit. So you been a bum since you were a kid? Where'd you grow up?"

"In a orphanage," he explained. "Out in California—way down in the south. Below what they call Southern California. I mean, where you can't hardly tell it from Mexico no more. You ever heard of Brawley, California—in Imperial Valley, down south of Salton Sea?"

I shook my head.

"Well, that's the closest place with a name to where I come up." He added: "In the orphanage there—that's where I done learned about cocksuckers. And black people. See, in a' orphanage, the two sexes is niggers-Mexicans-'n'-injuns—and whites. And in the orphanage where I was, there weren't but about ten, twelve white guys out of about seventy or eighty kids. Man, by the time I got out of that place at seventeen, I had so much brown and black dick shoved up my fuckin' asshole, I was about almost likin' it, I tell you." He meshed his huge hands, to frown across the park path. "You sure we can't get us no beer? It'd be better."

"I just want to suck your dick," I said. "I don't want to marry you."

"Yeah!" He barked a laugh. "I know what you mean!" Again he glanced over. "Though, you never know. Maybe I might want to marry *you*—then you might decide you just don't really mind it— 'cause a cocksucker usually likes it when some straight guy like me really likes him back."

"You're sure—with all the dick you've had up your ass—you're straight?"

"Yep." He sat back and nodded. "You'd think if you could turn some guy into a queer, that'd be the way to do it. But I guess that just goes to show you, y'are what y'are. Now I'll tell you, I don't regret it. It's a good thing to know how to do, take a dick up your ass. 'Specially if you're on the bum. I been all over the country since then. And I tell you somethin' else: if you got injuns an' niggers stickin' it up there a couple of times a day from the time you seven to the time you seventeen, then you goddamned well *know* how to do it!" He shrugged. "It don't turn me on. I don't never think about it when I beat off. I ain't never gone lookin' for it. But if some fellow wants to stick it up there—maybe slip me a few bucks for it—or, sometimes, I'll do it just to be obligin' 'cause he wants to get off." He shrugged again. "But at this point it just don't bother me none. Now what I like, see, is a big, nasty, smelly, runny, drippy, sweaty, funky black pussy! And I got a whole collection of 'em—" he tapped his forehead again— "right in here. It's been my experience—travelin' around, bummin' around—that most people is pretty nice. A guy in a truck who gives you a ride, he's horny so you tell him he can fuck your ass; when he's finished he usually says, 'Why, thank you, that's right obligin' of you' Some cocksucker wants to nurse on my dick while I lean back and do a little imaginin', well, I say, 'Jus' call me a piece o' shit and *I'm* much obliged.'" He looked up toward the trees. His immense hands joined over his groin, pushed down a little, pulled up a little. "I don't mean everybody walkin' around is some kind of saint. But the ones who don't know enough to smile and at least say, 'Thank you, you Piece o' Shit,' I just avoid 'em and go the other way."

"You sound kind of special," I said. "I'm surprised somebody hasn't snatched up your white ass and taken you home."

"Too much beer." He nodded deeply. "Besides, there ain't so many people think I'm *that* good-looking. Oh, it's happened to me a couple of times—so that I know when it's happenin', like with you. But for some goddamned reason—now, maybe it just could be 'cause I'm a dirty, smelly, clubbed-fingered, bald, barefoot bum with bad teeth—most people, even fuckin' cocksuckers, don't consider me all that much of a catch." He glanced at me a little slyly, took a breath, and let go of his crotch to spread his arms out along the bench back's worn green plank. "Come over here, next to me. Slide on up and lemme see you make your mouth into a cunt."

"Huh?"

"Come on." With his scraggly chin, he beckoned me closer.

I slid next to him. (Although his hair was receding a little and was thinning on top, I don't think it would ever have occurred to me to call him bald. But, as he'd mentioned it twice, I guess it worried him.) He put his arm around my shoulder, tugging me nearer. "Come on, now. Let's see that pussy-hole."

I frowned. "I'm not holding out on you," I said. "But frankly, I'm not really sure what you mean."

It was his turn to ask: "Huh? You mean you ain't never had to play pussy-face before? What the hell kind of cocksucker are you, anyway?" Though he still sounded friendly, he also sounded sincerely bewildered.

"You're just going to have to show me."

He threw back his head to laugh. "Well, if you don't know how, somebody's gotta. But I sure never thought I'd be showin' no nigger how to do somethin' like this!" His hand still making a gigantic epaulet on my far shoulder, he turned to face me. Some white stuff was caught in the inner corners of both blurred blue eyes. "You'd been in a orphanage like me, you'd learned about all this shit. Okay now; just hang them big old suckers wet and loose—" he turned out his own mouth, and I tried to imitate him—"There you go—you got it. Then you take your tongue and screw it 'bout as small as you can, up over your front teeth and press it against your upper lip." Now he made what I swear was the stupidest face I'd ever seen. "Sure," he admitted, when I broke and laughed, "it looks kind o' dumb when a white feller does it. But that's 'cause we just got these fuckin' slits for mouths. But you get a big-mouthed, black sonofabitch like you there—see, the tongue, that makes like a goddamned clit, right up there on the top. Hold on, just a second—yeah, now you doin' it right...." On my far shoulder, his hand slid up my neck. His fingers were sandpaper rough—and dry. They moved up over my cheek, then around to my mouth. "Yeah, bitch—there you go! Now you got a hole there that'll do for a funky black pussy just about any way. You wanna wiggle that clit a little?" His great fingers crossed over my mouth, to feel around, to probe within my lips, under my tongue. "That's so fuckin' sexy, man—it's funny, too. Ain't no real pussy I ever heard of could wiggle its clit. But you wiggle the tip of your tongue on my fingers, right while I got my hand in there, and it feels like too fuckin' much." One, then a second, finger slid suddenly and deeply into my mouth. "Oh, shit—bitch! That's one beautiful pussy, you got. Let me feel around in that fuckin' hole of yours." He closed his eyes, and his fingers probed deeper—they tasted surprisingly of salt. The white stuff—gray, really—stuck together a couple of his eyelash hairs, and looked like it was still soft. A lot of the stubbled pores on his cheek were large; dirt had collected in them. "I'm gonna finger-whip that pussy-hole up into a fuckin' lather. Then I'm gonna eat that nasty hole out for about twenty-minutes—then I'm gonna stick my dick in there and fuck it till it turns inside out and you can't walk away from here, but you gotta crawl on the ground!" A third finger suddenly slid into my mouth beside his other two, and the three of them began to move quickly and rapidly inside. "Oh, lemme hear that pussy make some sounds!"

I grunted a little.

"Yeah...!"

So I turned it into a kind of a moan.

"Oh, yeah, that's nice, bitch." His other hand joined the first one on my face, and he tried to push another finger in. "Don't loose that fuckin' clit for me—" Grinning, now, he blinked his mucus-stuck eyes open. "Shit, nigger, that's the nicest pussy I been in in a *real* long time. Look how it made me do—see how it got me?" He looked down.

I glanced at his lap, where there was now a tent in his pants.

"That's gonna be all yours, too, baby. You wanna take it out and play with it? You can feel it up, kiss it, suck on—"

"Wait a minute," I said.

He moved his head back, looking a little askance. "What's the matter?"

"Close your eyes for a second." I put my hand on his pants—and was surprised at the thickness of what I felt. I rubbed it a few times. "Just close your eyes a moment."

"Okay...baby." With a grin, he raised his face and let his lids slide down.

I reached forward and fingered the white stuff away from one corner. He pulled back. "What the fuck you—"

"Just cleaning up your eyes," I said. "You ever seen a dog with snot in the corners of his eyes? Well, that's what you got in yours. Eye-snot."

"Oh." He turned away. Raising his hands, he bent over and knuckled into his sockets. Again he looked up, blinking at me. "Any better?"

"The left one's okay. But do it again on the right."

He did.

Under my hand, his cock still hadn't gone down. There was something strangely hard at the front.

"How's this, now?" Over my wrist, he wiped his knuckles on his pants leg.

"It's funny," I said, "you Piece o' Shit: the dirt doesn't bother me, but the eye-snot *gets* to me!"

He laughed and turned toward me, both his hands going up to my face. "You never know—you may get so you like all of it." His left thumb brushed across my mouth, brushed back. I stuck my tongue tip up under and wiggled it. "Ah, man...this black bitch knows how to drive her honky crazy." He bent his gigantic thumb, pushed it into my mouth, and suddenly his own mouth opened and, tongue first, he covered mine, to dig deep into my mouth with it, right beside his thumb. I thrust back with my own tongue, feeling the dental wreckage along his gums—which he didn't seem to mind. After moments, he drew back. "You know, when you take that fucker out my pants, you're gonna have a little surprise."

"Little?" I gave it another squeeze. "I don't think so."

That made him laugh. "Why don't you go on take a look at it now, see what you think."

I glanced around, but there was no one within sight on the path.

His rough hands moved to my face again. "I have to tell you, now, my peter's a little on the unusual side—so I don't like to sneak up and spring it on folks when I'm too hot to turn back. Go on." He nodded down at himself. "Take it out and look."

Through the gritty denim, I could feel it was pretty fat. He took his hands away and put them out on the bench back again, while I turned to open his top button, then unzip him. It pushed right out. In its brush of brown hair, the fat cock slanted up, a kind of purplish brown, six or seven inches of it—but ahead of that, it bent sharply down!

I slid my hand forward on it, but after the bend the texture was much different—softer, only with hard places in it. "What the hell is—"

"That's a yoni. See, I been a real yoni man, almost since I got out of the orphanage."

"A yoni?"

"You know—foreskin, lace curtains. Yoni—what the injuns call it." I lifted his cock out his jeans: we're talking a good, fat, seven-inch dick, but with at least four *inches* more—maybe five—of foreskin off the end! (Underneath, though they were up real close to his body—as though his scrotum were just too small to hold them—his balls were big as a pair of oversized peaches!) But his skin wasn't just a limp five-inch sleeve: stuff inside it, hard or something, held it open, as wide as his cock. "I guess you ain't never seen a real bona fide yoni, the way the injuns do it, now."

"I guess I haven't," I said. "What in heaven's name is—"

"Right now I wear six yoni rings inside my skin. That's pretty good, ain't it?"

"Jesus…!"

"You wanna take a couple of 'em out and look at 'em? I'll tell you, some cocksuckers really get into 'em—like to take 'em out for me with their teeth!"

"That looks pretty incredible. It's like your *dick's* got a five-inch dick hanging off it!"

"Yeah…!" That tickled him. "That's about it! Here, lemme show you." He reached to take the end of the fleshy sleeve in his massive hand, then pressed his great thumb down, so that a shape inside bulged forward. "Go on, catch it for me—"

I got my hand under it, as an inch-and-half in diameter white ring slid from the end, to fall over in my palm.

"There you go!"

I lifted it up to look at it.

"Like I said, I wear me six of them yoni rings in there, now. The oldest three, there're real injun ones—one's turquoise, two is polished-up bone. Those was the first ones I got. Why I ain't never tried to sell 'em for beer, I'm damned if I know. Probably 'cause most people wouldn't know what they was, or what to do with 'em. The rest of 'em—the other three, well, they're just cut off from some old PVC coupling. Work just as well, though."

"What's the stuff all over it?"

"What the fuck you think it is?" He grinned at me. "You got you a good, grade-A quality goat here. And that's grade-A quality goat cheese! I mean, that's the *real* Gorgonzola."

"What I thought," I said. I turned the ring over, held it up, then put it in my mouth. "Not *bad*, Piece o' Shit!"

He barked another laugh. "Aw, man—I knew I had your number pegged, cocksucker. *Listen* to this nigger, how he don't like to see no eye-snot! Bitch, you gonna be suckin' the jam out my toes and eatin' the snot out my nostrils 'fore we're finished—it ain't like I never run into *your* kind before, you know!"

"Maybe I will." I smiled. "Maybe I won't. What's this yoni business—is that something they did to you at the orphanage, too?" The cheese was salty, grainy, and good.

"Naw, man. That was after I got out. Yoni—like I say, that's when I was staying with the injuns."

"California," I said, "always did sound like a pretty crazy place."

"This wasn't in California. This was up in Montana—after I hightailed out of that nuthouse. Well, they wasn't *exactly* injuns—except one of them. They was more like hippies. But they was all into this real heavy injun shit. There was one guy with 'em I guess was a real injun. If he wasn't Mexican or somethin'. But these guys was into pulling their foreskins down and stickin' these rings inside 'em. And I started out with a pretty healthy yoni of my own, even to begin with. Course it wasn't nowheres near as long as it is now. But if you got any skin on you at all, even wearin' one or two of 'em feels real sexy. It's the weight, I guess. There was even a couple of guys in with us what had started off kike-cut, you know? Man, why anybody would want to do that to a baby's dick, I wished I knew—that's fuckin' *sick*—cuttin' on some kid's pecker like that! I mean, that's got to be some kind of child abuse, don't you think? But then, every time I get me an opinion on *anything*, folks just tell me I'm some kind of madman. Anyway, it just took the kike-cut ones a little longer to start 'em stretchin' it and growin' it back again— that's all. And every time you put another one in, it stretches you out that much longer—till it grows and you got room for another one. There was one guy in the group—had a blond ponytail down below his ass, man, and used to wear twenty-*three* of these fuckin' yoni rings in his cock *all* the time! He had a fuckin' yoni on him down to his fuckin' knee—I'm not kiddin', either!" He held up an arm and ran one finger out along his forearm to indicate the length. "It was *that* long, just the skin on it—I swear—more than twice as long as his goddamned dick! He'd take 'em out and show 'em to you, every chance he got—let everybody stand around and watch him put 'em back in. He was kind of an exhibitionist, I think. But the more you played with it and pulled on it and put them rings in and out, the more it grew. Couple of times we all went to the movies in town, and sittin' right there in the theater, he'd open up his fly, whip it out, take out them rings, then slide 'em all back in, right in the seat in the goddamned movie, talkin' to me, talking to some of the other guys, with people walking on by him with their goddamned popcorn and large-sized Coca-Colas—he didn't fuckin' care! But it looked so strange, I guess, nobody could figure out *what* he was really doin'. So he never got caught. You know like them Africans, with the big lips—the ones what put them things in their mouth to make their lips even bigger, like shells or plates or somethin'?"

"The Ubangis."

"Yeah, man—that's what they're called? Well, I guess I just done the same thing to my dick. You know, them 'bangy niggers, they gotta have cocksuckers, too, I guess. Everybody else does—man, can you imagine gettin' a blowjob from one of them big-mouthed black suckers? That'd be somethin', wouldn't it? Wonder if I'll ever run into one of them to suck—or leastways to lip—on my yoni. Now, that's a picture, ain't it? Anyway, all those guys—and I admit it, I am, too—was *real* yoni-proud. Like I said, I only wear six of 'em today. But I bet it's more than *you* got!"

"By a couple of inches," I told him.

Minus the one ring, the end skin had fallen closed; at the place on his jeans, a wet spot darkened the cloth now. I ran my hand over his hefty haft, then pushed my middle finger within the broad cuff. Inside was slimy. "It's funny about us yoni guys—" he watched me play with his cock—"I mean, the ones of us who wear rings. We drip like motherfuckers, man—*all* the fuckin' time! The guy back there what first showed me how to put 'em in, he said it just went with the territory."

"Was he plowing your ass?" I asked.

He frowned. "Maybe he was—I don't even remember. Like I say, gettin' my asshole poked around in just don't mean that much to me. So I don't even keep track of it. He might've been. But you climb on me in the middle of the night, an' I'm just as likely not even to wake up while you fuckin' me—'ceptin' in the mornin', I'll probably have pissed the fuckin' bed. Somehow, gettin' some-thin' shoved up my hole when I'm asleep—or half-asleep—almost always makes me take a fuckin' piss. Never did know why—'cept that I wasn't never that good at holdin' my water, anyway. Half the time you see me, you gonna think I just wet my pants—nigger, you got a *nice* touch there! Keep that up. It feels good—don't *swallow* my fuckin' ring, now!"

"You got another one?" I took the first one out of my mouth.

"I got five more where that one's stashed. And the deeper down in they are, the more of that good stuff they got all over 'em."

I looked up and down the path.

"That's stoned cocksucker *candy!*" He nodded down at himself.

There was still nobody around.

Holding his dick, I started to bend over.

But he took my wrist and pulled my hand away. "You don't need to use anything but your mouth."

So I got another ring out, then a third one, and a fourth. When I'd sucked them clean of their salt curd, he said; "I think you bet-ter hand me those, now." He slid them into his pocket, as I went back for the last two. Working my tongue inside his immense, rumpled, cheese-filled folds, when my tongue tip finally worked in far enough to touch the head of his cock directly, he sighed, moved his knees wider, then said, sort of absently; "I think it's about time for me to *fuck* this bitch!" Standing now, not letting me lose him, he moved around in front of me. I put my arms around his hips. His pants had fallen below his ass. Those immense hands came down to cage my head. Now he pulled me back, his hard haft followed by those inches of skin that, limp now, fell from my mouth; he turned up my face, and dropped his mouth on mine—while I got his cock in both my hands and milked it forward with one, then the other. Bad teeth notwithstanding, he was a deep, serious spit-swapper. Once he raised his face to whisper, hoarsely, "A little cheese in that dirty hole gives that nasty cunt some *fine* flavor! Bitch, that's some *real* good eatin' pussy!" He went back to rooting in my gullet, both with tongue and fingers.

After a few minutes, he stood again and, with one hand, fed me his fat dick, with that five-inch rag on it long enough to fill up the rest of my mouth. Then he began to fuck. The odor of unwashed man filled the space between us—and as his crotch hair beat against my face and nose, in moments I found myself caught in the illusion that that space, that odor, was the universe.

Then, with acclimation, it faded—even while I tried to hold the smell.

In my mouth I tried to maneuver the skin around so that, first, it was to one side, then to the other. Then I began to let it ride back, fattening up his bloated shaft till it was even thicker, and the walnut of his cockhead, finally licked free of cheese, was completely out of its covering. Holding my face hard, he really began to hump.

I'd kind of lost track of the world, but I heard him say, suddenly, sharply, above me: "What the fuck you starin' at? Ain't you ever seen nobody get a blowjob before?"

I opened my eyes—I couldn't get away from him; he was holding my head too tight, but I twisted around enough to see beyond his hip. In a worn coat, an old black lady pulled along a shopping cart stuffed with papers and plastic sacks. She stared, she blinked, she bit her lip, and generally showed an absolutely hypnotized interest—without stopping walking, though.

It didn't halt him, so I took my cue from that. I lost her from sight—I guess she wandered on. In another three minutes, he began to shove in *harder*. He gasped now—his pants were down around his knees (no underpants on this guy), and I had his big balls in my hands. I rubbed the shaft behind them, where you could feel his dick's root curve up into his body. My hand went even farther back; his buttocks clamped my fingers. He was grunting, starting to cum.

I slid my hand back between his cheeks, pressing a finger toward his hole—and, surprised, slid two right inside him! Really, it didn't seem to make any difference. He shot. His last grunt was "Jesus Christ...!" Above, he bent over me, while the nutty savor of semen filled my mouth. And filled it. "Jesus, are you one *fine* black bitch!" Inside his ass, I wiggled my fingers. "Goddamn, nigger," he panted. "You could suck the chrome off a Mack truck's manifold...!" Which was when I realized that the flavor had changed: my mouth heated, salt flooded over my tongue, filled my throat.

I guess he realized what was happening the same time I did. I began to swallow—fast. He started laughing now, still holding my head. "Well, it's your own fuckin' fault, nigger—what'd you do, stick your finger up my ass when I shot? I done told you, that's gonna make me fuckin' pee, every fuckin' time!"

I took great gulps of his urine.

Loosening his grip on my head, he frowned down at me, still breathing hard. "Hey, you sure you can *take* all that, cocksucker? You come off it if you have to. Don't worry about getting some on my pants—that happens to me all the fuckin' time."

I shook my head, keeping my face in on his groin, and drank; and drank—and let it balloon my cheeks while I sucked in a breath through my nose—and drank more.

After he took about three more breaths, he began to rub my head again. His stream hadn't slowed at all. "Guess you *are* takin' it all." He rubbed; he patted. "That's a *good* cocksucker! Yeah, that's a good little cocksucker. Guess you do know how to service a feller." The pressure of his waters finally subsided. At last he stepped back—and splattered my face. "Oh, shit, man—I'm sorry! I thought I was done!" My fingers pulled from his butthole. Looking left and right, he reached down quickly and pulled up his jeans—his dick was still spurting—and pushed himself inside, inches of skin still flushing, dragging within his fly. Buttoning himself up, he looked about nervously; the lap of his pants darkened and grew wet.

He turned around and sat beside me on the bench. "Jesus, that was a good load I dropped. Boy, you really know how to make it good." He chuckled. "But when I'm payin' attention to my dick, you can drive a fuckin' Peterbilt up my hole and I probably ain't gonna even notice it. But it do make me piss—like I say, it's numb like that 'cause of all them niggers what was jammin' me when I was a kid in the orphanage. Anyway—thanks to you, cocksucker, I just had me one fine black bitch this afternoon—a *fine* black bitch!" Looking down at himself, he blinked at his pants. "Imagination..." Shaking his head, he laughed and rubbed down first one wet pant leg, then along the other.

I sat, looking at my two fingers that had just come out of his ass.

He saw them now, and suddenly put his hand under mine, lifted my hand toward my face, and declared, "Ah, clean that shit off, cocksucker!" As I slid my fingers into my mouth to suck them, he began to laugh. "And this is the cocksucker who's squeamish about a little eye-snot?" He crossed one leg over the other and began to run his great forefinger between his clubbed toes. "He's a fuckin' cheese hound—drinks my fuckin' piss like a trooper. Man, that's so funny, the way I can hardly tell whether I'm pissin' or cummin' anymore. You know, that all started with them yoni guys, too. The one I told you was probably a real injun? One thing he showed us how to do was beat off and as soon as you cum, start right in to pissin'. He said it felt real good—like you was cummin' and cummin' and cummin', on and on and on—till your piss run out. So we all was trying it. Pretty soon I got so as I could about do it. (We went to one of them dirty movies, I remember, and did that a couple of times. Man, we left the floor between them seats lookin' like an overflowed toilet'd stopped up!) But then, sometimes, I got so I'd be beatin' off and think I was gonna cum, only I'd surprise myself and start pissin' instead." He shook his head. "Sometimes, man, that's a fuckin' mess! But I warned you—so you don't got anybody but yourself to blame." He glanced over at me as I took my fingers out of my mouth. "Taste good?"

"Yeah." I shrugged. "It's not that bad."

"Probably don't taste like nothing, anyway. I'm usually pretty clean back there." He pushed his forefinger up against his nostril, wrinkling the big-pored skin of his nose. His finger was too thick to get inside, it looked like. But he dug around, and when he took his finger down, with a little snort, there was a green crust on it with something white, wet stuff blobbing from it. He held it up in front of me. "Go on—eat that."

"I will suck your dick," I said. "I'll drink your piss. I'll even lick out your asshole. But I will *not* eat your snot!"

"Your loss." He put his finger in his mouth, pulled it out—clean—and sat there, moving his tongue around inside his cheek, over the stubs of his teeth. "Goddamn, but I'm dry, after losin' all that water. Sure there ain't no way I could convince you to spring for a six-pack? Even just a couple of cans would be nice. I showed you a pretty good time, didn't I? You want to hang out with me some, I could get it up for you a couple or three more times before the day was out. We could drink a couple of cans, shoot the shit, swap lies—even party down again. I probably still know a couple of tricks you ain't never even tried yet." He went reaching into his pocket, to come out with his rings. Leaning forward, again he looked up and down the path. Satisfied that no one was coming, he sat back, pulled down his fly, and hauled himself out between the wet cloth. First the turquoise one, then the bone ones, he slipped them inside that humongous skin, working them back in as far as they could go. "One of the things I can do," he explained, sliding in the first of the plastic ones, "is tie a knot in that sucker. Then I jerk off, cum inside my yoni—two, maybe even three times. And I just leave it in there, all tied up like that. To ferment. If you like cheese, nigger, you can take me back to your place, let me grab a night's sleep, with a couple of loads knotted up in there overnight; then you can unloose that thing tomorrow mornin', while I'm still asleep, and just chow down on some really first-class Limburger—a couple of my loads, in there for a few hours with a little piss mixed in to start it goin', turns into something to make a cocksucker's mouth like yours just water." The last of the plastic rings opened up the front of his nozzle. "I done that before for lots of guys. Some of 'em even paid me for it, but I ain't even talkin' about stuff like that with you. I just want to have me some beer—and watch you have a good time eatin' out my cheesy old skin. You get me home, you gonna find out I'm a stoned cuddler, too. I just close my eyes, and, man, you turn into the biggest, nastiest, dirtiest black bitch—and I can eat out pussy and suck on that fuck-hole you got like it's goin' out of style. Like I say, I'm straight—you ain't *never* gonna find me with your dick in my mouth. I just can't *do* that. It don't sit right with me—not that there's anything wrong with anyone *else* doin' it. But I'll roll you over, put out a little imagination, an' eat out your black ass till the goddamn sun comes up. An', like I say, with me around, you always got a hole to fuck—if you don't mind a little piss on your mattress in the mornin'. But you already seen how that works by now. And one more thing, I'll tell ya, nigger, there ain't nothin' I like more'n wakin' up with my dick slidin' in an out of some black cocksucker's face. For a fuckin' can of beer—"

"Piece o' Shit?"

"Yeah, cocksucker?'

"What size shoes you wear anyway? I mean, if I were to find a pair—or run across some for you?"

"Biggest size you can get, then get a knife to slice the sides open. Leastways, that's in the summer. In the winter, I just cram 'em into whatever—and hurt like a sonofabitch!"

"And if I *did* go up and get us a six-pack, where would I find you when I got back?"

"Just a moment." He made like he was positioning himself on the bench. Then he moved his butt side to side a few times. "There. I just glued my ass to this here park bench—and *nothin's* gonna get me loose from it till you come back with that beer!"

"Well, in that case," I said, "I think I'm going to do that thing."

"You like Colt 45?" he asked as I stood.

"If that's your call, that's what it'll be."

"If you want, I'll come with you an' carry."

"I thought you just glued your ass to the bench."

"Well, then, I guess I'm stuck." He moved his broad feet out to balance on their heels. "The way I wet myself up, there"—he frowned at his lap—"I probably shouldn't try to go into no store or nothin' right now, anyway. You come in there with pissed-up pants and no shoes, they always throw you the fuck out. So I'll sit here and dry off a little…till you get back."

"Ten, fifteen minutes," I told him. "Twenty at the outside." I started up the path toward the Eighty-second Street entrance.

"Colt 45!" he called after me.

"You got it!" I grinned back over my shoulder at him, and kept going.

A Red Apple stood on Broadway just up from Eighty-second Street, but—open twenty-four hours—it was too expensive.

I went over to Amsterdam.

In those days, the bodega just across the avenue from my building sold sixteen-ounce beers for sixty-five cents a can and $3.75 a six-pack.

I was just coming out of the swinging glass door, thumb and forefinger hooked around the plastic straps, when across the street, coming up from the basement of my building, Jimmy—head dark as Darth Vader's above the his white T-shirt—waved at me.

I frowned.

Cigar angling from the corner of his mouth, he beckoned me over.

I thought about calling to him, "I've got to go, Jimmy." But then I figured, how much time could he take up?

The light changed, and I started across toward him. As I reached the corner, he called out: "You got a package, Mr. Marr. Federal Express—Saturday delivery, too. Here, I'll go down and get it for you. You can take it upstairs with your beer."

I held in my frustration, but there didn't seem to be any cause to explain to Jimmy that the beer wasn't *for* upstairs. And he was going down the basement steps already.

What he came back out with, however, was *three* packages: two bulging book mailers under one arm, Federal Express tapes and stickers all over them. The other was a carton that he lugged up by the twine it was tied with.

"Here you go, Mr. Marr. You want me to help you to get these into the hallway?"

I looked down at the beer in my hand. "Yeah, I guess so. If I'd known they were *this* big, Jimmy, I'd have asked you to keep them down there for me till I got home."

Jimmy pushed through the wrought iron gate and sat the carton on the sidewalk. "Since they come on Saturday," he said, "I thought maybe they was important."

"Yeah," I said. "Maybe." The return address, in pale blue carbon on the label, said: Irving Mossman.

So did the mailers.

Curious what he'd sent me, I was also eager to get back to Riverside. Jimmy handed me the mailers, switched the carton to his other hand, and carried it up the stoop and into the hall. Inside, I put the mailers and the beer on the radiator by the yellow wall. Then I took the carton, planning to lug it in one hand and the beer in the other. (I mean, beer is something you don't leave unattended in hallways in New York.) But—his steely cylinder of ash fallen to the tan tile just inside—the door was already closing behind Jimmy.

The carton was heavier than I thought.

"Next time you get something good," I said out loud, "bring it home *with* you, stupid!" Though, if I had, it would have been the first time I'd brought someone to the apartment since I'd moved there. "On the other hand"—now I was mumbling to myself— "wet mattresses. Maybe you better leave him in the park..." I hefted the carton with both hands. "Enjoy it—" I started up the next flight—"in the outdoors."

With a stop on every landing, it took me ten minutes to get it all the way up. And on the third, I realized I had to piss so badly my gut was paining; so I left the carton, barreled up to the apartment, got inside, and, straddling the toilet, let my clear waters splash down, while a burning glow bloomed around my body, that, till it quieted to simple relief, it would have been hard to place as either pleasure or pain. (Well, that's what happens when you piss for two.) I went back down, brought the box up the rest of the way, left it just inside the door, then hurried all the way down to the hall, and brought the mailers up under one arm, carrying the six-pack up in my other hand. By the time I got up the five flights the second time, I was winded.

I thought about just leaving the packages, taking the beer back down, and heading to the park again. But there was bound to be a letter in one of the mailers. I could open it, read it real quick.... I took the beer into the kitchen, opened the refrigerator door, saw there was no room to put it in, so opened the freezer and wedged the cans in on top of the ice trays. Then I went to the kitchen table, took the first of the mailers, spent three minutes looking for a way to tear it open, couldn't find one, and finally got out a knife and slit it down one side.

I slipped out several bound sheaves of paper, a couple of folders, a loose stack of Xerox copies—and no letter.

Well, I thought, maybe in the *other* one. Another five minutes, I figured, couldn't hurt—though by this time I'd been gone from the park, I realized, more than a half an hour. I slit the second mailer.

The first thing that came out was a manila envelope, with the butterfly clip's metal tongues pressed out flat through the hole . I lifted them up, opened the flap, and slid out the sheets with the university letterhead.

Dear John,

You probably won't be overly surprised at the news, but I've decided to put my biographical work on Timothy Hasler officially on hold. There's no reason this should place any restraints on your own project. Really, John, the more I've thought about it, the more I'm convinced that your work is actually more important than mine. Hasler was, as we know, an extraordinary intellect. And that intellect is what your project is dealing with. Whether that intellect was the world-class one that, a few years ago, a good number of us thought—well, the references to Hasler and his work have rather fallen off in the last year. Possibly that's our fault—or even mine. But one would like to think that if the work were *really* that interesting, then the work alone should keep pulling people back to it, even if one or two scholars—me, say, or even you—do not produce the illuminating exegesis we'd once envisioned.

Sometimes I wonder if, maybe—by this time—other people also know Hasler was gay; that is, it might be going around, if only by rumor, the *kind* of gay man he was. If it upsets me, perhaps it upsets these others; and rather than try to separate the sexual practices from the thinking, they are just turning away from the whole unhappy business and would rather not deal with it at all. At those times, I wonder why I should be the one left to wrestle with all this deeply unpleasant material.

Anyway.

Though I know you've been having your own troubles, I can't imagine your thesis has gotten stalled in the same morass that my project has run afoul of. But the fact is, whatever sort of intellect Hasler was, he was just not a very savory human being—however greathearted, witty, sympathetic, and inspiring a house guest Almira Adler found him in the sixties and seventies. Tell me, John, how can I write a meaningful biography of someone, when I find I've been walking through the streets for a couple of hours, muttering about him to myself: "He was an obnoxious little chink with an unbelievably nasty sex life. He was an obnoxious little chink with an unbelievably nasty..." It's awful, I know it. There's no excuse for thinking like that.

Still, that's how he strikes me.

At least at times. Sam [yes, did I say? Mossman had eventually divorced an already-estranged wife and married Sally-May Wallace: she'd been his graduate-student wife now for the last year and a half] thinks I'm doing the right thing.

In no way am I saying I'm abandoning the biography forever.

But I not going to pound myself over the head with my inability to go on with it anymore.

You know the sort of person I am, John. Most people don't find me short on compassion. Especially for sexual oddities. (Believe it or not, I have a couple of my own.) If two people love each other, if two people are committed to each other, if two people have each other's best interests at heart and want to join their lives to one another's, I would be a very small-minded man if I cared seriously that they happened to be of the same sex. Or even if their age difference were that great—hell, Sam is fourteen years younger than I am; and *we* love each other!

But what sort of compassion can I be expected to have for a man who writes an eight-page description in his journal about finding a Doberman loose in the park, bringing it home, feeding it, sucking its penis to orgasm four times, then turning it loose again (He wrote he wanted to get him back to the owner, but the dog got away from him when he took it out for a walk. So he said.), when I have not one bit of evidence that the account is anything but true?

What compassion can I have for a man who, once a week, bought a bottle of cheap wine, went out and hunted up an old black wino in the park, the two of them getting blitzed together, till he got the wino to urinate in his mouth? (He has the nerve to call this man his "friend." As far as I can tell, they didn't even know each other's names!)

What sort of compassion am I supposed to have for a man who fills up pages in his journal, fantasizing about sex with nightmarish creatures who aren't even human, but hideous demons who abuse him and ravish him in ways that—in these cases—I know are imaginary, because, otherwise, he would have been dead long before he was murdered?

But you can now see—see at least some of it—for yourself.

John, there's lots of things I've been meaning to send you—copies of notebooks, Xeroxes of papers, of documents, of letters, some by Hasler, some by his friends, some of Hasler's journals—for anywhere from months up to years. (Now, at least, with these papers, you have the chronology as I've managed to put it together so far.) Well, here they are. You are in the city where Hasler grew up, lived a good deal of his life—and died. Maybe these things will make more sense in such a landscape than they do here. But Hasler is just not someone whom I can any longer

That's when I stopped reading and put the letter down on the kitchen table, strode across to the refrigerator, opened the freezer, pulled the Colts free in a scattering of frost, and came back to the hall, swung through the door, and pulled it to after me.

I could read Mossman's self-righteous drivel some other time—I was *that* angry as I hurried back down the stairs!

On the stoop, I put the six-pack of Colt 45 under my arm. (They hadn't been in the freezer more than ten minutes and didn't feel all that cold.) At the corner, Jimmy took out his cigar stump and said, "Hey, where you going with that, Mr. Marr? That's some powerful stuff!"

"Right, Jimmy." I gave him a grin—"I'm going to go tie one on in Riverside Park"—and kept on across Amsterdam as the light changed; a block down, the cars began to move forward.

I left the Broadway corner, crossed the island, and made it to the far side, where a mother with a stroller was coming out of Burger King. It had to have been more than three-quarters of an hour since I'd left him.

Even with your ass glued down, waiting an hour for someone who says he'll be back in ten isn't that much fun—if my Piece o' Shit was still there at all. I hurried on toward West End, crossed the always-silent avenue, and continued down toward the trees and stone wall of the park.

I angled across the street toward the entrance at Eighty-third. As I reached the cobbled sidewalk, someone behind me said, "You! Hey!" in a voice I really didn't figure was for me. "Hey, you! Come on, turn the fuck around an' speak to me when I talk to you, faggot!"

Frowning, I kept going.

"Hey!"

Now I looked back.

The Hispanic guy with the green tank top and the bedroom slippers was hurrying up after me. "Hey, man! What you out doing...?" But at least he was smiling.

I shook my head, kept on going.

"Come on, faggot! Hey, how the fuck you doin'? What's happenin', man? You come back here to the park...?"

"I'm sorry," I said. "Really, I'm busy now and I—"

But even as I slowed to say that much, he grabbed my arm. "Naw, that's all right, man. Come on—talk to me! You come back to the park? You got some money for me now, we can do that thing like you wanted to, earlier. You know what I mean?" He looked around, stepped closer to me, reached down with the hand not holding me, and joggled his crotch. "We go in the park, find a spot in the bushes—I let you suck my dick. How much money you got?"

"Sorry," I said. "I don't have any money at all. We'll have to take a rain check on that." I tried to step away.

"You don't got no money? Ah, shit, man! Why you come back here if you don't got no fuckin' money? You tol' me you was gonna bring me some money! Fuckin' cocksucker—" He yanked my arm now, hard—as if he wanted it to hurt. "You got some fuckin' beer, though. You gonna give me some beer?"

"No. Sorry. The beer's not for you—" Again I tried to pull away; again he pulled me back around.

"You gimme that fuckin' beer, maybe I let you look at it. I ain't gonna let you suck on it—not just for some beer. But I let you look at it if you want. How's that? Gimme the beer now."

"Look," I said. "The beer isn't for you! Now get out of my face."

"Man, you're a fuckin' faggot!" He dodged ahead of me, where a wire trash basket stood near the park wall. Reaching behind it, without even looking, he pulled out a length of plank, half a dozen nails like quills in the business end. (My first thought was: How did he know it was there? With my second, I realized he'd put it there himself, for just such occasions.) "You don't got no money? You ain't gonna give me no fuckin' beer? Then what the fuck you doin' in the fuckin' park, cocksucker? Get the fuck on out of here! Go on, get the fuck out of here—you *hear* me! Go on, get *out* of here now!" He swung the plank at me; when I realized it wasn't a feint, I dodged back—and just escaped the end.

That's when two of the Colts chose to pull loose from the plastic strap and clunk to the ground, settling between the cobbles. I thought about trying to pick them up. (I thought about throwing the other four at him!) Then I thought I'd better let them lie.

"So what you gonna do now, cocksucker? Call a fuckin' cop? Go on, call a fuckin' cop! I don't give a shit!" There were, of course, no cops within sight. "You still wanna suck my dick?"

I stepped back again. Which inspired him to swing again—again I dodged back. I could probably get the plank away from him—he was holding it with the hand missing half his forefinger. But I didn't want to get my own hand or arm torn up by some rusty nails. The whole thing with this crazy one-ball Puerto Rican seemed ridiculous.

"Okay," I said. "I'm going!"

"You sure as fuck *are* goin', cocksucker. Get out—*now!*"

My four cans still in their loops, I stepped off the sidewalk, glanced about for cars, and sprinted to the other corner.

When I looked back at him, he had leaned the plank against a car bumper and was stooping to pick up one of the fallen cans. Standing now, he flipped the tab. White as an egret's plume, malt liquor sprayed the air. It wet his face, splattered his arms and shoulders, so that he turned sharply away.

On the other corner, I began to laugh.

Shaking off one hand, transferring the can to the other hand, shaking off the other, shaking his head and stepping back on the curb, the little guy exploded: "*Fuckin'* cocksucker!"

But not particularly at me.

I was thinking I could wait for him to go, or go away myself and come back in ten minutes—or half an hour.

But how long, I wondered, *was* my Piece o' Shit going to stay stuck?

The guy looked up and shouted, "And don't come back across this street, cocksucker! Or I'm gonna bust your fuckin' face!" Raising the froth-covered can, he drank.

Or, I thought, maybe it was time just to turn this whole adventure loose...

I walked back up toward West End Avenue, heading for Broadway.

When I was a third of the way up the block, I heard him call: "Hey, cocksucker—thanks for the beer!"

Muttering names to myself I wished I'd thought to shout at him, I kept going.

When I got home, I came into the apartment and slammed the door behind me—which, if you do that, doesn't lock.

Because of something in the set of the door, it just makes a loud noise and then floats open again. I had to go back and push it closed properly so that it would catch.

After that I sat in the dining room, drank one of the remaining Colts (Christ, that stuff tastes nasty!), got some tuna fish salad I'd made the night before out of the refrigerator and ate it, read at the rambling then-new Kripke—*On Rules and Private Language*—and didn't even pick up Mossman's letter—before I went to bed.

I could always read it tomorrow—

(At that point, the Hispanic with the plank and Mossman seemed to me blood brothers!)

—before I launched on a bout of Sunday typing.

At ten minutes to four—the glow-in-the-dark hands on the clock beside my bed told me—I woke. I got up, staggered down the hall to the bathroom to take a leak, in just the light from the air-shaft through the pebbled glass of the bathroom window. Still, when I started back, I felt pretty wide awake.

Turning into the bedroom, suddenly I flipped the light on, picked my jeans up off the floor, pulled them on, sat on the bed's rumpled edge to get on my socks, then my sneakers. I shrugged on an old zip-up sweatshirt, and went out in the hall (stopping first at the desk to get that last twenty), with the tingling feeling of some-one who, because of some unspecified emergency, had awakened much too fast.

Down on the stoop, I looked at the sky, black above the leaves of the block's maples, shingled nighttime gray and green by the cor-ner streetlight. I don't remember where I first read that 90 percent of all street crimes happen between six o'clock in the evening and eleven o'clock at night. (Among the apartment windows across the street, only three lights were on. As I looked, one went out.) But it had made me realize that, walking around at two, three, four in the morning, statistically I was safer than I would have been strolling home from an eight o'clock movie. Maybe it was a false security, but it was mine—and we New Yorkers treasure what we have.

I started for the corner of Amsterdam, heading again toward Riverside.

Although I might have been hoping, I certainly wasn't expecting the Piece o' Shit's "assglue" to hold for—hell, I'd left him around *three.*

It had been almost thirteen hours!

Still, if he was anywhere within five hundred yards of that bench, uptown or down, I had a chance of finding him. My plan? If I saw him, awake or asleep, drunk or sober, I was going to invite him home with me. At the twenty-four-hour Apple we'd pick up a *case* of Colt ! Wet mattresses? Well, I'd deal with that when and if it happened.

The Hispanic bully?

"I'm *not* going to run into him again!" I said aloud, as I turned the corner onto Riverside Drive. A breeze fingered my chest under my sweatshirt edge. "*That's* all there is to it!" Crossing into the park at Eighty-third Street, I believed it.

Did I *really* expect the Piece o' Shit just to be curled up on the same bench, sleeping? Still, of course, when I was about thirty feet away, the play of darkness over the planks for a few moments, for a few blinks, made me think someone *was* stretched out on it.

As I got closer, though, I saw that under the park's night lamps, the benches behind the playground where we'd fooled around that afternoon were empty. Searching up and down the park paths under night-lit trees, I must have gone past the spot we'd sat five times, if not six.

But he was gone. Really.

As I made wider and wider swings away, here and there on other paths I found a dozen guys asleep on other benches. Half of them had their shoes off; sneakers, running shoes, old loafers sat on the ground beside concrete stanchions or—in two cases—were wedged under some guy's head for a pillow. Faces turned from the light, almost all slept with fists thrust down between their thighs.

A guy wearing shoes, of course, was let out right there. The ones who'd taken them off, even when they slept away from any park lamp, I could pretty much tell weren't him with just a glance.

Before the sky lightens above the West Side, it gets a gray nap to it above the eastern trees and building roofs. Over the river, black hugged the water and nuzzled down among the night-glitter, save where here and there it was pried loose by Jersey's lights. In my mind, the specifics of my situation had given over to abstraction. Walking by the river, along the benches, by this time I wasn't even looking anymore—just walking and thinking: the kind of thinking you do when, if you're a kid, you believe maybe someday you'll cram all that thought into *The Systems of the World*; if you're an adult, though, you just call it thinking that isn't thinking at all, because it's so diffuse you know you probably couldn't understand it yourself an hour later, even if you wrote it down; it's never going to change anything you actually do, and nobody's ever going to know anything about it, anyway....

From one of the benches, somebody went: "*Pssst!*" As I walked by, I heard the whisper: "Hey, there, boy... *Pssst!*"

I stopped, looked over.

Pushing himself up on one elbow, with his white hair and the too-small T-shirt that showed his belly, the old black guy grinned at me. (His torn jacket was gone.) "You still out, lookin' around?"

"Yeah," I said. "I guess I am."

"You find what you're lookin' for, yet?"

"Found it," I said. "Then I let it get away. Now I'm looking for it again."

He sat all the way up, putting his feet—his big sneakers were on the bench beside him—in raggedy socks with holes in both toes and ankles, on the ground. "Ain't that the way it is, though?" Chuckling, he rubbed his stomach bulge. "Say, you still wanna suck me off?" His hand moved down over the twine holding his pants up to paw between his legs.

I thought a moment. Then I went over and sat on the bench beside him. "Pops, I'd be real obliged to you if you'd let me suck you off this morning!"

"Well, that'd be right nice. There ain't nobody out who'd see us now. Let me just get up here first and take me a piss." He rolled

to his feet and lumbered to the bench's end. "So I can enjoy it."
Fingering apart his fly, he began to urinate. "If you have to take a
piss, it don't feel as good when you cum."

"Can I come around there and drink that?"

"Huh?" He frowned back at me.

"Can I come around there and drink your piss?" I started up
off the bench, to get there before he finished—

"Drink my piss—? *Hell*, no, nigger! What you wanna do shit like
that for? That's nasty!"

I sat again and shrugged. "I was just asking."

He shook himself and turned back to the bench. "No, you just
do it normal like. I ain't into nothin' funny, now." He stopped to
rub one holey sock on the ground. "Got my goddamn foot wet.
Shit...! Hey, an' I ain't nothin' special in the pecker department,
either. But I do like to get it sucked on—and I think it's right nice
of you to wanna give an old nigger some pleasurin', boy." He lumbered up a few steps more. "But don't talk none of that nasty shit
no more!" He hadn't put it away: it was about four inches, maybe
four-and-a-half. He glanced down where I was looking. "It ain't
too clean. But it's all there. If you want it, it's yours."

"You want to stand up?" I asked. "Or sit down?"

He turned back to the bench. "If you don't mind—" he lowered
himself—"I'd just as soon sit down. You wanna kneel on here and
take it for me?"

"Sure thing." And I was around on my knees in front of him. He
had his hand in there to feed it to me; his skin was uncut and pretty tight over the head. The salty taste went all down it as he hardened. But when I finally got my tongue tip inside, he was
disconcertingly clean.

Still, his jeans had that funky smell (and gritty feel against my
cheek) they get when you've been wearing them a month or more.
I had my arms over his thighs. He dropped his hand on my hair and
I got to work. Really, I wanted to give him a good time. But, after
a minute, suddenly he was patting my head and whispering,
"Up...up...get on up, now! Got to get up!"

I came off, and he slid his hand under my arm to pull me, so that
in a movement—with just a little staggering—I was around and sitting beside him on the bench once more. "What's the matter...?"

"People comin'." He pulled his fly forward: his dick—like a black mole, that's what I thought—already soft again, jerked back into his pants. Inclining his head down the path, he whispered, "Ladies…"

I looked.

Down the asphalt beside the Hudson's rail, a dark form made its huddled way forward. Before I could make out a face in the graphite-colored dark, I was sure—from the creak of the shopping cart behind her—it was the black bag lady who had passed the Piece o' Shit while I'd been sucking him that afternoon. Another woman was with her, too. I could see her, as they neared: bonily thin, she was an awkwardly put-together white woman, who leaned over, talking heatedly to her black companion. The bag lady was still in a long overcoat. The white woman wore shorts and a T-shirt with some sort of picture on it I couldn't make out. Her voice whined across the morning:

"…so I told him right out, he ain't gonna stick his big black dick up my ass no more. I ain't his fuckin' bitch, no matter what he thinks! I mean, I'm fuckin' pregnant and I can't lose this fuckin' kid, or I won't *never* get on no welfare! So I told him, he could get himself fucked right there for all *I* cared. Then, you know, he tries to give me that shit of his about us gettin' fuckin' *high* together?" As they wandered past with the clanking cart, I could see the white woman's chipped nail polish on hands that were as dirty as her toes in their pink-rubber bathroom thongs. "I told him, get the fuck out of here with that shit! I mean, I'm gonna *have* this kid, and I can't be hangin' around with no deadbeat like him. Then they'll *never* gimme nothin'.…"

The black woman watched us—Pops and me—with the same blinking, lip-gnawing curiosity she'd had when she'd passed me earlier that day—so that my first thought, kind of startling, was that she recognized me from before. My second, however, was that her obsessed gaze, as she passed under the park lamp across from our bench, simply reflected the way the whole odd, awkward world struck her dark face.

"…now I tell you, this ain't no *prejudice* I'm talking about, now. This is just common sense—you hear what I'm sayin'? He don't have to go gettin' mad at me, just 'cause I got a chance to do somethin' now. He should just get the fuck out!" The feet on her sticklike legs hit the asphalt the way stilt ends might. Frayed and colorless cutoffs shook around thin thighs. (Where, I wondered,

in her gaunt, near-breastless body could a working womb lodge?)
Beyond them the Hudson flowed darkly between us and Jersey. "A
fuckin' black deadbeat with a goddamned big dick, and he thinks
he's hot shit or something! I ain't a fuckin' whore no more, see what
I'm sayin'? I do that shit, I can't give away the fuckin' money to no
fuckin' *man!* I can't afford it! So I'm sayin' to him, why don't he
just get *lost* and leave me the fuck alone, you know...?"

As they moved away, the black woman's silent progress beside
the river was as unarticulated as the cart she dragged.

Pops leaned toward me. "Ladies, now—see, you got to be
respectful of ladies. You can't let 'em see no shit like we be doin'."

Seriously, I thought about asking why.

When they were about ten feet on, though, I reached for his
pants again—he hadn't re-zipped. But his heavy hand dropped in
front of his crotch to hold me off. "Just give 'em another minute
to get around the turn there."

So I sat back again and waited.

Even after they'd disappeared, Pops leaned forward to look
some three, four times. (I was beginning to think this mouse-
dicked old man was, frankly, just wasting my morning.) At last,
though, he took his hand away, spread his knees a little, and said;
"You can go on and do it now."

So I took his dick out and kneeled between his holey socks
again, nuzzling inside his fly while he tugged the brass-toothed
cloth aside. His cock was like putting a very small potato in my
mouth; but it hardened as fast as it had gone soft. As I'd kneeled,
his hand went back to my head, fingers hooking behind. As I
sucked him, he began to add a rhythmic push to each bob of my
neck. Above me, he caught his breath like someone about to duck
under water. Then he let it out and caught it again. His other
hand went to my shoulder; his hips began to rock a little. It didn't
add much of a thrust—it wasn't to my sucking rhythm; and when
I speeded up to match his, his just slowed again. (If anything, it was
kind of distracting.) Once more, I heard him catch his breath.
Then he made a sound like, "...*Gggggghnnnnghnn...!*" and his
cock flushed its meager syrup.

I swallowed, cradling his cigar stub on my tongue. His fingers
relaxed on my head, then fell away.

"Okay." His hand left my shoulder. "That's it."

I gave his thighs a hug and dropped my face into his crotch, thrusting out my tongue to lick the raddled skin under his cock and the tight hair at the side of his scrotum.

"That's it," he repeated. "Did you hear me, down there? I'm finished now. Come on—get on up!"

I came off him. (Between my going down and backing away, he'd softened.) "Yeah. That was nice. Thanks."

"Not bad for a nigger my age," he said as I rocked back to my feet, using his knees to steady. I stood up, turned, then sat back beside him again. Sliding away from me a little, he pulled his rank jeans forward to get his cock inside. "Three weeks ago I had me my sixty-ninth birthday, too. You didn't know that, did you?"

"Belated happy birthday," I said.

"Yeah, that wasn't so bad for an ol' nigger."

"It was pretty good," I said.

"Thank you. That was real nice of you." He slid away more—though I hadn't tried to get next to him at all. "Maybe now I'll be able to catch me a little shut-eye, 'fore the sun come up."

We sat there another minute.

"I was just remembering," Pops said, as I was about to get up and walk on, "'bout the first time I ever got my dick sucked in this ol' park here—shit, it must've been twenty—no, more like thirty years ago. Maybe it was even thirty-five. I was on the bum then, too. It was the first time I come in here—I don't know why I'd never come in here before; nor why I chose to come in here just then. But it was in the middle of the day, I remember. An' I was sittin' out in the sun, on the benches, right down in front of one of them baseball diamonds they got down the way a bit. Some white guys was out there, playin' a baseball game. Most of 'em was white, anyway. An' while I'm sittin' there, looking back at 'em over my shoulder every once in a while, or just watchin' the river like now, this kid come up to me—little chink kid, thirteen, fourteen; slanty-eyed bastard, Chinese, I guess. Or Japanese, maybe. He come right to me an' he say, 'Lemme suck yo' dick.' Just about like you done, this afternoon—'cept he weren't a nigger, he was a chink. So I say, 'Okay, but where you gonna do it? I mean them guys is playin' baseball, right back there.' An' you know what he tells me? He tells me: 'That's all right—it don't make no difference. They come down here and play every week. They won't see nothin'.' And I say,

'What you mean, they won't see nothin'—they right *there* playin' baseball!' And this chink kid tells me: 'Look, there're two kinds of people in the world: there's baseball players. And there's cocksuckers. An' the baseball players just don't never even *see* the cocksuckers.' Then he tells me, besides, he done already sucked off *four* of the guys in the baseball team right where I'm sittin'! 'An' they wouldn't say nothin', even if they did see!'" Pops chuckled. "Smart little sonofabitch!"

"So then what happened?" I asked.

"What do you mean?'

"You let the kid suck you?"

"Yeah, I told him go ahead." He pushed himself back against the bench. "That little slanty-eyed chink was between my knees—got a mouthful of my juice in about a New York minute—man, could that kid suck dick! Back then, of course, I never did take very long." The memory seemed to tickle him. "'Course, back then, too, sometimes I'd do crazy shit like that. I thought it was funny—lettin' some chink suck my dick in broad daylight with everybody right out there in the park, playin' baseball. Guess I didn't know no better. But he was right."

"Nobody saw you—or said anything?"

"They was all baseball players."

I laughed. "Well, I was thinking something along the same lines, I guess, when those two, well...um, ladies came by."

"You got a point there, I suppose." He stretched his arm along the bench back, swinging his knees together and apart. (He hadn't zipped his fly; I wondered whether he wanted seconds.) "But then, you don't see a whole lot of ladies playin' baseball, neither."

"Well," I said, "I suppose *you* have a point, too." I stood. (But I wasn't up to seconds.) "Thanks for the load, Pops. That stuff's good for what ails you."

"I guess some people think so." He laughed, stretching his arms along the bench, pulling his soiled socks back beneath it. "An' it sure do feel good to get rid of a little of it, now and then. That was real nice of you, to pleasure up this ol' black bastard. Hope I'll see you again sometime."

"Sure. Maybe."

I started walking along the beside the river—doing, I suspect, the kinds of calculations you started a page ago: twenty years back,

Hasler would have been eighteen—but not only was he on the other side of the country then, he was just a bit too old for Pops's description. Thirty years ago, he would have been eight; but I just couldn't see even Timothy Hasler *that* precocious. (Thirty-five years ago, he would have been *three!*) Granted he was Korean—not Chinese or Japanese—it was still within the fairly large temporal window. But there was also the fact that Hasler's family—during that time—had lived in Brooklyn's Park Slope, so that Pops's story would have likely been a lot more relevant to my pursuits if it had taken place on the Promenade of Brooklyn Heights. Though Timothy had spent much of his last half-dozen years in this neighborhood, there wasn't much chance Pops's "slanty-eyed bastard" was my philosophical prodigy of twin-predicate logic and Nietzschean rhetoric.

Still, I thought, heading back around the playground, cocksuckers and baseball players...?

An insight like that might once have been worthy of *The Systems of the World*.

Outside the park wall, there were more benches, up and down Riverside Drive. Just up from me, one of them had a heap on it: another sleeping bum. Really, I thought, it was time to go home and give up. But maybe I could check out just a few more spots along the outside. In case.

When I got up to him, though, it was a young, immensely fat black guy, three times as big through the belly as Pops and grumbling in his sleep. At least I thought he was asleep. Only while I was looking down at him, he opened an eye and blinked at me—still grumbling.

So I walked away,

A few benches down, another guy was sleeping, feet toward me. They were bare, too. As I got nearer, I saw one of his slippers had fallen off his foot onto the bench. The other was down on the cobbles, about a foot away.

The slippers meant it probably wasn't *my* Piece o' Shit. But I went up closer, anyway. When I saw the tank top he was wearing, I recognized him—it made me breathe more quickly. My heart beat all up under my Adam's apple.

He was sleeping on his side, arms wrapped up over his head, so I couldn't see his face. But there was the plastic hospital band, and among the fingers hanging back over his hard little shoulder was his forefinger's stub.

I stepped away from him.

By the waist-high stone wall stood the wire trash basket.

In such situations, sometimes you move fast and don't think a lot. I stepped back again, reached behind the wire, grasped the plank, and brought it out. Nails caught the bottom of the receptacle to drag it a rasping inch—before the board came free.

He didn't move, though.

Hefting the wood, I stepped toward him. It would feel real good, I thought, to teach this scrawny motherfucker a lesson. (I'm glad he didn't shift in his sleep just then, because, from a combination of anger, fear, and—yes—revenge, I probably *would* have hit him!) Holding the plank by one end, I hefted the other in my other hand. I pictured him coming awake under the blow, his head turning up, my hitting him again and saying: "All right, you dickless bastard, maybe *this'll* teach you, when you have something to say to a cocksucker, to think twice about whether to be a little polite or not!"

The plank nails were pointed up.

I turned them over so that they would aim down. Then I said to myself: You know, this *isn't* who you are....

I mean, the fact is, I'm not a violent guy. I thought: Leave the fellow alone. Let him sleep, not knowing how close he came to getting hurt....

Then I thought: No, *he* really *ought* to know.

And then I thought: But you don't hit a sleeping man. (I also thought: Why the hell not?) In fact, you don't hit him at all unless he gets violent again. And *you've* got the plank....

I felt kind of tingly, as I figured: A little educational gesture isn't going to hurt this one. And maybe it'll make him think twice when he decides to terrorize the next cocksucker who comes up to him.

I turned the nails back up and laid the stick's end on his hip. And shook him with it. "Hey...!"

Whole and cut, his fingers twitched.

Then his body quivered.

It made me jerk the stick back.

I took a breath—and poked his hip again. "Hey—you one-nut wonder!"

Again he quivered. Then he made a sound for all the world like Pops shooting off his sixty-nine-year-old juice.

"I got your stick," I told him, "and I just want you to know I could beat the shit out of you right now if I wanted to."

The grunting resolved into a "...*Huh?*..." then started again.

Slowly, very slowly, he gathered himself, without looking up, feet flopping down to the cobbles, arms going round to hug himself. Back bent, he leaned way over. With just my eyes, I was looking down under the bench, trying to see in the dark if there was a pipe or a chain or a tire iron he might snatch up—

"Oh, *man!*" he rasped out, finally, still holding himself, head still down. "I'm fuckin' sick!"

"Well," I said, sure he was pretending, to make me lower the plank, "if I was a little meaner than I am, you might be even sicker!"

"They tol' me at the hospital, man, I couldn't drink no more. They tol' me if I drank anything, even a fuckin' beer, I was gonna *die....*" The words trailed off into a groan. "I said, then you gotta keep me *in* here. They said, 'Fuck you, get out of here, that's *your* problem.' I told 'em, 'You're killin' me, man, if that's the case. You're turnin' me loose to die—I mean, if I can't drink...'" He took a breath—or, rather, let out a gassy belch. "I only had two fuckin' cans of beer. Not even two—I lost half of one, 'cause it dropped on the ground."

"Look," I said. "I just want you to realize, *I'm* the cocksucker you stole the beer from!"

"I *didn't* steal it!" He rocked, still looking down, still clutching himself. "Cocksucker just dropped it when I was tryin' to run him out the park. Cocksuckers ain't supposed to be comin' over here, trying to take advantage of us, just 'cause we sick an' don't got no place to live..."

"I should have hit him," I said. "I really should have hit him. While he was asleep." Then I said: "Look up here a minute. I just want you to see something."

He didn't look.

With a jerk in his shoulders, and his head pulling even further down, what he did was...vomit—all over his knees, between his knees when they fell apart, all over his bare feet, and on the cobblestones between.

From his right knee, something ropy and black dripped down to his toes. More black stuff coiled in the puddle his turned-in foot rested in—one on its side. The nearest park light was two benches away, but by it I saw the maroon undercolor to the black stuff snaking his puke.

Still not looking up, he sat there, making hiccuppy sounds, as if he were giggling. But after a few moments, I realized it wasn't giggling at all. Another spasm hit: about a third as much spewed this time. "You gonna get me to the hospital?" he asked, at last, finally looking up. "Man, I'm fuckin' sick...."

"Look," I said. "A few hours ago, you were trying to whap a board full of nails into my side. Why the hell should I take you to the hospital?"

"'Cause I'm sick, man! I'm gonna *die* if somebody don't help me!" Another spasm caught him; again his head jerked down—but nothing came up. Blinking, he raised his face again. Puke slicked his chin; his sunken temples glimmered with sweat. Narrowing his eyes, his face screwed up with that myopic grimace. "You ain't the one," he said at last. "It wasn't you. That was *another* cocksucker..."

"No," I said. "I'm afraid it *was* me."

"Ain't nothin' wrong with cocksuckers, man. Some of them is good people—I know that. I mean, I *know* that! Last guy what got me to the hospital when I was sick was a cocksucker. He wanted to suck my dick at first, but when he found out how sick I was, man, he took me right over there! In a cab, too. Give me twenty dollars. I told him he could suck my dick if he wanted. Once we was in the emergency room, I told him, we could go into the bathroom"— actually he said "baff-room"—"and do it. He just said he'd collect from me some other time. I been waitin' around for him ever since. I thought maybe I could get some more money off him, you know?"

I looked at the plank in my hand.

Again he looked up, grimacing. "...that was *you*...?" He looked down again, to began poking around in his befouled lap, fiddling with his fly: a button broke, to fall against his pants leg. It stuck, to slide down the stuff there, maybe three inches—then stopped. With two fingers, from the wet cloth he pulled out the scrap of his sex. "That was you, huh? There it is, man. You wanna suck it? It's okay—if you just get me to the hospital." Then his stained and dripping fingers closed over himself, to slip on around his belly and hug; once more he bent way over, his breaths short and sharply drawn.

After a moment I turned and flung the plank over the park wall. As it spun away loudly through leaves, I had a surge of guilt: Jesus, I hope it doesn't fall on anyone asleep in there! From the sound it made, though, I don't think it did. "No." I turned back. "No, I'm afraid that *wasn't* me." I walked to the bench end and started for the curb.

"You ain't gonna get me to the hospital?"

"You're going to have to get there by yourself this time."

"I'm gonna *die*, man…!"

"That's all right."

I crossed over to the far corner and, for the third time in twenty hours, started up Eighty-second Street toward Broadway. Such as they were, the systems of the world function, I thought, so that educational gestures of a certain sort are wasted on some people. (I found the thought going through my mind again and again as I walked, the way that, when I was at school, something I wanted eventually to write down would cling, repeating and repeating, to memory.) And, like the Piece o' Shit said, you can't expect *everybody* to be a saint.

At least not me.

Above the buildings across Broadway, the eastern sky was light enough to suggest morning. By the time I reached my front stoop, the first sunlight was silver bright among Central Park's distant trees.

Upstairs in the apartment, I wandered from one end to the other a few times, picked up a few things and took them back into the rooms they belonged in, then, in the kitchen, washed a sinkful of dishes in the coppery light reflected from the windows over on the west side of Amsterdam Avenue.

Once I glanced over at Mossman's letter, still on the kitchen table—and *still* didn't pick it up. When I'd dried my hands, though, I took one of the sheaves of paper from the first mailer I'd opened yesterday and carried it into the living room, sat on the couch, and paged through.

It was Xerox copies of handwritten notebook pages. I could

make out the faint lines beneath the cursive script and—down one side—the holes and spiral binding. Though it was just random jottings, I was pretty sure it was from some notebook of Hasler's. I went through, purposely skipping the longer entries and reading only the shorter ones:

...I practice invention to the brink of intelligibility...

...for the last few days, out my kitchen window, down on the far corner of Amsterdam Avenue, the Plant of Paradise has been in bloom, with little clutches of yellow-green flowers all throughout its profusion of sumac-shaped leaves...

...There must be aspects to the universe that explain time and consciousness which, as of yet, we are all but unacquainted with—as the blind are unacquainted with color or the deaf with harmony....

...I started to sweat at dinner—got up, and took my blood pressure (the first of many times this evening). At any rate, I still have to send a revision of the last article to Dr. Weeks at Princeton...

...Two scruffy, near-spherical blackbirds with yellow needle bills were perched outside the window on the fire-escape rail in the gray New York morning, when the phone rang. It was a bored Dennis off in Harvey. We chatted a while—about everything from his cousin's upcoming gallbladder removal to those guys who were arrested for trying to blow up the Statue of Liberty (one of them, the newspaper said, was just released yesterday) to the cartons of books and general moving mess still strewn about my house. More coffee for me; then, on to work on the new article...

...Here in Ann Arbor the good weather and the snow pulse, one after the other—a day of one, a day of the other, now filling the streets with students, now all but emptying them of everything but wind...

Really, I wasn't paying a lot of attention to what I was reading. It was more like taking in a sentence here, another there.

...The daunting stack of index cards in their red rubber band that so far make up "The Mad Man" have sat by my bed, accusing me of their incompletion, now in Chicago, now at Breakers' Point, now in New York. 256 have so far been completed—though I haven't really worked on it in a couple of months...

...In four thousand years, writing has made of us a social animal to dwarf the bee and the ant...

...I'm beginning (not true; really, I've had inklings about the conclusion for six months now. But because I've actually gotten to the central transition material, I can start to think of it in terms of writerly articulation) to see the concluding movements of "The Mad Man." The very end—whether in social, if not personal, terms—I haven't decided on. That, to fix, I must work through the material. But at least now all seems do-able!...

..."Only as precipitates from memory are plot and character tangible; yet only in solution have either any emotive valency." (Leonard Knights)...

...The resonances of a word can not really be traced until it is written—if not on the page, then in the mind, or on the silent tongue...

...Must tell Dennis: he is the stronger personality. I can drive him away. But he can drive me crazy. I really need him more than he needs me...

...The captured spume of space foams in our ears...

So *that's* where that came from, I thought. Its familiarity made me read it over: it was on a page dated April 19, 1967, Breakers' Point. But even as I reread—really—I thought in a moment my eyes would close on their own, and shunt me off into that logical world where no logic applies. Had Tieck been this exhausted, I wondered, the first time he skimmed the *Blütenstaub*? And wondered, too, what trajectory had taken this notebook through Sam's old boyfriend's hands and finally into her present husband's. But I guess it's just a small world.

...I confess that I feel most of my life is lived behind a veil that separates me from the world. Every once in a while, at perfectly cliché moments—on certain summer nights or on cool spring mornings—I feel, yes, much closer to the world than usual. But the fact is, I consider that an illusion produced by the machine's running particularly well and so effacing its fundamental mediation a little more efficiently. Through the bathroom window the scent of burnt toast drifts up on cool air from the alleyway...

...We just went through a big, boring accumulation of cumulus. But we seem to be out the other side. I'm down to a coffee cup (my breakfast tray: a mushroom omelet made in a half-cookie mold, some salty potato shavings, and a sausage) and, at this point (8:30 A.M.), clouds have given out for a generally thin fog, through which I can just see the squared-off details of the land distantly below.

...It occurs to me that human beings, positioned where we are on the scale between the atomic and the galactic, must finally have an entirely distorted view of both "everything/infinity" and "nothing/no time."

...Books against books: *Don Quixote, Northanger Abbey, Madame Bovary*...

...There is a dark underside to the Golden Rule, "Do unto others as you would have them do unto you," and that is: "Do unto yourself as you would have others do unto themselves for your benefit." Thus, at the historical moment when that corollary is acknowledged to obtain, the "self" becomes a project...

...Honesty is the best policy; a policy is, after all, a strategy for living in the polis—in the city...

...Whitman's constant apostrophizing of his soul suggests an ever-split subject...

...History exists only when people disagree on what happened and debate it passionately and intelligently. When everyone agrees on what happened, there is only myth—and nothing is forgotten faster...

...In Riverside Park, when you sit on the benches and watch the Hudson flow, its myriad tiny wavelets move from left to right...

...Al and I have a sort of Hölderlinesque intimacy...

...*Wisdom is whole: the knowledge of how things are piloted in their courses by all other things*, is that wonderful Kentucky classics professor's translation of 'εν τὸ σοφόν·'επίστασθαι γνωμην 'οτεη κυβερνησαι παντα δια παντων. (Of course *nobody* knows what that 'οτεη means; we read it as though it were an archaic form of, or even a misprint for, 'όκη.) Siebert's translation of Diels, however, gives the fragment as *The wise is one thing only, to understand the thoughts that steer everything through everything.* Epigraph for "The Mad Man": παντα δια παντων...

...To live within the tethers of desire is—again and again—to be shocked at how far they have come loose from reason...

...To confuse a producing mechanism for a stabilizing mechanism is to create all the problems a mechanic might have confusing a gyroscope for an internal combustion engine, or a farmer might have who confuses his sack of fertilizer for a bag of seeds. In the field of human endeavor, language is a stabilizing mechanism, not a producing mechanism—regardless of what both artists and critics would prefer. This in no way contradicts the notion that the world is constituted entirely of language; i.e., that it is constituted by the structure of its stabilizing forces...

Then, somehow, *because* I was tired, I let my eyes move on through one of the longer entries and noticed that among the last of the words in it was (again) the word "Hudson." I moved my eyes back up the page, then across the previous page: And (again) I caught the word "park." Besides Riverside (where an hour back I'd been out adventuring) what other park in New York City was sided by the Hudson River? I turned to the beginning of the entry (there was no date) and began to reread—yes—the description which I've set as the proem of this book.

Don't go back and read it now.

Instead, remember what you can of it.

That's closer to the way that dawn reading struck me: something weird and fragmented, outside experience, unclear as to its purpose or its relevance to anything.

I read it once more. (Go on. If you want to: *now* you can look.) Its descriptive coherence was stronger. But I still couldn't claim to understand it.

I laid the sheaf of papers on the couch beside me, went into the kitchen, got a kitchen knife, came out in the hall and squatted by the carton that had come along with the two mailers, and cut the twine that bound it. When I started jockeying the knife along the carton edge, I could see more papers. I ripped the top back. Across the stacked papers lay a three-picture photo frame. From the center smiled Timothy Hasler. To the left was me—looking, I thought, scarifyingly young. Sure, I recognized my face. But at the same time, I thought, no, that's not the one that blinks back at me from the bathroom mirror these mornings when I go in to shave. (It wasn't that now I wore permanent, gas-permeable contacts, either.) Rather, it was the face of a twenty-two-year-old who still believed in the Systems of the World....

To the right, however, where Mossman's photo had once been, only backing cardboard showed in the satin oval.

I frowned.

I picked up the frame.

I looked at the back.

Metal tabs pressed into purple velveteen. One had broken off: like Mossman's photograph, it was gone.

I turned the frame over to the front, to frown at the absent image.

I stood up, took the frame into the kitchen, laid it on the table, and—after a few moments looking down at it—picked up Mossman's letter.

I walked with it into the living room, sat back on the couch, and looked at the pages without reading.

I was very tired. It would have been easy for me to go to sleep and put all this off till later. But, of course, by now I was curious.

I started at the beginning again.

The new stuff, when I reached it, was pretty much more of the same; over three pages Mossman complained about his undergraduate teaching load, a summer fellowship to Germany he'd applied for and not been given because, he was sure, of department politics, and a committee he had been assigned to for what he was certain were punitive reasons having to do with a speaker he'd wanted to come and talk at the university when Clapstone wanted someone else—followed by how much he missed my levelheadedness, my openness to new intellectual ideas, my enthusiasm and sympathy for real mental work (Sam was wonderful, of course; but still, we had a history together, he and I, that added something to our intellectual interchange, the sort that occasionally occurred between men, that could not be replaced)—nothing, in the least, to make me question my earlier identification of him and the pathetic bully in the park.

He didn't get around to mentioning the photograph until the second (of his three) postscript(s).

The first PS explained how he had mentioned me to the Old Poet—who had said (1) she was going to be coming to New York City later this year to do a reading at the 92nd Street YMHA and (2) she would not mind meeting me, if I wanted to get together with her while she was here. I could get in touch with her through somebody at the Y. She followed with a name (Grace something...?) and a phone number.

The third (PPPS) wanted to know if I knew anything about this strange "skin cancer" that a couple of doctors so far claimed was showing up only in gays and that people were now calling Acquired

Immune Deficiency Syndrome—or was it, perchance, just a hoax? That was what Mossman thought it probably was: hyped-up fall-out from the brouhaha over Legionnaires' disease from four or five years before—just to show you where I was, his letter was only the fourth or fifth time I'd ever heard of it.

But here was the second:

PPS—In the big carton, which presumably you haven't opened yet, right on top you'll find the pictures I framed so many years ago of you, Hasler, and me.

Mine's missing.

But, please, John, don't try to read anything meaningful into that—otherwise I can see you getting all upset to no purpose. (I know how you can be sensitive to these things. It goes with your particular sort of intelligence.) But Sam says it's her favorite picture of me from before we met—and begged me not to send it. I don't have the negative. So I decided I'd take the original out, get some copies made, then, when they came back, I'll send you one. You can replace it when it arrives. Indeed, if you want to look for symbolic significance, in three or four weeks (or months, if I'm lazy: sometimes these things do get away from you, you know how that is), when the replacement photo comes, you can take that as a likely sign I'm moving back toward the project.

As much as I complain, John, the fact is I've done too much work on this to let the *whole* thing slip away. Still, as I've explained, I need a space—even if just for a few weeks (or months)—when I can say, to myself, to Sam, to anyone who asks: "No. Right now I am not working on the Hasler biography." How much better that is than to say yes to the question, while melting inside—I mean something in my soul losing its form under the heat of the lie—because I *know* I'm not! Sam says it's got to be an improvement; I know she's right.

At any rate, in the light of new material, new facts, and the most recent defusion of Hasler's posthumous reputation, eventually I can start seriously rethinking what will be the most advantageous way to proceed.

In the light of Sunday morning, with my body truly exhausted but my mind preternaturally lucid, I thought: Irving, you're doing this all wrong—and you've been doing it wrong for years now. With someone like Timothy Hasler, you can't *gamble* on his fame like that! You read his work; you study it; you even teach it—and *you* decide if, within the systems of the world, that work is of major importance or not. If you decide it is, you write your book, and your essays, and your articles, and your lectures—in which you *say* just that! You write them because *you* believe in the work. You don't spend all your time looking around you, counting how many other people are saying this stuff is great—or not saying it. You don't keep counting the footnotes in which the name appears, wondering whether you should abandon the project because there aren't as many this year as last! When Thomas Beer wrote the 1923 biography in which he all but invented Stephen Crane, he didn't go out and count the references to *The Red Badge of Courage* that had appeared the year before, in order to decide whether he wanted to complete the project. (If he had, he would have come up with zilch!) Max Brod wrote his 1937 biography of Franz Kafka because he thought his late tubercular friend had written, back when he was alive, the strangest and most beautiful German stories he'd ever read, and that people had to know. When Lionel Trilling wrote his 1943 study of E. M. Forster, it's because he believed Forster had done something in his novels no American writer had done, and that America desperately needed to understand this—and that Trilling was capable of explaining it to them. The gamble, Irving Mossman, is *not* on Timothy Hasler. The gamble is on *you*. And right now, *you* don't think you're capable of telling—or, perhaps, even important enough to tell—the difference between "a first-class intellect" and "a world-class one." And if that's the case, you shouldn't be in the game!

Is three or four months going to bring you to the conclusion that this is *your* decision to make? Or are you going to go on pawing through philosophy journals and counting footnotes that mention Hasler and comparing them with the numbers from last year, finally to shake your head and decide you've bet on the wrong horse? Is thirty-year-old Sam going to be able to sit you down and, through gentle suggestion and creative listening, bring you to this point without sounding like an idealistic sophomore?

I looked up from the letter.

Faggots, I thought. Good people if you need something from them. Otherwise, bust 'em in the side with a fucking board.... Shaking my head, I got up, went into the dining room, lay Mossman's letter down on the plastic file box marked M, for later filing. Then I went into my bedroom.

I took off my jeans, shrugged out of my sweatshirt, and lay on the unmade bed. Fucking tired, I thought. And horny.

I took hold of my cock. (My basic pattern has pretty much been to go out, spread some joy throughout the world, then come home and—using *my* imagination, not unlike the Piece o' Shit—get mine.) Sadly, my parents had it cut. Still, it's a pretty good size: on a scale of small, medium, and large, I fall between the last two categories. Little guys always think it's *really* big. And really big guys are always quick to say, "Well, you sure can't call it *small.*"

Lying on my back, I began to pump. As the blood filled up the thickness in my hand, I thought about the hard little black cock, with its jet of aged juice, then the fat white one with a five-inch yoni, cheesy as a motherfucker, that followed a flood of cum with a flood of piss—at which point I spewed my own cum through my fingers and up my chest. I let myself relax, moving one slippery knuckle against another, on the softening meat of me....

In the dark, something, or maybe someone, licked my hand, my groin, my chest, my belly with a wet, wide tongue. But I was wedged up against the bedroom wall and was too tired, almost paralyzed, to roll away. Then somehow I *did* roll—the wall was down—and I turned over among chattering leaves.

Pushing up to my knees, I looked around.

Through branches I could see down to the backs of benches along the riverside path. Beyond the rail, the masts of small boats leaned together and apart behind the Seventy-ninth Street Marina's sagging wire fence. I walked forward, now pushing back a branch, now walking on the leafy stone steps between narrow rock walls, unsure whether I was ascending or descending.

My hand against a tree trunk, I stopped to gaze within the grotto. It stood, looking away from me, wings on their towering spines up in the high branches, its horned and tusked head not facing mine, its tail's barb near enough to the ground to rake up a line of dead leaves.

It wasn't fear, so much, as a kind of intellectual calculation. No, it was probably *not* good to be too near this thing, at this time, at this place. I turned and hurried up the street.

I had almost reached West End Avenue when, beyond the cars beside me, a taxi pulled to a stop, a pool of yellow around the light on its roof—the single illumination in the night.

The driver rolled his front window down and called, "You looking for a cab?"

Sometimes you do these things real fast, without thinking. "Yeah." I turned, starting between the bumpers of the parked cars. "Can you take somebody up to St. Luke's Emergency Room—at 116th and Amsterdam?"

"Take you—? Oh, I'm *sorry*..." Hanging one arm out the window, the driver was an Italian kid with curly black hair, black stubble all over cheek and chin, and a gold chain caught in the fur clawing out of his T-shirt neck.

"What are *you* sorry for? Can you *take* us?" I frowned at his consternation. Then I said: "What is it? You don't ordinarily stop for black guys?"

He looked me up and down. "Yeah...sometimes I don't. Okay— No, when I stopped, I *didn't* realize you were black!"

"Well," I told him, "when *you* stopped, I expected you to be some guy with a beard and a turban wrapped around his head, asking me directions in Punjabi."

"Yeah, well—" He sounded between belligerent and embarrassed. "You see an ordinary person, out this late in the city, a lot of times they're looking for a cab. I'm just trying to be helpful, do a good deed." Now he grinned. "But you sound like an okay guy."

"And right now I *need* somebody to do a good deed. What do you say?"

Still grinning, the kid sighed. "Yeah, okay."

"You want to back up to the corner? You can pull out by the park. I left him across the Drive, on one of the benches."

The kid sighed again. "Okay." I stood up, and in a darkness relieved only by a couple of streetlights much too far away, the cab started backwards down the street's gentle slope.

There was no other traffic out at all.

I started on foot after him. I wasn't looking forward to those puked-up pants, those vomit-smeared hands. Nor would I have been surprised if the cab, once it reversed onto the Drive, just took off. But it eased out and on across the street to wait under the trees by the park.

I crossed over, thinking: Basically, that's a good kid in there.

When I got to the curb and stepped up, the first thing I saw was that someone had already gotten the little Hispanic guy into his hospital pajamas and slippers. In a dark red robe he sat docilely on the bench near the wire trash basket, hands in his lap.

"Guess what," I said. "You're going up to the emergency room at St. Luke's."

"Oh...yeah...that's good." He didn't look up. "I gotta get up there...." He sounded drugged; or maybe, like he'd said, he was just dying.

It made me kind of anxious.

Out in the street, the cab rolled up toward us.

I sat, put my arm around his bathrobe back, and lifted. (On his far arm, my hand closed on something wet. But I ignored it.) The arm, under the maroon terrycloth sleeve, was surprisingly loose—like a very old man's.

Letting him lean on me, I got him up and to the curb. As I stepped off by the taxi's back door, I felt something wet my pants leg. It was running down my ankle.

As I got the door open with one hand, the driver looked at the window again: "Jesus, he's really *sick!* Did somebody *do* that to him?"

Looking down, I saw that the maroon of his robe—nearly a purple black—was, of course, blood. He was all smeared with it. So was I, now!

"I don't really know." I pushed him into the back seat of the taxi. He caught himself and actually got himself seated in there, half-falling out only once—I pushed him back in. "You just get him up to the emergency room at St. Luke's at 116th. Leave him off there—"

"You ain't goin' with us?" The Italian kid frowned out the cab window again. "Hey, I don't know about this, fella. That don't sound like a good idea—"

I was trying to close the door, but the little Hispanic guy was holding it open now, and leaning out. "You ain't comin' with me? Aw, man...I'm fuckin' sick—"

"Look," I said, still struggling to get the door closed. "It's a three-fifty cab ride. But if you take him up there for me—" I gave the Hispanic's shoulder a real good push and got him farther in and away from the door—"I'll give you—" I stood up, to step around the door and put one hand on the driver's open windowsill, while, with the other, I went into my pocket for my wallet—"my last twenty bucks—" thinking, as I got out my emergency twenty, even if I *did* find Piece o' Shit now, there'd be no case of Colt. Yeah, the whole thing was probably over.

I thrust the bill through the window.

"Man," the kid said, shaking his head while he took it. "You start out to do something nice for somebody, and it always gets so fuckin' complicated!"

"Well," I told him, "that's the way the Systems of the World work."

From the back, the Hispanic leaned out again. "It ain't no twenty bucks up to St. Luke's! He gonna gimme the change, ain't he—?"

"I seriously doubt it," I told him. "Hey, I'm closing the door, so get your hand back inside—unless you want to lose some more fingers." I got the door shut, then didn't even bother to look back at the driver, but began to walk quickly up the Drive, away from the back of the cab.

Once I glanced behind me.

The cab still sat there.

I paused for a moment, expecting to see the kid get out, come around, pull the Hispanic from the door and (with my twenty) take off. But I guess the kid was just nicer than I was. Once more he leaned from the window to call, "Hey, man…I really think it would be better if you went up there with us, you know?"

I took a couple of more steps away, backwards.

"You're pretty messed up yourself!" (I looked down to see that my sweatshirt was half-covered with black-red stain.) "Walkin' around like that, some cop sees you, especially a colored guy—and you don't know *what's* gonna happen…"

I shook my head. "No, that's okay. I'll—"

Then, somehow, I was in the back of the cab, without ever having really gotten in it; we were driving. The Hispanic was in his tank top and greens again. He'd fallen away from me, face against the cab's far window. His mouth was open against the glass, and as lights passed outside, I could see the faintest fog form and re-form on the pane, with his diminished breathing. His near knee was pressed against mine—but the stuff on it had pretty much dried. And I was thinking: "I don't like this. I don't really *like* this. I don't..."

Which was when I noticed we were driving downtown—not up. For some reason, I wondered, had the kid decided to take us to Bellevue, not St. Luke's? I was going to say something to him, but it was one of those taxis with the bulletproof shield between front and back, complete with metal grille. Bending forward to look through, I saw that beside the Italian kid driving, some other guy sat in the passenger seat.

"I don't *like* this," I said out loud.

But the Hispanic guy seemed asleep.

Just then, even through the plastic-and-metal partition, I heard the Italian kid exclaim: "Oh, *shit*...!"

We swerved, skidded, maybe spun—it was hard to see. I got thrown back, and immediately pushed forward, trying to look out the window. We were among trees, or something like them. And, waking, the Hispanic guy grabbed my arm again, pulling on it as if he wanted it to hurt: "Ah, man—you gotta help me, now...I'm gonna *die*, man, if you don't help me. I'm gonna die...." The thickest of those trees moved—and was an arm; and another, moving, was a...leg!

In the front, the Italian kid was wrestling the steering wheel. We rocked forward, then back, then forward. I realized I'd actually lost one of my shoes. You could hear the back wheels whining in dead leaves. I'd been sure my window was closed. But the next thing I knew, a clawed hand, eight, ten, fifteen times the size of anybody else's hand came through the window on an incredible arm. And so did an immense horned and tusked head! It made some sweeping gesture inside the car, and with a rend, rasp, and wrench of metal, the car's whole front end tore away and went hurtling forward into the trees, while, from the ground, leaves swirled up in front of us. I saw the bulletproof partition shatter and fall—and the Italian kid's head snap back, as well as the head of the guy on the passenger's side. Before the fragments disappeared in the foliage, with a sense of rightness that was unquestionable, I saw that the car front was no longer taxi yellow but bright blue.

The Hispanic guy was still pulling on my arm when the creature's great shoulder came around the front and these *other* giant fingers, blunt and nail-gnawed, grasped me around. The Hispanic guy was holding my sweatshirt sleeve. And some scrap of metal from the torn frame caught my pants leg. As I came out of the car in that titanic grip, my sweatshirt slipped off and my pants ripped away—with them went my other shoe.

The creature lifted me, naked, before his huge, inquiring head. Bending to the side, his wide tongue slathered out to lick my leg. Held aloft in the trees, looking up at the shadows of the wing spines, down at the hirsute mountains of his shoulders, I gasped—but his lick did not burn. It was only incredibly warm. The tongue passed, clinging, over my groin. Its warmth went all through my body, the way, sometimes, an orgasm will. But it wasn't an orgasm. It was simply warmth. The licking continued—a kind of absent-mindedness to it, not like someone tasting or testing a morsel of food, but the way a Labrador will lick your hand sometimes for minutes, in the middle of play. I blinked, just as the creature lowered me. For a moment I thought I might fall, or be flung away. But he thrust me behind him, pushed me up against one great buttock, and slid me over, beneath the scaled trunk of his tail. He was using me, like a farmer might use an old cob, to scratch his immense fundament. I felt myself jammed between the muscular walls of that canyon, thick with his excrement: it got in my mouth, my ears; and all I was aware of was a stench as pungent and rich as any horse barn. As I thrust out my tongue to turn it into taste, he pulled me free, bringing me, dizzy with his smell, with his flavor—and, yes, with the warmth of him—around in front.

Above, the horned head turned, looking one way, looking the other, eyes alive with circular fires, circles within circles, blood, gold, and orange, as he gazed off at aspects of the world I couldn't imagine.

That's when his piss struck. Torrential urine arched from the animal organ fleshed along his belly; again the astonishing warmth buried itself in my body. His monstrous waters ran from my left shoulder, down over his own great fingers, to flush my chest, stomach, and testicles, finally to flow down my left leg and fall from my foot, drenching leaves below.

I strained to get my face in his salt flow—I could just taste it with my chin dropped hugely and my tongue fully extended. I would have happily plunged my whole head into the flush. But, you understand, there was no more aim or intention in his voidings than there was with any other beast. Aim and intention, I knew, were elsewhere; and this accidental and arbitrary consecration, with the substance and essence—the bread and wine—of his body, was a gift like grace, that I could not have sought, but that only he could have given.

With the same absent extension, he raised me once more—to lick at me again, cheek and chest, groin and belly, surprised and—who knows—even mystified by my sudden change in flavor, the muscle's edge now a-slither between my buttocks, now moving in the crevice between its own thumb and my waist, finally the rug of his tongue entirely wrapping my flank.

Something—the sound of a car wreck?

He shifted his stance, lowered me once more, his interest having moved on for the moment.

If not a wreck, then something catastrophic and industrial.

He lowered me farther, making a growling thunder within his washtub neck, that I felt more than heard as the vibrations passed down the cables deep within the oak of his wrist. He stepped back. And back again.

His grip loosened. In a moment, I slipped free, but was able to clutch among the feathers ruffling the haunch over his left, lower claw, so that when those bird talons lifted, and I fell between them to the ground, I only scraped my hip and my hand a little.

Rolling to my feet, I thought: Whatever is frightening him, I'd be unbelievably foolish to stay and encounter what intimidates such a great, lazy lover. I turned in the cool wildness, and began to hurry—pebbles under my bare feet, small branches and ferns whipping my ankles and shins.

I rounded one tree, bent to take the turn around a boulder, pushed by the dining-room's door jamb, to come up short at the cluttered oak table.

Snatching it up, I almost laughed with relief.

Within the frame, there I was—on the left, where I was supposed to be.

In the middle was Hasler.

In the right-hand frame that had been empty, was a drawing of the creature, now like a Picasso minotaur, now like a Chagall bull.

As I stood, gasping for my breath, for moments it seemed a medieval hippogriff. For moments more it was some Doré denizen of Malabolge. Now with the authoritative marks of a Käthe Kollwitz, now with the fine hand of a Virgil Finlay, sometimes it appeared in color, sometimes in grisaille: the creature seemed to segue all periods of art, all artistic traditions. Yet the fact that the incredible energy of it was confined within the frame gave me the greatest relief.

The words from Marlowe's *Doctor Faustus,* "Metaphysics, thou hast ravished me!" in a woman's voice—distinctly it was Sally-May Mossman (née Wallace)—sounded out clearly, as, with that relieved sense, I woke—in bed, twisted in my sheet, wedged against the wall!

Freud has made famous a certain sort of dream from which we awake as from a total enigma, completely bewildered as to its sources, its significance wholly opaque. But there is another sort of dream that, while it may bewilder us through its course, nevertheless becomes completely and poignantly clear with the first return of reason.

The realization that arrived in that first second of waking was that my Good Samaritan taxi driver, from gold chain to curly black hair to daily three-o'clock shadow (he'd never had to wait till five) was—of course—Mike Ballagio. (The guy in the mortal seat beside him was Mike's long-since wheelchair-bound Long Island cousin, Vinny. Mike's Camaro had been, of course, blue....) And that, through the length of my dream's whole, unbelievably generous, second-chance encounter, neither Mike nor I had recognized each other across the mortal bourne—that I had not, the moment I saw him come to a stop and look out, pulled down my jeans on empty Eighty-second Street and thrust my black ass through the cab window against his always-horny, hungry guinea mouth—was the central and breath-stopping tragedy around which all the dream's other, too-clear oneiric significations would, of course, resolve (it was Mike who, after I had held him and jerked off, used to worm his way down me to lick the cream off my fingers, my belly, my nuts, while I drifted to sleep), from its simple-minded philosophical allegory to its simple wish fulfillment drama...*pace* Dr. F.

It was noon.

But I lay there, breathing deeply a full five minutes, heart about broken with the loss.

With its two remaining photographs (the right oval, yes, *still* empty), the frame lay on the *kitchen* table—not the dining room. Open, the carton stood on the floor beside one table leg. This is silly, I thought: No, you're not going to go looking for him again.

(If you do go down to Riverside Park—this sunny Sunday afternoon—it will just be for a pleasant stroll to soak up some Sunday sun.)

Chuckling to myself, still I left the apartment and started downstairs.

It was almost three o'clock, and both Amsterdam and Broadway were as busy with pedestrians as they were at mid-week.

There were even two people visible down West End Avenue when I crossed. You know, I really hoped the Spanish guy *had* gotten to the hospital—easy enough to say since I'd abandoned him to whatever nightmares of his own. But he didn't seem to be around. At Eighty-third Street, I turned into the park, swinging away from the water fountain and angling behind the playground.

He was sitting practically at the same spot, on the same bench, where I'd first seen him yesterday. A full shopping cart stood near him—and someone else sat with him. With his bare feet, half as broad, little toe (a misnomer on him) to big as they were toe to heel, his thinning, stringy hair, his immense hands—well, that he was there as though he hadn't really moved from yesterday made me wonder how elastic "assglue" actually was.

Neither Pops nor the Hispanic was with him. The person he sat with, one leg crossed over the other, and leaning forward, talking to her, was the black bag lady in her long coat.

My first thought was to run up, explain, apologize—then, maybe, smile and keep on my way. The urgency that had brought me out here three times now seemed appeased in all its particulars just by the sight of him—if not that strange and lingering dream. If he sees me, I thought, I may say something. But if he doesn't, I'll just walk past—

Which is when he looked up, grinned: "Hey, man—how you doin'? I guess somethin' must have tied you up yesterday, huh?

And you couldn't get back." With a hand on the old woman's shoulder, he stood. Then he started toward me. For the first time I noticed he was notably bowlegged. "How you doin'? You come back to say hello?"

I just stood—grinning, I guess. "Yeah, I...well, you probably wouldn't believe me if I told you what happened. I nearly got in a goddamned fight over that Colt 45. I'm not kidding—your Spanish friend stole a couple of cans from me and ran me out the park. I came back later, in the night. But you'd left by then."

"Yeah, I guess I had. That crazy Puerto Rican fella that was makin' all that noise yesterday? Them Puerto Ricans—they ain't like Mexicans. They're *crazy*, man! He ain't no fuckin' friend of *mine*—I swear, that motherfucker's crazy! They were tellin' him in the hospital he couldn't drink, and yesterday he was yellin' and carryin' on about how nobody could tell *him* what to do!"

"Yeah!" I said. "You better believe it!"

Reaching me, he hooked his hammer-handle fingers on my shoulder, stepped even closer, and said in a softer voice: "Hey, cocksucker, how you been? I thought you was gonna come back and swing on my yoni some more. Go on, reach between my legs and feel that fucker there—the front half's still hard! He must be missin' you!"

"Who's your friend?" I asked.

"She's a nice lady, now." He leaned toward me. "She got the nastiest, funkiest, smelliest black pussy I done had my face in for *years*. Nigger, when I had my hands all over your head yesterday, you musta changed my luck!"

I glanced at her. "Did you get some?"

"From about four o'clock this mornin' till after they opened up the restrooms down behind the runnin' track around eight-thirty"—he leaned closer to me, hand sliding to my neck—"we was back there in the bushes and she let me eat out that dirty ol' pussy of hers like it was goin' out of *style!*"

I clapped him on the shoulder. "Good for you, Piece o' Shit!"

"When I met her, she was sleeping under the overpass on some newspapers with this beat-up old white chick—man, she was tellin' me all about how she was pregnant and how she used to be a whore and how big her old man's black dick was, only she'd just kicked him out. I figured she had to want to get laid. Ain't no woman tell you all about her bein' a whore, the minute she wakes up, if she don't want you to fuck her now, do you think? But I just don't dig white women. You give me the choice between a twenty-year-old white woman and a fifty-year-old black one, and I'm gonna take the black bitch every time, man. So, soon as I could, I cut the old bitch out and we went off together with her goddamn cart creakin' and clankin' behind us. Man, when I finally got in there, her fuckin' panties was *stuck* to her—she was so nasty, I peeled 'em off with my lips, man—and the stink came up out of her like a piece of old liver! I went in there, tongue first, like an angel divin' through St. Peter's gates. Nigger, I was in *heaven!*" He grinned back. "You want me to show you how I ate her out, cocksucker? Go ahead, make a pussy for me!"

"I don't think we better do that right here—where she can see. After all," I said, "she's a lady and you have to have some respect."

"The *fuck* you do," he said. "Go ahead, let her see! When we was down in the bushes, some spic kid was hidin' out, just a little back from us, watchin' us and beatin' off for all he was worth." He gave me a big rotten-toothed grin. "I kind of wished it was you—but she don't mind."

"How do you know?" Though I remembered she'd seen us once already.

"Do it first. Then I'll tell ya'."

Feeling kind of silly, I got my mouth into that position, with my tongue screwed up.

"Now *wiggle* that clit for ya' old man...!" he rasped, before his other hand came up and took the other side of my face. He opened his mouth over mine, tongue lifting and lifting across mine. After a while, he backed away just a little. "Reach between my legs, bitch, and play with my pecker like you're dreamin' about sucking the cheese off all six of them goddamned yoni rings of mine!"

I put my hands between his legs. "*Shit*, man" I said. "You're really turned on like a motherfucker, aren't you?"

"Don't it turn you on, doin' this cocksucker shit in front of a woman now?"

"Um," I said. "Not like it does you, I guess."

"Man, she's a fuckin' nasty ol' whore. She gonna wet her fuckin' scuzzy undies even more than she already done, watchin' two guys like us, with you making like an even better bitch than she is!"

"How do you figure that?" I asked.

"You seen them dirty movies, that always got the lezzies in 'em, carryin' on—and how hot it turns most guys on? Well, women is the fuckin' same, man—they like to watch guys get it on with each other. Leastways, most of the women *I* ever been interested in do. Come on, lemme lick out that nasty hole of yours a little more. Think of you and me as two lezzies workin' out to keep some old fart hard in his drawers." Again his mouth covered mine; and his tongue—and his thumb—probed within.

I closed my eyes and just stood there, holding on to his hard crotch and letting him go snuffling and tongue-rooting in my mouth. Pretty soon the cloth between his legs had grown wet with his own leakage.

Finally, breathing hard, he moved his face away, blinking. (That white stuff was only in his left eye this afternoon. And, funny, it didn't bother me.) "She's one hot bitch, man—I mean for an old lady. She say she's fifty-five, but she gotta be sixty-nine!" He winked at me. "You know what I mean. Sixty-nine? Nigger, she got so excited while I was eatin' her out in the bushes this mornin', she done fuckin' started pissin' in my mouth. She just let it run, too—*just* like I done with you! Damn, nigger, that was some fine breakfast! Come on over here and say hello to my bitch."

"Hey, no...." I really was kind of embarrassed. "Why don't you go on back over there, and I'll catch you some other—"

"No, come on, cocksucker! See, maybe she'll let us take her back into the bushes some more." He had me by the wrist, in his great fingers. "Maybe I can get her to lemme eat her pussy out again, see, and you can suck on my dick while I do it—lick my ass out, if you want. If she let me fuck her some and drop a load in her hole, maybe she'll even let you eat it out her cunt after I'm finished!"

I just laughed. "Piece o' Shit," I said, "that's just too much for me this afternoon. You go on back there and be a gentleman. I'll go on and maybe catch you later—"

"Aw, come on, nigger. Don't be like that—" He tugged me back over to him. "I *know* she likes that homo shit."

"*How* do you know?"

"'Cause she ain't got up and run off yet—" he grinned— "while we been foolin' around here!"

She was still sitting on the bench edge, biting on her lower lip, watching us.

"Look," I said. "Let me go on, huh? You do your thing, you have to let me do mine."

The grin was just a smile now. "Well, okay. Yeah, I guess that's right." He let go my arm—and sighed. "Hey, nigger, don't lose me now."

"What do you mean?"

"Don't lose me, I said. You gonna run off, an' we ain't gonna never see each other again, probably. And that's too bad, 'cause we could really have some fun, you and me."

"You're having fun with her," I said. "You're straight. So isn't that better—for you?"

"Man, how long is a fine bitch like that gonna keep hangin' 'round with a piece of shit like me? I'm talkin' funny stuff to her now, keepin' her laughing a little, sayin' 'Oh, my!' and 'Ain't that interestin'.' But she could have any guy in this fuckin' park she wanted. That bitch ain't gonna keep with me for no length of time. An' she's bummin' around right now herself. So she can't buy me no beer. Tomorrow—or in an hour, or even when I get back over there, she ain't gonna wanna even look at this piece of shit no more. She done already let me eat her pussy, yeah. So I got it on store, man. In my mind. In my imagination. It's better there anyway, I guess." He shrugged. "But she tol' me she think my yoni looks all funny, and didn't even want to get near the fucker. Wouldn't suck it—wouldn't let me stick it in her hole—front or back. So I just had to play with it myself." He shrugged again. "Which ain't too different from what I usually do, what I mean?"

"Yeah," I said. "I think I do."

"But that's what I wanted you around for, cocksucker. To do the real work, down under the table, with your face in my lap, when I was up there, with my napkin tucked all into my collar, lookin' all smart like, an' my head between her bony knees, havin' me my tea! But she probably wouldn't go for that—unless, maybe, we got her drunk—if we all got drunk, that is. But you don't got any beer with you, now, do you?"

"I'm afraid I don't."

He sighed again. "Just don't lose me, now, cocksucker." He smiled, nodded, dropped his hand from my face, and took a step back. "You come on 'round and look me up again. We'll get that beer." He started back to the bench, then called over his shoulder.

"And have us a good time."

"Okay," I said. "I will." I even smiled and nodded to the woman. Who just stared—as he sat beside her again and started talking to her once more.

I went on down to the river.

The path by the water was full of dog walkers and Sunday-afternoon joggers and mothers rolling baby strollers and roller skaters wearing Walkmen and spandex and knee pads—with the occasional bum, sitting on the benches or wandering by.

It was a beautiful day.

On a couple of others, that summer, I did come back looking for him, maybe three or four times over the next week, week and a half. But I guess he—or he and the old woman—had gone from the park.

I didn't see either of them again.

Though a few weeks later I finally did get to suck off that young, immensely fat black guy whom I'd seen sleeping on the bench that night, grumbling to himself, who turned out to have an extraordinary dick—eleven fat inches, with a pair of wire-haired balls big as a couple of navel oranges—and who (while he stood among the trees and I kneeled in front of him, my arms about the oil drums of his denimed thighs, deep-throating him) stopped his grumble, as he came, to whisper, "...Oh, *yeah!*... Wow!" before he took up his half-internal complaint once more, and I was on my feet again and, after patting his frayed, oblivious, flanneled shoulder, walked out under the trees by the park wall, just as the evening streetlights came on.

PART TWO

THE
SLEEP
WALKERS

Change the currency.
—The Delphic Oracle to
Diogenes of Sinope (412–323 B.C.)

O, nun waren wir Nacht-Geweihte!
—*Tristan und Isolde,* II, ii.

In the years between 1982 and 1986, the world—that American hyperbole for urban U.S.A. plus the suburban residents concerned with what goes on there— changed. The cancer Mossman had mentioned in his third PS was not a skin cancer at all, but rather a cancer of the mesodermic capillary linings called "Kaposi's sarcoma"—till then almost unknown but, during those years, one of the most mentioned diseases in the American press. Soon, from time to time, I'd see men walking around the neighborhood with its purple lesions on arms, shins, and faces. Then, in papers like the *New York Native* and the *Village Voice*, it was joined by "pneumocystic carrini pneumonia" and "oral thrush" and "toxic plasmosis"; and, as statistics mounted from 3,000 to 6,000 to 20,000 to 60,000, we entered the age of Acquired Immune Deficiency Syndrome: AIDS.

At the same time, bums, hoboes, derelicts, and winos stopped being bums, hoboes, derelicts, and winos and became, rather, "the homeless"—or, if they were young enough, "runaways." Now grocery bags and milk cartons were stamped with the faces of missing children. And I remember how odd it struck me that this vast population of the marginal, the dispossessed, the underclass was now being defined in terms of that wholly distant and perfectly ephemeral social institution that, once on Christmas, once on Mother's Day, and once on my father's birthday (but, by her own wish, never on Mom's) I would take the ferry across to Staten Island to visit—"home."

For me that period began and ended with Timothy Hasler.

It started, of course—after two weeks of dipping in here and there—with a plunge into the papers in Mossman's carton, Mossman's mailers. That glutinous reading covered perhaps a third of it: it left me with an image, yes, of a very odd young man. But I was also struck with how different that image was from the one I'd gotten from Mossman's letter—or letters—and, indeed, Mossman's conversations over the years.

For one, I realized for the first time that Hasler was the most self-tortured of hypochondriacs. His whole life was subject to strange mental and physical jactitations that, in a moment—sometimes four and five times a week, sometimes two or three times a day—convinced him he was about to be the victim of a brain tumor, heart attack, stroke, or fatal neurological condition. Perhaps once or twice a year, he would descend on a doctor and—when pronounced in moderately good health—be free of such fears...for never more than three or four days!

But, from his own accounts, that was the longest period he went without such anxieties.

At first I was sure this must have dominated his conversation, all his friendships, probably making him an impossible person. But, as I went on through the papers Mossman had sent, now looking at a number of Hasler's letters to friends (in which no such anxieties were even mentioned), now coming across a number of cynical and self-deprecating passages among the journals, now finding a number of descriptions of Hasler by friends, written, apparently for Mossman, after Hasler's death (in which this aspect of his personality was not talked of at all; most of them never seemed to know it was there), I realized that more or less rigorously Hasler had kept his medical anxieties to himself—knowing they were groundless, yet experiencing them none the less intensely as constant, repeated, and inescapable terrors. That Hasler's outward personality and demeanor towards others were humorous, sensitive, and generally gentle, generous, and fun-loving (if sometimes heavily preoccupied), while—often—he was sure he was on the verge of a mortal heart attack or stroke, but that he refused to let (almost) any of his friends, and none of his acquaintances, know about them—well, it began to make him seem quite extraordinary!

Several passages in his journals discuss his syndrome. Some are rather moving. This one—characteristic—is particularly informative and succinct. The entry was made Christmas Eve, 1966, about 10:30 P.M., shortly after a particularly bad attack had made Timothy flee a ship's party and go cower, drenched with sweat, in his cabin, while on a boat from Marseilles to Venice. I take it up after some pages of pained description of the attack itself:

Hypochondria—and I've seen enough doctors, not to mention psychiatrists, in the last decade to know that's what it is. (My hand is still shaking, damn it! Will I or anyone else even be able to read my handwriting here in a week?) Free-floating anxiety in which the anxiety never floats *quite* as freely as all that! If it were just a matter of feeling ill, it wouldn't be so bad. Those rare times in my life I've actually been bedridden I look back on as quite pleasurable. But this is as if, from three times a week to three times a day, my body puts me under immediate sentence of death. It sends out signs and signals, little pains in the chest and ribs, tiny glitches in the perception, small dizzinesses, headaches, bodily quivers or changes in breath, rate of perspiration, or heartbeat, which my mind has no other choice but to interpret as the most direct and inexorable statement from an authority in the very heavens: "Within the next ten to twenty seconds, your heart will cease to beat—and you will *die!*" Or: "A clot has just torn from a vein's wall and even now rushes toward your brain, to plunge you, within seconds, into the night of death or languagelessness or paralysis!"

(Murderers who hear the voice of God demanding that they kill must experience their compulsions much the same way!)

Then it...doesn't happen.

But that doesn't prevent the horror accompanying it.

When I was fourteen or fifteen—then, if anything, the condition was worse than now—I used to consider suicide, just to release me (after one all-consuming passage of terror) from that so-immediate and so-repeated terror of dying.

Once, trying to laugh it off, I wrote:

> *Timor mortis conturbat me*
> Five to fifteen times a day....

All of us will have to live through the minutes, the seconds, the moments before our dying. If we're lucky, I suppose, we'll be so out of it, most of us won't even notice. But this is much closer to what the criminal who is strapped into the electric chair, or who has just had his neck fixed in the guillotine's wooden yoke must go through in the five to ten seconds before the current shoots, the blade falls. And, damn it, it's not fair! That it happens again and again and again and turns you into a wreck! It's always a surprise. If I am in front of a class or talking to other people, all I can allow myself is the pause of a moment, while for twenty, thirty-five, fifty seconds I look as if I've lost my train of thought. But that's better than shrieking and falling to the floor whimpering—which doesn't go over too well when people are around. Though sometimes that's actually what I've done—but less and less as I've gained more control (over my body, not my fear). You flee the room if you can—or at least withdraw unobtrusively, like tonight: I'd rather be alone when it happens than be with others, because at least if you're by yourself you don't have the added worry of *other* people realizing you're crazy. (*Me* knowing I'm crazy is bad enough!)

Perhaps the only thing that has been able to halt these endless rehearsals of death this odd combination of my mind and body endlessly puts me through is philosophy—for a few hours a day or so, when I'm actually working on a logic problem or writing up an idea.

And working on *Pascal, Nietzsche, Peirce* (O, blissfully remembered happiness!) could sometimes postpone it as much as three or four days!

Because it's philosophy I'm actually *doing* when I teach (even when it's reviewing someone else's), blessedly attacks have happened only two or three times in class now—and always during the business parts at the beginning or end.

How much of human accomplishment is, I wonder, a simple and direct attempt to stave off such mortal terror?

Outside my cabin portal I can hear the winter sea....

In two other entries to more or less the same effect (one three years before, while at Stilford; one two years later, at Breakers' Point), though neither is expressed so clearly, Hasler cites philosophy *and* the active pursuit of sex as capable of warding off—for a few hours, at least—his death fears.

What his journals told me of his sexuality made me wonder seriously about Mossman's reactions: yes, Hasler *was* gay. But what I read in those journal pages was an account of a fairly ordinary gay man with an obsessive fetish for men's bare feet! The sixties proliferation of long-haired, unshod young people in the bohemian sectors of our cities made those years into a holiday for Hasler. And, yes, he seemed to prefer his feet on the grubby side.

There were pages of mentions, as well as of descriptions, both telegraphic and detailed—by the eighteen-year-old Hasler, by the twenty-two-year-old, by the twenty-six-year-old, by the twenty-eight-year-old—of his glimpsing such unshod young men, of his following them for half a block, in some cases walking along near them for hours (or sitting across from them while they played their bongos or guitars or sold pot in Washington or Tompkins Squares—or, now, in North Beach or Venice, once he was in California; or, when he got to Europe, at one of the fountain's edges in the Piazza Navona, or on the low wall around Trafalgar Square); sometimes he even managed to start a conversation with one.

As far as I was able to tell, however, that's precisely what *was* behind what Mossman had once referred to in one of those early letters as "that undergraduate there was all that trouble over."

From some three fairly lengthy journal entries and a dozen briefer ones, written during twenty-year-old Hasler's second term as a graduate philosophy TA, this is what I've put together:

At Stilford, twenty-year-old undergraduate Peter Darmushklowsky had managed to put off his philosophy requirement till his junior year. Peter was a blond, blue-eyed, Polish-American bean-pole, who probably didn't shower quite as much as he should have (but perhaps that's only my addition), and who came to Hasler's discussion group about half the time in T-shirt and sandals, to sit at the far left of the front row, knees jabbing out the then-obligatory tears in his jeans—and the other half the time (or somewhat more than half) in jeans, T-shirt, and barefoot.

By his own admission, Hasler loathed the sandals. The logic was that sandals were worse than shoes because they *almost* left the foot bare, while covering this part and that part and generally obscuring the foot's overall form, suggesting a podical nudity never to be fulfilled. Shoes, as far as Hasler was concerned, were a nuisance; sandals were, "an obscenity that, really, all but turns my stomach!"

In-class flirting, at least on Hasler's part, went only as far as Timothy's commenting at the beginning of the third discussion class: "What, Mr. Darmushklowsky, sandals today? Why don't you take those off and get comfortable...?" to a few chuckles from the rest of the students, who'd noted Darmushklowsky's hippie ways. But apparently Pete immediately accepted the invitation , bending down, pulling loose the straps, and kicking the vulcanized soles with their interwoven leather web under his tubular chair, then sitting back to thrust out and cross his blocky ankles for all (or at least for Hasler) to view the cement-soiled balls of his feet, endearing him to Tim forever—even while he led the discussion on—as Darmushklowsky settled down to eat his lunch (recorded in the journal that evening): a container of Dannon strawberry yogurt, a waxed-paper bag of carrot and celery sticks, and an envelope full of pumpkin seeds.

Outside class?

Now Tim's journal recounts glimpses of Pete playing his guitar—barefoot—on a bench outside the student union ("one foot on the ground, one—should I say seductively?—up on the bench and thrust under his faded denim thigh, so that I could just see the bony mound, crossed by the wrinkle of one blue vein, of the upper instep—but no toes at all").

Now it recounts Tim's coming into the men's bathroom on the Stilford Union's first floor to find, among the college men entering and departing around them, Darmushklowsky, sans T-shirt (a bit on the yellow side, it hung over the sink edge) and, in Tim's telling phrase, "those big, bare feet of his just *swimming* all over the cracked blue and white floor tiles," the waist button on his jeans hanging open to hint at a glorious blond-haired pubis below, as Pete stood before the mirror, hands at the back of his neck, tugging and tucking the curls of his bronze rabbit's tail into its red rubber band.

That one kind of got to Tim. Without even saying hello, he fled the place for his office, locked the door, and masturbated—to worry over it for three more pages in his journal. Really, he had to get himself in hand! ("'In hand?' Well, no. I just *did* that, didn't I? *Not* in hand…!") This kind of thing just wouldn't *do*—though it left him without a hypochondriac attack for three wonderful days in which he put together the notes that were to become his fourth published article (turning on Hasler's critique of someone else's critique of John Austin): "How to Say Things with Words."

Eventually the boys became friends:

"Pete's got some very nice personality traits, actually. He's good-natured, if now and again on the moody side. (He's upset over his father's coming divorce. He likes his stepmother—that his cigar-smoking, San Jose construction contractor of a father is now tossing for a woman only five years older than Pete himself—much better than his real mother, whom he swears is both feebleminded and vicious!) Really, he's generous with his friends—and has lots of them. He likes to joke and hates exercise almost as much as I do. Maybe he's a little too lackadaisical about things he ought to take more seriously—perhaps I could take a lesson there and do the same!

"Generally different enough from me in his interests and ideas, he never makes me feel I'm wasting my time when I'm with him."

Yes, Irving, Timothy Hasler was *hopelessly* in love!

The "B" Tim finally ceded Pete for his contribution to the discussion class was, from what I can cull out, pretty much the mark Pete deserved—for which, I think, Tim gets points. (Confession: I gave Mike Ballagio an A that, no, he did *not* deserve at all! Much good it did him.) And a week after finals, Pete got together some four or five of his undergraduate friends, male and female; and, with a few of Tim's fellow graduate students, one of whom provided a van, over a Friday evening they moved Timothy from his attic

room on East Howard to the two basement rooms on South
Rushdale Tim was to occupy for his next two years at Stilford—for
the length of which moving job Darmushklowsky wore (without
socks) a pair of dirty, high-topped, once-bright-red basketball
sneakers.

And probably broke Tim's heart.

But then there was a pizza-and-beer fest after the last cartons of
books got carried down the basement steps, and, at about one in the
morning, Pete's guitar came out, the sneakers came off, and, as
Tim's journal recounts:

> ...with everybody watching, I took off my loafers and argyles
> and, right there, Pete and I had a session of something between
> footsie and foot wrestling. It was a roughhouse kind of thing—
> a big joke, of course, and everybody was laughing at it, at us.
> Including me. He was trying to play his new song, and I kept
> interrupting him, horsing around with his feet. He kept kick-
> ing me—and laughing—back. Mostly it was just silly—to
> everybody but *me*. (Certainly for *him*.) But that night, after
> they left and I went to bed, for the first time in a week I man-
> aged to get to sleep, not only deliriously happy, but without
> being struck once by the heart-pounding conviction that,
> somehow, before dawn I'd be dead.
>
> Really, the guy is nice! Just to take it on himself to round
> up Debbi [Darmushklowsky's blond, slate-eyed, almost
> silent—if Tim's description is to be trusted—girlfriend] and
> those guys in his band (well, they're *talking* about a band)
> and show up with them like that, to help me move what's got
> be a ton of books-and-their-bookshelves, not to mention the
> bed, the plants, and the pots and pans! I mean, I hadn't even
> asked him—just mentioned I'd be doing it this Friday evening
> when Soong could spare the van. (And, yes, we and the gai-
> jins got on remarkably well!) He just showed up with his
> crowd to help. I *am* overawed!

The "trouble" Irving referred to came the following September—
Darmushklowsky's senior year—and was occasioned by Hasler's
second published science fiction story, the first of the two that
feature the intergalactic minstrel, lanky and barefooted, guitar-

playing, raggedy-kneed, T-shirted Pete Flame—with his curly bronze rabbit's tail tucked at the back of his neck into its (right you are) red velatex band.

But there were a number of other identifying features, including some of Pete's characteristic turns of speech. As well, the lyrics of some of Flame's ballads were minusculely improved versions of Darmushklowsky's own song lyrics—and all of which were detailed and quoted in a third-page article in the *Stilford Student Chronicle* for September 23, 1964.

(Timothy pasted a copy into his journal: it was there among the Xeroxes. What sort of coincidence was it that predicted the day of his death, nine years on?)

The article describes Hasler as a "professor" in the University's philosophy department. Undergraduate Darmushklowsky, when interviewed, stated, no, until the student reporter came around, he'd had no idea that he'd been immortalized in the pages of the *Magazine of Fantasy and Science Fiction*. ("Yeah, Hasler used to be my prof. Last term. We were kind of friends—at least we used to be.") The idea of the stories didn't bother Pete so much. But the song lyrics did. Did that mean they were copyrighted by someone else now, and Pete couldn't record them if a record contract actually materialized? The reporter was sympathetic. For didn't this use of a recognizably real person in a fictional context represent a flagrant invasion of privacy? And if a *student* had used someone else's poems without attribution like that, would not that be considered the most blatant plagiarism by the University, worthy of instant dismissal? That professors could deal with students so cavalierly, stealing their work and doubtless getting well paid for it—lifting their very personalities for use in ridiculous commercial entertainments—well, it struck our reporter as appalling. What kind of double standard was the university now engaged in? Wasn't philosophy the domain of ethics? How sad, then, that the philosophy department chairman had declined to comment.

My first thought was simply that, reading the (first) article, there was no way you could tell that the two kids, Hasler and Darmushklowsky, were within six weeks of the same age—neither of them yet twenty-one. (Hasler's first, pithy comment in his journal, right after the pasted-in article's end, was: "I note they didn't interview *me*. And the reason they didn't get any comment from the chair is because our beloved leader is in Freiberg till September 7!")

Tim phoned Pete and apologized as best he could. He'd thought of it as a joke/surprise that Pete would *enjoy!* Pete was dubious and distant—and Tim was worried and surprised. ("...though, after that dumb article, I don't know why I should be. But I suppose I was hoping he'd take it better.") The problem was that a second "Pete Flame" story was due out in two weeks, this one in *Amazing.* Now Tim phoned the magazine's editorial offices to ask if there were time to change his hero's first name to "Bill" and his hair to black. He was told by the piqued secretary that the new issue had been printed last week and would be on the stands in days.

Then he was transferred to the editor:

"*What* was this guy's name, really? Darmushklowsky? And he's upset by 'Flame'? Frankly, it all sounds kind of 'fannish' to me. Chances are, you won't have to worry. For something like that to be libelous, he has to lose his job over it—or at least some money— or suffer some other material damages. Still, I'd watch out for that kind of thing in the future, young man...in case. When are we going to see your next story?"

With the appearance of the second 'Flame' saga, the *Student Chronicle* carried a second article—this one on page two:

The Further Adventures
of 'Peter Flame'!

Here the reporter did not seem to realize that both 'Flame' stories had been written and sold the previous spring. (Despite the article's title, nowhere in Hasler's texts is the hero ever called "Peter.") Rather, as far as the article's author was concerned, the "writing, sale, and publication" of the second, "only a month after the first (and only a week after our first article appeared)" was a flagrant and thoughtless flouting of the principles raised in the first article ("Certainly the author might have held off publishing his second invasion of senior Darmushklowsky's peace and privacy until some of the questions raised by your reporter last week were given a public hearing and resolved"), as well as an insult to the student press of America.

In a parenthesis at the article's end, the article acknowledges that the stories' writer was *not* a professor but a "Chinese-American [!] graduate philosophy instructor"—which, since Tim was only a TA, still got it wrong.

Nor, I note from my side, was there any mention in the articles of "Pete Flame"'s girlfriend in the tales, a beautiful, raven-haired, violet-eyed, brilliant, half-Korean girl, Diamonda, whose mother was an Italian countess (this in 24,000 A.D.!), and whose father was a warlord among a roving band of Korean-born space pirates, but who, before either story began, had been struck down by a dreaded wasting infection that meant Flame could never speak to her in person, but always had to communicate with her through an intricate arrangement of television screens, holographic projectors, and microphones, while her medically isolated and quarantined body actually drifted in a complex "nutrient healing tank," which she would never be able to leave, because without it she would die "of anaphylactic shock" within minutes of encountering the real world.

Their separation, Flame's and the beautiful, languishing Diamonda's, was the central tragedy of Flame's life. It is what had originally sent him, with his guitar, to wander among the stars.

Diamonda was sharp, witty, and gave old Pete some pretty good advice from time to time. And despite their wit, the scenes between them are still poignant. But one thing was certain: clearly she had little to do with blond, gray-eyed Debbi!

Make of it what you will.

Finally, Tim's journal recounts a real-life conversation between Tim and Pete, when Tim managed to get him alone in the student cafeteria. The account is compressed and succinct:

Got a chance to talk to Pete—in the cafeteria. Wish I could write it all out, but I'm too tired—and we went on a good two hours. But I feel a lot better. One thing he said was that he realized the only invasion of privacy was the damned newspaper's turning it all into such a big thing. Yes, it was a pain in his butt, all the kids in the dorm hall calling out to him, "Hey, Flame!" whenever he went past. But that was because of the articles, not the stories. None of them would have even know about it if the *Chronicle* hadn't interfered. (Well, I'm glad he realized *that!*) I hadn't known when I last talked to him on the phone—the evening the first article appeared—but apparently he never saw the first story! (I promised him a Xerox—since I've only got one copy of the magazine left myself: must go into the department early tomorrow and run one off!) But a day after the first article came out, there wasn't a copy left anywhere around!

That kind of hurts.

He said he liked the second, though: he thought Pete's solution was "pretty neat." (Which only means, despite his earlier protests, he's got *some* intuitive understanding—as long as you don't use fancy jargon—of Naming/Listing/Counting Theory. Plus the fact, of course, I'm not a bad popularizer.) Once I told him there wouldn't be any problem about the lyrics, he said he felt better. Apparently he liked my versions more than his.

So use them, I told him.

Pete: "Yeah. Maybe if they ever get on a record, we could split the money."

Me: "Don't be silly. I didn't split any money with you when I got paid for the stories. I wouldn't take anything from you. I changed one word here and two words there. It was just like me making a suggestion. That's all. It's still your song."

Pete said he was glad I felt that way. All the nonsense about copyrights had been something the reporter had suggested to him, with his talk about plagiarism, which Pete had said hadn't made a lot of sense to him anyway.

We said a lot of "you're a really good guy, and I'm sorry I messed things up for you"—the both of us. Pete said the reporter was an asshole and that Pete had told him it was kind of kicky to be portrayed as the hero of an SF space opera—but of course the reporter didn't write any of *that!*

After more of the same, Pete got up, finally, and with his split-along-the-top and held-together-by-rubber-bands-and-masking-tape black cardboard guitar case banging against the calf of his jeans, he ambled out through the cafeteria's green glass doors.

I confess, I'd been reading this whole account, vaguely curious as to whether Darmushklowsky had come to this last Tuesday-evening reconciliation shod or barefoot, and had resigned myself never to know, when, with a final two-word paragraph, Hasler cleared it up:

Fucking sandals!

From there Pete Darmushklowsky exits the cafeteria and Timothy Hasler's journal—if not Timothy Hasler's life and thoughts—into the remainder of his senior year, into, as it were, time and eternity.

There was some more discussion of it in the paper's letter column. And there was even an informal meeting with the department chairman (on September, 29). But there were no more articles.

Since Pete seemed to be appeased, I guess the whole thing, blew—more or less—over.

But where was the obsessive and degrading sexual eccentricity that had so disgusted Mossman—who, if anything, seemed as oblivious to Tim's foot fetishism as he was to his hypochondria—both of which, as far as I could see, were central to any understanding of Hasler's basic psychology.

Ah, *there* was the account of the dog sucking—which, as far as I could tell, was *surely* a piece of fiction! Like the description of the desiring dream monster of Riverside Park, it was much too polished, too "written," too arch and witty for me even to *consider* that it was possibly real. Besides, it took place in a large midwestern city called Pointcisme (*you* try to find it in any American gazetteer!), amidst a set of other entries that were all located in a small town in Massachusetts where Mossman's chronology has Hasler staying for some six weeks in 1968 and in which, from his other terse entries, he was probably bored out of his gourd enough to try writing such an exercise.

Oh, yes, and the name Tim claimed he found on the dog's collar tag was "Jurgen." But the fact is, there'd been a number of incidents back when I was taking his seminar which had convinced me that, whatever his teaching skills, in a number of areas Mossman was just style deaf.

No, I don't care *what* Irving thought: this was not a real account, but a kind of arch pornography.

As to the "old black wino" Mossman had mentioned from

Hasler's last months in New York, there was a barefoot (once again Mossman seemed to have missed *that* salient point), black homeless guy, whom Hasler had started talking to in Central Park, who, if Hasler would share a bottle of wine with him, would sit and talk with him and let Hasler massage his feet! (The "old" in the designation "old black wino" seems pretty much Mossman's addition. Hasler describes him as "beat up" and, from time to time, in rather bad shape. From *my* reading of the journal account [although, true, it doesn't say so in so many words], I picture him within a couple of years, one way or the other, of Hasler's own age—twenty-eight at the time.) As far as the urine drinking? Well, it's just as much there in Hasler's account of Central Park as it is in my account of my afternoon in Riverside. But, in Hasler's case, it seems to be something that the black guy forced on Hasler, rather sadistically (I use the term in as technical and as value-free a way as I can), and then only once, during their second—admittedly Ripple-drenched—encounter.

I quote:

"Man, you really like my feet, don't you?"

"Yes, I do—very much."

"Shit, I could probably piss in your fuckin' face, and if I said you had to do it, or I wouldn't let you play with my feet no more unless you let me, you probably *would* do it, now, wouldn't you?"

"Right now," I told him, "I probably would."

"I mean," he asked me, "could you get off on that?"

That's from Hasler's account of the conversation *preceding* the piss-drinking incident in the Central Park bushes. And from the conversation afterward:

I asked him: "Did that really turn you on?"

He sat there, holding his knees, looking at the bottle. After a while, he said: "Man, that's why I guess I'm a fuckin' drunk. You know what I mean? I mean, I always *liked* to do shit like that to people, ever since I was a kid. Piss on 'em. Shit on 'em. Hurt 'em sometimes. Sometimes cuss an' yell at 'em. Spank 'em." That made him grin up at me. "Lot o' people like to get spanked! Women, men—it don't matter. You spend all your time thinkin' about doin' shit like that to people, and you realize, man, I can't do stuff like that. That's wrong! So you get fuckin' drunk—and then you find somebody who *likes* doin' it! Or somebody who don't mind it—did you *like* it?"

"I kind of liked it," I said, "but I guess that's mainly because—well, I'm drunk; and, too, because I could tell you liked it and it was getting you off." I shrugged. "You've been letting me do stuff with you that I like: hold and kiss your feet."

"Yeah, that's what we gotta do, I suppose. Trade off." He turned around now and stuck his foot in my lap again. "A little of what you like. For a little of what I like." I took hold of it; and he went on: "But it would be better, see, if you *really* liked it." He moved his foot against my groin. "Drinking my piss, I mean. I mean, as much as you like my feet. You just didn't mind it 'cause we're friends, you and me. But you got some people who really like stuff like that. And that's always better—if you like doin' it, like I do."

End of entry.

Though two pages later, however, Hasler mentions he had never drunk piss before and probably wouldn't do it again—even though he was surprised to find there was "nothing particularly unpleasant about it; nor did I get at all ill."

And though, as far as I can tell, they had maybe a dozen foot-massage sessions in the park over as many evenings—and as many bottles of wine—this was, despite what Mossman's letter says, their only urolagniac encounter. I mean, if that was Mossman's idea of "an unbelievably nasty sex life," what in the world would he have thought of mine?

So you've had Mossman's basic picture of Hasler.

And now you have my revision.

Yes, while I was going through my reading, I often wondered whether a third reader—Sam, say, or, really, *anyone* else—would have come up with a picture as different from mine as mine was from Irving's. At the same time, Irving's blindness to Hasler's hypochondriacal anxiety, or Hasler's extraordinarily self-possessed way of dealing with that anxiety, or Mossman's inability to articulate Hasler's foot fetishism—which seemed to become, for Mossman, simply "an unbelievably nasty sex life"—confirmed something that I'd felt all along: Mossman *wasn't* the person to do a biography of someone like Hasler.

I'd also been struck with the irony that, for two years, my picture of Hasler as a gay man—thanks to Mossman's blindnesses—had been of a man rather like myself, in almost all his sexual, if not psychological, particulars. But what I was left with from these weeks of reading in the journals and papers Mossman had sent me was a picture of a man as different from me as it was possible to be.

I mean, start by comparing the objects of our two graduate-school romances: nigger-loving, asshole-eating, gay-activist, spread-eagled over the boiler pipes, car-crashing Mike Ballagio, and pumpkin seed-noshing, guitar-playing, fundamentally straight Peter Darmushklowsky. They probably both started off Catholic. But, as I see it, similarities end there.

And if his journals are an indication, Tim didn't even *know* where the cruisy john was at Stilford University!

If you had asked me to characterize Timothy Hasler from a biographical point of view (and, no, nobody had), I'd have said:

Given his hypochondriacal mortality terrors as well as his intense foot fetishism, Timothy Hasler starts as a man—and as a brilliant young philosopher—with very different relationships to death and sex from most of us.

And that means me as well as you: daily fears of dying don't soak my sheets with sweat every night. And though, yes, you'll find me on my knees getting my share of dick and pretty much actively digging anything that comes out of one when and where I can, you still won't find me in the park, woozy with wine, massaging some stranger's—or close friend's—feet like Christ with the lepers. (How, I found myself wondering, would Tim have related to the clubbed toes of my long-lost Piece o' Shit? They were grimy enough, certainly. But would their deformity have turned him on, turned him off, or left him indifferent? Frankly, there was little to let me know. There's even distinction among foot fetishists.) Let's face it, that man was a philosopher...! And, yes, I was beginning to see how and why.

Yet, as I continued through Hasler's papers, I began to wonder if there wasn't a bit of the Mossman in me, too. Irving's last letter had ended with all but a written Introduction to the Old Poet—certainly the most important person in Hasler's life in its last decade.

But the Saturday night of her reading at the 92nd Street Y, I spent the whole afternoon sitting in my living room, paging through the poems in *Mountain and Tower*. (Yes, it was raining. And, yes, I had a cold. [And I was supposed to be at a new temp Monday morning.] But—yes—I've gone to work with and in worse.) Then, suddenly, I was looking at my watch—it was 9:30!

Surely the reading was over.

I got up, went into the kitchen, looked in the refrigerator where I had put some take-out barbecued ribs the night before, and pulled them, in their translucent plastic container with the snap-on cover, out from their shelf.

Behind them were three unopened cans of Colt 45—which had been there, as another epoch would put it, ever so long....

Of course the next day I *didn't* call her as I'd been invited to. That I'd missed her reading made speaking to her in person seem, somehow, impossible.

The center of the period about which I'm writing was, of course, that odd spring of 1984, which began in late April, when I turned on the six o'clock news and sat down in the living room to see the announcement by Secretary of Health and Human Services, Margaret Heckler of the isolation of HTLV III (that would soon be known simply as HIV) by Robert Gallo, and ended when I was over at the American Museum of Natural History later that June, looking at the traveling exhibit on "Lucy," the First Lady of Hominids, when I ran into my friend Pheldon (who'd had been at some of those dinner parties I mentioned at the start of Part One), and now told me: "Did you see the papers this morning? Michel Foucault died...!"

I asked, like pretty much everyone else who'd read his interview in the *Voice* about being gay, when last he'd been in the country teaching, "Was it AIDS...?"

"It must have been...they said something about a neurological infection. But they haven't said so officially."

They wouldn't, of course, until more than seven years later.

It was the near side of the same summer, when I got a letter—
not from Irving, but from Sally-May Mossman!

I read it on my living-room couch after work on a Thursday
night, while I ate from a plastic container of salad I'd gotten from
the newly installed salad bar in the Korean vegetable stand two
blocks south on Amsterdam and chicken and fried rice out of a
Styrofoam container from the little Chinese take-out place that had
just opened up across the street beside the bodega.

October 3, 1984

Dear John,

    I know Irving writes you fairly regularly—so I'm sure he's
at least hinted, if he hasn't outright told you, that things
haven't been going all that well between us in the last year....

The last letter I'd gotten from Irving had come with the two
mailers and the carton—more than a year ago now. The only two
times I remember him even mentioning Sam in a letter were from
the ones I've quoted. I mean, in the closings, there'd never even been
any "Sam and I send you our best," so that I'd almost stopped fantasizing his pity for—perhaps he'd call it sensitivity to—his gay
acquaintance who would never know the joys of heterosexual domes-
ticity.

    ...Irving always was the writer in the family [Sally-May went
on], and I probably do myself more damage than not by envy-
ing him the larger world that always seems to put him in
touch with, *vis-à-vis* my own horizons—limited, I confess, by
what is probably no more than my own laziness, to something even smaller than those of most faculty wives here at the
college.

    Well, he's away for three weeks—I could just as easily write
"We're apart for three weeks." That would probably tell you
more of what's happening; but I found myself thinking about
almost a dozen onetime friends of ours, of mine, and I decided this time I wasn't going to just sit around, remembering,
feeling sorry for myself for what's drifted into the past: I would
actually write a letter, however short, to each of you.

    I won't spend pages crying over my own situation, which

after all is not as bad as it might be. (I mean, he's promised he won't *see* the auburn-haired little bitch again, except in class; and, for whatever stupid reason, this time I believe him.) More to the point, I haven't got the energy to write out the details to even one of you, much less to you all—though Lord knows, it's a pretty usual story.

You can fill it in.

But I do think of you all, sometimes very warmly—particularly you, John, because you're gay and this AIDS business that we keep reading about here sounds just so terrible. (A graduate student in my old stamping grounds, anthropology, withdrew from school last term because he had it—and that really got people rattled!) Irving says he thinks that Foucault's death wasn't Acquired Immune Deficiency Syndrome at all, but that it's just people trying to lump him in with a lot of other promiscuous gay men. What do you think? But philosophers just don't carry on the way you apparently have to in order to get it (at least, that's what Irving says). At any rate, because we love you, stay safe and healthy, John—and watch out.

It occurs to me—I don't know whether you see it this way or not—that AIDS has put gay men into a situation that women have occupied since the beginning of time: where every sexual act has the potential for life or death—though, of course, in the case of women, the life is not theirs so much as it is that of a potential and unknown child.

At any rate, if Irving knew I was writing, he'd want me to send along his best. So, in that funny way,

Best from us both,
Sam (Mossman)

I couldn't begin to tell you why Sally-May's letter bothered me. At first I thought simply to ignore it; but, like I did for the Hispanic guy I hadn't taken up to St. Luke's that night, I felt sorry for her: it seemed particularly sad she so overestimated the communication that took place between her husband and me on personal matters. And, because of that, I felt sorry for Irving, too.

"I didn't even know black guys *could* be gay…!" There was no more connection between the Sam who had blurted that to me back in the student cafeteria and the Sam who'd just urged me to stay safe from AIDS than there was between the John in Mossman's three photographs and the John who had just read Sam's letter.

But also, of course, I was angry.

I was angry that the replacement photo had never arrived.

I was angry over Mossman's misguided view of what Timothy Hasler meant to the world; I was snarled in so many half-hearted years of work, that my thesis was probably growing less and less acceptable, anywhere and everywhere.

And because of that anger, two weeks later I sat down, dated a letter "October 20, 1984" and began to write:

Dear Sam,

Sorry it's taken so long to answer yours of October 3. Probably it's a strange time for us all. I was particularly taken with your comments about AIDS. Suddenly it raised in me an urge to talk about some things in my own life.

You haven't asked to know them.

They may not interest you at all.

But they want to be told. (I want to tell them.) Something about me yearns to put my communication with someone or other on a new footing—that seems, somehow, in this time, this situation, important. So here's some of what I've been doing over the last few months—it's up to you whether you want to share it with Irving or not.

In a sense this letter starts from the shared concern between me and Irving: Timothy Hasler. But what impels it, more than anything, is my realization of all those things Hasler and I share that Irving doesn't. That, at least, is the insight that fell to me as it began. But it ends—and this is specifically what your AIDS comment took me to—with the realization of a certain separation.

Some months ago, I went down to "GSA Night" at the Mineshaft—stayed out till six-thirty in the morning. (Rare for nine-to-five me.) On the first Wednesday of each month, my friend Pheldon told me, GSA (the Golden Shower Association) sponsors a Wet Night—catering to guys with a taste for recycled beer. "Since from time to time you've said you were interested in that kind of thing," said Pheldon, leaning on the counter of the Fiesta, "go on down there and check it out. I did. It wasn't that bad. Here's the address."

So I did.

The bar's in what must have been, at one time, the second floor of a warehouse. A couple of stairways angle down to the first floor, where there's also a bar. At one time or another, that space must been a garage. The lower floor's concrete, with half a dozen built-in drains. Water hoses, in green or black coils, hang here and there on the dark wooden or brick walls near old-fashioned spigots with iron handles. In the largest room are three bathtubs. Under dim blue and orange bar lights, they just sit there. In some of the other rooms is a variety of slings, tables, and—yes—washbasins.

On Wet Night the upstairs opens at nine, and for fifteen dollars you get all the beer you can drink till midnight. In the upstairs bar, there's a room to check your clothes. (About three-quarters of the guys in line do. But not wholly sure of what was coming up, I didn't.) For fifty cents extra, you can rent an old jockstrap, if you want. You go downstairs, get your beer free from the two hardworking bartenders there, drink it, and...

After three different guys just walked up to me while I was standing in a corner, whipped it out, and started peeing on the leg of my jeans—like big fucking dogs!—I began to realize why so many of them had opted to get rid of their clothes.

Well, you see some pretty strange stuff—in those rooms where it's light enough to see. I started out pretty much on the "pitching" end of things. I guess that's only natural with a bunch of guys you've never seen before. (I thought I might have some trouble in that department, but after the fourth or fifth beer, I lost my inhibitions—since it was going on all around me.) Generally, it's fairly quiet there, considering forty or fifty men are moving around and drinking beer. Every once and a while, in one of the darker back rooms, you hear an echoing slap—from someone getting his butt smacked. Sometimes you'll hear a couple of guys laugh. But generally everyone kind of whispers—or at least talks pretty softly, especially once you get away from the beer counter. And, of course, there's the general trickle and chatter of spilling urine—sometimes louder, sometimes fainter.

Purposely I'd worn my rattiest pair of jeans and an old green work shirt. To be accurate, I hadn't know about the clothes check when I arrived, so I kept my clothes on for most it. But, if anything, that seemed to make me more attractive to the committed pitchers in the crowd. Once, in a *sotto voce* conversation with a little pudgy blond guy, I was told about the clothes-check place upstairs. "Well," I said. "Next time, I guess." But I was already sopping from my chest to my pants cuffs. Inside my sneakers, it felt as if I was walking on wet sponges. Finally I had to take my shirt off. (Some of these guys aim high!) I stuffed it behind a folded-up Ping-Pong table that was leaning against one brick wall on one of the hallways.

Finally I decided I'd better take my turn in the barrel—that is, one of the tubs—since that was really what I'd come for. That night I did at least one thing I'd never done before: I got in a bathtub while some nine guys (with several more standing around) drifted over, unbuttoned their flies (the ones who weren't already naked or in jockstraps; zippers, I guess, are not too popular with these guys), and let go all over me. You know what it feels like, to be pissed on by nine guys at once while you lie spread-eagled on your back in a bathtub, Sam—I mean, more than anything else?

It feels warm!

At one o'clock they closed the downstairs for cleaning—shooed everybody up the brick-walled stairs into the upper bar. The work lights were all on and the hoses were coming off the wall when I left the place.

About ten minutes after they'd locked the door to the downstairs area, though, I remembered that my shirt was still down behind the Ping-Pong table. The upstairs bartender—as shirtless as was I, but in a studded black leather body harness—told me I had to wait till the whole bar closed; then he'd let me down there to see if I could retrieve it.

So I sat down at the counter, to drink my first beer of the evening that I paid for out of pocket. Miracle of miracles, only the edges of my money in my wallet were actually wet. A little lively, wiry older guy was there, who, like me, also had no shirt on—but I think that's the way he'd come. He just wore jeans, a big, silver, longhorned belt buckle, and cowboy boots. Bowlegged and a little unsteady, he was strutting around the bar and wanted to joke around with everybody. Some tattoos were blearily visible in the white hair over his arms, and he had this twangy southwestern drawl. He looked like a remarkably well-preserved fifty or fifty-five and, I thought he was kind of cute. But when he went up to two fellows at the bar (both of them still just in jockstraps), put a hand on each of their shoulders, and proposed loudly that they all go off in the back and have a threesome—well, first the two guys were clearly into each other and were equally clearly put out at his intrusion. Finally one said "no" loudly and firmly—and I realized most of the customers there were finding the old guy a real pain in the ass.

But I went over to start a conversation with him; he told me— hanging onto my shoulder—that tonight was his sixtieth (!) birthday. He was celebrating, and he was out (I quote) "to show as many of these young cocksuckers what I can do as would be interested." He seemed disappointed that so few of us were taking him up on his offer.

Boxes and crates were piled up at the back of the bar, and after I bought him a birthday beer, he went over and climbed up to sit there, knees wide, horny hands on them, banging his boot heels on the boxes below, and me (with my own beer bottle raised before my bared pectorals—moderately okay from my morning push-ups, I guess—like a protective sword between us) standing in front of him and looking up at the snarled white hair over his suntanned chest and, above that, his wrinkled brown-red neck.

"I mean," he explained to me, "I'm a fuckin' trucker. No joke—a real one, with a real *truck*—parked outside right down the street. No kiddin', boy! It's no eighteen-wheeler or nothin'; it's just an old Dodge Cube. I work pretty much between New England and Maryland. But I always stop off here when I'm coming through the city—especially on Wet Nights, if I can make it. I've had some pretty good times here—usually I make out like a fuckin' bandit. But I don't know what it is tonight. All the cocksuckers is supposed to be crazy for goddamn truckers, and here I am—horny, hung, and ready for bear—and can't get a taker nowhere! It's enough to make a birthday boy break down and cry!"

"I'll suck you off," I said.

"Yeah?" He brightened up. "You will? Hey, how about that! Well, let's see what you can do, boy." And he set the beer I'd bought him down, pulled open his fly, and tugged out a respectable, uncut six-incher. While I was working on him (his jeans were still wet from his stint downstairs—as were mine) and he was holding my head, the bartender came up to us and said, "Come on, Tex." (This old fart was actually called—at least in the bar—"Tex"!) "Take this guy in the grope-room in back or into the men's room or something. You been here enough times to know you're not supposed to do it out front here, with everybody walking around. Even if you *are* an exhibitionist!"

"I know, I know," Tex said. "But this cocksucker's good. It won't take me long. Just gimme a minute—just a minute, now!"

"Okay, but if I come back here and there's a fuckin' puddle on the floor in front of these crates, I'll eighty-six your hillbilly ass out of here for good! I'm not kidding, now—birthday or no birthday, you hear me? The stuff you like to do is downstairs —and it's over with for the night, anyway!"

Then the bartender walked away.

And Tex, still holding my head, said, "Fuck him! Suck my dick, black boy!"

So I did; and in two minutes, he grunted, "Oh, shit...!" and dropped a small, lumpy, old man's load. I sat there milking him with my mouth. He sat above me there, breathing hard. As I started to pull off him, he caught my head with one hand. "Aw, come on now. I saw you downstairs. I know what you come in here for tonight. You just lemme get my breath back, and I'll give it to you. You can take it all, now—can't you? Just don't spill any—then I really *will* be in some trouble. You heard the bartender—we just can't leave no mess up here on the floor like you can downstairs. But you'll take it for me, won't you, cocksucker?"

From his movements now, I could tell he'd upended his bottle of beer; then, with his softening dick still in my mouth, he began to pee. It wasn't very salty, but it flowed and flowed, long, warm, and hard. I drank. And I didn't spill anything. Finishing, he sighed, "Boy, that felt good!" His hand relaxed on my head as, at last, I came off him. "That was some birthday present you give the old man." He held down his hand. "Wanna shake?"

So I shook his hand. His palm was sandpaper rough, and his fingers gripped me hard. Without letting go, he leaned down and said:

"Gimme a kiss."

So I stood up on tiptoe; he bent way down—and thrust his tongue way the hell into my mouth. I thrust mine back; and from the slippery hardness it hit, behind his teeth and under his palate, I realized those were dentures that had filled his friendly grin. Finally he sat back, wet-lipped and smiling. "Now, that's what I call a real happy birthday! If you don't catch a little of what you pitch, you can't really appreciate it, now, can you? You better get on to the men's room, 'fore you fuckin' bust!"

"Yeah," I said. "I was thinking on the same lines."

"If you're still up for it," he said, "you should try the Real Men's Room."

I wasn't sure what he meant, as he patted my head and I turned to go across the bar floor. Three or four people who had been watching us—one stopped masturbating to put his cock inside his leather pants—turned away.

The rest rooms were marked Men's and Women's. But over the woodburned panel that hung on the women's-room door, someone had taped a piece of paper on which was scrawled in Magic Marker: "real men's room."

I opened the door—on a space with three commodes in it. Two were occupied. On one sat a small, muscular blond guy. He was just in a jockstrap, which was down around the ankles of his basketball sneakers. In front of him stood a black guy, about forty, maybe forty-five-years-old. He was about 6'3" and, though not particularly muscular, big. I mean, he weighed a good 250, 280 pounds. (He had glasses on and a baseball cap with the visor turned to the back of his head—which I assumed was from some time spent sucking cock downstairs.) From his stubby, uncut dick, protruding from dark fingers like a still-darker sausage, a full stream of yellow glittered, like a golden staple between it and the little white guy's open mouth.

It kind of surprised me.

I decided I'd sit down myself, though, and take up the one free commode. Moments after I did, I realized there *weren't* any urinals in here. We—the ones of us who were sitting—were it. And just to confirm that, three more guys came in as I was settling: one took up his place in front of the other man sitting next to me, a bony fellow with a black leather hat on, black boots, and not much else.

Two more took their places in front of me—one a pretty good-looking fellow with a brown beard who'd obviously done some working out with weights; he had on a leather vest and jeans. The guy in line behind him was in marine fatigues and shirtless. (But he looked more like Phyllis Diller than a marine.) The bearded man unbuttoned his fly, pulled out both cock and balls—from a moment's stagger, I realized he was drunk—and just began to piss in my face, letting me get it in my mouth.

This guy had a real horse bladder, and the pressure of his water was immense—greater than I'd thought somebody pissing could muster. Swaying in front of me, as I gulped and gulped him, he looked over his shoulder and motioned to the kind-of-ugly-looking guy in the fatigues, "Come on up here, man, and piss in this guy's face with me, huh? He loves it! Look at him." The guy stepped up and, in a minute, I had both cockheads in my mouth, with their vastly differing flows.

I don't know why. Maybe it was because this was the first time I'd done anything like this—I mean, in a bar, in a controlled situation, where all (or most) of the people who'd come were into the same thing—but I found myself with the obsession not to spill any.

The guy on the commode next to me, every once in a while, would hold the cock delivering into him in his hand, sit back, and play it over his face and chest, letting it waterfall down between his legs, over his dick and balls, and into the toilet. Then he'd go back to drinking. But I—*and*, I realized, the little white brick shithouse on the other end—were not about to lose a drop.

I had about a six-minute rest before the next three guys came in. I took them, one right after the other. Just before I finished the last—a squat Puerto Rican, who grinned down at me all through it, nodding drunkenly, approvingly—I felt an overwhelming urge to shit. Since I was on a commode, I let it go. It was shit, yeah, but it was awfully loud, a whole lot of it, and very wet. And not a full two minutes after I'd reached back to flush, I had to go again. This one was even wetter.

Two more guys—and I took them.

A couple of minutes later, old Horse Bladder pushed through the door again: the big, bearded fellow with the leather vest and the muscles. In the thirty-five minutes since he'd been in here before, he hadn't gotten any soberer. His cock—as I saw this time—was (as I already knew) fairly sizable: cut—but pretty raggedly. And he had some of the most pronounced veins webbing his shaft I'd ever seen. At one place on the side, one seemed to have ruptured beneath the skin, to form a smooth little dime-sized planetarium. But it didn't seem to bother him. He grabbed my head with one hand, more to steady himself than anything else, and thrust his cock, already spilling tasteless waters out its quarter-inch slit, hot on my face, hot in my mouth. "Oh, shit...!" he grunted. "I didn't think I was gonna make it, man!" and leaned with one fist on the wall behind me—while I felt my asshole open up again: below, it let a stream that everyone could hear roaring into the toilet.

It came out me like a fire hose.

What had happened was that, I realized, all my sphincters had simply opened up and were letting liquid through and out as fast as it came in! Nor had it been traumatic—or even vaguely painful.

Damn, I thought; I'm going to have the cleanest gut in Manhattan!

When he was finished, Horse patted my face with his wet hand. "Thanks, fella. See you again in a little bit."

But, frankly, as he left, I wasn't sure I was up to another half hour in here.

I wiped myself—really, I was completely clean—pulled up my pants (still pretty wet from downstairs), and—had to go again! So I pulled them down again, sat once more, and hosed out another quart.

Then I wiped and pulled up my pants a second time. The bony guy in the boots and black cap had gotten up and gone by now, but it looked like the little muscular white fellow in the jockstrap was still going strong. One guy stood with his dick in the fellow's mouth; one guy waited in line behind him—even though the other commode was free.

I pushed out the rest room, back into the bar.

The first thing I noticed was that the place had pretty much cleared out—there were maybe a third as many guys at the bar as there'd been when I'd gone in. Horse Bladder was still at the counter, in his leather vest, talking to somebody. I came over beside some character in full leather I didn't even remember seeing before and sat on a stool. The bartender immediately came up to me with a beer. "Tex bought you this—he said to give it to you when you came out."

"Oh," I said. "Did he go yet?"

"Nope." The bartender nodded toward the counter's end.

I looked but didn't see anybody—at first. Then I noticed, up on that pile of crates and boxes, somebody stretched out on his back. The toes of a pair of cowboy boots pointed toward the beamed ceiling, a few feet overhead. The bartender repeated, "He said he wanted to buy you a drink before he fell out."

"Oh," I repeated. "Uh...thanks."

I looked at the clock. It was a couple of minutes after 3:00. I'd gone into the Real Men's Room just a bit before 1:00—though, if you'd asked me, I would have sworn I'd been in there closer to one hour than two.

I put a forearm on either side the bottle, and wondered whether I should drink it. Should the urge hit, I was all set to scoot back into the john and lose more water. Finally, though, I picked up the bottle and took a swallow…and realized, as I set it back down, that I felt…good!

Incredibly good!

And peaceful.

And content.

I didn't feel any need to talk to anyone. The feeling that gets you up, looking for this and that, that starts you off doing one thing or the other, just to have something to do, was in abeyance—an abeyance I usually associate with tiredness; only, though it was after 3:00 in the morning, I didn't *feel* tired.

I thought about that strange and rarely attainable condition Heidegger called "meditative thinking" and wondered if this was it.

I was sitting there, the time going just as unconsciously for me now as it had been in the Real Men's Room, when suddenly a big, heavy arm landed around my shoulder, and a big, bearded face pushed up into mine. "Oh, man—there you are. I was hoping it was you! I'm ready, man—I'm about to fucking bust. You gonna take it for me…?"

I was startled. But I didn't even pull away. "Hey, I'm sorry." I smiled. "But I think I've had my full—"

"Oh, no, man! You gotta take it for me," Horse insisted, shaking his head drunkenly. "There isn't anybody left in the bathroom. And I gotta piss so bad I'm about to bust. You know, I can't piss in the fucking toilet—not in a place like this. That's the rule, you know? Tonight. I mean, that's *my* rule. I gotta do it on somebody, in somebody—please, baby. Lemme piss in your face. You know you love it, you know you want it! And I'm not gonna make it if I have to hold it too much longer—"

Though I'd never said it, I knew what he was talking about: it was the same voice speaking in him that—in me—had said I had to drink it all. "Okay," I said. "Yeah, sure. I'm just afraid I'm going to shit out piss all over myself again if I drink any more—"

"That's okay, guy. That's okay, I'll help you.…" And he was forcing me down from the stool, pulling at his fly.

I got his big, veiny meat before he started. I was holding on to his leg with one arm and a rung of the bar stool with my other hand. While I was kneeling there, somebody else came up. And a western drawl: "Oh, shit—is this cocksucker still workin' out? 'Cause, Jesus—I gotta take me one wicked piss. I just woke up back there—an' I gotta piss like a fuckin' racehorse, boy—"

Swaying above me, Horse said thickly: "Well, come on. Stick it in his mouth and piss, you scrawny-ass motherfucker! You can see he's taking it!" Hands moved over my head, and a moment later a second, uncut cock prodded and pushed in beside Horse's—and let go!

"Jesus Christ, Tex—? What the fuck...ah, come *on*, guys!" It was the bartender again. "Who you got down there? Will you let him up, man? I told you, you can't do that up here in the bar. That's for downstairs. Or in the men's room!"

"Get the fuck out of my face," Horse grunted. "If I make a mess, then you can say somethin' to me. But I know my piss drinkers, man. And that's not this one's style." He bent over me a little. "Is it, cocksucker—it better not be! Or we're gonna be in deep shit!"

Tex just chuckled.

"I swear," the bartender said, "I'm gonna kick the both of you out of here—shit, it's time to go, anyway. All right, drink up! Mugs and bottles and glasses on the bar, guys!"

I drank.

Tex said: "*He's* sure drinkin' up, ain't he?"

"Drink up and turn 'em in, guys!" I heard the bartender call again. "All in, now. All in!"

Tex finished first. His dick slid out from beside Horse's thicker, longer tool. The cleaning lights came on about twenty-five seconds before Horse finished. *Five* seconds before he pulled his dick out my face, I felt that pressure building in my ass.

As soon as I was off, I rasped, "Oh, shit, guys...I think we've got an emergency!"

Maybe it was the look on my face.

Maybe it was my tone of voice—

"Uh-oh," Horse said. "Come on, Tex. We gotta get this cocksucker into the bathroom." They both were over me, lifting me by the arms, dragging me, practically carrying me across the room. Clearly they had a good idea what was going on—like they'd both been here before.

They pushed into the john with me. Horse was pulling at my

pants. "Let it go, guy. Just let it go...." A moment later, my ass hit the toilet ring, already splashing loudly below.

Sitting there, my butt spurting water like a stuck balloon, I began to laugh. "Well, I guess we made it...!"

The whole thing just seemed crazily comic.

Tex squatted beside me, rubbing my belly. "How you feelin' there now, boy?" He seemed to think it was pretty funny, too. But Horse was swaying again, like maybe he was too drunk to find it funny. His hand on my back, he rubbed down, up, rubbed a few more times, and the next time went right on down, over my buttocks, through the commode ring and under my ass; he moved his hand around in the hosing waters—once even stuck a finger three joints up into my spilling hole. Which made me laugh more.

I leaned against his jeans. (And I still had that same good feeling. I wondered if, in their drunkenness, Horse and Tex did, too.) Horse's pants lap was wet, as though he'd had some trouble holding it in for a while now. Or maybe it was left over from downstairs.

Still bending over me, Horse looked at his big wet hand. "Cocksucker, you're clean as a fuckin' whistle!" I was still smiling; suddenly he thrust his forefinger into his mouth between his mustache and beard, then the second; then, surprising me equally, he dropped his hand to my face and ran his third into my mouth; he followed that with his little finger. "If you don't catch a little of what you pitch," he said when he'd finished sucking off his fingers, "you can't really appreciate it."

"Yeah," Tex said. "That's what I told 'im, before."

Horse stood, wiping his hand on his weight-lifter's chest. He pushed his vest back enough for me to see a really thick-gauge tit-ring piercing a nipple five or six times the size of the nipple you'd see on most guys—five or six times the size of mine, anyway. Still rubbing, absently he moved his vest back from the right side one. No ring. But his male teat in its quarter-sized aureole was still big as some women's.

When I stopped spurting, and the sound died beneath me, Tex asked me, "You okay now?"

"Yeah, I think so."

"Good." Horse took a breath. "'Cause I gotta get home. I have to be at work at eight-thirty this morning." He staggered a moment, then stood up. "I'm a computer programmer, working on electronic music—only now I double as a sound engineer at Columbia Records. And *just* don't ask me," though, drunk as he was, I wasn't sure *what* I wasn't suppose to ask, unless it was, What are you doing here...? "Hey, man—thanks for everything," he said, with that alcoholic seriousness of someone who has managed to rise to some emergency. "Especially that last one—that was the important one, you know? Thinking about all the piss you had in your belly, guy—and how you *still* took mine: man, I'll be beatin' off to that one for a long time!"

"Yeah," I said. But I was grinning again. "Good. I'm glad...."

I think Tex was fixing to stay in there with me, but Horse gave him a kind of push on the back of the head: "Come on, old man— get on out of here. Let the guy get himself together, huh?"

"Oh, yeah..." Tex said and stood. "Yeah, boy. Okay. You get yourself together. You okay now...?"

I nodded.

The two of them left.

And you know, I felt even better?

When I came out this time, Horse was gone. The bar's work lights were still bright around the place. Tex was lingering at the door.

I went over to the bartender, who, behind the counter, in his studded leather jock and his body harness, was dunking glasses in one sink, twisting them on the pair of brushes in the next, and then moving them to the rinsing sink. As soon as I went up, he said: "You see, man—these guys are always trying to abuse the place here. You gotta follow the rules. Or we won't be able to do it no more. At least they didn't mess up the floor—but there's a place for everything. And you still have to follow the rules."

"Sure," I said. "I understand that."

"I know it wasn't your fault. Some of these guys just don't really give you a chance to say no. Still, you gotta be kind of firm with 'em—some of these piss masters. For their own good—and yours. I mean, you like this shit; I like it too. I'm not trying to be holier-than-thou. But—still—you gotta obey the rules."

"Look," I said. "Before, you said that when you were closing up, you'd let me go downstairs to see if I could find my shirt...?"

He looked up, frowned, then seemed to remember. "Oh, yeah. That's right." He wiped his hands on a towel. "Come on, then."

I followed him to a door that had been locked for the last few hours; after he unlocked it (with a key on the ring at the side of his leather jock), I followed him downstairs.

He turned on some more bright work lights. I found the Ping-Pong table in a hallway in the back, but when I pulled it away from the wall, my shirt wasn't there.

"You know," he said, while we walked back up the brick-walled steps, "when they hose that place out, after the guys get finished with it, they really hose it down good. The walls, the ceiling, every-thing—then they slop a couple of barrels full of disinfectant around—and hose it out again. Anything that's in there, it goes out as garbage. I mean, you can understand that, can't you?"

"Yeah," I said. "Sure. I understand."

Then, when we were coming out between the raw brick walls into the upper bar again: "You see, we don't have it set up to clean out upstairs the way we can clean it out down here. We don't got the hoses and stuff. That's why we have the rules we do."

"Yeah," I said.

Tex was gone now. Besides the two bartenders, I was the last person to leave.

But when I got outside though, on the porch, with the meat hooks off under the awning to the left, Tex was waiting on the sidewalk—still shirtless (like me), in just his jeans and boots.

"Hey," he said. "I got my truck. You going to Brooklyn, or maybe down toward Canal Street—I'll give you a ride, boy! I can't stay over or nothin'. But we can go in my truck! You like that? You like to ride in a real trucker's truck? It's all mine, too—all paid for over three years ago now. Ain't a big one. But it's mine."

I grinned. "Thanks, Tex. I'd appreciate that. But I'm heading uptown."

"Oh...." He looked really sorry. "Well, then. I gotta get going, too. I'm gonna be late as it is, boy. I should have been out of here and back on the road by midnight. And it's fuckin' four in the god-damn morning!"

"Hey, Tex," I said. "I was just wondering. Did anybody ever tell you that weren't supposed to call black guys 'boy'?"

"Oh, shit...!" Tex said, looking down and stepping aside. "Just about once every six weeks as far back as I can fuckin' remember—and, well, goddamn it, I must be gettin' fuckin' senile already—" he reached up and scratched his short brush of white hair—" 'cause I never can fuckin' remember it! Look—" he raised a hand in front of his face, rough palm toward me—"I swear up and down, if it makes you feel any better, I sure don't mean no offense by it. So help me, I ain't callin' you boy 'cause you a nigger; I'm callin' you 'boy' 'cause to me you look like a fuckin' *kid!* Believe me, I ain't out to offend no niggers! It's my fuckin' *birthday*, man! I just wanna have a good time! Hey, why would I be out to hurt some nigger's feelin's after a blowjob like that? And if I did, so help me, I'm sorry, I'm sorry, I'm *sorry*—!"

"Okay, *okay!*" I said. "Okay!"

"Why am I gonna go out and try to make people feel bad on my fuckin' birthday? That's fuckin' *crazy*, ain't it? I'm just tryin' to have me a good time, gettin' my dick sucked, tryin' to let you have a good time swingin' on my meat—that's all! There wasn't nothin' bad meant by it! I swear, up, down, sideways, and on my momma's grave! I didn't mean nothin', not a thing, I tell you—"

"*Okay!*"

He looked at me, with a kind of child's bewilderment in his aging face, dropped his hand he'd been fending me off with, and thrust it out to shake. "No offense then, nigger...?"

It kind of made me start. Then I laughed. "No offense, you fart-faced old toothless piss-drippin' scumbag honky!"

He grabbed my hand as I raised it, and pumped it hard, laughing too, and, with his other hand grasped my bare shoulder. "That's more like it, boy! Hey, I don't give a fuck if I'm late. I'll give you a ride up to wherever you live anyway—four hours late now, a fifth ain't gonna kill me! You just gotta point me in the right direction. When we get to the truck, I'll even pop my teeth and suck *your* dick for you—you can blow your big black load right down my throat. You sucked *my* dick; I done pissed in your mouth—twice! And I'll suck *your* fuckin' dick, nigger—without my teeth, too. How you gonna think I'm fuckin' prejudiced after that, *huh?* Come on, now. We'll—"

"That's okay," I said. "You have to get on. And so do I."

"Naw, come *on!* I'd be *right* obliged to suck your dick, boy. You gave me a real good suck—two of 'em. And you don't find a toothless cocksucker like me every day—I can make that meat of yours feel *real* good, nigger!"

I laughed because there was nothing else to do. "Thanks. But maybe when you come through the next time. Okay?"

"Well—I guess if you gotta go. And, well, yeah—I should be gettin' along, too, I suppose. Okay. Maybe I'll see you next time I'm through." He ducked his white-haired head. "G'night! Hey—and thanks again for my birthday blowjob! That was real nice!" He turned down the nighttime city sidewalk, heading—shirtless and bowlegged—toward the corner.

I turned and walked the other way.

How does a black guy in a pair of urine-soaked jeans, with no shirt, two blocks from the waterfront, get a cab, I wondered, at 4:00 in the morning?

But on the corner, I saw the Number 11 bus that runs right up Amsterdam Avenue.

I had some change in my pocket. I hurried across the street, made for the bus's open door—wondering whether the driver would say anything.

I climbed up and funneled my ninety cents off my fingers into change box.

The driver frowned up at me from under his visor and said, "*Jesus*, nigger—a rough night, huh?" But he was another black guy.

I smiled, nodded. "Yeah…rough night." That was the good feeling speaking; I wonder if the driver heard any of it. Or, really, if Tex had?

"It looks like it." Then he shook his head and went back to looking out the windshield.

But maybe when you're feeling that good—and looking that bad—it has to be a private thing.

I walked to the back of the bus, sat, and leaned forward on my knees—I was the only passenger.

After waiting another thirty seconds, the driver leaned forward to take the wheel, pushed the pedal that thunked the doors closed and, hauling the wheel around, pulled from the curb to start the whining bus uptown.

A few weeks later, after getting out of work at an office on Fifty-seventh Street, I stopped into the Grotto movie theater on Eighth Avenue; you can usually find some action there, and it's still only three dollars.

I'd just finished blowing a rather thinnish man in a maroon shirt, sitting down toward the front of the balcony in a little row of double seats they have there (especially for sex, you'd almost assume), when I saw Pheldon. We drifted together and stood in the back, talking a bit about what was available and what was not. It was Pheldon's day off, and he'd been there since the afternoon. I had my briefcase with me—and Phel, who lives only three blocks away from me and gets off at the same subway stop I do, said: "I'm about to leave. But if you want to hang out here a little longer, I'll take your briefcase home and give it to your super. Then you don't have to worry about someone snatching it when you've got your face buried in some number's lap!"

"You're a good friend, Phel," I said.

So he took it and went off.

Shortly after that, I went downstairs to the bathroom. There was a youngish (nineteen? twenty-one?) Guardian Angel standing around—in a black beret, rather than the traditional red one. He was white. (Most Guardian Angels are Hispanic or black.) Half a head shorter than I was, he was a scrawny little nail biter, in the kind of jeans that were bleached by the company that made them to look as if they'd been well, well washed. As soon as I came in, he started talking to me, complaining about a migraine headache. He'd had it for three days. He'd even been to the hospital emergency room about it. They had told him to rest and drink liquids. But he didn't understand how drinking liquids was going to help a goddamn headache—though that's why he was hanging around down here with the water cooler. He explained that he had to go on subway patrol the next evening "between seven and eleven," to help the police patrol for muggers and the like.

"Yeah," I said. "I thought maybe you were on duty when I saw you down here. I figured now they're sending in Guardian Angels to make sure the johns of dirty movies are safe for cocksuckers and for queens who want to take it up the ass—not bad, I thought."

He seemed to think that was pretty funny.

On the one hand, the Angels are pretty close to a vigilante organization. Still, given the amount of violence in the city, most New Yorkers think that the Guardian Angels are generally a Good Thing. And when I look up on a subway and see two of them standing by the subway doors, arms folded, in their red berets and white

T-shirts and raccoon's tails, I think most of us feel a little better.

The kid told me he hoped his headache would be gone by tomorrow evening, when he went on duty. I said I hoped so too, and went back upstairs. I checked out the orchestra a couple of times, but not much was going on except the good-looking little PR guy who sits down at the front—all day every day—jerking off and chain-smoking. He's friendly enough and doesn't mind the gay activity around him. He even grins and says hi to those of us he knows. But he isn't into getting his dick sucked—except, as far as I can tell, about once every ten months. And that's only because probably some guy's offered him money.

When I went upstairs, though, I saw the Angel again (basically I made out his black beret), sitting next to the wall in the balcony's first row. I sat down two seats away from him. Three minutes later, he made some comment to the dark about the porn movie on the screen—something about one of the buxom porn star's "Pop-Tart" tits. And soon we were talking again. ("Come on," he said. "Move over here, so we don't have to shout at each other." And I moved—so that we were only *one* seat apart now.) He was from Ohio and had come to New York about a year ago specifically to be a Guardian Angel, after seeing them on a news program, then reading about them in some magazine. I asked: "How do you get involved with the Guardian Angels?"

"Well, anybody can join," he explained. "You just have to be over sixteen. And *you* certainly look over sixteen," which made me laugh. I explained I was just curious and wasn't thinking of it for myself. That surprised him—understandably, I suppose, since in his world the Angels were the Most Important Things There Were. His name was Mark. He said the theater's darkness had rested his eyes and improved his headache. He was looking for an all-night movie to sleep in.

"This one closes at midnight," I told him.

"It does? Aw, shit. You mean I gotta go out and find *another* one?"

I told him about a twenty-four hour movie—the Hesperus—just down the street was cheaper than this one.

"Yeah, somebody told me about that. That's the one I thought I was going into when I came in here. I guess that's 'cause they were on the same block."

I gave him the appropriate warnings about sleeping in the movies: the guys who go around with razor blades, slitting people's pockets and lifting wallets and change.

He explained to me how his favorite parts in the porn movies were the cum shots. (Just as he was telling me, the film obliged us with one—all over the blond heroine's buttocks. "Man," he said, "now that *really* turns me on!") His old lady, he went on to explain, was in the hospital, with blood clots and a cardiac infection. (I wonder if he meant infarction.) It seemed at this point like such a setup that I couldn't resist coming back with the classic line: "Then what are you doing for pussy while your old lady is out of commission?" (Am I making an unnecessarily fine point here adding that "pussy," "old lady," and "out of commission" were all terms *he'd* introduced into the conversation, two or three times each—before I decided they were up for grabs. When I say setup, I *mean* setup.)

He grinned over at me with his weasely little face under its day of stubble and drawled: "Anyone and everyone I can!"

So I moved over to the seat beside him—while we were both still laughing. But we still went on talking for a while. More comments about the movie, while we sat with our feet on the iron rail running along the balcony's rim. A couple of times he hit my knee at some particularly ludicrous part of the film. A couple of times I obligingly hit his back. There was some brief discussion of comparable techniques of men and women at fellatio. (Me: "Then who do you think does it better?" He: "Oh, women. Definitely. Sure. Really." Me: "Suppose I gave you some evidence to prove you wrong?" He: "Well, shit, man—I'm just talkin' about in the movies. Like up there. I don't mean in real life or nothin'.") When it finally came out of his jeans, it was a thick and solid nine inches—one of these little guys who turns out to be all dick, if you know what I mean. While I sucked him, I learned he was also a head holder—which I like. During the buildup to his orgasm, I felt his leg under my chest start to shake. Then, his feet still on the rail, he lifted his butt from the seat cushion, still clutching my head, his whole body quivering. When he was finished, he seemed perfectly content to sit there, rubbing the back of my head, his meat gone soft but still filling my mouth. I thought perhaps he was going to start pissing. But, the truth is, as much as I like that, you just don't find that every time you go down on a dick. Even the best of them. Finally, when I got up, I told him, "You're quite a little stud!"

In perfect seriousness, he frowned over at me. "Little! You call what I got *little?*"

Which made me laugh again. "I was just referring to your…age," I told him. "Compared to mine, that is." Pheldon had just taken me out to dinner for my twenty-fifth birthday about six weeks before, and I was still feeling a little self-conscious about it—but that's *another* story.

"Oh." Then he said: "Hey, you got three dollars?" He added quickly: "This ain't a hustle, man. I ain't no hustler. I'm a Guardian Angel, and Angels don't do shit like that. But just as a friend, I mean. But, since I gotta get out of here and find another movie to sleep in—you know what I mean? I just thought maybe…"

I did feel slightly as if I was being hustled. Still, there I was, in suit and tie; and there he was, with no place to stay for the night. "If I have it in change," I told him, "it's yours." So I went into my pocket and, there in my palm, picking over quarters, nickels, and dimes, I got together two dollars and seventy-five cents and funneled it, chinking, into his cupped hands. "Aw, thanks, man! Really, thanks!" He lifted his ass from the seat again and got the change into his jeans pocket. "I can always get a quarter from *somewhere.*" (I was surprised neither one of us had dropped any on the floor.) "Really—thanks!"

A minute later, I heard faint snoring—Mark had fallen asleep with his head against the wall. Although his dick was back in his pants, he still hadn't zipped his fly, which made a pair of miniature roller-coaster tracks, one beside the other, in the screen's quarter-light.

My watch said it was about seven-fifty.

So I left and went home.

The next day after work, I strolled to Forty-second Street and was—again—walking up Eighth Avenue in the after-work crowds, when I saw him coming up the far sidewalk as I was crossing Forty-third Street. Same beret; same T-shirt. And certainly same jeans and sneakers. Ambling up—just a bit slower than all the hurrying New Yorkers around him—he picked at a sore on his chin with the nubs of his fingers. Over the pimples, his stubble was a day longer.

"Mark…!"

He turned and squinted, like someone in pain. Obviously he didn't recognize me (that day I'd gone into work with just a sports shirt and no tie or jacket, though I still wore slacks), until I said, "I met you in the movies yesterday?"

"Oh, yeah," he said. "The colored fella."

"How're you doing?" I asked. "How's your headache?"

He shook his head. "About the same. I took a whole bottle of Bayer, too. And it didn't do no good. And that was a damned dollar fifty-eight!"

I asked him if he was eating.

"Oh, yeah…" he said, as if that was no particular problem.

" 'Cause I've got most of a whole roast chicken at home I did last night, if you wanted to come up and get some dinner…?" Somehow, running into him the second time, I felt more expansive.

"Naw, naw—I gotta go on subway patrol in about an hour. I don't got time to go nowhere and eat."

"Oh," I said. "Are you staying anywhere…?"

"Yeah," he said. "Tonight I got some friends down there…in the Times Square Motor Hotel…?" He pointed along the street at the sign hanging off the building—which figures in the story of Pheldon and my birthday dinner. (But, as I said, I'm not telling that one.)

"Okay," I said. "Well, good to run into you.…"

"Yeah," he said. And started walking once more.

I went on up toward the Grotto. You run into someone like that twice in two days in the same neighborhood in New York, and you just assume that you'll run into them again. But, with Mark, I haven't.

A little while ago, I phoned Pheldon and said: "I believe we're coming up on another Wet Night. You're the guy who told me about it. Want to go down there with me?"

There was a considered pause at the other end of the line. "I think of you as a social friend," said the familiar voice with its faint West Indian flavoring (though Pheldon has not been anywhere near Montego Bay since he was fourteen). "Sunday brunch and all that. I'm not sure if I'm ready for you to see me wallowing in the tubs of depravity."

"Pheldon…" I said.

"Since it doesn't start till nine," he said, "I'll meet you at the Fiesta at eight. We'll have a drink, then go on down together."

"Okay," I said. "Wednesday—at the Fiesta. At eight."

For some reason, that Wednesday (one of the problems with temp work) they let us go just before four o'clock So I went up to the Strip and decided to hang out that afternoon in the balcony of the Cameo—a porn-film palace on the other side of Eighth Avenue only a trifle less sleazy than the Grotto.

I'd gone down to the men's room to take a leak; when I came back up to the balcony, sitting in the seat beside where I'd been sitting (he must have come in while I was downstairs) was this butch-looking red-bearded guy about twenty-nine. Ordinarily I'd have sat at least a seat away from him, but it really *had* been where I'd been sitting before. So I sat beside him. Not fifteen seconds later, there was a warm knee (his) against a warm knee (mine). I put a warm hand (mine) on a hot crotch (his), thinking we were about to really get it on—but, after a minute, he leaned over toward me and whispered: "Maybe we better not. There're too many people around." In the Cameo balcony (where three blowjobs were going on within sight), ordinarily I'd just have assumed this was his polite way of saying, "Sorry, I've just changed my mind. One of us should probably take a hike." But as he leaned to say it, he put his hand on my shoulder, his callused palm moving against my neck; and his lips brushed my ear, which made me think, well, maybe…. His hand came down from my shoulder to take mine again: the fingers were work-hardened; also, I realized, he didn't have very good teeth at all. And, I confess, there's something about guys with bad teeth—this one's four front ones had about rotted away.

An hour later, I'd learned that this fellow: one, necked like a motherfucker, teeth or no; two, he was hung, if not like a horse at least like a respectable (cut) pony also he was extraordinarily affectionate. At one point, I recall, he took my cock in his rough hand and settled down against me. "Jesus," he whispered, "that feels awful good to hold onto." Such things in the midst of "impersonal" sex kind of wipe me out. Over the next hour, I found out that he was a carpenter who lived in New Jersey with his (well, you can't win 'em all) mother. More unbelievably, he had never been to any of the theaters here on the Strip before—or so he said. He'd been working as an assistant on a job about three blocks to the west; lacking some lumber, they'd broken off work early and the head carpenter had driven back up to New Rochelle. Instead of going to the Port Authority and catching the Short Line back to Elizabeth, New Jersey, he'd wandered up here and come into one of the dirty movies on a lark. Once I pointed out to him the action going on in the seats around us, though ("Jesus, Christ, man—I didn't see *any* of this when I first come in here! I guess if you don't know it's happening, you just don't see it." Baseball players.), he had my cock out of my chinos and into his throat in no time, his arms around my waist, and his head working in my lap.

Once he came off me. "Jesus, man, I hope you don't take offense at this. But I like sucking black dick more than just about anything in the world!" He was down on his knees now, wedged between me and the back of the seats in front of me, holding mine up against his bearded face. "About the only thing better than sucking on one of these things—a nice big black cock—would be sucking on *two* of them! Or maybe three or four..." I just chuckled, locked my hands around the back of his head, and pulled him forward again.

Like I said, usually I'm the guy who gets the load and takes the good memories home to replay them later. I mean, to get *my* load a cocksucker has to be good, not in a rush, sensitive to where I'm at in my excitement, and affectionate: well, at five-thirty, I dropped five squirts of cream into this guy's face that had him hugging me like the thankful cocksucker he was. ("So what would you like two black guys to do to you?" I whispered to him as I helped him get up. He shrugged in my arms, rubbing his beard against my cheek: "I don't know. Just about anything. Fuck me. Stick it in my mouth. Piss on me—anything, man." Now he pulled away—just a little: "I don't mean in any SM way. I mean, friendly-like—the way we're doin'. Doin' it because they *liked* doin' it—because it got them off too, you know?") At quarter to six, bucking his ass off the seat and making enough noise to start some of the queens three rows away giggling (but, I knew, with envy), he gave me an equal load back. A couple of guys a row away applauded—which made him laugh. At quarter past, we were still going after each other's tonsils, tongue first.

"Hey," he said, finally backing up for air. "We really been in here for a while now. You think maybe we could go out for a couple of beers? There's another theater I used to go to, about four blocks down and over on Broadway. It's usually got a lot less people in it than here. We could have some real privacy if we went there. ...Maybe after we drank a few together...?"

"Sure, little guy...."

"Aw, man," he said, nuzzling his beard in my neck, "don't call me that. It gives me a hard-on again...!"

So we left the theater and went up to Smith's, the Irish hot-plate bar on the northwest corner of Forty-fourth and Eighth. Buying alternate rounds of draft, among the lingering crowd of heavy-drinking workingmen left and right, we talked for another hour. More of the guy's story came out: his name was Dave. He was an ex-alcoholic. Well, he wasn't really sure just how ex- he was anymore. Recently he'd been chairing his local A.A. meetings, but about three weeks back, he'd fallen off the wagon. Ther'd been a couple of binges, but nothing yet that had made him miss any work. Tomorrow or the day after, he was going back and get himself straight again. Bisexual by his own judgment, over the last few years he'd been finding himself moving more and more toward men—and what did it signify, he wondered, that it was black men he was most interested in?

"I mean, *are* there black guys who just want to make it with white people—white men?"

Thinking of Pheldon, who, by his own characterization, is a snow-queen, I told him, "Yes. There are."

The racial predilection seemed to have nothing to do with his heterosexual experience. "You know what the hottest thing that ever happened to me was? It was when I was about twenty-five, and I was hitchhiking back home from somewhere down south. Back then, I wouldn't have even said I was bisexual. Back then, I thought of myself as fuckin' *straight*, man! Anyway, this fellow picked me up—a black guy, actually. Big mother, too. Though, at that time, I was hardly even thinking about things like that. But there in his car we got to talkin', jokin' around, and finally he told me he wanted me to come home and fuck his *wife!* At first I thought he was kidding. Then I realize he's serious. Then he tells me that his wife is white—man, I mean, there we are in Georgia or Mississippi or someplace! And when I get to his house—and he had a real nice house, too—this woman is a Cheryl Tiegs look-alike! I'm not kidding. And I fucked her—with him right there, messin' around with us both, beatin' off and feelin' us both up. Man, this woman had some tits! And a mouth that wouldn't quit. And she *loved* gettin' fucked by some strange fella her old man dragged home off the highway! I still jerk off to that one...only now, I imagine *all* the black guys I see around, in there with me. And sometimes I'm the one who just watches, or plays around with them, you know? And sometimes they get after me...." He shook his head, the shift in his own sexual fantasies a real mystery to him.

He went on to explain that he liked big family holidays. But he could put on weight real fast. "A week of holiday eating, man, and I can put on twenty-five, thirty-five pounds. I'm not kidding, man. It's incredible." To me he looked pretty solid, but there were eight or nine pounds, mostly beer, he probably would have been happier without.

By seven-thirty it looked as if we were going to do more beer drinking and talking than anything else, so I made the suggestion that had been drifting in and out of my mind since before we'd left the theater. "So you'd like to get pissed on by a couple of black guys—like me, maybe, and a friend?"

He looked up from his beer mug, gray eyes suddenly gone real big.

"I mean, you're interested in water sports?"

Now he frowned. "Water sports?" His naïveté was sincere. "You mean like water polo and stuff?"

I just laughed—and described Wet Night at the Mineshaft. Dave's first comment, before any of the sexual stuff seemed to register, was "All the beer you can drink? For how much—fifteen dollars? The way I can put it away, man, that's a pretty good deal."

"Well," I said, "I'm going down there with a friend of mine in a little while—another black guy. You fellows might even like each other. His name is Pheldon. He's West Indian."

"Gee. Some of them West Indian guys," Dave said, describing Pheldon almost perfectly, "are *real* black, aren't they?"

I just grinned. Not smiled—grinned.

"Well...I can't say I haven't thought about it," he admitted finally. "Sure. I'd like to go and at least check it out."

So we left Smith's, walked up to Forty-sixth Street, and went around to the Fiesta, where, in his motorcycle jacket and no shirt under it, black jeans, and engineer's boots, Pheldon, who is a muscular, blue-black, 6'2", thirty-five-year-old photographic librarian for a major city newspaper, was leaning over the counter edge, engaging La Veuve—the bartender—in a round of jokes:

"Did you hear the one about the groom who couldn't find his bride? He forgot where he'd laid her last...."

"How do they separate the men from the boys in Greenwich Village? With a crowbar...."

"Kid goes to his dad and asks, 'Dad, can I have ten dollars to get myself a guinea pig?' His father says, 'Here's fifteen. Go get yourself a nice Irish girl....'"

That last one put Dave practically on the floor. So I assume his and Pheldon's friendship started on a positive note.

"Nice to meet you, man. You're a new friend of John's...?"

I'd come in chinos and sports shirt this time—while carpenter Dave was in plaster and paint-splotched corduroys, orange construction shoes, and a plaid shirt rolled up his forearms.

I explained to Phel that Dave was a friend I'd just met in the movies—

"The Cameo? Oh, I *see*...!"

—who wanted to check out Wet Night downtown.

"Now did this cocksucker"—Pheldon put one hand on Dave's shoulder and leaned close—"who rode home on a bus in pissdrenched jeans and no shirt at four in the morning last month, because he's just a *little* slow about some things, tell you what you're supposed to do about your clothing when you get there?"

Dave looked back at me, questioning. "Yeah...about the clothes check?"

"Good."

The Fiesta is not that far down from the Pit—yes, where Timothy Hasler was killed. And though I still don't like going in there, I'd at least figured out by now the ecological deployment of gay bars along the Strip. The Pit was the hard-core hustling bar. When both the johns and the hustlers got tired of the hard sell, they drifted down here to the Fiesta—for what I guess you could call soft-core hustling.

A couple of times, Dave asked: "This is really a hustling bar, huh? It seems pretty nice." (Calling the Fiesta "nice"—I mean, it's still pretty sleazy—made me wonder what kind of bars Dave usually went into.) "You mean all these guys are really *hustling?* Well, what do you know!" But some people really are just both nice *and* naïve.

We stayed for another few rounds, and when Dave dutifully paid for his, Pheldon laughed: "Now have you ever seen anyone who looks as hot as he does pay for a round a drinks in here in your life?" which I'm afraid went over Dave's head.

A bit after eight-thirty, the three of us got on the subway, rode down to Fourteenth Street, and walked down the empty cobbled streets toward the waterfront, by concrete porches under the meat warehouses' hook-hung awnings. At the Mineshaft's narrow doorway, we joined the GSA line—of about twenty-five, thirty guys—though it already went in and up the stairs to the second floor.

About five-to-nine, they let us start filing up.

The leather-capped cashier at the upstairs desk asked: "You're here for the GSA party?"

"Three of us," Pheldon said.

"All right." One after the other, as we shelled out, he stamped the back of my hand with a (waterproof?) marker. That made a slightly smeared, luminescent yellow-green star over the brown ligaments as my hand passed before a cold violet tube of black light, becoming invisible when I lifted it to look—a new wrinkle since last time. "So, if you want to go out for a little while, maybe visit another bar," the cashier explained to my frown, "you can come back in here and we know you've already paid. Right through there." He reached out to stamp the others.

Inside, men were lining up at the clothes check on the right side of the bar. One of the upstairs bartenders wore studded gauntlets and a metal-studded jockstrap like last time. The other was in lederhosen, with engineer boots and a black leather SS cap—though neither was the guy who'd given Tex and Horse the hard time, or who'd let me go down to look for my hosed-out shirt. Somehow ending up several guys ahead of us in line, Phel got rid of his coat and pants real fast and had already gone down. So behind Dave, I said, "You don't *have* to check your clothes. But I've been here once before, and I didn't. Take my advice and leave them up here. You'll be happier."

"I'm checkin' 'em! I'm checkin' 'em!" Dave hopped on one foot, corduroy pants around one ankle, plaid shirt already off one shoulder. Then he glanced up at me. "You're just gonna go down there completely *naked?*"

"Except my shoes," I said.

"Okay." Dave handed his clothes through the window. We put the elastic check tags around our wrists.

Besides his orange work boots and socks, though, Dave kept on a pair of brand-new-looking Fruit of the Loom briefs—which I'd gotten down once as far as his knees and twice as far as his ankles, back in the Cameo.

He turned to follow me into the narrow brick stairwell, a hand on either wall.

At the downstairs bar, though still generally subdued, there was more talk and laughter than last time. Once a big guy reached past me, leather vest swinging back from a pumped-up chest with a thick tit-ring through an outsized nipple. "Hey, there." I said, as he came back with a can of Schmidt's.

The big, bearded guy looked down, then grinned. "Oh, how you doin' there?"

"Back again," I said. "Seems I can't stay away."

"Know what you mean," Horse told me.

I introduced him to Dave (Pheldon was off somewhere in the back already)—and learned that Horse's *actual* name was Kelly. We talked some more—he was explaining something technical to me about sound patching, when suddenly he stopped and put his arm around my shoulder. With his other hand, he reached down and pressed low on his belly—tonight, besides his vest, he was wearing just a rented jockstrap and, like Phel, black engineer boots. "The pressure's kind of building up in there—in a minute, I'm gonna have to get off in the back and let some of this out." He took a breath. "You and me, last time we were here, we had a good time together, didn't we?"

"Yeah," I said. "We did—"

"The thing is," he looked down, then up, "the way I like to work it is not to do any serious messing around with the same guy—or guys—two Wet Nights in a row. You know what I mean? I like to spread it around, use different guys each time."

"Oh," I said, "yeah. Sure."

"It's just one of my rules. Tonight. For this place."

I nodded.

"Look," he said. "Three, maybe five months from now—we'll run into each other here. Then we'll get it on again. But that's just how I like to do it, you understand?"

"Sure," I repeated. "Yeah, I can dig that." I was a little surprised—and though I wasn't really thinking about any marathon piss-drinking session yet myself, I confess, I was a little disappointed.

He gave me another grin and a heavy pat on the shoulder. Then he took up his beer can and walked away from the bar. I turned back to Dave, who was on his second beer. "Come on," I said. "Let me take you back into the tub room and show you around."

"Okay." He picked up his beer and we moved away, through one of the brick arches, into a hall that led to the dim rooms in the back. A couple of times we started to make out again—doing pretty ordinary things to each other, while the sound of trickling water or—occasionally—a smack on someone's buttocks resonated around us. Once we found ourselves in a tight little circle with three other guys, playing with ourselves, now reaching out to feel each other up. Then one, another, and another—including Dave, cock out the leg of his drawers, and me—began to urinate. Warm, messy, fun—still, it was on the tame side. But Dave's briefs got soaked to near-transparency. And he kept grinning over at me as though the whole thing were pretty wiggy, so I guess it was a good introduction.

I left him at one of the tubs, watching some guy still in a business suit take it from the guys clustering around him, both clothed and naked: seven, eight, ten streams soaked his pin-striped lapels, his Gucci tie, poured into the open fly of his natty slacks.

"I'm going to move around a little," I whispered. "I'll see you in a bit."

Dave nodded in the half-dark. "Yeah. Okay...." and I drifted away.

Fifteen minutes later, I was back at the downstairs bar for a refill on beer. Thirty seconds later, with a (wet, rough) hand on my shoulder, Dave joined me. "Man, this is pretty fuckin' wild!" He finished one can, put it down, leaned over, pulled one back from the four the bartender set out, and upended it for a long swallow. "I seen some stuff here tonight like I never seen before in my whole fuckin' life! There was one corner, where they had this leather...thing.

Like a big swing. On chains. And one guy was in it, on his back, with his legs up in the air; and another guy had his whole goddamned *hand* up the guy's ass! I mean, to here...!" And, with one hand coming down halfway up his forearm, Dave demonstrated the depth. "That's fuckin' unbelievable! The guy with his fist up the other guy's ass was black, too. The guy takin' it was white." Dave shook his head. "That was fuckin' something. I don't know if I'm ready for that, yet." He took another drink of beer. "But it sure was somethin' to see!" He put the beer back on the aluminum counter. "I counted about nine colored guys here—not counting Puerto Ricans." Dave, wouldn't you know, had counted. "They ever have *more* black guys than this here?"

"I haven't been here that often." I shrugged. "So I couldn't tell you—but somehow I doubt it, though."

"You're all pretty nice-lookin'," Dave said. "It ain't sayin' nothin' bad about you, but I'd give almost any one of 'em I've seen here tonight a tumble—"

I ruffled his hair. "You'd tumble with any nigger who looked at you, wouldn't you, white boy?"

He grinned at me like a redheaded puppy.

At which point, having gotten rid of all his clothes, Pheldon stepped up and said, "So, how do you like being someplace where, any moment, someone may just walk up and"—letting go, he turned left, then right, to blitz the bellies, thighs, or buttocks of me, Dave—and everyone within four feet—"piss all over you!"

I laughed, as did the guys on either side of us. But Dave leaped back as though he'd stepped on a tack, bumping into one guy, making another spill half a can of beer, foaming down his hand to the puddled concrete. After saying "I'm sorry" a lot, "Oh, gee, fella, I'm sorry," Dave stepped back up, grinning and embarrassed. "Man, I don't know. I don't know..." he kept saying. "I don't know about this. I know I'm gonna come back here. Yeah, I know that. But I don't know...I mean, if I'm really ready for all this. But it's real interesting."

Cannonball-shouldered, mahogany-hipped Pheldon grabbed Dave by the back of the head and pulled him up close—beer splashed on them both. "Didn't I hear you say something about wanting a nigger to piss all *over* you, white boy?"

"Oh, Jesus...!" Dave grinned with idiot pleasure. "*Jesus*, man!"

Later, moving through the back rooms, in a blue-lit corner I came on Phel and Dave getting it on together. As I stopped to watch, Phel bent Dave's head back, deep-kissing him. Dave had his eyes closed, but Phel was blinking, eyes like ivory lozenges under the blue light.

And he saw me.

Now he began to push Dave down, as thought he wanted him to go down on his dick. "Shit," Phel said, breathing hard and hoarsely. "I think I'm gonna *piss* on this honky motherfucker! That'd really make me feel good." He turned back and beckoned to me. "Hey, bro'—come on over here, and piss in this white motherfucker's face with me."

I'd actually been carrying a pretty full bladder toward the tubs in the back, to see if anyone was in there who needed spritzing. But now I stepped up beside Phel, who put his arm around my shoulder.

Phel let go his stream.

Piss hit Dave on the cheek—he was sitting against the wall now. He shook his head once, but didn't try to get out of Phel's way. Dave reached for my cock—his rough carpenter's grip felt good and familiar. I let go—not as strongly as I might have, because just his hand had gotten me half-hard. But it arched out and struck his shoulder, to run down his chest. With his other hand, Dave began to rub the sheeting urine around.

"Go ahead, nigger," Phel repeated. "Piss on that white motherfucker! Look at him—that white boy *loves* nigger piss! Don't you, honky?"

Blinking up at us, Dave nodded. His mouth was open. Some of mine, then some of Phel's, got into it. When it did, Dave swallowed. But he wasn't into drinking it all, the way I'd been. He rubbed it over his chest, over his face, down his belly. One hand went under his briefs and he pulled out his cock. Balls slipping over the sopping rope his briefs had rolled into, he began jerking off.

Then a voice, real deep, said, "You pissin' in the sonofabitch's face, nigger? Just a second, here—lemme throw some juice at the white motherfucker, too!"

I looked up. It was the tall, 250-, 280-pound black with the glasses, whom I'd last seen, last month, urinating in the white guy's mouth when I'd first come into the Real Men's Room. His baseball cap was again on backward. He wedged up on the other side of Phel—he still had a beer can in one hand—and let go. In three waves of his cock, he wet Dave down from the bridge of his nose to his nuts.

Dave put his head back against the brick and beat his cock harder, looking up at one of us and, then the other.

Phel ran out first.

Still beating, Dave lurched forward on his knees and took Phel's dick in his mouth. His wet hand held my thigh. He came off Phel to go to the new man, who was still pissing—he gave the guy's thick, spurting dick three sucks, then he coughed or something. Urine erupted from Dave's mouth; it ran out his nose, too.

Again Dave fell back against the wall, wiping at his face with one hand, still beating his meat with the other.

In a voice deep as Darth Vader's and as country as Stepin Fetchit's, the new man intoned, "Suck that big black dick, white boy! You got three pieces of prime nigger meat here—don't you let it go to waste now!" And Dave lurched forward, now getting the new guy again for half a dozen sucks.

"Hey, there, little guy," I told said, "you're doin' real good there. Keep it up!"

Increasing his speed, now Dave moved on to Pheldon (the only one of us who, with his ten-and-a-half downcurved, uncut, graphite-blue inches, anyone could say had a *really* big black dick), to give him another dozen sucks.

Finally, he was back on my eight-inch, cut, mahogany prong. Inside his warm mouth, I felt my growing hard-on stop my stream.

The feeling it gave me was funny: suddenly I was overcome by a sense of just how happy the little white cocksucker was, with three black guys pissing all over him, with my black dick down his throat and two more prodding at his mouth.

I felt myself start to cum.

Because it's unusual for me to get off like that, though, and because I'd already cum with him once, I thought it was going to be one of those half-orgasms that starts but doesn't go all the way. I readied myself for it to peter out at the halfway point— like a sneeze that doesn't happen.

Pheldon was still holding me. Around beside Dave, the other

man had wedged his leg against him and reached down to take Dave's pale shoulder in his dark, thick hand; his piss was still running, breaking over his own heavy fingers, dribbling down Dave's chest, getting all on my leg, too, where a wet Dave was hugging my thigh—warm and kind of electric.

Suddenly, instead of fading, my orgasm moved to new level—it *wasn't* going to stop! It kept on blooming! Then I kind of exploded inside Dave's throat. "Goddamn...!" I reached down and clutched his head.

He was still beating down there. His face was caught between my groin and Pheldon's. His free hand was groping for the other man's cock now.

Dave began to grunt.

Pheldon said, a little incredulous: "You *came*...?"

I nodded, taking a deep breath.

"God *damn*...!" Pheldon said, with both appreciation and envy.

Phel strengthened his grip around my waist. With his free hand, he hefted up his shift and began to pump. His fist was up against Dave's face, and he hit Dave's ear half a dozen times, so that I could see Dave's head jerk, and feel it through his mouth on my softening dick, till it slipped free.

Maybe it was just a theatrical gesture for Pheldon, but Dave raised his face; his tongue came out his mouth, blobbed with my cream; cum ran down the side of his chin onto his beard. With his eyes closed, Dave strained his tongue out and down to get the spilled jism back in.

"Look at that honky suck scum!" the big guy said. "Go on, Jim, make yourself feel good! Cum in his fuckin' honky face...!"

I reached over to hold Pheldon's balls; Dave's free hand was already there.

Leaning forward now, one hand on the brick, Pheldon shot. Some got in Dave's mouth; some splattered his cheek. Now Dave took about three-quarters of Pheldon's dick while Phel's dark fingers pumped the base, beating Dave's mouth.

Pheldon whispered, "Jesus H. *Christ*...!" and, using the wall, pushed himself upright again.

Dave collapsed away from all three of us.

His fist at his groin was pumping too fast to see. Leaning on brick, Dave's face strained up—with his bad teeth in the center of

a grimace that was either pure pain or pure something else....
His grunts became a gasp.

Dave shot—up over his belly, spilling down his fist. Gasping, he moved his other hand from Phel's stomach to mine—then back to the third man's. He had finally finished urinating.

The big guy said, "Guess your white boy's all right down there, now." He gave Phel and me a grin, patted Dave's shoulder. "That was real nice there, honky." He stood up, and reached an open palm across to me.

Still breathing hard and kind of out of it, Pheldon just looked.

But I gave him (a very low) high five.

"Yeah...!" The big man said, and took another swallow of beer. "Ain't nothin' like peein' on a white boy, is there?" Nodding to us, he turned—"It just makes *everybody* feel good, don't it? Okay, fellas, so long—" and lumbered out of the light.

From the floor, Dave said, "Jesus!"

"Need a hand up there?" Phel reached down to lift Dave. "That's a cryin' shame, boy. I thought I was gonna get that load out of you. And there it is all over your belly."

"Yeah," Dave said.

I gave him a hand, too.

"What am I gonna do with this shit, now? I mean it's a shame to waste it."

"Isn't much you can do with it now," I said.

Still hanging on me, Dave said, "Usually I eat mine—when I beat off by myself. When I'm alone, I mean. I started that when I was a kid."

"Huh? Really?" Phel asked. "Well, knock yourself out. It won't be the strangest thing I've ever seen."

"You don't mind?" Dave asked.

I just laughed and, still supporting him, shook my head.

Hanging on me with one arm, Dave brought his other hand to his mouth and took a big lick across the back. Then he turned his hand over and ran the little finger, then his forefinger, into his mouth.

Letting my speech get a little blacker than it usually was, I said, "Cum and nigger piss—that should be a real treat for you, honky."

"Yeah." Dave grinned at me. "It is. Want some?"

"Why not?" I said. Dave held his hand up to my face, and I licked the mucus off his palm—surprised again at how hard carpentering had made it. "Good stuff."

"Oh, man," Pheldon said. He'd stepped away from Dave now. "Will you two fuckers cut it out? Let's go get a beer, huh?"

So we came out the arch and went back to the aluminum counter. (Pheldon never did arrive, though. Some guy in a leather harness got into that black dick of his while he was passing by; so he looked at us, smiled, shrugged, and we left him in the hallway.) At the bar, hopping now on one orange construction shoe, now on the other (both darkened with urine), Dave finally tugged off his briefs. "My socks are fuckin' scrungy, man!" He shook his head.

"So are everybody's, pretty much," I said.

Dave still had Pheldon's cum all over the left side of his face. But I didn't say anything. While he swigged at another beer, it made him look even cuter.

As usual, they closed the downstairs at midnight.

Upstairs, after he got back into his corduroys and shirt, and, when the bartender said something ("What's that on your cheek, guy?" "Oh, shit, man—this? Oh, Jesus—lemme get a napkin here. Oh, *shit*, you mean I been walkin' around with *cum* on my face all night? Oh, *man*...!"), wiped off his cheek and beard with a square bar napkin, Dave stayed through one more beer.

"But I got to go to work tomorrow," he told us. "And that's after I get back up to Port Authority and catch a late bus out to New Jersey!"

I gave Dave my number. Enthusiastically, he gave me his.

Pheldon, I noticed, abstained from this ritual.

"Now, my mom's name is Pat Collins," Dave explained. "In Elizabeth, New Jersey. So even if you lose it, you can still get me through Information." On his way out, he flung the wet wad of his briefs down into the green oil drum standing in the corner, with the ruffled collar of a plastic garbage bag flowering its rim. "I sure as hell ain't never gonna wear *those* things again!" Then, with a grin and a head shake, he went out the door for the stairs.

"Damn," Pheldon said. "If I was as much into black piss as that boy is, *I'd* have taken 'em back to Jersey with me as a souvenir."

"He probably would have if they were yours," I said. "Or mine."

"Well, yeah," Pheldon said. "There's that." And, still naked,

Pheldon turned to move away, like a broad-shouldered black scarecrow, toward the bar's darker half.

Again, I stayed till closing.

Got into a couple of pretty wild scenes up there, too—this time, all within the rules. One—no kidding—involved the big black guy with the voice (I got his actual load) *and* Horse Bladder Kelly, who, by the night's end, was too drunk or too desperate to remember me, or his own rules, or something. Anyway, I had even more fun that time than I did the first. And, by the end of it, I was feeling just as good as before.

When the upstairs bartenders starting calling, "All in," I ferreted Pheldon out of the shadows, and (in all my clothes this time) rode uptown with him on the bus.

(The only problem, as Dave had said, was wet shoes and socks.)

We got off at Seventy-ninth Street and, as Thursday broke indigo and copper over the trees away toward Central Park, we went into a coffee shop just opening up and had ourselves an immense breakfast of pancakes, eggs, sausage, juice, and coffee.

On the other side of the booth's seafoam blue Formica table, back in his motorcycle jacket, Pheldon leaned toward me. "I think our friendship, John, has entered a new phase. And I would really be upset if this changed anything—I mean, because of it."

I frowned. "Oh, come on, Phel," I said. "I've seen your big black dick before tonight."

"But—before—*only* in photographs…of that orgy I had at my place last Christmas. To which you were *not* invited. And this is certainly the first time you've ever seen me dump my load all over some hungry dinge-queen's mug! I'd feel just awful, though, if the next time we went to brunch, there were these long and awkward silences because your mind was elsewhere and the ordinary demands of civility and gossip had suddenly become too great a strain."

I grinned. "Don't worry, Phel. That's not me."

"I hope it isn't," he said, sitting back and lifting a triangle of toast to take a very large bite. "Although most of my affections go toward the Daves of this world—as I have never made a secret of, at least from you—the fact is, John, I don't *have* a lot of black, gay men friends. You mean a lot to me."

"He was cute as a button," I said. "I kind of got off, sharing him with you. And *he* sure liked it."

"You did?" Pheldon asked, surprised. "You know, we really *are* friends, aren't we?"

"Even if we never get undressed in each other's presence again. Feel better now?"

Under his leather cap, Phel cocked his head. "You're a sweetheart!"

I laughed and held up my cup for the squat Greek waiter passing by to pour me more decaf.

Phel said he was going into the newspaper library early—

"Like *that?*"

"Nobody'll be there when I get in. Besides, after six years I've about got them trained—and I have a change of clothes at work, anyway."

—and he would stay till around noon, then come home early and take a nap.

I made halfhearted noises about going in today myself.

Good as I was feeling, though, when I got home I called in to work and told them I'd be out that day. With temp work, you can do that a little easier than at a regular job.

I'd been waiting for Dave to call. But now I decided, what the hell—I'd call him. (I'd always assumed that was the prerogative of the younger guy—and I was a couple of years down on him.) After work one evening, I phoned the number he'd given me—to find, after four or five tries, it wasn't even a New Jersey exchange.

I was a little surprised at that.

So then I called Information like he'd said.

There was no Pat Collins in Elizabeth, New Jersey.

Now people are always giving out phony numbers and phony names in sexual situations—a couple of times I've done it myself. But I hadn't been badgering him for his. I'd just given him mine and he'd volunteered his own back.

A couple more calls to the New Jersey operator, and I found out that there were only three Pat Collinses in the entire area code—none even close to Elizabeth.

One turned out to be an older guy.

One was a woman who'd never heard of Dave and didn't sound old enough to be mother of anyone older than three.

And the last one was no longer in service.

If I had to characterize Dave with only, say, three words, I would say good-hearted, affectionate, and naïve. But it was disappointing to find that the naïveté extended to his feeling that, just as a matter of course, he had to give out phony names and addresses to everyone he met.

"Well," said Pheldon, "I kind of had a feeling about the guy. That's why I didn't offer him mine—although I certainly had the urge."

"You mean you picked up on the kind of guy he was?"

"I had a feeling," Phel repeated.

Me? Talk about naïve.

But, as I figured when I thought about it later (and, when we got to talk about it later, Pheldon agreed), the guy was probably scared.

An alcoholic working-class white guy from New Jersey, who, at twenty-nine or so, realizes he's turning gay, that he likes to make it with black guys, and that he wants them to piss all over him, well—especially if he's also basically a nice, affectionate guy—in this country that guy has a lot to be scared of!

And I don't mean big, obliging niggers, either.

Sam, I've been writing this letter, as you might imagine, over a number of days now. Rereading it tonight, I've been wondering if there isn't, finally, something wrong with my portraits so far—of me, of the men I have sex with, of those I see having sex around me. It's not that any particular detail within them is untrue. (You have no idea how I've tried to discipline my account here and keep it strictly to the observed!) Rather, as the incidents from which such portraits are constructed pass in life, they occur in a context that, because I have, yes, omitted it, I feel falsifies them. The point is that, in these depressed sections of the city I've been describing, there is life. (And very much the life I recount.) But it functions under incomparable silences, in streets full of strangers, snarled in a net of degradation that, to specify with some rhetorical color (the old men in baggy suits with their adjustable aluminum canes still bearing the blue sticker, "Property of Bellevue Hospital," or the anorexic six-foot drag queen in shorts and bandanna, standing on the movie-house steps, giggling over a peach in her hand and hiccuping, "Oh, mah' Lord, this is a peach! Isn't this a peach? I could hit somebody with this peach and do damage!") is to distort it by the very gesture that takes the oppressively general and represents it as the humanized specific.

Just to take the few blocks on and off Eighth Avenue that cradle within them the Grotto, the Agape, the Hesperus, the Cameo, the Fiesta, and the Pit:

In those doorways, bars, porn-magazine and peep-show shops, the movie theaters where sight itself is so dimmed, in such theatrical darkness true vision is simply and largely absent. In one sense all the encounters that occur here take place on some vast and dreary Audenesque plain where a thousand people mill, where no one knows anyone else, and there is nowhere to sit down. Someone new coming here might never see some of the encounters I've described: there is such effort to hide them. Any exchange resembling real conversation takes place quietly and ceases when a stranger walks by.

The bourgeois visitor always goes home with reports of this area's violence, but that is to repress all mention and memory of what is truly terrifying here: the vast stasis, the immense periods of time—hours, days, weeks—when *nothing* happens, when psychic immobility reigns in the lives of those stalled here at an intensity people at jobs, people in families just cannot conceive of.

It's meaningful that, with the Strip below it, Hell's Kitchen a block to the west, the theater district just to the east, and midtown Manhattan right above it, this particular area has no name of its own—certainly no name that I, Pheldon, Mark, La Veuve, or any of the other people who, monetarily or emotionally, live in or off it all share and can use to speak about it in common. (Outsiders tend to call it by any of the names above—"Theater District," "Hell's Kitchen," "the Strip"—depending from which area they approach it, always feeling, as they pass into it and out of it, that something is nominally wrong—even as the city fathers from time to time write in the papers about tearing it down or destroying it.) When I made this point to him, Phel suggested, "What about calling it the Midtown Mausoleum and Take-out Service...?" But when it finally does develop some geographical sobriquet with which the tourists who stroll out of the Milford Plaza or straggle over from the theater to catch the uptown bus on Eighth Avenue can think about it fondly or fearfully in private, then it will no longer be the same place.

Talking about it with us one day at the Fiesta just before planting an upside down tumbler on the bar before us both (i.e., buying both Phel and me a drink on the house), La Veuve told us, "You know, you're right. Now I remember, about eight or nine years ago, a bunch of the regulars at the bars here started calling it the Minnesota Strip—because that summer four or five farm boys turned up hustling at the Pit who started out in—or at least came by way of—Minnesota. But that name only lasted a season. You're right—it doesn't really *have* a name. Or, at least, it doesn't seem to be able to keep one when it gets one."

Let me try, then, Sam, for a more generalized collection of—well, snapshots, instead of portraits. Let me move from the narrative totality I've been so far seeking to another, more abstract narrative level that might, finally, be more revealing.

Whether angry, fearful, or content (and there are those), the women who come here are insistently passive in a way that should be deeply studied by feminist analysts. (This immobility was, for example, the real object of a group such as Women Against Pornography. And this area is precisely where they had their "shows" and organized their "tours," even as they were unable to grasp and grapple with the pornographic figure—because their true object was the ground that informed it—until they finally wandered away in muddled paranoia to persecute other feminists with better analytical tools than they.) When these knots are truly untied and teased apart for serious view, then real understanding of the psychosocial calamity in which we live may finally begin.

Outside the residence hotels (where the alcoholics and the drug addicts and the crippled and the mad and, yes, the merely poor and confused try to hide with dignity, sometimes succeeding heroically, sometimes failing at a degree of pathos unimaginable to someone who does not pass the momentarily open door of some twelfth-floor room, packed with newspapers and trash, floor to ceiling, in which a seventy-year-old woman lives), when we speak of women, we are seldom speaking about more than 10 percent of any visible group. That means, of course, that in *some* places, like the Times Square Motor Hotel, in its elevators, in its halls, in its high-ceilinged and gilt-molded lobby, in the hive of rooms above, when we speak of women we are speaking about 85 percent or more of the population!

In her forties and living at the Times Square for (I overheard her say) the last three years, Dodie looks more like sixty. Her pale face seems as if it has been smashed up and put back together hastily, a little makeup applied hurriedly to hide—ineffectually—the damages. Chain-smoking, in a small black hat, she sat all last night at the bar in Smith's, on the other side of the partition from the hot-plate counter, sipping gin and tonic, the only woman in a bar full of workmen, or men who would like to be through working, discussing her alcoholism with insight and intelligence, dispensing sympathy to every masculine problem presented her. One could wonder why I say such a woman seems "passive." She could as easily be called a gutsy, ballsy woman. She disagrees, she argues, she laughs loudly, she has strong opinions. Her sympathy? Isn't it simply the compassion of a middle-aged woman who's lived a hard life? But listen: she is sympathetic to every idea that is presented. All her considerable ire and hostility is reserved for whatever or whoever is absent. Were Governor Long sitting on one side of her and Reverend King on the other, she would be equally supportive of both (solely because both were male and there)—and equally and articulately against what each of them disapproved of (because it was not there).

It is not that her sympathy—or her antipathy—is false.

Or even hypocritical.

It is that neither, in their particular deployment of presence and absence, is finally sufficient. To deal with this world, certain things and ideas that are present must be said no to. Certain things that are absent must be hailed and hauled into play. And that is what it is almost impossible to imagine ballsy, gutsy Dodie ever doing.

In the Cameo, the hefty brown Puerto Rican woman arrives with her equally hefty brown boyfriend of five years. She's forty. He's thirty-three. They come to the theater so that he can get turned on so that later they can return to her furnished room on Forty-seventh Street, between Ninth and Tenth avenues and he can get it up; again, the same passivity. Yes, there are both white and black and young and middle-aged versions of this same couple, who, from time to time, come to the Cameo, the Grotto. Their relation may be more or less stable, their ages may be higher or lower; but all seek the same essential psychic commodity.

Black, white, Oriental, Hispanic, the high-school and college girls come with their necessarily protective boy or boys, simply to see what a dirty movie is. They, and even more so the boys with them, are, for the same reason as the girls, the ones before whom everyone else in the theaters grows silent. (We all feel that society—all that surrounds this strip of conflicting absences, this construct of desire at its darkest and lightest, all that finally secretes the discrete and shabby elements that, together, make up this space, so that somehow it is a part of, as much as it is apart from, the world—was built for them.) Sometimes the boys come here alone, for the same innocent reason as the girls it renders so much more, however momentarily, immobile: to see what's going on. Is it resentment we feel or just an endless and confusing separation? (Alienation?) Perhaps all the males (and indeed some of the females) on this side simply feel we should *be* them.

But the women conduct us to the truly less comfortable portraits.

I do not know this man's name, but he is as frequently at the movies as I am. Perhaps thirty-five, he usually wears a T-shirt and sneakers but never jeans: always a pair of old slacks, of which he has several. Over the two or three years I've seen him, his hair has thinned a little. More than half the time he has had a beard. (I fantasize that he is a good-looking bus driver, who probably works out of the Ninth Avenue garages up around Fifty-fourth Street—on an evening shift, possibly, which keeps his days free for the porn shows. But the chances are just as great that he is on some kind of welfare, or even that he does intermittent labor or "shape-up" work.) He stands near the back of the theater or just in the stairwell where he can still see the screen, his penis out of his pants and ill-concealed under a light jacket or, on colder days, a sweater folded over one arm, intermittently masturbating. Only if one of the homosexuals (like myself) pays him too concerted attention will he turn himself out of the line of sight or move to another location. When there is a couple present in the audience, he will contrive to sit two or three seats away from the woman and jerk himself with diminished motions, penis hidden only behind his free hand (which quivers while the other pulls and pulls), staring at her—until she glances at him, where-upon he looks away and hides himself again. Once I stood with him in the stairwell area of the Cameo with half a dozen other men. Most of us were masturbating, not really quite getting off on each other. For him, this was license to masturbate as well, though his interest was entirely in the actresses on-screen.

A couple who had been sitting in the balcony decided to leave. (He white with a short, muscular, well-knit body, she black, overweight, and in tight, electrically colored clothing somewhere between "punk" and prostitute.) Most of us hid our privates as, in the three-quarter dark (and certainly oblivious to the activity around), the white man led the black woman through those of us gathered there.

The man I've described hid himself too, instinctively, as one does in such situations, responding to what the rest of us were doing by the same mechanism by which a pigeon will fly when the group flies, and so an entire flock will take off, flapping—all at once it seems—at the flight of one, all, apparently, equally astonished. But realizing, with a look around him, why, an instant later he uncovered himself and, with the shoulders of his T-shirt back against the dirty blue wall (recently the management has repainted the same wall a fresh yellow), he rocked his hips forward so that his half-erect penis brushed the hip of the heavy young woman's satin toreador pants...closed his eyes, drew a quick breath, and settled his own hands before his genitals again, as, unknowing, unseeing, the woman hurried behind her boyfriend downstairs into the lobby's light.

Why is this portrait disturbing? Because I like this man. I don't mean just sexually—although once, perhaps a year ago, he let me play with that same semierect penis for some ten minutes, while we waited, silent in the dark, for the projectionist to fix the film (he is totally uninterested in blowjobs), whereupon he grew bored and walked away, terminating all physical contact between us ever since; and, as far as I've seen, all physical contact between him and any other male there. (He wants to be touched gently, almost ticklingly soft, not only on his genitals, but anywhere on his body. And only the men—or women—who, by trial and error have discovered that, will he put up with.) I like his reticence, his general carriage and personal demeanor, although—really rather rare for someone I've seen that many times—we have never exchanged an actual spoken word. And frankly I am uncomfortable liking him.

For on those areas of the social map where people, with the

word "pervert," refer to a man basically heterosexual (not quite a homosexual, not quite an obscene phone caller, not quite a flasher, not quite a fetishist, not quite a rapist and certainly not an ax murderer), he is what they mean.

He has as many black and white and Hispanic relatives as does the Puerto Rican couple. One such—though he doesn't show up as frequently—is a white laborer of about twenty (possibly nineteen; certainly no older than I am), with tousled brown hair, who arrives at the movies after lunch in his soiled greens with two or three six-packs in a brown bag. Braver than the other, he will usually sit directly next to the woman in a couple to masturbate. (Rarely does anyone ever complain—so rarely, in fact, it's inconceivable some are not excited by the flashers around, so that even here some psychosexual exchange can occur.) Having already arrived drunk, over the next hours he will drink himself into insensibility, whereupon one or two shadowy figures will drift to his slumped, snoring form and, with razors, slit his pants open to pick out any loose bills, small change, or his wallet. When he wakes, he staggers from the theater, pants ruined and thready at both hips. The rip-offs—which plague perhaps one out of three men who fall asleep here—seem to be a part of the ritual for him. It's probably what keeps his visits so infrequent.

Once, bringing in three cans of Colt 45 with me from home, I drank one and, before I left, stopped at his seat and handed him the remaining two, still bound in plastic loops. He took them and, without looking at me, whispered, "Thank you!" then bent to stash them noisily in the brown bag with his other cans still under his theater chair.

Little Black Joe is perhaps the same age as this workman. But he is one of the most physically beautiful men I've ever seen. Certainly he had a year or two of weight lifting somewhere recent in the adolescence he has not quite left behind. He sells loose joints in the balcony and the restroom of the Cameo—and occasionally hustles. For as much of the year as he can, he wears sleeveless shirts or tank tops, stylish clean jeans, blue running shoes. He is nearly jockey short, and his totally unblemished face and arms are the color of bittersweet chocolate. There is nothing grubby about him—and, oddly, nothing effeminate. Indeed, his black masculinity is as saturated and as natural as his sales banter with the clients he sells his dope to. He also pimps for some of the younger black and Hispanic queens who hustle the older men in the theater.

Once, as I started down the Cameo's stairwell, I saw him at the turning, deeply kissing a young Spanish queen (a sixteen-year-old boy, most probably still in high school, who, with no classes after lunch, rushed there in a frenzy of seersucker and cologne). Joe stepped back. The other boy's thin arms dragged limply away from Joe's molded and muscled shoulders. Suddenly Joe's small hand whipped—*crack!*—across her face. (His cock, out of his fly, bobbed before the boy's belly, an accusing black finger, reversing all usual Freudian symbology): "You know you workin' for *me*, bitch!" he hissed, between full, smiling lips.

Rubbing her jaw, the queen (who, though small, is still half a head taller than Joe) whined, "You know, you don't have to *do* that!" then slipped from him to continue down the stairs.

As I came down, Joe pushed his still erect penis back into his pants and, indifferently, started up.

At the stairs' bottom, still rubbing her jaw, the queen joined two others, who had observed from below what I'd observed from above. "You know, I really think that guy is just kind of a little bit crazy!" she declared. "I really think he's a little crazy!"

Accepting her judgment, I've more or less avoided Joe since. Perhaps three times in two years, I've seen him the center of some altercation that has grown in one part of the Cameo balcony or the other, bringing members of the audience to their feet, staring in the dark. No blows have ever been exchanged in these, however, only loud words.

But the truth is, even though I avoid him, I like Joe too—though it is impossible for me to think of him as good, or trustworthy, or reliable. (Maybe I would if I were, as he is, into drugs.) But since I am here only for the sex, there is nothing he has that I particularly want.

Once, when I had just come into the theater and was standing at the back of the aisle, waiting for my eyes to adjust, someone brushed by me. I looked up into a gaunt black face with fire-engine red lips aglimmer with gloss: "Hi...!" came a light and throaty whisper. "Want a blowjob...?"

As I grinned and shook my head, I reached up to squeeze a

bony shoulder under lace. "No thanks..." I whispered back. "I think we're both here looking for the same thing."

"Oh...!" The face nodded, still smiling.

Black lace rustled by me: light caught on the heel of a black pump as she moved off down the aisle.

She cannot be over nineteen and is probably a few years younger. Since then, I have seen her maybe ten times. Mostly she's been in her lace dress and makeup; perhaps three times, she has arrived as a very thin, gawky, and uncomfortable boy. All the time, however, she still says "hi" to me in that sweet, dazzled voice.

I say "hello" back.

And we part.

Sometimes I see him gazing wishfully at the older transsexuals who move about the aisles, most of them black, as we are, their surgical breasts displayed in net or lace shirts or simply bared in open blouses—male genitals bound tightly under Ace bandages between their legs before the women's underpants are slipped on: most of them can only afford the upper half of the operation.

Another man I like.

What makes these men disturbing? Why is it disturbing to feel camaraderie with them? I suppose because there is no economy that reconciles my actions around them with my emotional response to them, as well as my intellectual convictions about who they are as political/ethical beings. The greatest good for the greatest number? Most of them can be mildly annoying to someone at one time or another. But given any ten days in their lives, including their time here, you will not find them annoying *any*one. Yet the boys for whom society is made (as well as the city fathers a few of those boys will manage to become) would prefer that none of them existed—with a passion that dwarfs their merely sadistic delight in leering after the female prostitutes patrolling the avenue outside.

We are guilty that we are not them—are not those boys destined to run the systems and cities of the world: that puts a rift between us. They, on the other hand, are terrified, lest through some inexplicable accident, some magic happenstance of sympathy or contagion, they might become us. In most of them, we know, that terror can be repressed before adolescent curiosity. But we also know that that terror, given the license of adult exercise in the

darkness of unquestioned moral right, can assume murderous proportions: our deviance, our abnormalities, our perversions are
needed to define, to create, to constitute them and make them
visible to each other and to themselves.

The descriptions I've just given you are not tales to displace or
replace the stories of Tex and Mark and Pheldon and Dave. Rather,
they are tales to be superimposed on those earlier stories. The
first were tales of things I've done. The second recount what I've
seen around me in the interstices of doing them. Neither set is
complete without the other.

The polemicist in me, of course, would rather talk only about
those encounters that are satisfying, that display true humanity, community, *bonhomie* (highlighted with the terminal nostalgia of imper-
manence)—and display it openly and unambiguously. But, equally
true, to separate them as I have done here is to falsify them almost as
much as to omit them. I wonder if I, having committed this exercise
in context, I can now move closer to some sort of integration.

As I walked down the aisle, a stocky businessman in his early
thirties with glasses looked at me from his seat and, minutes later,
when I walked back, was still looking. So I moved in before his knees
and sat beside him. After a few minutes of fooling around (this guy,
as I said to Phel the next day, was fucking hung!), he said: "Let's
move someplace darker. It's too easy to see us here."

I explained to him the situation's optics: "You can easily see
three rows around you—and ten rows away you can't. So ten rows
away always looks darker, no matter where you are. And wherever you're sitting, it always looks too light."

"*Mmm,*" he said. But he still wanted to move. After picking up
his attaché case and moving us to two different locations in the balcony, he said, "You know, I think you're right."

"I know I am," I said. "Now I want you to look very carefully
over there...." And I proceeded to point out six people in the
process of giving/getting head.

He laughed out loud. "You know, I was up here for half an hour
before, and I didn't see any of this."

I smiled.

And blew him.

(Turning a baseball player into a cocksucker...Sorry, Sam, but
you probably won't get that.)

Afterwards he told me that it was his first time here. But not, I'm sure, his last. "The people are very nice here," he said as he was leaving. "They really act pretty nice to you, don't they?"

They do.

It is not, of course, a businessman's hangout, and the attaché cases are few and far between. In general, so are ties, leather shoes, and dress shirts. Because of this, about a week ago, when, with curly black hair and dressed in black slacks and a white dress shirt with the sleeves rolled up to his forearms, a tall young man came into the balcony, I noticed him. He sat down in the front row of the balcony's back section. As I passed, he kept looking at me. In my jeans and an old pair of running shoes, I sat next to him a little dubiously. I put my leg against his, my hand on his polyestered thigh. He smiled and put his hand on my crotch. No, this was not his first time here. He was very much into mutual sex, which can be a mixed blessing as far as real pleasure is concerned, but which nevertheless promotes a good feeling between people. Once, the uniformed security guard the theater's hired recently (to discourage the razor-blade rip-offs I told you about before) stopped in front of us. "Okay, guys. Take it somewhere else." We looked up and the guard walked on.

"What, does he just want us to get our feet out of the aisle?" my partner asked.

"I think so," I said.

So we moved back a row of seats. At one point, with my head in his lap, I took hold of his hand and was surprised to find it the hard hand of a laborer; I'd thought he was some kind of East Side office worker. Apparently not. In general, along with Dave and Mark, I count these among my most pleasant recent encounters.

Which reminds me of a third encounter, equally pleasant though more complex. Sometime last winter nearly a year ago, I saw a Hispanic—about the same age as the last man I just described—sitting in the front row of the Cameo, in a brown leather jacket and knitted cap, masturbating. I sat a few seats away from him, finally moved a seat or two closer. He had very large hands and a kind of bemused expression as he stared up the screen. He also had a comparatively unique method of gripping his sizable, uncut meat—thumb buried down in his fist, so that his thumb knuckle kept brushing what would have been the upper part of his glans when his considerable skin was wedged back. Finally I leaned over and asked if he wanted to do anything. "Sure," he said. "But I'm hustling."

"Oh," I said, then got up and moved away, since I wasn't interested in paying. Later, I saw a heavyset white-haired man sitting with him. Apparently he'd found a customer. Over the next hour they both must have had a fairly good time, too. Between rounds, when the white head would disappear in the younger man's lap, both of them spent a lot of time laughing.

Over the next year I glimpsed him about three or four times, but I never approached him again.

Then, perhaps a week ago, as I was about to leave the Grotto, I saw him come in. On a whim, I lingered in the theater and finally walked down the aisle. He was sitting under one of the lights. He had taken his jacket off and was wearing sneakers, maroon pants, and a colorful shirt, though faded and frayed at collar, shoulder, and elbow. His pants were open. (His thumb was still tucked down in his fist.) I sat down directly beside him. This time there was no talk of hustling. But I learned very quickly what had provoked all the laughter of a year back. He was very into giving instructions. Once I started sucking his sizable uncut cock, he began to intone softly: "…very slow…yeah, real slow. Slower…okay, like that…no, stop for a second…. That's right, now a little faster…yeah, faster…. No, slower now…." Once I took hold of his big hand and, in the same way I'd been surprised by the hardness of the last guy's hand at the Cameo, I was surprised by the softness of those large brown fingers. "Lick it for a while. No, wait…I don't wanna do nothin' until we get to a good part in the movie…. Okay. Go on…. You can do it faster now…. Yeah, that feels real nice." Fortunately he had an ironic sense of the ludicrousness of his detailed urgings and pacings. So we both laughed. "Real funny, huh? Well, yeah…go on…. Hey, I'm gonna squirt now… I'm squirtin'—! Squirtin'—! Squirtin'! Ah, that was nice! Real nice!" He shot a fourth gout. "Good!" He followed with a fifth. "Yeah!" And a little sixth, final spill. "Wow!—that felt good!"

Sitting up, I said: "I liked it, too." I patted his thigh. "I hope we run into each other again."

"Me, too!"

I—or at least the polemicist in me does—think of the above

three encounters as among the nicest. Yet they are neither typical nor are they among, say, the half-dozen most sexually exciting ones I recall from the hundred-plus the last year has provided. Yet their general good feeling, the acceptability of the persons or their emotions, and the sense of exchange on more than just a physical level are parameters for something that I suppose is simply easier to speak of than certain other aspects of such a life.

Not only easier to speak of, but it also has its real importance—important enough so that when such encounters as the above three—as opposed to any of the others I've described—cease, one seeks out other cruising grounds. Several times since high school I've abandoned one area of the city for another, when forces I will never comprehend drive down the number of such accessible, satisfying exchanges, whose satisfaction is always, Sam, measured on a (or on several) scale(s) more complex than the sexual. Yet, in all cases, a dismal, gray, and unresponsive ground is the incomprehensible template against which they occur, not throwing them into relief so much as providing a necessary obscurity to their outlines, making them bearable, even possible (making them hard or impossible for we who indulge in them to speak of in any terms *save* the sexual, even as they are, in their actuality, wholly social), in a world that largely denies they exist.

But *could* this entire dithyramb of depression and recovering optimism be merely response to losing Dave?

Two weeks ago, Pheldon phoned me. "No more Wet Nights."

"Huh?" I said.

"No more Wet Nights. GSA is discontinuing its golden-shower parties."

"Why?" I asked.

"It's this AIDS stuff. The word out now is no exchanging of bodily fluids. And I don't think you can do more in the line of fluid exchange than the guys on Wet Night get into!"

"Shit," I said. "They really think that it can be passed by...pee and stuff?" And didn't know quite how to finish.

"Did you know a guy named Kelly?" Pheldon asked. "White guy. Very sweet fellow, really."

"Big? Muscle builder almost? Beard—and one tit-ring? Sure, I saw him at both Wet Nights."

"Nicely built," Pheldon said. "But not what you'd call big. Beard, yes. And *two* tit-rings—not one."

I frowned into the phone. "Well, maybe—"

"Also, you wouldn't have seen him at Wet Night. He's a regular at the Mineshaft—or used to be. But I don't think he was ever into piss. Tit torture was his thing. He used to leave there every night, he told me, with both tits lacerated and bleeding. But you wouldn't have seen him there in the last couple of months, anyway. Anyway, he's got it."

"How did he get it?"

"Well, you know—open cuts and blood and stuff. I'm *sure* that's how he picked it up."

"What about getting fucked?" I asked. "That's what they say is probably the major way it's spread."

"Kelly told me he almost *never* gets fucked. Maybe once or twice and year—no more. And if that business about repeated sexual contacts is true, then that probably wouldn't be the way for him."

"*Mmm,*" I said, because I couldn't think of anything else.

Since Margaret Heckler's April announcement of the discovery of the AIDS virus, a summer has intervened, Sam. We're now well into the opening of winter.

There's been a whole lot of brouhaha since, about whether or not they've got the right virus, or whether it's a virus at all. But, I confess, though I still read the opposing theories that saturate the *New York Native* and from time to time spill over into the *Voice*, I'm convinced. The rest is too hysterical and has too much of the feel of the lunatic about it.

But what I want to tell you about now is something that happened to me two Saturday afternoons ago. And, frankly and simply, it was the most dramatic thing that's ever happened to me in my life—the second Saturday in November.

As you know, I'm not a very "mystical" person. Yet the density and feel of it was as close as I, personally, will probably ever get to a mystical experience—which is to say, the feelings, the conclusions, the grounding, and the process of it all were immensely and solidly real. The difficulty of writing that solid reality has, more than anything else, till now controlled the extent of all the introductory material that has preceded it, as it controls what I already know must turn out an inadequate attempt to go on and tell you about it from here.

Like so many mystical things, Sam, what "happened" was simple:

It will sound—I hope it sounds—much like what I've already written about. And because, now, thanks to what I've written already, you're more familiar with it than you would have been without those pages, you'll be able to pay attention to the upcoming ones in a way that is less dazzled by sensationalism—or salaciousness.

I'll try and tell it to you the way I still haven't been able to tell it to Phel yet.

Listen, Sam—

On Saturday at about noon, in my grungy beige winter coat and my tan watch cap, I took the subway down to Fourteenth Street and Union Square. But instead of walking west toward the waterfront, I walked east past the large hole in the ground that was once S. Klein-on-the-Square department store, walked by the dark green shell of the old Lüchow's Restaurant, passed the boarded-up Palladium (once the New York Academy of Music) and Julian's Billiard Parlor—a still-thriving upstairs pool hall, which has been there for fifty years or more—and over to Third Avenue. Then I turned the corner to walk down to Variety Photoplays. From the old suited-and-tied Puerto Rican cashier with the thin white hair who has been mumbling and arguing in that glass booth of his for what seems like a hundred years now, I bought my $2.25 ticket.

Six months ago, they had taped a sign inside the glass: "We're sorry about raising our price. But at $2.25 we're still a bargain," which, of course, is true. Three years ago when I was twenty and home on summer vacation, they upped their price from $1.50 to $1.75.

A clutch of four or five Puerto Ricans, between twenty-five and forty years old, have managed the theater since I was in high school. As usual, they were all talking just inside the door. I gave my yellow ticket to the man in the black shirt on the stool. He tore it and handed me back the stub; and I wandered across the small lobby's worn maroon floor and into the vestibule of the theater proper—an upright water fountain, a soda machine, a door at each side—to stroll into the darkness down the right hand aisle.

From the back, I recognized one of my regulars of the last eight months or so. Physically he's an immense man. That's tall and fat. Puerto Rican, he sports a white-flecked beard and wears glasses. From his huge, hard hands, I know he does some kind of physical labor. Every Saturday morning at eleven-thirty, he arrives at the Variety, practically by the clock. From time to time we talk; from these miniconversations, I know he's married, though he has no kids. He lives somewhere in the Bronx. Still, I don't know his first name—nor he mine. He's rather good-natured and not particularly bright. I don't mean he exhibits Dave's sort of naïveté. *Any* group of normal men and women would find this guy slow.

He always sits one in from the aisle in about the same seat, each week. And he was in his usual position.

I sat down beside him. He glanced over, recognized me, put a barrel of an arm around my shoulder, and said, "How you doin'?" and went on to make some comment about what the actress on the screen *really* needed.

His particular thing is to spend ten minutes or so "talkin' dirty" about the porn movie in progress in front of us—which turns him on as much as, or more than, the movie itself. Finally he begins to dig in the mountainous darkness that is his lap and belly, getting his jeans apart, pulling his uncircumcised cock, always flavored with his body's salts, free of the white folds of his size forty-six briefs; and I go down to suck that hard finger of flesh till, a hand splayed on the back of my head, he presses my face into his gut and, grunting, jets his juice into me. I enjoy him a lot.

When I finish, he always says, "Oh, man! That was *real* good! You did that real good this time." He's both enthusiastic and friendly.

This time when I came up and looked around, I noticed that sitting in the row just behind us, well forward in his seat, was a slight, effeminate Hispanic in a beret and glasses, the collar of his pea jacket turned up around his neck and some kind of tote bag slung over his shoulder. The beret had the exact opposite effect it had had on the head of Angel Mark, where it had looked quite butch and scruffy. This one, though the same black, looked affected and like a gesture at some sort of effeminate styling. He'd been sitting forward, intently watching us.

Fundamentally, I don't mind that sort of thing, depending on the "tone of voice" in which it's done; if you really don't like to be watched, you don't come to such a place. If you want to sit a seat away and masturbate, it's fine by me and even lends something to the atmosphere. But just to lean over someone's shoulder and *leer* is, I think, bad form. Often it bespeaks someone who is looking for an opening to move in and take over—which is a no-no. And it can add the dampening aura of the deprived, desperate, and needy to an otherwise pleasant encounter.

Five minutes later, when I stood up, immediately this guy scooted around and into the seat I'd vacated; and I heard my big Spanish friend say gruffly, "Hey, no! I don't *want* to no more. Didn't you see? I just *done* it already!" And a moment later, looking about through his glasses and nursing his bag below his forearm, the thin little guy got up and hurried down the aisle toward the men's-room door in its recessed alcove to the left of the screen, which, illegally, still has a dime paybox on it, under the yellow light.

As I walked down the aisle, toward the corner of the center section I recognized a guy in his mid-twenties toward whom I've always felt rather friendly. He's thin, Irish (I can bet if I learned his name, it would be Billy, Joe, or Mike), almost scrawny, with many attributes of a junkie—save that he dresses a little too well. He usually wears some kind of sweater over a white dress shirt and black slacks or jeans, with only his incredibly worn basketball sneakers and his always-grubby hands and dirty fingernails setting him apart from the somewhat preppy look he aspires to. One night about six months ago, describing him to Pheldon, I said he had "a lost-wax face," which I thought pretty much captured him. But Phel, who is usually pretty swift, turned up his hands, looked blank, and said: "I haven't the faintest idea *what* you mean." Well, it refers to a casting method for metal sculpture. But there's a quality to his features as if they'd all been molded sharply from some white wax that had eventually been drained and blunted by an external heat, then set in that softened form by an internal chill that had more recently seized his body.

He's almost as much of a Saturday-morning regular as my big Puerto Rican. He always brings in one or two quart bottles of Bud in a paper sack—sometimes he has them in a small knapsack. He sits somewhere in the first six rows of the orchestra, opens his pants, fly, belt, and upper button, rucks his shirt and sweater halfway up his pallid belly, slouches down with his knees wide against the back of the seat before him, and masturbates furiously, usually to completion three or four times over a four- or five-hour visit, drinking his beer between bouts. He starts off very shy of other people, pulling his pants closed quickly if anyone comes near him or looks. But once he gets into his thing (and through his first bottle), he becomes both friendly and uninhibited—even something of an exhibitionist to the older men who, slowly but inevitably, move in to sit around him, a couple of seats or rows away. The second time I saw him, sometime last spring, we got into quite a conversation. I was sitting in his row, two seats away, also jerking off, when the projector broke down for some ten minutes. The house lights came on. And along with the rest of the audience, we complained volubly, now shouting out to the whole house, now wisecracking to each other—without missing a stroke, either of us, while other guys around the theater occasionally looked over at us and laughed.

Indeed, I wondered then if that were part of his trip. (But I suspect, rather, it's part of mine.) This guy's particular kink, which bewildered me the first few times I saw it but which finally I think I've read right, is this: just before he cums, he pulls his shirt down over his erect penis, gives a few rubs at it through his clothes—and shoots all over himself, but under the cloth. Almost immediately, then, he falls asleep for up to half an hour, head to the side, lank hair straggling his bony forehead, small mouth open...all heightening the junkie-like impression.

Finally he wakes, yawns, stretches, watches the movie a few more minutes, then, eyes still fixed to the screen, pulls apart his pants again and starts to milk his cock, now overhand, now underhand, now overhand again pausing a few moments to massage his nuts (which are bigger than you'd expect from his six-and-half-inch dick), and, getting his rhythm, finally starts jerking again in earnest.

I've seen him there maybe six times. The time after the shouting session at the broken projector, I asked him if I could blow him. He asked me if I could give him any money. I told him I didn't have any.

He let me do it anyway. He was salty and took a good twenty minutes to cum. (To shoot his load manually takes him sometimes upward of forty.) Afterward he said I was very good. Only once did I ever seen him accept a blowjob from someone else—though I know he gets lots of offers. That time it was from an older guy, and there was a major argument between them afterward about money, that brought one of the Puerto Rican guys from the front down the aisle swinging a flashlight back and forth. More recently he's tended to wave away anyone who tries to sit directly beside him or comes on to him to do more than watch.

As he finished up—sweater yanked down, hand rubbing quickly over the knit where you could just make out the rod of his dick under cloth, then a little quiver, followed by a big breath released slowly, as he settled farther down in the chair, head moving to the side like a creature looking over to peer into the pit of his own slumber (he must like the feel of it running down his stomach, under there)—I went on around the front row and back up the other aisle, without bothering him.

Out in the lobby, I went up the narrow stairs to the balcony, by the posters for the various porn films to come over the next month that no one ever looks at, but which the management shifts around religiously week to week. ("Next Tuesday!" "Next Wednesday!" proclaim the permanent letters over the blue-painted frames.) On Sundays and Mondays the Variety's double feature always includes one nonporn film (back when I was a kid and still living on Staten Island, I actually came over here once to Manhattan to see Peckinpah's *The Ballad of Cable Hogue* and not for sex, which probably made me unique in that day's audience); those posters are there, too—though now I'm almost strictly a Saturday visitor. The nonporn relief used to be very nice, actually, when, years back, I would come into the neighborhood from home. But it's a drag if you only come down there to cruise.

The Variety's balcony—about a quarter the size of the orchestra—is where most of the action is. The open area behind the seats on the right-hand side of the projection booth is sometimes referred to as the "lounge" by longtime patrons. And since I started coming here at seventeen, I guess that counts for me. A filthy skylight is set in the roof above it; here and there you can just see through the dirt that's collected over the ages.

The Variety is, incidentally, the second-oldest functioning theater building in New York City.

Sitting in the front row, down in what no doubt was once the loge, off to the side sat a tall guy in his late twenties/early thirties. I'd already seen him wandering about the theater two or three times downstairs. He wore a black leather jacket, black jeans, and a black plastic cap. But it wasn't your standard motorcycle drag that signals SM interests; rather, he seemed some East Village local who was simply into the "punk" look you see all up and down the streets of the neighborhood outside.

He was playing with himself.

I slipped in beside him—I'd been sure he was wearing black pants when I'd seen him before. But now he was in white ones—then, no, I realized seconds later: his pants *were* black, but he'd pushed them all down around his ankles, so that his pale legs were what I saw!

On the balcony's flat rim stood a paper bag, the top of a beer can showing over its edge. Occasionally he picked it up and drank. He had a broad forehead, large eyes set far apart, and a full mouth. Indeed, the distance between his eyes verged on deformity: his face was vaguely dwarflike—though, as I said, he was quite tall: 6'3" or more. The pants around his ankles suggested he was open for just about anything. So I reached over and touched his leg. He didn't stop me or move away. So I moved to sit beside him.

He was really hung, too.

Two things I found out about him quickly. First, the way he squirmed whenever I got near them, his testicles were ticklish; so I left them alone. Second, he had two polyps—they might even have been warts—on his penis: one right under the glans, one farther down the shaft. I blew him anyway. The one on the shaft felt funny, sliding in and out the corner of my mouth. I wondered whether it made for problems with other people. I eventually got a finger up his ass; he liked that, as long as I didn't joggle his balls. After a few moments—I guess when he decided I knew what I was doing—he really got into it.

Big balls, little load.

I don't know if that's a pattern, but the thought returned to me when he squirted his teaspoon. But however much it was, he sure enjoyed getting rid of it.

I sat up and gave him a pat on his leg. He took another swig from his beer can—but didn't pull his pants up; I left without either of us saying anything, to wander the balcony a little more and see what was going on.

In their late thirties to early seventies, eighteen or nineteen men stood around under the skylight in "the lounge." (Twenty-five, and the dark, dirty space—in which inevitably someone has peed against the back wall—is really crowded.) A couple of blowjobs were going on in the corners. A couple of guys were watching and masturbating. But the feeling was—as it so often is here—that not much was happening. Off near one wall stood an old ice-cream freezer—white enamel sides and shiny steel top with rounded corners, then square black lids set along the top, of the sort that used to be in old-fashioned drugstores—like Tom Fordes' in Harlem, before they pulled it down. Sometime back when I first started coming to the Variety, the freezer used to be down in the lobby, right where the guy now sits on his stool, taking tickets, and you could buy ice-cream cones…for about three or four months, till it was acknowledged that ice cream just wasn't what people were coming there for, and the freezer, disconnected, had been moved up here.

(I swear, some of the men walking round it today were there when I made my first visit when I was a teenager.)

Standing behind the freezer, wearing only a zip-up jacket and a pair of pink-framed glasses, a pudgy black guy leaned forward with his elbows on the top, watching the men ambling about quietly, intently, slowly. (Near him some bald guy in granny glasses was smoking the inevitable cigar.) Like the guy out on the balcony, his pants were either way down around his shoes or completely off, so that his buttocks were available to anyone who wanted to wedge in behind him. Maybe once an hour, there would be a taker. In my mind, the archetypal servicer of these guys leaning over the freezer is some stubble-cheeked, thickset Puerto Rican gorilla of around thirty-five, with fraying thermal underwear showing at his neck, a soiled blue sweatshirt over that, and a tattered denim jacket on top of it all (maybe in a baseball cap and his black hair held back by a three-times-rolled-up rubber band), belt buckle flapping and clinking at his hips as he humps for all he's worth, panting, and grunting, now and again, "*¡Hay de mios…!*"—though certainly I've seen enough guys, white, black, and, yes, Asian, pitching and catching on that freezer. And I can remember a couple of times, when I first started coming here and was just feeling lazy, sitting out in the balcony, letting two or three guys suck on my dick till they got tired, then coming back here to finish up and off, in whoever happened to be bent over and waiting.

A guy very much like the archetypal pitcher—Puerto Rican, thermal underwear, baseball cap, denim jacket—sat on the freezer's end, staring around the shoulders of the men in front of him, down over the half-wall at the edge, where, on the screen, you could still see the movie. I found myself watching him pretty intently; every once in a while he'd dig at his crotch—I really wanted to suck his dick. But every time I moved up, he definitely turned away. So finally I thought: things are going much too well today for me to court this overt rejection. I shouldered to the narrow gateway in the forward wall to walk down the steps between the seats, busy with the coming and going traffic.

Before I went downstairs, I looked over again toward the balcony front, to the side where the guy in the cap and no pants I'd blown was sitting. I could see the tan jacket of another man, hunkered down over his lap: he was already working out again!

I went back down through the lobby and into the orchestra. Strolling down the aisle, I noticed Billy/Joe/Mike was awake and once more pumping his dick. The seats near him still were mostly free. I went on down to the front row, walked across in front of the screen, came up the other aisle, and slid in to sit a seat away from him in his row, opened my coat, undid my jeans, took hold of my cock, first in one hand, then in the other, and started jerking along with him. I kept up pretty exactly to his rhythm, which, with certain guys, is a turn-on—I've never understood quite why. Not stopping, he glanced at me a couple of times. After about five minutes (now I got faster than him), I shot a load all over my hand and wiped it on the seat edge between my legs. Then, just holding myself and not really rubbing too much, I watched him till about ten or fifteen minutes later he reached his own, nervous, quickly-covered finish—and, with his four or five rubs through his sweater (and doubtless cum running down his belly underneath, only seconds beyond it)—sank back in the wooden theater chair and into sleep, one sneakered foot now up over the wooden seat back in front.

As I glanced around, something going on a row behind, which I'd noticed out the corner of my eye, cleared now: the small

Hispanic with the beret and bag was just moving over beside a blond guy with a full lumberjack-style beard; the little guy bent down, and, as his head disappeared, the white guy put his hand up on the seat back beside me: the man himself was pretty sizable, but his fingers were incredibly small—as well as clean, neat, and hairless. His hands seemed only a little more than half the size they should be: really, it was one step from a deformity—though otherwise he was attractive enough.

I looked around a few moments more, then left my seat to prowl further. I went to the john to see what was going on, rattling the door and waiting for someone already inside to let me in—though with all the action in the theater proper, people tend only to look at each other in that narrow space (painted maroon, a sink at one side along with two urinals and a commode at the end). I walked up and down the aisles a few more times, noting the irregular pattern in which some of the lights were on and some were out in their holders on the night blue walls. When I went upstairs again, the guy in the cap and jacket was still in the front row, alone now. On a whim, I moved to sit a few seats away. His pants were still down, and he was jerking off.

I moved over next to him, put the notebook I was carrying with me (the only thing I've left out is the three times I sat down and made some jottings on what was going on: but otherwise how do you think I would recall these details) on the floor to kneel on this time, got down, and sucked his mouth-filling dick—with its two polyps—again. He seemed even more into it than before. Holding tightly to my shoulders, again he came in my mouth. As he let go, I swallowed and sat up on the seat. "You're really working out today," I told him. "How many times have you gotten off here, anyway?"

He looked over at me, a little surprised that I was talking, I suppose. "A few," he said. "Yeah, I got off a few times today." Then he reached down and pulled his jeans up over his knees, lifted his buttocks from the seat, and slid his pants under them.

"Who knows?" I said. "Keep it up, and maybe you'll shoot a few more." But he looked like he was about finished. "See you around." I got up and moved out of the row.

A woman (I'm pretty sure she's not a transsexual, but sometimes you just don't know) works the Variety regularly, asking

twenty dollars for a blowjob and often taking ten. A blonde somewhere around thirty-five, she wears jeans, white boots, and a blouse
which she leaves spectacularly unbuttoned over generous breasts.
I would think, by now, she'd recognize me, but perhaps every third
time I cum, she accosts me with a smile and "You wanna go out?"
which means going off with her to the theater's side seats for her
to give me a quick suck. As I was coming down the stairs, she
turned to me with her line. I smiled. "Sorry, not today." (Is this the
tenth time I've told her this over as many weeks?) "By the way,
you know I see you here almost every time I come. What's your
name?"

She smiled, quite pleased, leaned forward and touched my shoulder with red-nailed fingers. In the yellowish light, her knuckles
were puffy and mottled from the cold outside—or drugs. "My name
is Linda," she said with the inflection of someone giving me a
friendly business tip.

"I'm John," I said. "Nice to meet you. I'll probably see you
around next time."

Downstairs once more, as I was coming down the aisle, I saw the
bearded blond with the small hands was by himself again; he was jog-
gling the crotch of his pants while he watched the movie. I sat down
beside him. He didn't stop. But when I put my hand on the leg of
his jeans, he shook his head a little and pushed my hand away. So I
got up again—consoling myself with the fact that his miniature
hands were really so off-putting that if I'd ended up blowing him,
or even letting him blow me, it would have been largely an act of
charity. I'd been in the theater by this time not quite two hours. Why
didn't I leave, I thought, and see what was new on the shelves of the
St. Mark's Bookstore.

So I got up, walked up the aisle again, out into the bright lobby—
squinting a little—and out onto loud Third Avenue. A block down,
at the parking lot, I turned inside to go take a leak against the back
wall of the maintenance shack. As I was coming out between the
mangy tufts of city grass, I saw the tall man in the leather cap and
jacket whom I'd blown twice in the balcony crossing the street
toward me. But he went right past, and we didn't speak.

A few blocks down, as I turned onto St. Mark's Place, on the
out-thrust facade, with its four arched windows and stone pilasters,
the bronze plaque still explained that, in the 1830s, James Fenimore

Cooper had had a farmhouse on the site. The St. Mark's Baths had been closed down a while now. Pheldon says the fact that I never went while they were opened probably means I'm not really gay or something.

In the St. Mark's Bookstore, beside the cashier on the shelf of new titles, was the trade paperback of *Mountain and Tower*—the first time I'd seen it. It must have come out that week. More than a year ago I'd sprung for the hardcover. But, like most graduate students, I find that till a book is in paperback, I don't believe it's real. Back in the '60s, the Old Poet—Almira Adler—like just about every other poet in the world I guess, taught a workshop at the St. Mark's Poetry Project right up the street at the St. Mark's Church. There's a poem from that period, dedicated to Ted Berrigan, clearly about her and Tim Hasler going to Gem Spa on the corner of Eighth Street and Second Avenue to drink vanilla egg creams together. The poem's title is also its first line:

"When I and the Young Philosopher..."

Somehow the book opened to that one as soon as I picked it up. I read it over—it's kind of cute. So, in honor of Tim and Adler (and simply because of the way I was feeling), I put the book back on the shelf, walked up to the little candy store with all the newspapers out on the counter in front, went inside and, as I've done many times before, bought a commemorative egg cream to drink on my way to the subway.

Just as I stepped out the door, the same guy I'd blown came barreling around the corner, so that for a moment we stood, quite astonished, no more than eight inches from each other, face to face: under the visor of his black plastic cap, he blinked his wide-set eyes (at that moment, for the first time, I realized he may have been Puerto Rican, or possibly even a very light black guy), then ducked away, out of the arena of our mutual shock, that held the space on the street corner, I like to think, like some quivering entity of its own, for a second or two even after he'd rushed away and I'd started back toward Third Avenue, drinking my egg cream with a straw through the plastic top, till the foam chattered at the bottom of the waxed cardboard container and I tossed it into green dumpster at the curb.

That is the account of what happened during my most mystical of mystical experiences: kind of an average day of cruising, for someone my age. A Saturday afternoon not so active as some, but a good deal more active than others. In terms of general satisfaction, I'd say it just made it into the upper half.

But the inner drama, which till now I've rigorously omitted from this account, Sam, and which we must now reinscribe over it all—what makes the whole few hours so important—was simply (yet most complexly) this: when I entered the Variety Photoplays Theater, doubtless, like half the men there, I was terrified of AIDS. As I walked around the theater, doing what I did, like most of the men there, I thought about AIDS constantly and intently and obsessively. But when I left (and in this aspect alone, perhaps my experience is—not unique—but certainly rare), I no longer had any fear of the disease.

At all.

Concern? Yes. Of course I retain that. But I spent the whole time, as I roamed the theater, orchestra, balcony, and lounge, doing all the things I've recounted to you, thinking with a violence and a life-and-death committedness it will be hard to convey. Certainly, telling you the result of that thought is that the fear—the dull, so reasonable, yet so crippling terror a part of my life and the lives of so many gay men for two and a half, if not three and a half years—has vanished, does not give you the process's mechanics or affect.

When sex is so available and plays such a large part in life, sexual activity ends up fulfilling many, many psychological functions—as chosen recreations often do: it helps you deal with any number of tensions and becomes a stabilizing and balancing force—and it provides an object for as much or as little intellectual analysis as anyone by temperament might require. (Sex and death, William Butler Yeats wrote somewhere, are the only subjects truly mysterious enough to engage the serious mind.) Still, when life tensions get high, it's almost impossible to avoid the logic: Well, I probably have it anyway. I might as well go out and do at least some of what I was doing before. At this period, people who cruise with any frequency are not gambling on the possibility of avoiding it. Largely, they are gambling on what strikes them as the much higher probability that they already have it—so that, in terms of their *own* eventual health, their activity makes no difference. The argument is there at one level or another of consciousness in us all, believe me, who do.

Yet another of the strongest realizations I had while walking up and down one or another aisle of the Variety was that this was precisely what the situation was for me—indeed, for so many gay men—when I first started cruising as an adolescent, living at home on Staten Island. AIDS had put us in the same situation I'd been in when the only information I had about homosexuality was what I'd found in an outdated psychology book by Erich Fromm from the 1950s on a shelf of the local library, whose appendix told me that to indulge one's homosexual urges was to foredoom oneself to an unavoidable career of alcoholism, devoid of any "rewarding" or "mature" relationships (whether sexual or any other kind), with an almost-certain probability of suicide sooner or later! It was a non-win situation, in which to be concerned about it at all was, in itself, to be doomed; thus I went out into the world carrying a mantle of death and resignation as heavy as Childe Harold's. And what relieved it was not the political flowering of gay rights—which, frankly, seemed so distant from me I wasn't even sure if what I did (I mean, I didn't have a "life partner"; I wasn't *dreaming* about "coming out"; I wasn't a happy homosexual—I was scared shit-less!) was even concerned with what they were doing. But it was only through a few years of doing what I was doing and looking at the people I was doing it with, many of whom seemed no less happy than anyone else, that I began to ask that most empowering of questions: Could all these people around me be both crazy and damned? When one is dealing with the satisfaction of an appetite, you relegate the Erich Fromms *et alia* to the place where one stores those abstractions that don't particularly relate to the systems of the world around you.

I did that.

And I ceased, somehow, to be terrified.

(It was only when I ceased to be terrified that I could even pick up a flyer, a pamphlet, a book about Gay Liberation and read it. And, by then, I was already converted, as it were.)

Somehow, moving around in the Variety, I ceased to be terrified again.

When I got home, Sam, I was felt so extraordinarily elated that I ran up the steps like a kid, dashed into the apartment here, and slammed to door behind me. (Gave myself quite a scare, too—when, later, at three o'clock in the morning, I got up to go to the

bathroom, came out in the hall, and saw the apartment door standing wide open. It took me three minutes to figure out what had happened: if you slam the door in my place, it doesn't catch, but just
stays open and sometimes swings in. I looked through all four
rooms of the apartment for prowlers before I went back to sleep.
There weren't any.)

But the psychological problem for those of us who cruise is
complex—and though I've put real effort into curtailing and mod-
ifying my cruising habits in the light of AIDS, the fact is I've never,
for more than a month at a time, been able to cut out sex entirely; at best, I've reduced those three hundred-plus contacts a year
to a frequency that, if I could keep it up, would still total more
than a hundred a year anyway. One thing I realized and realized
articulately that afternoon, even as I realized it was something
that most commentators trying to get a handle on the situation
seem to miss absolutely: Because of AIDS's seven- to thirty-six-
month incubation period, those of us who have traditionally lived
our lives at three hundred-plus sexual partners a year move through
our lives today not afraid that we might catch AIDS: rather, we
move through life fully and continually oppressed by the suspicion that we must already have it!

I think you can understand from the number of physical acts
I've recounted that you need only have a couple of sessions a week
like the one I've just described, to log over three hundred partners
a year. I've talked to guys in the offices I work in who are really
actively searching for sex all the time—who make much more use
than I do of the far-more-than-a-hundred-such locations in the
city, including theaters, public restrooms, peep shows, park areas,
bars, and baths—whose sexual contacts number four or five times
what mine do. I remember the good-looking kid, currently living
on unemployment insurance and who occasionally ends up on
Pheldon's living-room couch, who, just about a month ago, when
Pheldon was bringing in the coffee, suddenly announced, "I just figured it out! I've swallowed between three hundred fifty and four hundred loads of cum in the last three *weeks* alone!"

The medical aspect of the situation is, of course, very different
between the two situations—though the etiology of AIDS is aston-
ishingly similar to the etiology of homosexuality itself in the conservative view, that sees it as a disease, i.e., a sickness that can be

carried about asymptomatically for years, until eventually it appears as a sudden and deadly weakening of the system that leaves one a victim of every possible evil contractible.

What preceded my vanquishing of terror last month ran, in précis, something like this: Given the statistics both of the disease and my own sexual history, the chances are high that I have been exposed to it. More and more it looks like a two-population situation, with one population, most probably the larger, largely immune, or at least highly resistant, to the disease—though there is no way to tell which population you belong to.

I know I'm resistant to hepatitis B.

I seem to have a strong resistance to herpes.

If low-grade exposure to the disease over a period of time can produce an immunity, chances are I've acquired it.

I've never used poppers (other than half a dozen times in my early youth when I experimented with them and found out I didn't like them): I don't smoke. Today I drink only occasionally but not at all heavily, and my yearly checkups regularly pronounce me healthy—including two I went to last year specifically worried about AIDS. My own precautions include limiting myself as best I can to a circle of regulars. And the last time I took it up the ass was just over ten years ago.

(Anecdotal evidence has it that passive buggery [or "Greek Passive" as they say in the Personal Ads] is, indeed, the major form of contagion. And is there anything in this account that applies to the men who are as obsessive about anal gratification as I am about oral...?) A couple of times for a week or two I gave up swallowing and spat out all the cum I took. But, you can see, from what I've just recounted, that's not been my general pattern at all. I don't cruise when I've got a cold or am feeling physically run-down. And (this last my own little quirk which may be pure superstition) I don't suck within three hours of brushing my teeth in the morning; and I don't brush my teeth within six hours of sucking, as the minuscule sores connected with bleeding gums are a regular point of circulatory-system infections, so that, in this case, that just seems to be asking for it.

How has AIDS affected the cruising scene? As far as I can tell, there are fewer people out—by about 10 or 15 percent. But those there seem more serious in their sexual pursuits. The ones who just stand around, thinking about doing something (and, maybe, if something really excites them, getting down, but otherwise just drifting about, taking up space), have ceased to come out because the epidemic has scared them off.

I started this letter in October. It's now November 1984, Sam. In three days, it will be December. And what I am writing to you now is what it seems reasonable (or, more accurately, what it is possible, because possibility is what my revelation was all about) for a gay black man, with a degree in philosophy and three years of graduate school to think about AIDS right now. I have to put this historical disclaimer on all this because one of the things we have all seen is how incredibly fast possibility changes in this situation. A year ago, we didn't even have a virus for it. Two years before that, it didn't even have a name. In a year, or six years, if not in six months, what I'm saying here may look, in the light of new medical knowledge, like rampant superstition and raging ignorance.

I hope it does.

The thing that I am terribly aware of—and here I get as close to the center of the mystical aspect of the experience as I ever will be able to in words—is that, until much more is known, there is no earthly way I can, with any degree of responsibility, recommend the logic of these precautions to anyone else with any sort of suggestion of even probable safety. They are all entirely a blind gamble. Still—until much more is known—any course of action is more or less a gamble—even unto cutting out all sex entirely. And in such a situation all of us must put up our own stakes and know that the outcome can be death—that, indeed, 43 percent of the over seven thousand men and women to come down with AIDS to date are already dead; and that, yes, for those of us living in New York, a couple of thousand of those cases have occurred in our own incredibly sexually busy backyard.

Yet it is the realization that one is gambling, and gambling on one's own—rather than seeking some possible certain knowledge, some knowable belief in how intelligent or in how idiotic the chances are—that obliterates the terror.

You know, Sam, as, with my egg cream, I wandered across St. Mark's Place and my thought processes, as it were, began to return to earth, I thought about Tim Hasler. Because what I had just gone through, I realized, was an experience that Hasler had never had—could never have had. Neither the material for the experience nor my particular resolutions of it could possibly have been his. And this experience—rather than some homily like "Hasler was a gay man before the age of AIDS"—was what set an incredible historical, fundamental abyss between us. Because sex (from the orgy to the isolated act of masturbation) is an inchoate part of people's lives, and only in incredibly unusual circumstances do the people give it up (even when they say they do, even when they understand they must), that means I would maneuver my way on, through history, farther and farther away from Tim. It was an interesting thing to consider—with the taste of a vanilla egg cream in my mouth, certainly not so different from the taste Hasler and Adler had enjoyed one spring day twenty years before.

And yet, because of the change of context, their situation—his situation—was entirely different.

Well, for better or worse, Sam, I've chosen my course. (Can one write this without resorting to such appalling clichés?) What I learned that Saturday was that it *was* a possible course for me. In a year or ten years or twenty, its results can be judged and, in such a statistical context where it is compared with many other courses, as well as the results of research, it can become part of what others may then reasonably call "knowledge"…but it very possibly may never be "knowledge" for me. What I must live with—and quite possibly die with—is a certain sense of its reasonableness, a certain sense of its risk, knowing my "sense" of both are absolutely without experimental foundation; and, somehow because of it (is this what existentialism was about?), I can now live without any basic terror or basic hope.

Intellectually, needless to say, I hope for (and would, indeed, work for in any way I could) a cure, an alleviation, a scientific certainty as soon as a reasonable path toward one were pointed out to me. Of course.

Still, within the realm of my own chosen gamble, the obliteration of terror allows me to act as sensibly as I can, given those limits. In the weeks since this revelation occurred, I probably have gone out less than I did before—and have enjoyed myself more when I did.

Yes, there is a New Feeling of Power and Strength.

And one of the odder fallouts of that is that, a couple of nights ago, at the Fiesta, I got into a really odd argument with Pheldon. I suspect it has to do with the abuse of power on my part—which is to say, if I go around trying to push my revelations on other people, then it is slips across the very iffy border that separates revelation from what, yes, I'm willing to call insanity. But let me not bore you with details, but only say I think it got satisfactorily resolved by us both.

Still, I feel like a stronger person.

At any rate, the experience itself in the Variety felt, through the course of its two hours and the hour right after, as though my whole brain were untying itself, neuron by neuron, thought fragment by thought fragment, if not synapse by synapse—and reweaving itself into a new pattern, in which the heavy, nervous, and interminably obsessive, wheedling *fear* of AIDS that has been a part of my life in one form or another since a year before it was *called* AIDS—over three years now, I realize!—was simply no longer there, the way an ugly, unfunctional, and depressing room, with its shredding wallpaper, broken light fixtures, and cracked molding, vanishes when the house that contained it is at last pulled down.

I don't know if you can follow this. I really wonder, Sam, what all this has got to look like to somebody so outside this particular life as yourself. But it all feels very sane and good. Or, at least, it feels as sane as I can be, right here, right now, at this moment in medical history.

Though you may think me mad.

It's ten days later; this letter is still unmailed. But Pheldon called me again. "Kelly died yesterday afternoon."

I didn't know exactly what to say, so there was a long silence. Even though I knew by now that Pheldon's Kelly was not my Kelly, it was hard *not* to keep on picturing big, bearded Horse Bladder somewhere on a wheeled, white-sheeted gurney.

Finally Pheldon said "I saw him three days ago in the hospital. I wasn't really ready for it—the man looked like a corpse already when I went in; he was down to about a hundred ten pounds— and Kelly's at least six feet tall....John, this stuff is scary. I mean..." and couldn't say *what* he meant.

We talked about twenty minutes longer, anyway. On regular nights at the Mineshaft, Pheldon explained, some guys had started coming by, distributing condoms. There were even people there giving demonstrations of sex for the regular customers, using condoms and showing how they could avoid exchanging fluids.

"A blowjob with a condom?" I said. "That sounds about as exciting as sucking off a pencil eraser."

"Yeah, well..." Pheldon said. "But you didn't see Kelly."

When I got off the phone, I thought about Dave again. Not because I particularly missed him—though, I suppose, I did, a little. If I had gotten through to him, I thought, it would just have been one other thing for the little guy to be scared of.

I said, Sam, that this letter was sparked by your comment about AIDS. It occurs to me, reading it over, that it may only seem that a few lines concern this odd and awful illness. But, reading it over, I see every line of it is about the disease. That's because I don't think anyone *can* really understand what AIDS means in the gay community until she or he has some understanding of the field and function—the range, the mechanics—of the sexual landscape AIDS has entered into. And that means having a clear view of the sexual activity available; and that means understanding both the camaraderie and good will that exists in so much of it—as well as the barriers to social communication that fall, like those between a scared white man and, yes, a scared black man, like Dave and me—as well as it means understanding the friendship, and its rather unusual nature, that might grow between me and a Pheldon.

I just learned that the city finally closed the Mineshaft down: that gay group Pheldon told me about on the phone, which I believe is associated with the Gay Men's Health Crisis, has been promulgating what it calls "safe sex," that entails wearing condoms, no exchange of bodily fluids, and more inventive ways of enjoying yourself with another man: one of its slogans is "On you, not in you." Not only did they descend on the Mineshaft, like I said, but they also hit the St. Mark's Baths (among other places) before they were closed. They were apparently giving active and specific demonstrations of how to follow their guidelines. I've described the Mineshaft to you and what goes on. These guys weren't just handing out leaflets. They weren't just showing you how to put on a condom. They were doing live, active, hands-on sexual demonstrations, that people could take part in and follow, right then and there. I never saw them, but Pheldon did. I gather they were pretty impressive—and pretty hot. But all this got back to the city fathers, who were outraged. These guys invited the city fathers to come down and see—and take part! Newspapers that never had been concerned before that there was actual sex going on at these places now became outraged that there were live sex demonstrations going on. To quell this moral outrage, they closed the bar down. Also the baths—where the demonstrators had also arrived with their exhibitions. On the one hand, as you might imagine, I am wholly in sympathy with the demonstrators. The closing of these places is a murderous act by the city—not because of anything necessarily to be learned from the "safe sex" demonstrations about AIDS, but because it drives thousands of gay men from a fairly protected environment out into far more dangerous venues, where robbery, murder, and general queer-bashings are far more common. For all my sympathy with them, however, let me note that their particular option—condoms, no fluid exchanges—while I feel it is just as valid as mine, still, is *not* mine; indeed, it's not lots of people's.

I've never yet sucked off a dick with a condom on it, and I'm not particularly anxious to start!

From a couple of things you said in your letter, Sam (I thought I'd better reread it before I wind things up), I think you think that Irving shares much more with me than he does. Certainly I've never written him anything like the sort of things I've just recounted to you in these pages. I confess, the fact of your misevaluation (and the fact that I do not), make me said. But then it occurred to me, I'd always just assumed unquestioningly that all the things in Irving's letters to me—almost exclusively about Timothy Hasler—were things he'd already talked about with you, i.e., that since you and Irving first married, you'd probably heard an awful lot about Hasler.

Well before you were married, you once told me about a boyfriend of yours, who got to clean out Hasler's office drawers at Stilford; so I just assumed that, on whatever passing level, you have your own interest in Irving's (and my) philosophical obsession.

But just as you were mistaken about Irving's confidence in me, I might even be presumptuous about his in you. Still, part of the point of all this is that—thanks to AIDS, as you mention it in your letter—the gay male world has changed, changed in some catastrophic ways, changed in some directly material ways, but also changed as a way of thinking, both by gay men and by the whole greater society of men and women of all sorts around them. The gay world of Timothy Hasler—a man who, after all, is not a full dozen years dead—doesn't exist anymore. And that means we cannot rush to judge him without exploring—exploring both with sympathy and disinterest—his world that is gone. But I would hate it, Sam, if you misread my effort to chronicle how my world has changed around me—so that it bears only the most complex and difficult relation to Tim's—as if it were an effort to explain, say, Tim's world.

I would also hate it, Sam, if, after reading this letter, you decided you now knew all about *me!* Remember: it doesn't talk about my work—either the work I do that I think of as serious and meaningful, connected with Hasler or philosophy, or even the day-to-day office work I do that pays my rent and keeps me fed—as well as lets me get to the Variety, the Cameo, and the Grotto for what may, finally, be a few too many times a month, a couple or three times a week.

You won't learn from this letter, Sam, my three favorite tracks on Prince's *1999* or which Duran Duran cassette I've practically worn out playing; you won't learn Pheldon's opinion of Gay Men of African Descent, whose meeting he went to three months ago and about which he talked to me on the phone for over an hour and a half; you won't learn how much damage I think the country will suffer under this, its second term of Reagan, about to begin, nor will you learn about the various letters I wrote to my alma mater (and yours, and Pheldon's, and Hasler's) demanding that their trustees divest themselves of their South African holdings, or the number of hours a month I put in transcribing for the Black Oral History Project up at the Schomburg; or how many evenings I've sat in Caesar's Pizza down the block, watching MTV on their corner set—or why, four weeks ago, I gave my own TV set away to Angel and have decided to live without one. (It didn't work that well, anyway.) No, that's just not what this letter is about.

It doesn't tell you what I think of the books I read or the movies I see. It doesn't tell you how I greet Mrs. Conkling or Mr. Espedrosa on the stairwell or what I—or, indeed, Pheldon and I—talk about when we go to Angel's for dinner or what I say to my father when he calls me, usually about every second or third Sunday evening.

It tells you nothing about the Christmas bottle of Myers's Rum I give to Jimmy every winter or the ten bucks I leave for my postman, Max, in a holiday envelope at New Year's.

There's a model for the "self" that has as much to do with the way we misunderstand each other as it does with what we understand: each person is assumed to have a public life, a private life, and a secret life. And the relation between them is assumed to be that the public stands before the private, as the private stands before the secret, each masking the ones behind from view. Much the same notion: the secret self resides within the private self, which resides within the clearly public self. Such a model holds that to delve through to the private or to the secret is to explain and obviate the public area we've just passed through to reach them. Well, I would also hate for you to think I was telling you here about my private self—much less my secret self.

Because the fact is, what you do at bars and in movie houses is public—not private. And to the extent that it controls your subsequent behavior, the revelations you have, silently, in the aisles of a darkened movie house on Third Avenue should be just as public as the sex demonstrations at the baths. The fact that, yes, there are people I suppose I wouldn't particularly want to know about some of what I've told you is, itself, a public and political problem—not a private and personal one. In the best of all possible worlds, such things wouldn't *be* problems—and it's in that spirit, Sam, with an eye to making such a situation eventually a reality, that I send this letter.

Reading it over yet again, I realize I would hate it equally if, after reading it there at school, you thought, "Now I understand the gay experience." (Much better take away from it intimations of all the things you *don't* understand about this world I've been writing of.) Of course there's the obvious—even self-evident—point that I haven't mentioned gay women at all in this—whose experience is other than ours in almost every aspect. But to highlight that is to obscure a less-obvious point: even in New York City, a white guy who goes to East Side bars and bathhouses has a very different experience of the gay world than I do in, say, the back of various West Side porn movies, with the occasional stop off to jaw with Phel or Lewey or La Veuve at the Fiesta. Another black who cruises the subway johns and stops off at highway rest areas has a very different experience of the gay world from either of us. A gay man Tex's age can follow right behind a gay man Dave's, at a place like the Mineshaft, and have an experience of the gay world entirely different still. And a gay black kid growing up in rural Kentucky is going to have a very different experience of the world from a gay black kid growing up in East Philadelphia.

I've met several gay men who have had only a single sexual experience in the course of their entire, long, long lives—and, in a couple of cases, I've met a gay man who'd had no overt and actual sexual experiences with men at all! Also I've met gay men whose actively sexual lives make my own look quite calm and placid by comparison.

The gay experience, then...?

I can only smile, even while I try to explain that all of these I've mentioned are going to be different still from the gay experience of the white guy with the mustache, the plaid shirt, and the button-fly jeans (about whom you probably say, "Really? Him...?") that you can see out in College Town at brunch on Sunday.

Sam, I hope this hasn't been too demanding.

Best in Friendship,
Old and New,
John Marr

I started my letter on October 20. I finished it some ten days beyond Thanksgiving—sealing it, addressing it, and carrying it to the Eighty-second Street post office and mailing it all the same morning. Delighted to get it off my hands and out of my hair, I stalked over to Broadway, in my jeans and bomber jacket, and turned down the aisle of Christmas trees in corded bondage against the wooden racks on the outside of the street, to hurry by the newsstand and around in front of the First Baptist Church on the corner ("1891" in foot-and-a-half-high founding numerals to the right of the steps), and down to the IRT kiosk , to begin a day of almost-frantic cruising.

In the first weeks of winter, the cruising in New York City dries rather spectacularly up.

At the Variety, at the Hesperus, at the Cameo, at the Grotto, and even around the bathrooms of the Port Authority, nobody seemed to be out—and the few who were were not particularly interested in me. For the whole day I had to dwell with the irony: I had mailed Sam my description of, my paean to, my celebration of the city's sexual abundance on a day it far more resembled a sexual desert. Well, that happens. But it's bad for the soul.

I ended up sitting till very late in the Harem (where I almost never went)—wondering how I'd managed to go through over twenty dollars on cheap porno houses without eating anything but a gyro on pita. I had two what I guess you'd call "encounters"; but the time they took and their generally low level of interest on my part—and on the other guys'—meant they were more frustrating than not.

Sometime after midnight, I came back uptown on the No. 1, and got out at Seventy-ninth Street.

At certain hours in the first and blowy days of early winter, the city goes static. Air ceases to move; winds pause for an hour. In your apartment, the ventilating crack you've left in the bedroom window is suddenly and wholly inadequate, and you fling up the sash to leave the opening as wide as if you were in the midst of the city's breezeless summer sauna.

As, with half a dozen others, I walked up out of the kiosk on the east side of Broadway, this guy on his knees in a heavy coat, his face scabby and filthy, turned an expectant smile up to the passing people. His hair was stringy, and he didn't look any older than I was.

Clutching a cloth hat, occasionally he thrust it out. He moved to one side three or four steps—still on his knees—then to the other, pushing his hat toward this one, then toward that one. The kneeling was so extreme, it took moments to realize he wanted people to put money in it.

The temperature was in the upper forties. Broadway was still darkened here and there by a brief rain that had fallen while I'd been in the movie. Little else moved in those postmidnight minutes.

I pawed at my pocket and went in to feel crumpled bills which I wasn't about to give him. I dug further for change. What came out (as I managed not to pull the paper money loose) was three quarter-sized subway tokens—which, at a ninety cents a shot, I wasn't going to give him either.

I dug in again.

The change I dragged out this time was a nickel, a dime, and four pennies. I sighed, smiled, shook my head in apology, and dumped the nineteen cents into his cap.

"...bless you, sir," he said—though at first I thought it was some nonsense formula or possibly even an Eastern chant: *Bleshusuh*...(No, he was white.) "God bless you, sir." On his knees, he moved away over the sidewalk to someone else.

His whole lower trousers were in strings where they'd worn away from his crawling the pavement. In what shape, I wondered, were the knees and shins themselves, from scurrying around like that on cement?

I turned away from him because he was really repellent.

Would it be absurd, I thought, instead of going home, to wander down to Riverside Park and walk beside the leafless trees by the postmidnight river, keeping an eye out up and down the waterside walk for someone amenable to sex? With the great window of the toy store behind me, dark now despite their Christmas trappings, I crossed west over Broadway, over the island, toward the First Baptist.

On the steps, one fellow slept, headless in a bundle of dirt-stained quilting—probably once someone's down coat. Two black guys stood at the foot, over by the Christmas trees that made a narrow aisle up the sidewalk. They swayed together, not talking.

Below the sleeper, a white guy sat. He was wearing just about what I was—only anyone would have known that he was homeless.

And I was not.

Though zipped to his neck, with the leather flap buttoned across it, *his* bomber jacket was too big. The scars and the dirt and the worn spots across the rumpled leather spoke of something recently thrown out. He was scrawny, with much facial stubble. Dirt smeared his forehead. Dirt showed through the hairs on his jaw. He looked at me looking at him—and smiled.

I slowed—and smiled back. Because nothing had happened that day. And you never know.

About forty—which is by no means too old for me—he had a fundamentally good-looking face; but there was a gauntness to it that, to me, was a turn-off. (I prefer my guys on the meaty side.) He ran his hands out to the end of his knees; a tear across the denim showed darker denim beneath. A palm's width bald spot to the front, he let his head fall to the side. Then his smile got this mock belligerence to it. "Hey!" His chin jerked toward me. "...cock-sucker!"

That's when I looked at his feet: his high-topped basketball sneakers were split left and right to let his absurdly broad feet spill out of both sides. Pushing out, his feet were in gray wool socks, the top layer torn. But by the corner light, I saw more layers under-neath—even though, on his right foot, two toes pushed through.

I went to the bottom step, walked up the two that curved out from the lower porch. He sat on the upper, watching me.

I looked down at him. "Hey, you Piece o' Shit!"

The smile opened into a rotten-toothed grin of recognition. "I *thought* that was you, nigger! Sit down!" He patted the concrete. "Sit down—sit down, man. How you been? Nice to see a friendly face, even yours!" As I sat, his grin grew in warmth. "Didn't I *tell* you you wouldn't be able to scrape me off your shoe, once you stepped in this turd?"

"Where've you been?" I asked him. "I haven't seen you—it's over a *year*, guy! You go back to California?"

"California, shit!" He rubbed his thigh with a hand whose mas-sive fingers I remembered as big as that, but not so bony. "Where the hell *have* I been? Oh, yeah—I went to Boston for a while. For a while? I guess I was up there six goddamn months. When I got back, I hung out in the Village. I don't know why—nothin' goin' on down there. I just come up here a couple days ago."

"You know," I told him, "I wouldn't even have recognized you, apart from those clodhoppers of yours!"

He sat back, somewhat between surprised and mock offended—"Naw—" and pulled a hand down over his stubbled jaw. "Just 'cause I'm growin' a beard?"

"Oh," I said. "Is *that* what you're doing?" To me it looked like five or six days without shaving by someone who didn't have to—more than every third day, anyway.

"Well," he said, "since I'm losin' it on the top, I decided to let it grow out on the bottom."

"No, really," I said. "I wouldn't have recognized you there—you've lost some weight."

"Me?" he said. "I always lose weight in the winter!"

"Sure," I said. "But somebody'll think you have AIDS or something." This was still '84, remember, when, in certain circles, you could joke about it.

"Now how the *fuck*—" he dropped his hand on my knee—"am *I* supposed to get AIDS?" He narrowed his eyes, bent closer, and spoke more softly. "I ain't no fuckin' faggot—like *you!*" He sat back, shrugging, smiling. "I'm heterosexual."

"Well," I said, "heterosexuals have been getting it too, my friend."

"You ever *knowed* one who got it?" The question accused all print and media knowledge not confirmed by experience. "I mean one who wasn't a fuckin' druggie—usin' dirty needles? And you know me, I'm into beer—not wine, not smack, not coke, not needles! Yeah, I know, I lost some weight. But I ain't been eatin' too good. I probably'll get cancer, before I get AIDS."

I shook my head. "With all the stuff you were bragging about to me a year ago that went up *your* ass, maybe you ought to think about that again—"

He raised his other hand before his face, dropping all the fingers except the fore, to silence me: "Now," his voice was quiet again, "we don't *talk* about what goes up *my* ass—"

"Right!" I put my hand on top of his. " 'Cause you're a heterosexual Piece o' Shit." I thought it was funny. "And I'm a black cocksucker. What *I* want to talk about is your big cheesy cock—and whether or not you wanna get it sucked on. Because I've been running around like a madman all day, looking for dick and not finding any; and I would *really* appreciate getting a little something in my mouth before I go to bed."

"Shit," he said disparagingly, "I *always* wanna get my dick sucked." He dragged his other hand back to his crotch and squeezed. "Can I ask you a favor, though? Now, I don't want you to think of this as hustling—'cause I hate a fuckin' hustler. And I just don't like to do that. But there's this breakfast place that these folks been runnin', down on Forty-eighth Street—over by Amsterdam: I think it's still Tenth Avenue down there. For sixty-nine cents, they give you a *real* good breakfast—eggs, coffee, toast. Bacon and stuff. Fried potatoes—and the potatoes are *good*, too! Better than a lot of these greasy spoons where they just boil 'em up and throw 'em on the back of the grill. It's for bums—like me. It opens up at five-thirty in the morning. They run it till eight. Then they close for the day. But you got to have sixty-nine cents. It ain't even the food, man: these people are *nice* to you. They say hello, and how you doin'. Got one old guy in there, him and me always shoot the shit—'nother bum, like me. But it's bein' inside, and bein' able to sit down. And talk to somebody at the table over a good cup o' coffee, if you know someone in there. You get yourself set on somethin' like that—and you just know it would make you *feel* better. Anyway, since I decided I wanted to go there tomorrow morning and get me a good breakfast, I been sittin' here thinkin' about gettin' up and walkin' over to the corner there beside the subway—and arguin' with some other guy who's gonna come along and tell me it's *his* corner (even at fuckin' one o'clock in the mornin', I *know* it), and how he wants me to get the fuck out—I ain't even got a cup! Then I gotta go an' horn in on Dirty John's turf across the street, and I don't like to do that to the poor slob—he's religious crazy and got it rough enough. And I'm thinkin' about walkin' up and down here, gettin' dimes and nickels—and there ain't nobody out at this hour anyway. And leavin' my cardboard here just means it's gonna be stole when I get back. It's funny, man, once the Christmas trees go up—" he nodded toward the black draperies of pines, crowding the block beside us—"nobody's got a thing to spare. And places where you could bum up three bucks in an hour, you can't make shit. And, man—

"I *just* don't wanna do it!

"I'm tired. My feet hurt—and I'm horny as a motherfucker, but that's par for the course with me. I'm gonna be over there tryin' to get sixty-nine cents from the people out tonight, and some other bum is gonna steal my cardboard from over here. And, well—man: I ain't even asked you for any beer this time—I already had my beer for the day. But if you would loan me a dollar, I swear you can suck my dick from now till it's time for me to go to breakfast!"

I laughed. "Look, I'm between offices—I don't have to go in to work. Come on home with me, Piece o' Shit. I'll cook you up a good breakfast: eggs, coffee, toast. Everything but the fried pota-toes—I don't have any potatoes in the house. But you can have it whenever you want it—now, *or* tomorrow morning. I'll even serve it to you in bed—"

"That's nice." He nodded. "That's real nice of you. You're a *right* fine guy, cocksucker—I knowed that from when we got togeth-er before. And I know you're tryin' to be nice. But all I want's a dol-lar—really, sixty-nine cents'll do it. And I would *love* to have my dick sucked—I want my dick sucked *real* bad—*you* know what it looks like, don't you? You swung on my crank before."

"Your yoni? Sure—that's why I'm sitting here rubbing up against you like this."

"Nigger—" he beamed—"it would be an *honor* to have you suck my dick! It would mean I could go to sleep feelin' *good!* It would mean I'll enjoy my breakfast that much more, when I get to it. But I'm out here—I got my cardboard for the night over there. You was goin' in that direction, up where I guess you live. I gotta go down *that* way, where the breakfast place is. I don't wanna carry around no ten feet of cardboard. Another time, I'd say, that's just great, and come over to your place in a minute. But right now I just want sixty-nine cents; I wanna get my dick sucked—and I wanna go to sleep. When I get up, I can go down and get me my break-fast—"

"*Okay!*" I said. "Sure." The fact is, I was on the tired side myself. "I understand. Yeah, I got a dollar for you—" I sighed— "you Piece o' Shit."

"I love you, man!" He flung his arm around my shoulder and buried his stubbly face in my neck. "You're fuckin' great, man." Smelling like that, he must have been drinking beer all day and most of the night—probably *another* reason he didn't want to trudge in torn-open sneakers to my place. "You're fuckin' beautiful! We gonna have some fun." The ruined leather of his sleeve slid over the back of my neck.

"Okay, now—!" With a hand on his shoulder, I tried to pull a bit away. "Okay! Where're we going to do this, huh? Over in the park? Is there a doorway someplace down there…?

"Do it right here." He sat back, looking around the church-porch steps. "It'll be okay."

"We're on the corner of Seventy-ninth Street and Broadway," I said. "What do you mean, 'right here'?"

"It's after midnight," he said. "Ain't nobody out."

"There's him," I pointed to the guy sleeping on the steps above us—"and him and him. And the newsstand guys over there. Cops are going to be walking by. And the two guys staying up in the trees back in there—?"

"It's all right," he repeated. "I got my cardboard. We get under that, nobody'll see. They may see your feet stickin' out the bottom. But I beat off under there three times yesterday afternoon: nobody could see me—and nobody ever said shit." He eased forward to stand. "Come on. I'll show you."

Frowning, I stood up behind him—then turned to look up at the church facade.

Above the left-hand sixteen-paneled door was carved: IF THOU SHALT CONFESS WITH THY MOUTH THE LORD JESUS, AND SHALT BELIEVE which didn't make sense, until I realized it was just the first half of what was carved over the *right*-hand sixteen-paneled door: IN THINE HEART THAT GOD HATH RAISED HIM FROM THE DEAD, THOU SHALT BE SAVED.

He'd gone over to the other side of the steps where a large piece of cardboard lay, the size of a mattress carton. It was folded up flat, but he unfolded it: three sections still hung together.

I walked over to see what he was doing.

"Come on, get in there. We make that like a little pup tent over us. They stole my blanket this mornin'. But it ain't windy out nohow. Two of us together, we can actually get warm. Come on, get in there and hunker down. I'll get in there with you, lick out your pussy a little while—" He reached up and, so gently, touched his wide fingertips to my lips— "then I can undo my jeans—I got two pair of 'em on, right now, but the zipper don't even work on the ones I got underneath—and you can slide down and plug my dick into your face as long as you fuckin' want...you fuckin' nigger black bitch pussy!" Stepping around from one foot to the other, he looked really excited.

I glanced around me. But nobody was paying any attention to what was going on here on the steps.

I got down on the length of cardboard while he held the edge in his hands. Under my palms, I could feel the corrugations beneath the top tan layer. The cardboard was a lot warmer than the concrete. I stretched out my legs. Piece o' Shit swung the big pieces up and over me, wrapping me about in shadow.

"All right?" At the triangular head, I saw him squat while a truck came around the corner at Seventy-ninth, and, from behind his knee, threw a blade from its headlight that cut, without heat or sound, across my eyes, through the carton's insides, and, for moments, lit my hand enough to see the ridges of my dark knuckles, my fingers splayed over the lighter tan. I straightened myself and got as far back as I could (we were right up against the next step) to let him push first his legs, then his hips, and then his upper body into what felt like a triangular cardboard coffin, six feet long with three-foot sides. "You okay?"

I said, "Yeah."

"Get on top of me, if you want." He slid down till his head was inside. "You remember that special kiss I taught you how to do? Didn't know I liked to be on the bottom with my bitch sometimes, did you?" The top of his head was about three inches from the edge of the cardboard. Anybody who came up, bent down, and looked in the top or bottom could have seen us. But then, who was going to? I lay on top of him, while his tongue moved up and into my mouth, our spit ran back and forth, and I probed the bony wreckage of his gum, my cock hard in my jeans. I could feel his— hard—too. He seemed really to enjoy lying under me, his arms around me. "You're really comfortable?" I asked him.

He grinned up at me, then raised his face to mine—"Sure, man. You keepin' me warm"—to kiss some more.

We got pretty heated up in there. After about fifteen minutes, he whispered at me, "You wanna get on down and suck me?" So I worked my way down—my feet coming out the bottom. He wiggled himself up an inch. My hands and his played at his crotch, opening the top button, zipping down the fly, pulling back one flap of sweat-infused denim, then another—then another (I reached down into my own pocket for one of those crumpled bills. I knew it was a single: it was change from a gyro sandwich I'd brought on Eighth Avenue), then one more. "What you doin' in my pocket?" he whispered down to me. "Ain't nothin' in there."

"I'm sliding a dollar in it," I told him. "For your breakfast."

"Aw, *thanks*, man!" Another headlight swept through the night, and lit him putting his head back, thrusting out his stubbled chin. "That's gonna be beautiful!" he spoke out to the night.

In one hand, he lifted his cock for me, the hose of his skin hanging down (the bulge of two rings actually visible when the next headlight passed), probing for my mouth. It was still hard. Beneath tented cardboard, I took it in. I'd remembered it as thicker—I mean, my mouth remembered. (Cocksuckers will understand: throat, lips, and tongue have a memory of their own.) But, inside me, that extraordinary skin, longer than a penny wrapper, was like the chewy finger on a leather glove. I guess he only had two of his rings in. I figured I wouldn't ask what had happened to the other four. I got to work getting them out—with just my mouth. His hand was down there, waiting to receive them after I'd sucked them free of cheese. Then I got to *work!* After five minutes, with only the gentlest bucking of his hips, he loosed a load.

Still holding him in my mouth, I tried to pull his pants farther down his hips, aiming to get a finger or two up his ass to make him piss. He probably figured what I was doing, though—and pulled them back up. "Yeah, you like piss, don't you?" he whispered down under the cardboard. "I can give you some. Just a minute—" But already within me his urine had began to flow. I drank him—and between his gripping legs rubbed myself on the cardboard. (I wonder what twitchings my shoes were doing out the bottom.) And came in my pants.

When he finished running, I gulped a great breath and came off him long enough to whisper up toward his head, "Jesus! We've been under here twenty minutes! You mean to say nobody out there has come over, or said something, or looked up here funny, in all that time?"

At his end of the triangle, he shrugged. "I don't know. I ain't payin' any attention to anything outside, except you—and what's in my imagination!"

I laughed. "Oh...I see!"

"Hey, I can probably go one more, if you wanna keep suckin'. It's chilly out there—and it's hot in here." He fingered my lips' edge and in my mouth. "It feels *real* good, cocksucker."

I started sucking again.

Though remaining stiff as a tower (with a wind sock hanging off it), he *didn't* cum a second time.

Soon I realized his hands had gone completely still. It occurred to me that he'd fallen asleep. I lay my head over on his hip, hooking my fingers around his pants, pulling them down a little from his loins. His jacket had ridden up his naked belly. I didn't think he had on a shirt or anything under it.

Under the cardboard, I thought: Now this is what I'd wanted with the Piece o' Shit that night two summers back, when I'd searched for him in Riverside Park—

That's when another truck came around the corner—and another headlight speared our cardboard tent. Light flooded down across his pale flesh, with its crinkled pubic hair, just before my face—

I frowned. And raised my head. His cock, soft now, pulled from my mouth.

If you've seen them, they're pretty recognizable. And, as I said, in the summer, I'd seen a fair number, on guys just walking around in the street. Also, there was Angel's roommate, Sandy, when Phel and Lewey and I had come to dinner that night at Angel's apartment—and the five of us had had a really nice time, even though Sandy, Angel's ex-lover of three years ago, was blotched with Kaposi lesions all over both arms and legs—with two on his face. (Did we talk about it with him? For a polite twenty minutes, yes— then rigorously changed the subject.) It *could* have been a purple birthmark, about the size of an irregular silver dollar...

I waited for another headlight—and, of course, no truck came by. Then I muttered, "This is ridiculous...!" I started to wiggle backward and out the bottom of the cardboard—but the newel wall to the steps was in my way. "Ah, shit...!" Suddenly I pushed up. On my head and back, the cardboard rode up over us, and fell outward—settling on chill air, down over the porch steps. I stood, expecting him to open his eyes, leap up, and protest: What are you doing...? What's the matter with...? But he was sunk in the most turgid of post-orgasmic slumbers. The two layers of jeans gaped wide, balls and cock free.

I looked around. The guy on the upper step with his head in the quilt still slept. The two black guys had gone.

By the street lamp, though, it was easy to see that, yes, on the pale skin of his hip, most of a purple blotch showed from under the filthy, flapped-down cloth.

There was another just below his rucked-up bomber jacket.

His face was to the church. Both hands were on the cardboard at his sides. I stepped forward, then kneeled beside him again.

The buttoned tab across his neck came loose easily. Taking his collar in my hands, in a motion I unzipped his jacket to the waist, where it fell apart. No, he *didn't* have anything on under it—

Cancer is named for the crab. And my first thought was that a handful of quarter-sized sand-dollar crabs had been strewn over his chest and belly.

At least five, at any rate.

My lower lip clenched between my teeth had started to hurt from the pressure.

So I released it and let out a kind of grunt. Really, seeing the lesions on him was like being hit.

On my knees I scampered—like the guy I'd given the change to across the street—back along the cardboard. I yanked up one of his jean cuffs—and the cuff beneath that. His calf was thin enough so that the layered pants leg slid up easily. His soiled sock had bunched down anyway over his deformedly large foot. In the hair there, on his dirty shin, if I saw one, I saw four purple bruiselike marks, some round like quarters, some oval like mussel shell, and others more irregular.

I've mentioned the smears on his face? Now I crawled/sprinted to the other end of the cardboard to look down at his sleeping features—Lord, he slept soundly! Nor was I being very gentle at this point.

I wanted him to wake up so I could say, "You piece of shit, what the fuck do you think you're *doing!*" I wanted him to wake up so he could say, "Hey, man, those *aren't* what you think they are—" and give me a reasonable and rational explanation.

The one on his forehead was, yes, just dirt.

But the one under the stubble on his chin—once I moved around to get myself out of the streetlight—was purple, with a clear edge to it, like the others. And, as I said, I'd *sat* across the table from Sandy last summer and joked with him and pretty much pretended to ignore them for the evening (even as I'd examined them with photographic attention), three months before Angel called Phel from Sandy's folks' place in Connecticut to say that Sandy had died.

With the cardboard now open, another passing headlight made blindingly clear *all* I'd seen on his pale flesh. I looked up—

On the far side of Broadway, a policeman was just starting across the street.

I pushed to my feet, stepped over him, hurried down the two steps and started for the corner newsstand. Why, you want to know, didn't I just sprint away among the Christmas trees? I was actually on my way *to* the policeman, to say something to him! When he was on the island in the middle of the avenue and I was about ten feet from it, suddenly I realized: This is crazy!

I stopped looking at the cop, put my hands in my pockets, dropped my head, and hurried at a different angle, on across the avenue—yes, he looked at me.

I almost ran up the block toward Amsterdam. About ten feet in, close to the wall, I turned to look back.

The policeman was walking directly up the church steps, toward the Piece o' Shit—who slept obliviously on the opened-out carton. Then the cop did something to him with his foot. I wonder whether he saw the lesions. Or if he had any idea what they were.

Suddenly Piece o' Shit rolled one way, rolled the other to push himself up to sit. Looking up at the cop, looking down at himself, he grabbed his jacket and began to tug it around him, tried futilely to drag his pants up over himself—

Fighting twenty different impulses to flee, I stayed—long enough to see that the cop wasn't hitting him. (And if he had, what would I have done, save send a troubled PS off to Sam?—though witness has its use.) But he roused the Piece o' Shit to his feet, so that he stumbled down the church steps, clutching up his clothes, dragging behind his cardboard.

Then I turned and ran the rest of the way up the block. At the corner, I went to the gutter, leaned over it, and, holding on to the edge of a wire-rimmed trash basket, I stuck a forefinger as far down my throat as I could—cursing myself for every second I'd lingered to observe. I stood there trying quite a while, too. But when you've spent years damping your gag reflex, you just don't get it back like that.

I couldn't bring up a thing.

Turning at last, my mouth open and taking great breaths every three or four steps, I walked up Amsterdam Avenue.

"Some people are saying," Pheldon said on the phone (it was two o'clock in the morning), "you can't get it through oral sex. Or, at any rate, you're not very likely to."

I'd used mouthwash about six times, then actually drunk down three capfuls of Scope.

"*Phel*don—!" I said.

"They say kissing is pretty much okay—except they advise against *heavy* kissing."

"This," I said, "was pretty much the heaviest kissing you can do!"

"Oh...well." He sounded vaguely put out. I don't blame him.

"Phel," I actually said, "just be here for me a little bit. I know there's nothing you can do. Just let me talk to you for a while—"

"Sure, baby," he said. "Talk. But I mean, you know as well as I do you're not going to get anything just from *touching* someone's Kaposi lesions."

"What about inadvertently sucking on one for ten or fifteen minutes?"

"Oh, come on, John! Gimme a *break*—!"

"What in the world was I thinking of? I mean, he'd lost so much weight, I didn't even *recognize* him when I saw him—"

"What you have to do," Pheldon said, "is go to a doctor and get one of those antibody tests they're talking about. At least if you want to find out whether you have it or not."

After a moment, I said, "Yes." Then; "*That's* what I have to do." Then I said, "Would *you* want to know if you had it?"

He was quiet a while. Then he said: "Yes. Before we lost Sandy, I might not really have been sure. But, yes, now I'd want to know."

I didn't get the test.

First I didn't do it because I read something about its taking some time for you to develop the antibodies, so that a test within a day or two of infection would likely turn up negative—when you were actually on your way to being positive. Then I put if off because I got incredibly busy with what I will shortly be telling you about.

Then…I just didn't do it.

I never saw my Piece o' Shit again, which—this early in the book—makes a pretty unsatisfactory conclusion for a character in a novel. But then, "unsatisfactory conclusions" is what AIDS seems to be about. You ask me what I think? Especially now—after all this time? I think it was AIDS with Kaposi's. I think he's dead. And if he made it to a hospital and anybody bothered to ask him, I believe he died swelling the statistics of heterosexual cases. (Looking rueful, with the frown of those whose sentences are real: "I just didn't think heterosexuals could get it. Since you tell me they can, I know better now. I must've picked it up from some black bitch out there I was fuckin'." In his imagination.) Whatever he thought he was excused from, it's yet another lie that will kill people who are not him.

But did this test the "New Power and Strength" I'd written of to Sam? It *was* my new power and strength! And if you're unsure exactly what that means…well, so am I. But it's what I mumbled to myself that kept me as close to sane as I was during the next days, weeks, months.

A momentary replay:

First I gave you my new picture of Timothy Hasler.

Now I've given you something of a new picture of me.

Yes, they both began with my intense identification with Hasler. But certainly they were resolving into clear and distinct differences.

Besides the psychological ones, what I realized now was that Hasler was a man—like so many other men and women who make up that extraordinary construction called history—who had lived and died before the age of AIDS. Indeed, so many biographies have to be not just *The Life of…* but *The Life and Times of…*; it was becoming clear that soon the lives—at least the sexual lives—of those who had lived in an age that was, no, not more innocent than ours, yet by the same token as different from ours in its outlines and articulations as sexual ages could be, would be all but incomprehensible to those coming after.

I sent Sam that letter the first week in December. I didn't real-

ly expect an answer—and got none. But the first change in my picture of Hasler began toward the winter's end, with a postcard showing a Vermont covered bridge in glorious autumnal colors, the
message side busy with difficult-to-read scrawl, including a phone
number and return address in western Massachusetts:

March 7, 1985

Dear Mr. Marr,

I have heard from a friend of a friend that you want to
contact any onetime friends, students, or professional colleagues of Tim Hasler. Though I qualify only in the first two
categories (and one of those is iffy) I'd be pleased to talk with
you, if you like. Give me a call at my home at the above number—or drop a line, if you'd prefer.

Warm regards,
Peter Darmushklowsky

At least after ten minutes of squinting at it, I was pretty *sure*
the last name was "Darmushklowsky." Though, as I said, the handwriting left it none too certain. But who else was there with the first
name Peter and a last name that long beginning with D, who had
been such a part of Hasler's life?

My first phone call got me a woman's voice, young-sounding and
delicate, with a quality close to an accent and not quite an accent
at once. No, Mr. Darmushklowsky wasn't in. If I could leave a
number, however, he'd call back.

The man's voice that returned my call was as large, friendly,
and outgoing as the woman's had been reserved and petite: "Hi,
Darmushklowsky here... Oh, yes, Mr. Marr. You got my postcard.
Well, if you're still interested in Tim—Tim Hasler—I knew him
out in California. Oh, yes, he was very into philosophy. Heard he
made quite a reputation in his field, before he died. Yes, the death
was just awful. I hadn't seen him for years by then, of course. But
Tim was just too good a person for that sort of end. No, I'd be
happy to talk with you about him...."

I had to ask: "I was wondering, Mr. Darmushklowsky, if an
acquaintance of mine—a friend, actually, a Professor Irving
Mossman—had ever contacted you before about Hasler."

A big, generous laugh: "Sure, he did—that was back when I was in California, of course—just about seven or eight years after Tim's death. But somehow we never really got together. That was four, five years ago. But we just kept missing each other—half a dozen times, too. Then, the last time I called him, he told me that, actually, he wasn't really working on Hasler just then—said he probably would be again, but just wasn't right now. Frankly, I kind of got the feeling by then he didn't want to be bothered.

"But it turns out one of my recent clients, who's at the university down in Springfield, was a friend of Professor Mossman's. And he remembered Irving mentioning something about one or another of his students who was also interested in Tim.

"I don't know, Mr. Marr—but there was some stuff I wanted to talk about. Then Mossman put it off; and I put it off; and suddenly—a couple of weeks back—I realized it had been put off for getting on to years now. And that just seemed a little to long.

"So my client called Irving—and came back with your name."

"I see," I said.

Turned out *we* missed each other twice.

Darmushklowsky's nascent software business (wouldn't you know) would be bringing him to New York the next weekend. After he finished his business in the morning, he and I would get together for a long lunchtime talk. I called Cathy at Temp Time, my agency, and asked if she could work it so my job switch left that as my free day. First she told me, "No,"—then she called back fifteen minutes later and said it was okay. But that morning there was a call at six-thirty: "Darmushklowsky here. Look, John, I didn't get any sleep at *all* last night. Some business friends of mine, we tied one on. And I just walked into my hotel room two minutes ago. The chances are I'll be back in the city a couple of weeks from now. Would you mind if we canceled for today and tried again on my next trip in…?"

A couple of weeks later, *I* called *him*. "You know, Mr. Darmush-klowsky—"

"Hey, not bad! You said it right—"

"Thank you. Mr. Darmushklowsky—?"

"If it's hard for you, please. Just call me Pete. Everybody calls me Pete. I'm not kidding; we've been married six years, and Sue still can't say my name right three times in a row—and it's hers, now!" Big laugh. "Now what is it I can do for you, John?"

"I was thinking, Pete: you aren't really that far from me. I have some friends in Northampton who can't be more than an hour from you—with whom I could stay overnight. Maybe the answer is for me to take the bus up there and spend an afternoon with you—"

"Hey, now, you wouldn't have to stay with your friends. If you were willing to come, Sue and I would be delighted to put you up for a night or two...."

Only I was the one who had to call up and cancel this time. The Tuesday before the Saturday I was to go (the last Saturday in the month), my mom went into the hospital with a (fortunately minor) heart attack; and, after bouncing back and forth to the hospital half a dozen times in less than that number of days, that weekend I had to go out to Staten Island and cook for Dad.

"Pete, I'm *really* sorry—"

"No, no. I understand, John. Of course!"

Two weeks later, however, on a mid-April weekend, after five and a half hours, I got off the bus at Pittsfield.

There at the little Massachusetts bus stop, over three steps toward one another, while we went from not knowing who each other was to questioning frowns, to smiles, Peter Darmushklowsky certainly did a better job than Mike in my dream of not looking *too* surprised that the guy in the sports jacket with the briefcase was on the black side. And I thought: so this is that long-haired beanpole. He'd filled out into a bear! And the hair, white at temples and walrus mustache, was, over his small, neat head, near-military short.

Darmushklowsky wore tan slacks, cordovan shoes, and a blue thermal vest over a green plaid shirt—though it was a balmy afternoon.

Even before the next three steps, though, and his hand came out to shake, I was struck: He seemed so much older than I was! And he was the same age as Timothy Hasler! I'd pictured both, I realized now, as occupying some nebulously ephebic never-never age between nineteen and twenty-five. But if Hasler had lived, I realized, this (I did some quick figuring: I guess about...forty-one) is precisely how old he would be!

"Hello—John Marr? Pete!" And we were shaking hands. "It's real nice of you to come all the way up here, John. Picked a real nice day, too. Come on, meet Sue; and we'll run you out to the house. Want me to carry that for you?" He pointed to my overnight bag on the strap over my shoulders. "You've been lugging that all the way up from New York—" which was, of course, ridiculous. It had been in the rack above my seat till five minutes ago. "Here you go—" and in an easy swoop, he lifted the strap over my head and, at the same time, swept my briefcase up and away.

"Oh, really…you don't have to—" Then I was trotting behind him.

"I'm parked right around here."

What I was thinking now, as I crossed the parking lot's tarmac, was that a good number of academic philosophers, with fairly megacephalic reputations, were a good deal older than Darmushklowsky/Hasler. Save some fluke MacArthur "genius" award, or an anomalous Kripke-like ascendancy, for a philosopher of Hasler's reputation to be *only* as old as Hasler would have been, even if he were alive, pretty unusual.

As long as I'd been dealing with Hasler, immediately upon meeting a contemporary of his I felt certain very basic facts falling into their proper proportions and place. Really, it was kind of interesting to pluck Peter Darmushklowsky back out of time and eternity, as it were, and say hello—even if nothing overly interesting came of our actual talk.

Pete stopped by the front window of a very new, very green Buick. Immediately the pane began to sink into the door. "John Marr, this is my wife, Sue…?"

I'd heard her name three times. Still, my image of Pete's mate was the steel-eyed, silent Debbi. The face smiling up at me from behind the glare-streaked glass was petite, black-eyed, and Asian—most certainly Japanese, with traditional black bangs straight across the forehead. "Hello, Mr. Marr. How nice of you to come up and visit Pete and me."

"Oh, call me John…please—"

"Did you have a good ride on the bus, John? It's an awfully long trip. Pete always drives me down to the city if I have to go. But once he couldn't and I had to take the bus. It seemed to go on *forever!*"

Protesting that the trip was fine, I got into the back. Pete slid my overnight bag and briefcase in after me, then loped around to the driver's side, got in, turned on the ignition, and we rolled down one small town street after another, that quickly gave way to country road.

"You are a professor," Sue said brightly from the front of the car, "interested in Pete's old friend, Tim? I think they liked each other very much. Pete tells me they were very close. It's sad that he died so young. Pete says that he was a very brilliant boy. He knew all about philosophy. But that is not something I know very much about at all."

"Not a professor," I said. "Just a graduate student—really, at this point just an interested researcher. But, yes, I'm hoping to get some material for my thesis in philosophy."

Laughing, Pete went around a curve. "Now, like I told you, I won't be able to help you out too much with anything about Tim and his philosophy work." (He hadn't told me that at all, actually. Not that I'd expected it.) "That stuff Tim was into, that was all beyond me. To me it always looked more like mathematics, anyway. But we were friends, and I can talk some about being friends with him. That's the part I can do."

Up through the drinks and the barbecued steaks Pete forked about on the black enamel and aluminum Weber grill—"Looks like the starship *Enterprise*, doesn't it?"—while Sue supplied a huge wooden bowl of salad, boiled corn on the cob, and a broccoli and carrot casserole au gratin from their small but efficient kitchen, the talk stayed pretty general, however.

When we'd all but finished, Pete returned from the back porch with another couple of Heinekens: "Now, you must have some specific questions, John...." He handed me my third.

As if that was her cue, Sue stood, and from the wicker lawn table picked up a black tray which held the remains of our hefty Saturday afternoon dinner. "I have some things to do in the house. I will leave you two here in the garden—" and their three layers of backyard really *was* a garden, most of it Sue's doing, I'd been told earlier, in some detail—"to talk about Tim." And she was up the brick steps by a bank of fuchsia, heather, and irises.

Sitting now in wooden chairs with rope webs, Pete and I were practically facing one another.

"You know what really impressed me first about Tim?" Darmushklowsky looked at his beer bottle, turning it in one large, almost-glowingly-pink hand; there was dim gold in the early evening light across the garden.

"No," I said, holding onto mine. "Please tell me."

"Well, you know that I started out as a student of Tim's in one of his discussion classes for my undergraduate philosophy requirement. We all recognized that he was young to be a teacher, though I didn't realize he was six weeks younger than I was until sometime later. That same term, there was some graduate seminar that he was giving regular lectures in, every week—"

"Hanson's 'Problems with Mathematical Models of Monistic and Dualistic Systems' seminar?"

"Yeah, that's what it was called—I remember now. And if you really wanted to know about the advanced work Tim was doing, those guys in there with him are the ones you should probably start by looking up—I think Tim said, once, there were only six people in it beside Professor Hanson. And Tim got to do most of the talking. Our class was just some undergraduate discussion group for one of the cattle-call survey-requirement courses he was leading to make some money. When I said my status as a student of Tim's was on the iffy side, that's what I meant. But, anyway, from the very first day in our class, Tim never mispronounced my name. Or felt he had to make any kind of joke about it." Darmushklowsky chuckled. "I'm a California Polack, and I had to put up with a lot of that, growing up out there. And though it took me three months to realize it, Tim was just a kid like I was, and he had a pretty good sense of humor. But with Tim my name was never something to joke about—not that I really minded when people did. Because they did it all the time. But, I suppose, I *did* appreciate it when people—like Tim—*didn't*."

I said, "Tim was very fond of you."

"*Mmm.*" Pete nodded. "Once the class was over, and we stopped being teacher and student and just became friends, we both liked each other a lot. We were very different, of course. I mean, Tim really *was* a genius. Sometimes it used to kind of scare me. That somebody as smart as Tim, already a professor—well, not a *real* professor, but at least a teacher—in college, could like somebody like me...? I mean, I did okay, but I was never anybody's brain. I asked him about that once. You know what he told me? It's always stayed with me. One day, when we were sitting around, and he was asking me stuff about what I was doing—with my music, I think—I just came out and asked, 'How come somebody as smart as you wants to hang around with a lazy lummox like me?'

"He looked at me for a minute. Then he said, 'You really want to know?'

"I said, 'Sure, I want to know. That's why I asked'—though, I remember wondering if I would really like what he was going to tell me.

" 'Look,' he said. 'I'm so much smarter than anybody you see around here—you, the other students, the graduate students, *and* the professors—if I only made friends with people who were as smart as I was, I wouldn't have *any* friends. At all. So, looking for people who know, say, *half* the things I know already doesn't even interest me. What I look for in a friend is someone who's different from me. The more different the person is, the more I'll learn from him. The more he'll come up with surprising takes on ideas and things and situations. I don't like you because you're smart— *or* stupid. I like you because we're different.'

"Isn't that something?" Pete took a swallow of beer. "Like I said, it's stayed with me. And generally *I'm* a liker—I mean, I like all sorts of people. People who do all sorts of things. All kinds of people. And when I make a new friend—like you, say—I think of what Tim said about the most interesting friends being the most different from you."

"From one point of view," I said, "it's a rather arrogant thing to say."

"Well, Tim didn't *say* it arrogantly." Pete shrugged. "Besides, he *was* the smartest person I'd ever met before—if not since."

I smiled and drank from my own bottle. "He liked you very much," I said again.

"We both liked each other—a lot."

"I have copies of his journals from 1964—the year the two of you were friends. They start from the first time Tim noticed you in his discussion class. They go right up to the end of the business with the Flame stories."

"Oh, yes. 'Pete Flame.' I thought they were pretty good—it's kind of flattering to be turned into an intergalactic hero."

"We've found the first eighteen typed pages of a third 'Flame' story among Hasler's papers. But apparently he never finished it."

"There was a third one?" Darmushklowsky raised an eyebrow. "Now I didn't know that. He must have stopped it once the whole student newspaper business started. That was really an awful thing.

Nobody remembers it now, but there were threats of hearings before the school ombudsman, and Tim was called in to see the chairman of his department. Oh, it was just a lot of nonsense. But a lot of it was ugly nonsense. And a lot of it hurt—it hurt Tim, I know. And it hurt me—thick as my skin is. But the stories themselves, I liked them—I was flattered, just like I was flattered by Tim's friendship. And this asshole of a senior reporter kept on trying to change it into some kind of exploitation of the students by the faculty." Pete shook his head again. "Finally, yeah, it did kind of queer our friendship after a while—I didn't want it to. Tim didn't want it to—he worked real hard to make sure it didn't. But I was leaving school that year anyway. Maybe any two people would have had to work harder than we were ready to, to keep up our friendship—even without the trouble over those stories."

"From both Tim's journals and the stories themselves, I get the impression that the Pete Flame stories are really kind of love letters to you."

"Yes." Darmushklowsky put the bottle on his knee. "They were."

"And they were, if I may say so, rather elegant and charming love letters at that."

Pete chuckled. "Yes. They were that. And maybe that's why it was so sad—so unpleasant—to have people try to turn them into something else. But also, maybe that was the aspect of them that upset everybody in the first place. It was just there, under the surface, annoying those creeps at the school, who couldn't quite put their fingers on what it was."

"I'd never thought about it from that point of view," I said. "That's interesting. You may have a point."

"You know what Tim was actually in love with, about me?" Asked so bluntly, it surprised me.

So I answered: "Your feet."

Pete raised one white eyebrow; he seemed surprised I *had* an answer. "Yes. That's right—my big, clumsy feet. And back then they probably stunk, too. But then," he added, "you said you have his journals. I suppose that's in there."

I nodded. "I'd be happy to leave a copy of them with you. I brought one in case, after we talked, you wanted to read it. They might jar your memory about other things—if we have a second session."

"Well," and Pete went back to considering his Heineken, "I'm not sure I really want to do that—read his journals. Tim never showed them to me. If there were things in there he'd wanted me to see, he probably would have—at the time." He slid his cordovan shoes out in the grass and crossed his ankles. It was easy to imagine the same gesture by the twenty-year-old junior at the first row's far left. "On the other hand, it's been a long time. Tim's dead. And I'm older." He frowned. "I can't really imagine there being anything in there that would make me feel *too* much different about him...."

"I don't think there is," I said; though I was also thinking of Mossman. "At least, not if you already knew *that* about him. As I said before, Tim was simply very fond of you. May I ask you something?"

"Sure."

"Did you figure it out—about how he felt about your feet—the night you and your friends moved him from East Howard to Rushdale? That's the night you had the foot-wrestling thing together, at the new basement apartment. Is that when you picked up on it?"

Pete frowned now. "When was that? When he moved? Goodness, no! I knew a long time before that."

"Do you remember when, exactly, it hit you?"

"It never 'hit' me," Darmushklowsky said. "Tim told me—I think it was the day after the marks were in. He said he wanted to talk to me about something. We went for a walk—and he told me. I've thought about it a lot of times since—it always struck me as a very brave thing to do."

That was a surprise. "You mean the two of you...talked about it?"

"Several times."

"I'll admit," I said. "I didn't realize that. It's not in the journal."

Pete shrugged, as if to say he couldn't be responsible for everything that was or wasn't there. "Well, we did."

"I suppose," I said, "nothing compelled him to put *everything* that happened to him of importance into his journal. It wasn't a real diary. For more than half the days there're no entries at all. Still— you say you knew about it. Because he told you. And from time to time the two of you talked about it. How did it make you feel?"

Pete shrugged again. "I don't think I was really bothered by it.

It was mostly just interesting—another fascinating thing about this incredibly strange, incredibly interesting, incredibly smart Korean kid—Korean-American, I mean." Here Pete chuckled again. "But other than an occasional session of foot wrestling like that—and when we did it, yeah, I knew exactly why—he never did anything else about it…I mean, really. I thought it was funny. But if he got something out of it, it didn't bother me. He certainly never touched me in any other way. He never put his hands on me—I mean, on other parts of my body. Tried to feel me up or anything like that." Darmushklowsky put his head to the side. "And other men have, John—and I don't go in for it, either. I mean, when I was a year out of college, I hitchhiked back and forth across this country—and had to do my share of arguing with the damned truck drivers to keep their hands off—get them to leave me the hell alone! No, I don't have any complaints to make about Tim Hasler on those grounds."

"Sounds like you don't have any complaints about him at all," I offered into the considered silence. "Did you have any feelings, at the time, perhaps, about the way he worked himself into the Flame stories—as the beautiful Diamonda? Or was that just part of the joking?"

"Pete's girlfriend?" Darmushklowsky frowned again. Hearing him use his own name in the third person was kind of disorienting. The silence went on a long time—and added to the feel of displacement. A breeze rose, roaring among the trees, then stilled. "You know," he said at last, looking thoughtful. "There was all sorts of stuff I'd planned to tell you, about me, about Tim, right at the beginning. I'd planned it back as far as when your friend Mossman first called me. Then, just talking like we've been, somehow we got away from it—I don't know exactly how. We're talking all about Tim, which is what you're interested in, I know. You didn't come up here to learn strange things about Pete Darmushklowsky. But I realize from what you just said, there're a couple of things you misunderstand. Diamonda wasn't Tim." He waited a moment, then went on. "I don't think Tim was *that* kind of gay guy."

"She wasn't Debbi, was she…?"

"Debbi who?" he asked.

"Your girlfriend Debbi."

"Oh, my friend, Debbi. Back at school. No. She certainly wasn't *Debbi!*" He started to take another swallow from the bottle, then set it on the table beside us. "The fact is, John, Tim Hasler was an extraordinary guy—an extraordinary man. And I haven't told you why. But, to tell you, I have to tell you about both Tim and me."

"Please go ahead," I said. Yes, I was prepared for the confession of some late-adolescent sexual liaison that would obviate the recent overbutch protests about hitching and truck drivers. But what Peter Darmushklowsky told me was this:

"In many ways, John, I'm a very ordinary guy. But there are other ways in which, I suppose, I'm not. All my life—at least all my life since puberty—I've been fascinated by Asian women. Though I could tell you a dozen incidents in its development, I certainly couldn't tell you how it started. But by the time I was old enough to know what sex was, I knew that Chinese women, Japanese women, Korean women—for me, that's just what women *were*. White women—or even black women—to me it was as if, at least in terms of sexual attractiveness, they weren't even the right gender. My father was in construction, just down from Frisco, on the outskirts of San Jose. And the idea of his son having an Asian girl-friend was not one that would have gone over big with him. I found that out my first year in high school, when, as innocently as you could with someone you thought was the most beautiful and sensual and heavenly creature on God's earth, I walked back to my house with a Japanese girl in my class—and had to put up with a solid year of teasing from my old man. By the time I was fifteen, I knew I couldn't talk about it, I couldn't let anybody know. If I had pictures of Asian women, I had to hide them under bland old airbrushed *Playboy* centerfolds. I thought I was weird. I thought I was sick. I thought I was damned and would go to Hell—while I believed in Hell. And what going to college meant for me—once I stopped believing in Hell—was that there was an Asian—and also an Asian-American—student community that, perhaps, I could make some sort of contact with and, maybe, just *maybe*, manage to get an Asian girlfriend. For one or two dates. Possibly the rest of my life?—oh, no! I didn't dare *think* about it! And when Tim made the first overtures of friendship toward me, I fell all over him, trying to make him my friend—yeah, sure, because I was flattered having a genius for a buddy; but also in the hopes that I could meet other Asian students—yes, especially girls—through him.

"And I did, too.

"Probably I was as subtle about it as he was about my big old clodhoppers.

"In fact I was so hopelessly, heart-stoppingly, completely terrified of my own pursuits, I never even noticed his thing with my feet—*until* he told me about it. At the same time he told me about my own thing.

"Up until then, you understand, I really thought nobody knew! If an Oriental"—he laughed—"nobody said Asian back then: if an *Asian* woman went by, I'd stop in the street and turn around and stare with, literally, my mouth hanging. And it wasn't like some damned construction worker ogling a pretty girl and whistling and elbowing all his friends—that's just a performance for the other guys! But me, to the extent I'd thought about it at all, I figured what I was doing was so strange and unusual and inspired by feelings so unknown to anyone else that most people wouldn't even realize what I was turning in the street to look at—so that I was safe from detection, like a madman slowing down on the sidewalk to perform his own private, personal, and incomprehensible ritual. Believe me, nobody could have been more shocked than I was, when Tim and I were walking together across the grass and he said, 'Pete, I've noticed something about you...'" Pete laughed again. "Well, not only did he tell me that he'd figured it out— like, I suppose, at that point, anyone could have missed it—but he also told me that it was...all right! And that I should go for it. And that he would help me! And that he felt the same way about my feet as I felt about Oriental girls—like I say, people used the term 'Oriental' back then, and nobody ever raised an eyebrow. I was really just about falling all over myself with hope and nervousness and expectations and anxiety and...you see, I guess this is the only way to put it. I was something of an asshole with girls. All girls, really—Asian or any other kind. I think it had to do with the fact that I was sure I would never get the kind of girl I wanted. And at the same time, I wanted one—a wonderful, beautiful, Asian one—so incredibly badly. And Tim was the first guy—hell, the first person— to sit me down and explain to me that, first, I could *have* what I wanted, and, second, that the only person who was keeping me from getting what I wanted was me.

"Possibly it was because he was gay, but Tim got along with girls pretty well—a lot better than I did. And he was perfectly happy to put a little effort into setting me up with a date here and there with one or another of the Asian girls he knew—most of them were Japanese, even though he was Korean. And he was also very patient in explaining to me what I'd done wrong—for the first few times, he was very careful to put it in cultural terms: Well, Japanese girls were just not brought up to understand X, Y, or Z— which would usually be some asinine thing I'd managed to do. But finally it dawned on me—I'm not a genius, but I'm not an idiot either—that *no* girls were brought up to appreciate the kinds of tricks I liked to pull. Indeed, most *guys* wouldn't put up with them either; the only reason Tim did was because—well, you say you read his journals. It's probably all in there."

"Actually," I said, "it's not. Along with the fact that you knew about his foot fetishism, and that the both of you talked about it, there's no mention of your being particularly attracted to Asian women."

Pete cocked his head and looked at me—unbelievingly, I realized. After a while, his eyes left mine, and a few moments later, he said: "Well, you say I surprised you. You've kind of surprised me back. All I can figure out then, is maybe…well, Tim was gay. I was straight. Tim was into guys' feet. I was into women. True, the women I was into were Oriental—Asian. But basically my problem may have seemed so small compared to his that he didn't think it was even *worth* jotting down!" He laughed and shook his head.

"That's possible," I said. "From what I gather, Tim was a pretty civilized guy."

"And I was a long-haired hippie madman, back then." Pete laughed again. "Civilized—that's one way to put it. But quite honestly, though, I think that I'm a reasonable and happy man today, and that I'm married to Sue—and very happily, I might add— basically *because* of ideas about what we were allowed to do in this world that I'd never realized before and that Tim first introduced me to. And I think I'm *still* married to Sue, if you know what I mean, because of ways that he suggested that a person act with another person that he cares about, that he loves, that he wants to stay with him. That's all part of philosophy, isn't it? At least it is to me. I mean it seems to me that it *ought* to be, if it isn't."

"Perhaps," I said, "it's just part of the systems of the world." But he didn't seem to need me to explain the personal reference.

"Yeah," he said. "But, like I say, John, Tim was a really extra-ordinary guy. And I just wanted to give you a little idea of how. Diamonda—?" he looked up at me—"she wasn't supposed to be Tim. *I* knew who she was as soon as I got to that part. And it really hit me, too. She was the girl I'd always wanted—and the girl it was always so hard for me to have. The stuff that kept us—that kept Pete and Diamonda—apart, that was, like they say in the college lit classes, a metaphor. That's all. A metaphor for what kept me away from the real Asian girls I kept seeing in the distance and was always trying to get to meet, to get them to see that I wasn't the total clowning asshole I always felt I had to act like as soon as I got within ten feet of one, because if she saw what I *really* felt, she'd think I was as bad and stupid and evil for wanting her as my father would have…. But Diamonda, well, she always believed in Pete. And Pete, thank God, maybe because Tim put an image of Diamonda in his stories for me to hold onto, believed that it was *possible* for her to be real—if not then, then someday. Do you see what I mean?

"If those stories were love letters, Diamonda was certainly the reason why they were as goddamn elegant as they were. Because he was saying, because *I* love *you*, it's all right for *you* to love somebody else…."

"I see," I said. "Yes, it makes sense. But—yes—it's all quite new to me. It's also just possible, as far as the journals were concerned, that Tim left out certain things because he was afraid if someone else found them, it might compromise him—or, indeed, embarrass you."

"That's possible," Pete said. "People sure didn't carry on back then about being gay and stuff the way they do now. Yeah—I guess that makes sense." He sat forward a little. "You know, I'd really *like* to take a look at Tim's journals—from that time. If you have them, I'll take a look at them tonight. If they jog my memory, I'll make some notes. We can talk about them some more tomorrow."

Shortly we went in from the garden. I got the pages from my briefcase for him—and, much later that night, when I got up and left my room to go out to the bathroom, I saw a light on down-stairs. On a whim, I went down six steps to look. It came from the office, where I saw Pete, through the open door, still up, in robe and pajamas, sitting at his desk, turning pages.

In the kitchen the next morning, Sue broke out bagels, orange juice, butter, cream cheese—"Did you have a good sleep? I always worry about how comfortable that mattress really is"—smoked salmon, cantaloupe, prosciutto, sticky buns.

"It'll be kind of mix-and-match this morning." Pete brought over the steaming pot from the black-and-white Braun coffee maker.

"We're getting rid of the leavings for the week," Sue said. "You've been elected to help."

Darmushklowsky didn't even wait for me to bring up the subject. "That was really fascinating—and made me think a lot, too—Tim's journals."

"It certainly did," Sue said. "I thought you would never let me get to sleep. He talked my ear off till after three in the morning!"

"First off, I suppose, there were the little things he got wrong. Not many of them—at least that I can detect at this distance. But one place, I remember, he's got me eating pumpkin seeds in his class! I *hate* pumpkin seeds—always have. Always will. Along with the yogurt and the carrot sticks, what I used to bring in there was a little waxed paper bag full of *pistachio* nuts!

"It was pistachio nuts practically every day. I remember my fingers would get all pink from them." He chuckled, poured coffee into the blocky ceramic mugs Sue had set out, first for me, then for Sue, then for himself. "*Pumpkin* seeds!" He put the coffeepot on a bronze trivet. "I'm sure if you'd asked him when I'd been in the class three more weeks, even he would have realized pumpkin seeds was a mistake." Now he looked around at Sue, at me. "I mean, it's not a big one. But he was so accurate an observer, to get something like that wrong." He laughed. "Pumpkin seeds...! I suppose the real thing that struck me, though, more than anything else, was how much he left out. I mean, reading it over just started my mind boiling—remembering this, remembering that. Stuff that probably wouldn't mean anything to anybody—most of it. Probably, not even to Tim. I don't even mean him never writing anything down about me and my...peculiarities; but about so many other things. Like the way I used to play the guitar all the time, whenever I was around people, so they couldn't talk or anything—and never play a song all the way through, mind you. Just tootling. And don't talk about asking me to *stop!* Until people got sick of me—they would get up and sneak away just to be shut of me!" He laughed. "It was because I was afraid of having a real conversation with people, I guess. But nobody else could, either. Today I don't even *own* a guitar—the guy who was going to be a rock-and-roll star and write songs and make fifty gold records...you know, another Bob Dylan." He laughed. "And you said, for instance, yesterday, that the journal pages go up to the *end* of the business about the Flame stories. But it only goes through the first two weeks of it—unless there were some pages missing at the end...?"

"No," I said. "That's all he wrote about it."

"Well," he said, "it certainly didn't end *there!* It went for months—and got a whole lot uglier than that, too. At one point Tim was told he would be suspended from all teaching in the future. And I know there was a while he was considering transferring to another university—did you know that?"

"No, I didn't." I wondered whether Mossman had.

"And it was certainly hell on me. When everybody is telling you that somebody you think of as your good buddy has abused you and exploited you and plagiarized you—"

"And you know he's a pervert who has unnatural feelings for you—"

"Yes, that's right. You don't know *how* you're supposed to feel about him after a while. But until now I've never told any one about those 'unnatural' feelings. I stuck with him—I really did. I don't know if he ever knew just how much I did—I even got in a fight once I never told him about. But that was because *he* was walking around with a black eye when some guys jumped on him."

This was news; and I'm sure Mossman hadn't known things had gone to the brawling stage.

"I mean," Darmushklowsky explained, "after the student paper got it straightened out that he *wasn't* a professor, the whole thing developed an incredibly racist side: having to do with the foreign TAs, especially Nationalist Chinese and Japanese ones. Some of them had some trouble with their English, and when they were assigned to teach classes, the students really resented it. That Tim, personally, was just as American as anyone else at that school—well *that* got away from people pretty fast. By the end of it, my name was mud with half—well, more accurately about a third—of the Asian-American kids at Stilford—who, frankly, were the only people I gave a damn *what* they thought of me...do you know about any of this?"

I had to shake my head.

"Well, it was a pretty rough thing to go through. I hope you understand what I've told you—and that you won't make anything out of it that you shouldn't. Not about me, so much. I never did care too much what people had to say about me. And I still don't. But I mean about Tim."

"All I can tell you," I said, "is that I have great respect and great sympathy for Tim Hasler. You said you thought he was an extraordinary man. Well, so do I. And you've only alerted me to ways he was extraordinary beyond the ones I was already aware of. And I have a great deal of respect for you for talking so openly to me about him—and about yourself."

Now Darmushklowsky put his arm around Sue's diminutive shoulders. "The other thing, of course—the thing that was the real surprise—was simply that I really hadn't known how bad Tim had it for me. Last night, when I opened those pages up at the desk, just from the way you'd talked, I figured I was in for a pretty easy trip down memory lane—you know, it was even a surprise to me that I recognized his *handwriting*. He never wrote me letters or anything. But just from his written comments on the head of the papers I did for him in class, as soon as I looked at the first page, I realized I still knew his handwriting!" He took a long sip of coffee, steam wreathing before his nose and eyes. "At any rate, like I was saying yesterday, I knew Tim liked my feet. And I knew he liked me in a serious, even sexual, way. We used to joke about it. And he knew that I wasn't turned on by guys at all. I mean, it wasn't even something that seemed bad to me back then. It just seemed silly. But that his feelings were as intense as they were—well, *that* came as kind of a shock! I mean, when he had to run up into his office and beat off, just because he'd seen me, barefoot in the boys' john—"

And do you know, I'd forgotten *that* particular entry was in there?

"—well, *that* one I wasn't ready for! The fact is, John, I think if I'd have known at the time he felt that strongly, I probably *would* have done something with him—sexual, the way he wanted. I mean,

I know what it's like to want someone till you're half-blind with it and can't stand up. And you think you won't be able to go on breathing. And it feels like somebody's punched you in the stomach, and you hope nobody will say anything because you can't even talk." He gave Sue's shoulder a squeeze. "And I know what it's like to have that person say yes, and give themselves to you... I probably could have done that for Tim." He shrugged. "It wouldn't have been any skin off my ass."

"But wouldn't it have made a difference," Sue asked, from within the arc of his arm, "whether, say, I gave myself to you just to be nice? Or I gave myself to you because I wanted you back—which I did very much?"

"Sweetheart, you could have given yourself to me because you loved me, or because you liked me, or by accident—or because you happened to think it was a cute idea—and I'd have been incredibly, eternally grateful *any* way it happened!"

"You see," Sue said, "that's the thing I never understand about men. If I loved someone like that, the way you say Tim was in love with you, the only way I could accept you physically was if I knew you loved me back. I couldn't take your body just because you thought it was a nice thing to do, or a kind thing, or a friendly gesture between the boys—one of whom was just overly horny." Sue shook her head. "Maybe it's different with men and women. I know everybody says it is."

I smiled. "Well, to know that Pete *does* feel that way about you, that means you know he really loves you." Saying it, I thought it sounded awfully sappy.

"Yes." Sue reached over and took Darmushklowsky's large hand in her small one. "I know that." (It didn't sound sappy when *she* said it, though.) "That's still not what I mean." But she didn't seem ready to explain any further.

"I don't mean you should do something like that—go to bed with somebody—if you hate the idea, or it turns your stomach—if it makes you sick." Pete shook his head a little. "If I thought you felt that way about it, no, I couldn't accept physical love from you either. And if I'd felt that way about it, I don't believe Tim would have been able to accept physical love from me. He loved me; he didn't want to *rape* me! But, hell—John, I was telling you yesterday about arguing with a couple of truck drivers to stay off me, when I used to hitchhike? Well, like I told Sue, long ago, the fact is, a couple of others—not many, but three, no, four, actually—I *didn't* argue with. And they were complete strangers." Shrugging, he glanced down at his wife, who sat, listening, blinking, smiling—clearly, this was one of the things they'd talked about last night. "If I'm going to do it with a guy, I would rather have done it with someone who was a friend than someone who was a goddamn stranger—just for a meal or a motel room, like I did. Does that make sense?" which he aimed down at Sue (who still smiled, who was still silent). Pete went on: "I mean, what the hell difference would it have made to me if me and Tim had laid around naked together a couple of times and I'd let him slobber all over my toes—or whatever the hell he wanted to do with them. Hold 'em, suck 'em, jerk off on 'em—or what have you." He grimaced. "You see...the fact is, without the naked part...and this was something else I was thinking about, I mean, just remembering. In the very back of my mind: I guess I...did let Tim do that, or something like it. A couple of times, too—while I pretended I was really interested in something else. Probably playing the guitar. I mean, I know we never got undressed with one another. And I can't even really remember what the situation was—or where we were." He snorted. "Probably it was at his place, after we got him moved in. But for all I know, it could have been in a goddamn classroom after everybody else had left—or maybe it was even in his office, when we were suppose to be going over some work and I broke out my ax instead to play a song for him I'd only about half put together. But the fact is, I can *remember* what Tim's tongue felt like between my toes—it tickled, that's how it felt! You know, I said this to Sue last night. If a woman on a date let some guy carry on like that without stopping him, getting himself all worked up over her, while she pretended it wasn't really happening and with her mind off on something else, counting the pigeons and wondering where he was going to take her for dinner, I'd call her a first-class bitch!" He snorted again.

"If a teacher got you as a student alone in his office," I said, "and started making love to your feet—or any other part of you—you could also call it sexual harassment."

"*Mmm,*" Pete said. "Yeah, well maybe. Still, I know what *I'd* call it." He shook his head again. "Christ, when I was a kid, I was really something, wasn't I?" Now he pulled a bagel off the plate. "But the point is, it didn't *mean* anything to me. Really, for the change it made in our relationship, it could just as easily never have happened. We were just as good friends afterwards as before. So I just wish I'd understood it more—maybe gone with it more, so I really *would* have known more of what it meant to him. Then— I don't know—maybe it would have meant more to me."

"Well," I said. "It was a very long time ago. It's over now—"

"—and Tim's long dead," Pete finished. A chill spring sun burned in the window. "Right. Sure. But if, by being a little more sensitive, I could have avoided hurting him—and being insensitive to people is something I'm good at—well...I just wish I had. Sexual fucking *harassment?* Good God, he was scared to death! I may be insensitive, but I'm sure not *that* insensitive! And this is the guy who, as far as I'm concerned, is majorly responsible for my being a deeply, deeply—" he gave Sue another hug—"happy man today. I'm sorry: to read what Tim was feeling, and what he said about it, and what he did about it, any other way—like sexual harassment— that's *my* idea of perverted!"

Sue glanced up at her husband. I had a moment's impression that she was not as convinced as he was—that, indeed, she was still making up her mind.

"You know," I said, "whether you're right or wrong, to admit some of this, Pete, or even to talk about it in this way, makes you a rather remarkable man yourself."

"I'm just an asshole." Pete gave me a grin. "I'm known for saying outrageous things all over the place—aren't I, honey? Not just to you, John—to lots of people. Really, I wish you were special. But you're not. But, hell, that's the way I feel. One way or the other, it just wouldn't have been that big a deal. I mean, it wouldn't have been for me. I just hope it wasn't for him." He raised the bagel and bit. "Well, at least Tim didn't have to go through this AIDS business. And sexual harassment charges? Jesus, that's *all* he would have needed, on top of all that other nonsense back then!" Shaking his head again, Pete munched his bagel, sipped his coffee. "Another thing that got me, though—while I was reading: all the things that he could have said about me, things that wouldn't have been too good at all. And he didn't. Most of the things he put down were actually about the *nice* things I did—and I just don't remember myself quite that way. I mean, I *did* the things he said. Sure. But I pulled so much other shit, like the stuff I just told you about, I'm surprised he even noticed *any* of the good stuff."

"Just one question, Pete," I said. "A couple of times you've referred to yourself as a 'madman.' I was just wondering if—" Then I paused. "Oh, never mind. It relates to something else in Tim's journal, but from much later. And I want to think about what you've just told me. Should the other become important, I can always phone you about it."

"Sure." Pete lifted his mug to finish up his coffee, sun cutting blue ceramic into a shadowed and a shiny half. "You know—" he put the mug again on the table—"I said Tim was an extraordinary man. And he was. And you said he was civilized. Which he was. We all know he was a genius and stuff. But is there any way, if you write about him, you could let people know just how fucking *nice* the guy was—I mean, to me? The way he wrote about me. And just being my friend, I mean?"

Riding back on the bus to the city, I thought about the untrustworthiness of journals. Thoreau's? Banneker's? Katherine Mansfield's? Emerson's? It wasn't even that they were selective—since selectivity implies a pattern; once you know what that pattern is, you know something about your subject. Rather, I realized, at least in the case of Tim Hasler, his journals were arbitrary.

I also thought about Mossman. And his "obnoxious little chink with an unbelievably nasty sex life." Is it sexual harassment if, like Pete Darmushklowsky, you don't think it is? Is it sexual harassment if you barely remember it—and it's just brought back by not being actually being mentioned in a journal that circles around it?

Tim's journal pages were filled with rich and suggestive information about himself. But there was no single situation about which I could be sure they were exhaustive.

Whatever I thought of his judgments, was this the sort of problem that had driven Mossman, more sensitive to certain aspects of it than I, from the project?

About the rest of the "Flame" business, probably it was too ugly, or too oppressive, or finally just too complicated for Tim to go on chronicling. From some of the things that Pete had gone on to outline in the next hour, above and beyond what Tim had written down, recounting the whole of the situation could easily have been a book in itself! Of course (black eyes not withstanding), maybe it hadn't been as bad for Tim as the rest of Darmushklowsky's account had made it seem—which might have explained why there was no more about it in those pages. But quite as possibly it could have been even worse—which might also have accounted for the absence of further mention.

But it is always odd to discover the ways in which desire fuels the systems of the world.

Let's return to the March Pete's first postcard arrived. Depressed over a complicated incident that really has nothing to do with this story (an older woman at work, a very young Burmese kitten she wanted someone—not me, but another woman temp-worker named Lillian—to cat-sit for, sixty dollars I'd loaned her, and a misunderstanding about the date of her plane trip to Puerto Rico), I went down to walk in the park. Sitting on a bench with my jacket open, I saw this guy—clearly homeless—glancing at me from the edge of the underpass down to the steps that led to the marina.

So I looked at him. He didn't look away.

(I've probably got it; if he goes in for unprotected sex, he's probably got it too...)

Tony was a ham-handed little bull of a fellow, a few years older than me, with a hoarse voice, curly red hair and beard, and a big grin—most of the time—for everybody; he had a fat, stubby cock with a generous Irish foreskin; that first time I sucked him off, beneath a park underpass, nuzzling between the flaps of his perfectly foul sheepskin jacket, he asked me, "You don't mind I got them warts on my dick?"

"There are only three of them," I said, on my knees, looking up.

"Some guys see 'em, and they just take off—think they're gonna catch 'em or something." Leaning against the curved wall of the underpass, he took one fist out of his coat pocket, rubbed at his nose, that—broken a couple of times, I guess—was broader than mine.

"You keep a lot of cheese under your skin," I told him. "That's enough to keep me suckin', warts or no."

He grinned down. "Really? You like dick cheese? Shit—I'll keep my curtains *full* of that stuff for you, if you want, from now on.

That's easy enough to do."

And he did.

A week later when I first brought him up to my apartment here, (I'm not going to say anything if he doesn't...) after we rolled around on the living room floor and I'd sucked him off, and, on the faded maroon rug, we'd fallen asleep, I woke from another odd dream of Ballagio, to find Tony with his nose shoved between my buttocks and his tongue drilling comfortably in my asshole. One of the things I really got to appreciate about him over the next month was that he never invited himself up to see me— but four times out of five, when I ran into him panhandling beside the news kiosk on Seventy-ninth Street, if I asked him to come up, he would. He always got a pretty good dinner out of it—with a bottle of wine. Which he liked.

When I mentioned to him that I appreciated his tact, he told me, "I'm a homeless guy, professor—" his nickname for me, once he found out I was getting my Ph.D.—"I know how I gotta act. If I started droppin' around here anytime I wanted, pretty soon you wouldn't have the time of day for me. Besides, I got a couple of friends in this neighborhood besides *you*, you know."

Soon we had a regular routine. When we met outside, we'd go over to the park and (if we made it that far; a couple of times I just did him in a doorway down on a side street) I'd suck him off. It was convenient for me to bring him upstairs, after a lot of sloppy kissing we'd do a sixty-nine thing on the rug, where I'd lie on my back and suck on his dick while he'd lie on top of me, my legs hooked back under his tattooed arms, while he ate out my ass and humped my face till he came.

I remember two odd incidents with Tony. Once, when it was still cold and I'd met him by the kiosk about seven o'clock in the evening and we were going over to the park, he said he wanted to try something different. Instead of just ducking into the first bushes there, he took me down to the park's jogging field, where a lone woman in purple shorts, mittens, and a ski cap was thumping heavily around and around the track. "I'm gonna take off all my clothes, professor, and lie down out here on my back in the grass. Then you gonna pull your pants down and sit on my face—"

"Tony, it's cold!"

"I know. But *I'm* the only one who's gotta get naked. Not you."

"But somebody's going to see—"

"Nobody's gonna say nothing. She's the only one running around, and I bet she won't even notice. Besides, if you see somebody comin' over, you just take off. I'll be the one naked," he repeated. "You'll still have your clothes on. Nothin's gonna happen to you if—"

"Tony, I don't—"

"*Please*, professor! It won't take me no time. You won't even have to touch me—I'll shoot all by myself, probably." He hung onto the arm of my overcoat. "We come all the way down here. Come on. Please?"

"Well, maybe, then—"

So this little brick shithouse drops his ratty coat, pulls off his filthy sweater, unbuttons a plaid shirt whose collar was grease black (though, below the line of the sweater neck, it suddenly became reasonably clean-looking), he peeled off a long-sleeved, waffle-knit undershirt as gray as if it had been rolled in powdered graphite from a chest hairy as rusty Brillo (a panther stalked the red jungle of one biceps; a dragon coiled about a skull on his other forearm. Here and there, amateur jailhouse work in Bic blue, said "Fuck You & Your Momma's Jammy!" and, behind his left flank, "I'm Ruff, Tuff, Eat Nigger Shit for Breakfast, and Piss Battery Acid!" On his right was an erect cock and a pair of balls below, above which it said, "Suck My Dick!" On his chest another, "Eat Shit!"— but all the graffitti on this john-stall wall of a man was blurred in copper), then kicked off his sneakers—even standing in the middle of grassy field, with a cool breeze blowing, I got a whiff of those feet of his—a size larger than mine on this guy a whole head shorter. Then, sitting on the ground, he pulled off his pants.

I kind of watched the runner, wondering if we looked to her like a couple of guys changing into a running clothes. But finally I rucked my coat back, pushed my gray wool slacks down to mid-thigh, and straddled Tony where he lay on his back—and squatted. In front of me, his stubby dick jutted up and to the left, like a leaning tower— of Zenid, of Pisa, of Babel—its warts three crusted knoblets. Without a hint of an erection myself, I began to grind my butt on his mouth, while he speared me with his tongue. His rough hands gripped my buttocks and were tender with them. I was contemplating taking hold of him to give him a couple of helpful pulls (just to hurry him along), but, in less than three minutes, apparently by doing no more that flexing his big stubby toes—while I let out a long grumbling fart—he spewed up his pearly slop from his loose cuff, all over the red carpeting on his gut. Some dribbled (over a tattooed Star of David shattering a blue swastika) down his hip.

A few more thrusts from his tongue—and, below my coat, he patted my left cheek. So I stood, pulling up my slacks as I did so.

Tony pushed up on one elbow. "Hey, thanks, professor!" He grinned with glistening nose and lips. "That was great!" Some grass was caught in his hair; a dead leaf stuck to his side. "You're really the best, man!"

The runner was at the track's far end, bouncing along to whatever music issued from her Walkman's yellow headphones—staring at the ground receding under her.

"You should probably take off now. I'm gonna get up and walk around the park naked for a while. I could get me in trouble over that. So you don't need to be around."

I started. "Hey, *Tony*—"

"Naw, I do that sometimes. It's stimulatin'. It makes me feel kind of like I'm alive, you know?"

Then, because I really liked the little fucker, I said: "You want me to come with you—maybe run interference for you? Look out for cops, at least?"

"Hey, thanks, professor!" He grinned. "But, naw—that's okay. It's better if I'm by myself. If the cops stop me, I just tell 'em somebody beat me up and stole all my clothes—least, that's what I plan. I never had to do it, yet." Now he got his feet under him and stood, reaching down to wipe some of the cum off his belly. On his thick, grubby fingers, he held it up and pushed it against my mouth. "That's for you—I know you like it."

I sucked his cum, cooling now, from his big hand. "Thanks, Tony." It was funny, I hadn't felt anything sexual, really, in the whole encounter. Still, it was a friendly thing to do.

"Aren't you cold, Tony?"

"As a *mother*fucker!" The little guy grinned. "But it feels kind of good, too. It gets me—like I say…stimulated. Know what I mean?"

I just took a breath—as, in the evening light, the runner passed maybe twenty yards from us; she still hadn't noticed that Tony was naked.

"I'll piss on you, if you want, professor." Then he stepped back, frowned. "Oh—but you got your good workin' clothes on. Maybe we better do that some other time, then."

"Yeah, I guess so," I said. "But thanks."

Tony turned and started walking heavily across the field, bare feet like pieces of meat flopping on the grass. I followed after him. "You're just going to leave your clothes like that?"

"*Shit!*" With a big, grimy hand, Tony rubbed one hairy pectoral. "They're so fuckin' scuzzy, nobody's gonna take them things. If I hid 'em, somebody'd find 'em and steal 'em. If I leave 'em lying out in the open like that, though, people'll think somebody must've pissed on 'em, or shit in 'em, or somethin' worse—and they'll leave 'em alone. I'll be back here in a hour or so—they'll still be here. If they ain't...?" He shrugged, then reached down to paw beneath his nuts.

At the gate to the running field, I realized: "That's a *policeman*—Tony! Down *there*...!"

In his navy blue uniform, the officer (black, and on the heavy side) was walking under one the park lights that had come on since we'd gone into the track.

"Then you better get the fuck on out of here, professor, 'fore you get in trouble hangin' out with me!"

And I'm afraid I took him at his word and hurried on ahead, to hear him, standing beside the gate, chuckling behind me in the three-quarter dark.

After I passed the policeman myself, about a minute later I stopped walking and looked carefully back. The officer was somewhere off in the shadow, while—thirty yards behind—Tony walked forward, thickset, stolid as a little bull, ambling bowlegged along beside the benches, passing under the same lamp I'd seen the officer by, the light bright on his hair and beard in that chill night, naked for anyone to see.

He saw me looking back, raised his hand, then—grinning—lowered it to his genitals, set his feet wide, grasped his dick, and began making vigorous beat-off gestures.

I just shook my head, turned away (yes, I was laughing—though I was worried) and hurried up toward the steps beside the marina—where four men and two women with their leashed collies and Dobermans, coming down, turned in my direction.

I went past them—and didn't stay to see what they did when they reached my friend back there.

Would he duck off the road at the last minute, as he saw them near...?

Or maybe sit on a bench, one leg crossed over the other, hand splayed down his groin...?

Or stand there in the light, playing with himself...?

The next two times I saw Tony on the street, we went off to the park again. ("How often do you do that shit anyway, like you did last time?" I asked him.

("What do you mean?" Tony asked. "Do what?"—as though he *really* didn't know what I was talking about.

(Then he winked. "Not that much." He shrugged.) And this time was just like before. Another couple of times, I had him up to the house again. He was a funny little fucker. But he was good sex.

Then, on April 25, 1985 (ten days after I returned from visiting Pete and Sue: I'll never forget it), I had Tony up to the house yet again: the second odd incident.

While in the kitchen, still in his sheepskin (he'd never take his coat off till after he'd eaten, at which point, usually unasked, he'd strip naked for the rest of his stay: *you* explain it), wolfing down pork chops and gravy and the turnip greens I'd brought back in one of Mom's aluminum icebox dishes from the last trip out to Staten Island, pushing them all into his mouth with pieces of my Italian bread, Tony said he had something "personal" he wanted to ask me—before we got down to sex. I said sure. He explained to me how he wanted to go down to Florida for a while and could I maybe afford to buy him a bus ticket. I told him I didn't think I could do that. I was surprised when he actually tried to argue me out of the money.

We had sex—he worked like a dog, getting me to cum—twice; but didn't shoot his own load. Then he brought up the bus ticket again. When it was clear I wasn't going to fork over the fifty-nine dollars, at three o'clock in the morning he decided to leave—to go see somebody else he knew in the neighborhood from whom he might be able to hustle up the ticket money.

But could he take a shower first.

Sure.

In my living room again, wiping at himself with a towel, he stopped to examine his thick, hirsute thigh. "Looks like I got me some kind of rash."

I went over and looked. On his pale skin, below the copper fuzz, was a Pleiades of purplish pimples.

"That's funny," I said. "I've got kind of the same thing, here just above my ankle." I'd noticed it just after we'd rolled out of bed, actually.

I mean, save the darkness of my skin, they looked exactly the same as his.

Tony got his clothes on: "You sure you can't give me a twenty— or even a ten toward my ticket, professor?"

"Tony—really, I'm sorry. I'm good for a meal—a blowjob. And I like to get my ass licked out just about as much as you like to chow down on it, you ass-eatin' lace-curtains honky punk!" I reached out and, as he stood in the doorway, ruffled his red hair. (Within his scruffy beard, he grinned.) "But I can't do money. I'm a poor nigger—white man. Not a rich one."

"You're a good nigger, professor." With his thick, soft fingers, he touched my cheek—still damp from the last of his urine. "You *still* good," and he turned to start down the stairs. I closed the door behind him.

Three days later, the pimples had all but joined—and, absently looking at my other leg, I realized a similar configuration was starting there. A week later, I had two darkish spots on my right leg: one the size of a quarter, one the size of a nickel. Low on my left shin, I had another the size of a dime.

On my dark skin, I kept looking for any bluish or purplish or violet undertones—as there certainly had been on Tony's Caucasian pale flesh.

If you are a gay man, though, you know what lesions on the lower legs mean: Kaposi's.

A couple of days later, I saw Tony again (he still hadn't made it south), while I was coming home from the subway. "Hey, Tony. Do you remember that rash you had on your thigh when you were last up at my house?"

"Yeah? What about it?"

"What's happened to it?"

"I don't know. A couple of days later, it was gone." He shrugged.

"I thought at first I was gonna get some more warts—on my leg this time. About four or five years ago, some came out on my hand. Only after a while, they fell off." Then he frowned. "But this didn't look like warts or anything—really."

"No," I said. "It doesn't."

(Should I mention AIDS, I thought. Well, he hadn't...)

That night, as I sat on the edge of my bed, examining the marks on my shins, clearly it *wasn't* gone on me.

Finally I sat up and looked at the wall.

So, I thought, I've got it. At last.

Most of the articles by then were talking about three years as the maximum survival time. But once you had it, there were no cures.

I remember clearly asking myself:

What is it you really want to *do* with your life?

Because what you should do is go ahead and *do* that—till you get too sick. Then you can take whatever steps are necessary.

I didn't go to a doctor. (But the day I decided not to, I *did* look for Tony to tell him I was pretty sure what I had—and that perhaps he should get himself checked out at the city's health facilities. But he must have managed to get his ticket. I didn't see him again for a long time.) Seven weeks later I finished my first article on Timothy Hasler: twenty-eight typed pages, it was about my visit to Pete Darmushklowsky, the "Flame" stories, and the brouhaha in '64 back at Stilford, journal quotes, university paper articles, black-eyes, brawls, and all. I sent it up to Pete for checking, who said I had it pretty well down. It wasn't scholarly. It was an account for a general reader and was published in a gay magazine that paid me $175.00. But by the time it appeared, I'd written two more articles on Hasler. The technical one about the relationship between the philosophy and the science fiction stories (based on those very first notes I'd shown to Irving, five years ago) was published in a science fiction "fanzine," of all places. It got me three letters from professional academic philosophers, all congratulatory. It made me smile, because there certainly wasn't any *philosophy* journal where I could have published it.

At about that time I remember thinking how funny it was: although I knew the layout of Hasler's five rooms as well as I knew my own, I had no idea *which* room he'd used for his bedroom, *which* room he'd used for his living room—so I couldn't tell you whether he had to walk sixteen feet to the bathroom each morning (like Hilda downstairs) or twenty-seven feet (like me). On the other hand, when he took his jeans down to Mrs. Espedrosa to mend, I knew how every step of that journey would have looked to him. The stairwell walls had been painted blue back then, not the yellow they were now. (Jimmy swore his predecessor—there had been two supers since Hasler had lived here—had told him that the previous paint job [blue] had gone at least seventeen years without a change of color.) At the time, there'd been no gunmetal gray linoleum on the steps, with the aluminum edging. Rather, the wooden stairs had been painted a dark brown, with a rubber scuff mat nailed to each one ("...like the last stairwell, above you, up to the roof? That's the way it used to be like, all the way down...") Now, in suit and tie, Mr. Espedrosa pointed out to me across Amsterdam Avenue: "The bodega on the corner was still there, yes; though at the time it was owned by a very nice Colombian woman, Señora Colon. She used to give everybody in the neighborhood credit—she kept the accounts in a black-and-white-marbled school notebook. It was always in pencil, so she could erase it when you paid her at the end of the week, or the month. I'm sure that young Chinese fellow—" I'd given up explaining he was Korean—"had an account with her. We did—everybody did. But the people who own it now don't do that stuff no more. Where the Yellow Rose Café is now there used to be a Chinese laundry. Where the Chinese takeout place is now, that used to be the Havana–San Juan Dry Cleaners—no. No, wait—that was before it moved from across the street on the corner there, where the gift store is now. (Now he's around on Eighty-third Street, I think.) Before that—oh, yes, of course, it was the Beacon Paint Store. Next door to that was an upholstery shop—after that was a lamp store for a while, before it became that restaurant there now. And somewhere over there, between them, was a *botanica de fe*...do you know what that is? There aren't very many of them today."

"Yeah." I smiled. "I'm a New Yorker too. That's like a Puerto Rican head shop."

Which made him laugh. "Years and years ago, as far back as the sixties, I would guess, some kids painted in big letters right on the wall of the St. Agnes Public Library, there in the middle of the block, FAGGOT CRAZY CROSS. I have no idea what it meant. But it was right beside the steps there. For years—till they sandblasted the whole building, I guess it was the summer before you came. But everybody in the S apartments, if you looked out your windows, ten, fifteen years ago, that's what you saw."

And why should anyone be interested in what Hasler saw out of his New York City windows—or where he went to have his jeans sewn?

Well, in Hasler's fourth published SF story, "Mirror of the Mighty," the young Mage Apparent (the secondary hero) seeks out the archives in the basement of the library "beside the Sign of the Crazy Cross." (The tale, you'll recall, implies it's an evil, troubling sign, whose meaning is lost in history, though it still makes the residents of the neighborhood "hurry by, trying not to see it...") And in the same story, the main hero, Dunston Wong, after a comic episode in which he gets his pants ripped by the villain, takes them to be patched at the home of a woman "who worked on an ancient electrical/mechanical fabric mender that hummed and chattered at the end of a hall set with magical and historical icons, framed in glass and silver, that spoke of another culture, like a distortion of one Wong had, sometime in his past, vaguely known": the pictures on the Espedrosas' dim white walls had not changed, I'm sure, for twenty years.

(And for those of you who didn't read my fanzine piece, "Mirror of the Mighty" is directly related to the article "Formal Parameters of Informality," written at about the same time.)

But I wrote about all of this in still another an essay that surveyed what we did and what we didn't know at this point about Timothy Hasler and his world.

I wrote three other essays, too; all but one were printed.

I sent copies—not as they were written, but as they appeared in print—to Irving. With the second, he sent me a postcard: "Many thanks for the copy of your articles," it said. "Hope to respond in more detail soon." But that was all I heard. There was no mention of Sam, nor of my letter to her—as there had never been any answer from Sam herself.

I wrote four *more* articles about Tim.

The one on the relation between Adler's "Meridian" and Hasler's twin predicate-logic papers, besides sending to Irving, I sent to Breakers' Point. A month later, I got a letter from the Old Poet:

Dear Mr. Marr,

Thank you for the article on Tim and me.

I confess, old biddy that I've become, I thought your conclusion 180 degrees ass-backwards. But the first three quarters of your argument were rich and provocative. Given the
quality of most of what I read about us, you're not doing so
badly. Perhaps someday when you are out this way—or if I
should get to New York again—we might sit down together
and discuss it. Several years ago, you were impressively rec-
ommended to me. In your article you come very close to living up to it.

All best wishes,
Almira

I filed that one—and pasted a Xerox of it inside the front of my
hardcover of *Mountain and Tower*.

About that time the editor of a paperback book company wrote
me, then phoned. They wanted to do a collection of Tim's science
fiction stories. It was my fanzine article, of all things, that had
given him the idea. We decided to include the incomplete "Flame"
fragment and the other incomplete tale as appendices. A well-
known science-fiction writer named Aranlyde (I confess, I'd never
heard of him; but apparently, because for a while he'd taught at a
southwestern university, he had some particular cachet among
more intellectual SF readers) was retained to do an introduction.
Aranlyde and I had lunch together; I talked generally about Hasler.
Aranlyde drank negronis and took notes in a brown spiral notebook.
I loaned him a copy of *Pascal, Nietzsche, Peirce* and some articles—
Tim's and mine. (Aranlyde had a Xerox of all the stories, of course.)
Three weeks later, along with the book and articles, in a manila
book mailer, he sent me back a copy of his "Introduction."

Certainly, it's one of the liveliest pieces ever written on Timothy
Hasler. Factually, it was about three-quarters all right—though
he'd gotten some of the most basic things wrong: things that really surprised me, too. From something I'd said about Hasler's
hypochondria, for example, he'd picked up the notion that Tim had
spent some weeks, if not months, in a mental hospital—which was
just not true, though he'd had an endless string of psychotherapists,

of many schools and persuasions, from his twelfth year to his twenty-fifth. But Aranlyde also managed to get some anecdotes from Hasler's two sisters—which, I'll be frank, made me wonder why *I'd* never thought to mine Hasler's family. (Somehow, I'd always assumed Irving had done it already.) I sent him my notes on his piece, suggestions, and outright corrections. A week later in the mail I got back a much-improved version.

I vetted that one, too. This time my comments were minimal enough to give them to him over the phone.

The version that came back, two weeks later, was really very good—and I felt practically like a co-author. The afternoon it arrived, I got a phone call from the editor at the publishing house. Aranlyde had all but insisted I be invited to provide an "Afterword" of my own.

So I did: not a very technical explanation of how actions in general in Hasler's stories could stand for predicates in particular in his philosophical explorations.

Then there were three days when nobody was sure what the name of the book was going to be. Someone in the publisher's office, whose name I never learned, thought we should call it *Nightrise*, after Hasler's first short-short story from *Fantastic* (March 1963); it had appeared days before his eighteenth birthday, and is really quite a clever little paradox of a tale. The reason for using it as the title was because, consciously on fledgling Hasler's part, it recalled the title of an extraordinarily well-known science-fiction story, on which it is a brief and clever take. (Suppose a planet in a complex orbit about several stars moves among them so that the hemisphere with land on it has only a single day of actual daylight in a thousand years of night....) Myself, I thought that was a good reason *not* to use it.

Aranlyde suggested sensibly enough we call the book *The Black Comet*, after the last, longest, and—he and I agreed—the best of the Hasler stories (I will talk more about that one later; it explains several things you've been wondering about till now), though, Aranlyde commented to me cynically over the phone, they were just as likely to call it *Salvation*, which is the *second*-longest story in the book and, as far as I could see, the weakest: it's the only one where the abstract logical considerations simply swamp the plot, so that there just doesn't seem to be much of a story there at all.

Really, I wouldn't be surprised if it turned out actual pages, if not some whole scenes, were missing from the published version. It's the one we don't have any manuscript for at all.

My choice for the title was *Flame!*—since Pete Flame appeared as the hero in two of the stories and also in one of the fragments we used as an appendix; as well, he was the subject of much of Aranlyde's and my fore and final pieces. Also, major fires figure in two of the other tales; and the other, non–"Pete Flame" unfinished story, that comprised the second appendix, was called "The Flames of Jarondok"—in that case, the Flames of Jarondok is the name of a Thuggee-like gang of interplanetary criminals, one of whom (a double agent) is our hero. Aranlyde said he had no objections to my title—in fact, he rather preferred it to *The Black Comet*. The only thing to recommend his own choice was that his was slightly more commercial—but (he said) it would be rather nice to set such considerations aside for this volume.

Only *then* I got a call from Matt, the in-house editor: "Isn't it possible that that fellow, Darmush-what-ever-his-name-is, might object to all these stories being brought up again after all this time, especially under the name of the hero that he was so upset over when he was in school? I was talking to our legal department and—"

"Mr. Darmushklowsky never objected to the *stories,*" I explained. "He knows about the project and is quite supportive of the whole thing."

"Sure—you told us that before, I know. Still, it would be nice if we had something in writing.…"

So I phoned Pete, who burst out laughing. "That's the dumbest thing I've *ever* heard! I told you, I *like* the stories! Why should I have any objection if they call the book *Flame!*? I mean, it's not like they're calling the book *Darmushklowsky!* And even if they were, I swear, I wouldn't mind! Look, I'll phone your editor there and tell him it's all—no! I've got a free morning. I'll do the whole thing up right for you: I'll write a gloriously enthusiastic letter, officially waiving all my 'rights to the name.' I'll tell 'em what a wonderful idea I think the book *and* the title are. I'll have five copies made up, all of them signed by a notary public—that should take me about an hour or two. Then I'll phone your editor, *read* it to him, and tell him that it's coming. And I will put the copies in the mail, at overnight-express postage, so they'll get them tomorrow—and they can file them in the various places around the office where they keep such things…with their legal department! And I will do all this for Tim—well, for you, too, John. 'Cause I think you're a pretty good guy!" Laughing again, Pete muttered, "Boy, is *this* ridiculous…!"

But that's exactly what Peter Darmushklowsky did. My copy came by express mail the next day. Actually, it was a pretty nice letter.

And the title was *Flame!*

By this time, I had published eight articles about Hasler, counting the lengthy technical one in the fanzine. My general take in all of them was not that Hasler was the most important philosopher of the middle twentieth century, but that to me, as a gay man and a culturally marginal man in racist America, as a philosophical enthusiast, he was an interesting and important figure.

Sex?

For the first five weeks of this regime I didn't have any—save beating off. (Before, I'd finally convinced myself I didn't have it. Now that I was sure I did, I was of course a carrier.) Then—even before I met Tony—I fell spectacularly off the wagon. And when I broke out and went wild, I forgave Piece o' Shit a hundred times. Whether he assumed that he was straight and the sarcoma he had did not mean AIDS, or whether he assumed I was just another cocksucker and already had it anyway, I forgave him. That's when I learned the idea of total abstinence in terms of AIDS was preposterous advice. (That's when I learned that he hadn't done it for the sixty-nine cents, but for the kissing, the cuddling, the blowjob.) With occasional efforts to cut back, soon I was at my usual three or four contacts two or three times a week. My justification? That everyone I was having unprotected sex with around the city—and I never had any other kind—probably had it, too. (And if they didn't, they'd long-since decided to take the same gamble I had back in the Variety.) But the fact is, when those used to regular sex have regular sex available, they have it. It's no more complicated than that. You can put if off a few hours, a few days, a few weeks. But beyond that, you are out of the precinct of morals and into the land of hormones, which have developed evolutionarily to make sure morals will *never* stand against them. That's how they work.

That's what they're for. And they fall on the body like Niagara. They erupt in it like Etna.

In 1988 *Flame! The Science Fiction Tales of Timothy Hasler* appeared, with Aranlyde's "Introduction"—and an "Afterword" by John Marr.

The two "lesions" on my ankle had joined into an island a little larger than a silver dollar. Four or five smaller ones blotched my right leg; there was still only one on the left. And, in general, I felt no sicker than I had three years before. Also I was six pounds heavier.

I can't believe it was just the academic philosophical community that snapped *Flame!* up and put it into a second printing inside a month—that community isn't big enough. But the fact that, two months later, Gerald Jonas said nice things about it in the *New York Times Book Review* probably helped it into a third.

(Sometime near my twenty-seventh birthday, the Variety Photoplays movie house was closed by the city—the Eighth Avenue houses were still going strong: there was even a new one: the Beverly.)

The same month Hasler's *Flame!* appeared, I made an appointment with a dermatologist.

On the afternoon of June 10, 1988, Dr. Mark Schuyler on West End Avenue explained that these flaky patches of skin had nothing to do with Kaposi's but that, as far as he could tell, I had a psoriasis-like condition on the lower legs that would likely clear up with daily applications of some unbelievably expensive hydrocortisone cream, covered each night with Saran Wrap held in place with adhesive tape, alternating with applications of a tar-based gunk that looked like petroleum jelly. I should expect it to take about six weeks to two months to go away (I had let it go, after all, three years!)—and, indeed, intermittently it might return.

If it did, I should just repeat the treatment.

"I'd like to get an HIV test, while I'm at it." I told him.

"Certainly," he said. "I'll take the blood from you here, and you can bring it down to the testing facilities yourself." He gave me the Lower Manhattan address.

I rode downtown on the subway and left the blood off with them that afternoon. A week later, Dr. Schuyler called me into his office to give me the negative results in person.

But what I thought about as I walked up to Albert's Pharmacy on Eighty-sixth Street to get my tar-and-hydrocortisone proscription was my revelation at the Variety of three years before. I don't think I've ever been more grateful for it than I was that day. Without it, instead of writing those articles, likely I would have committed suicide.

I'm not a brave man.

And certainly it was one of the things I'd considered most seriously when I'd first been certain I had AIDS.

PART
THREE

MASTERS OF THE DAY

Man needs what is most eil in him for what
is best in him. The secret for harvesting from
existence the greatest fruitfulness and the
greatest enjoyment is—to live dangerously.
—Nietzsche

Habet acht! Habet acht!
Schon weicht dem Tag die Nacht.
—*Tristan und Isolde,* II, ii.

June 15, 1989

Dear John,

This should probably be a letter at least as long as the one you wrote me five years ago! But it will end up fairly short, I'm sure.

After all too many stabs at getting back together, Irving's and my divorce came through last week. (We've been—more or less—separated since the start of '87. But I assume you knew that.)

[I hadn't.]

Write Irving. Though he began this adventure in his late forties, he's closer now to sixty than to fifty and I think—finally—it's been harder on him than on me. At least I have a (surprise!) girlfriend, named Regan, with whom I have been getting along smashingly for the last six months. She's brilliant, Jewish, and was born in Brazil, has all sorts of wonderful ideas for all sorts of wonderful projects in Women's Studies, that sometimes she has just the teensiest trouble carrying through on. (In some ways, I suppose, rather like Irving—no! Perish the thought!) She's deeply into post-structuralism, Marxist literary theory, magic realism, that sort of thing; but best of all, she's a great person!

Irving's undergraduate redhead dropped him, however (two years after graduating—as anyone but Irving could have predicted), like the proverbial hot potato; that was in late '86 (possibly the beginning of '87) and if rumor is to be trusted, no one has yet picked up the pieces.

I should warn you, Irving's feelings about your Hasler articles are ambivalent, to say the least! But I know he's incredibly happy you sent them to him immediately, so that he can always say he's read them when anyone else brings one of them up. They're not scholarly—that's his most frequent complaint.

They're not supposed to be, is the most frequent response he gets to that one. At which point, he grinds his teeth, looks at the ground, grimaces, and shakes his head like a man in deep and considered confusion. (This means to his colleagues, as I'm sure you know, he's *working*—on the philosophical aspects of the problem, that is.) Clapstone even proposed an argument that, for a while, brought Irving around to your side completely: part of the value of your articles, suggested Our August Chair, is that Hasler never got his Ph.D., and much of his "popular" work (*Flame!*) was marginal to scholarly pursuits. Since you with your articles, Clapstone pointed out, occupy an identical position, what better place is there from which to approach Timothy Hasler?

In private, Irving has pointed out to me that you've practically started a Hasler revival on your own! This past year, he says, there were more references to Hasler in scholarly articles, not only in the philosophy journals, but also in English journals (usually having to do with Hasler and Adler) and Gay Studies pieces (where Hasler seems to be on his way to becoming the quintessential gay philosopher after Wittgenstein), with a little bit of cultural diversity thrown in.

Every other Thursday, Irving is willing to acknowledge that this is 85 percent your fault.

The department is getting ready, at any rate, to promote

Good Old Irv to full professor at last—as compensation for the pain his divorce has caused, that's how I figure. (I'm a bitch: I know it. But *you* know the philosophy department here—and it hasn't changed much since you left.) More generously, it's *their* totally misplaced, I'm afraid, attempt to pick up the pieces. I've actually heard someone say it will improve his self-esteem immeasurably! Also, in a way, I think it's to compensate him for the success of your articles—since (though to give him credit, he has never suggested any such thing) everyone *knows* that all the basic work behind what you've written on Hasler was initially Irving's... *Ahem!*

There's another edition of *Formal Conjunctions/Informal Disjunctions* due out next year, to which Irving has been asked to contribute a new "Introduction." The Department plan seems to be that this (which, he tells me, he has not even started work on, by the bye) will be the piece justifying his promotion. Given the length of time he's been a Hasler scholar, departmental consensus is that his thoughts on the topic will certainly have sufficiently ripened: surely with this (they've all agreed, before the fact—at Clapstone's urging) Irving can *not* be publishing prematurely.

Change of subject:

When I first got that 110-page tome you sent me, frankly, John, I thought you'd gone round the bend. I was sure you'd totally lost it—not because of the content, but because you'd decided to send such a thing to *me!* After reading twenty pages, I wrote you off as this madman who, at one time, back when he was sane, I used to know. Then a lot of things happened.

Regan says I should tell you about them—like my coming out, for one thing. Also I met a whole lot of people doing AIDS work who were connected with the school here. About a year later, after telling Regan about it (before we were really lovers), I picked the thing up and read it again. One end to the other. It didn't seem anywhere near as strange/crazed as it had. Not too long ago, a kid here almost got in trouble for distributing an article that I'm enclosing with this letter. Probably you've seen it: "Risk Factors for Seroconversion to Human Immunodeficiency Virus Among Male Homosexuals: Results from the Multicenter AIDS Cohort Study" by

Kingsley, Kaslow, Rinaldo, *et alia*, from *The Lancet* for Saturday, February 14, 1987. Although the medical stuff in your '84 letter is really out of cloud-cuckoo land, my friend, the article (from a study completed three years later) may suggest some of the reasons why you're still HIV-negative—assuming you still are.

At any rate, just last week I read your letter over yet again—and at this point it seems to me quite a document—though, I might add, a document from a time as distant to people concerned with AIDS today as Hasler's world seemed to you in '84.

Still, some of your subsequent Hasler articles convinced me that if I *did* write you, I would still be talking to a sane and reasonable entity.

Really, the best of luck to you in all you do. Regan says you sound like a really interesting guy, and she hopes she gets a chance to meet you.

Although they're not particularly scholarly—at least the ones I've read, and thus aren't chapters for a thesis—nevertheless the articles suggest you're on the way to having yourself a book. But then, I don't know how many of them I haven't seen. Communication with Irving have been notably intermittent, especially the last six months.

Well, this letter *has* turned out to be longer than I intended—in fact, it's the longest one I've written since I wrote you last in '84!

Love and stuff,
in New Friendship,
Sam

If Sam—along with the rest of the country—had become more knowledgeable about male homosexuality, she was still a bit naïve about the mechanics of fame—though perhaps that was still a bit of what came to her, even after the divorce, through Irving.

Eighty-five percent of the Timothy Hasler revival was because Aranlyde, even before *Flame!* appeared, was commissioned by a friend of his at *Turn* magazine to do a piece called "Postmodern Masters of the American Academic World Today," which was a superficial, but at least readable, account of American (or currently American-based) university personalities: Appiah, Baker, Eagleton, Felman, Gallup, Gates, Haraway, Jameson, Johnson, Rorty, Sedgewick, and Spivak. (Now *you* argue about who else should, and who shouldn't, be on the list.) Actually, he did it rather well. But in it, for eccentric reasons of his own, Aranlyde decided to devote equal space with these others to the Korean-American graduate student, who, though he'd died violently some fifteen years before, had "left a body of work which specialists in natural language philosophy have been fascinated with since the beginning, and is still attracting new thinkers by its incredibly rich, intricate, and provocative reasoning." Hasler's story is an attractive one—it always has been. And Aranlyde, after his own *Flame!* introduction, could tell it well—and he did.

That same month Edwin Schaliapin—the guy who wrote the introduction to the '78 reissue of *Pascal, Nietzsche, Peirce*, remember?—published a long article in *Philosophy Today* on Hasler that, frankly, pretty much fulfilled the task, precisely and succinctly, Irving had set for my thesis five years back. But it did more. In its conclusion, it stated (and I realized as I read it, Schaliapin was, once again, right):

> What have come to be called "Hasler grammars," and even more so "Hasler structures," are undeniably interesting. Whether they will remain interesting very much longer is, however, moot. But what is inchoate to Hasler's work, from beginning to end—what he best represents—is the realization that large-scale, messy, informal systems are necessary in order to develop, on top of them, precise, hard-edged, tractable systems—or, more accurately, structures that are so informal that it is questionable whether they can be called systematic at all are prerequisites for those structures that can, indeed, be recognized as systems in the first place. The first three-quarters of our century have been dominated by the unquestioned conviction that the world worked the other way around: that reality was built up of atomic perceptions, that language was built up from the meanings and grammatical potentials associated with individual words. Hasler's work—and more so the polemic Hasler's work represents—

positions itself diametrically against this idea. For Hasler, clear and specific counting is basically a refinement of generalized, messy pointing, or even random flailing. The human mind and possibly nature herself master generalized, messy pointing, inexact indication, and flailing well before they learn to individuate and count. And this is the larger, overarching idea that makes many of the dense and difficult details in Hasler's intricate logical arguments make sense.

Now that's the kind of insight you go away from, thinking: I've been reading and rereading this stuff for ten years now. Why didn't it ever strike *me* that way before?

Nor did it hurt the "Hasler Revival" that the same month, Almira Adler, smiling from her wheelchair, had her picture on the cover of *The American Poetry Review*.

My articles may have inspired Aranlyde to what I thought, frankly, was a rashness near the lunatic—including the deceased Hasler in with those living and lively academic moguls. But, at the same time, my articles were there for anyone who wanted to pursue his piece farther than the presumptions of mass illiteracy and packagable "Great Ideas" that were the parameters of *Turn*. That people in our Philosophy Department were happier talking about me than about *Turn* was simply because I was a known factor. And that, I'm afraid, is all.

A week after I got Sam's letter, I wrote a longish letter to Mossman. I won't quote it. But in it I said what is perfectly true: I owed all my interest and most of my knowledge of Timothy Hasler to him and his generosity. If I could acknowledge this in some way in any upcoming articles—or in any book that might grow from this, I would like to—if, indeed, he wouldn't mind. I thanked him for giving me such an incredibly important part of my life, and wished him the best.

In those three years when I'd assumed my death was only months away, the world had changed again. The Fiesta had closed down and become a Realvalue Locksmith: from time to time I'd stop at the gated plate glass on Forty-sixth Street and gaze in at the wooden walls, black and mirrored two years before, now white pegboard on the right and hung with ranks of key blanks, padlocks, and hasps, the new black-and-white vinyl floor, the bar counter replaced by a commercial desk almost equally as long, a cash register some-where in the back. The three thousand, then six thousand, then eight thousand who had contracted AIDS in '84 and '85—and who, for three years, I'd been convinced I'd joined—were now some vague and unimaginable statistic like eighty-five thousand, ninety-five thousand. Twice in one year, three times in another, I'd been asked to attend a university conference and present a paper on Timothy Hasler. Wanting to write something wonderful and new each time, I confess, I'd ended up using one or another sec-tion of that long technical piece from the fanzine—more or less spiced with anecdotes from the other published pieces, depend-ing on how many laughs I thought the audience would need in order to swallow the rest.

In 1986, Pheldon and I and pretty much every black person I knew—I mean my parents came in from Staten Island for this one, only to be surprised that it was something *I'd* be interested in—managed to beg, buy, borrow, or steal tickets to the New York State Theater at Lincoln Center to see Anthony Davis's opera *X: The Life and Times of Malcolm X* (libretto by *Village Voice* writer Thulani Davis). Bewildering white writers, the event filled the papers for a week before and a week after: it's an experience to see, in a theater space like that filled with black people, all of us rise to our feet applauding not a political revolution, but the repre-sentation of such a revolution in the most sophisticated of musical terms. I got a bootleg tape two weeks later and, for the next three months, listened to *X* again and again, alternating with *Parsifal*, till I could pretty much hum along, as it were, with both. Then, in 1988, on a whim Phel and I got a dozen people together one night to go down on that mild November's election eve to stand around watching the national debt go up on the light-board at Avenue of the Americas and Forty-second Street. First we giggled; then we were silent; finally we wandered away in bemused confusion, won-dering what trillions of dollars actually *were*. And sometime among all that, I had my first and single sexual encounter with someone wearing a condom.

Oh, there had been two or three older guys who, in an attempt to blow me, had fumbled out a rubber and tried to get it over my cock. (I'd pat their hands, smile, and get up and leave.) But this was the first—and only time—it went as far as an orgasm.

He was a high-school kid. (I don't particularly like kids.)

Leaning back against the wall of the well, he gave me a heavy cruise, clutching the crotch of his jeans, while I was leaving the rest room on the second floor of the Port Authority Bus Station. (I never cruise the Port Authority unless I'm going somewhere on a bus or—in this case—coming back from someplace: friends in New Jersey, but that's not part of this story.)

Stocky, stolid, he looked incredibly eager. (In twenty years, I remember thinking, that guy will actually be sexy. But now he couldn't have been more than eighteen.)

A butch little number, he seemed wholly ignorant of the ordinary means and modes of pickups. When he motioned me over to talk to him, I asked him what he wanted. Someone had told him about the bus station; it was the first time he'd ever been here. But he came on as if he were about to pass out from terminal horniness: "Let's go do it, man! Anywhere! Anywhere you want!"

Yes, I was flattered he wanted me.

I told him I would take him to a movie theater. We walked up crowded, autumnal Eighth Avenue together. I paid his way into the Grotto.

He chose a seat directly under a wall light and, pulling down the zipper on his stiff new Levi's, took out an erect cock and, digging in the pocket of his bulky gray jacket, got out a foil-wrapped condom. I just sighed—while he tore open the blue package, dropped the foil into the theater floor's liquid dark, and unrolled the sheath down the short, thick length of himself. (I've probably got it; and he probably doesn't...) His cock had the same proportions he had.

At that point, I told him, "You know, the truth is, I really don't have time for this. But if you just sit around here like that with your dick out, someone will want to suck you off within five minutes—"

But he grabbed my arm. "No, man! Please. *You* do it!"

So I bent over, took him in my mouth: the little rubber end filled on my third suck. As I sat up, he still gripped my arm. "You gonna give me all your money now?"

"Huh?"

"You're gonna give me your money now!" he repeated.

"I don't understand." I decided to play a little dumber than I was.

"Money! Money!" He shook my arm. "You got to give me the money you owe me—now!"

"Look, friend," I said. "I don't owe you any money. If that's what you're into, you have to set that up *before* you get started." I yanked my arm away and slipped out into the aisle.

Don't you know the bastard shoved himself into his pants and came after me?

We actually had a struggle in the lobby. I got away again and out the theater's glass door. But he pushed out after me into the street. Again he grabbed me: "Look, man, I'm a dangerous guy! You don't believe me? You don't believe I'd hurt you—look! Look!" He went pawing in his pocket, to pull out a much-folded paper. "See, this is my court paper. I got to go to court. So I don't give a fuck about you—I'll hurt you in a minute! The police gimme this, 'cause I got to go to court!"

Which is when the bus came. I yanked my arm away again and vaulted up the rubber steps to explode at the driver: "Close the damned *door!* There's a *mad* man out there!"

But he already had. We rolled away. Down on the sidewalk, looking in through the windows and holding his police court paper, the kid followed after the bus half a dozen steps before stopping, belligerent but confounded.

Shaken, I went back to a seat, thinking: Yeah, sure. Safe sex...

And to tease apart the meaning to these and suchlike adventures, Phel and I took to meeting for our occasional drink in Cats, a bar out on Eighth Avenue, between the Agapé and the Hesperus, just down from the Grotto.

It was that first week toward the end of June '90 when, as I looked out the living-room window, I could see, down on Amsterdam, that finally New Yorkers had relaxed into their shorts and short sleeves, deciding spring really had settled into summer. I had watched myself turn twenty-nine—the age of Hasler at his death—then thirty, when I was a year beyond Hasler. Only last month, I'd turned thirty-one: two years older than Hasler had ever been. Surely I was beyond whatever had been so dangerous as to bring about his destruction.

"Phel," I said, "I'm probably going to take a little walk. And maybe I'll drop in to see you, later this afternoon."

"All right," he said, at the other end of the phone. "I'll probably be here."

Earlier, the weather report had been something about possible showers, but then I stepped out on the stoop, looked up at pale, lucid blue—and just laughed. The air above and between apartment buildings was drenched in sunlight.

In a way, it started like something out of a Mack Sennett comedy. As I was crossing Broadway, from the Burger King's glass door, I saw this guy in his maroon uniform something between shove and throw this kid, who was wearing neither shirt nor shoes: "Now get the fuck *out* of here—!"

The kid—that is to say, he looked about twenty—hit the sidewalk staggering, stumbled into the wire trash basket on the corner. Both he and the basket went over into the street.

For a moment, twisting around, he half sat on it; then, as it rolled, he slid down. That would have hurt anyone's back, and the kid went: "*Arrhhhh!*"

Right behind the uniformed guy who had given him the toss stood a man in a dress shirt with a maroon tie that had the Burger King insignia on it—the manager—who called now, upset: "You're a fucking pervert, is what you are! We've got women in here. And kids, man! Get the hell out. And don't come *back* in here—I'm serious, now! You keep *away* from this place!" He rubbed a finger nervously under his nose; then, with a hand on the uniformed worker's shoulder, he inside.

The kid slipped down all the way, so he was sitting in the street—as the basket rolled away from behind him, I heard his head go back against the wire. Then he went over, to lie on his side.

His big hands were very dirty. So were his feet.

He was white. (Both the uniformed guy at the Burger King and the manager weren't.) His hair was curly and brown, on the stringy side, and getting on toward neck length.

I saw, up on the curb, a couple of people passing look down at him. But nobody stopped.

The basket reversed its direction and rolled back up against him—spilling trash all the way; one end swung around his head and clunked against the curb.

Through reflex, I grabbed up the metal rim and yanked the trash basket upright. The kid turned over now. Across pimples and freckles on his back, a red lattice from where he'd rolled down the metal marked his shoulder and flank with crossed diagonals.

Lifting the trash basket had been automatic. With the kid, though, it wasn't. About to step over his outstretched arm, I looked down: he had big, heavy feet and hands; and, as I looked, his broad fingers curled up. Short and dirt dark, of a length beyond the quick exactly that of the thickness a medium-point felt-tipped pen would make, pressed to the paper, had it marked the forward rims of his nickel-and dime-sized nails, those nails were neither long nor short. His street life would with time, I suspected, take them down farther. I walked seven, eight, nine steps along the curb and beyond him.

Then I thought, What the fuck is *wrong* with you?

I turned around—and didn't go back to him.

I stood, looking, while he kind of rocked in the gutter and, after a moment, drew up one knee. He was wearing a pair of dark blue pants (not jeans), dirty to the point where I wondered if they weren't really black; and too big. He straightened his leg again.

Another clutch of people walked by—six guys in different-colored shorts, talking together, who didn't even glance down.

Thinking about going over to help him, while the sunlight clutched the back of my neck like warm fingers, I actually felt scared: that coldness at the throat's base when you're about to do something no one else is doing, or wants to do, or would approve of if *you* did: the feeling before swiping something or starting to sing in the street or going over to help some homeless guy tossed out on the sidewalk.

I *hate* that feeling more than anything.

I walked back to the corner, stepped off the curb over black water trickling in the gutter, and squatted. "You okay?"

The kid got his head up, to feel around on the tarmac with one palm. "I hit my back...on that fuckin'..." He pushed himself further up, and grimaced.

One middle tooth was broken halfway off, unevenly.

"On the trash basket," I said. "Does it hurt?"

Then the guy in the maroon uniform, lurking inside Burger King's glass door, opened it again and leaned out. "Don't *help* that guy, man! He's a fuckin' pervert!"

"Well," I said, loudly over my shoulder, "so am I. I suck a lot of dick, myself."

The guy in the uniform didn't look put out so much as confused. Frowning, shaking his head in his yellow cap, he stepped back inside and let the door swing closed.

I shook my head, too.

The kid moved his shoulder. "I don't think I broke it." He was trying to grin: I realized that was supposed to be a joke. His gray-green eyes were set within dark lashes. Against his spring sunburn, his eyes looked a little startled, and a little crazy. The face around them was one of those weasely white-guy faces, though he was fairly muscular in a lean and stretched-out way.

He got one knee up, swung the other around underneath, and with one hand clawed down at his crotch.

"What were you doing inside that got them so twisted out of shape?" I asked.

"I wasn't doin' nothin', man." He kept rubbing. "I was scratchin' my dick, that's all!"

"Can you get up?" I asked.

"Yeah." He put his other hand on my shoulder. "I think so."

With an arm around his waist, I helped him stand, getting him back to the curb.

"Yeah," he repeated. "I'm okay." But he didn't let go of my shoulder.

"You go in there for something to eat?" I asked.

"Sure," he said. "But I couldn't get nothin'—I was just sitting there, waiting for somebody to finish."

I'd seen the Burger King gambit: a homeless person goes in, sits in the corner, and when a few people leave without busing their places, he or she quickly circuits the tables, picking up any half-eaten Whoppers, burgers, or red cardboard holders of french fries—to leave moments later and stand on the corner, where we stood now, shoving the food in her or his mouth, chewing doggedly. Sometimes you'd see the idea get to one of them, who'd suddenly turn and throw the rest into the trash basket (the wire one the kid had knocked over), and scuttle off. Sometimes, yes, it was because they'd eaten enough. But sometimes you could see them realize they were standing on a corner, eating junk-food that kids and their mothers and off-duty policemen and old men with pensions had half-chewed—and they couldn't put any more in their mouths. I said: "You want some cold cuts, man? Some fruit, maybe a piece of cake or something? I'll get you something from the Red Apple over there."

"Yeah?" He had a kind of smell, like the inside of a closet where leather coats and old shoes had been stored. "That'd be real nice of you, man." He was still holding onto my shoulder and leaning close. " 'Course, what'd be even nicer is if you got us a couple of bottles of beer—the big bottles, you know? Forty ounces? That's the cheapest way to get it."

I looked at him a moment. He was about half a head shorter than I was. His expression was confused and hopeful and cocky and scared—even as he held on to me. I said: "Okay—beer. And...what? Bologna? Salami?"

"Bologna, man! That's my fuckin' favorite!"

"You got it. Come on, wait for me outside the store over there."

"Oh, man!" As we started across the street, he released me. "You really gonna get us some eats and some beer? Man, that's real nice of you. That's *real* nice."

"Don't worry," I told him, as we stepped up the far corner. "I'll take it out in trade."

He barked a laugh, reached over and squeezed my shoulder again: "You got it!"

"You wait here," I said. "I'll be out in five minutes."

At the gate-covered door, I glanced back.

He'd gotten down on the sidewalk beside the building, big fingers splayed on hot pavement. With people walking around him on the sunny avenue, he was doing push-ups!

Inside, the air conditioning was knife cold. I got a yellow plastic package of bologna from a row of packaged cold cuts hanging on a white wall, and two hard rolls from a clear plastic bin behind the checkout counters, a couple of nectarines from beside a slope of summer citrus, and two Bud tallboy six-packs—substantially more than in a pair of forty-ounce bottles.

Behind a ratty little black guy returning two red, white, and blue plastic shopping bags full of cans, I paid the sixteen dollars it came to for them at the checkout line (and realized I'd expected it to be about two dollars less; but that was Red Apple; fortunately I'd just come from my bank's ATM machine), and after the sullen, overweight cashier in the scarlet uniform and the big gold (plastic) earrings loaded them into a paper bag for me, I carried them through an aisle whose walls and floor were shaled with fliers and trampled sale newspapers. The electric door was still not working when I shouldered back out into summer.

Leaning against the plate-glass window backed with red-and-white "sale" signs, the kid had his outer arm down between his legs, moving it up and down as though he were scratching his flank with his elbow. Blinking in the shadow of the supermarket's marquee, he stood up: "Shit"—he looked at the bag—"you got a fuckin' *week's* worth of groceries!"

"Lunch," I said. "That's all. Let's go over to the park—where we can stretch out and get comfortable."

"Oh, yeah." He fell in beside me, hooking his hand over my shoulder again. "Want me to carry?"

We turned the corner, heading toward Riverside. "Sure." I handed the him the bag. "Here you go."

He took it, looking in the top. "Hey, you *really* got some beer!" He looked up at me, surprised.

"That's what you asked for."

"Yeah," he said. "But I wasn't sure you were really gonna do it." Holding the bag against his naked chest with both arms, he moved up beside me till his arm was pressed against mine, hotter than the sunlight. "Were you serious about takin' it out in trade—that thing you told the guy, about suckin' dick?"

"Never more serious in my life."

"God *damn!*" He hefted the grocery sack once more. "I guess I fuckin' lucked out today!" Now the sack went to his far arm, and for the third time, with the near hand, he grasped my shoulder. "Thing is, I'll tell you now, I don't usually go with most cocksuckers," he explained. "Not that I got anything against it, man. I mean, I *love* to get my dick sucked—more'n just about anything! But most cocksuckers, man, they suck you once, maybe twice if you're lucky. Then it's 'So long',"—his hand left my shoulder to flip on ahead—" 'See ya'!" It came back. "And that just drives me crazy, man! I need it three, four—" He scowled and shook his head—"maybe even five, six times. Or I just can't take it. I go a little crazy, you know what I mean? I mean, you ain't like that, are you? You bought all this food and beer. You wanna hang out together for a while, do me a few fuckin' times, huh? Right? Otherwise, you wouldn't've bought all this shit! Just once, man, and it makes me feel goddamned awful. I mean, it makes me feel like I'm sick—I shouldn't have even got started, you know what I mean?" We neared the corner of West End Avenue, as usual all but deserted. "I mean, I got a big dick. Cocksuckers are always tellin' me what a great dick I got. Got me some big balls, too." As we reached the sunny corner, he looked up and down the street. "Here—lemme show you!" Again his hand dropped from my shoulder; with thick, dirt-dark fingers, he pulled down the brass tab on his zipper, and, with a slight bend of the knees stuck his hand inside his fly, to haul out a...fucking sausage—uncut. A pair of nuts tumbled out beneath, bigger—I'm not kidding—than the two nectarines in my bag. (And the nectarines weren't small.) His cock—soft—was too long to stash in one of the sixteen-ounce beer cans, nor would there have been much leeway in the diameter, getting it in. He held up his meat by the middle for me to see. "How you like that?" He let it all flop down, still out his pants, and gripped my shoulder again—my heart had started to thud, real loud, in my chest, from the surprise. "Cocksucker told me a long time ago, man, if you wanna impress a faggot, just take it out and show what you got. It don't matter where—come on. We got the light."

I had to glance back—and there *were* people passing behind us. But, true, no one was crossing toward us from the opposite corner. We walked out into the street.

At the end of the next block, though, somebody *was* coming up: a middle-aged woman pushed a flabbily frail-looking man in a wheelchair.

"That's...impressive," I said. "But don't you think you'd better put it away for now?"

"Why?" He leaned closer: "Reach down and grab hold of it! You wanna put it away for me, you can—or you can play with it till we get to the park."

I reached down and took it—really, I was going to shove it back into his pants. But two things stopped me: one, it was incredibly warm—warmer than the sunlight around us. And two, it felt like twice the size I knew it was. But that's probably because I just hadn't spent a whole lot of time walking down the street holding some homeless kid's ten-inch-plus wanger.

"Oh, yeah, man...that feels real good. It's nice to have somebody playin' with your dick, just walkin' out in the street like this."

In my hand, I felt it growing, thickening, lifting—one of those whose natural curve was down instead of up. As we walked, his balls moved under my knuckles.

"That's a dick-and-a-half, ain't it, now?"

"Shit!" I said, hefting him in my hand: "Your cock is so heavy!" It sounded inane; but it felt as weighty as something rubber, filled with hot water.

We reached the far corner.

"Yeah, I know."

In front of us, the wheelchair was still three-quarters down the block. I glanced up. The sun shone full on us, a plate of silver polished too bright to look at. Really, I *started* to push it back in, but the kid leaned over to whisper: "Don't put it away yet, cocksucker. This is a really beautiful day, man. And it feels so good out today—"

"—you think you'll leave it out today," I finished for him.

We'd started down the next block before the park. "That's about where it's at," he said to me. "Hold the fucker for me, man. They ain't gonna see it, I swear!" It was pushing my fingers apart, still getting bigger. But by now, I was afraid to look down at it because I thought I might direct the attention of the woman and the man in the wheelchair toward it—who were about thirty feet in front of us now—if I glanced.

My hand tingled up and down both my sides. I couldn't tell you if I was breathing or not.

And the kid wasn't talking anymore, just holding the bag of beer with one hand and my shoulder with the other.

My hand on his cock began to feel as if it wasn't there—I mean I could feel *him*, like the humongous trunk of some baby elephant. But I couldn't feel my hand *on* it.

And, like that, I watched this guy with a few blades of gray hair combed across his freckled scalp, wearing thick tortoiseshell glasses, and a black yarmulke on the back of his head, roll up to us in his wheelchair, pushed by this woman in a gray sweater held corner to corner by one of those little pearl chains with a jeweled dog on one side, till they were not three feet away from us on the sidewalk—while somebody thumped rhythmically below my Adam's apple with a forefinger.

Then, without anyone's pointing, or screaming, or sputtering, or even widening their eyes—really, they hadn't looked at *all!*—they were behind us.

I breathed: "...fucking baseball players!"

Moving my hand down his rigid shaft—feeling poured back into my fingers—I fingered the glans inside a foreskin that slid as loosely over the head as parachute cloth might over a golfball; I managed to say, "What the fuck were you *doing* in that Burger King anyway, that got you kicked out?"

"I told you." Again he leaned over to whisper. "Just scratchin' my dick."

"Was it inside your pants or outside"—I sneezed, but it was the sun and nervousness—"when you were scratching it?"

"Started off inside," he told me. "But pretty soon, I guess I pulled it on out—I was beatin' off, where I was sitting, with it under the table in the corner there. Two little girls across from me was watchin' me—and like to bust out gigglin'. One of 'em had her hand down between her legs. I thought she was maybe doin' it, too."

"Would that have turned you on?" I asked.

"Shit," he said. "Anybody doin' it turns me on. An' women can do it a lot easier, too—some of them can just do it by pressing their legs together. Did you know that?"

"No," I said. "Actually, I didn't."

"When I was in the hospital, some girl told me she could do it that way. But in the Burger King back there, this one woman was just starin' and starin'! When I took it out, under the table, and started shuckin' on it, I thought she was really gettin' into it. I think she *was*, too. 'Cause she just watched me, about three whole minutes—*before* she went up to the counter and told the manager. That's when they threw me out."

I laughed. "I think the guy who threw you out of there had to be one jealous motherfucker."

"Yeah, I know," he said. "People've been tellin' me that for years. Even one of the doctors, he told me that. It was suppose to be a joke the way he said it. But I don't think it's a joke, man. I think it's serious. I mean, all my life, *everybody* wants to look at my dick—they always asking me to see it. Because I got such a big one—kids and people, they're always askin' me to take a look at how big it is. This one wants to know how fat my balls are. That one wants to see how far I can shoot my load. The other one wants to know if I use one hand or two hands to beat off—*I* like to use three! Or maybe two and a cocksucker's mouth—that's best!" He grinned over at me. "And I *like* people to see my dick—I *love* playin' with my dick, man. I'm crazy about playin' with my dick. I play with my dick all fuckin' day long—or maybe have somebody else play with it, like you—"

Just then, these three guys came around the far corner—three black kids in baseball caps and baggy jeans. And I lost it. I pulled his cock up (which, since the wheelchair guy had passed, was half-soft again), jabbed it back into his fly, and snatched my hand away.

He just chuckled and went on. "I used to play with my dick so much, they put me in the crazy hospital—twice! That's where the doctor told me other guys were jealous of it, which was half the reason it was always gettin' me in trouble—but they don't got to be jealous of it! All they got to do is fall down on their knees and *suck* it! Then we'll *all* be happy, see?"

"Where was this hospital?" I asked.

"Up near Hyde Park. But my mom lives out in Brooklyn—that's where I'm from."

"I never would have guessed." But his "th's" were closer to "d's" and his "r" had the flatness of those raised on the other side of the river. (The "oi" for "i" exchange, of course, these days you only hear in old movies: probably it has something to do with the homogenization of language by television.)

"Least she used to live out there. I ain't seen her in the longest time. First time they put me away, I was fourteen. I thought they was punishin' me—at first. Then I realized I could sit around my room and beat off all I wanted, all day long. I figured I had it pretty good. By that time, I knew some guys liked to suck on it. Back when I was a kid, I thought it was just *old* guys! Really, I thought that was what old guys was for. *That* was pretty stupid, huh? But I learned quick, no matter what I did, the *doctors* didn't seem to mind—so I'd go in to see a new one with my hand already in my pants, playin' with it. I'd be in the office there playin' with it, and some doctor would ask me, 'Does that feel good?' I'd say, 'Yeah!' Another one wanted to know what would happen to me if I stopped playin' with it. I said, 'I dunno. But I don't plan to find out anytime soon.' Another one said if I didn't stop playin' with it, I couldn't come back and talk to her no more. I said, 'That's all right.' I mean, what would *you* rather do—beat off or talk to some fat old woman with glasses and a purple birthmark all up her jaw? I got this one real old doctor, and I asked him if he would suck it for me. He asked me why. And I told him, 'Cause it *feels* good, motherfucker!'"

One of the three guys coming toward us suddenly kind of stared—then laughed and started pointing. Then they pretty much all started looking and laughing. As they passed, one of them gave us a thumbs-up sign.

The kid was just grinning. I was wondering what that was all about, when I looked down at his pants:

"Oh, Jesus—"

Though I'd put his cock back in his pants, his nuts were still protruding out his fly (the curve of his dick like a third ball on top of the lower two) in their cloud of bronze brown hair.

"—will you put those things *away!*"

"Whatever turns you on!" He dropped his hand from my shoulder, hooked his thumb in his fly, and flipped his balls back in. Then his hand was up again—though he *still* hadn't zipped his pants. "One of the doctors, he told me: 'You ask everyone you meet to suck your dick. Why do you do that?' I told him, ' 'Cause I really like to get it sucked. Besides, a whole lot of people say 'yes!' He says to me, 'Don't you realize that's very hostile?' I told him, 'Man, that ain't hostile, that's hopeful!'"

I laughed now. "Well, you didn't ask *me.*"

"I didn't *have* to ask you," he said. "It was the first thing you said you was gonna do. Plus you got us some beer and some bologna. Man, I figured I lucked out. You know—" As we reached the corner, he lowered his tone. "—a lot of you stoned cocksuckers, the kind that come and just say right out, I wanna suck your dick, man, they like it if you take a piss in their mouths. I mean, I've had guys who like to drink the piss right out my fuckin' spout!"

As we walked across the street together, I asked, "Do guys who just come up and say, 'Hey, will you suck my dick?'—do *they* like to piss in a guy's mouth?"

He grinned at me. "*I* sure as fuck do!"

"Well, I don't think that's going to be a problem with you and me," I said. "I'll drink your piss like it was going out of style."

"Oh, man!" He reached between his legs like he was adjusting himself—only, through his pants, he grabbed himself and pulled on it; and pulled on it two, three, four more times. "I was pretty sure you was my kind of cocksucker. And I noticed I didn't have to argue you into gettin' no beer—that's always a good sign."

Stepping between some cars, we started toward the curb. (And he kept pulling.) "Oh, shit!" Looking down, he stopped. "I don't think I can make this." A windshield must have shattered here, because the mounded asphalt on the curb was thick with the pea-sized nuggets shatterproof glass makes when it shatters.

I looked at the kid's bare feet. "Come on. Let's go around a little further."

He was still tugging at his pants as we backed from between the cars. We walked around a pair of Dodges and a Chrysler before we turned in to try for the sidewalk again.

"The first time I was in, they turned me out the hospital right at New Year's—that was the year before last," he told me. We stepped between cars again: a handful of years back, the city had torn up all the little six-sided paving stones from the walkway beside the park and replaced them with a blobby concoction of macadam and gravel spread unevenly up to—and sometimes slopped on top of—the cobblestones still squaring the trees and lining the benches' stanchions. "I had me a coat—but I don't think I had me no shirt under it. I don't usually wear no shirt"—on the sidewalk now, we turned toward Seventy-ninth Street—"but I got me a bottle of beer. I'd panhandled me up a couple of bucks. I was down on Times Square, you know, where all the people hang out. And after I finished my beer, I stood around in the middle of that crowd, with everybody pressin' up against me—and I pissed in my pants! You ever do that—piss on yourself in a crowd?"

"No." Lots of broken glass lay over the sidewalk's graphite-colored mounds. I watched the kid lengthen one step or shorten another, to avoid curved shards. "No, I never did that."

"It feels pretty good, man." He was still pulling at the shape in his crotch. "I had hot piss in both sneakers, man. It was really nice—"

"Until it began to cool off?"

"No, it was *still* nice! It feels sexy, you know? But then I got me another bottle and took it into one of them dirty movies—on Eighth Avenue?"

"Now, that I've done," I told him.

He hefted the grocery bag higher on his chest. "I went and sat on the side, opened my coat—under one of the lights, so people walkin' by could see I didn't have no shirt on under it: you wanna get your dick sucked, you gotta show some skin. So I drank me some more beer, then I closed my eyes and put my head against the wall and pretended to be asleep. Pretty soon someone sits down next to me, and there's this hand feelin' around between my legs. But soon as he feels my pants are all wet, he gets up and scoots. Two more of 'em come by—felt me up and run off. I don't even open my eyes. But finally somebody sits down and puts his hand there—and don't take it away. He's feelin' my big dick and rubbin' my fat old nuts, and don't seem to care about the piss at all.

"So I open my eyes and look over at him.

"It's this white-haired old nigger—scrawny little black guy in a navy pea jacket, about a hundred years old. Well, maybe sixty, sixty-five. So I lean over and whisper to him, 'I sure hope you wanna suck my fuckin' dick!' He grins and nods at me—this little old black guy. But he has these big, rough hands. I told him, 'I'm afraid I pissed all over myself. Hope you don't mind.' He shakes his head, still grinnin'. So I say, 'I just might do it again, too—while you're suckin' on it!' And he asks me, 'You want me to take ma teeth out?' And I tell him, 'Gee, Pops—would ya?' 'Cause you can't get a better blowjob than from some old guy with all his teeth out! So Pops flips them pink-and-white suckers out his black old mouth and sticks 'em in his pocket. And he goes down on my dick like a trooper. Man, he sucked my cock till they put us out at six o'clock the next morning. I really like that, see? A cocksucker what'll let me stash my dick in his face and leave it there till it really gets to feelin' at home. He got down on the floor between my legs, with his head in my lap. I sat there, drank my beer, and watched the movie—while that black bastard come all over my sneakers. A couple of times I took me a good long piss in his mouth—he really liked that, too. The first time he swallowed everything—didn't miss a drop. An' I bent over an' told him, 'You don't have to swallow it *all*, man! Gotta let *some* of it spill around my balls, ya know what I mean?' And he did too, cause the next time I had the warmest, wettest balls in New York City! That nigger's mouth was hot, man! I swear, I must've come ten, twelve times—"

"Hey, come *on*—" (He stopped near the waist-high wall.) "You don't have to bullshit me, now," I told him. "I like you fine just the way you are—"

The kid put the grocery bag down on the broad stone. "I ain't bullshittin' you, man! I swear, that's the way I like to do it; ten or twelve loads in a cocksucker what'll stick on my dick for a few hours—maybe seven or eight. That ain't nothin'!" He parked his butt on the wall's edge and swung around to put one big, dirty foot up there with him. "Once, man, I had my hands down on his head and was humpin' that old man's face, only I guess he must a' gone to sleep, if you can imagine that; 'cause when I came, he started coughin' and stuff—and cum run all out his fuckin' nose, all over me. But he *still* wouldn't turn loose my dick! I guess he just woke up, that's all. The next time"—the kid had his hand in his lap, working again—"when he said he was tired, I took my dick out of his mouth and jerked off all over his face for that one—that's cool, too." I glanced down: his dick was out of his pants *again!* He sat there, lifting his fist up his towering prong—dropping it again, lifting it again; sitting on the wall, grinning at me. Hunched over the way he was, it went well over halfway up his chest!

I looked left and right. Yes, there *were* people walking toward us and away in both directions—I hoped to hell they were *confirmed* baseball players! I was about to tell him to put it away again—

"I was about ready to marry that old nigger—I swear, man! I was hopin' he was gonna ask me to come home with him in the worst way. But once they turned on the lights to clean out the movie theater and got us up out of there, he cut me loose—I guess nobody wants some crazy snaggletoothed fucker who plays with himself all the time and stinks like dried piss, I don't care *how* big his dick is!" He grinned at me, broken-toothed.

"Well," I said, angling around to the side, to get in the way of whatever the people coming up might see, "maybe he was just a little scared of you—I mean, he's some old black guy. And you're this white kid—"

"Man"—still rubbing his dick, he narrowed his eyes up at me with his head to the side—"how the fuck you suppose to know I'm white? That's fuckin' presumptuous! There're black people as light as I am—don't you know that?"

I frowned at him. But this kid looked *so* white...

"I mean"—and he looked down at himself, dropping his fist into his hair, to waggle himself side to side—"does this look like some white guy's dick to you?"

"Yeah," I said. "More or less—"

"What's that joke they say, man? What's twelve inches long, two inches across, and white?"

"What?"

"Not a fuckin' *thing*, man! You know that. Well, this here is eleven inches when it's soft. Some guy told me it was fifteen-and-a-half hard. He measured it—in fact, a couple of other people took a ruler to it. How could I be white and have a dick like *this*?"

People were coming up by the park wall in the other direction, too—

"I figure that's about half Polack and about half nigger—with maybe some Italian or Scottish or something thrown in." He gave it a few vigorous rubs. "I heard they got some big cocks on 'em, sometimes."

—but they were a little farther away.

"Look," I said, "it's certainly a *big* white dick—it's a Johnny Wadd dick. It's a Moby Dick dick. But it still looks like a *white* dick to me."

He laughed; and took my shoulder once more with his free hand. "Come on," he said. Then he lifted his other foot up on the wall, turned himself around, releasing me, and moved to the back, to put his legs over—and, cock out like a flagpole, pushed off, to drop out of sight. I heard him crash in leaves below.

The grocery bag sat on the stones.

A moment later, his soiled hands—both of them—reached up above the stone wall. (He was too far down for me to see his head.) One hand snapped its fingers. "Gimme the beer," I heard him. "Then get your black ass on over here, sucker!"

I lifted the bag up and handed it to him, then sat on the wall, brought my sneakers up on the stone, and turned to the trees and foliage that was the park. I moved forward to the wall's edge, put one shoe down, glanced down. Inside, six or seven feet below, the leaf-strewn ground at the wall's bottom was actually the top of a thickly wooded slope that dropped away into the park and toward the river—only more than fifteen feet off, nothing was visible through the trees.

Down behind the wall, the kid was dragging over this big piece of cardboard—like a large air-conditioner carton come open—with the grocery bag sitting on one end of it. Now he grinned up at me.

I pushed off, landed on the cardboard, went down to my knees—lost my balance, and went over on my seat, flailing.

The kid stood, grinning down. The top button on his pants already opened, he pushed the waist down to his thighs, to his knees, then got one leg out completely. "Pretty neat, huh?" He gestured around the woods, backed by seven feet of black stone running off left and right.

On the street, it had been hot. Here, under the trees, it was just warm. I could smell leaves and dust and stuff, which wasn't so bad, here on New York's edge.

His cock was in his hand again, and he pulled on it, overhand and down. "My mother was Scottish—or Irish, or somethin' like that. I think. But I don't know who the fuck my dad was. He *could*'ve been some black guy, though—I don't know," which kind of came out of the blue, till I realized he was finishing up our conversation from above.

The grocery bag still lay on the cardboard's corner.

"He was probably just one of these little guys who are all dick," I said, from where I was sitting. "You just inherited it—in spades!"

"Yeah." His other foot kicked free; the pants fell to the cardboard. "Man, I just don't like wearin' no fuckin' clothes if I don't fuckin' have to—you know what I mean?"

In a pile there next to his big, dirt-grayed right foot, his pants looked even filthier than they had when he'd worn them. But that's because you just don't usually see people wearing clothes that dirty, and I'd been cleaning them up a little in my mind. He planted his grimed, oversized heels apart, and stood in front of me, grinning down and pulling at his cock. "Nice, huh? You like it?"

I smiled; I nodded.

Suddenly he turned away. "Wanna see a shitty ass, man?" He bent over and the paper bag scrunched and chattered as he rummaged for a beer. "Take a look at mine. Go on—spread it open and take a sniff."

I got up on my knees on the cardboard.

With one hand now, he reached back to tug aside one buttock, reddened with half a dozen pimples. Disembodied like that, pawing at his scrawny butt, his fingers looked immense; I was struck all over again how large his hands—and feet, and (though I couldn't see it that moment) dick—really were.

I said, "Jesus—"

Within the crevice's length was a brown black crust, matted to his hair either side and cracked across and up and down, like some dried mud road. I couldn't even *see* his asshole!

"Somethin', huh? You can sniff it, but keep your tongue out of that shit trough, okay? I keep it like that for a friend of mine."

"Don't you ever wipe yourself—"

"Not no more—" Now he stood, turned back around—and the head of his dick, curving down, hit my cheek. "He said I don't have to ever use no more toilet paper—" (Yes, he said "terlit," and that one always gets me) "—as long as he's around. I kind of like that." He took it in his great fingers and began to massage it inside its generous skin. In his other hand he had a beer can. "Here—open that for me?"

Reaching up, I pulled the tab on the can. A little spray cooled my left cheek. "I hope he pays you a lot of money."

"Naw," the kid said. "This is another homeless guy—like me. I wouldn't take no money, anyway—not no more than a penny. And he just likes to eat shit—that's all. I sleep up here, usually, and he comes around, every night—pulls down my pants, and laps out my shit-hole till it's clean as can be." He raised his can and took a drink, while his large, soiled knuckles, working on his cockhead, brushed my cheek. "Dirty as it is when I go to sleep, every morning I wake up with the cleanest asshole you ever seen. That's real nice, man, havin' someone come up at night and eat out your ass. Sometimes, when he wakes me up doin' it, I jerk off a couple of times while he's down there lickin' it out. So we got an agreement—I don't wipe my ass no more when I take me a shit. I don't even go in the shitter now—it's like pissin' on myself. It feels sexy. I just go and sit somewhere, on a bench or something, and pull my pants down, and take me a shit. I like to sit in it, and wriggle around a little—and beat off a few times, you know? I do that in the morning, before anybody gets up. Then, at night, this guy comes around and cleans me up. Pretty cool, huh?"

"If it's your thing," I told him.

"He don't suck no dick though. That's the only thing wrong with him. But—hey, now I got you, don't I have to worry about that. Come on," he said, looking down at me. "Give my big old dick a kiss."

So I did. Very gently, on its heavily veined side.

Immediately he squatted in of front of me, still pulling at himself. "Now, why don't we have some of that there bologna and drink some beer together; then we can really have some fun." He took another swig from his tallboy. "It's better, though, if I just beat off the first time—you can watch, I don't care—just to get some of the pressure off, you know? Then you can have everything else that comes out of this all-day sucker, man. I mean, once I get rid of that first load, it's all yours." Now he dropped to sit—right in front of me. His foot went right into my jeans crotch. While he reached over for the grocery bag, through my jeans he kneaded my hard cock with his toes.

He dragged the bag back and came out with a roll. "Here, you want this?" He handed it to me, pulled out the other one. Now he put his beer can down on the cardboard; and, holding the bag rim with one hand, he went in with the other.

He came out with the yellow plastic bologna package, already ripping it apart. He fingered out a slice, which collapsed into a bologna-colored flower that he shoved into his mouth, pulled out a second slice—his balls, out of their hairy cloud, in front of him on the cardboard, were the color of the lunch meat—and shoved that in with the first, then tore off a bite of roll. Chewing, he looked at me again—and asked, through crumbs: "You want some?"

"Sure," I peeled a round slice off the pile from under the transparent plastic cylinder he'd ripped apart. "When's the last time you ate, anyway?"

He shrugged, grinned— "I dunno"—and chewed. "Yesterday, sometime. Out here on the street, you can't pay too much attention to when you eat or not. Otherwise,you get pretty unhappy. Know what I mean?"

"Yeah." I nodded. "I guess so."

"But I could tell you everywhere I jerked off—in the park and out of it, in the last three days!" He turned to swipe up his beer can again. The bologna package was lying beside his knee. His roll, a third of it eaten, was on the other side of him. His leg was still jackknifed up between us. "About three o'clock in the morning, I did it sitting out on the bench on the island in the middle of Broadway. Right in front of the Burger King, where we was before. Two people come by while I was doin' it, but there weren't no policemen. So they just looked for a little bit and didn't say nothing." His toes were still moving through my pants. He took another swallow—and I reached forward to brush crumbs off his chin; then a few others off his chest.

"Go on—that's right." He grinned his broken-toothed grin. "You can touch me. Anywhere you want—that's okay. Put your hand under my balls and tickle 'em."

I eased forward a little more and slid my hand beneath his heavy testicles, which were too big for my palm, so the one on the right kept rolling out between my thumb and forefinger, and I would thumb it back; my hands aren't particularly small, either.

He drank some more beer—we were close enough that I had to lean back to let him raise the can between us.

His other hand was down on the thick shaft of him, a knot of knuckles and fingers and nails and rough, soiled callus, rising on his long, long cock, and falling again; and rising again; and falling.

"You wanna suck my dick, doncha?"

I nodded.

"You wanna suck it so bad you can already taste my fuckin' cheese, right?" His voiced dropped to a tone like troubled gravel. "It tastes salty, man. That's the kind of dick taste you like, don't ya', cocksucker?"

I nodded again.

"You're a fuckin' scummy-mouthed cocksucker, ain't you?" His fist moved faster. "Ain't you?"

"Right. You got it." I put my hand on his shoulder; I moved the other one under his balls.

"Oh, yeah...that's nice. I wanna come for you, cocksucker. I wanna come for you a lot—a whole lot of times. I wanna come in your mouth; I wanna come in your face; I wanna come all over your nigger-nappy hair—" He looked down at himself; his hand was moving fast enough now so that the details had vanished.

I felt something cold; he'd put the beer can up against my face, to pull me closer.

"It feels real good, jerkin' off for you, man—this is probably the biggest fuckin' dick you'll ever suck on. And I been learnin' how to make cocksuckers feel good ever since I was a fuckin' kid, man. Since that's about all I fuckin' *can* do, I'm really into doin' that good. Jesus, playin' with this big dick feels so good!" He looked up at me again. I could see his jaw shaking with the movement in his right shoulder. I could feel his quickening rhythm through his foot against my groin. "I love to jerk on my dick, man—all the fuckin' time, all day long, all year long. That's all I ever wanna ever do, man—jerk off and fuck some cocksucker's face. Comin' feels so fuckin' good, man! It feels *soooo* fuckin' good! Lemme see some tongue—lemme see that hole I'm gonna be stickin' this big old fucker in, that's right—open it up and lemme see that nasty black suck-hole. Show me how you gonna lick around under it, and tickle my balls with your tongue—that's right. Oh, man, that's fuckin' hot! That's fuckin' hot, 'sucker—that's really turnin' me on. Man, this fucker's gonna shoot in a goddamned minute, 'sucker! It's gonna shoot like a motherfucker!" Now his face was down, now it was up. He was hunched over, beating hard as he could—only then the beating got even harder. "Oh, shit! Oh, fuckin' shit...that's so fuckin'...fuckin' horny, man! Fuckin' horny motherfucker!"

If somebody took a two-thirds-cup measure from the row of decreasing-sized aluminum cups I have hanging over my sink, filled it half up with egg white and half with heavy cream, mixed them, then—just as if I weren't there sitting in front of him—flung it on the kid in three tosses—splurt! splat! splop!—that's what his triple shot was like.

Like four BBs, hot drops hit my jaw and chin.

Cum ran down the kid's forehead from his hair. A big blob of it covered the left corner of his mouth. A line of it beaded from his right eye's upper lashes to the lower, to streak on down his cheek. His chest was splattered all over—a glob covering his left nipple eased away from his teat, down his ribs. I looked at his bronze bush, speckled and draped with mucus. Still stiff, his whole dick was slick with it. Pearls of cum rolled over his knuckles, down the back of his fist. Cum puddled under his balls, in my palm.

Breathing hard, opening his green eyes, he grinned at me again. "...and you got about half a dozen more of them loads to come, the next one right inside your face!" He thrust out his tongue to lick cum from the corner of his mouth. "What you laughin' at, nigger?

You got cum on *your* face, too!" He took three more deep breaths. "You can have this load, if you want—somebody's gotta eat it. You, me..." He sounded matter-of-fact about it. "Go on. Stuff's too good to waste—and it makes you healthy. Some guy told me that when I was a kid. Go on—eat it off me."

I looked down. On his jackknifed leg, cum slid in two trickles down his calf. On the instep of his foot, and strung across the dirty knuckles of the first three of his big toes, still working on my crotch, were two globs of it.

I felt the beer can, still cold on my neck, pull me forward. And looked up—and licked the blob off the corner of his mouth. His breath was bologna and something else. And he turned to stick out his tongue against mine. The heel of his thumb slid—rough as some cement worker's—over the back of my neck as I lowered to lick some of it off his chest. He was salty—strong salts, too. Above me, I heard him say, "You're gettin' close to the good part, now."

The beer can left my neck. I saw him set it on the cardboard. A moment on, he reached between his legs with his free hand (the other, cum-bright, worked slowly on the base of his still-erect meat) and pulled my hand out from beneath his nuts. As he sat back, he raised my melanin-dark fingers in his dirt-grayed ones, to drop his face into the pearly smear roiling there. I felt his tongue, warmer and softer than any cat's, lap the pinker palm. And lap again. And again. His lips dozed together, now at the heel, now at the ball, and now in the pooled center. The wet wad of his tongue nudged between my knuckles, slipped across the skin stretched from forefinger to thumb, flicked my wrist where some had rolled. Looking up as he licked, he blinked. Then he raised his face, slick from nose to chin. "You eat cum, and it keeps you from gettin' sick. I guess that's why cocksuckers suck cock, huh? And livin' out in the park, you gotta keep real healthy. I don't suck no cock, man. I am *not* a cocksucker! But I'll eat cum—especially my own. Sometimes I drink my own piss, too. Though somebody else eatin' it and drinking for me is really better, you know?" He chuckled suddenly. "I'm a fuckin' pervert, like the guy said!" Dropped his face to my hand to lap once more, then let it go.

I reached down to take his foot in my hands—and lifted it from my crotch. The sole was rough as board. Inside my pants, my groin tingled where the pressure of him had been. As I raised his big, dirty foot, he went back, to lean on one elbow. (The other hand was still at his own cock. And that cock was still slick with cum and hard and curving toward me.) His toenails were the same worn-down length as the nails on his fingers, with the same dirt beneath. I glanced up at him. Quite seriously, he watched me as I dropped my mouth to eat the cum off his foot.

"You wanna suck my toes, man, that'd be great. I love to get my toes sucked."

"I know someone who really would have liked you," I said. But, then, how would I have explained to a kid like this about Hasler? (But then, maybe I wouldn't have had to.) His toes were rough—and salty, too. I moved on up to what drooled his calf.

He was leaning back on the cardboard, waving his cock from side to side—"See, it's waitin' for you, 'sucker. And it ain't gone soft at all. Get the cheese first, now—oh, shit!"

That was when I dropped my mouth over his cum-slicked head and pushed beneath his skin with my tongue. Troweling smegma from where it was packed thick in the trough circling beneath his glans, I took him all the way down to his scummy fist. (Above, I heard him gargle more beer.) His hand left his cock. And I went down another inch, to where his wet hair pushed against my face—and though my throat was completely blocked, it still wasn't all the way. With wet fingers on my right cheek and dry ones on my left, and his thumbs over my brow, he held my head, and we rolled to the side. He began to hump, at first only filling my throat with half or three-quarters of that fifteen-inch shaft. But after a few plunges, I got a big breath in and thrust my face all the way into his crotch, taking it to the base—"Oh, *shit*, man!" and let him get in four, five, six total thrusts, before I backed off again, to get in another breath.

Pretty soon, we got this pattern, with him taking five or six three-quarter thrusts, while I breathed—and then six or seven full thrusts, to the root—while I didn't. About the second cycle of that, he grunted, "Don't let me kill you now, cocksucker! You're too fuckin' good; and I done almost choked a couple of cocksuckers by accident!"

I just nodded, and we kept it up that way. It was pretty intense. But the kid knew what he was doing. I guess if you have meat on you like that, you learn—or you *do* kill a few cocksuckers!

His speed increased.

Then one hand came away from my head, the other slipped behind it; he grabbed the base of his cock and began to slam in hard with each blow. His fist made a collar I couldn't get past, but even so I was taking nine of fifteen inches, each thrust, every thrust. You just assume—at least I do—that most guys' second loads are going to take twice as long as their first one. But it wasn't the case with this kid. He shot—I felt it in the back of my throat. He pulled out, squirted twice in the front of my mouth—and, I swear, fucking filled it up. Then he went deep in and squirted again. I swallowed, and gasped, and cum rolled out over the bony knot of his fist.

He was taking big, deep gasps—when he released his cock and brought his hand up to his face. Without letting his shaft go, I looked up. Lying on his side, he licked the stuff off his fingers; maybe, with him, there was always going to be some extra. Near his shoulder, two beer cans lay on their sides, empty, by a half-eaten roll. A little ways away, another stood upright on the cardboard. Finishing with his fingers, he reached over, got the upright can, and took a long swallow—while I wondered where the hell he'd gotten time to drink a whole second can of beer.

But then, I'd been pretty busy down there.

He put the can down, got my head in both his hands again, and rolled over on his back—not letting me go, so that I rolled over on top of his legs. I had gotten my jeans open, and they were halfway down my ass, but that was all. Now he brought one foot up against my cock, so that it lay up along the crevice between his rough sole and his calf. I began to rub—but gently—while he moved his hands, again one wet and one dry, over my face. "Man...now that was a...good suck," he said between gasps.

I took his cock in my hand and came off it (he gave a little grunt), and began to run my hand up and down it, holding it pretty tight. (He let the gasp out, in a comfortable sort of sigh.) "You said you used to drink your own piss," I said. "How did you do that?"

"What do you mean, how?"

"Tell me about it."

He raised his head to look down at me; then he put it back on the cardboard. "I dunno. I'd get me an old cardboard milk container, and open it up, rinse it out—and go down where all the benches are, by the river. I'd sit there, with all the people, usually not too far from the comfort station. Then, when I had to take a leak, I'd stand up, take a couple of steps from the bench out in the road, flip my dick out, and piss into my container. Usually I'd have a fuckin' hard-on, but I'm lucky; I can piss pretty much just as easy, whether it's hard or soft. I don't know why, but somehow if you're pissin' into something—a bottle or a milk carton or something, nobody ever stops you. You can be in the middle of the goddamn street. Policemen can even be walkin' by, and as long as you're pissin' into something, they won't say nothin'. I wonder why that is?" Lying on his back, he thrust a forefinger, thick as some plumbing tool, into his nostril, dug around, came out with something, and, while I watched, ate it. "Anyway, I'd fill up my milk carton with piss—for me, it's gotta be a quart container. A pint won't hold all my juice, most of the time. Then I'd go back, sit on the bench, wait a few seconds, then take me a big drink out of my carton." He dug in his nose again, found something else in there, and ate that. "You don't wanna wait too long, so it'll still be hot. But then I'd kind of look around and see who was watchin' me." He went back to digging in his nose again.

"What the fuck are you doing?" I asked, from where my head was, down at his crotch.

He glanced down, paused, finger in nose. "What do you mean?"

"What the fuck are you doing?"

"Huh? I'm eatin' my fuckin' snot. What does it look like? You want some? It's good—it's real salty."

"Oh, shit!" I said.

"Naw, come on," he said; this time, with what he scraped out, he thrust his big hand down toward me. "There you go—I just forgot for a moment. I know how to take care of my cocksuckers, man."

I was actually going to take it. But I didn't get a chance to. He pushed his finger into my mouth.

And it was salty.

And it *was* good.

"A couple of years ago," he went on, "there was one guy I used to see in the park here—always dressed real nice. Older guy. He lived right up on Riverside Drive, he said. Said he was an executive in a bank or somethin'." He pulled his big finger out of my mouth and went back up to digging in his nose. "About the second time I did that—pissed in a milk carton, down by the benches, well, he comes over to me, sits right beside me, and says, 'Sure is hot today. I could use a drink of that, if you wouldn't mind.' I asked, 'You know what it is?' And he said, 'Sure. I saw you pissin' in there. That's your piss.' I said, 'Okay, motherfucker. Have a swig—on me.' So he took a long swallow, and said, 'Good stuff.' Then we sat there, passin' it back and forth and shootin' the shit; we talked all sorts of crazy stuff—he was a pretty interesting guy. He tried to gimme some money, too, the first time. But I said, 'Shit, how'm I'm gonna take ten bucks for a couple of swigs from a milk carton full of piss?' We did that about five or six times, too—but that was a few summers ago. I ain't seen him in the park this time. I wonder if he's still all right. But maybe he don't live there no more."

"Did you ask *him* to suck your dick?"

It's funny how even when you can't see somebody's face, sometimes you can hear them grin. "Yup! He said he'd try, and we went into the comfort station there, together. He was kind of scared, though—which is fuckin' stupid 'cause that's what everybody in the place is there for. Only, when it cleared out, he couldn't get it in his mouth. My dick was too fuckin' big! For him to get it in his mouth. I peed on him, though. He said he'd like that, so I did it. But you see, he was this white guy—he wasn't no big-mouthed, woolly-headed nigger like you!" He reached down and roughed my hair; and laughed. "Hey, you rubbin' like that on my leg—don't come yet, will you? Wait till I shoot another load, huh? You come, and you gonna wanna take a rest for a while—I know how you guys are. But I still gotta go some before I can really relax. Here, I got something for you!" And from the head of his cock, still stiff in my flexing fist, from its loose collar of skin, water lifted in a sparkling arch!

I went down on his full yellow stream—and he was holding my head again, wrapping one leg around my shoulder. "Let it spill a little, man, like I told you—all over my balls." Both his hands were wet, now. But I think that was my face. "That's right…that's right…" By now I had both my hands full of his scrawny ass, too, fingertips in his crack (something dry crumbled under them and powdered out), but, hugging him into my face, I didn't care.

Even before his urine ran out, he'd begun to hump. He remembered our rhythm, too. And in three more minutes, he'd shot *another* load—I swear it was as big or bigger than his first. Cum exploded out my mouth, even as I tried to swallow it.

His hands were down there, fingering what ran down his balls up and back up into my mouth, or lifting his big, dripping knuckles to his own mouth. "Oh, shit, man—that was real good. That was fuckin' beautiful, cocksucker!" Once more he rolled me on top of his legs; once more he pulled his foot up against my cock. "You can shoot now...I'm ready to take five." He was breathing hard. I mean the kid put twice the energy most guys do into shooting; and then shot three times as much as anyone I'd ever seen before.

I began to rub—and tasted urine again.

I shot all over his foot.

Yeah, I thought; this kid could have made Tim—or, I suppose, *anyone* who didn't mind a little grub and grunge—happy.

Finally his cock lost about half its hard. I came off him; his whole belly was wet.

There was a little puddle of urine over the blackened whorls within his belly button.

So I licked it out.

Which made him laugh.

He was sitting up now—drinking his fifth can of beer. Again, I hadn't seen him get through the fourth, but four lay empty on the cardboard.

Soon as I rolled off him, the first thing he did was reach down with all his fingers together and wipe my jism from his blackened instep and then run his fingers into his mouth. (He could only get three into it at a time. "Some black kid was lookin' down over the wall at us, a little while ago. I guess you didn't see him. But that's what got me off the last time. I guess I'm kind of an exhibitionist, sort of." He said it like a considered admission.

"Yeah," I said. "I'd noticed."

He thumbed up some more of my cum off his leg and ate that. "Nigger cum, man—that's the best kind. That's gotta be the healthiest."

I was breathing pretty hard, too, though it was only my first load. "Glad you like it."

"I mean, for makin' you strong and keepin' you from gettin' sick and stuff. Don't you figure?"

"Well, I never—"

But he was pulling over the grocery bag. He jammed another slice of bologna into his mouth. "You want a beer?" He pulled another can loose from its plastic loop and thrust it toward me.

"Sure." I took it.

"And some bologna?"

I opened my mouth and leaned forward.

He started to put it in, then looked down and laughed. Arching forward over his big nuts, his dick was still half-erect. He draped the bologna slice over the head of his cock. "Eat it off my fuckin' dick!"

So I went down between his legs—and while I was getting it in my mouth, he started peeing again. So I got piss down my neck and on my shirt; and the bologna was pretty salty. When I came up, we were both laughing; I popped my beer can and took a swallow.

He looked around, found the roll, and ate more of that. "Hey," he said. "Tell me something."

I was scratching between my legs, where it had grown sweaty with my pants still on. (I was thinking about taking them off.) "Sure."

"What's your name?"

"John," I told him. "What do they call *you?*"

"Crazy Joey," he said. "That's 'cause I was in the fuckin' crazy hospital. Out on the street, you been in the crazy hospital, and they call you 'crazy.' Crazy Joey. A couple of years ago, one guy used to call me Joey-who-needs-a-bath. Every time he saw me, that's what he'd call me: 'Hey, Joey-who-needs-a-bath!' Which is funny, 'cause my name ain't even Joe. It's Mencus. But just like they call everybody 'crazy' who's been in the crazy hospital, they call everybody who's got a hard name or a funny name or a foreign name Joe or Joey—or John. So they call me Crazy Joey. I don't mind it.... Hey, John?"

"What?"

"I wanted to ask you something—that I don't ever ask nobody till after I dropped my third load in 'im—Mad Man Mike, he told me that. Mad Man Mike and me, we're real tight, see. But I wouldn't even mention his name to you till I'd come three times with you—at least. He told me, sometimes the second time you shoot a load into a cocksucker's face, then they've had enough and they're gonna get up and run off, and you never see 'em again. Guys like him and me, see, we can't take shit like that. Mad Man Mike, he says I'm just like him, when he was a kid. And he told me, don't even bother sayin' anything personal to somebody before the third load—with me, it's three loads and some piss, too. Maybe it's that way with him—he ain't never said. But we're just alike, him and me. Anyway, I wanted to ask—"

"What did you want to ask?"

"Can I turn you out?"

I took another swallow of beer. "What do you mean?"

"Would you like for me to turn you out? Don't you know what it means to turn somebody out?"

"I'm not sure," I said. "I don't think so."

"You know, like when a guy's workin' a bitch, see? And he wants to show her what a good whore she is; so he goes and gets all his friends, see? And they all come up and fuck her—they take turns. Or sometimes they do it all at once. After that, the bitch knows she's really a part of everything that's goin' on with 'em, 'cause she's fucked all the guys at the same time. That's turnin' a bitch out."

"I've heard the term," I said. "But I'm still not exactly sure—"

"I got friends." He nodded deeply. "I got some friends in this park. I could go get some of 'em, bring 'em back here—I could be back in twenty minutes, I bet. And we could all party down—'cause you're a good cocksucker, man. I mean, I know they'd like it. Mad Man Mike—like I say, man: you like me, I know you'd like him. We're real tight, and we like pretty much most of the same stuff, him and me. He knows a whole lot, too, about how to get over, if you're after this kind of stuff. And I was tellin' you about my friend, who likes to eat shit? And Big Buck? He's another black guy—but he's real nice. He's got a big black cheesy dick. You like to suck me, you'd like to suck him—wouldn't you?"

"Well, I don't know," I said. "It sound kind of complicated, for right now—"

"It ain't complicated. I'd put my pants on, and run right down there—I know where these guys hang out. They like to party just as much as I do." He was standing up now and reached down for his filthy trousers.

"Hold on, now," I said. "Come on, Crazy Joey—there." I reached up and took hold of his cock.

With his pants on one leg, he stopped and grinned down. "Oh, shit..." he said. "The nigger done got me by my fuckin' dick again!"

It had gone down halfway, but not all the way. As I rubbed it though, it began to swell. "You're supposed to be able to come ten times. Let me see you make number four."

"*Awwww...*" he said, real fondly. He turned around to face me, still holding his beer. "Suck it, nigger..."

So, on my knees in front of him, I got his fourth load in what, I swear, had to be under an hour and a quarter since we'd been together.

Sometime in it, his pants came off again. Sitting beside me, after he was finished, he flung an empty beer can off into the trees and asked me: "You ready to go again?"

"Are *you?*"

"*Yeah*, man!" He put his arm around me, and pulled me over. For about three minutes we sat there, wiggling our tongues inside each other's mouths. Then he was pushing me down on him, and his schlong rose up again to prod my face.

We did it three more times after that! Between numbers six and seven, we both lay down beside each other on the cardboard and talked awhile—him mostly about being in the "crazy hospital" and some about living on the street. But he didn't bring up turning me out anymore—for which, I guess, he got points.

"I have to take a leak," I told him.

"Go ahead," he said. "The world's your fuckin' toilet, nigger! And don't forget it—that's what Mad Man Mike says."

Laughing, I got up, went to the edge of the cardboard, and began to pee off the edge into the leaves. A minute later, I felt something behind me; then Joey's hands came around in front of me and joined in my stream. His chin was propped up on my shoulder behind me (and the downcurve of his dick was pressed between my buttocks), and he was washing his hands in my piss. It was a little messy, but it was kind of sweet.

Afterwards, he told me, sucking first one finger, then another, "I piss on my hands every day, man—makes 'em hard. You ever notice how most homeless guys, they have real soft hands, man? Real soft—that's 'cause there's nothin' for 'em to do out here." (Indeed, it was something I *had* noticed.) "But you piss on 'em, and it keeps 'em rough. For jerkin' off. But sometimes you gotta use someone else's piss besides yours—to change the chemicals and stuff, I guess. That makes sense, don't it? Nigger piss, if you can get it. That's cause it's stronger, or something... Like nigger cum. You know anything about that?"

I had to allow I didn't.

"Now, man, I love a nice soft, wet mouth to stick my dick into. But when I beat off, I need me a little friction, know what I mean? That's why I got to keep my hands on the rough side. You gonna suck me off again, now?"

Before we did it this time, I told him, "My jaw is sore, guy!" And it was, the whole underside—but, for some reason, more on the left than on the right.

"Yeah," he said. "But you love it."

"I do."

"And you wanna see if I can really make another load—all in one afternoon, don't you?"

I nodded. "Yeah."

"So you're gonna suck on my big, nasty dick one more time before you go."

"If you're really horny, why don't you beat off one more time—"

"I will if you'll get down there and make love to my balls and dickhead while I'm beatin', man. I wanna see you lickin' on it and lovin' it for me."

So I did. And ten minutes later, lying there, grunting and bucking his butt up from the cardboard (dried shit in a kind of black powder on the cardboard made a line beneath his ass), while I pressed my face into his groin and his fist banged at my mouth and cheek, he shot all over my forehead and left eye and ear. Again his heavy, rough fingers wiped it off my face and pushed it into my mouth. He didn't seem to want any of his own anymore.

By this time, I'd noticed, there was hardly any dirt left on his hands—I mean even his nails were clean. Which was a sobering thought.

He rolled a little to the side and slid his cock into my mouth again along with his scummy fingers; after I'd sucked them clean, his hands came up to cage my head and he started humping my face *again*—and, hugging my head practically into his stomach, ten minutes later grunted out *another* load!

When we got our breath back, I told him, "I think I'm going to have to go. I mean, if you're okay…?"

"Sure," he said. "I can stand it now, I guess. I'm gonna have to jerk off a couple of times more before I go to sleep tonight. But at least now I won't get all sick and crazy." We sat together on the cardboard, him still naked; I'd pulled my pants up to go with the last one—then come inside them, when he'd really got to working on this last one. He said, "But you're going to look for me again, ain't you?"

"I…yeah, I think so."

" 'Cause now you know what I can do. Right? I ain't bad for a fuckin' pervert, am I?"

"No," I said. "You're pretty good."

"You'll see me around, in the park—sometimes out on Broadway, panhandling sometimes. If they don't clap my ass in the crazy hospital again, for pullin' on my dick. But Mad Man Mike, he says I just gotta do what he says, and they'll stay off me. They ain't caught me now for a whole long time—almost three months."

"Yeah," I said. "Well, then, you probably should listen to him."

I stood up.

"Got something for you, to take with you. For a present." He stood, too. Now he bent down and picked up one of the beer cans, emptied it over his mouth, then turned it up and shook out the last few drops.

Lowering it between his legs and holding his schlong, he aimed for the hole and let his glittering waters go, into the opening; pee roared on the can's bottom. As it filled, the roar grew higher, rising like something not quite a musical note. Then it bubbled over the top, wetting his fingers; so he just moved it aside—dropped his dick—and kept on pissing, stream swinging back and forth from splattering from his right foot to the puddling cardboard between.

He held up the can. "Since we're out of cold ones, you just gonna have to make do with a hot one." He took a swig from the can, then held it out to me. "I'll tell you"—his urine still chattered on the cardboard—"it don't taste like nothin', though."

I took it. The can was wonderfully warm. I drank some. "Beer piss." I shrugged. At this point, yeah, it was like drinking hot water. "But at least it's yours."

He pointed off behind me. "You go down along the wall about a hundred yards—" his dick was just dripping now from the skin: drip-drip-drip-drip-drip-drip…drip-drip…drip-drip…drip…drip… drip—"and it gets low enough so you can climb right back over it."

"What are you going to do?" I asked him.

"Beat off…a couple of more times. Maybe take a nap. Whatever."

"Okay." I looked down at his feet—the left one wet with urine—standing on the piss-darkened cardboard where we'd just been lying. In one large stream and three small ones, urine rolled off the edge. And, yes, I thought about Timothy Hasler. But I didn't get down and kiss his foot or anything, which is probably what Tim would have done. Or thought about doing.

I turned, stepped off the cardboard's frayed edge, and started along beside the park's inner wall. Once I looked back.

He'd stretched out on the cardboard—again doing push-ups!

Crossing Amsterdam Avenue, I was drinking the last of his urine from the can, when, in the middle of the street, one of the homeless Hispanic guys always hanging around the church down the block called to me, "Hey! You ain't supposed to be drinking that on the street...!" It was the heavy guy, who always wore the filthy red cap with the visor pointed backward; he kind of startled me, staggering unsteadily toward me. I got a face full of his winey breath. "You ain't suppose to be drinkin' no beer on the street! Gotta have it in a paper bag—or the cops'll bust ya', man...! You got to go to the bodega over there, ask him for a little paper bag—he give it to you, man. He's nice. You put that in the bag, now—then you be all right, you hear me?"

I just grinned, shook my head, and walked on. (Where those aluminum-colored clouds had come from that now grayed half the sky, I didn't know.) I tossed the can in the wire basket on the corner, and some other homeless black guy in a red cap with a plastic garbage bag over his shoulder swung around and went in after it.

The first raindrops peppered my face and the brown-painted stoop as I reached the door.

By the time I got upstairs and looked out my kitchen window, it had become a real cloudburst. It wasn't six o'clock yet, but it was dark enough for late evening, on its way to night. Outside, Amsterdam Avenue simply exploded with rain.

I made myself a cup of coffee, sat at the kitchen table—and thought about going to look for Crazy Joey, offering the guy at least a place to stay out of the wet. But, frankly, it was raining too hard for me to go back out. And I'd probably have no more luck finding Joey in the rain than I'd had finding a Piece o' Shit that first night five years ago.

I took my coffee in the front room, sat down by another streaked window, picked up the receiver, and punched some buttons on the phone. "Hi, Phel? I'm sorry I didn't get by. But it was such a nice day out—and then the rain and everything—"

"That's okay, babes," Phel told me. "I was out for about an hour myself, earlier. I thought maybe you'd come by when I wasn't here and I'd missed you..."

After we hung up, I sat by the water-beaded pane, thinking: That was about the most interesting, if not the best, sex I'd had in three or four years. I'm not going to put it in a journal. I'm not going to write about it in a letter—and I probably won't even mention it to Pheldon. So how would you go about researching something like that in someone's life?

I looked over at the eleven plastic file boxes—maroon, blue, gray—in two rows along the foot of the bookshelf: more than half of them were filled with material on Hasler.

Suppose I was researching, not the life of some genius philosopher with his books and articles and a wake of articulate friends and acquaintances, but rather, a homeless kid in and out of mental hospitals for chronic masturbation and indecent exposure? (I mean, maybe twice in my life I've seen some guy with a dick that big, jerking off at the movies; but, without making a big thing of it, Crazy Joey's was—yes—the largest I'd ever gotten a chance to wrestle with, as it were, in person.) How would I even start?

A notice in the *New York Times Book Review*? ("I would appreciate hearing from anyone with letters or reminiscences of a mule-dicked white kid called Crazy Joey, or—sometimes—Joey-who-needs-a-bath, late of Brooklyn by way of the state mental hospital at Hyde Park, with green eyes, a broken front tooth, and shit in his ass-crack.") Did you go back to the Burger King and ask the manager: "That young man you tossed out of here for masturbating over in the corner last week? While you were throwing him out, he didn't happen to mention his last name or his patient file number from when he was last confined a year or so back, did he?" His real first name, he'd said, was something beginning with M?

Researching Crazy Joey would make researching Mike Ballagio—much less Tim Hasler—look like (my dad would say) "Chopsticks."

As I drank my coffee, gazing out at the streetlights behind the glittering slant of droplets, the downpour smashed into Amsterdam's tarmac—and an unsettling image came to me: naked on his cardboard, the rain decomposing it into mulch around him, Crazy Joey, cross-legged, jerked furiously—rainwater running out his hair, pouring over his shoulders, cascading his hunched-over back, washing his vertebrae's' knobs away, softening his weasely featured face, blunting his knees, dissolving his peach-sized testicles, leaching the green from his eyes, melting away the whites like Lifesavers, sucking at him till he was running, flowing, washing away in the downpour, till there was nothing but his dick and his fist around it, pumping, then only the pistoning of his fist on his cock, when even cock and fist had dissolved to just the pulse, pulse, pulse...

The rain went on all night: really, lying in bed, listening to it— it smacked on the loose window glass at the foot of my bed—I decided that the image was worthy of one of the farther-out entries from Hasler's journals:

A pulse, faintly but firmly repeating, inches from the ground, over some decomposed cardboard below the park's wall, through the night, under sluicing leaves...

Yes, I knew it was only to compensate for the impossibility of the real task I'd envisioned, had anyone ever thought to undertake it. And yet...

Two weeks later, it was raining when I got the phone call:

"Is this Mr. John Marr?" said a kind of clanking woman's voice.

"Yes?"

"This is Almira Adler. I've been under the impression, on and off, that you were about to get in touch with me for what seems to be getting on to several years now. When you sent me your article on 'Meridian,' I sent you, I recall, a rather curt note back. I hope I didn't offend you, and thus dissuade you from—"

"Oh, no!" I said. "No! Not at all. On the contrary, I took it as a compliment!"

"That's very nice of you. Not everybody would—though, indeed, that's how I intended it. Mr. Marr—would you come and see me? I'm calling from California now, but I'm flying into New York on Saturday night. I'll be in the city all Sunday—then I'll be in and out of the city for the next four days. Readings—Harvard, Amherst,

Wellesley...I make this request as an old and infirm woman, asking a favor. You can certainly say no—"

"But I'd be delighted to meet you!" I said. "Really, my not getting in touch with you has just been a kind of shyness—and, yes, I suppose, indolence on my part. But I'd love to make amends. There are so many things I'd like to talk to you about!"

"And there are things I have to speak with you about as well." Her brassy voice had developed a kind of smile in it. (What does a smile sound like over the phone?) "A friend of mine is letting me use her town house while I'm in the city. So if you come Sunday then, for brunch—if that's all right..." She gave me an East Seventy-third Street address.

"I really look forward to meeting you."

"Thank you," she said. "Brunch for me is anywhere between eleven-thirty and twelve. Till Sunday, then."

When I say that I had questions for the Old Poet, you must understand: behind the big file boxes, there were half a dozen smaller plastic boxes full of index cards; one of them held 174 cards, each one with some point I'd wanted to raise at one time or another with Almira Adler—though, the truth is, I hadn't added a card to it for more than four years.

On Saturday night—it was raining again—I pulled the Adler box out from behind the files, sat at the round oak table, and began to flip through some of them.

My first thought was just how silly so many of those questions sounded after all this time. Most were about chronology—where she had been with Hasler when; but Irving's twelve-page "Chronology" (at the bottom of the big carton) had cleared up 85 percent of those. As for the other 15 percent ("Would you happen to remember the precise date you got back from Spain in May of '71 to Breakers' Point and found Tim already there waiting for you?"), they were just not the sort she was likely to have on the top of her head—at brunch seventeen years later.

A lot were interpretive questions, having to do with various of her poems—whether this or that image was a reference to, or a source for, something in one of Hasler's articles. Those I'd simply be too embarrassed to ask, at least on our first meeting. Finally, however, I decided on three questions for the Old Poet—and only if they worked into the conversation.

The first had to do with an eighteen-line poem that had always intrigued me. Adler had written it, I gather, in the late sixties, and the title was in Greek: Περὶ φυσεως. Phel (whom you didn't know had an undergraduate degree in classics from the University of Tennessee, did you?) had translated it for me years ago: "On Nature" (or "Concerning the Natural" or "About Nature"). The irony seemed to be that the poem's topic felt completely artificial. The poet and a young man are in a dark old cellar, full of ancient toys and bric-a-brac—possibly of a library or a bookstore. The young man is, I was sure, Timothy Hasler. ("...I despair / before the cliché of his black / ice-and-almond eyes...") The two look together through dust-covered shelves, until finally they find a manuscript that the young man, at any rate, is excited over. He reads a line from it out loud: "The universe is guided by the foot..."

End of poem.

I'd always had a suspicion that something was going on there, and that it concerned Tim. Tomorrow at brunch, I decided, would be as good a chance as any to ask.

My second question had to do with a phrase you've encountered several times—and have already wondered about—in the course of this telling: "The Mad Man." The reason you haven't encountered more about it here than you have, however, is that if you were an actual Hasler scholar, familiar with the manuscripts, you'd pretty much think you *knew* what the phrase meant—at least when Hasler used it in his journals, a couple of which entries I've quoted for you at the end of Part I.

On the first page of the typescript of "The Black Comet," the longest (and the best, remember) of Hasler's science fiction stories, just below the title, in Hasler's hand, are the words: "The Mad Man," which have been hatched through—though they're still easily legible. Clearly, then, "The Mad Man" was a subtitle, or possibly an alternate title, for "The Black Comet," later omitted or discarded. For in that breakneck galactic adventure, with Lance Chung racing to find the secret of the Star Barons before the return, through its seventy-six year orbit, of the Black Comet— which will signal the Silver Marauders to begin their campaign of terror among the moons of Callisto VII's third gas giant—at one point, when Lance is hunting through the ruins of Silicon City, he sees a madman staggering and raving in the wreckage of that once-great center of miniature electronic production. Then again, at the end, after Lance has restored order among the satellites, and Silicon City is likewise being restored to its former state of glass-and-aluminum glory, Lance sees the madman staggering away, raving through the streets, toward (presumably) Center Section for rehabilitation.

Except...those are the *only* two appearances of any madman in the story; he isn't even really a character, just a sort of narrative decoration, a kind of passing symbol—though of what, it's not particularly easy to say.

Nor is the phrase really written directly *under* the title, when you actually look (regardless of what Aranlyde says in his *Flame!* introduction: "...at one time, apparently, Hasler thought of subtitling the story "The Mad Man" but later crossed it out on the manuscript...." Pfft!): it's slanted, and somewhat off to the left—as though it might have been a note made absently on the paper, *then* crossed out.

Considering the above, one could easily say: since the madman is such a small part of the tale, that's as good a reason as any for Hasler to have abandoned his subtitle. But since the phrase was written in (surely) *after* the manuscript was typed—and the story was told—why even consider it? And if it *is* an extraneous note, what is it a note about?

That—at any rate—was what I intended to ask Adler, fully expecting her to confirm that, indeed, it was only a subtitle, as I'd first thought, and nothing other.

My third question was the most general: five years ago, when she had first decided to cooperate with Irving Mossman, Adler had come up with all sorts of journals and letters and papers Tim had left with her—most of what Irving sent me in Xerox copy. I wanted to ask her if she still held any material back. I planned to be hugely diplomatic: if there was material she had and was still unsure about sharing, I wanted her to know I wholly respected that. But if she could tell me what period it was from, what time it concerned, then I would know at least in what periods lay the gaps in my knowledge.

For the rest, I decided, I'd be as friendly as possible and try to learn as best I could what she wanted of me. (The last thing I did before I went to bed was to go through my files and take out a

Xerox of each of my eight Hasler articles and put them into a manila folder to take with me the next morning—wondering if I would actually be brave enough to give them to a poet with a Pulitzer Prize!) Running over wordings for my three questions, that night I drifted to sleep.

At eleven thirty-five, I rang the bell beside the blank gray door on the black-and-beige facade (the folder under my arm), realizing, as I did so, that it was a private house.

A young woman in brown slacks, a white blouse, and of my own dark complexion answered. "Yes? Can I help you?" Her hair was pulled tightly back, her earrings were large and polished copper, and her accent was a good deal more West Indian than Phel's.

"I'm here to see Miss Adler."

"Certainly. You're Mr. Marr, then?"

"That's right."

"Come right in. She's downstairs in the back." She stood aside to let me into a foyer whose walls were hung with abstract paintings, and in three of whose corners (why not four, I don't know) were large, certainly original, abstract sculptures. "She's expecting you." I was just about to ask, *And what's* your *name?* when it hit me that, however elegant this young woman looked, she was a domestic—not a member of the family. I tried to remember the last time I'd *been* in a house with a cleaning woman, much less a maid, and let her take the lead, to follow her through the next room— a stairway rose up out of it to the right—as traditional in its furnishings as the paintings and sculptures in the foyer were contemporary. But we were only in it the time it took to cross it. In the next room, a broad stairway led down. Below, in front of its landing, a comfortable distance across a tawny rug, set with a small, pudgy couch and several hassocks, was a glass wall, one of whose sliding panels was rolled back.

We went down.

Out in a small New York backyard—no, this was not a yard; it was a brick-walled garden—a woman sat in a wheelchair, near a table and turned somewhat away from me, reading. Her hair was puffy, curly and red. She had on glasses and wore a silver-gray sweater against a chill that simply wasn't to be felt in such an enclosed space at this time of year.

We stepped out onto the walkway, its flags clutched at the edge with ivy.

It's an odd feeling to walk into a garden and realize that the six-foot mobile drifting slowly below the hook sticking out over the shrubs in the corner is a *real* Calder, that the four-foot painted plaster sneaker collapsing elegantly beside the rhododendrons is a *real* Oldenburg.

"Miss Adler, Mr. Marr is here."

The head came up, the book was left in the lap, and the large hands dropped to the wheel's inner rim; the chair turned. "Thank you, Miss McIntyre. That's so good of you to bring him down here. Mr. Marr!"

The chair shot forward; then, ahead of her, her hand was out in the air.

I took it, shook it—as the chair stopped.

Beside me Miss McIntyre laughed. "Mrs. Bacojson, she tell her to call me Bevy. I tell her to call me Bevy. But she always call me Miss McIntyre."

The Old Poet beamed at us. "You call me Miss Adler, dear; and I call you Miss McIntyre—that's only fair. Mr. Marr, how good of you to come see me on a Sunday morning. Would you like a drink? A mimosa? A Bloody Mary? Let me warn you, *I'm* having a martini!" The book in her lap was a trade paperback whose cover showed a power-cable pylon above a dark hill, a pastel bay in the distance backed with mountains and sunset clouds. Its title was *What*, and its author someone named Silliman. "Or, if you'd prefer coffee or tea?"

"Miss Adler, you want anything, you just ring the button. I'll be in the pantry. And you say you and Mr. Marr will want your brunch in…half an hour?"

Adler looked at me, with a nod of mock consideration, as if to say, "That would seem about right…?"

"Fine with me," I said.

"Then, in half an hour, we'll have it! Do sit down—do sit down! Since I'm always sitting myself, forget there aren't chairs around for other people. Now let's see—"

"Here." I got a wrought-iron-backed chair from under the glass-topped table, on which a whole bar had been set up, as well as a drip coffee maker with a pot on its warmer steaming around the carafe's chromium cover.

I put my article folder down on the chair's gray blue cushion. "Now a mimosa," I said, "that's orange juice and champagne?"

"Right. The juice is in the pitcher there—"

Obviously, I saw as I poured it, it had been freshly squeezed. Open in the ice bucket, the champagne was Taittinger. (No Freixenet within *sight!*) While I took my tulip glass, bubbling at its golden brim, to sit on my folder, Bevy McIntyre disappeared somewhere beyond glass walls. I said, "This is a beautiful place."

"It's awfully convenient of Maggy to let me use it while she's in the Caribbean. I mean, with the whole house staff at my disposal. Maggy and I were at Radcliffe together: I was on scholarship—and she adores modern art! If all of New York were like this, I might move here. But you're curious why I wanted to talk to you."

"Yes. Very much so."

"And doubtless you have questions you want to ask me."

I nodded. "Yes, I do."

"What are they?"

"Well…eh," I sipped. I laughed. "If you really want to know, just like that, I'll tell you: You wrote an eighteen-line poem, back in the late sixties, with a Greek title: *'Peri Phuseos'*—'On Nature.' In it, you—that is to say, the poet—and a young man are in the basement of some cluttered shop, going through old books and papers, and the young man finds something that excites him. I've always assumed that the young man was Timothy Hasler?"

With her elbows on the wheelchair's arms, Adler joined the tips of her fingers. "You assume correctly."

"I was wondering if there was anything else you might tell me about the poem—perhaps about the significance of the title. It suggests some sort of irony, that—well, perhaps I don't fully understand."

She leaned back and looked at me askance. "Now I had heard that you were a student of philosophy—like Timothy. Surely the title didn't escape you?"

I frowned.

" *'Peri Phuseos'*—'On Nature,' as you say—is the title of the lost treatise of Heraclitus. Presumably the hundred-ten odd fragments that are all we have of Heraclitus's work come—most of them—from the *Peri Phuseos.* "

Now I laughed. "You know, I just wasn't thinking in that direction." At one point, yes, I *had* known that. But, I confess, I hadn't known it for a long, long time. "Then the last line," I said, "that the young man reads from it: 'All things are guided by the foot.' That must be a play on the Heraclitus fragment, 'All things are guided by the lightning,' or '...by Zeus's Power,' or '...by Zeus's bolt,' or '...by God's power," or however you choose to translate it."

"That's right. As I recall, when I wrote it, Tim and I were in New York together, back when I was at the Poetry Project at St. Mark's. Tim and I had gone book hunting among those wonderful secondhand book shops—there were still half a dozen of them left back then, on Fourth Avenue. Tim was talking about the Heraclitus—and the lost philosophical treatise. And how, perhaps, someday, somebody might be looking in the lower shelves of a place such as we were in and actually come across it. Then he pretended he'd found it—it was terribly funny. Only, when he started reading out the lines with recognizable fragments, they were all wrong and mixed up. Yes, like, 'All things are guided by the foot,' instead of 'by the lightning.' At the time it was very funny and made us both laugh a lot. Talking about it after all these years, it sounds sophomoric. But, yes, that's what the poem was about."

" '...guided by the foot,'" I repeated. "Well, that certainly makes sense in terms of Tim."

"It was just a bit of nonsense he came up with, on the spur of the moment."

"Of course," I said. "But then, given his thing about feet, it's rather meaningful nonsense, don't you think?"

She frowned. "Meaningful? In what way?"

"Well, I just mean..." Then I frowned back. "Well, you knew of course that Tim was gay. And I guess, with his thing for men's feet, I just meant that, for Tim, yes, all things might well have been guided—for him—by the foot...so to speak."

"Yes, of course I knew Tim was gay. But, no, I *didn't* know anything about...well, that he had a thing for...*feet*, as you just told me!"

"Oh!" I *was* surprised. "Well, there's great a deal about it in his journals—all through them, in fact." I said it carefully, though.

"Ah," she said. "Well, of course, I never *read* Tim's journals while he was living. And, indeed, though, after he died, I read a page or two of the ones he'd…left with me, I could never bring myself to sit down and really read them through—I mean, he hadn't given me permission to do that. You see, we were very close, Tim and I. Very close—far too close for me to betray his trust in me by doing something like that."

"So Tim's"—I took another sip of my mimosa, realizing that this was not at all going to be a conversation like the one I'd had with Darmushklowsky—"foot fetishism was never something he talked about with you."

"Sex in general was something Tim and I didn't discuss—very much. I'm sure he felt it was a kindness to me. And, frankly, it was as a kindness from him that I accepted that reticence. Foot fetishism? Until this moment, I would never have thought about it in terms of Tim. I'm not sure I want to start!"

"What *did* you talk about?"

She smiled. "Poetry." She reached for her broadly flared glass, from the table beside her, with its chill sea of vodka, and sipped. "And philosophy."

"But of course," I said, and realized that, presented with the obvious, I felt I had nowhere to go. "Perhaps," I said, "you should tell me what you wanted to ask *me* about?"

She looked at her lap. She raised her eyes and, through her glasses, looked a bit above me. Then her eyes—dark and fine—dropped to catch mine:

"I want to know who killed Tim—and why."

When I remained silent, she went on:

"In your researches, you wouldn't have happened to have found out, would you?"

"No." I shook my head. "I know some of the circumstances—but, really, in this case, I'd be very surprised if I knew anything more than you."

"He was stabbed to death in a parking lot behind a gay bar called the Pit. And it was not a *nice* gay bar," Adler said. "It was an evil place, full of evil young men trading on the desires of pathetic older men—that's how it was described to me by someone who went there and came back to tell me about it. And though I didn't say anything, I was perfectly furious at Roger for talking about it that way, because I really felt that if Tim *had* gone there—for any reason whatsoever—to reduce it to such absurd and moralistic terms was to preclude ever finding out actually *what* went on!" She took a deep breath.

"The police never found out who did it." Saying that, I felt I was reading a line out of a really poor detective novel. But we always revert to received language when we're at a loss.

"In a place like that—though I've never been there—I suspect the police are not very likely to find out very much anyway. Have you ever made inquiries, Mr. Marr?"

I shook my head. "It's been years. And I—well, I somehow never thought—I mean..."

"*Would* you make them?" she asked. "For me, if I asked—if I begged you to?"

"But why, after all this time, do you—"

"If I don't find out how Tim really died, Mr. Marr," she said, "I'm afraid I shall go to my own grave convinced that *I* killed him! And I don't know whether I could stand that." Again she raised her eyes to mine—then raised her martini.

I don't know why I felt so accused. But because I couldn't look at her, I watched the bright apostrophe of lemon peel rocking in her glass. "That's a very harsh thing to say about yourself." In California where she'd come from, it occurred to me, it was three hours earlier. I tried to think about drinking martinis before nine in the morning. "You were in Breakers' Point, California. Tim was killed here in New York. In what way do you feel responsible?"

"Well, you went quite to the center of it with your very first question, Mr. Marr. Tim and I were very good friends, over many years...well, over eight years." She paused. "Though it seemed like many years when it was happening, when I look back on it now, it seems all too brief a period. While he was alive, I would have easily called Tim my best friend. And on more than one occasion he told me that I was *his* closest friend. Yet the fact is, I was never very accepting of Tim's sexuality—though I never would have said that at the time. After all, I accepted *him*, didn't I, even though he *was* gay? Shit"—and I was startled to hear this sixty-year-old woman spit out the scatologue—"five out of six of my male friends were— and *are*—gay! I'm something of a fag hag—and have been one pretty much most of my life: fag hag—that's the term they used ten or twelve years ago. Do they still?"

"Perhaps," I said. "Not as much as they used to."

She *humphed*. "I first met Tim when I was doing a reading tour, going to various colleges, doing poetry workshops and giving talks. Stilford was the second or third on my itinerary, back in March of '64—"

"'Sixty-five," I suggested; then wished I had remained silent; but really, for better or for worse I'd almost memorized Mossman's chronology.

She hesitated. "Yes…I suppose it *was* '65, now you mention it— since it was a year before I was in New York, at the Poetry Project. And that was *definitely* '66." (I was glad the correction—unnecessary, since *I'd* remembered the proper date, even if she hadn't— hadn't derailed her. I resolved to be quieter.) "I'd given a reading at Stilford, and at the reception afterwards there was this wonderfully charming, intelligent, fun, and attentive Oriental young man of about twenty-one or twenty-two, with whom I just had *so* much fun! I've been in this wheelchair since I was nine years old; and he was perfectly happy to wheel me everywhere—and joke about it! Which was a lot better than the *very* morose woman they'd first assigned to get me up and down curbs and over thresholds. Then he showed up in my poetry workshop the next day, and I discovered, somewhat to my embarrassment, that he wasn't a poet at all, but a philosopher. Though I must admit, he was extraordinarily well read in poetry. As I recall, afterward we got into this wonderful discussion of Ashbery's *Tennis Court Oath*, which hadn't yet come out in the '67 edition. There was only that little Wesleyan book, from '62. That's when I'd first read it—in '62 or '63; but he'd just gotten hold of it a few months before, and was absolutely on his ear over it. 'There was no turning back but the end was in sight,' I remember, he kept quoting; and 'Naked men pray the ground and chew it with their hands.' I mean, back then, outside of New York, you just didn't *find* youngsters who knew about, much less who liked, poetry of that sort. Do you know Novalis's remark about the division between the poet and philosopher being only apparent and to the disadvantage of both? Novalis goes on to say that such a separation is a sign of disease and of a sickly constitution—one presumes he means in the society that accepts such a division. Well, I remember thinking that Tim was a marvelous sign for the health of the whole society—it *was* the sixties, of course. At that time, you saw such signs everywhere you turned. A little later, one of the other teachers told me some more about him—that he was something of a celebrity in his own right, already having been rather a prodigy. (And he *was* from New York, after all—which probably explains some of it.) He'd just been in some awful trouble at the university over some stories that he'd published—they actually turned out just to be a couple of dreadful science fiction tales in some ghastly pulp magazines. He was supposed to have been accused of plagiarizing something from one of his own students—not that he did, I'm sure. I can't believe Tim would ever have done *anything* like that! But it had gotten quite out of hand, I gather. Though Tim was the sort of person who just attracted attention with pretty much everything he did. I invited him to come down and see me at the Point. And he did—three times over that first spring and summer. And we always had a marvelous time—I hope some day *you* get a chance to visit. The Sur is such a wonderfully therapeutic landscape.

"But there is an incident I remember—from his second or third visit. And, no, I'm really not sure which it was. My friend Roger was also out at the Point with us—Roger's a painter, and is my age—actually a little older. And gay. It was Roger who, after a day or two, first told me that Tim was queer—that's the term we used back them. I was really quite surprised! He just looked at me and said, 'Well, you've done it again, dear,' meaning that my new young friend, about whom I was so insistently enthusiastic, was, like Roger, another gay man. On the last day of his visit, Tim came to me and asked if, the next time he came up, he could bring a friend with him. I recall it even now—someone called Pete. I just assumed this Pete was a boyfriend of his, and if they both came up, they'd be off together all the time, and I'd hardly see either of them, or they'd be locked up in their room all afternoon doing things that would just embarrass you if you glimpsed them through the window (and the guest rooms are completely glass on one side, so you can't very well *miss* what goes on in them, when you roll past)—or whatever. And heaven help me if they got into some tiff, with one not wanting to do this just because the other did, and me in the middle. So I said, with my biggest smile, 'Absolutely not, darling. While you're here, I want you all to myself!' He looked quite surprised—that was probably the first time I'd ever said no to him about anything. But he seemed to recover fairly quickly—or at least I thought he did. I think I mentioned it to Roger later, and we had a little laugh over it.

"But a little after that—in the evening, when they were out on the deck, and I was coming to join them for drinks, I was still inside and heard them talking—they didn't realize I was there. Tim was saying to Roger, something like, 'I just wanted Pete to come up because I thought she would really *like* him. I'm so awfully fond of him myself. And he's fun, he's obliging, and he plays the guitar—' Goodness, that's *all* I needed—some postadolescent guitar picker, plunking around the house all day and making conversation impossible!

"Then Roger said, I can hear him just as clearly, 'You have to understand, Tim; Almira is just a bit jealous of her friends. While you're with her, she wants all your attention—and she doesn't want it diluted among other people.' And you know, Mr. Marr, I sat there, in my wheelchair, just beyond the door, shocked!"

I frowned.

"What Roger had just said to Tim was almost exactly what I had said to him; yet it seemed to me, back then, as different as black from white. When I said I didn't want to share him, I was sure Tim would understand it as a joke, and realize what I really meant, underneath it. But when *Roger* said I was jealous, I was stunned! Because I realized he believed it. And I realized that Tim would probably believe it too, now!"

I asked: "What *did* you mean, then?"

"I was"—her brassy voice took on a querulous tone, and I wondered if she had had more than that single martini this morning—"I was…well, *protecting* him—at least that's what I thought I was doing: I was protecting him from his own perversions. Good Lord, I'd had enough heterosexual couples out to visit me at the Point. But I wouldn't have dreamed of having a gay couple there. Breakers' Point is beautiful, it's healthy, it's inspiring—"

"It's California, huh?" I smiled when I said it, though, and tried to say it gently.

"Very much so." But now she chuckled. "Oh, this was two years before Stonewall! And I suppose that I had somehow incorporated it into my vision as a place where these poor, wonderful, brilliant—but, I was sure, deeply wounded—creatures could come, and I would hold their sickness at bay, by refusing to let any sign of it within the grounds. And I had considered myself so incredibly witty and diplomatic by disguising it as a kind of flippant jealousy. Only here, someone as close to me as Roger was taking that protestation of jealousy at face value—and, what's more, passing it on to someone—Tim—that I already knew I wanted to be a very good friend."

"If Tim had asked to bring a girlfriend with him next time he visited"—I hazarded—"that is, if he had been straight and had asked you—?"

Sitting back in her chair, Adler raised her martini glass in both strong hands like a chalice before her. "I would have said, 'By all means! Have her on the next bus up. And we'll all have a wonderful picnic together, as soon as she arrives!'" She said it like Pandarus or Rosalind pronouncing an epilogue to Shakespeare.

"You say you wanted to protect Tim. Did you want to protect yourself, a bit—perhaps from what your neighbors might think if they realized you were having gay couples out to visit?"

"Breakers' Point doesn't *have* any neighbors—at least, not within hollering distance! That's one of the things that's so wonderful about it. Really, I wished I *had* felt that way! But I didn't. If it had just been some personal fear, it would have been more forgivable. But really it was just this notion that I could do something for them—especially for someone like Tim, because he was so young— by discouraging him from pursuing men, at least when he was around me!"

"Miss Adler—"

"Oh"—she threw a hand out at me, letting her wrist break—"I like you very much, and you must call me Al. That's what Tim called me. That's what my students have always called me. Please—"

"Al—" I smiled. "I'm going to leave you a bunch of articles, eight of them, I've written—about Tim. One of them is about Tim and Pete—the young man he wanted to bring to meet you out at Breakers' Point, in '65. Was he Tim's boyfriend, back then? Not exactly. Right now he's a happily married software designer, who lives with his Japanese wife in Massachusetts. But if you read what I've written on Tim so far, then you'll know pretty much what I know. You'll also learn that *I'm* gay...."

"Yes, Professor Mossman was rather quick to tell me that, when he was first recommending you."

"And I think, considering both what you've asked me to do, as well as what you've already told me about your own relationship with Tim, that's only fair. More than fair, I think it's imperative. Because if I'm to find out anything on the lines you've asked, there's probably a lot more that I'll have to understand—that I'll have to ask."

"I've read two of your articles. Professor Mossman gave them to me when I made much the same request of him, before he explained he was no longer working on Hasler's 'Life' and referred me to you. But neither one of them was about anyone named Pete—though I rather liked them."

"Thank you."

"If you're at all like Professor Mossman, you've come with a whole list of your own questions, though."

"Not a lot," I said. "Did you ever meet *any* of Tim's lovers?"

Only when she shook her head, negatively, did I realize that I had asked a question not on my list of three.

Then I suddenly thought to ask a question that, again, quite crazily I realized, had never been asked by Mossman, certainly, and so, I supposed, had never been asked by me: "Did Tim *have* any lovers…lasting relationships, I mean?" And while I sat there, waiting for her to answer, I actually felt my cheeks heat and myself grow momentarily dizzy with the maniacal presumptions of those who undertake research: I was twenty-seven and hadn't really had one.

Why should Tim Hasler…?

"Before—I think—I know he had…well, one. Though I never met him. But I remember him mentioning to me—it must have been just after he got back from Chicago—that a friend was staying with him. Then, a few weeks later, he mentioned his friend again—whom I realized was still there. I didn't think anything of it, I just thought it was some school friend who was rooming with him while he was visiting New York. Then, a couple of months on, he said something about getting home to his friend yet again. And I said, 'He's been staying with you quite a long time.' And Tim smiled, with a sort of knowing smile, and said, 'Yes, it's been quite wonderful!' And suddenly it struck me that this *was* a lover he was talking about. Then, perhaps six months later, when Tim and Roger were both visiting, while I was wheeling myself into the room, I heard Tim telling Roger, 'Well, we finally separated about three weeks ago. It was kind of messy at first—and I was terribly down. It's so odd being a bachelor again. But I'm holding together, I suppose'—some comment like that. And I realized that whatever the affair had been, it was over! But nobody ever said any more about it—at least to me. But, yes, it was a little surprising to learn that someone as close as Tim and I were could have gone through a whole live-in romance—even one that lasted less than a year—without my really knowing anything about it."

"Do you remember the person's name?"

"I think his name was…you know I *don't* remember it, after all this time. I don't think Tim *said* the name to me more than once or twice. David, Donald, Denton…or maybe something else entirely? Was it Michael? Was it Billy? But, again, I'm not sure. What I always used to try to do, you understand, when anything like that came up—with Tim, or with Roger, or, indeed, with any of my gay male friends, was *not* to think about it! If I could put it out of my mind, then perhaps they could put it out of theirs. And when I realized, say, that it was something that Tim and Roger discussed anyway, when I was out of the room, I felt a sort of failure—that, somehow, I was letting them down and had to try harder."

"How did it make you feel—how does it make you feel now—to know, for instance, that your best friend was a foot fetishist? And that you didn't know it?"

She laughed. "Mr. Marr, we're talking about the epoch of the faked orgasm! At that time, husbands didn't know things that were going on—or not going on, as the case may be—in their wives' *bodies* while they were in the midst of the sexual act itself! I daresay there were thousands of *wives* who didn't know that their husbands were shoe fetishists! It could very easily be something you didn't know about a friend—so it's just not something you can make me feel guilty over today, given the times back then. It only means you're young and weren't there—or don't remember them very well."

"There are no references to live-in love affairs all through Tim's journals." I shrugged. "There is a fair number of descriptions of casual sex. But nothing about long-term affairs or enduring sexual relationships. But then, there's no reference to a live-in roommate, during the year he came back from Chicago, either."

"I'm not surprised." The yellow twist was now merely a flaw at the all-but-empty glass's vortex. "Again, you must remember the times—especially the times before '69. And even in the two or three years after. I said I wanted to protect Tim by keeping all overt mentions of homosexuality out of our relationship. If Tim cared for somebody, cared for him in a truly committed fashion, he might well have wanted to protect him in the same way—"

"But I don't—"

"Protect him from blackmail—that was still possible, remember, for someone who wasn't, as they say today, out. And he may also have felt that, at the same time, he was protecting him in that odd way that I spoke of. If you did have a relation with someone about whom you cared, you might very possibly never mention it—in a journal—simply from fear that it might be discovered, misunderstood, and misused—to hurt you and, even more, hurt the person you loved."

"That makes a kind of sense," I said. I don't know why I felt uncomfortable with it, though. And I decided I'd better get back to my own plan. "One of the things I was going to ask you was if you new anything about 'The Mad Man'—the subtitle for 'The Black Comet.'"

She nodded slowly, smiling. "Oh, yes—one of Tim's stories. We corrected the galleys together for that one, out at Breakers' Point, the last time he was there."

"It was the last of the stories he published while he was alive. 'The Mad Man' was written on the title page of the manuscript, under the typed title, like a subhead."

She considered a moment. "I had a friend once, many years ago, a fellow I met in Europe, actually, who told me: 'One must listen to madmen—they are becoming increasingly rare.' I haven't seen him in more than twenty years. But I wonder what he'd think now, when our country's squares and avenues are full of them, and they stand, filthy and gibbering, barely able to hold out their cups, practically on every street corner."

"Today," I said, "you have to be more careful to watch out for counterfeits. If everyone I heard called mad around me really was, the world would run as a *very* odd machine. The fact is, not all of those men and women *are* mad. The statistics, if you're interested, are that about a third suffer from some form of mental problem. Another third suffer from drug and/or alcohol abuse. And a third are there because they haven't got any money and can't afford to be anywhere else."

"I'm sure you're right," she said. "But that's rather ghastly in the land of the free, the home of the brave." She looked around on her lap, as though searching for papers or pages. "—I'm glad it wasn't like that when Tim was here—" but they were not there. "There's a madman in Tim's story, isn't there?" She looked at me again.

"Yes," I said. "But he plays a very small part."

Again she looked down. "What I remember is this—but let's have them bring in that brunch! Or I'll be so sloshed there won't be any talking to me!" Reaching over to the table again, she lifted a small black plastic rectangle that looked like a TV set's remote control. After looking at it a moment, she sort of collapsed back in her chair. "My father always had a housekeeper. I have a woman who comes in twice a week and does cleaning and shopping for me out at Breakers' Point. But, really, though I love Maggy like a sister, the idea of *ringing* for servants...I find that appalling!"

I said (and tried to sound nonthreatening, even friendly): "You have to be used to servants in order to prefer calling them by one method rather than by another."

Glancing at me, she smiled oddly. "You're very sharp, Mr. Marr. I like that." Then she bounced her forefinger on some button on the black plastic. (In another room—the pantry—I heard a buzzer growl.) "I didn't eat *anything* on the plane last night— I'm famished!"

Less than a minute later, two dark-skinned women in gray uniforms with white aprons—neither of them Bevy—came out into the garden with a large tray that held a platter of scrambled eggs and dish of small sticky buns and one of bacon and sausages and a bowl of strawberries and fresh pineapple chunks and a platter of smoked salmon and sliced cucumbers and a bowl of incredibly rich yogurt— at my first taste I thought it was pure cream. "This is quite a feast!"

One of the women was still trying to position the little fold-out table in front of Adler's bulky chair. "Really, that's fine! No, that's fine! I'm quite used to it, eating with it there." At last she backed away about a foot, turned the chair to the bar table, and, with a despairing air, poured another martini from the pitcher there, from which a bamboo stirrer thrust up, topped by a gold ram's head.

The women left. (By the time they did, I was fairly sure neither they nor Bevy had cooked any of the stuff requiring cooking. Who, I wondered, in this day and age, keeps a staff of four live-ins—especially when they're in another country?)

Back at the table, with her refilled martini glass (and only some strawberries and two strips of bacon on her plate), Adler told me, "The last summer Tim came to see me, he asked me—again—whether he could bring out a friend." She looked pensive for a moment. "He did it the first time he came. He did it the last time. But never any others. You know, things really had changed: Stonewall had happened—and we'd certainly talked about it. And that time I very nearly said yes. But then, you see, that had never *been* part of our relationship. I asked him, I remember: 'Is this someone you're involved with?' He nodded. And I said, 'I don't know, Tim. I'd probably be more comfortable if you didn't.' 'Of course,' he said, bubbly and happy as usual. 'I understand perfectly!' And I thought it was over. But—and I had the impression he'd planned what he was going to say next—he told me: 'That means I'll only able to stay between a week and ten days—rather than the whole summer, the way we talked about. I'll have to get back to the city. You understand, don't you?' Now it was my turn to say, 'Of course,' though really I was a little hurt; perhaps by now I *was* jealous—in precisely the way Roger had once suggested. 'But you have to stay the whole ten—eleven or twelve if you can.' 'Ten,' he said. 'But they'll be a wonderful ten, Al. I promise.' He really was sweet that way. So we arranged that he would come out for ten days toward the beginning of June—then fly back to New York." Again she was quiet a while, above untasted strawberries and bacon. "And so Tim came out to see me at Breakers' Point for ten days." She sighed. "And was murdered in that bar back in New York, not a full three months later. But there, you wanted to know how I could feel responsible for Tim's death, thousands of miles away on the other side of the country?" And her eyes came up again to mine. "If I'd been a little more accepting—a little less jealous—and said, 'Yes, of course you can bring your friend out for the summer. We'll all have a wonderful time together, the three of us. And when Roger comes up, he'll join us—and so will Stan, and Gene, and Maggy...' and Tim had stayed through till it was time for him to return to classes at Stilford. Well, if I'd done that, Tim might very well be alive today."

She forked a strawberry from the plate, ate it, put down her fork with the finality of breakfast over, and lifted her glass again. "But you'd asked about 'The Mad Man.' "

I took another sticky bun—then got up and made myself another mimosa.

She waited till I was seated again.

"I'm sorry," I said. "Go on."

"I'd always ragged Tim unmercifully about his science fiction stories. I don't think I ever read more than two and a half of them—but his sense of prose, at least when he was writing that stuff, was this Gosh! Wow! Blammy! pulp-magazine hyperbole, like something out of the nineteen thirties! There was something in practically every other paragraph to make you laugh out loud! But I suppose, after I got over being angry at him, I was feeling guilty about having cut off our summer together like that. The day after he arrived, he mentioned he was expecting galleys of a new story—and had given them my address. And, sure enough, after two days, there was a special delivery—" She stopped. " 'Special delivery'—now, *there's* a term you don't hear much anymore! But there was a special delivery postal truck at the gate: Tim's galleys had arrived. As he was bringing them in, I told him, 'I'll help you with those.' 'Oh, you don't have to,' he said—I know he knew how I felt about them. 'No,' I told him. 'I want to. I'm not going to tease you about them, either. I'd really like to help.' 'Well,' he said, 'it would be nice to have another set of eyes go over them before it was published.' So, a little later, he brought them in, and we set ourselves up on the porch at the back of the tower, there on the stone table. He had the original typescript, and the long, flimsy galley sheets, in that narrow-column print the magazines used.

" 'They want us to make as few changes as possible,' he told me. 'So, if you see something that you think is a mistake, check it against the original typescript. I can have a handful of author's corrections, but not many more.' We got started reading. He went faster than I did, of course, so while he read the first galley sheet, I just waited—till he went on to the second. Actually it was great fun, and I think perhaps this story was better than the others I'd read."

"It's really quite good." I smiled.

"I don't know whether I'd say *that*." She smiled back. "But it wasn't quite as *painful* as the others—though it may just have been because of the attention I was paying to it. I made half a dozen suggestions—you know: that he choose *one* of the three adjectives he'd appended to some helpless noun and omit the other two. And we managed to get a couple of sentences close to something resembling parallel structure without moving *too* much type. I remember, Tim was one of those people who always wrote 'different than,' rather than 'different from'—and it used to drive me up the wall! Though I notice even the *New York Times* lets 'different than' slide by these days." She sighed. "And nobody thinks of the *Times* as an arbiter of English usage anymore, anyway..." She shrugged. "Some days I just feel more and more of a mastodon. Tim was wonderfully sweet about accepting my suggestions."

"I'm sure they were good ones."

She shrugged again. "It was a beautiful morning, sitting there with him on the porch, being quiet together and reading galleys—listening to a sandpiper rattling around in the sword grass outside. I was just sitting out there yesterday, before I started off for the airport, thinking about that morning in 1973. It was almost as if, if I'd looked up at the proper moment, I might have caught Tim, still there—it was a moment, really, that you wanted to go on and on. And, I like to fancy, somewhere, perhaps it is....

"Tim finished before I did, and once I glanced up to watch him. He had his pencil out, and he reached over to where the original manuscript lay between us on the table—and he wrote 'The Mad Man' across it, under the title. Then, immediately, he crossed it out with a handful of slant lines." She took a long, slow drink.

After a moment, I asked, "Did he say anything?"

"No."

"Did you ask anything?"

She shook her head again. "No."

"Then it was just a thought for a possible subtitle—that went in and out of his head that morning. He jotted it down—and immediately crossed it out."

"Possibly," she said. "Possibly it was a thought about something else entirely, and he just used the manuscript to jot it down on—before he crossed it out."

I nodded. "I knew it was written on the manuscript after the story was typed up. But I didn't realize that it came after it was set in type and the galleys were corrected. You really make it sound like one of those mysteries of flickering consciousness we'll be unable to fathom."

"Possibly."

"The only thing," I said, "is that, from time to time he refers in his journals to 'The Mad Man'—something he's writing. Do you think that might have been his private name for *The Black Comet?*"

She smiled. She shrugged. Clearly that was her answer.

"May I ask you one more question?"

"Certainly."

"Tim left an incredible amount of stuff—journals and letter drafts and papers—with you. Manuscripts and things. Indeed, there's so much, I get the impression he must have been storing things with you for years."

"Do you?" She took a breath. "Tim left nothing with me—save the letters he sent me. As close as we were in some ways, as you can now understand, a great deal of his life was completely closed to me—very possibly because I wanted it that way. But for just that reason, Tim would probably never have left a journal—or some piece of writing that touched on his private life—with me. He didn't trust me, if you like. He didn't want to offend me—or shock me, perhaps. Or alienate a friend."

"Than how did you get all the stuff you passed on to Irving Mossman?"

"Your Professor Mossman made the same assumption you did." She looked thoughtful. "It's only natural, I suppose. And I certainly didn't do anything to disabuse him of the notion. But that's because, at that time, I felt I didn't want to know anything at *all* about Tim's death. It was part of the ugly and tragic sector of his life I had nothing to do with—and I wanted it to stay that way. But Tim's reputation as an important philosopher had started several years before he died, and he was very happy about it. He wrote several of his articles during his visits with me at the Point. It was only because of the attention he'd started to receive from a small group of academic philosophers that he was reinstated in graduate school and given another teaching assistantship for that autumn. And he was excited by and about his own work—you asked me what we talked about? Well, his work was a great deal of it, toward the end. Tim thought what he was doing was important—I think he'd be a little amused at the parts of it people find important today. But Tim believed in his own work quite as much as—or more than—any of the commentators who've come after him.

"The night he was killed, here in New York, his wallet was stolen. But he had a small address book inside his jacket pocket. And the New York police were simply going through it, phoning everybody in it, to identify him. So I got a call, on the morning of the twenty-third: they were calling from New York because someone had been murdered and my name and address was in a green pocket address book in his suit jacket. Well, already I knew who it was. Then they said that he was Oriental, a man about thirty..."

She shook her head, a small shudder.

"If they had his address book, they must have called his relatives."

"He didn't keep his sisters' numbers and addresses in his book. Probably he knew them too well. So the police were stuck with a weird gaggle of artists and philosophers, pretty much scattered all over the country. I don't know how many people they called that first morning, but—"

"Adler," I said. "You were probably on the first page."

"I'd never thought of that!" She shook her head again. "But I was going to say that I'm pretty sure, if they did call twenty or thirty people, the particular twenty or thirty they called—all of them professional philosophers or artists of some sort—had as much to do with the initial little surge in Tim's reputation as anything else. Those were the names he kept in that book."

"I see." My plate was down to bacon, which I really like and always eat last. "Then how did you get hold of the material?"

"Roger," she said. "His studio was in New York City at the time. I phoned him immediately—the police had phoned him only moments before. I told him it was imperative that he go to Tim's apartment, bribe the super with up to a hundred dollars if he had to—I would get it back to him—but get the key to Tim's, get in there, and get as many of Tim's papers as possible and ship them out to me. I mean, I've known people far more famous than Tim who've died and you wouldn't believe they had ever existed at all. When lonely old Wystan Auden died, his apartment down on St. Mark's Place was left wide open for a year! People were walking in and out of it, taking letters, paper, even furniture. I don't think the estate executors ever *did* get down there to check it over for papers! Well, Roger took his van up to Eighty-second Street—it cost him, I gather, the full hundred. But three weeks later, I received three cartons of Tim's papers: the ones I gave copies of to Professor Mossman five years ago."

"The ones he passed on Xerox copies of to me," I said. "Did you pass them all on to Mossman? Or are there perhaps some more—"

"Please," she said. "Would you let me finish this—it's not an easy thing to tell. But if you're going to help me, you'd better know this."

"Of course."

"The night the papers arrived, I got a call from Roger. 'Yes,' I told him, 'I'd just received them that morning.' 'Getting them wasn't very easy,' he told me. 'I don't mean bribing the super, either. Do you want to hear the details? They're not very pretty.' 'Of course I do,' I told him. And I really thought I did. 'It's probably going to be very hard on you,' he said. 'But you may just want to know, for Tim's sake.'" She looked down, looked up, looked at me. "The super wanted to go in with him, to make sure Roger was taking only papers. But when the super opened the door and they got four or five steps down the hall, the super said, 'Christ, I'm not cleaning *this* place out!' Apparently the stench was overwhelming. 'I really thought,' Roger told me, 'we were going to find another body in here, decaying somewhere. Tim's apartment was a sty...a shambles, an abattoir.' The paint was hanging in sheets from the ceiling, in what Roger said looked like water damage. Furniture was overturned! Books were off the shelves, clothes were out of the closets—and a pile of them had apparently been urinated on and defecated on—repeatedly! Food was strewn about—he said there was a roast beef rotting in an armchair in a crust of blood! Roger said that excrement was smeared over the walls! A mirror was broken near the wall. Another one leaned against a couch—excrement had been stuck on both. Furniture was overturned. Books had been pulled from the shelves. There were a couple of stains on the carpet that Roger thought were blood, but they were apparently fairly small—thank God! The stench suggested that every corner had been used for a urinal. The word '*Ekpyrosis*' had been written in shit, twice on the walls and once on the inside of a window. Roger said he didn't think one person could have done it all. He said five or six people might have produced that much excrement and filth if they'd worked at it every day for a week. In the bedroom, he said, the mattress was drenched—certainly with urine. The sheet, fouled, had been pulled off. There were signs that someone had gotten dressed recently—probably Tim. And the super said he'd seen Tim go out of the building the previous day looking perfectly ordinary—though, Roger said, the idea of somebody actually *living* in there was almost unbelievable!"

I said: "Good *Lord!*"

"Tim's papers, Roger told me, were, if anything, fairly easy to find—once he realized that they were in the boxes in the back room. There were two cartons of notebooks, a box of manuscripts, and several piles of fugitive papers. Tim had quite a library, as you might have imagined; and I'd even said something about getting Tim's books. But Roger said a third or more of the volumes had simply been ruined. Roger had to take the papers down himself. The super refused to touch the boxes, even though, somehow, they seemed to have escaped most of the vandalism. Only a corner of one of them, Roger told me, was wet."

"That," I said, "is pretty amazing. I know this was a long time ago, and I certainly believe what you're saying. But is there any chance of my talking directly to Roger about this? I mean, if you still want me to…make inquiries, perhaps there's something that I might get from him that he overlooked in telling you—out of delicacy, or possibly just because he forgot it or he—"

She interrupted me. "Roger died a little over a year ago—fourteen months, to be exact—of AIDS. He was with me out at Breakers' Point. He wanted to die there. *I* wanted him to die there. The last few weeks, however, it became too difficult, taking care of him. So we moved—both of us—for his last days, into a hospice, north about forty miles. It was a very beautiful place—but, no, it wasn't the Point."

"Oh!" And I thought, so this is the first time—then, I stopped and thought: looked at properly, it's the second—AIDS has impinged on Hasler studies. "Was Tim a particularly messy person?" I asked. (When I said it, it sounded perfectly silly.) "I mean, there are some people who live simply extraordinarily slovenly lives. I'm just wondering, perhaps—I don't mean to imply that what you described could ordinarily—"

Her voice took on the querulousness again. "He wasn't what I believe they call 'piss-elegant.' But Tim was clean, he was civilized…"

"What I mean, I suppose, is: had you ever been in the apartment yourself before?"

"*Many* times!" she declared. "I went to dinner there, with him, every time I was in New York. I'm not a strict vegetarian, by any means." With her fork, she indicated the uneaten strip of bacon on her plate. "But I tend a bit in that direction. And Tim would always fix a fresh asparagus dinner for me, if he could get it—from the Fairway down on Broadway. I quite loved it, and it was almost a ritual with us. Yes, it was a run-down building, but inside was a warm, charming apartment, with lots of bookcases and wonderful books!"

"I see," I said.

"An abattoir," she repeated. "A sty…"

"It sounds to me, Al—"(I would have been *so* much happier calling that woman Miss Adler; and she could call me Mr. Marr till the cows came home: I like being called "Mister.") "—as if you've decided, at long last, to explore a very odd part of the world. It's a part that lots of people would find simply deranged, disgusting, and without interest—even lots of gay men—no matter which of their friends had been caught up in it. I don't have any problems understanding why it's taken you this long to decide that you wanted to learn the unpleasant and clearly sad details about something that happened in that world. But in the course of coming to this decision, you must have decided that Timothy was really quite important to you. If I asked you why Tim was so important, could you tell me?"

She took a long breath, recovering, I guess, from the description of Hasler's apartment. "You *are* very sharp, Mr. Marr. I must have been interviewed a dozen times in the last three years, and at least a third of the interviewers felt obliged to sound very knowing about the relation between Hasler's philosophy and Adler's poetry. But you're the first person who has ever asked the question that simply and succinctly. Myself, I've always wondered why people don't— because it has such a simple answer. A lot of my early poems try to get back to that place before thoughts are clothed in language. Very early on in our friendship, when Tim and I were talking about this, he said to me, 'Al, that's perfectly silly. Thoughts are *never* not clothed in language—or, rather, that's not the relation between thought and words: the relation between a body and a suit of clothes. Thought is part of language. But everything we perceive, either through our senses, or through our bodily feelings, or through sitting in the dark with our eyes closed, remembering or thinking or figuring, *is* the linguistic signified. The whole range of human perceptions, of subject and object, *is* the "meaning" part of language. So a thought doesn't come "without words." It comes first as simple language—simple meanings, if you will. Then, what we call "thinking about it" is just the arrival of *more* complex language that elaborates on it—that's all. Once the elaborated language has come, we remember the simpler language as somehow prelinguistic. But it isn't.' Then he said, 'It would be very useful for a poet to remember that simpler language in which a thought or feeling first arrived. But to look for a thought *before* language is to look for something that isn't there.' And I cannot tell you, Mr. Marr, what a useful insight that was. For a poet. I would like to think all my poetry since that discussion has, to some extent or the other, reflected it."

I nodded. Than I asked, "Did you tell any of this to Professor Mossman—I mean, about the state of Tim's apartment at the time he was killed?"

"Some of it," she said. "I didn't tell him that Roger had taken the papers. I let him believe Tim had left them with me. But I told him I had a firsthand account of Tim's apartment on the day after he was killed. And I described it for him—yes."

Now I grew pensive. "He never told any of this to me."

"I asked him not to," Adler said. Her second martini was finished. "I told him I would rather tell you about it myself. I felt it was a delicate subject—and it is. As they pass from person to person, things can get very distorted—especially things of this sort. That's when he said he would write you and have you get in touch with me. But you never came to my reading—I believe that night I'd left a ticket for you at the door."

"I'm very sorry," I said.

"But it was raining," she concluded. "And I'm not sure if, at that point, I was ready to ask you what I've asked you to do now, anyway."

Walking up the steps to my fifth-floor apartment, I stopped on four and looked at Hilda Conkling's door. A year or so ago, when I'd last been inside her apartment, it had looked exactly like mine: walls and bookshelves painted, floors scraped and polyurethaned. I tried to imagine entering it, sixteen years before that, to find the filth and stench Adler had described.

Had Roger and the super—two before Jimmy—smelled any of it in the hall?

How long had it been that way—and what, indeed, were the steps in the transformation between an apartment where you would happily invite a wheelchair-bound poet for a fresh asparagus dinner (How, I wondered, did she make it up these steps? Roger and Tim carried her, of course—I found out later) and the sink of filth Roger had walked in on the morning after Tim Hasler had been stabbed down at the Pit off Times Square?

How much, I wondered, of what Adler had told me, as I turned to go up the last flight, had prompted Irving's distaste for Hasler? How much of that had influenced his reading of the graphic few sexual encounters here and there in Hasler's journals that so revolted him?

Reaching my own door, I went inside.

The first thing I did was go to my own little clutch of books on Heraclitus and, in a concordance, look up "*Ekpyrosis.*" Yes, it was—as I'd suspected—a term in the pre-Socratic philosopher's vocabulary: it meant "conflagration" or "apocalypse," and, as used by the philosopher, is generally assumed to refer to the end of the universe, when everything, according to Heraclitus, would collapse into fire.

Should I, I wondered, *be* the person to explore such a world—for Almira Adler or anyone else?

I though about it on my trip out to the store and thought about it some more when came back and decided to take a nap. I was thinking about it when I got up and decided to call Phel—with whom I did *not* discuss it. But, half an hour later, when I put the phone down, I wondered if the fact that I wasn't really comfortable talking about it with Pheldon wasn't something that I ought to take into consideration in making my decision. I was thinking about it an hour later when I went out again to visit four of the neighborhood's bookstores, during which visits resolutely I bought nothing; I was coming out of the Gryphon Book Shop, when I heard the clink of change in a cardboard coffee-to-go cup. I looked up—

He was just as stocky, just as grubby. Through his red hair, though, and at the sides of his beard, a gust of ash had blown (really, that's the first thing I thought), lightening streaks in it to gray. Ahead of me, a couple of college kids dropped some change in his cup and strode by, happy with the beggar's mumbled blessing.

I slowed. "Hey," I said, "you with the warts on your cheesy fat dick! How long have you been back around here?"

Tony turned to me—cup out. Then, within his beard, his grin bloomed. He lowered the cup again. "How're you doin', professor? I wondered if I was gonna run into you. But I figured you probably wasn't living around here no more."

"No, I'm still in the same place."

"Hey professor, it's real good to run into you!" He frowned, suddenly, pulled back, and raised one big hand to touch a knuckle to my temple. "Now what the fuck is *that?* You mean to tell me, I go away from here for a couple or three years, and when I get back, you gone and gotten *older?* That ain't right, man. We ain't *supposed* to get older, now—not us. That ain't supposed to happen to you and me!"

I just laughed—yes, I'd gotten these gray spots on my temples in the last year (my dad was gray by the time he was twenty-five); but not as much gray as Tony, a handful of years my senior, had picked up.

"You been in Florida?"

"I been lots of places, professor—never did get to Florida, though. But I got out to Seattle—and got me into jail!"

"Jail?" I said. "What for?"

He gave a humph. "Guess it won't hurt none to tell you, but you got to keep it to yourself, now. For walkin' around naked at three o'clock in the mornin' in Pioneer Square."

"You gotta watch out for that stuff, Tony," I told him. "We like you around this neighborhood—when you do that stuff, you have to be careful."

"I *am* careful, man," Tony said. "Most of the time—damn, professor. A whole lot in this neighborhood has changed so much. The Burger King's all different—" which was true: they'd redone the whole inside a couple of years back, getting rid of the Pepto-Bismol-colored fiberglass booths and putting in a salad bar, then getting rid of that, and putting in all these little plant holders on these new white-and-green partitions. "They closed down the Red Apple," which had happened only the week after I'd gone with Crazy Joey to the park; but that meant Tony hadn't been here in the city that long at all. "The store across Broadway, from the Burger King, that Town House thing—"

"Town House West," I said.

"That's all closed up. And the Chinese restaurant on the other side of Eighty-second Street—that's gone now. Didn't we get some food there, you and me, once?"

"Perla del Sur," I said. "That's right—we did. All those Chinese kids who waited table there, first they went uptown—now I don't know where they are."

"I could go in there sometimes, when they was closing, and they'd give me something. But it's closed up now. And all these fuckin' college kids is running around—"

"Yeah, it's changed a lot, Tony. You been over to Amsterdam Avenue, where I live? They've got all these college bars opening up there, now. Friday and Saturday nights, it's like goddamned Fort Lauderdale. But there's a lot of panhandling going on."

"Yeah!" Tony said. "They're all fuckin' black guys, though—not that I got a thing against 'em, professor! You know that. It's just surprising to see how it's all changed. That kids' bookstore—it ain't here no more, either."

"Eeyore's? Yes, it's gone."

"The guy who run that, he was always *real* nice to me. Real nice, professor." He shook his head. "I liked to look at some of them kids' books, too. So what you been up to?"

"If I told you, Tony, you probably wouldn't believe me. Talking to an Old Poet today."

"Spring is here," Tony declaimed, "the grass is riz! I wonder where the flowers is. My feet is long-fellows, man!"

"Right!" I laughed. "But we were talking about a guy, used to live in my building, just downstairs from me. The only thing I can figure out is that he got real heavy into urine and excrement—he started off into guys' feet. But got his rooms all smeared up with crap, and somebody pissed all over his place. He got murdered, see. Stabbed in a gay bar downtown. But when they went into his apartment, it was—well, man, it was like somebody had emptied a couple of dozen toilet bowls all over everything."

Tony didn't say a thing—he just looked at me.

Then he said, "You were on the edge of some of that shit your-self, weren't you?" He nodded. "Me, too. You got a little deeper into it, maybe—since I went off to Seattle?"

I shrugged. "What about you?"

He gave me a shrug back. "We should get together again, you and me, professor. We could go over to the park, if you want—"

"Yeah," I said. "The next time I see you, we'll do that, Tony. Or you can come up to my place, grab some chow. Like you used to. Right now, though, I'm kind of running."

"Sure, professor. Next time…"

I put my hand on his wide, thick shoulder, so far below mine. The sleeve of his jacket, completely loose from the shoulder, was pinned there with half a dozen safety pins. "The guy who got killed, Tony, that was seventeen years ago. So it doesn't really mean anything now."

Tony nodded. Then he surprised the shit out of me: "That was the Korean guy, that philosopher you was researching—who used to live downstairs from you? You told me about him once—how you were studying him and everything. About how he liked to play with guys' feet—an' how he was what you was gonna be a profes-sor in. I met a bunch of guys like that. They like my feet 'cause they stink so bad!"

"Jesus, Tony!" I said. "You remember that?"

He nodded.

Because I certainly didn't remember telling him—though, obvi-ously, at some point, when Tony had come up and we'd been rolling around on the rug in front of all the file boxes, he must have asked what was in them—and I must have told him.

"We'll get together soon, you and me. At the park, at my place—hey, I missed you, you fuck-faced old scumbag!"

He opened his mouth, wobbled his tongue inside it in a perfectly obscene gesture. "I missed your black ass, too, nigger. Hey, I got somethin' to show you. If you're into this new stuff, maybe you're gonna like it." Sticking his cup into his pocket, he made a fist and brought it up sharply, as if to punch me. But the broad fingers, with their haze of red, hung before me. Now he brought the other fist up, faked another punch—and both fists hung there. In the orange light from Gryphon's window, books askew on the shelves there, I saw, tattooed across the four wide knuckles of his left hand. S H I T. Across the right was P I S S. Holding them up before my face, he said: "You know, how everybody's always tellin' you, man, don't get anything tattooed on your hands or on your face? You do that, an' you ain't never gonna get any kind of a job. Well, shit, man"—Tony's hands came forward and lowered, one to my left shoulder, one to my right—"in three weeks I'm gonna be thirty-four fuckin' years old, professor! And I know damned well I ain't never gonna be too much more than what I am now—so I figured it wouldn't be so bad if I advertised a little: what I got"—his right hand left my shoulder to give my jaw, with his fist, a flyweight tap— "and what I want." Then his left did the same.

"Yeah—" I said. "Well...we're gonna get together, Tony—you and me. Soon." I squeezed his shoulder, turned around; and I was still thinking about the whole business Adler had asked me to explore when I got upstairs again, to read only four and a half pages of a book I'd been meaning to read for four years: Appiah's 1986 argument, *For Truth in Semantics*. But I stopped, thinking: So there *are* some people I can talk to this about. (That made me feel a little better.) But just not Pheldon—not right now. By then, of course, I'd decided "no" and "yes" to Adler's request, several times, and for several chains of reasons complex enough to tax the systems of the world.

Anticipating dreams of the winged and roc-clawed phantasm, with its human foot and nail-bitten fist, who lumbered, splattering urine and erupting fecal matter through Hasler's journals, voiding and drenching in the apartment below, flinging clothes from the closets, dragging bedding from the mattress, overturning tables, breaking mirrors, sweeping books from the shelves, transforming the cozy clutter of the student and philosopher's retreat and study into an apocalypse of piss and shit, I drifted to sleep—but slept the night in an uninterrupted and revivifying instant, signed only by morning.

And that day—Monday—I began (again) another week as a very ordinary temp-worker.

There's always this odd day in spring when—even though it may have been going on for a couple of weeks—you realize it's six-fif-teen and the sun is *still* out.

On Friday, Cathy at the agency had said the new job was in a jeans-and-sneakers office. So, that Monday, I wore jeans and sneakers, and I was still wearing them on the way home.

On Broadway's island, they'd put out a refuse drum—dented metal, dark green, its rolled rim rusted, one side kicked in angrily as with a knee. A thick and hirsute giant, he loomed, with his curly hair, curly beard—both gray-shot brown—in a blue sweatshirt, the bottom of which hung high above the stretched-out waist of his woolen pants, too tight and too hot for summer. The refuse can's rim hit *me* at belly-button level. On his green woolen pants, it was just above mid-thigh. Stockily built, he slowed at the island's curb, in his big, dirty running shoes. With one fist he rubbed the rug of his flank, under the soiled sweatshirt—hair chestnut and wiry, up his belly and chest, over his collar, and all around his thick neck to meld with his rumpled beard.

The beltless green pants were low on that broad gut, pelt thickening toward pubic density at the pants' waist—low enough on his hips (three inches below the sweatshirt's bottom) so that if he'd been standing with his back to me, I could have seen inches of fur clamped in his buttocks' bevel. He bent over the drum's rim and swept a hand with a dessert-plate-sized palm down through what was inside.

After a few moments of paper scrunching and bottles hitting each other and the metal wall, he came out with something gray and white and catsup-dabbed (the Burger King was just on the far corner behind me) in a colophoned sheet of flapping wrapping. Metal rim on his hip, he punched burger and bun into his mouth with fingers thicker than hammer hafts. His knuckles were big as walnuts. Broad as quarters on the fore joints, his nails were gnawed well back of the crowns, to strips of horn, lined at ballooning crowns and thickened, cracked cuticle with black.

I glanced down at his pants cuffs, backs trod away to wet fray. One cuff was torn and flapped away from the huge hock of his ankle: he wore no socks. This skin there, under the hair, was as gray as that on his hairy hands.

Shoulders hunched forward, head lowered, somewhere still high in the air, he chewed.

Two women passed, one in a stylish T-shirt.

The other—with a tight summer top on—moved her gaze across

his chest as though the dark meadow of it were glass, not muscle and fur and flesh.

A man with an attaché case and wearing a light gray suit stepped between us—glanced up at him, glanced away.

The four o'clock sky (because it was Friday, they had let us off early) was gathering up aluminum colored clouds for another summer shower.

Finished, he dropped the paper, which hit the rim and—surprise—balanced there, caught in some matrix of its own creases, now about to fall out on the street, now about to tip into the drum...again it rocked outward with a breeze I could just feel on my fingers.

I turned, to see where he was going.

Though the light hadn't changed, he started across the street—two cars shot by him—and lumbered up onto the corner, to pass the King and continue on toward Riverside.

I looked back at the paper, still caught on the can's edge.

I'd thought to step forward and glance at what he'd fished his food from.

But I know what's in a refuse can, and I decided: No, not today—feeling, I confess, queasy, I turned to cross the avenue in the other direction.

On the south side of Eighty-second Street, across from Holy Trinity, a newer and an older apartment building are joined by a narrow wrought-iron gate. Its decorative terra-cotta transom makes it part of the older. Someone had taken a four-foot piece of plywood, wired it up against the scrolled bars, then spray-painted over it in foot-and-a-half-high letters:

I AM THE DOOR!

It set me chuckling as I walked up to the corner.

When I got across Amsterdam, Tony was sitting on my stoop. He was eating something in a large piece of French bread, the shoulder of his green work shirt leaning against brown concrete. (Last night's jacket had gone.) A diagonal shadow cut his scruffy red beard.

With big, dirty fingers, bearing their letters from night into the day, he pushed the bread, crumbling, at his mouth, and sat up, chewing.

"What you eatin' there, Tony? Something good?"

"Just some shit I got over in the park."

What squeezed out the back of the crumbling crust was too brown for meat loaf, too dark for peanut butter. But what the do-good organizations were passing out these days, I decided I'd better not question: I thought of the big guy I'd just seen eating out of the refuse can. Tony turned the sandwich around and went in for another bite, heavy fingers leaving valleys in the crust, as though it had been struck with little baseball bats.

"Hey, I was pretty sure this was where you lived, professor. I figured if I hung out over here long enough, I might even catch you."

"Good to see you, Tony." Rugged little fuckers like that are always a turn-on for me; and, I'm sorry, the older they get, the more of a turn-on they get—I was looking at the white that shadowed the sides of all that red, hanging off his face.

"Hey, you know what else they changed, professor?" which left me a little bewildered, until I remembered our conversation from the night before.

"No, Tony. What?"

"That other fuckin' Chinese place, that used to be right down on Eighty-first Street an' Amsterdam? The one that gave Dirty John the broken glass in his food—it's gone, too."

"Broken glass?" I frowned. "What was that about?"

"You remember Dirty John. He used to hang out on Seventy-ninth early on Saturday and Sunday morning—this bald guy, though he wasn't that old. Younger than me—he was always on his knees? He was real religious—he was always tellin' us how it wasn't people what was givin' us money, it was God? He would come up to the people on his knees—and always said God bless you?"

"Vaguely," I said. And wondered if I did.

"I wouldn't think anybody would forget Dirty John. He was pretty colorful. Anyway—though, when that place down there first opened up as a Chinese restaurant—it was called Snoozy's..."

"Fozy's! That's right. I remember it."

"Yeah—Fozy's. Anyway, it was a couple of years ago—John went up there just when they were closing and asked them if they had any food for him. So they put up a quart of Lo Mein or something and brought it out from the back. He said thank you and God bless you, like he always did—and took it outside to eat. He opened it up and took a mouthful and bit down on a piece of broken glass. Cut his gum and the inside of his cheek, too. Man, his mouth was really bleedin'—they'd mixed up the noodles with all this broken glass!"

"Jesus!" I said. "That ought to be illegal. I mean, did he do anything?"

"He took it to the police station down there." Tony nodded toward the precinct at the other end of the block. "They told him he'd have to press formal charges or to get the hell out of there."

"Did he?"

"You ever seen Dirty John? He couldn't hardly put two sentences together, except to say 'God bless you, sir…God bless you, ma'am.' How's somebody like that gonna press charges? I saw him when he was coming from the police station that night—right down on Eightieth Street, goin' back to the park. They'd told him to keep the container of noodles for evidence and bring it back the next day when there was somebody there who could take his report—like he had a goddamned icebox he could go put it in? How you gonna keep a carton of noodles for three weeks—or three months—if you're homeless, while you're waiting for them to set up a fuckin' trial? He was cryin', man, he was so fuckin' angry! And his mouth started bleeding again—while he was trying to explain it to me. He felt like they were trying to kill him, and he couldn't get any satisfaction. From the police or anybody." Tony moved one running shoe to the step below. Some of the dirt on the shoe was where the rubber had worn from the cloth beneath and the cloth had turned black. And some was just scuff and grime. "I sat listening to him cry for a couple of hours. It's funny—the restaurant's gone, now. Dirty John is gone. And probably nobody even remembers the fuckin' glass in the noodles." He took a breath. "But that's what we gotta put up with out here sometimes, professor."

A history of homelessness on the Upper West Side for the last decade. How would you go about researching it?

In the green cloth of Tony's pants, his cock—which, when I'd first met him, I'd decided must keep a permanent hard-on ("Naw," he'd said, real deadpan. [It just came back to me, like that!] "Just when I'm around you")—made its usual tent off-center from his fly.

"Hey, professor?" Tony looked up, gap-toothed and serious. "You and me is friends, right? An' you know a lot of shit. Can I ask you somethin'? I mean, somethin' personal, like?"

"Sure," I said. "You can ask." I remembered Tony's last personal request: basically, homeless people seem to ask you for money. "Don't be surprised if I can't do anything for you, though."

Tony patted the step beside him: another nail biter—*is* it more prevalent among the homeless? I sat—and got a smell as if someone had just laid a royal fart. But I ignored it. You learn to, if you're going to hang around with these guys. (Bitten nails or, I suppose, long claws that never get cut. Since, I confess, the latter turns me off, I'm just more likely to associate with the former.) "Now seriously, professor"—Tony leaned toward me—"how many times can a guy jerk off in a day, before he starts to hurt himself—or go a little crazy? Or get sick?"

"Gee, Tony," I said. "I don't know. Four, five—maybe six."

"Shit," Tony said. "Five or six ain't gonna hurt you none! I know that—I been doin' *that* all my life, and I ain't crazy...yet!"

I laughed. "Well, yeah. I guess I was thinking about myself too. I don't know, Tony. Why'd you ask?"

" 'Cause I got a friend, this guy—over in the park. Nice guy, too—a homeless guy, like me. Only he beats his meat all day long, just about. I mean, he's gotta be doin' it fifteen, sixteen times a day—at *least!* Sixteen times?" Tony frowned. "I mean shootin' a load, too. In fact it's gotta be a lot more than that, because I was hanging out with him, when he must have done it ten times in three or four hours! So that's like, maybe, twenty or even thirty times in a day—*Shit!*" Tony frowned, awed by his own calculations.

"Is he all right?" I was thinking, of course, that Tony must have run into Crazy Joey. "I mean, is he healthy and everything?"

"Well, he's a big fuckin' guy," Tony said, which made me frown. "Makes about two and a half of me and you put together."

Which let Crazy Joey out of the picture, since he was about Tony's height—and thinner. "He seems okay. He drinks—but then, everybody out here does that. But he's a nice guy—he gave me this sandwich." Tony shoved the rest of it in his mouth. "I just don't want nothin' bad to happen to him." He chewed. "But all he does is pull his pecker—*all* day long!"

I glanced again at the tent in Tony's pants—which was now wet in an irregular blot at the peak. Tony was a dripper of the first order.

He looked at me, mocking indignation. "What *you* lookin' at, professor?"

"You with your permanent hard-on. All this talk about beating off, I was wondering if you were angling for a blowjob."

"Me?" Tony grinned. "I don't have to angle with you, professor. If I want me a blowjob, I just gotta pull it out, stick it in your face, and hump till I lose my juice—right?"

Now I laughed. "That's about it." I nodded.

Tony moved one hand around over his belly and glanced at me. "Come on," I said. "We'll go inside, okay? In the back, down the stairs—like we did that once." I don't know why I was weary of bringing him up to the apartment—since he'd been there half a dozen times before. "And I can do you." Only not in the last couple of years.

Tony just grinned as he pushed up from the steps. He took hold of my hand in his thick, soft fingers, and I got up and we went into the vestibule.

As I put the key in the door and twisted, Tony crowded up behind me. "Man, I'm fuckin' horny!" he rasped, surprisingly close to my ear. "You gonna give this old cheesy cock a workout? Since I seen you last night, professor, I ain't even skinned it back once—I remember how you like it."

I glanced down behind me.

Tony was pulling at his crotch.

"Take it out, motherfucker," I told him. "I'll show you what I can do, right here—in case you don't remember."

He laughed, and pressed up against me, getting his fingers in his fly. "I remember." He pulled the brass teeth apart as the door came open. We both went in.

In the back, under the stairs, a doorway went down to the cellar. Jimmy had the whole file of five buildings to take care of. In the cellar three up, he had made himself something between an office and a nest—so he almost never came into ours.

I pulled open the creaking door and started down. When I was halfway to the bottom, behind me Tony said: "Hey...come on!"

I turned.

Tony stood two steps above me. Broad as a small Idaho potato, his cock was out and hard. "It's pretty fuckin' dirty," he whispered, roughly, warmly. I dropped to my knees on the dusty stair between. The smell of his lived-in pants filled my face.

Mouth opened, hands going on his knees, I threw my head at him.

As my lips struck hair, pressed the thick flesh beneath the hair, struck the pubic bone beneath the flesh, Tony caught my head and grunted, "Oh, fuck!"

Tony's cock pegged my mouth, its head wedged in my throat. I moved my throat around it. Without words now, he grunted again. But it meant the same as "Oh, fuck!"

Sucking Tony always made me think of sucking on a bullfrog. Part of that was the warts—he still had the three old hard ones, up and down the fat shaft. He went into my mouth, all salty and thick, and I felt two drag within my lips. His loose cheese-laden skin, was full of thick, waxy curd, some of it creamy with his leakage—half-pee, half-come—and some like dried putty, packed under his glans. His palms flattened on my cheeks, hot over my ears, closing out air and sound. In the cellar steps' half-dark, he pulled my head into him, his gut cushioning my forehead with its red mat.

I put my arms around his ass, and he began to hump my face, taking big breaths and holding them four or five thrusts, then gasping in another.

I like responding to a guy's dick.

With men I've sucked off repeatedly, like Tony, I keep track of what they enjoy. It's interesting to have that information come back to you, along with the familiarity of the meat in your mouth—especially when it hasn't been there for more than a year. Do they like it tight or loose? How much tongue work? Is the head very sensitive or not? About how long will they take? Half the knowledge, you can't really talk about. It's something your body—your head, your tongue, your arms, your neck—knows, about rhythm, about tightness and tension, about pacing. With Tony, for instance, I remembered that, after I've gotten pretty far along, once all his skin worked back, if I worried the spot just under the wart on the rim of the his glans with my tongue tip, I could practically control when he shot. (If I did it too early, it didn't do anything.) Lots of cocksuckers are always sucking some fantasy dick. But what I'm into is making the real dick on the real man I'm really sucking feel real good—as *that* guy defines good. Tony liked it wet and tight, with lots of affection—which, with his knees against my chest, his hands all over my head, he returned amply.

Though I've never actually timed him, Tony was a four-minute man, who got his hump in a rising line of thrusting, grunting, and face fucking—which now he'd started to do: while his pants slid farther and farther down his heavy legs, I jabbed my tongue at the spot under his glans' wart. "Oh, *shit!*" he whispered, stumbled on the stairs, and, clutching my head and shivering, came. The muscles in his left leg shook.

I steadied him and rubbed his left thigh, hard.

Slowly his gasps, as he held my head, became regular.

Finally, hands still over my ears, he straightened up. "I'm gonna do somethin' nasty to you, now, nigger." Within the thick wash of its own syrup, save for the small, hard warts on it, his broad cock had gone half soft. Above his belt on my forehead, I felt his stomach tighten. Urine jetted in the back of my mouth, flooded to the fore—and the thing as nice as remembering, after a long interval, how some dick likes to get sucked and doing it, is to have some dick remember what *you* like and doing it.

I swallowed.

"Oh, yeah," he rasped. "Let it stay in there, around my cock. Maybe let some of it spill, real hot, down my balls." A familiar enough request.

So I did.

And felt Tony's big nuts relax in their sack, lengthening down my chin. Reaching up, I moved my fingers over the roll of flesh between his legs behind his balls—clear of the balls themselves. They were kind of sensitive, I remembered. And Tony didn't really like them played with it. Another jet ballooned my cheeks with liquid heat—and another memory: whether in my mouth or against the side of a building, Tony never let his piss run—rather, he pissed like a dog, in four or five big, messy spurts. And, if he was outside, he'd put himself away, then find another spot twenty feet off, and leave another four or five splatters. Again I swallowed, even as I let my lips go loose, to feel piss run down my chin, to drip, drip…drip.

Running his hands over my head, Tony sighed, "Oh, shit!" and erupted a third mouthful.

While I swallowed, he gave me a fourth—then suddenly pulled

out, turning toward the rail, spurting my face and getting pee in my left eye. "Hey..."

I pulled back a little. The step's corner cut into my knee. Over the edge, down on the concrete, Tony's urine splattered.

"Hey," I repeated. "Why'd you pull out?"

Standing with his hip in my face now, Tony laughed. "Some for you, man—but I gotta save some for me, too."

From the movement of his heavy forearms—and the variation in the sound of his copious waters on the floor below (concrete, cardboard, a pile of wood?)—I realized that he was rubbing his hands together in his stream.

"What the fuck you doing, man?" I pushed up to stand. "You're wasting that shit!"

"That's so I can get my hands hard," he told me. "I'm a big guy—not tall, I know. But I'm big. I'm tired of having soft hands like a fuckin' sissy."

I frowned. Like his warts and his sensitive balls were old, wanting to spill piss *on* his balls was new for Tony; so was this. "You been hanging out with a kid in the park called Crazy Joey?" I asked.

Tony glanced down at me. The light was behind and above him from the half-opened door. He shook his head a little. "Naw...?" It was vaguely questioning.

But I shrugged. "I was just wondering," convinced he was lying and wondering why.

His water quieted; then he started another gush; it quieted again; then another, breaking on his intertwined fists, splattering away beyond the rail.

"You're a fucking dog, Tony," I told him.

I could hear—if not see—him grin. "Yeah."

I stepped around behind him, leaning my hands on his muscular back, to start up the steps.

When I reached the door, I stepped up on the landing and stopped between the door and the jamb. Without looking back, I dropped my hands to undo my belt. "Dog," I said, "eat out my black ass."

Below, his piss ceased sounding. His sneakers thudded on the board steps behind, coming up. Looking at the bubbled and mottled yellow paint that blistered the wall three feet in front of me, I pushed down my jeans.

His big fingers touched my ass. Then, leading with his tongue, his face pushed between my buttocks. I took the weight off my right leg, to let him get deeper. His fingers were still wet—and now, along with his tongue, one slid into me.

His face went back. Behind me he whispered, "Nigger, you got some shit in there!"

"You want it?"

Like an answer, his face smashed in between again. So I pushed. At first I thought it was his finger inside me that made me feel I had to go. But then I felt something move. I pushed again. Inside me, beside his turning finger, something moved as he dug. His finger came out—and something else come out. "Got the fucker!" And his face was back between my buttocks, tongue spearing and swabbing, swabbing and spearing my rectum.

Above, someone was coming down the stairs.

I started to step back in the doorway, but Tony wasn't going to let me go. To see me, though, you would have had to come around under the steps and actually look—and most people leaving the building don't do that. I made a wager with myself that I would just stand there—and if whoever it was came in to look, I'd deal with that when it happened.

When the footsteps started down the last flight, right above us, Tony stopped licking.

The footsteps reached the bottom, changed timbre as they started forward across the tile floor. Because of the heels, I was sure it was a woman. Five steps across the tile, they stopped—probably it was just to check for the keys, adjust a package, or look at a watch. They started again—and went out the front door.

Moments later, Tony stepped up beside me, to stand beside me in the cellar doorway.

He was breathing fairly hard. Not as long as mine, but long enough and almost twice as thick, his dick was still out his pants, curving away and down, half-hard—as was mine.

I reached over and took it in my hand. His lap was blotched wet all around it.

Tony brought his hand forward: a length of shit, fatter at one end, ragged at the other, lay across his palm. He ran his fingers under my cock, so that my dick lay across it beside the turd. "Damn!" he said. "I give me another six months, maybe a year—and I swear I'm gonna be suckin' niggers' dicks by then, man. Look, they're about the same fuckin' color, ain't it?"

I laughed. "That's good nigger shit, dog. You better fuckin' eat that!"

Tony took his hand away from my dick. But he was grinning. With his other hand now he put himself back in his pants, pulled up the zipper. (I pulled up my pants and buckled my belt.) "Come on," he said. "We better get out of here."

I closed the cellar door behind us, and followed Tony over the tile floor to the vestibule, and out through the wooden door with curtained window.

On the stoop, I sat down—while Tony looked around absently, he was kind of hefting the turd in one hand, as if he wasn't really thinking about it.

"Sit the fuck down, dog!" I said. "Sit *down!*"

Tony glanced down at me, then sat beside me. I moved my leg up against his, slid over so my arm was against him. "Look at that, man—go ahead. Look at it."

Tony put one hand below the other and—left hand supporting his right—gazed at the turd: rich brown, pungent, kind of knobby, and probably still warm on his palm with my own inner heat.

"Tony," I said. "Dog—you're a fuckin' scumbag, you know? You're probably one of the lowest things in the world. You're so low, you'd eat a fuckin' piece of shit right out of a nigger's ass—go on. You could eat it—it would even turn me on."

He stared at the turd. "Would it turn you on to see me do it?"

"You wanna make a nigger come in his pants?" I said—surprising myself.

"I like people to watch me do stuff—walk around naked. Eat pieces of dog shit and stuff. Especially if it gets 'em off."

"And that's better than dog shit," I said. "That's fresh nigger shit. You ask fifty guys what the lowest thing in the world is. They'll tell you, it's a cocksucker. Ask them what's lower than a cocksucker, and they'll tell you it's a nigger cocksucker—right? And that's a nigger cocksucker's *shit*—that you're gonna eat! You'd eat a nigger cocksucker's shit—which makes you the fucking lowest scumbag around, right? Well, see, not only is it a nigger cocksucker's shit, man. It was a nigger cocksucker who was sucking on *your* fucking dick, drinking *your* fucking piss! That means it's gotta be even fuckin' *lower*—and the only way you could be lower than that, dog, is if you ate that fuckin' shit. Scarfed it all down. In front of the fuckin' nigger." I put my arm around his back and squeezed the far helmet of his hard shoulder. "Then you'll be so fuckin' low that if you rang the goddamned nigger's doorbell and he answered it, the door would swing right over your head—you'd be that low! Go on, you fuckin' homeless shit-eatin' scumbag—"

Tony dropped his face and shoved it into his mouth—his jaw worked rapidly, under his red beard. Now he pushed more of it in, with two fingers of one hand, then with two fingers of the other.

"Goddamn, man"—with my arm around Tony's broad shoulders— "that's great—man! That's really fuckin' low—it really looks fuckin' good."

And, you know, my dick had gone from half-hard to almost-painful inside my jeans.

Tony sat there, beside me, looking down, chewing.

I said: "Hey, scumbag!"

He looked over at me.

With my arm still around him, suddenly I thrust my face into his, my mouth over his mouth. His mouth opened under mine, and his eyes closed. Both of his arms went around me, hard. And he was shaking. His forearm was hard around behind my neck.

Then suddenly it hit me: I'm sitting there, with a bum, on my stoop on Eighty-second Street, our tongues working furiously inside each other's mouths, while he still has a face full of my turd.

And I shot my load in my pants—and, as, over the next thirty seconds, I got my breath back, still kissing him (and Tony still clinging onto me like a man drowning), I heard somebody walk past; and then somebody else in the other direction.

But this is New York.

When I blinked my eyes open, Tony's green-blue eyes were wide.

I sat back. He let his arms fall from around my shoulders. (Now he leaned forward, to see who it was who'd passed. But I figured I'd rather not know.) He reached up and rubbed his rumpled red walrus down over his face, his fingers going around to furrow his white-brushed red. "Man," he said, after a moment. "I could taste my fuckin' piss, still in your mouth." He looked around.

A policeman walked by, going down toward the precinct at the block's end.

"It made me come again, professor. Shit, and I ain't even into piss—shit, yeah. I can do shit all day till I fuckin' puke. But not piss—except when I taste my own in somebody else's mouth, I guess. On top of some good shit."

I sucked on my lower lip, then my upper—to get what I had in there down. "Me, too—I came, I mean."

Tony turned back forward, raised his big, empty hands, and rubbed them together. "How did you learn all about that stuff, professor?"

"What do you mean?"

"What you was sayin' there—the way you got me off?"

"I read it," I told him.

"In a book?" he said, surprised.

"No—off your fucking hands." I pointed to his fingers, which he turned over now—with the letters tattooed across his knuckles. "You got it written, right there."

He looked down at them a while.

"Hey, Tony, how long you actually been eating shit?" I asked. "I mean, last time you were around here, you weren't actually eating it, were you?"

He shrugged. "I don't know." He held up the hand with the S, H, I, and T. "I been thinkin' about it all my life. But I just started doin' it." He shrugged again. "A couple of years, now—I guess." He frowned, as if it were hard to remember. "Right after I got these."

"You got the tattoos first?"

"Yeah." Then he said, "I used to do it when I was a kid. All the time. Dog shit. Nigger shit—like you say, that's the best. There was a black maintenance man in the school I went to; I used to come in early and follow him into the john, all the time—see if I could catch what he left in the shitter. But then I stopped—and started doin' all that other crazy stuff. Takin' my clothes off—beatin' off where people could see me." (Just then, chewing his cigar, Jimmy came down the street and turned up the stoop beside us. I raised my hand to him and nodded, without really turning away from Tony—who only paused for a moment, as Jimmy went into the vestibule behind us.) "I always really liked you, professor—'cause of the way you was into piss and stuff. Now, you know, piss never was my thing—catchin', I mean. I don't mind pitchin'—in fact, I really *like* to pitch. That's why I was so surprised, shootin' a second load like that just now. With you. But you know, I always figured because I liked to do all that kinky stuff, that's why I'd always be a homeless fucker. A fuckin' bum. When I was a kid, once, my older sister caught me, eatin' dog doo-doo—a really great dog, too. I loved that dog—belonged to our next-door neighbor. A real friendly black Labrador. But when my sister saw me eatin' his shit, she wouldn't let me back in the house. For a whole night—our parents was away that night. And she wouldn't let me back in. So I took my clothes off and walked around the streets all night. Buck naked. And nobody caught me, neither. I guess that's the first time I figured it out—that if I was gonna do stuff like that, I pretty much had to be a bum. Especially wantin' people to see me all the time. I always had to be ready to get carted off to the fuckin' hoosegow. But then, a few years back, when we first met up, you and me—here you was, into piss—almost as fuckin' kinky as I was. And you had a place to stay—*you* had a job and everything.

"I mean, you got a home—that you could keep up." Tony shook his head thoughtfully. "Now, me—maybe it's too late for me to ever have that. 'Cause I just opted to go without, you know what I mean? But, you know, professor? Once I met you, I really started thinking about that."

"Well," I said, "I'm not an exhibitionist, Tony—but exhibitionists do turn me on, I guess. Watching guys eat shit—that brings something out in me. Yeah…I guess it did."

"How many times you get to do that?" Tony asked.

Now I looked at him. "Actually," I said, "you're the first."

"But then, how?"

"Like you said, I been thinking about it, I guess."

Tony shook his head. "We're a fuckin' pair, you and me, professor."

"I guess we are." Then I said: "Tony, you're into shit—and stuff. I'm into piss—and stuff."

"I'm into you," Tony said. "And you're sort of into me, I guess. Ain't you?"

"Yeah. But I was wondering. What do you think that's all about—piss and shit? Wanting to roll around in it—eat it, drink it?"

"I thought about the shit part," Tony said. "A lot. I think it has something to do with death."

"Huh?"

"When you die, you rot—go back into ook and yuk and decayed shit—before you just dry up and blow away. That's pretty grim to think about. So, I guess, somehow, getting into shit, eating it and stuff, bein' low-down and all, that's like getting closer to being dead. Making it more natural, more ordinary. It's warm, ordinary, pleasurable. It makes life easier—because it makes the idea of dying, as much as we can really think about it, easier."

"Tony," I said. "This is all *your* idea?"

He nodded. "Um-hum."

"That would," I said, "have been worth a whole chapter in *Beyond the Pleasure Principle.*"

"You think I'm right?"

"I have no idea, Tony, but I haven't ever heard a better one."

"I don't think I've ever heard *anybody* try to figure out before. I got a couple of guys over in the park what shit for me, regular-like. I saved up my panhandling money for three days, once, and got me a big plastic jar of that Metamucil stuff, and give it to them so their shit would have some form to it—and come out regular."

I started to say, *Tony, please! Spare me!* Then I thought: But who knows when I'll need to know stuff like that.

"—so it still comes out looking like shit," Tony added emphatically, "and not like mud. They take it for me pretty regular, too." Then he chuckled. "So you read all that stuff, about me likin' to be low-down and all, off my fuckin' hands? I'm glad I got these tattoos, then."

"You're having a better time since you got them?"

Tony shrugged. "Yeah. There was a nigger in Seattle—he'd shit, then we'd smear it all over his dick, and he'd let me eat it off him. He'd always come while I was doin' it. He swore up and down he'd have me suckin' cock in a week like a regular cocksucker. But it was just the shit and it being so fuckin' low. Professor, when you explained to me just how fuckin' low I was, that was really good. It was like somebody was watchin' me, all of a sudden, who really understood it. I liked that a lot. The nigger was the guy what told me about somebody with tattoos like this on his hands.

So I decided, like I told you—what the fuck. I got me a Bic pen and a needle, like they do in the jailhouse. And I—"

"Goddamned, motherfuckin' *animals!*" Jimmy exploded out of the vestibule door behind us.

I actually jumped.

He came down the steps, cigar stub quivering between his yellow teeth. "I fuckin' don't understand it! Why somebody gonna come in the fuckin' house, go in the fuckin' cellar, man, and piss all over the goddamn floor! What kind of fuckin' people we *got* out here, today? Do it in the fuckin' gutter, man. Or in the fuckin' street! Man, it's these fuckin' homeless guys—though how the fuck they get in here, I sure wished the hell I knew."

"What happened?" I asked, in feigned innocence.

"These fuckin' homeless assholes, they don't got no respect for anybody. They come in here, piss in the hall—now one of them must have gone down in the cellar and peed all over the cartons I had down beside the stairs. You can fuckin' smell it."

"Hey," I said, "that sounds like some of these kids, maybe. Maybe last night, coming in when the bars closed. All the crazy college kids—?"

"Who's gonna let 'em in last night?"

"You know, Jimmy," I said. "They ring all the bells, and somebody lets 'em in."

"Yeah," Jimmy said. "And that's how the fuckin' homeless guys do it, too." He stood over near the tree, shaking his head. "Shit!" His cigar stump shaking.

With his hands on his knees, Tony said, "I guess I'm gonna go on back over to the park, professor."

"Yeah, Tony," I said. "Good to see you—you come on back, soon."

His stolid little form thicker in every limb than mine, Tony stood up in his soiled clothes, to squint at the sky. His lap was still wet. He started walking toward the corner.

I looked back to say something appeasing to Jimmy, but he was already gone, up the street in the other direction. Feeling kind of stupid, I touched my shirt, which was still wet around my collar and down to my pocket. I got up, went inside, and started upstairs.

PART
FOUR

PLACE OF EXCREMENT

Nun weiss ich, wenn der letzte Morgen sein wird—wenn das Licht nicht mehr die Nacht und die Liebe scheucht— wenn der Schlummer ewig und nur Ein unerschöpflicher Traum sein wird. Himmlische Müdigkeit fühl ich in mir. —Weit und ermüdend ward mir die Wallfahrt zum heiligen Grabe, drünkend das Kreuz. Die kristallane Woge, die gemeinen Sinnen unvernehmlich, in des Hügels dunkeln Schoss quillt, an dessen Fuss die irdiche Flut bricht, wer sie gekostet, wer oben stand auf dem Grenzgebürge der Welt, und hinübersah in das neue Land, in der Nacht Wohnsitz—warlich der kehrt micht in das Treiben der Welt zurück, in das Land, wo das Licht in ewiger Unruh hauset.
—Novalis, Hymnen an die Nacht, IV

T

he remainder of this tale is a love story.

When they're happening to you, not when you're hearing them, love stories are funny and scary and kind of unbelievable and turn your head around because they make you do and think and say things you'd never otherwise do or say. This one was, in that sense, classic. Just like I'll never forget the day I decided I had AIDS (that April 25, with Tony), I'll never forget the day *this* part of the story started: it was about three weeks after having my cellar session on Tony's return, with Jimmy getting all upset. We'd gone through a loud, sweaty July Fourth, on which Pheldon turned up with barbecued ribs and chicken and potato salad and champagne, half a dozen friends and a van (driven by Lewey, the redheaded sanitation worker), and we all went on this picnic up at Bear Mountain, which was only moderately crazily crowded that year.

The day I'm talking about was, however, Tuesday, July 18; I remember because it was also the day I decided to do something about Almira Adler's request.

At work (back in suit and tie, in that blue-walled, anonymous office with three names, the last one joined to the first two by an ampersand), I wondered whether, if I wanted to go to the Pit and ask about what had happened on September 23, 1973, I'd do better with lots of people there (maybe some who even went back that far) or with only a few (that is, when somebody might have time to talk to me). Tuesday is the deadest night in any bar. But I decided to go that night.

The office chat was of rain that evening. I didn't have an umbrella. Go home first then, I decided, change, and come back downtown. When I got out at my subway stop and, minutes later, turned from Broadway's crush up Eighty-second, it was a warm quarter to seven. The light had a bronzy gloom, that might, yes have meant rain.

A quarter of the way down the block, he stood—fists in his sweatshirt's pouches, looking across at the church. (You remember him: the big guy on the Broadway island who'd fished the hamburger from the refuse can...) I neared: he was standing before the small gateway blocking the alley between the two apartment buildings—the one the wag had wired a piece of plywood over and spray-painted across it I AM THE DOOR!

Weighted down by his fists, his sweatshirt was open over his chest's forest, his gut's rug. As I got closer and closer to him, things kept striking me:

The front was torn almost free from one of his running shoes, so that, with the upper flopped over to the side, I saw a big, naked foot, in the rubber rim, the broad nails picked back about as far—I suddenly remembered—as his fingernails had been. Now he took one fist from his sweatshirt, raised it to his mouth, and began to chip at his nails with his lower teeth, while he watched me over his knuckles. Thirty-three? Thirty-five? For some reason, with his beard and his rumpled hair, behind his fist he smiled—at me; or maybe he was just a bear who smiled a lot.

I smiled back.

He nodded, still gnawing, still smiling.

Within his wool pants, his other hand moved around toward his groin. For a moment, I glimpsed in outline what hung there—which was considerable. Inside his pants he scratched himself; and watched me. And smiled.

Walking on to the corner, I wondered if that had been some sort of a come-on. The light lifted behind the dark grille to WALK, and I crossed the street.

Up in the apartment, I changed my clothes. While I was in the bedroom, tugging off slacks and pulling on jeans, I thought: Here's the whole, busy replacing vinyl with tape and worrying if it's going to have to go through the whole process again a year or so from now with the new, silver CDs; since the Berlin Wall tumbled last November, millions are paused for the leap into cyberspace, where everything glitters and soars, but nothing dribbles or squishes; the summer is getting into spandex and roller blades; the number of AIDS cases is now within a stone's throw, one way or the other, of 100,000; a while ago, the Variety had been closed down because, said an article in the *Daily News,* "158 acts of unsafe sex" had been observed there by a plainclothes inspector over— what? Twenty minutes? I'd seen workers just last week, gutting the building and starting in on its refurbishment. (Even the Grotto had suffered a brief attempt to heterosexualize its operations, instituted and advertised by the management, called "lap dancing"; fortunately, it failed miserably, and things were now back to normal.) And only last week Phel called me to tell me that, as a black intellectual, I must pay more serious attention to rap, because, if nothing else, it's a black art that's *verbal;* but what does all this mean to a homeless white guy, not to mention all the other black ones down by law and out on the street in one torn sneaker, who may never have had occasion to call anything "marvelous," "excellent" or "awesome" in their lives? At the same time, I was rehearsing what I was going to be saying in half an hour down at the Pit: "Excuse me, but do you remember anybody who might have been working here in the early seventies...? When that murder happened...?"

With my umbrella, I came down again. When I stepped out on the stoop, it had started to rain—not hard, but steadily. The umbrella was a collapsible black Taiwanese thing. But because the evening was warm, I didn't put it up.

At the corner I crossed Amsterdam.

No longer standing, he sat, leaning forward on his knees, on a stoop at a building beside the gate. As I came down the block, he looked around at me. Again, this smile broke out on his bearded face. He looked right at me, too.

Water gemmed his hair. It was hard to tell what was glister and what was just the gray that brushed his head and beard as though a house painter's hand smeared with white paint had swiped him.

Again, I smiled back—and slowed.

I noticed one hand was back between his legs. Some of his hair was wetted to his forehead in little blades. Under his arms, a patch of his sweatshirt was still dry. But water glittered in his beard, over his mustache, on his eyelashes. I'd already decided, running into him this second time, I would speak: Hello...? How're you doing...? (Can I suck your dick? No, I'd leave that to our next encounter.) Kind of wet to be sitting out here? But the hand back in the shadow between his legs was moving, moving...moving, a rhythmic moving. On his thick forearm, hair lay down on the blocky muscles. The rolled-up sweatshirt was a tight band. Hanging over one knee in front, the hock of his wrist was thicker than both of mine.

I said, inanely: "What're you doing sitting out here in the rain?"

His hand kept working back in the shadow of his belly and lap. He kept on smiling. And, in a rough and slow voice, he said, "Sitting, here, getting, wet, and playing, with myself." The smile didn't break.

I swallowed. Because I was surprised.

As I stood there, my mouth went kind of dry and droplets ran down my forehead. "Bet it feels good."

"Sure do." He moved his shoulders up. "Wanna see?"

"Okay," I said, "Sure."

Sitting back, he let his knees fall wide: loose from his fly was a cock as thick as Tony's and more than a couple of inches longer. An inch wide and two-and-a-half inches long, a leathery cuff dangled off the end—and, while it wasn't the freakish five-and-a-half-inch skin the Piece o' Shit had had hanging from his meat, it was enough to send me back six years to that sunny Saturday in the park.

In the rain, he pulled his dick forward, first overhand, then underhand. I looked at it; the cuff waggled.

"Jesus," I said, "what have you been doing? Wearing yoni rings in that thing?"

His smile got sort of lopsided; he let his head drop to the side. "Now what you know about yoni rings?"

"Nothing," I said. "Really. I just knew somebody once who was into them. How *else* are you going to get a skin that long?"

"I used to wear 'em," he said. "Back when I was in a yoni club. You ever in one of them?"

"No. Like I said, just somebody I knew. Was your club in—" I tried to dredge up what little I remembered about the business— "in Montana?"

"Naw," he said. "We was in Florida, when I had me a job down there—shape-up; but I was workin' pretty regular then. I only wore 'em for about a year. Well, a year and a half—but only a year regular. I was up to where I could hold two in by themselves—three, if I used some adhesive tape around the edge. Then, when I went back on the bum, it got too much trouble. I think the fucker's shrunk back half an inch. long."

But some of them guys had skins on 'em eight, twelve, sixteen inches "Yeah, I've heard."

"They was wearin' *their* rings for years. Once I went on the bum again, I got lazy. You're the first person who wasn't in a club who just seen my dick and knowed right away how I got my skin like that." He sat up real tall now, to look up and down the street.

Probably because of the rain, though, no one was coming.

I can be disarmingly straightforward about sex; but when someone comes on that forward to me, myself I disarm pretty quick. "Um, eh—" I said, trying to think of something to say. "You looking to get that sucked on?"

"Sure." His big fingers urged *all* that skin back enough for me to glimpse the finger-width slit up the broad mushroom of its head; he slid it forward again. "You wanna suck it, that'd be nice." He leaned again on his knees, so that his working fist and the cock thrust out of it retreated in the shadow of his darkly furred gut. "What I'm really lookin' for, though"—as he leaned forward, his smile broke apart; under it were all sorts of expectations and don't-give-a-fuck belligerence and even some fear, at the same time as all of a big man's vulnerability—"is to find me a nigger to piss on..."

I swallowed. The thud, thud, thud inside my chest got so heavy that I staggered a little—I don't know whether he saw me.

His free hand left his knee and reached out; and I could see his fingers were very rough, for all the rainwater. "Man, I need to piss on a nigger so bad I could just about cry."

So I blinked and said: "Go ahead."

Now he patted the wet step next to him; I wasn't sure if he'd heard.

Frowning a moment, I stepped up on the stoop and sat beside him on the stone—and felt my jeans' seat soak.

"See across there—" he gestured with the hand not working in the darkness of him—"that church?"

Above the visual stutter of its concrete steps, Holy Trinity had recently polished its eight bronze doors (the two single ones on the ends, the three pairs in the middle, under their half-waffle irons of concrete tracery), three still open for summer.

"I could take you over there." His hand came back to fall on my knee, beside his. He rubbed my leg a couple of times, tightened his grip on my jeans. "We could go inside. Down by the altar—ain't nobody in there, now. Pissing on a nigger in church, that'd really be something, wouldn't it? Or we could go down into the subway. You go up to the far end of the station, where nobody would see us—except if a train was coming in. Then it would only be who-ever was lookin' out the window. And they'd whip all down to the other end of the station, so they couldn't do anything anyway." He rubbed his immense hand on my leg again. " 'Course, if you don't mind people seein', we could do it right down on Broadway in the fuckin' Burger King. You go in there, get some french fries and a hamburger, and just be sitting there, eating—then this big, hairy, stupid motherfucker—me, I mean—comes in like somebody you ain't never seen before, and walks up to the table you're eat-ing at, pulls out his dick, and pisses right in your fucking *face*, nig-ger—all over your fuckin' hamburger! All over the table—right in your fuckin' french fries—and when you look up, surprised, this guy aims his piss right *in* your fuckin' mouth. You ever had something like that happen to you? What'd you think you'd do if somebody like me did that to you?"

"I don't know." I took a breath. "Probably I'd say, 'Hey, thanks, fella!' Then, if the bread wasn't too wet, I'd go on eating my ham-burger. I mean, I don't like a soggy bun on my hamburger—"

"Jesus, nigger—!" He barked a laugh. "You're too much!"

"What would *you* do, once you did it?"

He leaned forward again, still pulling on himself. "I don't know. I never had quite the nerve to do *that*, I mean. Yet. Or the black fella who wanted me to do it. I mean, not at the same time." He leaned closer to me. "But if I got me a nigger like that, I probably wouldn't want to turn him loose for a long time, man. A long time." He sat back again and frowned up at the sky. "God's pissin' on both of us now," he said. "The two of us. Right here."

"No, he isn't," I said. "Piss is warm. At least when it hits you. This isn't cold—it's a nice rain. But it's not warm."

He looked up and kind of chuckled. Then he said, "Yeah. I guess you're right."

I put the folded-up umbrella beside me on the step. "Come on, get up," I told him. "Turn around here."

He pushed himself upright—he was easily 6'4", if not taller. And thick, from his hips and gut to his chest and shoulders. He turned to face me. I leaned forward and forward, from the step and into a crouch—and when I took his dick in my mouth, he went, "Oh, *fuck*, man...!" I took hold of his legs. And began to suck him. Once I squeezed his head with my tongue: the cheese slid out into his leathery ruffle. "Shit, man...!" The rain peppered the back of my neck; it tickled my forehead. "Hey, if somebody walks by—"

I came off his thick, rod long enough to say, "Fuck them—unless it's a cop. You're too big, fella—nobody's gonna mess with you!"

He chuckled again—and slid his heavily skinned cock, thick as some flashlight handle, back into my face. "Yeah. That's true."

About three-quarters of a minute later, somebody *did* walk by, head down and hurrying in the rain—but I don't think realized what we were doing.

Baseball players.

I lifted my hand to the broad back of his. His turned, took hold of mine in his huge fingers; clearly more comfortable, he settled his feet wider apart. "You suck that good, little guy."

I raised my hand to his fly, got in under his heavy, hairy nuts, while I troweled my tongue once more beneath the broad shelf of his glans, deep within his thick and cheesy skin.

"You like to clean out all that shit, huh? Glad I kept it in there for you."

His big nuts were warm and heavy in my hand, and, when I pulled them out, hung down a good eight inches in their furry sack.

"You can swing on those fuckers a little—if you want." His other

hand settled like a great cap on my head, moving with my pumping motion, speeding me up a few moments, then slowing me. I
gathered the length of his sack in my hand and let my arm depend
from it with its own weight, hair out the top tickling my fist, his
nuts' bulge smooth around the bottom. "Yeah, put some weight on
'em. That's good."

I kept sucking.

A few minutes later, he said, "Yeah..." again; then, "I'm gonna
piss in your face, little guy. You ready for me to pee in your mouth,
you cocksuckin' nigger scumbag?"

Sucking, I nodded.

"Nigger, you're a low-down fuckin' jigaboo bastard." He gave
my head a little push with his hand, without its coming away.
"*Drink* my fuckin' piss!" And from the hard shaft I felt a trickle, then
a flow, then a flood of hot salts.

I swallowed. It was incredibly hot—without burning.

"That's it, you fuckin' scumbag! *Suck* my dick while I piss in
you, nigger."

At which point, somebody else passing said, "Hey—" Multiple
steps sounded on the wet concrete. "Jesus—it's some homeless
guy gettin' a blowjob from another one—right out on the street!
Just like that! Man, in this fucking city, I guess you see *everything*,
now...!"

I pulled back and off his dick—his hand came down from my
head to grasp his outthrust penis and spray me, lap, chest, and
face; I turned away enough to see the couple passing; the woman
looked back.

His urine hit my face again—and she kind of jumped, turning
quickly, to hurry off beneath her boyfriend's umbrella. And because
that thing feels so good plugged into your head, I threw myself back
on his cock again. He grunted, receiving the heat of me around him,
in the rain. Still holding his cock, his fingers pushed against my
mouth as I went down. Then they opened against my face, to
move, rough as wood or stone, up my cheek, back to my head,
over my hair. Forceful waters pressed within. "You suck a good
dick, nigger—and drink that stuff like it's yours. Here—" He leaned
back once more, to come out of my mouth, cockhead falling an inch.
Piss hit my chin with its heat. His stream struck my chest. Inside
my shirt, piss dribbled to my belly.

I took a couple of deep breaths.

"Drink some more, nigger...!"

So I caught him in my mouth again, and drank. And the last of his waters ran out. He moved his legs again, and I fell to pistoning rhythmically on his cock, seeking for his pressure, his pace, the speed that would loose his semen.

"Hold on, cocksucker...!" He came out of my mouth, and turned quickly to sit again on the stoop beside me. (I sat back down myself.) Again he leaned forward, to gesture with his head up the street, and growled, "Fuckin' cops..."

Though only one policeman came—quickly—down the street in a graphite gray rain-cloak, cap visor sticking out from under his hood. A moment later, a very thin man walking a nervous, wet Weimaraner turned up the steps we were sitting on, to climb the stoop and push inside through the door. Then two women walked by with umbrellas. The rain fell from the July evening, still wedged here and there with the last, brassy light.

"You want me to finish you off?" I said, up to the big guy's shoulder.

He grinned. "It felt pretty good...but I just take too long to cum." Then he added: "I'm just not too smart..." which seemed a non sequitur.

I was going to say something about what did brains have to do with coming. But there was something about the way he said it that made me look at him.

He said: "When I was in school, in the second grade, they said I was a slow learner—borderline retard. Even niggers can call *me* dumb." He looked pleased, even proud.

"Yeah?" I smiled. "You must be pretty dumb, then."

On his bearded face, the smile came on again like a streetlight. "Yeah!" From the movement of his sweatshirt's shoulder, I could tell his hand was working back down between his legs.

I said: "You're probably too dumb to pour piss out of a boot."

While his big smile broke apart into a pure grin, he sat back and opened his legs again. His cock was still up. His fist was a blur on it.

"Man," I said, "you're so fuckin' stupid, you don't even know enough to come in out of the rain. You're probably the stupidest whitey running around homeless in this fucking neighborhood.

You're so fucking stupid you'd piss on a nigger in the middle of the street then let him suck your fucking dick. You fucking retard—they don't make 'em any stupider than you, do they?"

He grunted—grunted again.

"You're one dumb sonofabitch, aren't you—you fucking dummy!"

He grunted a third time. "Yeah...take it, if you want it...!"

So I leaned over his leg, got half a dozen fists in my face, before his other hand clamped the back of my head and he pushed me down on him. Within my mouth, he erupted his thick and copious juice. Rocking forward over me, he held me to him with both hands, both arms. (And, of course, somebody else came by—but I don't know what they thought, seeing me with my head in his crotch and him leaning over me like that.) His great breaths got further apart—and quieter. Finally, he let me up.

With one hand on his big shoulder, I said: "It didn't take you all *that* long."

He was still breathing hard, though. "It don't, when somebody gets ahold of my thing like that. You picked up on that pretty fast."

I shrugged. "You don't really seem like you're that retarded, either."

"I'm pretty okay, I guess," he said. "I can't read and write—but I'm not stupid." He ran both his hands out to his knees, and back. "I sure ain't as stupid as they told me I was in the second grade. If I was *that* fuckin' stupid, I'd be dead! I was just raised different, is all. Me, I think I'm pretty smart, for what I gotta do with it. I get over, man—like you black fellas say. Hey, you know this little guy who hangs out in the park—got a beard like mine, only it's red—and more curly? Name's Tony?"

"Yeah," I said. "Sure!"

"Well, he said if I was to get my nut off with you tonight, I was to tell you that you owed him a penny."

Now I was the one who grinned. "You mean *Tony* sent you over here—for me? How'd you know who I was?"

"You're the guy Tony calls the professor." He leaned forward again, and pointed up the street. "Right? You live right across Amsterdam Avenue—in the first house there?"

"Yeah. But how—?"

"Tony said to look out for a black guy, about thirty—he said a good-looking black guy, too." He gave me another grin. "He said you would probably come on to me, if I looked like I was halfway interested. Tony said you were into some of the same things I was—piss and stuff."

"Well," I said. "I guess he knows if anyone does."

"It's nice," he said, "to meet somebody new, and get each other off like that—" Then he frowned. "Did you get off?"

"Naw," I said. "But that's okay."

"Aw, man! I thought you got your nut, back when you were drinking my piss."

"Don't worry," I said. "It'll be something nice to think about later—"

"Naw, man. I want you to get yours, too. I mean, you pulled a nice load out of me. It'd only be fair. You can do pretty much anything you want with me, man. I'm easy. I like to get mine—and I like the person I'm with to get his too. I could go another round—a couple of cans of beer, and I'll piss all over you some more. Pissing on black guys is a real thing with me—that's why Tony said I should come look for you. I already almost got in trouble about it, over in the park. I mean, *I* thought the nigger would like it. I could—"

I stopped him with a hand on his tree trunk of a leg. "Look, that's nice of you—what's your name?"

"Leaky. But some guys I make it with, they call me Dummy." He smiled at me. "I guess you figured it out—I kind of like that one. Not that I mind the other one either."

I grinned back. "Look, Dummy," I said. "I'm supposed to be going somewhere tonight—I probably won't be back for a couple of hours. It would be really nice if we could get together some other time so that—" Then I frowned. " 'Leaky' 's got to be a nickname, too, doesn't it? Just for curiosity, I was wondering what your real name was, unless it's none of my business—"

"Leaky," he repeated; then he chuckled. "That's what my old man named me. Leaky. A lot of the time, I don't even tell people that. For a while I used to tell them my name was 'Larry'—but then I'd go through the same thing, with social workers and stuff, 'cause they'd always want to write it down 'Lawrence.' So finally, I decided, what the fuck. My name *was* Leaky, so that's what I'd tell anybody who asked me. It sure ain't 'Lawrence'! Look: I shot my load.

You didn't. If we get together again, I can make it up to you. How about that?"

"Fine," I said. "I'd like that."

But he was frowning now. "You're going someplace...like *that?*"

"I'm pretty well soaked through—but it's just a bar." I wondered if I should go home, get some dry clothes, and start again. Or maybe even put it off to another night. "I'll be all right." The rain, I figured, would dilute the pee; it was still in the high seventies, low eighties—and there was something kind of fun, I confess, about going into a place like the Pit right after I'd had a workout like this. "I just have to ask some people a few questions."

He sighed. "Okay—it's nice to meet you, professor...little guy..." He turned to me, stuck out his big grubby hand. "...nigger." We shook.

"Good to meet you too, Leaky...Dummy." My hand, which is not small, was lost in his.

Then his other arm went around me, and he pulled me against him, my face against his wide, hairy chest, beside the brass teeth in his sweatshirt. I hugged him back. With one hand now, he rubbed the top of my head. In a kind of rough voice, he said, "I'll see you around, piss face..."

I dropped one hand between his legs. "Leaky...?" I felt him move inside the wet wool of his pants.

He chuckled. As we turned loose, he said, "I ain't even kissed you—and I love to neck and kiss and swap spit and stuff. Well, I guess we got to save something for next time."

I grinned. "Yeah..."

I left him sitting on the stoop. Rain sluiced the sidewalk, like molten glass, into the gutter. In the drizzle, I started down toward Broadway.

Sopping as I was, I decided the air conditioning on the subway (if I got a car where it was working) might be a bit much. So, at Broadway, on the downtown side of Seventy-ninth Street, across from the First Baptist, I waited for a bus (fingering a token out of the folds of a wet jeans pocket is a chore!); when it pulled up, I got on—to realize, as I sat beside the droplet-sequined window, that I'd left my umbrella, rolled up, on the stoop where Leaky and I'd been sitting.

Sometimes you're just lucky. The bus was cool enough to take the damp out of the air, so that my clothes actually got noticeably drier on the trip down. Though, when I stood up to get off, in the blue plastic hollow of the seat where I'd been sitting a puddled surface shivered to the engine. I turned for the door. As I stepped outside at the corner of Fifty-first, the air was warmer than on the bus—and the rain, down to a warm mist, cut to nothing by the time I reached the middle of the next block. I walked over to Ninth Avenue and down.

Yes, my clothes were damp. But they weren't dripping wet, when I reached the Pit. Nor was I.

Outside the place, wearing a sleeveless undershirt, a pair of baggy camouflage fatigues and high-topped combat boots, a blond kid leaned against the brick wall beside the door, arms folded, head down. He could have been anywhere between nineteen and twenty-two.

It was easy to assume that he was waiting for the two guys talking over near the curb by the garbage can: one was tall, curly-headed, and Hispanic, in a sweatshirt unzipped over a bald chest. His hand was on the shoulder of a shorter, dark-haired white kid, with a muscular build and one of those athletic shirts, white and red down to his rib cage, fishnet hanging below that and out of his jeans. The two of them, bending together, whispered of exchanges of dope, of women, of fabulous formulas that controlled the neighborhood's glittering dreams of power.

I stepped down to the entrance, pushed open the black door with its dark glass panes, and walked into the black interior, with its mirrors, its orange lights across the ceiling. The entrance was crowded with a trio of archaic phone booths on the left, a cigarette machine on the right. Above that hung one of the monitors for the jukebox video—where, as I looked up, the camera swooped through a burned-out neighborhood, in which, now in this rotted-out window and again against that broken wall, long-haired musicians twonged and boinged at heavy-metal intensity.

The counter and its customers stretched away on the right. On the left a row of stools sat along the wall, till the place opened up in the back for a pool table under a low-hanging ceiling lamp, another mini-bar, and doors here and there, to the bathroom, to the kitchen; and—presumably—to the parking lot out back.

If you go to the Pit three times, and somebody asks you to

describe it, you'll probably say something like the following: "The johns—the middle-aged and older men—sit at the bar, some of them in suits and ties, some dressed more sportily. The younger hustlers—the working men—sit along the wall, while the johns check them out either directly or by means of the mirror behind the bottles stacked at the bar's back. Now and again some hustler will join a john he already knows at the bar in conversation; or johns and hustlers will both go off into the back area to start conversations around the pool table, making their contacts there." Only then, when you come in the *fourth* time, looking for that pattern you just so carefully articulated, you notice a twenty-year-old muscle builder at the bar, clearly a hustler, nursing a rum and Coke between two older men who are paying him no mind whatsoever. Over by the wall, two tall, white-haired gentlemen, one in a tie, one in a sheepskin jacket, sit on stools either side of a voluble Puerto Rican kid, who's keeping them entertained with a cascade of loud stories about his cousin Luis. Another kid has been invited to the bar, where he and a john are talking intently. Still another, with a baseball cap turned backward and baggy jeans, wanders from the back to the front, and leaves—while in the back, shooting pool, is some guy, who, though he's wearing what looks like a high-school jacket and is pretty slender, with just a black T-shirt under it, is nevertheless—you see each time he turns to face you—in his late forties, if not early fifties. Certainly *he's* too old to be working—isn't he? But why is he dressed like that, acting like one of the working men, rather than a customer? (Though, to me, he was probably the sexiest-looking guy in the place, which makes you wonder...) Finally, sitting toward the back of the bar, a brown-skinned figure dressed in black lace and sable sequins flips a cigarette ash into an ashtray with the tap of a red-nailed finger—throwing *all* the systems of the world into question. Indeed, you realize now, the pattern you first intuited is only a reduction of a vast number of exceptions to itself that, at any moment, make up the customer configuration.

And, from half a dozen years before, I remembered Dave, back when the Fiesta was open, asking, "You mean all these guys are really *hustling*?"

I found a spot at the bar. I asked an Irish-looking bartender, who had a kind of youthful face in the half-light, but, up nearer, I saw was in his late forties: "Excuse me...?"

With a smile, he leaned both hands, far apart, on the bar. "What can I get you?"

"Is there anyone here who'd have information about some things that might have gone on here, oh, seventeen or eighteen years ago?"

"Sure," he said. "The owner. You want to talk to her?"

"If I could."

"She was just about to leave, I think." Now he stood up and looked toward the back. "Hey! Is Aline back there?"

A brassy voice came out of the bar's shadowed and mirrored depths: "She's in the goddamned shitter, honey—what do you want her for?"

This was apparently some sort of joke that set everybody laughing. The bartender turned back to me. "Maybe in a couple of minutes. What would you like to drink?"

"Eh," I said, "vodka and tonic."

"You got it." A glass with ice emerged from below the counter. The bartender turned to swing a bottle of vodka from its place before the back mirror, to start pouring mid-swing. The bottle was back in place by the end of his circuit. Now he picked up a siphon attached to a gooseneck, and pressed a clear plastic button, the light within momentarily aglow on the underside of his thumb.

"Lime?" he asked. "Lemon?"

"Lime," I said.

He scooped up a green and gray tetrahedron from a white plastic tray, squeezed it, dashed it down with a splash, and slid it to me on a square napkin. "Two ninety-five—or do you want to start a tab?"

"That's okay," I said, and went digging in my damp jeans for my wallet.

He took my damp and rumpled bills; as he returned to clack my nickel on the bar, a hand landed on my shoulder: "Now, honey—" it was the same brassy voice that had shouted out a moment before, and so I understood the joke "—what can I do for you?"

"Hello!" I turned to her.

Towering, blonde, and massive, she wore a blouse as loose and large as something from Erda's maternity wardrobe, from prehistoric Willendorf. Through some trick of gestalt shift, she looked the same age as she had the first time I'd come here, just back from school and living in Manhattan for the first time. Below, she wore shiny patent-leather shoes and dark pants—that must have had at least a forty-eight or fifty waist.

"You're Aline, the owner?" In the other bars throughout the neighborhood, people were always mentioning her, telling which working man she'd just eighty-sixed, what acid comeback she'd made to whichever caustic queen who'd decided to trade repartee. How old, I wondered, had she been seventeen years ago: twenty-five? thirty? thirty-five?

"Me and Johnny—but we don't want *him* to know. So we *call* it mine." She smiled, and we shook hands.

Her hand small, her palm dry, like a woman's who did a lot of housework. "You wanted to ask me something?"

"Yes," I said. "I wanted to get some information—any information you had, about something that happened here, seventeen or eighteen years back. A young man was killed, stabbed to death—either in here, or in the parking lot just outside. He was twenty-nine years old—and a Korean. Korean-American. His name was Timothy Hasler, and he was a fairly well-known philosopher, even then. But he's become even more well-known since his death. No one was ever tried for his murder. But people are more and more interested in Hasler today, and we're trying to…well, collect as much information about how he died as we can."

For the beat of five, she looked at me, perfectly blank. Then she said, "Are you sure that was here? A lot of stuff goes on in this neighborhood. Seventeen or eighteen years ago? There were a lot of bars back then that are closed now—a lot rougher than this place ever was. The Haymarket. O'Neill's. That's the kind of thing that was more likely to have happened over there than here."

I frowned.

"Eighteen years ago—"

"Seventeen, actually," I corrected.

"Whatever." She went on: "That's a long time—I don't even know if I was around here then."

"When did you become owner of the Pit?" I asked.

"Late sixties, early seventies," she said.

"This happened," I said, "on September 23rd, 1973—it was somewhere after one in the morning. So it was really a continuation of September 22nd—"

"Well, then—" she nodded "—I would have been here. But I don't remember anything like that. That really sounds like something that would have happened in another place. Probably the Haymarket—they were always having set-tos over there. Or maybe it was one of the places that used to be over on Tenth Avenue. Some of them were pretty savage—you know, the closer you go to the river, the wilder it gets. They had some pretty rough spots over there. But we always tried to keep it cool in here—that's why we're still around." Then she frowned. "How old did you say this kid was?"

"He wasn't a kid," I said. "He was twenty-nine."

"Now," she said, "you see? We never had a lot of people that age hanging out around here. We have a lot of people over thirty-five—over forty, actually. We get a lot of kids under twenty-five. Just look around—you'll see what I mean. The kind of place this is hasn't really changed all that much since we got started. But we just don't have many customers your age—in that twenty-six- to thirty-six-year-old range. You should ask around and try to find out about some of them other places—that are closed down now. And didn't you say it was out in the parking lot? You know, ever since we been here, there've been people getting ripped off in that lot, getting roughed up, getting stabbed, getting shot—I mean two or three times a month. I don't even pay any attention to it anymore. But that doesn't have nothing to do with us, honey." She shook her head with a firm frown. "I'm afraid I don't know anything about what you're talkin'. That was a long time ago—and it probably didn't have nothing to do with us, anyway."

I said, "I'm pretty sure it was here."

"Naw." She shook her head with a small, definite shake. "That wasn't here. Look, the next drink's on the house—hey, Donny?" With her elbow on the bar, she leaned across it. "This guy's next drink is on me!" Now she pulled back. "But you're not going to learn anything about stuff like that. It's too long ago. Nobody remembers that kind of shit. *Ehhh!*" She gave a little shiver, that moved all through her bulk. "Who'd want to! I gotta go. I like to get out of here before the animals arrive." She started away, then turned back again, to lift a hand in which I saw a bunch of car keys, one between her rather girlish fingers: this smile was actually a nice one: "Down here we don't have too long a memory. It's probably better that way." She turned, like a silken tank, to move majestically toward the door—while Donny (I assume that was the bartender's name) came over and put a tumbler upside down in front of me on the counter.

"For your next drink," he said; and moved off.

The other bartender was only about three feet away—an older guy, well knit, in a blue sweater with a V neck showing a snarl of white hair on his chest; around his beret the hair was a darker and richer brown than Leaky's, who was at least fifteen years his junior—which, only after another minute of sipping, did I realize meant it was dyed. He moved away to do some work. I looked around, feeling a little lost. When my eyes swept past his—he was back, looking at me—he gave me a mellow smile. He picked up a rag—and did not wipe the bar around the three-quarters empty basket of popcorn in front of me. "Aline sure gave *you* the brush-off. What were you asking her about, anyway?"

"Something that happened here. I guess she just didn't want to tell me about it."

"Management...!" he said, with a moue and a hand flipped at me on a wrist that broke dramatically. "She has to be like that. But she likes you—I don't know why."

"How long have you worked here?" I asked.

"Not steadily," he said. "But I'll tell you, I was a porter here the day Aline opened this place, Monday, October 13th, 1969—we started out as a pure exploitation of Stonewall. Nothing more, and nothing less. And by the first of the year, I was tending bar pretty regularly. Sometimes I've been away, but I always seem to come back."

"Well," I said, "there was a murder here—"

"There've been several!"

"A guy named Timothy Hasler—a Korean-American, twenty-nine years old. He was stabbed—"

"Oh, my God—" The bartender looked askance at me. "You're not really trying to find out about *that* one, are you? Our first murder was three weeks after we opened. A black kid named Willie, who started beating on a john named Edward Sloan, who had a heart attack—right *there*, not three feet away from where you're standing. Willie did three years for manslaughter. Now wouldn't you prefer to hear about that? Aline thought she was going to get closed down for sure, with something like that so soon after we opened up. But the parking-lot trick worked—since, I guess, it was the first time we tried it."

"Parking-lot trick?"

"If something happens to somebody, you do *not* leave 'em lying on the floor in here. You take them outside into the parking lot out back—*then* you call the police. Then you get some kid to say they were out back there and saw the body—and came in here shouting to call the cops. It's humane—I mean, we don't just *leave* them there. Are you sure you wouldn't rather hear about the June '80 robbery—that's the one that everybody gets such a kick out of! And I was working here the day *that* one happened. So were two phone repairmen, the same afternoon. About four o'clock these guys came in here with—my dear—a double-barreled *shot*gun! They made all the customers lie down on the floor. Then they made me go through and collect all the money and the wallets. And I'm cooperating, too—I'm being just as nice, and moving them toward the door, see, while I do it. I just wanted them out of here in the *worst* way, you know what I mean? Well, I've got them about halfway toward the door, and wouldn't you know, this crazy queen, lying down on the floor in the back, suddenly shouts out, 'Oh, I got another twenty, in my pocket here!' Like they were gonna go back and check?" He lowered his face, raised his eyebrows. "Well, of course they *did* go back—and got that poor shit's last twenty. Then they said I should lay down on the floor, too. And I said, 'Well, I don't think there's any *room.*' It was crowded in here, that afternoon. But he hits me on the shoulder with the gun barrel— hard, too." He raised both hands like a kid gesturing "I give up." "Well, one of the phone repairmen was down on the floor right where I was standing—you talk about a cute pair of buns? So I lay down *right* on top of them, my dear. And they left." Laughing, he slapped the bar. "Then I called up Aline and told her, 'Honey, we been robbed at gunpoint. And I'm going to have a drink, shut the place down—and go *home!*'" He laughed again. "Oh, I'll tell you anything you want to know about this place. But I can't imagine you really want to hear about that Hasler business, now..."

"Yes, I do. Very much."

He leaned forward, put his hand on my forearm. "You're not some kind of cop—or a detective, or a newspaper reporter? Are you?"

"No." I shook my head. Then I thought, why not? "I'm a graduate student, doing a Ph.D. thesis in philosophy. Hasler was a philosopher—and I want to find out how he died."

He looked at me for a few moments—and I recalled the blank look Aline had given me. "Well, you don't *look* like a city father trying to shut us down."

The tall gray-haired man sitting beside me, who (I'd thought) wasn't even vaguely listening, said, "They don't make those in black, dear."

The bartender pulled back sharply. "Oh, yes they do. They certainly *do!* Tell me." He leaned toward me again. "When did you suck your last dick?"

I laughed. "You really want to know?"

"I would not have asked if I didn't."

"Actually," I said, "about forty minutes ago. This homeless guy—uptown. In the rain."

"Oh, my *dear*—!" His hand went to his throat, to fiddle there for a surprised moment. "I think I'll buy you a drink myself! Look, I don't know how much you know about this place. But you really have asked about a strange one—"

"You were here when it happened?"

"I was here that evening. A little after midnight, I went over to Tenth Avenue with some friends. And about one-thirty Philly Dan came running into the bar I was in, to tell me that this Chinese fellow had just gotten stabbed here in the Pit. Korean—*I* know! But nobody knew it at the time. So I came back. The police were here by then, and I helped close up the place. And of course nobody had anything else to talk about for the next three weeks. So—no, I *wasn't* here when it actually *happened*. But I was here just before—and just after."

"Do you know who did it? Or what it was about?"

He gave me the blank look again that brought back Aline's first stare.

"What did people *say* happened?"

"Well, I was also there when the Chinese—Korean—fellow came in: I noticed him right away. Like Aline said, we don't get many guys that age. Nor do we get that many Orientals—at least we didn't back in 1973—though only two weeks ago, we were thinking of starting a Japanese businessman's night here. We don't see any for a month. Then, suddenly, we get twelve at a time—and, sometimes, they can become very..."—He snapped his fingers above his head like a Spanish dancer—"gay! The problem, of course, wasn't him—your Korean friend. It was the guy he brought in with him. I realized there was going to be trouble as soon as I saw him."

"There was someone with him that night?"

"Oh, yes. This tall fellow—blond, I believe. Well built. And..." Here he stopped.

"Then what happened?"

"Well, how much *do* you know about places like this? Not much, I'd gather, from the way you came on with Aline. Or me."

"I used to go to the Fiesta fairly frequently, before it closed—"

"And now sometimes you hang out at Cats," he finished. "That's what I would have figured. But the Pit, see, is a hard-core hustling bar. That's all it's here for. That's all the people here are here for. Oh, like anyplace else, it's got a few guys who just hang out and watch the action. But this isn't Cats. And it sure isn't the Fiesta!"

I looked around. "It doesn't look too busy right now."

"Yeah? You hang around for another hour, hour and a half. Even on Tuesday night, once you get past nine o'clock, nine-thirty, this place makes the New York Stock Exchange look like a Sunday-school picnic. You talk about philosophy—really it's a matter of the philosophy of a place like this. If philosophy's what you'd call it."

"I'm kind of lost."

"You see," he said, "this place is a lot of older men who think the only way they can get anything worth having sexually is to pay for it. And the kids who come here are all kids who want to get paid—need to get paid. Some of them are supporting a habit, yeah. But it's astonishing how many of them have a wife and a kid that they're taking care of by coming in here on Thursday, Friday, Saturday night and going home with somebody a couple or three times in an evening. I know more than one kid who put himself though school this way—though, the truth is, most of them are just out to prove how big and bad they are. They *can* do it—so they *do* do it. But the thing that makes this whole place possible is a belief that sex—the kind of sex that gets sold here—is scarce. Because it's scarce, it's valuable. And because it's valuable, it goes for good prices. Now suppose, one day, you had some guy come in here—twenty, twenty-one, twenty-two: young, good body, nice-looking. But the thing about him was he didn't think sex was scarce at all. He thought it was all over the place. He didn't mind older guys—'cause he liked all sorts of guys, young, old, and everybody in between. As far as sex, he's one of these guys who lives his life with his hand in his pocket, playing with himself. And whipping it out and giving it to one of these..." he looked left and right, then leaned forward again to whisper, under his breath "old cocksuckers here, well he just thinks that the most fun you could possibly have in an evening. Money? He'd pay *them* to suck on it, if he thought they wanted it! So what happens if one of these guys comes in, starts hanging out here, huh?"

"I guess it kind of upsets the system—at least the one this place operates on."

"You better *believe* it does!" He pulled back. "Something like that happens, it generates a lot of hostility. Especially from the kids working here. Fast, too. I mean you could even say it was the principle of the thing—you ready for your next drink?"

Looking down, I was a little surprised I was. But I guess it's all the ice they put in the glass that makes the drink go so quickly.

He hailed Donny, and pointed down at my glass—and while Donny came to fill it, he went down to take care of some customers on his half of the bar. Then he was back: "It's funny that we don't get more of them, I suppose. As long as I been here, it seems to me to average out about three of these guys walking in here over any four-year period. By this time, I know enough not to even let 'em hang around for five minutes. A lot of times, they're pretty beat up—but we always have our share of those, too. Usually though, it's drugs, not sex. And to most of the fellas sitting at the bar, anyone under twenty-five looks good. Half of them are right out of some mental hospital. I actually *knew* one, once—when I was younger and a lot more naïve. Let him stay at my place for about two weeks—he didn't have any place else to be. *Child* abuse? The stories that kid told me about the things that had happened to him when he was a child—well, you tell me about how you got your little pink asshole—or your black ass—" he leaned forward, with a conspiratorial wink—"diddled half a dozen times by the priest after choir practice and a lollipop for your pains, and I'll tell you, it happened to me too, honey: and I loved every saintly centimeter he shoved into me—I just wished it was a little longer. But I have neither time nor sympathy for bullshit like that."

I smiled, feeling uncomfortable with his pronouncement. "It never happened to me," I said. "I'm not Catholic."

"Well, you know what I mean. But you have to keep a sense of proportion about these things, don't you think? How can you get seriously twisted out of shape by things like that, when you know what's really going on out here to some of these children—I feel sorry for them. I really do. But one of them comes in here, after he's gotten roughed up by the cops for beating off on the street corner at three in the afternoon—that was the last one, about a year back—and they think that finally *this* is someplace they can make out. Well, I go straight up to them and tell them they have to leave—no, baby! Not in five minutes. You're out of here. Now! It's for their own protection."

"Really."

"If one comes in when it's crowded, sometimes I can miss him for a half an hour or so. But, in twenty minutes, one of those guys in here throws off the whole chemistry of this place."

"How can you tell if somebody just walking in is one of them?"

He gave me a withering look. "I'm talking about the guys that everybody else in the world thinks of as perverts. I mean, if some kid walks in here and can't keep his hands off his crotch, and has a stupid shit-eating grin, and the next the thing you know he's got some old white-haired guy in the corner, and you know no money is going to change hands—I mean, ten times a night, some kid, sitting at the bar, is going to pull his pecker out and show it off to the old man sitting next to him, just to let him know what he's got. You can't do anything about that in a place like this. But if some kid's sitting at the bar, looking stupid and his arm is moving below the bar, real steady, and half a dozen guys are trying to get a look at him, without me or Aline or the waiter or somebody who works here seeing them—well, *then* you got a problem!"

I laughed. The bartender nodded at me knowingly.

"But that's who your friend Hasler brought in with him that night. There *was* hostility—there *were* problems. *Christ*, there were problems! And the Korean fellow just got in the way of them—maybe because he brought the kid in, that's why he ended up buying it. Now, I wasn't here. So the precise mechanics, I'm not real clear on. Say—" and he drew the word out, lengthily and thoughtfully—"you know who you ought to talk to? Apple

Blossom—Ronnie Apple. He was here the night it happened. I mean, we must have talked about it nonstop over the whole next three weeks! He doesn't come in a lot anymore. But he drops in from time to time. You say this is going to get you your Ph.D?"

"Well, it'll make my getting it a little easier."

"Okay. I'm going to do my bit for affirmative action. Look, write your phone number down here." He handed me a card. "Next time Blossom comes in, I'll ask him if he wants to talk to you about it. And if he says okay, I'll give you a call, and you can set up a time to talk."

"He was in the bar? When it happened."

"He said he saw the whole thing. And though she is a charac-ter—and some of these queens want to be in the center of every-thing—still, I don't think she's a hopeless liar." He handed me a pencil. As I wrote, he said with a leer: "Now they're all going to think you're my new trick for the month!"

I looked up and smiled. "Say, thanks a lot. Really!"

"I haven't done anything for you yet, dear. And paper's cheap. Right back behind the pool table, that's where your friend was stabbed. As soon as it happened, a bunch of guys dragged him out in the parking lot out back, and dropped him on the ground. I told you: Aline has got this thing—as soon as anyone is really hurt, out they go! Unless it's *real* cold. Anyway, that's when they called the police. Of course, after all these years, the police pret-ty well know: if it happens anywhere within fifty feet of this place, they assume it *did* happen right here—even if it didn't, some-times. Aline's seen this place through some rough times. But she and Jimmy have some very good connections. And, in some ways, the coppers figure the Pit's a kind of calming influence on the neighborhood."

"Then she really knew what I was talking about?"

"She wasn't here at all the night it happened." He shrugged. "I can vouch for that. It was a Saturday—and she stays away from this place like the plague on weekends. She *might* have forgotten. A lot's gone on here."

"What happened to the fellow who Hasler brought with him?"

"Oh, he was cut!" He nodded again. "But he was scared too, I guess; and he made it out the back. As did the person who did the stabbing."

"It's funny," I said. "This is something I've been interested in for years. But I've learned more about it this evening than I have since I first got interested in Hasler." I took a breath. "Now I have to figure out how to explain the details to somebody else. I'm really anxious to talk with your friend—Apple Blossom?"

"Ronnie! Apple Blossom is just between you and me—you know what I mean. But you just let me get you together with him. He'll tell you the details of the whole thing. We're all getting to that age where we like the idea of young people getting interested in what happened to us. Most of the kids in this place couldn't care less. They're the one's who're selling—not us."

"I'm going to go in the back," I said, "and walk around the pool table—maybe step out into the parking lot outside. Just to see where it happened."

"The door to the parking lot's locked. Aline's kept it that way for over ten years—except on those sultry summer nights, all too common I'm afraid, when our air conditioning is on the fritz. Then it's the only way to get a breeze through here. Or, of course, when we have to open it all of a sudden to get someone out."

"Oh." I got up from the bar chair.

"I wouldn't be surprised if it was because of the Hasler killing that she started locking it."

I left the counter, went into the back, and walked around the pool table, anyway. Behind it was a black door from which the brazen eye of a lock barrel stared at my chest: the door had no handle—I assumed it went to the lot.

Between the pool table and the door, I looked at the black floorboards, wondering if there were eighteen-year-old bloodstains under the paint. Then I went and left the talkative bartender a three-dollar tip.

"Why, thank you! You're not going to let me buy you that drink? Stick around for it. You give the place some class—" again he leaned forward—"which is what we say to all the cute numbers who come in here. Really, though. We like for our new customers to have a good time—at least on the first night. We want you to come back. On me—really. That was a vodka and tonic—?"

"Maybe next time," I said.

He said, smiling: "Maybe next time I won't feel like buying you one."

I couldn't think of anything to say. So I just laughed. And left.

Riding the subway home, again I thought about me and Timothy Hasler. Yes, it was the Tonys, and the Crazy Joeys, and the Leakys that I went for. But as different as Tim and I were, as different as we'd started out, that seemed what Hasler had ended up with. Who, I wondered, was this street pervert who couldn't keep his hands off his dick, who'd come with Hasler down to the Pit and whose sexual carryings-on had precipitated Tim's death? Walking back up Broadway, I looked across at the corner of Eighty-second Street: the idea of a Burger King as less violent in its response to that sort of deranged sexuality than the Pit was weird—even as it made its own reactionarily deranged sense. (I turned up Eighty-second Street for Amsterdam.) Then there was the distressing fact of Hasler's apartment, from which Tim—or Tim and his friend—had emerged that night to go down there—

Why somebody should think that just because some guy's homeless, he's got nothing to do but sit around (in the rain, even) and wait around for some guy with a roof overhead to come by is unbelievably presumptuous. Yet, when I realized Leaky was nowhere on the block, I felt the same disappointment that, six years ago, had driven me out into the park three times in a night to find my first yoni. In front of the little gate across from the church, I stopped and looked at the plywood wired up across the bars. Three amoeboid patches still wetted it, and for a moment I imagined the beast of Hasler's journal, crouched before it, splattering it with his urine. Stepping up to it, I read over the spray-painted letters... Then I bent to touch the grain with my forefinger—low, on one wide wet spot down near my knee. A moment later, standing, I touched my finger to my tongue, hoping, I guess, for some faint salts.

But it was only rainwater.

"You," I said out loud, "are the door. Yeah—*sure* you are."

Then I walked to the corner.

Something large and dark lay on the vestibule floor—someone was sleeping up in there!

First I stopped, then I hurried up the stoop steps.

He was curled, fetal position, blue sweatshirt hood pulled over his head. Ten inches of hairy flesh showed above the waist of his pants (that woolen cloth, far too heavy for this weather), below his sweatshirt bottom. Sleeping with his back against the wall across from the one with the mailboxes, he had pulled his rough, soiled hands up loosely before his face. Faintly, he snored.

My folded umbrella lay on the floor against his belly hair.

In the warm night, my clothes had pretty much dried. I reached down to feel whether his sweatshirt was still damp—to see I was standing in a yellowish puddle, over some two thirds of the vestibule's white tiles.

Suddenly, it kind of got to me: this big, grubby guy, who'd come over at Tony's behest, trying to have a good time, trying to make sure I did. "Leaky...?"

He lay, curled in the puddle of his own piss.

I squatted down now. "Hey, Leaky...Dummy? You stupid asshole," I said, "you gone and pissed all over yourself—you fuckin' idiot!"

In his sleep, suddenly he thrust one hand down between his legs, pulling and prodding at his soaked fly—which wasn't zipped.

"Hey, stupid...!"

His big hand got into his pants and, inside, he pulled at himself—eyes still closed. Within the salted chestnut hair of his beard, his lips hung faintly apart. Then, suddenly, he heaved in a breath. And blinked.

"Hey, Dummy," I said. "You okay...?"

He looked up, blankly, blinking.

Then he said, "Aw, man...you come back? You left your umbrella—"

"Yeah," I said. "I just got here. You stupid asshole, you pissed all over yourself!"

"Yeah." He grinned. "I do that a lot sometimes...pretty much since I was a kid. That's how I got my name."

I said: "You want to come upstairs with me? We could fool around some more—I could get you something to eat. And you could sleep on something a little softer than these hallway tiles."

"Sure," he said. He pushed up from the ground. "That'd be nice. You want to?"

"Yeah. You want some beer?"

"Man!" he said. "Now that *would* be nice!" Frowning down, he lifted one great hand from the flooded floor, looked at his huge wet fingers—then licked his palm broadly and made a face up at me. "Sure as hell *is* piss. We get some beer, after a while it won't taste like nothing. I mean my piss. It'll just be like fuckin' warm water, you know?"

"Yeah," I said. "I know."

Suddenly he pushed his wet hand in my face. "Try some of the good stuff, while it's still got some flavor!" Thrusting his fingers in my mouth, he practically knocked me over—but I kept my balance.

As he stood, I stood up beside him.

"You like it when I do shit like that? I gotta ask—" he grinned— "the first couple of times, just so I'll know. After I learn, though, then I'll just do it—or I won't. You like it?"

The taste was bitter and salt, and, yes, it startled me. (I remembered what Tony had once said about exhibitionism and stimulation. I remembered hoping for that same taste from the plywood—but having tasted it, yes, everything was brighter, clearer, sharper.) I took a breath. "Yeah," I said. "I like it."

He shrugged. "It's only piss. It don't hurt you—you know that."

I said: "The Korean place is open all night down the street. We'll get a case."

"Man!" Leaky said. "You're fuckin' serious, ain't you?"

I shrugged. "Come on. You carry half; I'll carry half."

"I'll carry the whole fuckin' thing, man," he said. "I don't mind."

A wet stain darkened the side of his pants, waist to cuff; and the whole right arm of his sweatshirt was soaked. He unzipped it now and let his hood fall back. "It's funny," he told me; we started down the stoop steps. "It don't matter how hot it gets, I have to zip the fucker up—or take the whole fuckin' thing off—if I want to fall asleep. I can't sleep with it just flappin' around me like that. Here's your umbrella—" he picked it up, gripping it full—"if you still want it?"

"Yeah, sure," I said. "Here." I started to take it from him gingerly. Then I just grasped the little club of folded-up wet black cloth—and held it the way Leaky had.

Leaky carried the case of tallboys on his blue sweatshirt's shoulder back from the all-night Korean vegetable market.

"You sure you want to carry the whole thing?" We turned down the nighttime street. "You don't have to. We can break it in half—"

"I don't mind. I'm a big, dumb ox—that's what I'm for. Lugging stuff around. I'm okay."

"That's probably because you're so fucking stupid."

He shook his head and pushed his free hand into his open fly, to work on himself. "Nigger, you an' me gonna get along real good." Now he hauled himself out, three-quarters hard, and milked his cock forward a few times, then (he sucked a breath through his teeth), while we walked, shook the two free inches of skin on the end, and put it back inside.

I thought about what the bartender had said about the kids flashing their dicks in the bar. But there was no one else on the street.

With my keys, I opened the door, and he hauled the case, in his falling-apart shoes, ahead of me up the stairs. One step above me, his butt was at my eye level. I could see the top three inches of the hairy crack between his buttocks, and the whorls as the fur rose on either side of the small of his back. On the fifth floor, I opened the umbrella and left it on the floor by the hall wall to dry. Leaky stood back while I opened the apartment door.

"Where you want this?" He stepped in behind me.

"Put it in the kitchen," I said, "down beside the refrigerator."

In the kitchen, he tipped it down, caught it in both hands, and swung it to the maroon vinyl before my refrigerator, then dropped to his knees and ripped the cardboard top off the carton in one motion. Still kneeling, he opened the refrigerator door and, with meticulous care, while I watched, took out each can and put it on the bottom shelf. Closing the refrigerator door, he stood—and the cardboard case was suddenly in the air, was torn in half, torn in half again, the pieces all collapsing behind his meaty fingers, as he pulled them back first against his chest, then his hairy gut.

He handed the folded cardboard to me; I put it in the green rubber garbage can in the kitchen corner, while he asked me: "Maybe we should have a couple of those?"

"Sure."

So he opened the refrigerator again, leaned over, and, with one hand, took out two. He stood up, and while the door swung closed, he began to bite at the nails on his other.

I took one from him and opened it—then opened his, when

he held it out to me. His fingers were just too thick to get under the tab.

"Come on," he said. "You can climb on top of me and fuck my belly till you fill my hairy ol' belly button with cum. Then you can lick it out." He let me go first down the hall, with a hand on my shoulder, hanging down from somewhere in the dark heavens.

The beer was cold and good.

In the living room, I said: "Have a seat—on the couch there, that's comfortable." He walked over and let himself down, then sat back with his beer can balanced on one of his wide-spread knees. His fly was still open. Inside I could see dark hair and, deep within it, his cock's thick base.

I sat in the chair across from him in the corner.

"You actually read all these fuckin' books?" He looked around at the shelves.

"Most of them."

He pursed his lips and nodded. "That's why Tony calls you the professor, huh? Me—" he shook his head—"I don't know how to read and write, myself. I told you that, though, didn't I? But that's 'cause nobody ever really taught me. My daddy didn't send me to school until second grade. He said he forgot how old you was supposed to be before you was supposed to go—which is why I missed out on first. That's when they did all these tests on me what said I was stupid—I'll tell you, the way they was comin' in vans to pick me up, takin' me all over here, drivin' me down to there. And lettin' me talk to this one and that one—I seen more doctors and social workers and what-all—well, I guess I thought being stupid must be pretty important, if they did all that shit for you. I wonder if that's why it turns me on, somebody talkin' about it to me, like...well, you know. Maybe because all that was happenin' about the time I started pullin' my dick. Once they left me in the back of the van by myself for a couple of hours 'cause the guy what was supposed to give me the tests wasn't there yet, and I beat off three times, 'cause I didn't have nothin' else to do. And I ate it so they wouldn't find the cum. Another time, I was in a doctor's office and two doctors in the other room was talking about this other kid, and joking about how stupid he was, the two of them together—and I got so hot I shot in my pants. Later on, I used to think about that and pretend they was talkin' about me, when I jerked my pecker.

But after all the tests, I never went back to *third* grade. So I guess I just got beyond the age where you can learn it—readin', I mean."

"You could learn," I said. "You might be somewhat dyslexic—but there're ways to get around that, even."

"Yeah?"

"Yeah."

"Go piss in yourself." He grinned. "Naw—you wait for me to do it. We'll both have more fun that way. Hey, you wanna take my shoes off for me? I got some big, smelly feet, man—I'd like to rub 'em in your face, too. Relax 'em."

"Sure," I said.

I drank some more beer, stood up, started over—

"But—" he lifted his can—"you could get me another one of these. This one's empty. I go through these things pretty fast, at least the first two or three."

"Okay," I said. "I'll bring you back two, then."

"Good idea."

Back in the living room, I gave him one. He lay the other beside him on the couch. I dropped down to the floor, cross-legged, and moved his foot out toward me. "How do you manage to find shoes that fit?"

"I don't," he said, "most of the time. These're a little tight. Leastways the right one. That's why I had to open it up. Some woman gave me these—said they belonged to her ex-boyfriend. He was a professional basketball player. When I do get a pair I can get into, I wear 'em till the fuckers fall off me. Then I gotta go barefoot till I get some more. If I get small ones—size thirteen or fourteen—I cut the backs open, sometimes. But, shit, it's easier to go barefoot, actually." On the sneaker that was pretty much torn off, the dirt-blackened laces (they'd once been white) were pretty knotted up together. While I picked at it, he leaned over to look. "That one's been airing out," he said. "So it probably don't smell as much."

Under the flapping upper, I rubbed his immense, soiled toes, with their picked-back nails—and wondered how all this would have struck Tim Hasler.

Above me, he kind of *prrrred*—and took another tug from his beer.

The shoe came off—his foot came out of it. The surrounding

rubber had taken the shape of toes and ball. I bent down to sniff—and he obligingly raised his foot for me. "It smells," I said. His sole was board-rough, like I'd expect someone's who was going bare-foot to be. "Not much. But it smells—good."

I put it down and turned to the other.

There was still a bow in the lace; I pulled it loose. The little length of lace that had been in the knot was a lighter gray than the blackened length around it. His gray ankle, thick as a small pork shoulder, slid out the ragged top—and with his foot came a stench like vinegar and dirty laundry and maybe the smell you get in an old spice cabinet—only nine or ten time stronger.

"Jesus...!" It was enough to make me blink.

"That's the one," he said.

The running shoe fell over on its side. He flexed his toes.

I put a forefinger between the big one and the one over, and rubbed—hard.

"Aw, shit, man—!" He gave a grunt that just went on and on and on that, for the length of it, I couldn't tell if it were pain or plea-sure. "*Arrrrrhhhh...feels fuckin' good!*"

I moved my forefinger on between the next two toes.

Dirt and dead skin came out, first in chunks, then in rolls.

As I rubbed, above me he made these roiling growls, with his eyes closed, that I'd imagine out of a rutting grizzly. "Once, man—" his eyes were still closed—"they picked me up for hitchhiking, and put my ass in jail. And there was this piece of chain hanging off the wall by a nail. I took my sneakers off—I'd been walking in them dogs for three or four days steady, I guess—and I got that chain between my toes and started running my foot up and down, scratching the skin between them with it. It felt so fuckin' good—only, five minutes later, I opened my eyes, and don't you know the fuckin' chain was all bloody? I'd done tore up my fucking foot on that thing, scratching it, and didn't even know." He opened his eyes, took another pull from his tallboy (in *his* hand, it looked like a twelve-ounce can), and glanced down again. "But that sure feels good, nigger." I finished between the little toe and the toe over—his nail on his little toe was larger than the nail on my fore-finger—what wasn't picked away.

Then I went to scratch between the toes of his other foot.

"Funny." He grinned. "*That* one feels good, too!" And while I scratched his cracked, callused foot, he lifted the other one and put it against my face, turned the sole in, and rubbed.

I closed my eyes, and let the smell wrap all around me, filling me (was this the sort of thing, I wondered, that made Hasler happy), and fading—even as I tried to hold onto it, the way scents and tastes and even colors sometimes will when they engulf you.

"You like to do for a big, dirty guy like me, don't you?"

I nodded.

"That's good. That's the way it should be—for you and me, I mean. An' I like a nigger doing for me—little things: getting me a fucking beer, opening it for me, rubbing my feet, playing with my balls when I beat off, lickin' the cheese from out my fuckin' yoni when my dick gets *too* fuckin' filthy, going to sleep with my dick in his mouth so I don't have to worry about pissing the goddamned bed. Waking up, with a nigger sucking on my big, hard dick—fucker's always up when I wake up in the morning. Ain't nothin' nicer than waking up with some nigger sucking on your dick, so you can just lie there and drop the first one of the day without even having to think about how you gonna get off the first time." His foot came around to my face, covering my mouth. On my mouth, his sole was rough as sandpaper. (This, I thought, was probably what Timothy Hasler would have considered heaven. And the truth is, it wasn't that bad.) With the edge of his foot, he rocked my head back and forth. "Man, about the best thing in the world is to have you a nigger you can piss on, anytime you want. I'd do anything for that—I swear, just about anything if it meant having that permanent-like. And one who's real smart and can call me stupid, too...!"

His foot slipped to my shoulder.

And as I opened my eyes, he reached down, scooped his big hand under my arm, and tugged me up—he'd unzipped his sweatshirt. Both his beer cans were on the floor. And his dick was out his pants in his fist as he pulled me up—"Get some of this, motherfucker"—and he pushed my head against his dick. As I got it in my mouth, he flooded it with hot, tasteless urine.

A moment later, he was dragging me farther up against him. Then I was pretty much on top of him; he had his arms around me, his face was against mine; and his big tongue probed inside my mouth. I probed in return—some of his back teeth were in rough shape.

I got my pants open and down as far as my thighs. His cock lay between us like a small log. I got my dick alongside his and began to rub. With the hair and the heat of him, gone sweaty in the warm apartment, his groin was pleasingly rough; his arms made a cage of flesh and muscle and fur around me; I got one hand under his head, in his hair; he wrapped one leg over me. (His head was propped on the arm of the couch. His extended leg went well over the other arm.) His tongue kept trying to spear as far down my throat as he could, and as I rubbed against him, the sweat lubricating us suddenly became a rush of heat—suddenly, in the hair of him, my belly slid against his, gone wet and hot. He was peeing on himself. I sucked on his tongue and, into his rushing water, shot all over his belly.

Without taking his tongue out my mouth, he began to laugh. Reaching down, I felt urine running over his gut fur. Now one of his hands left my back, to slide his fingers between us. They moved around the head of my dick, still sensitive, then came out and up to my face—there was something wet on his fingers, that now he pushed between our faces, first one into my mouth, then the other. The sound of his breath—our paired breaths—between us, was a roar.

Opening my eyes, I saw his—dark brown—were open.

Around his tongue I tried to swallow the scum he'd fed me.

Then suddenly I pulled away, pushed back: his cock, still hard, still hosed a ravine up across his stomach hair, shed away either side the rill. Bending, I reached for it, thrust it in my mouth, and, threading his skin over my tongue, drank. And drank.

And drank. (I heard him sigh; I felt him move his butt over. Under my hand, the wool of his pants was wet.) And drank.

When he finished, both hands had come to cage my head, and he pulled me up to lie against him again, over the slippery place between his gut and mine where some of my cum still was.

"Tony told me," he whispered roughly, "that if you brung me upstairs and got your own nut off, then I was to tell him you owed him a whole nickel. But don't you pay that redheaded fucker no nickel for me! You pay him a fucking penny—like he first said."

"Where—" but I wasn't really listening—"did you learn to do that?"

"I had myself a good teacher." He was smiling again. "I think we kind of messed up your couch a little. But it's just fucking beer piss. The first three or four times, once it dries, you can't even smell it."

"Well, I guess...oh, fuck it," I said. "I probably should have christened it years ago." And, yes, I was remembering the Piece o' Shit I'd never got up here.

"You stay on top of me," he said, "and you won't have to worry about lyin' on no wet spot."

Which made me laugh.

His hand went behind my head and his tongue thrust into my mouth again, and moved around in it, slow and firm. We looked at each other, open-eyed and blinking, while we did it. For a long time. Then he took his mouth away from mine. "Sometime or other, I'd like to take a shower. But you tell me when. I can tell, you probably don't want me to do it now."

"In the morning," I said. "How's that?"

"Fine with me. You have a good time with me, nigger. Have a real good time—please?"

"You," I said, "are a strange guy."

"Yeah?" he said. "Why?"

"Just the way you come on. Leaky...Leaky what?"

"Leaky Sowps."

"...Sowps?"

"Yeah. Sowps. S-O-W-P-S...I can spell *that* one. I can even write it out. With both hands. My daddy's Billy Sowps. Just like when I started using 'Larry,' they always wanted to make it 'Lawrence,' they was always trying to make my daddy into William Sowps. But he ain't no William. He's a Billy. And he named me Leaky."

"What about your mother?"

He sucked his teeth. "She didn't name me nothin'...!"

"Leaky Sowps—from...? Where are you from, anyway, Leaky?"

"I been all over, man. I don't think there's a fuckin' state in the union, leastways the northern half of it, I ain't hitched in. I do not like the South though. I was born there. I been back down there a few times—Florida, Georgia, Alabama. But, you know, I can't take the way they treat black people. I'm serious. You'd think with me, gettin' off on black guys what get off on bein' called 'nigger' and stuff, that wouldn't make somebody like me blink an eye. But I can't take it. It fucking turns my stomach—not that it's that much better up here. But maybe I'm just used to the way it happens up here—and at least everybody isn't jokin' about lynchin' 'em up and cuttin' their balls off and expecting you to laugh your head off. So now I guess you really think I'm strange."

"No," I said. "Actually it kind of makes sense—at least to me."

"It don't make no sense to me."

"Well—" I thought of explaining Freud's idea about the way perversions were the opposite of character neuroses. But that would probably be better for another time. "You like black guys. Even if it's just to piss on."

"Shit," he said, "I like 'em for a lot more than that!" His arms tightened around me.

"Anyway," I said, "it makes sense to me that, if you like some group sexually, and want them to be around and happy and fuck with you a lot, you might be concerned with how they're treated socially—and politically."

"Guys who like to fuck women," he answered, "usually treat women like shit. But, then, I could never understand that either."

"Well," I said, "heterosexuals were always kind of beyond me."

I felt his chin come down to brush the top of my head. He said, "*I'm* heterosexual," with some indignation.

"Jesus," I said. "another one?"

"I don't mind fuckin' women. They just don't seem to like fuckin' me. Hell, I'll pretty much fuck with anybody what'll buy me a beer. Last woman what bought me a beer was three—four, five...Hell, *six* years ago now! And she made it pretty clear she didn't wanna fuck. I'd've fucked her if she wanted. I'd've pissed on her, too—and wiggled my big toe up her pussy till she cum. But she wasn't into that."

I laughed. "You were going to tell me where you started out."

"Now you gonna make me tell you my whole life story?"

"Sure. Go on."

"If it gets you off." He chuckled. "You know, there was this guy, once. Picked me up when I was hitching, had me tell him about things what happened to me when I was a kid—and he'd listen and beat off. Must've cum about four times that night—we were in a motel in Nevada. I kind of liked him, actually." He shrugged. " 'Nother nigger. What you wanna know?"

"Where'd you start off, like I said. Where're you from?"

"Well, *you* never heard of it." He *humphed*. "You know where Speilman, Lydia, and Fair Play, Maryland, are? Fair Play—that's *two* words: Fair Play. Name's bigger than the damned town."

I frowned.

"Nearest real town is Martinsburg, West Virginia, over the state line. Nearest real city *in* Maryland is Hagerstown."

"Hagerstown—*maybe* I've heard of that...?"

"Well, I wasn't born in Speilman, Lydia, *or* Fair Play. I was born about fifteen miles outside 'em. You probably heard of Antietam."

"Where they had the Civil War battle—in Virginia...?"

"That's about an hour's drive in your pickup from where I come up. We're between Antietam Creek and the Conococheague."

"I wouldn't have taken you for a hillbilly. Cowboy, yeah. But hillbilly, no."

"All the same fuckin' thing." He slid his arms back around me. "You comfortable, little guy?"

I remembered the kid—Crazy Joey—*I'd* called little guy, and put my head down on Leaky's chest. "Yeah." The hair made a brown forest before my lower eye.

"Remember how I was doing with my foot before?"

I nodded against him.

"We have us a humpbacked nigger at home that I used to get off like that every fuckin' time. He'd suck my feet. And he'd rub his black dick against my foot—yeah, we went barefoot most of the goddamn year. Then he'd cum all over my toes, pretty much regular-like. It tickled my old man, too. I had dried nigger cum between my toes practically all year long I was down home."

I laughed. "Are you serious?"

He shrugged. "You said you wanted to hear."

"Go on."

He chuckled. "Blacky—I love that crook-backed nigger." I heard him move his head on the couch arm. He sucked his lips, remembering. "That was his name. You know what the first thing I remember is? When I was almost a baby, like? It was my daddy, standing up on the porch, drinking a beer, his dick in his hand, pissing on me—where I was standing, down in the grass. I couldn't have been three years old. I maybe even still had on a diaper—though I probably didn't have on nothin'. I remember I was laughin'. He's playing that big stream of his all over my belly, up in my face, down to my knees, on my shoulders—and all this warm pee is running down all over me—me and my old man, today, we both piss like fuckin' racehorses. My daddy and me, we had the same momma—only she ran off, right after I was born. My daddy was only a kid hisself when I come along. Billy Sowps. But he was a big sonofabitch, too. My momma—and his—was a drunk hillbilly whore. That's what my daddy said. That was Sarena—what my daddy said her name was. I never knowed her—" I could hear his voice sliding even closer to the Maryland/West Virginia border. "My daddy told me her name was Sarena Sowps and she loved to fuck more 'n just about anything, till I come along. But after that, she didn't like the idea of her own son gettin' after her pussy no more. So she run off, with this Polack truck driver that had started hangin' around the place, when I was about two and a half years old. He may've been a cousin or somethin'. But I don't think he was a Sowps. My daddy, he was the one what pretty much raised me. But I loved that crazy ol' fuck. That's what we all called him: Ol' Fuck. He was Billy Sowps, but we called him Ol' Fuck. And he raised me pretty good—him and Big Nigg."

"Wait a minute, now—" I raised my head to my chin. "Are you sure this guy was really your father? Maybe he was big brother, or a cousin, that, once your momma left, was stuck with raising you—so he just had you calling him 'daddy.'"

"You want to hear how I was raised? Or you want to tell it yourself? You got a *lot* of strange family stories from around those parts. Everybody lives a half a mile, a mile, three miles away from anybody else, back in the woods—and a lot of shit goes on."

"Go on." I put my head back down.

"My daddy and Big Nigg both run away from the reform school together. They both got put there when they was about eleven. They was best friends—jack-off buddies, actually. And they hitched home to my mom's farm—my dad's mom. Sarena. I guess pretty soon they both started fuckin' on her. Both of 'em always said she was just a drunk ol' whore. Daddy always said that if Big Nigg hadn't been such an asshole nigger, I'd probably come out a nigger myself. They said she used to suck 'em off at the same time in the kitchen. Then daddy would stick it in her pussy and Big Nigg would shove it up her asshole and they'd go to town. Ol' Fuck—

that's what Big Nigg always called my daddy: "Hey, y'ole fuck!"—
I swear, that's what I thought his name was. Until he told me once
his real name was Billy. Like mine was Leaky. But I guess the Ol'
Fuck and Big Nigg used to screw daddy's momma all over that little shit-ass dirt farm, out there in the woods. And once she began
to swell up with me, they was both real interested in what I was
gonna turn out to be. 'Cause sometimes they traded off holes, you
know. They weren't what you'd call exclusive. It was just druthers.

"Once I was born, they told me, she hung around till I was
about two and a half years old. Then her and her Polack cousin, they
run off and left him and Nigg to do whatever the fuck they wanted with me. I told you about daddy takin' a pee on me from the
porch? Well, it couldn't have been much later—I was playing
naked in some mud back in the yard. And Big Nigg was back sitting with Dad up there, and they was goin' through a case of tallboys—an' I heard Daddy tell him, 'Wanna see somethin' funny,
Nigg? Watch this. Hey, you little shit. Come on over here.' So I
come over. An' Dad, he put his big boots down on the porch floor,
and he's scratchin' his hairy chest, and he pulls down the zipper on
his jeans, stands up and as I come running—there he goes again:
whizzin' all over me. 'See,' Dad says. 'Look at the little shit, laughin' there; see how he likes it.' Well, that just about broke Nigg up,
laughing, and the next thing I know, he's sayin', 'Oh, shit, I gotta
try this,' and he's standing up, barefooted like he usually was, and
hauls his black mule-fucker out his pants, and he spurts out this
arch o' gold, and both of 'em is standin' there, laughin' and pissin'
all over me, and I don't know which one of the three of us is havin'
a better time!

"Nigg and my Daddy were about as close as two guys could be
that weren't suckin' on each other's dicks or pumpin' each other's
butts. If they'd been doin' that, I would've seen it, 'cause all three
of us slept on the same mattress on the floor. I look at it now, and
I don't know how Daddy stood it, 'cause me and Nigg was both bed
wetters too—unless he kind of liked wakin' up in a pissy bed. The
three of us slept up there in that attic room on that goddamn mattress and it smelled something fierce. Sometimes Nigg or Daddy
would hose it off. Funny, whenever I was staying there, though, I
never minded it. But a couple of times, when I come back from the
State Home, and I'd go in there for the first time, I'd wonder how

the fuck they stood it—until I'd slept there a couple of nights. Then it was like I'd never been away. If it happened to me once, it happened to me two or three times a week: I'd wake up with Nigg hosing all over me and snorin' at the same time—even when I hadn't done pissed in the bed myself. And none of us got out the bed in the morning without beatin' off. I probably saw 'em do everything—but I never caught 'em suckin' or fuckin' each other or anything like that.

"Both of them was stoned scum eaters, though. That's how they got to be friends, back when they were back in reform school; Nigg caught Dad beatin' off, and saw that he ate his own cum when he finished—just like Nigg always did. So, without being faggots or cocksuckers or nothin', they got to be real close, an' sharin' their cum with each other—then with me when I come along. An' I'll tell you, nigger, I still scarf down most of mine, 'less I can lay it deep in some cocksucker's face. Most of the time we did that shit up in the room, when we was in bed. But sometimes like that we'd get into it right out on the porch in the sunlight and everything. But you see—" his arms tightened across my back again—"I just wanted you to understand, that I know what some of this shit is about. I been in it all my life, see. I know what hot piss feels like. I know what eatin' scum tastes like. We're different, you an' me. I'm more into pitchin'. You're a little more into catchin'. But the only difference with that is that the pitchers usually got into it a little earlier—we're always catchin' first, when we're kids. That's what turns us into pitchers. But we ain't that different—understand?"

I nodded. "The only thing that bothers me," I said, "is you're talking about some real serious child abuse there, Leaky. You know that?"

"Pissin' on a little kid in the summer in the yard ain't child abuse. It's a fuckin' game—I mean, if you hose 'im off afterward."

"No, Leaky, you just can't—"

"Yeah? Can't what?" he asked. "Your fuckin' *dick* is hard."

"It got hard because I felt yours get hard under me."

"Yours got hard first—that's why mine stiffened up."

"Well, I don't remember whose got hard first. But, I mean, if all that stuff here really happened, how does it make you feel?"

"My talkin' shit like that—" and suddenly he rolled to the side, still holding me; I thought I was going to fall on the floor, but at the same time, he rucked himself back, so that I was on the wet couch. Under my hip and arm and shoulder, it was cold. "Does that bother *you?*"

"No," I said. "It doesn't, really. But—"

"'Cause that's me, man. That's my life. If it bothers you, I'm sorry. But it's the only life I had—I don't know what yours was like."

"I just was wondering, if—well, how much it bothered *you.*"

I felt him shrug beneath me on the couch.

"I mean, you're sure you're not exaggerating a little—I mean, because we're fucking around together?"

"Nigger, some weird things go on, up in those mountains. Some of them are a lot weirder than that."

"It's just that usually people who go through things like that—with a parent or an adult—aren't so blasé about it."

"You must know a lot of 'em, then..."

"Well, no—but you read things—"

"At the State Home, I knew a lot of kids. And a lot of shit happened to me there that was worse than anything that happened to me with Big Nigg and Daddy. At least when I was with my daddy and Big Nigg, nobody ever tied me down and fucked me up the ass. Nobody ever busted my face open 'cause I didn't wanna suck no dick—or locked me up in a fuckin' cement cellar room with no lights and—"

"Leaky—!"

He shrugged again. "That's why I run away and went back. My daddy and Big Nigg loved me, man. Somebody hurt me, or did somethin' to me, and they would've come after 'em with a fuckin' shotgun! They were good people, man—Nigg and my daddy. Just because they're two ignorant hillbillies, just 'cause one of them is white and the other's black, just 'cause they lived on a poor little shit-ass dirt farm where the fuckin' house always smelled like piss, that don't mean they weren't good people. Or would steal from you. Or would do you in. Or anything like that. You don't believe the shit I'm telling you—?"

"I didn't say—Of *course* they're good people! They're your parents, and you loved them, Leaky! There are good people all over the place." I shrugged. "This evening, before I came home and found you, I was at this gay hustler bar, downtown—called the Pit? I was looking for some information—about a guy named Hasler, who got killed there seventeen years ago, now. And the bartender told me everything he knew. And he told me he was going to get a friend of his, named Ronnie Apple, who was there the night it happened. And he'd call me when he came in and we'd set up a time to talk."

Leaky *humphed*. "Ronnie Apple? That sounds like candy apples. My daddy bought me a candy apple at the county fair once. There're good people down where I come from—"

"And there're good people sleeping over in the park on the benches. And there're good people down at the Pit down on Fiftieth Street. And there're good people—"

"—who take some big, smelly fuckin' hillbilly bum upstairs they found lyin' in a doorway, sleepin' in his own piss. Yeah, I know." He squeezed me again. "I know that, little guy. I know that." After a few moments more, he said, "You wanted to know about me? This is the fuckin' truth, nigger. Don't talk about no child abuse. I was raised by my daddy and a nigger what he met in reform school. And if we *didn't* have the same mom, why's he gonna go tellin' me shit like that? Huh? And they beat off—all the time, just about. And so did I, once I learned how! They ate their own goddamned cum—'cause they thought it made you strong, or something. And they taught me to eat mine. And I still eat mine, too—unless I'm givin' it to somebody else to eat for me…that I like enough to give it to. Piss, shit, cum, snot, cockcheese—all that stuff: see, that's like a present, little guy. That's like a present that comes from inside you. Inside your own body. I mean: how am I gonna give somebody somethin' more personal than my own cum, my own piss, my own spit, my own shit?"

"You have a point," I said.

"I got a point?" Mock seriousness ghosted his smile. But I was so close to his face, I wasn't sure I was reading it right. "Then, if I got a point—get me a fuckin' beer, nigger!"

"O-*kay!*" I pushed up to stand above him. He settled back on the couch, put one big hand under his head and, with the other, furrowed through his chest's dark meadow, wet now, and grinned up—Jesus, he was a big galoot.

"Man—lyin' on a wet, cold couch? This is like fuckin' home!"

I turned and went into the kitchen.

Squatting in front of the icebox, with a beer in my hand, suddenly I frowned—because till then I'd been grinning so hard that the muscles in my cheek had almost cramped. Why, I wondered, does some big, homeless hillbilly with smelly feet, who can't hold his water, saying, "Get me a fuckin' beer, nigger," make me so happy that I could hardly see what was in front of me on the icebox shelves?

When I came back in, he'd shucked his pants (in a pile on the floor) and his sweatshirt (under the back of his head over the sofa arm). With his big, dirty hand, he rubbed his hairy nuts around, cock flopping back and forth, while I came over and popped the tab on the beer can for him. I held it out.

He took it, elbowing up to take a swig, then lay down and patted his stomach. "Climb on top, little guy—but whyn't you take those clothes off, first?"

So I toed off my sneakers, dropped my jeans, shrugged my shirt, and lay out on him again.

"Yeah…" he said.

His hairy gut was surprisingly firm.

"I like to be on the bottom, sometimes. Especially with a little nigger like you, who ain't too heavy." Putting the beer on the back of the sofa, he folded his arms over me.

"I'm five-eight," I said. "I'm not that little. You're just a very *big* guy."

"Yeah?" He laughed. "Hey, you want me to tell you 'bout the nigger we used to have—I don't mean Big Nigg. I mean the black cocksucker we had when I got back from the state home?"

"The humpback?"

"Yeah—that's right."

"Sure." I settled again, my face on his side.

"That was Big Nigg's brother. He was about ten or twelve years younger than Nigg and a couple of years older than me—he'd been in the crazy hospital, I guess—" Leaky lifted his leg beside mine and rubbed the back of his hard sole over my calf—which had been just itching, I swear. (When he put his foot back down, I was wondering whether he could read minds!) "Big Nigg's family didn't live but about twenty miles away from us. And every couple of months, he'd go off and see 'em—sometimes for a couple of days—

hang out with his folks at home. But one day, when he come back, I heard him talkin' to my daddy. "You dumb ol' fuck, we gotta *do* somethin'! They gonna *kill* that nigger if we let him go on home. Big Daddy—" that was Big Nigg's pa—"don't want no humpbacked nigger cocksucker hanging around his place. He gonna tie that boy up in barbed wire and use his damned head for baseball practice! I seen him do shit like that when he thought he had a no-account nigger on his hands! And just 'cause it's his own son, that ain't gonna stop him. Naw, see, we could bring that blubber-lipped bastard over here an' have us some fun, you an' me. Give 'im a place to stay, some food to eat, an' some dick to suck on. I just gotta get to him 'fore he get home and Big Daddy kill the hump-backed little fuck.'

"Later that night, when we was all lyin' in bed together on the big mattress upstairs, and I guess they thought I was asleep, I could feel Daddy up against me, and I could tell he was pullin' on his big ol' peter—his arm movin' against my back, and while he's beatin' off, he's askin' Nigg, 'You sure this humpback brother of yours really likes to suck dick?'

" 'Aw, man,' Big Nigg says, 'he likes to suck dick more'n just about anything in the world. I used to feed him my big black meat just about every chance I get. You remember that white kid in the reformatory school with us, everybody used to call 'Lips'? You remember how he used to beg all the guys to piss in his mouth, then suck us all off, one right after the other? Well, that's how Blacky is. And 'cause he's got you and the little shit there, he be happy as a possum in a pie. I know for a fact he really likes suckin' white dick.'

" 'He like to get roughed up a little, an' called names an' stuff?' Daddy asked.

" 'Sure. I told you, you ofay asshole, he's just *like* Lips. 'Ceptin' he's black and my brother and got a crookback on him. Look, you gotta break the little turd here into gettin' his dick sucked. He been shootin' his load all over this mattress an' everybody on it a couple of times a day since he come home—"

" 'Most of the time, he just drunk an' pissin' the bed—like you an' me,' Daddy tells Nigg. At which point, still pretending to be asleep, I turn over, lean up against Daddy, and let whizz. An' he says, 'Ah, shit! There he goes again!' and I feel 'im jerkin' on his wang just a little harder—really, I think they liked shit like that. Anyway, Nigg is sayin':

" 'Blacky'll mouth-train the boy. And instead of all of us pissin' the bed up every night, Blacky'll hear us start to spurt, an' he'll be down on that dick like a shot!'

" 'Yeah?'

" 'Yeah!' Nigg says.

"And Daddy laughs and says, 'Well, maybe we should get the black bastard over here!'

"Big Nigg went off the next day—and a couple of days later, he was back with Blacky. I was behind the house, foolin' around inside the pickup engine, but I heard somethin' around the other side. So I stand up and wander around to see, just as they came walkin' in, under the trees, Big Nigg first and grinnin', with this other nigger behind him, in overalls, one strap goin' over his broad black shoulder, the other strap not there at all. Then I realized he was humpbacked—and bowlegged, too; and barefoot—big feet on him; and big hands. Almost big as mine and Daddy's. And a face like a bulldog's, and black like the metal on the motor case inside the truck chassis. He hung just a little behind Nigg, lookin' all around. And on the porch, Daddy took a long swig of beer, propped his can on his thigh, reared back in his chair, and said, 'Howdy, there....'

"Big Nigg he just laughs and says, 'Well, I got the black bastard here for us, you cheesy white motherfucker.' Blacky steps up beside him—he's big, like his brother, but he don't look but three or four years older than me—maybe twenty-two, maybe twenty-four. Big Nigg drops his hand on his brother's hump. "This is my brother, Blacky—best nigger cocksucker in this fuckin' county! An' Blacky, this is my jerk-off buddy—I call him the ol' fuck. And that there's our boy, Leaky.' Big Nigg grins over at me, where I'm standing at the end of the porch.

"Dad stands up on the porch edge, with his plaid shirt hanging open, and rubbin' his hairy gut and says, 'So, Nigg tells me you like to suck dick.'

"Blacky looks up at my dad real serious, like: 'Yessuh!'

" 'You like to nurse on a big white, nasty dick?'

" 'Yessuh! Very much, suh!'

" 'What about suckin' nigger dick?' Dad asks.

" 'Oh, yes, suh!' Blacky finally grins over at his brother; Big Nigg just lets out a whoop. And Blacky says, 'That too, suh!'

" 'Then just come on over here, nigger,' Dad says, ' 'cause I wanna show you some *real* nasty dick.' He drops the front chair legs to the boards, reaches forward and puts his beer can on the porch rail, sits back and pulls down the zipper on his fly, sticks his hand inside—and flips out his dick and his nuts. You know what mine look like, so just imagine them about the same way—except not all the skin.

"Anyway, Blacky steps up to the porch edge to look.

" 'I mean,' Daddy says, 'I gave up washin' this thing a long time ago, nigger. I mean, you wanna see some fuckin' cheese...?' Dad looks down at himself. Blacky's getting closer and closer, and now he reaches slowly out, through the porch rail, and takes Daddy's hairy balls in his big black hand. I stepped up, too, to watch. Daddy says to him, 'You skin that fucker back, nigger, an' the cheese'll drop out on the fuckin' ground—hey!' And he chuckles—'I bet you never seen a dick that fat with hair growin' that far down it.' 'Cause Daddy's got hair growin' halfway down his cock, just like me.

"Blacky started to say something.

"But what happened next was kind of like a silver burst, sparkling from the head of my dad's dick in the sunlight.

" 'Oh, shit!' Daddy begins to chuckle again.

"Blacky just froze.

"And Daddy says, 'I guess I just gone an' peed in your fuckin' face, now, didn't I, nigger? Well, you got to know, ain't nobody in this family ever been able to hold his water real well. Pissed in your face? Is that what I just did, nigger?' "

"And Blacky looks up at my daddy with—I seen it now—the biggest smile on his pug-gorilla mug a nigger could get, piss dribblin' over his cheek and down his lips. 'Yessuh!' he says. 'You sure did, suh!' He ran his tongue over his lower lip and out the corner of his mouth; that's when I saw he didn't have no front teeth—at least no upper ones. The first time I seen Blacky smile like that, with daddy's dickhead hanging out over the porch rail at him, it was like lookin' at this stoned black sunrise. Blacky's two side teeth just dropped down beside this pink gap, where his front teeth must have been one time, inside this big, happy smile. There was drops all over his black face, like diamonds on tar in the sun, with the hickory leaves rustlin' overhead. Standin' there, lookin' down at him, grinnin' at my daddy's dick, what had just pissed on him—seein' that nigger smile, like the Lord himself had just stepped out of heaven, his face covered with pee and that close to my daddy's cock, well, that's when I got my first hard-on over the idea of pissin' on a nigger! Man, I'll never forget it. Right there, I fell in love with that black so-and-so. I knew that black sonofabitch was gonna be suckin' on my daddy's dick in a second; I knew it from the way he was craddlin' Daddy's big, hairy nuts, and from the way he was lookin' at that fat cock, downcurved to the right—like mine—and I wanted him to be suckin' on *my* dick so bad—and I wanted him to be tastin' my pee and my cum and smilin' 'cause it was *my* piss he was lickin' off his big black lips—that I put one hand in my pocket through the tear—I used to tear the bottoms out of all my right-hand jean pockets, when I was at home—and grabbed hold of myself and just held on for dear life!

"Well, Blacky takes dad's prong in his mouth all the way to the fuckin' root, nigger!

"To the *root!*

"Big Nigg's steppin' up now to the other side of 'em—he's so proud of this scummy-mouthed cocksucker brother of his, and what he done brought around the farm, and horny besides. He's watchin' his brother suckin' off my pop—he's about to bust.

"While he's givin' my pop a blowjob, Blacky gets his far hand up on my pop's jeans—and suddenly I feel that nigger's other hand take ahold of *mine*—Oh, shit!

"Not the one in my pants—the other one. It was kind of...well, electric, you know. 'Cause suddenly I realized that after he finished suckin' on my daddy, I was gonna be next! And that, just standing there, like the big old stupid sonofabitch I was, in just my jeans and no shirt, barefoot and smeared up with car grease—I'd been out in the back, workin' on the pickup motor—and this black bastard wanted to suck on my dick next! That without even having really looked at me, this nigger wanted my big ol' hairy pecker in his mouth—I guess Big Nigg had told him about how Daddy wanted to get me mouth-trained. Well, I tell you, I was one happy trainee. So I just stand there, holdin' my dick in my pants and watchin' him get my daddy's nut off. Once he took hold of my hand, I started pullin' on myself a little; then I realized if I kept that up, I was gonna shoot. So I let go and took my hand out my pocket and just stood there watchin', and bittin' on my nails, as happy as a shoat in a shitpile, 'cause I knew now, however much he worked on daddy or Big Nigg, that nigger was *mine!*

"Daddy shot his wad pretty quick. An' Blacky didn't even get to stand up straight before Big Nigg swung up on the porch with his black hog sticker out and, a moment on, buried it in his brother's face.

"Daddy crossed his arms, with his wet meat still loose, a-dangle and glistening over his hairy low-hangers, and tells me: 'Black bastard's pretty good. I guess he's about ready for you. You wanna try 'im?'

"Yeah! Sure!' I said, steppin' from one foot to the other. That nigger's *still* holdin' my hand.

" 'Think I'm gonna hose out his suckhole for you first, though.'

"Blacky got Big Nigg's nut with a couple of grunts and a loud, 'Oh, shit...!' which is *usually* how Big Nigg dropped his load.

Blacky sat back on the grass now, and Daddy's stepped around the rail (grabbin' up the beer can, up-ending it over his face, and pouring the last of it in, then flings it off across the yard, where there's about five hundred of the fuckers in a pile against the garage) and comes down from the porch, his dick still in his big, blunt fist. 'Look up here a minute an' show me that nasty suckhole of yours, nigger.'

" 'Yeah,' says Nigg. 'Let's see it, boy!' He was kind of steppin' around, too.

"Blacky opens his mouth.

"And Daddy lets loose with a fuckin' fire hose worth of piss. A moment later, Nigg was beside him, and turns on his own Niagara. And I'm just watchin', *still* holdin' that nigger's hand, and feelin' hot as a slice of bacon burnin' on a griddle. Blacky's takin' pretty much all of it, too. Some's bubblin' up between where his front teeth ought to be and runnin' out over his cheeks and his chin. But not much.

" 'Jesus,' Daddy says, 'nigger, you look good down there!'

"And Big Nigg tells him, 'See, y'ol' fuck? That nigger's our own personal urinal, man! He's a fuckin' humpbacked, liver-lipped outhouse on two legs! I done told 'im, while we was comin' up here, that white cocksucker, Lips, what used to drink our piss back at the reformatory ain't nothin' to what this nigger can do! Right?'

" 'You better believe it, nigger,' Daddy says. And he stirs his stream around in the caldron of Blacky's mouth; piss is bubblin' yellow out at the corners and foamin' inside those truck-tire suckers, between his two side teeth and up over his gums. Sometimes Daddy would spritz him in his face, and sometimes Big Nigg would point his stream down into Blacky's lap, where he's foolin' with himself with his free hand, now. And I guess I must've been remembering how good it felt to be a little bitty kid with the two of them pissin' all over me. But the way he's blinkin' up at Dad and Big Nigg, like they was two faces o' God an' he just been let into heaven, it looked like that humpback bastard was havin' more fun than any fuckin' kid in the whole world, and it was all I could do not to edge in there, pull my pisser out and spurt some down there myself. But I finished workin' on my nails and reached back into my pocket and held onto my dick again, pullin' on it every now and then, but not enough to make it shoot, and stood there, holding his hand and starin' down, with my own mouth hangin' open like a crazy fool's— pretty soon first Dad, then Nigg, runs out of piss. Blacky's pretty wet down, by now. But when he turned that pug-ugly black face, with the piss drippin' off his chin and running down the side of his big nose, to look at me—I don't know why I didn't shoot in my hand. He was like a big black woolly-headed dog down there, still grinnin', with his tongue hangin' out—which is not some joke. It *was* really hangin' out, to the side of his mouth now. And kinda twitchin'. Me, I'm so excited, I started to pee in my pants, man— which, as you know, happens to me a lot.

"And Nigg says, 'You still want somethin' good, you better get Leaky, now—look at his pants gettin' wet there. He's pissin' himself, he's so turned on! *Look* at that—' I mean, you tell me a fuckin' joke and if you really start me laughin', the next thing you know I'll be peein' all over myself. Or sometimes if I'm cryin' about somethin', too, for that matter—which is kind of weird. But I'm like that.

"Anyway, you know what that nigger done?

"Still holdin' hands, he comes for me now, on his knees, and leans his face against my dirty jeans, and begins to lick where it's gettin' wet—oh, shit! I just squat down a little to let him get to it easier. Then we get my fly open and it comes out, blastin' piss in his fuckin' face, and then it's inside his face, in that hot hole, runnin' like the Conococheague in a summer flood! I grab his head and start to humpin'—oh, shit! I love the way his hair feels, when you're holdin' a nigger's head and humpin', man—like you're snatchin' at a shaggy old coconut that's gonna break open all full of the sweetest white milk! And his throat is goin', 'cause I can feel him drinkin'. And I'm rubbin' his head and his hump and holdin' this nigger into my dick like it was the end of the world and we was the last two people in it, and I can feel his tongue workin' on the underside of my cock, and below my balls, where my piss is runnin' hot, and he's suckin' that thing all down deep in his face, man, and I can't fuckin' hardly see. I mean, if I ever been fuckin' crazy, man, that's gotta be the time. Daddy's laughin' and holdin' me up, and Big Nigg is got his hand down on his brother's scratchy head, and pushin' him into me..." Then, somehow, Leaky's mouth found mine, or mine found his. And, straddling the log of his dick, pressed up hard against my belly, I humped his hairy gut till I shot again.

After a few lazy minutes, Leaky said: "Is that number two, or number three for you?"

"Eh..." I said, "Number two, I think. Hey—," and I pushed back from him, on my knees.

Immediately he smeared up my load on his fingers, took a big lick, then thrust his hand into my face, fingers splayed across it. "Finish that shit, nigger."

I licked, but, kind of startled, also pulled back.

"—I was gonna say," I said, beside him with one foot on a spot where the carpet was wet, one foot where it was dry, "why don't we go in the bedroom. That's got to be more comfortable than this old couch."

"Anywhere you want—" And he pushed himself up to sit. Before he stood, though, he looked at me—and laughed. "Hey, you know you look good with cum all over your face. Don't wipe it off. Just bend down here and gimme another kiss."

So I did. And pretty soon we were holding each other and necking on the couch. "Leaky," I said. "How old did you say you were when all this nonsense with Blacky was goin' on—I mean when he first came to you father's place?"

He pulled back a little now. "Didn't I tell you, man?" He grinned at me now. "Free, white, and over twenty-one. God's honest truth."

I frowned. "What do you mean?"

"Everything I done told you about, I was at least twenty-one when it happened."

"It sounded to me," I said, "like you were a lot younger."

"Yeah? Well, I don't want you talkin' no shit about no fuckin' child abuse no more! So I was over twenty-one for all of it. Understand?"

"Well, look, if it really happened, I don't mean that—"

"It happened. You think I'd make all this shit up, just to get you off? Naw, nigger. I'm tryin' to explain somethin' to you here."

He stood up.

Frowning, I stood up after him.

Then we walked out of the living room, across the hall (with a quick trip to the kitchen to get Leaky another beer), and into the bedroom. "You know," Leaky told me, "after that was all over, like I was tellin' you, that first day Blacky come, and I was the last one what shot my nut in his face, we're all standin' around together, Big Nigg and Daddy got their arms around each other's shoulders, an' I'm holdin' onto Blacky, and we're both still breathin' hard. Daddy's in his big work shoes, and the other three of us is barefoot; an' Daddy asks Blacky, 'So how you think you gonna like it here, nigger, servicin' the three of us? We got enough dick to keep your face full a while?'

" 'Oh, yes, suh!' Blacky says, and grins big as he can grin. 'Oh, yes. I really like it here, suh!'

"And Daddy says, 'And what's all this 'suh' shit, nigger? You ain't got to call nobody around here, 'sir'! I'm gonna be callin' you all sorts of black nigger turd-eatin' mule-suckin' humpbacked scumbag shit—you mind about the humpbacked part? 'Cause, if you do, we can chuck that. But you ain't gonna get out of any of the rest.'

" 'And Blacky say, 'No, suh. That's all right, suh. I don't care what you call me. I got a humpback, and they ain't nothin' I can do about it. It don't bother me nobody talkin' about it—least not like you do. Or Nigg do.'

"And Daddy says, 'Good. 'Cause you're part of the family now. You got your big brother here—' he nodded toward Nigg— 'and Leaky's your little brother, now.' He nodded to me; though I towered over him by as much as Daddy did. (I tell you, the notion of havin' a brother like Blacky put a pretty big grin on my face that afternoon.) 'You go around callin' people 'sir,' that's gonna be downright odd. I hear what Nigg calls you—and it ain't 'suh.' Nigg don't call nobody 'sir,' here. Leaky don't call nobody 'sir.' Here— why don't you go on and try callin' me a drunken ol' white moth-erfuckin' scum-suckin' piece of maggoty mule shit. 'Cause that's closer to it, now. Go on, say it.'

" 'Suh…?' Blacky asks, his eyes kind of wide.

" 'See,' Big Nigg says to him. 'I told you, you dumb cocksuck-er. Go on, he ain't gonna bite ya. He ain't like them white men in the crazy hospital. You go on do what he says, now.'

"And Blacky kind of glances at me, then at Big Nigg, and he swal-lows; then he says, kinda low, and lookin' down, 'You a' ol' fuck, scum-suckin', piece of mule shit…suh!'

"Which starts Daddy and Big Nigg off laughin' again—and when Blacky looks up and smiles, I started laughin' too. 'Well, he's *almost* got it,' Big Nigg is sayin', slappin' his knees. "Not quite. But almost.'

" 'Just needs a little more work,' Daddy says, 'an' maybe a little more goddamned dick!'

"Now you're really sure," Leaky said, as though he wasn't chang-ing the subject completely, "that you want me in here with you, sleepin'?"

We stood, looking down at the bed.

Because it was so hot, I had only pulled up the top sheet over the striped fitted bottom.

"You see," he said, "the thing I guess I'm still tryin' to tell you is, I don't know how long you been into this shit, but I probably been in it a lot longer—all this stuff like you like, that's just home to me. Lemme tell you: we can get a couple of them plastic garbage sacks you got in the kitchen, open 'em out, put some newspapers out on top of them; you can sleep in the bed like you always do, and I'll sleep right down next to you on the floor here. I don't mind. That's pretty much how I sleep whenever I'm indoors, lest I'm back home, where nobody cares who pisses up the fuckin' bed."

I thought a moment. Then I told him: "Look, like you said, since it's going to be just beer piss, the first couple of times won't really hurt it any."

"It'll be nice and warm at first, but when you wake up, it's gonna be kind of cold and damp."

"In this heat," I said, "that could be a blessing."

"And when it's cold and damp," he went on, "there's only one way to get it nice and warm again." He grinned at me.

I smiled back. "Well," I said, "maybe it'll start to be just a little like home to you."

He turned around and sat on the bed, pushed himself back—now he turned around, got one of the pillows, and propped it in the corner. Then he scooted back against it, kind of half-sitting, with his long legs diagonally over the sheet. (His feet really were pretty grubby.) "Come on, then, little guy; crawl up here between my legs, where you belong. Get yourself comfortable." I turned the light off, and before I climbed on the bed with him, I bent over to take a whiff; his hard foot came up against my face again. Breathing in, I crawled around it, practically into his great, hard, warm hands. "Hey, you little black bastard," he said, twisting around. "Stick your tongue in my asshole a minute, huh?"

Surprised, I wedged my face forward, as he pushed his butt back against me. As I stuck out my tongue into his hot crevice, I heard and smelled and felt him fart—the wrinkled bud of flesh centered in his hairy crevice suddenly relaxed, puckered—and honked. "There. Now that felt good." His big leg slid back over my head.

"Candy apples," I said.

"What?" he asked.

"Your ass tastes like a candy apple—without the sugar. But it's got a fuckin' apple taste to it."

"Yeah?"

"I was just thinking about that guy," I said thoughtfully, "I'm supposed to talk to at the Pit, Ronnie—about Hasler."

"That the one who got killed?"

"Yeah." I pushed my face into his crotch, and he pulled his dick up where I could get to it.

"I guess," he said, equally thoughtfully, "it was when I was in Florida, in that yoni club. You get used to them things hanging off your dick; now I'm more comfortable with someone tuggin' on the fucker than I am just lettin' it alone. But maybe I was always a *little* like that, which is why I got in the club in the first place."

So I held onto it, with its collar of fur, and tugged a little. "Yeah. It's real nice to have a nigger down there, where he can get to you, soon as you or him need to. You said that Pit place was a hustler bar?

You stay out of there, nigger. You don't need no fuckin' hustlers, man. That's stupid, people payin' money for stuff like that. Somebody took me in one of them places once, and the only thing that happened was that somebody got into a fuckin' fight and knocked another guy's tooth loose in his fuckin' head. Hey, you know, later, when Blacky had been on the farm a while, my daddy asked him what had happened to *his* teeth. We was all drinkin' beer and eatin' greens—and sweet potatoes, right out the fire—for our dinner, sittin' around in the yard, when Blacky told us that Big Daddy had busted 'em out his mouth years ago, when he caught Blacky under their porch, suckin' off their dog. And Big Nigg just shook his head. And Daddy says, 'I don't hold with no daddy beatin' on his kid like that, I don't give a fuck *what* the hell he's suckin' on.'

"'It was a nice dog, too,' Blacky said. 'Big Daddy went and clubbed its head in too—kilt it right dead. I thought he was gonna do the same thing to me. But he just knocked my teeth out.'

"Daddy says, 'Now, that just ain't right.'

"And Big Nigg say, 'Now you know why *I* don't stay there no more. That nigger's crazy—Big Daddy, I mean. And it ain't like he cares none—he just wants everybody out of the way, so he can do what the fuck he want with the women still around there—my momma, her sister, our sisters, too. That's why I brought Blacky over here.'

"And Blacky says, 'We sure eat better here.'

"And I say, 'I bet you drink better, too.' 'Cause I'm feelin' the beer buildin' up already.

"About three weeks later, it was, Daddy come home with a big old part-Labrador, part-wolfhound, general all-around mutt puppy. 'We gonna call him Little Fuck,' my daddy said, ' 'cause he's the biggest Little Fuck I ever seen!' And pretty soon, we'd all get around and watch Blacky suck him off—sometimes I'd squat out back by the truck, with all 120 pounds of Little Fuck on his side with his back leg up, and his tail sweepin' back and forth in the dust, and I'd shuck on his dickskin till it got big—Daddy was Ol' Fuck and the dog was Little Fuck—rubbing that dog dick until that red, raw dog meat pushed on out from his hairy skin. Then I'd call Blacky: 'Hey, nigger. Little Fuck here's got somethin' for ya.' And Blacky'd come, grinnin', and hunker down with one hand on the hubcap, and one in the gravel, and call out, 'Hey, y'ol scum-suckin' fucks, you wanna watch a nigger suck off a dog?' Then, while Big Nigg and Daddy would come around to take a look, an' maybe one of 'em or the other'd take out his dick an' beat off over it, Blacky'd get that dog dick in his mouth, gettin' his big lips over that wet peach-sized ball that swells up near the back of a dog's dick when he's gonna cum. Blacky'd work on that dog till he'd start howlin' for his life, then he'd finish suckin' him off—and move right over onto me, 'cause it got me drippin' hot to watch the nigger go after the dog. And Little Fuck would lick my hand, or sometimes my nuts, while Blacky was suckin' my prick at the same time. We never cut that hound; and it was still just as gentle as it could be! That dog loved Blacky, and Blacky loved that dog—the only thing was, Blacky could never get the dog to piss in his mouth. Me and that dog was both mouth-trained to a nigger real early. And we all—Daddy, Big Nigg, me, an' Blacky, too—spent three months tryin' to figure out how to train that mutt to pee in that nigger's mouth. Best we got him, though, was so that sometimes he'd come over and pee on the ankle of your jeans. But that was all...."

Rubbing my head while he talked, Leaky went quiet now. In my mouth, his dick had grown hard, gone half-soft, hardened again, and softened once more. His hand stopped; above me his breathing changed. And suddenly, in my mouth, I felt the rush of heat, the current of his urine. Pulling myself up, I swallowed and swallowed—and swallowed.

Above me, he mumbled, "Oh, shit...!" jerking awake. Then he said, "Oh—you got it?" And his leg, which had jackknifed up, slid out again. He kept running. I kept swallowing.

Leaky sighed.

And probably went back to sleep, even while his waters ran inside me. After a while, he stopped peeing. But the quiet, slightly raw breathing went on. His gut lifted and dropped my forehead. I lay there, his furry warmth against me, feeling very much like someone who was in his right and proper place; the feeling was much like the peace I remembered from that night down at the old, now-closed-up Mineshaft.

A kind of physical relaxation comes after orgasm, which is wonderful and satisfying and makes you fall into the heaviest of sleeps—but that's not what I'm talking about here; although, because I'd just dropped a second load twenty minutes ago, that might have had something to do with it. But there's another, psychological peace, which, were I religious, I'd describe by saying it feels like you're doing what God intended you to do, like you're occupying the space God intended you to occupy. Perhaps it's the feeling of desire—not want, or need, or yearning, but desire itself—satisfied. Finally satisfied. Not a God believer, I'm willing to accept the God in that feeling as a metaphor. Yet, it seemed to me, here I'd found the point where metaphor and the thing it's a metaphor for *might* be one. Lying there, I thought: people feel guilty about *wanting* to do stuff like this. But this is the reward of actually *doing* it, of finding someone who wants to do it with you: the fantasies of it may be drenched in shame, but the act culminates in the knowledge that no one has been harmed, no one has been wounded, no one has been wronged. (Leaky was like having, I thought, your own personal Mineshaft in bed with you.) Could two, I wondered, or, indeed, even more people, feel this in the same way, over one encounter? Was this—here—the "home" Leaky's scabrous childhood was trying to reach for in its deranged accounting?

I realized I had to take a piss myself.

Moving back on the bed from between Leaky's legs—my feet were already off it (I smelled his feet go by)—I stood, turned, and walked out by my half-open closet door, into the hall, and down to the bathroom—where the night light by the mirror inside lay a blade from the ajar door across the hall's floorboards. Inside, I sat on the commode—even *though* I just had to pee.

When I was finished, I stood up, went into the hall and back to the bedroom.

When I got on the bed, like it happens with big men, Leaky was sleeping all over it. When I pushed him hard enough, he rolled away, still sleep. I kneaded a pillow up under my chin, and pretty soon there was a hairy big arm and a wonderfully heavy leg over my back: he'd spread out again; and I just happened to be under him. I guess I went to sleep like that—only then, in a moment, there was a something on top of me. I heard Leaky grunting, felt his weight, felt his arms clutching me—he'd climbed on top. His dick was wedged in the crevice of my butt (running along the crack), and he was humping and grunting hard as he could. His hand was under my face, and now I took two of his big fingers into my mouth, and held onto his forearm hard. "Yeah...do it, man," I grunted, under him.

"You all right..?" he asked, without breaking his rhythm.

"Yeah, you dumb, fuck-face... stupid asshole idiot, low-down moron, mule-brained dumb-ass..." Then I had to breathe.

He gave my head a squeeze.

"...stupid dummy—"

His semen shot up the small of my back. With a great gasp, he stopped, shook, and relaxed over me. "Yeah, that was fuckin' good..."

"You okay, Dummy?" I asked.

Somewhere in the dark, I know he nodded.

Now, as he rolled to the side, his hand moved over my back, and then, slimy with his cum, was between us. In the dark I licked and sucked his hard, salty fingers, encountering his tongue with mine, encountering it again while his other hand grabbed my head and held it there, so that finally, with two of his fingers again in my mouth, we deep-kissed in the dark. At last he whispered, "Move on down where you belong, little guy..." I slid down till my face was at the forest of his crotch and got both my legs around one of his. He was still hard. Before I could ask about it, he said, " 'Cause you ain't cum again yet. Go on. Suck it, you pee-guzzlin' scum-sucker! You can hump my leg like Little Fuck used to do." So I sucked, and, while he held my head, the last quarter-can of beer his kidneys had filtered filled my mouth—and I came on his hairy shin.

"One of us better eat that shit..." he growled. But before either of us could get to it, his other leg went over my back. Still hugging him into me again, I heard his breathing change. His hand slipped over my face. Realizing he'd fallen asleep, I fell asleep.

Grasping the rail, I stepped over the drain to start up the subway's concrete steps. After I came around another landing, though, I realized, above the third floor, I was passing Hilda Conkling's door. I looked down, but the stairs had already become stone, leaves either side. A breeze played in the night air above me, behind me, as I mounted the mountain flank's rocky crevice. Above, in the flicker of summer fire and lightning, I could see him perched on his giant buttocks. One vast and feathered claw reached down half a dozen steps. His human knee was jackknifed high against the clouds. Above his horned and shadowed brow, the spined movement of his wings slid across moon-blasted cloud. As I climbed, entering his smell, like a stable with its fecal pungency, he reached his clawed hand down to grasp my shoulder, while his man-foot extended to hook me with his great picked toes beneath my arm, and lifted, my feet scrabbling over dirt-banked roots to keep me upright as the last stone steps gave out. On his peak, he pressed my face against his immense and doggy groin, his huge and bristled sheath erupting sudden, scalding salts, glittering and bubbling in my face, with his extraordinary warmth, like something given up from within the earth, from within the city's highest buildings, from the mountain itself—

—and woke long enough to feel, in the dark, my face still in his groin, my hand between his legs, that turned to press his buttocks toward me; grunting but not waking, he arched his groin into me, while his heavy cock once more poured its night water hot against my lower cheek. (One of my feet was well over the bed's end. The other leg was bent on it.) I moved my other hand hurriedly up to lift him, loose and hotter than the night, against my face, drank of him in my dry mouth, and finally lay his length, warm and hosing between us, between us. Above me in the bed, his breath had the evenness of the soundest sleeper's. Before he ran out, his hand came down against my face—fell there in his sleep, actually, hard enough to surprise me. But as I licked the urine running along his massive thumb, his breathing rhythm carried me across that startling moment, back within the sleep that moments ago we'd shared, that his piss had propelled me out of that—now—its cessation welcomed me again within.

The next day I got up at about eight. (Tink. Tankle.) In the kitchen, I loaded the very cheap Melitta coffee maker—that had been a present from Pheldon—with a filter and six scoops of Bustelo; and I poured water for nine cups into the transparent hopper. Then I pushed the switch on, and, as the toggle's plastic rectangle went red, made my way, naked, into the living room. Standing by the window, I dialed the agency. "I'm afraid I won't be coming into the office today."

"Are you sure, darling?" Cathy asked me. "You've been taking an awful lot of days off recently, John—" which, having nothing to do with any of what I've recounted, was true.

"Yeah," I said. "I'm sure. But thanks for reminding me."

"Okay," she said. "But you're very close to that point where Dorothy will move your name to the bottom of the Assignment List—I don't know why I'm telling you this."

"Because you're fundamentally a nice person, Cathy."

"Yeah," she said. "So long."

I went back into the bedroom to stand, looking down on this mound of man, asleep, a bear in my bed. He lay facing me, knees bunched up and one huge foot, still in its mottled sock of grime, pushing down the other. I bent over to smell his feet. A night free of his shoes had leached the bite from the odor, but they were still rich and pungent. As I stood, he let—without waking—an ass-flapping fart. And I dropped one knee to the mattress, to lean across him without touching his furry flank. And breathed. His stench rose, not particularly pleasant—rather, vegetative and rotten: yet my dick lifted forward between my legs.

I moved back to stand again.

And just looked.

His baggy balls dangled his thigh's furry barrel. Enlarged (though not in any way erect) with the morning's warmth, in its hank of hair his cock lolled across them. No great stains scored the sheet with yellow and jagged edges (like a comic-book balloon from the mouth of a monster or an electronic speaker—though I decided, probably, soon there'd be one, or three, or many, lapping the panel of our encounter). But I saw the one circle, dark and a dinner plate's diameter, like a gray Frisbee he'd rolled half onto, its center directly below his wrinkled skin, for surely only minutes before (it hadn't been there when I'd left...?), he'd let some lazy half-cup of his urine run.

I bent again, this time to smell his breath (there were three beer cans on the floor, one upright; two had tinked and tankled over when I'd gotten up to call in), and wondered if—as it whispered out, engulfing me—this was what people in love with alcoholics loved. As I opened my eyes—

—he opened his eyes and, with one hand (because they were so big, for moments, unbalanced, I thought he'd grabbed my head with both), pulled my face against his and filled my mouth with his morning tongue, rooting up like an inverted oak grown wild for the sun's magma, and I thrust out a hand and caught the sheet beside him (for some reason, there—was it summer sweat or drying piss—the cloth *was* damp beneath my hand) and lowered myself against him. His tongue probed and ran under my upper lip, on both sides of the flesh holding it to the gum in the middle, then under my lower. When I was rubbing my dick on his belly, he loosed his mouth from my mine long enough to say, "Shit, there ain't nothin' tastes better in the mornin' then a nigger what's been suckin' dick all night."

"What are you trying to do?" I asked him. "Turn into a bottle of mouthwash?"

"Why the fuck not?"

"You," I said, "are the fucking stupidest, fucking dumbest, most fucking mindless and ignorant white asshole I ever did know. Shit, you are one stupid, crazy, moronic, brainless mother—"

His whole body heaved up at me (before I could say "fucker"), while his arms wrapped me. His cock began rubbing under my belly. His tongue filled my mouth again (while, this time, I filled his back) and, within the next fifty seconds, we both came together (first of the six times we did so over many, many years. Yes, I remember them all—not because they were that wonderful, but rather because they were so easy and we seemed to get so far into so many other things. But that's getting ahead of the story). "Jesus, little guy—get down there and lick that shit up. Then come gimme some fuckin' scum in your mouth, huh?"

While I pushed back to move down to the saturated hair of his groin, out in the kitchen the coffee maker began to spit and warble its terminal splutterings.

"You want a big breakfast?"

"Sure, if you can make it."

Out of the plastic bag I kept in the stew pot under the table, I took some potatoes, peeled and diced them. With some Puritan oil, they got fried—with onions butter-fried in a separate pan. And there were these mushrooms I had in the icebox, that I sautéed and added. Meanwhile I finished off by cooking the last package of bacon I had.

He sat at the kitchen table, big hands locked across his belly, bare toes splayed around the table legs, grinning and watching and clearly appreciating and not saying anything except, now and again, "Shit, that smells nice."

"How you like your eggs, stupid?"

"Scramble 'em—that's good. You mind makin' me three or four?"

For the two of us, I made six.

When I sat down at the end of the table, he picked up his fork in his fist, lowered his face almost to the plate and scooped in one big forkful—his other hand had moved to the table. (Thumb out from his forefinger, and on the paisley cloth, the span was as large as the plate, no kidding.) Now he put down the fork on the plate's edge and asked: "Hey, I'll eat with company manners if you *want*, but if it's okay with you, you mind if I eat like I do at home...?"

"You eat any way you want," I told him.

"Okay then. Come on, nigger, get over here beside me—"

I started to move my chair around the table.

"No, you don't need your fuckin' chair. Lemme feed you like I used to do Blacky at home. Sit on the floor by my chair here."

I wasn't really sure what he wanted. So I stood up—while he scooped up a pile of eggs on his fingers and pushed them into his mouth. "Shit, that's good," he said through the mouthful.

He motioned me down on the floor by his chair. "Come on—this is how I used to do that humpbacked nigger down home. Come on, sit on the floor. Him and the dog. Come on, now—" and as I dropped cross-legged beside the chair—above, I heard him pull my plate across the table toward his—suddenly his hand, again full of egg and potatoes, dropped in front of my face. I opened my mouth, and he thrust his fingers in.

One handful for himself, one handful for me—pausing to chew a remarkably long time, considering the size of handfuls that he took (or fed me) at a time. "This is how Nigg and my daddy used to feed me when I was a kid. And how I used to feed Blacky, once he come to stay with us." His hand came down to grip my shoulder, then rub it. "Only you don't got no hump—which is okay, too. Ain't this more homey-like?" Sitting there, him in the chair and me beside him on the floor, eating toast and potatoes and bacon and scrambled eggs from his hand, immense fingers prodding food into my mouth, we still actually had a real conversation about the efforts of the New York Transit System to keep itself going, since apparently he'd slept on the subways for a week, earlier in the year, when it had been colder: "Before I got to the park, once it warmed up."

Finally, with his great, greasy nubs gripping the familiar blue ceramic rim, the strips of his gnawed nails outlined in black, he handed me down a cup of coffee. (I take it with milk; this one came black, but I really didn't care.) I held the warm cup in both hands and, my head against his hairy hip over the chair's side (while, from time to time, he rubbed my head, my face, my neck), I found myself—glancing now and again at my own cock—almost painfully erect. Finally, I reached up over his leg.

Then, because his was as hard as mine, I put the cup on the floor and crawled around his left knee, under the table, to take him in my mouth. "*God* damn, nigger," he rumbled above me, locking both his hands behind my head, "it sure as hell never took *Blacky* that fuckin' long! I was beginnin' to think you didn't like me no more!" Taking a big breath, the callused and horny edges of his feet hugging my shins, he began to pump my face.

"...Some guys, see, want a fuckin' cigarette after they eat. Me, I just wanna drop a load!"

In bed again, hours later, I woke to go down on his drowsing cock. He woke with it already hard and moving in my mouth. "Yeah, nigger—now, this is what life's about!" After he came, when I suggested we go out for a walk, he said, "Okay, let's do that!"

Back in our clothes, as we were walking down the stairs, I told him: "We could go down to Robins, on Thirty-eighth Street—you know, just below the Port Authority—and I could get you a pair of jeans. Those damned wool pants you got on, besides being pretty raunchy, are just too *small*, Leaky; and, in this weather, they've got to be uncomfortable. While we're down there, we could go to one of the dirty movies—you said something about being heterosexual, if I remember. You can watch some guys fuck some women, and I can suck you off some more."

"Yeah?" he asked me. "You can do that in the dirty movies?"

"In some of them," I said. "We'll take in a six-pack of beer."

"Shit, man. I didn't know they'd let you do that."

"You've just been to the wrong movies," I told him.

"I ain't never been to *any* of 'em." Then, as we went out on the stoop, he said, "Hey, you really wanna get me somethin'?"

"I want to get you some pants," I said. "That you'll be more comfortable in."

"I'm pretty comfortable in these," he said. "I'm kind of used to them by now. But if you really want to get me somethin' that I'd like…" His look went from sheepish to uncomfortable, then back.

I wondered what sort of wristwatch or Walkman or whatever he wanted that I really wouldn't want to spring for.

"It ain't expensive, man. But it would sure make me feel good."

A bottle of crack, I wondered. Some pot? Vodka? Pills—

"They got this pet store right down on the corner there. I seen it when I first come up. I don't think it'd even cost as much a pair of jeans—you think you could buy me a dog collar?"

"A what?"

"You know," he said. "A dog collar. That I could wear on my neck. It don't have to have my name on it or anything. We stay together awhile, maybe we could get the name later. But just you givin' it to me, that would make me know you owned me, like. And I'd feel better. If I knew I was your fucking dog."

"Leaky"—I looked up at this six-four, ragged gorilla, back in his foul sweatshirt, again unzipped, and his too-small pants with his gut pushing over the waist—"if we got a dog collar, *I* should be the one wearing it. Not you. I'm pretty clearly the bottom in this relationship, don't you think?"

"Shit," he said. "It don't matter *who* wears it—and it would be fuckin' stupid for *you* to wear it. You got the money, you got the house, you the one in charge."

"You guys put a collar on Blacky?"

"Daddy put one on him. Just like on Little Fuck. I mean…" He paused. Then he said, "I done cum with you three times, ain't I? And you shot three loads over me, right?"

"At least," I said. "It's more like five apiece, I think…"

"Well, right now, Mad Man Mike, he say Tony owns me." (And because of how extraordinarily strange things had been going since the night before, I thought neither of Hasler nor of Joey.) " 'Cause he gave me a penny, before I come here. But you'd give him that for me, wouldn't you?"

I wasn't sure what he was talkin' about. But I said, "Sure—I'd probably give him a whole nickel!"

As we reached the corner, Leaky grinned. "Yeah? Well, that's nice to know. But until you get a chance to pay Tony his penny, it would sure make me feel better if I was wearin' a collar. I mean, that's how we did it at home."

I looked at him.

Then I said, "Come on."

When I'd first gotten to this neighborhood, it had been a check-cashing place. But that had moved north. And now it was a pet store.

I crossed the street, Leaky beside me taking one step to my two.

"I'm gonna wait here," he said, "outside."

"Is there any kind you particularly want?'

"You got to get me the fuckin' collar," he said. "You have to pick it out."

"Right." I nodded. "Okay—I'll see you in a few minutes."

I pushed open the glass door.

A wall of gourmet pet food cans, a tower of sleeping baskets, wicker and plush, the cedar scent—off beyond the counter, on a reddish pegboard, with metal hooks and brackets sticking out, were various styles of dog collars.

I walked up to the board, looking over the kinds hanging here.

The first one I took down—they only had two in that style—was a wide, spiked affair, for some kind of monster guard dog. Fingering the rough edging to the black-dyed leather, with, even-ly along it, twenty-seven (I counted: nine rows of three) molded, four-sided, half-inch spikes, I grinned—but put it back.

I took down a choke chain and hefted its jingling weight in my palm.

I looked at some five more—kind of liking the fourth: a wide collar, stained deep brown, with a good brass buckle and a hefty brass ring, as well as a copper plate for a name. Then I put them all back—and turned, rather sharply, from the board, to take three steps away and stand, startled, in the middle of the floor.

Suddenly it had hit me what I was doing.

All this stuff about paying a penny, about collars—suddenly it was all frightening. My heart beat, thudded, banged against the insides of my ribs. You crazy black bastard, I mouthed to myself. *What* are you getting into?

Then, hearing myself, I laughed. (The kid at the cash register looked up from a sale just over to a woman wearing a red halter.) I turned back to the board, took down the collar I wanted to see on Leaky (the brown one), and went to the counter—piled high with pink and yellow plush catnip mice and small red rubber bones. With spiky black hair and a black sleeveless shirt, the kid—whom I'd first thought was a boy—took my money ($8.95 plus tax) and the collar, and put it in a bag.

"That must be quite a dog you've got there. That could fit an Irish wolfhound." She smiled.

I grinned back. "Oh, it's not for me." I took the change from my ten. "It's for a friend." Immediately I thought of adding: —*for a friend's dog.* Then I decided to let it hang.

"Well." She cocked her head. "You and your friend have fun."

Still feeling scared, but grinning, I left the shop.

The air was warm and—for a moment—still. The street was loud with traffic. A late garbage truck turned onto the avenue, to roll behind where Leaky stood by the lamppost. Clinging to the side rail with dirty red rubber gloves, the loader wore an open green work shirt, blowing suddenly back from a sunburned belly covered with bronze hair almost as thick as Leaky's. For a moment it looked like Lewey, and I even started to wave and smile—

But it wasn't—and the truck's white flanks moved away.

Leaky's sweatshirt blew to the side, too.

I walked toward him. Taking the collar out of the bag, I tossed the brown paper into the wire trash receptacle. He glanced down at it as I did. (I thought: I've seen him eat from such things...) There was no grin on his face, now. I looked up at this tall, thick fellow, his hair starting to gray, his beard rumpled and his face still overshadowed with dirt. (He never *had* gotten that shower.) His eyes narrowed in the sun, their gaze both easy and vacant. I stepped right up in front of him, looked down at the collar in my hands, and started to open it. While I undid the buckle, I could smell him. While I stood there, both his hands went to his lap; with thick fingers he pulled at his crotch.

I lifted the collar—as I put it around his hairy neck, under his beard, he raised his chin. For a moment, I wondered whether I'd

gotten it too small. But, turning it around, the buckle tongue went
through the third hole, though his neck must have been half again
the diameter of mine (and I take a fifteen and a half). Pushing
one finger under it, I moved it along to make sure it wasn't too
tight.

I dropped my hand. "How's that feel?"

He took a slow breath. "Like I'm a fuckin' human being what
means something to somebody else again—for the first time in a
fuckin' *long* time, man. Even if you sell me off tomorrow or just
kick me out tonight, this feels pretty good. Like now I'm where
I'm suppose to be. And I got to thank you for it, too."

"I don't think," I said, "I could kick you out, after just putting
something like that around your neck."

"Makes you feel better too, don't it?" He grinned.

"It would be a real head-fuck," I said, "if this is what buying and
selling slaves turned out to be all about."

"No," he said, like some kind of teacher. "That's about makin'
people what don't got nothin' do all the fuckin' work. This is
somethin' else."

"Well, yes," I said. "It makes me feel better."

We went downtown on the subway, and though we didn't get to
Robins "—Why don't you wait before you go buyin' me any shit
till after you see whether you like what you got me already, huh?
I mean, at least give it a few days."—we got a six-pack and, holding it low in a plastic bag, I bought us two tickets to the Grotto.

"They really got movies of people doin' shit like that?" Leaky
looked down at the pictures on the montage outside. "I seen that
in magazines and stuff. But I didn't know they had 'em in the
movies, too." As we walked into the balcony, and the theater's
video projection showed a bucking ass over a heaving cunt across
the screen, Leaky whispered down at me, "That's fuckin' weird..."

"Does it turn you on?"

"Yeah, man! I got me a big hard-on already! Come on and sit
down, so you can play with it for me."

I confess, the combination of his naïveté about the movies themselves, coupled with his complete lack of inhibitions about sex in
public—you'd think he'd been coming here for years—tickled me.

We—or rather he—went through three tallboys out of the six-pack. Then he said, "Just a second. They got a bathroom down-stairs?"

I nodded. He was up and moving toward the door, before I could stop him.

But three minutes later, he came across the front of the aisle, loping and kind of bowlegged, to say, "Hey, nigger, look here—"

In the theater's dark, I wasn't sure what he was doing, his hands at his waist. Then—piss splashed my face.

I pulled back, trying to control my surprise.

"You fuckin' nigger scumbag..." he rasped. "You goddamn cock-suckin' black sonofabitch...*Drink* my fuckin' piss, you low-down no-account shit-suckin' nigger shithole..."

A dark, bad-mouthing giant, half before the screen, legs plant-ed wide, he played his cock across my face, stepped closer, got his knee on the seat beside me, and pushed into my mouth with his saline eruption, pulled out again, and played it over me again.

"Hey, man!" one of the three other morning patrons called from the balcony's back. "Why don't you sit the fuck down, huh? You in the way!"

"Hey, motherfucker!" Leaky barked into the darkness. "I'll sit the fuck down when I finish' pissin' in my friend's face, here! You got a problem with that?" Then, in a lower guttural: "Open your fuckin' mouth, nigger!"

I caught my arms around his hips and sucked him in, till I coughed and he laughed. Piss came out my nose. I lost his cock, and he grabbed my head and rubbed his streaming hose across my face, while I managed to get my breath back. Then got him again.

"You fuckin' black scumbag..." he kept on, bending over me. His hands never left my head while he dropped into the chair beside me and, his arm around my shoulders, bent above me to thrust his tongue within my mouth.

"I'm gonna do that to you someday in the fuckin' Burger King, little guy," he told me, beard moving with his mouth on my wet ear. (A year and a half later, he walked in when I was eating a dou-ble-Whopper, and did. They just let him march out afterward, all of them scared as shit—and were incredibly solicitous of me, with apologies and outraged exclamations. We met back on my stoop and laughed for forty minutes, before we could get it together to go upstairs.) "When I do that to you in the fuckin' church, nigger, that's probably gonna mean we're married or somethin'."

(But we never did do that.)

"When you went down to the bathroom," I told him, "I thought you'd decided on your company manners here."

"So did I—until I got down there. Then I thought, what the fuck, and come back up."

The Hispanic midget, Shorty, one of the three people in the balcony, came down the aisle now, stepped across to us, and said, "You know, if somebody tell on you downstairs, they gonna throw you out, you do stuff like that." He folded his arms across the chest of his short-sleeved shirt and looked down—almost sadly—at the floor "That's no good. That's nasty." I liked Shorty, but sometimes I think he must *live* in the theater, because since he'd come back from Peru, about two years ago, I hardly ever saw him not here.

Leaky said: "Then don't tell."

"Yeah, well," Shorty said. "Okay..."

We sat there, through two more cans of beer and two more orgasms for Leaky. During one, when he had his pants down under his ass, and was leaning back just jerking off, an old guy leaning on an aluminum cane, like they give you in the city hospitals, came over and stood about three feet from us, to watch. Leaky had one hand around my shoulder, and two fingers moving in my mouth, for all the world like he was feeling up a pussy, while with his other hand he jerked. Without breaking rhythm, he grinned over at the old guy and nodded—

—and, grunting, a moment later, shot all over his belly and his hand. Raising his fingers, he licked some off, then moved his dripping fingers over for me to have some. "Man, that's good, ain't it?"

I nodded, and sucked two, then a third, of his fingers clean.

Now he leaned across me and lifted his hand toward the old guy. "You want some, Pops? You standin' there lookin' thirsty. An' I shot me a *big* load!"

The old guy just laughed. Then, with a surprised *For me?*-smile, he touched his wrinkled white shirtfront with long, knobby fingers.

"Take a lick there, y'old scumbag." Leaky grinned, pushing his hand toward the old guy again. "I know you want some! It's just cum. It ain't gonna hurt you."

With his fringe of white hair become a filigree of black, silhouetted before the grunting and thrusting shapes on the screen with
their green-rimmed flesh and their poster colors gone off, the old
guy lowered his head. To me it looked as if he kissed the back of
Leaky's hand.

"Go on," Leaky said. "Take yourself a big lick. That stuff is
good, Pops. It'll put hair on your chest. Make you young again."

The fellow laughed. "Thank you," he said, smiling widely, turning unsteadily, on his cane to move off. "Thank you very much."

Turning back, lowering his head, and slurping his tongue across
his palm, Leaky said, "That's probably the first real taste of cum
other than his own that old fuck's gotten in a coon's age."

"Hair on your chest—is that where all yours comes from?"

He laughed. "Here..." Again he pushed the callused edge of his
palm against my mouth. "We got any more beer?"

An hour later, I was between his knees (jeans wet through from
knee to cuff), on the balcony floor, while he gave up another load
into my mouth—my sucking punctuated only once, without comment, by his urine. Looking at the screen, he helped pull me up to
take a seat beside him. "Shit"—Haloed in hair, his flickering face
stared full forward—"I didn't *know* they made movies like this!" (I
don't think he'd actually twigged to the fact that this was a video
projection, not just a funny-looking film.)

"Didn't the guys in your yoni club ever tell you about this stuff?"

"Not down in Florida, they didn't." He sighed, and let himself
spread out in the theater seat again; and, arms behind me and out
along the seat back, he farted. "This is really somethin', little guy.
I like this place. It's nice here. You think we can come back sometime soon?"

"You stupid scumbag," I whispered to him, "anytime you want!"

Leaning forward again, he dropped his far arm into his lap to take
his cock and milk it, slowly and absently, between the tree trunks
of his thighs, in their binding of wrinkled wool.

That night I cooked pork chops and mashed potatoes and cab-
bage and turnips—and got fed them pretty much the way I'd been
fed breakfast. The last six-pack in the case kept us going till after
midnight. When we came into the bedroom, I sniffed for the
remains of the previous night.

"You won't be able to smell it for a day or two," he said soberly, sitting on the edge of the bed. "When you do, though, maybe you gonna wish you hadn't."

We talked, and necked, and rolled around, and slept, and necked some more, and talked some more. In the dark, he told me stories about sexual things that happened to him while at the State Home and out on the road hitchhiking, that made what he'd already told me of Big Nigg, Blacky, Billy, and Little Fuck sound like an Osmond family picnic. We talked about AIDS. I told him about Kelly. I told him about the Piece o' Shit. ("I would've killed that sucker, man!" "Well, the point is, I don't have it." He just grumbled.) And he told me about a guy who'd picked him up hitchhiking, who had it, with whom he'd stayed for two weeks. "This guy was *really* into piss, man—white guy, too. Made me fill up his fuckin' bathtub with it. Over three or four days. He took baths in it, too. Even let me shit in it a couple of times. I stuck everything up his fuckin' asshole except my dick. My foot. Coke bottles. My fist. Then he give me a hundred dollars and told me we probably wouldn't see each other again. He was a real good guy, too." I told him about Pheldon and Lewey and Angel and Sandy and, when the window started to go light, all about a new idea I had for another thesis topic I'd been toying with almost three months now, involving the later parts of Russell and Whitehead (*Principia* post-§56), and its implications for the theory of Definite Descriptions and its use in the resolution of the set-of-all-sets paradox and the antinomies, which, while it *does* relate indirectly to Hasler's work, still took Hasler out of the central spotlight of my intellectual concern, because, at least to me, by now Hasler had become more of a fascinating hobby than the working center of my world (the new thesis was actually most of the reason for all the missed work days, when, two months back, I really made a stab at seeing if I could reconstitute my committee on this side of the country, using the various people who had switched universities since then, and getting another couple of members), till finally I said: "Hey, Leaky—are you following any of this?"

"Some of it," he said. "It's interesting. But now I know when you call me a stupid fuck, you really mean it! I like listening to you talk about things I don't understand. It gets me hard. Hey, why don't you ask me a whole lot of questions I couldn't possibly answer—about philosophy and history and shit. I could probably cum that way without even touchin' myself," and, rolling over on his back, his cock lifted in the half-dark.

A couple of hours later, I was in the living room again.

"Cathy," I said into the phone, "why don't we say I just won't be in to the office till Monday. How's that? From then on, I promise I'll be back on schedule."

"You're pushing it, sweetheart," she said. "But you already know that. And Dorothy isn't interested in excuses. But I've got you down."

I went back inside, bent over and kissed the uninscribed name tag on his collar and crawled over him, when he turned onto his back, caught me by my shoulders, and pushed me down between his legs....

Sometime after eleven o'clock, we were lying in the middle of the living-room floor together. He'd just given me *my* first blowjob; and I'd cum in his mouth like a trooper. I said, "I don't know—somehow I just didn't think you were into sucking dick."

"Nigger," he said, "ain't you got it figured out yet? I'm into anything you are. Now, I'll tell you, I ain't into *talkin'* about suckin' dick too much—me doin' it, that is. But that's somethin' else. You own me, now, nigger." Grinning broadly, he raised his chin to finger the collar. "So you can suck my dick, drink my piss, lick my asshole, or—the fact is—do anything else you fuckin' want. Okay? You want to stick your dick in my face, do it, little guy."

And, shortly, I was dozing against him and thinking that there certainly wasn't anything I hadn't already done with him that I could figure to do further, when he said, "Hey, scumbag—I wanna do somethin' with you."

"Huh?" I said. "What?"

"I wanna turn you out."

"What do you mean?"

"You a stoned cocksucker, right?"

I nodded.

"Well, I know about cocksuckers, man. There ain't no cocksucker that can be really satisfied with just one dick—I don't care how good it is."

"Yours is pretty good, Leaky."

"I know. But that's how I know a couple or three others wouldn't hurt you none. Don't you ever go out and suck three or four in a day?"

"Sure," I said. "Sometimes five or six."

"Well, see?" He pushed my shoulder with the back of his hand.

"And I wouldn't be no proper top stud, if I *didn't* know that." He pushed up to sit cross-legged beside me. "So how about me goin' out and roundin' up some of them guys from the park—bringin' 'em back here, and really lettin' you and us work out. It'd get me off somethin' fierce, watchin' you suck some other dicks than mine."

"Leaky," I said, "if it turns you on—go do it!"

"Don't worry, it'll turn *you* on, too! I know the kind of scumbag cocksucker you are." He uncrossed his legs, to lumber erect, still pulling absently at his wanger. "Oh, man—you just great, nigger. It probably won't take me half an hour to find the guys I'm lookin' for. You just wait here. I'll be back—lemme hold a twenty, so I can bring back some more fuckin' beer?"

"You got it," I said. "My wallet's in my pants." There were three twenties left from the five I'd gotten from our last trip to the ATM machine. "Take two."

On the couch (the cushions were off on the floor; one was pretty wet by now) he sat, pulling on his woolen pants, pushing his feet into his running shoes. ("I don't even know why I bother with this one. I should probably just go barefoot." But he tied the laces on the torn-open one anyway. Two feet away, half under the couch, one of my own was sticking out.) His dog collar was almost hidden in the hair growing on his scrub pail of a neck. Carrying his sweatshirt with him, he went into the hall.

I heard the door close.

Sitting there, I pulled my knees up, hooked my arms around them, and tried to put the excesses of the last twenty or thirty hours in some prospective. Why, I wondered, had I said yes so easily to Leaky when, six weeks ago, I'd been so reluctant to say it to Crazy Joey? Certainly I trusted Leaky more than Joey. But it occurred to me, though I remembered clearly this had all started on Tuesday, July 18th, I had no idea now whether it was Thursday or Friday. I sat almost ten minutes, there on the living-room floor, frowning at nothing and trying to think about it.

I thought about calling Pheldon, but the idea crumbled when I tried to imagine what I'd say.

Are you happy now? I asked myself.

The answer: I'm a little scared, now he's gone off.

No, not scared. It's just that he's not where he ought to be, and I'm not where I ought to be. I'm not between his legs with his dick in my face. But then, of course, *he* was still within the circle of the collar I'd given him—maybe we both needed one? Or perhaps I was just scared that my own routine and rigid world systems had lost their edge and order in the last forty hours.

Then it hit me: You haven't even checked the mail!

You could, I thought, do that.

But I sat another ten minutes.

Then I got up, hunted my jeans out of the bedroom and pulled them on—it was warm enough that I didn't need a shirt. But when I got to the apartment door, I stood there with one hand on the knob, one hand against the yellow paint. Then I went back into my room, got a T-shirt from the pile in the corner, a blue one with a red circle on the front that Phel had given me last Christmas (I don't think it was clean) and slipped it over my head; then I went to the apartment door again, stepped outside, and started, barefoot, down the stairs.

Would I look particularly odd, I thought, if one of the other tenants saw me?

None of them did, though. But I guess noon isn't a time a lot of people go in and out of this building.

Opening the vestibule door, for a moment I couldn't remember what I'd come down for. Then, when I saw the mailboxes, I took a breath, reached in my pocket, and got my keys.

Standing on the tile, while the leaves rustled in sunlight above the sidewalk outside, when I turned the small key in the lock on the striated door, half a dozen interfolded letters and flyers nearly fell out. A couple more were wedged inside—and a package.

Wrapped in brown paper, and taped with packing tape, it was about seven inches by five by five.

When I got it out with the other letters, the return address read:

Almira Adler
Breakers' Point, CA

The wrong size and shape for a book, it didn't weigh quite a pound. Locking the mailbox, I shouldered back through the vestibule door while looking through the other pieces. All but two were second-class junk. One of the remaining ones was a Con Ed bill.

The thing to do, I thought, was to go to the corner and dump the junk mail in the trash basket there; I had enough paper upstairs. It wasn't just my bare feet, though; I felt I didn't want to be seen.

Plodding back up the steps, with the grit of the linoleum underfoot, I thought: is all this good for you? It leaves you kind of raw and unshielded to the world—so that it's more comfortable thinking of yourself as a "you" than as an "I."

At the door, I realized that, for a moment, I'd forgotten about the packages in my hand the same way that, minutes before, I'd forgotten the purpose of my trip downstairs to the mailbox. Squinting to get the key in the lock, I thought: it could just be the amount of beer I'd drunk in the last days.

Stepping inside, for the first time I smelled the faint ammoniac odor of urine. And something else. Even though Leaky wasn't in the apartment, it was Leaky's feet—which, even more than the piss (after all, I'd been kind of ready for that), surprised me. I pushed the door closed behind me, but didn't lock it, and walked up the hall into the living room.

On the round oak table, I put down the mail. Frowning at Adler's package, I turned it over—then went, got a scissors, returned, and shoved the blade through the wrapping paper and began to cut it open along one taped edge. I turned it at the corner, cut along one more edge. Then I pulled the wrapping back.

Inside was a letter, folded around what turned out to be a five-inch stack of old-looking index cards, crossed and recrossed in rubber bands. Three of the bands were yellow and pitted, as though they were years old and, likely, would break as soon as I took them off. (Hours later, they did.) Some newer, red ones had been put around the pile more recently, surely as a precaution.

I took the letter off—and remembered what Pete Darmushklowsky had said about recognizing Hasler's handwriting.

Beneath the rubber band, in that handwriting that till now I'd only seen in Xerox after Xerox copy of journal pages, I read: "Consider for epigraph to The Mad Man, Part One" and, on a line below that: παντα δια παντων.

That fragment of a (Heraclitus) fragment; "*All things [are guided] by all other things....*"

I put the bound cards on the table, picked up the letter, and opened out its creases—then realized I had to go to the bathroom....

There, I just sat, forearms on my knees, looking at the faces forming and dissolving in the squiggles on the shower curtain—most with beards, too—or looked at the shadows over the granulated glass window, where, outside, some pigeons trotted about on the sill.

Now and again they cooed.

Minutes later, I came back in, picked the letter up from the table, and read it.

July 17, 1990

Dear John Marr,

First let me say how much I enjoyed our brunch get-together at Maggy Bacojson's two weeks ago. I hope you won't feel patronized when I tell you that you struck me as an eminently civilized young man—and that I could not feel better about entrusting you with the delicate, probably unpleasant, and perhaps even dangerous question of Tim's death...is it really seventeen years ago now?

(I only hope, along with my own desire not to prosecute, but only to learn, time will have sapped the remaining dangers from the tragic business.)

At brunch, you asked if I had any more of Tim's papers.

Though you did not ask, I want to reassure you now: I never destroyed any of Tim's writings. I come from that generation horrified by the accounts in Maurois and Marchand of the destruction of Byron's journals—and perhaps even more so by Henry James's deranged, if understandable, defense of that destruction in The Aspern Papers—haven't we all heard it re-resound, if not in Auden's exhortation to his correspondents, then via Winnerton's conflagration in Barnes's barbarically written, but, intriguingly conceived, recent Parrot-ing of Flaubert?

Still, I felt quite reluctant—from the same urges I've already described to you, to avoid the unpleasant sides of Tim's life—to mention these, that I send you now. In their then-new rubber bands, this pack of 296 index cards (I assume that's how many there are; they are numbered and that is the number written and circled on the upper right-hand corner of the last) arrived at Breakers' Point in the first carton of manuscripts, papers, and journals Roger sent me after they were retrieved from Tim's apartment in '73. Then, I read some dozen or dozen and a half of them, decided that I would never read any further, and returned them to their original bands. There seemed no point in my perusing them more.

But you must believe me when I tell you that—after seventeen years—I did not remember the opening cards very well at all. Only after meeting you and finishing my set of East Coast readings, did I decide, on my return to California, to look into the carton again—pretty much emptied of it contents and sent to Professor Mossman some years before. Of course I now noticed, on the top card in the pack, the phrase that particularly interested you, in the line about the proposed epigraph.

I have now at least skimmed the entire set of cards.

There is no card devoted only to a title; thus you can understand how I'd never fixed the packet in my mind by a title. Nevertheless, having skimmed them, I am now sure that these cards are your Mad Man—that is to say, they are either a draft of a project Tim thought of as having that title, or they are the surviving notes (surely the only ones) toward such a project.

If there is material among them that will help explain Tim's death, you must ferret it out. But I am inclined to feel that they only chronicle some of the less savory, more debased moments of Tim's history—and whether late in that life or early, right now I am not prepared to say.

But since you were specifically curious about them, I send them on. Yes, I have had my assistant make a Xerox of them all, though, from looking over the sheets he returned with from the Copy Center, I'm afraid he's done rather a messy job. Thus, I entreat you, take care of them: the originals are now yours.

Hoping to hear from you when it is convenient, I have been and remain

Yours truly,
Almira Adler

I put the letter down by the bound cards and, frowning, wandered into the hall. What I wondered, to the point it slowed me as I walked barefoot on the hall's dark and worn wood planks, was: what is contained in that most innocent of closings, "Yours truly"? I am truly yours. I belong to you. And that belonging I mark with the terrible sign of "truth." Thus you are my owner. You own me.

I have put a collar on you that allows you to roam and, because the collar is a *true* sign of belonging, of ownership, of the genitive in its possessive mode, lets you return…to what comforts, what privileges, what rights, what responsibilities, what violences?

Historical, political, and bloody, in a land built on slavery, what appalling connections were inscribed within that phatic figure?

The bell rang from downstairs.

I murmured, "Yours truly…"

In the kitchen on the side of the old walled-up dumbwaiter, I rang the buzzer that would open the downstairs door.

What, within the systems of the world, I pondered, turning away, turned and returned eternally, posited about and around possession, truth, and the home—position and thesis, opposition and antithesis—among which I occupied one place and a man whom the world called homeless occupied the Other (a landing down, footsteps hurried up), even as I had dreamed of bringing him across the boundary between, into mine, through whatever marks he assigned me to assign him…

There was a knock on the door.

Without waiting for my answer, it burst in. "Hey, man! Look what I got!" Leaky grinned down, ducking beneath the lintel. On one shoulder he carried a case of beer: red print declared it Bud. On his hip, he held a tub of fried chicken. "I got Crazy Joey with me; and Mad Man Mike—hey, come on in! Guys, check out this scumbag nigger cocksucker here! He's real good—I tell you, *real* good!"

"Hey, look, it *is* the guy I was tellin' you about!" Crazy Joey's Brooklyn twang cut around from behind Leaky. "I told you, that's who I thought it was. The guy who brought me the beer and the bologna when we was foolin' around over in the park—after I got kicked out of that fuckin' place on Broadway—"

But Leaky was already saying (to me, I realized), "And Big Buck's gonna be up here. I pushed that little button on the side of the door down there so it would stay open and he could get right on in here." (Which everybody in the apartment building does, though Jimmy is always adamant about us not doing it.) "And your friend Tony's gonna be up soon, too. You just remember to give him his fuckin' penny, okay? Hey—" the case swung from his shoulder, to land, on edge, loudly on the hall floor—"this is Crazy Joey—but you guys already met, huh? And this is Mad Man Mike—he's real good people, man. He's somethin' else—the Mad Man, here!"

Still barefoot, Joey wore a shirt (of sorts) at least. Without buttons, it hung over his hard, small-muscled chest, as open as Leaky's sweatshirt (Leaky was wearing it again). "Mad Man Mike, man, he say he knows this place." Joey bopped up to me, with his broken-toothed grin, goodwill, and camaraderie.

Kneeling by the beer, Leaky said, "Mad Man says he's been here before, a long time ago. Hey—" which was back over his shoulder.

"The Mad Man, man, he knows a lot of shit." Joey hooked one soiled hand on my shoulder. "He's a great guy, man—" His other was already within his open fly. "Hey, Mad Man, this nigger can *really* suck some dick—you gonna see. He was the guy I wanted to turn out. I bet he gonna get a dozen loads out of you. The Mad Man, he say—" Joey turned back to me, to breathe his raunchy breath in my face—"he knows this place." Again he turned to call: "What'd you say, Mad Man—what was it, fifteen, twenty years ago?" And back to me: "I told you about Mad Man Mike, right? When you was suckin' my dick over in the park—after they throwed me out that fuckin' Burger King on Broadway. It wasn't your place, though—the Mad Man said the guy he used to know who lived here, he was downstairs."

"What you mean?" The hollow voice filled the hall like a liquid, like a solid. "How come you told him about me? Didn't I *tell* you not to tell nobody—"

"But it was after he shot his load three times all over me—like you said, Mad Man! Mad Man Mike, he said nobody should ever talk to nobody else about him, till they shoot three wads with you. We did that, didn't we, sucker? Me and the Mad Man, man—we real tight. I always do what the fuck the Mad Man says, you know? 'Cause he's the guy who fuckin' keeps me alive and out of the fuckin' crazy hospital!"

"The way you cum, you little scumbag"—I thought of a rasp,

working slowly over stone, in the center of some vast and vibrant metal drum—"you should make it *six* fuckin' times! You cum the way I fuckin' do, so you should make it six."

"You want me to make it six?" Joey said. "Shit, if that's what you say, Mad Man, I'll do it!" Now he turned back to me. "They ain't caught me now since before I run into you—that's 'cause I been doin' what Mad Man Mike tells me to. I know I got to do that, if I'm gonna make it out here and not get stuck back in no fuckin' crazy hospital, man. Me and Mad Man Mike, we just alike." Joey's horse dick was out his pants; his fist milked on it with the nervousness of the totally deranged. "He told me, man, he was just like me when he was a fuckin' kid. Is that right? Is that right, Mad Man...?"

Leaky dropped down on one knee to set the beer case over flat, putting the fried-chicken tub on the floor beside it. Though it was the same colors, it wasn't Colonel Sanders, but something called Pudgie's!

Standing behind Leaky (he wasn't as *thick* as Leaky. But he was as tall—or taller), he wore a blue shirt gone almost brown with dirt. Its sleeves were gone. His arms looked like sacks of sulfurous tan rock. He was a towering, light-skinned black guy, I saw now, with steel-wool tight, nappy yellow hair. There was a good deal of it, tufting out in peaks here and there of the blocky forms of his head. He had a broad, froglike face—older than Leaky by six or seven years, I figured. But he hadn't started to gray the way Leaky had.

People who get their muscles from work outside (from construction work to chain gangs) and people who get them from workouts inside (from barbells and Nautilus sessions) show fundamental differences between their bodies. The indoor exerciser controls the time of his or her routines and thus molds her or his body's expansion toward some preset perfection, whereas someone whose forearms, thighs, shoulders, and flanks harden from work in the wild is shaped *by* that work to whatever angle and form and muscle labor hurls at him or her.

Leaky was a big, strong, comfortable bear—with the hair and thick skin and the beer-gut bulge and the grin within his beard to sign an out-of-work worker made for comfort.

At least an inch and a half taller than Leaky's 6'4", Mad Man Mike was massive, with the imperfect, angled muscularity and massiveness of someone years at a time outdoors—though he probably weighed twenty pounds less than Leaky, he was just as broad, and his muscles all showed their edges and ridges and moorings. His skin flung me back to a memory of the thinnest layer knifed from that grimy bar of yellow kitchen soap I'd once found on the cabinet under my grandmother's sink, when we'd visited her in rural Kentucky when I was nine.

If the Mad Man took a deep breath, I thought, there in the hall, his shirt would rip in a dozen places! While I thought it, Mike's hands, like cuts of golden meat gone gray, hooked the front of his shirt, one high, one low, and—slowly and perfectly naturally—pulled it apart. The snaps that still held came opened, and he shouldered out of it and let it fall beside him on the hall floor. "This the cocksucker, huh?" His voice was soft and raspy—and *still* filled the whole hall. A large scar jagged his left pectoral. The spare hair on his sternum snarled like curled wires. From under bony brows, he looked at me with eyes a yellow-green. "I'll give you a penny for a piece of that." The expression that, on those stony features, passed for a grin, flickered forward among them, like an animal emerging a moment from rocks, then retreated within. "That nigger look like he worth a penny to me."

"Go on, Mad Man." On one knee, Leaky pulled the top up from the beer carton. "You take my nigger inside there and check him out. He's a real good suck, man. I'll bring in some beer."

A dirty rope held up Mike's pants. Some of the loops were broken. The zipper had probably busted long ago: a large triangle of cloth flapped down, revealing a span of dirty thigh, one side of his wiry pubic bush, the folded arch in the flesh beside it, and enough of the right side of his penis to know he had one. How, I wondered, had he gotten here through the streets, unless he'd held it up with his hand—as I've seen any number of crazy guys clutch them, wandering the city.

He wasn't clutching it now.

With one hand, he reached within his gaping flap. With the other, as he came forward, he reached for me. (Outside in the hall, I heard more footsteps rushing up.) I've described both Leakey's and Crazy Joey's hands as big; and they were. But you took Joey's and put the thickest leather gloves over them, you might have a set of hands the size of Mad Man Mike's. When the fingers moved, you were surprised they could. They made you think of small clubs, and didn't feel like they were alive. The nails were horned arenas, all but the one on his little finger half again the area of (and broader than) subway tokens. They extended to the fingers' ends, but with no projecting scimitars. The daily labors of his survival had worn them down, not to the quick, but still prevented them from any extension. Seeing his, I couldn't help picturing Leaky's, which might easily have been arenas as broad; but since childhood Leaky's dental demolition had chipped at and blasted up and stripped away more than the first three quarters of each, so that, even though they were as wide or wider, on Leaky's fingers the flesh before them had hardened and broadened and risen, till his great nubs were incapable of picking up beer can tabs, dropped coins, dimes to quarters, or needles and paper clips to be lifted from any smooth surface—services that, after the first day with me, he no longer even tried, but immediately looked at me to do.

When the Mad Man touched my neck—certainly no more roughly than Leaky—it felt like a stone or a tree branch fallen against me.

With the hand at his waist, he pulled free his dick.

"See, man!" Crazy Joey, beside us and pulling on his own mule cock, exclaimed. "The Mad Man's got a fuckin' dick on him bigger'n mine! Remember, you said I couldn't be a black guy 'cause no nigger could be my old man. Bet Mad Man Mike could've been my old man—that's why I got this big fucker down between my legs. I wouldn't be surprised if Mad Man Mike was fuckin' on my momma, years ago. Our eyes is the same color." Gray-green for Joey, yellow-green for Mike. "He could be my dad, easy. Then I'd be a nigger—and you said I couldn't be! But I *could* be—if Mad Man Mike was my pop!"

If I'd seen it somewhere else, probably I'd have had to phone someone, or write it down, or draw a picture of it. Pheldon had entertained a passion for John Holmes pornos, and I'd seen quite of collection of them—and his passion had survived, even been excited by, the sordid business of Holmes's supposed murder of six people in an L. A. cocaine slaying, and which his death from AIDS had only raised from the sordid to that of acceptable martyr. In a book like this you just can't *say* someone's was the biggest cock you've ever seen. Because in a book like this, calling something the biggest cock you've ever seen doesn't mean anything. It's been said too many times...

His fist ran out to the end of it. His fingers flipped wide, his hand snatched back under to the pair of gnarled and near-black avocado pears that were his nuts, in their tuft of steel wool gone rusty. His fist ran out to the end of it again. The fingers flipped wide, snatched back. His fist ran out to the end of it, flipped, snatched back—

With some guys, it's the downstroke that's the business one. With others, it's the upstroke. Mad Man Mike was an upstroke man—and my throat was trying to learn that, even as my mouth was telling my brain, hey, how the fuck are you gonna *fit* that thing in your face...?

"Hey, I got up here—nobody saw me!" The voice was familiar; I glanced up, to see Tony come through the door, with all his red hair, with his green work shirt that had gotten enough dirtier since the last time I saw him to make me realize that—the *last* time I saw him—he must have just come from some charity-clothes hand-out. "Hey, Mad Man, is this the place you meant—that you was tellin' us about? The professor here, you don't mean you knew *him* for twenty years now, do you?"

"Hey, Tony, man"—Leaky stood now, a six-pack in each hand—"help me get these things to the kitchen—"

"No, I told you," Mad Man's voice rumbled above me. "This was sixteen, maybe seventeen years ago now. It was this building, but it was downstairs—an Oriental fella. From Korea—"

I was actually gonna say something *then*—but Leaky was over me. "Man, will you give fuckin' Tony his fuckin' *penny*—please, little guy! I can't stand this no more, you know what I mean? I gotta get me free and clear and be yours, now."

"—Huh?" I had already reached in my pocket.

"It's just a fuckin' penny. That's all. Go on, he's in the kitchen, puttin' the beer away."

"Mad Man...?" Saying it, I felt I spoke to the primal past itself, already knowing what I did about him. "Just a moment. I'll be..." and pulled away from him, from under that hard hand that tried to hold me, down the hall toward the door they'd all just come in, then turned suddenly to the left, into the kitchen.

Crouched behind the refrigerator door, Tony was pulling the

cans from the plastic loops and pushing them onto the lower shelf. He looked around the door at me, grinning: "Hey, I guess it all worked out, between you and Leaky, huh? That's fuckin' somethin', man. That's great!"

Pawing in my pocket, I came up with a handful of change. "Leaky said I was suppose to give you some...some change?"

He stood, grinning at me. "How you doin', professor. Oh, yeah—this is gonna be fun. Hey—no, man—"

Because I tried to dump the whole handful of change into his palm.

"No, just a penny. That's all you owe me. I'm fuckin' glad to get over all this shit. That's right—here, I'll take it. Just a penny..."

"Tony," I said. "Why am I doing this?"

"Huh?"

"Leaky said you'd paid a penny for him?"

"—yeah, when I bought him from Mad Man Mike."

"—and now I have to give you a penny *back?*"

"Yeah." He held the coin, copper tarnished nearly black, up between his big fingers. "Now you've bought him from me. He's officially yours now. We got beer—did they get the chicken?"

"Yeah," I said. "Inside. Tony, why am I doing this?"

"Huh? I don't know—Oh, I see. You mean...well, I guess it's some sort of game—Mad Man Mike's game."

"Huh?"

"Mad Man Mike, he figured it out. I *guess* it's like a game. Only it works—it worked for Leaky, didn't it? It worked for me, too—that's what he paid for me."

"Paid who?"

"Mad Man Mike—he paid a penny for me. Can you imagine that? I thought it was all a lot of shit, really. But it really made me feel fuckin' better, man."

"Who did he pay?"

"Me, man!"

I made some gesture with my hand full of the nickels, pennies, quarters, and dimes that had come loose from my pocket. And Tony, misunderstanding me, raised his hand to halt me—

"—No, professor. Mad Man Mike, he explained it to us, a long time ago. Just a penny—you can't sell a person for no more than that."

"Why—?" Which was not the start of the question Tony chose to answer:

"I guess it's 'cause of how you were talkin' to me, once…about bein' so fuckin' low? He said that the thing you buy and sell, when you buy some scumbag this way, it don't got nothin' to do with what some one can *do*—I mean, how much he's *worth* out there. It just has to do with…I don't know. Owning."

"Hey—" which was Leaky, who, a hand on either jamb, was hanging in the kitchen doorway. "He pay you off for me, yet?"

"Yep," Tony said. "Got my penny right here." It went into Tony's pocket. "And I'm keepin' this one, too."

"Come on, guys," I said. "This is fucking *crazy*—"

"Aw, man," Leaky said. "Then this is really mine, now." His bearded grin filled up his face, filled the whole kitchen. One hand came down to thumb along the dog collar around his neck. "Hey," he called over his shoulder. "Anybody want a fuckin' beer? Come on, scumbag—the Mad Man wants to check you out." A moment later, with his familiar arm around my shoulder, he was moving me again down the hall.

Mad Man Mike was waiting in the doorway to the living room, and his own hand received my arm, as Leaky's hand left my shoulder. "Mad Man, you wanted a cocksucker who could drink your fuckin' piss, man? This nigger drinks piss the way Tony scarfs up your fuckin' shit, man. We can trade, Mad Man, or I'll pay you a fuckin' penny for Tony and you can buy this cocksucker from me to use him like you want for a while—"

While Mad Man Mike pushed or pulled me around into the living room, leaving Leaky behind, the Mad Man's other hand still worked on what angled free of his pants.

Crazy Joey came around with us, though: "See, man, the Mad Man's dick is just like mine. Both of 'em curve the same fuckin' way—ain't that somethin'? But you see, me and the Mad Man is just alike—"

"Get the fuck out of here!" Mad Man Mike raised his hand to Joey.

"Yeah, Mad Man! Sure, I'll be right outside, if you need me—"

"Get yourself a fuckin' beer, huh?"

"Oh, yeah!" Crazy Joey gave a big grin, pulled back from the living-room door, and loped off down the hall.

"You're the Mad Man," I started. "I was wondering if I could ask—"

"You could help me out, is what you could do." Mad Man Mike's hand moved farther around my shoulder. "Shut the fuck up now, and listen." His face bent toward mine. "See, you gotta understand about me." The rasping filled my ear, my whole head. "I got these kind of rules, you know what I mean? It's kind of funny, like, but you see I ain't never pissed in a fuckin' urinal for more than ten years. Or shit in a fuckin' shitter, either. I just can't do it—you know what I mean?" While I looked up at his face, just below my vision his hand kept up its movement along his immense member. "I can't do that, man. Tony, now, see, he's real good for me. Every fuckin' day, nigger, I shit in his fuckin' face—and he, you know, he eats it for me. He's beautiful. So, you see, if I had two of you fuckin' scumbags, one to eat my fuckin' shit, one to drink my fuckin' piss, I'd be okay, you know what I mean...?"

"Yeah...sure, but I—"

Which was when I felt the warmth and water at my waist. I looked down, started to pull away—

"No, man." His great arm pulled me forward. "I'm just pissin' on you, nigger—it ain't nothin'. That's good nigger piss—a nigger pissin' on a nigger. A fuckin' revolutionary act! Just me takin' a fuckin' piss on you, here in your fuckin'—what's this? Your fuckin' livin' room? Leaky, man, he said you was fuckin' good, cocksucker." His arm weighed down on me. "Go on. Get on down. Lemme piss in your fuckin' face. Go on. Leaky don't mind—he said he'd sell you to me, for a penny. You know? That's all. Try it! Go on, get the fuck down—"

My knees broke, and I went down on my knees on the rug.

"Yeah...!" His urine splattered and burned my eyes, welled in my mouth. It wasn't beer piss, either. "You look fuckin' good down there, you black sonofabitch! You look as fuckin' good drinkin' piss, nigger, as that redheaded mick looks when he's scarfin' down my fuckin' turds." My arms went around his hips. From the movement of his pants against his blocky buttocks, I realized they were torn down the rear seam; my fingers went over the right edge and felt the bare skin of one cheek. "I gotta save 'em for that shit-mouthed scumbag—yeah, that's right! Drink it—hey, Tony? Come here! Don't he look fuckin' good?"

I heard Tony's familiar chuckle, from the door. "Jesus, Mad Man—"

Mad Man Mike stepped suddenly back. Stream dying, it traced a wet sickle over my rug. "Okay, boy—now you go get yourself a fuckin' beer, too. Is that okay? You like the flavor? You like the temperature? You like the smell and the feel...?"

"Yeah. Sure—but I just wanted—"

"Good! Me and Leaky'll work this out. Hey, you dumb-ass stupid motherfucker"—his bellow startled me—"get on in here and bring me somethin' to drink!"

Tony at the door was already holding a can down beside the thigh of his baggy jeans.

"Come on, you shit-eatin' bastard. I saved something for you, so when I got the both of you here, I could try you out together—" Mad Man Mike backed away across the rug, and suddenly dropped to a squat. His naked forearms went over the knobs of his knees, and he grinned up at Tony. "Come on over here, little guy." And I wondered which of us had started calling which of us by that name first.

In a squat, Mad Man Mike moved to one side, then the other, flexing his feet inside his collapsed shoes—I could see the leather move: what I suspect had at one time been a good pair of black combat boots.

His gas broke free—then something wet. "Come on, look down here, sucker. Wanna watch it fall?"

Tony took a big swig, then practically fell on his knees, then dropped even lower, to stare into the space between the Mad Man's split seam and the rug.

"*Ehhhh*—there it *goes!* Good one for you, Tony boy. Big thick one, ain't it? You fuckin' low enough to eat that shit? Come on, are you fuckin' low enough—?"

In the hall I turned toward the kitchen, wanting to get close to Leaky again; everything I felt by now was happening not in words but in urges and sensations and feelings. "Hey, man—" Crazy Joey's hand hooked my shoulder as I walked. (I glanced over; his T-shirt had gone the same way as Mad Man Mike's old work shirt.) "—you gonna suck my dick, ain't you? I mean, three or four times? That's how you gotta do with me and the Mad Man. We're like that, him and me—"

"Yeah," I said. "Yeah, Joey, that's right—"

Leaky came from the kitchen with a beer in one hand, a piece of chicken between his thumb and forefinger, which he was just taking a bite of; suddenly I ran toward him. And threw my arms around him. He caught me, laughing: "Hey, what the fuck is the matter with you...?" He bent down; I felt the cold cans against my neck. His warm hand splayed on the small of my back, up under my T-shirt. "*Hey*, now, little guy. What you want, now—" I smelled the chicken he chewed.

My left leg and buttock were shaking. So were my right shoulder and arm. Against his beard, I growled, "I want to suck all their cocks—I want to suck all your fucking dicks, till you cum all over me, five or ten times. Then you piss all over me—"

When he spoke, his inflection may have been a response to calm my intensity, or perhaps he was just infected by it: "That's *just* what we gonna do—" My bare feet had come off the ground: he set me down: "Come on, we go see the Mad Man. He gonna set you up—"

"Leaky," I said, still shaking. Because my leg was still quivering, I thought I was going to fall. "I have to talk to him—"

Leaky's free hand now went to my face, then he put his knuckles back against my shirt, and grinned. "Shit, nigger—he done broke you in already, didn't he? He ain't been here but a minute—"

"What—?" and realized he meant my urine-wet T-shirt, the piss on my face. "No, I mean I have to talk to him. I know who he is—"

"Yeah," Leaky said. Still holding me, we started up the hall. "When I told him about you, and where you lived, at first he said he thought he knew who *you* was. But when we come over here, he said it was someone else he knew what used to live here. Some chink what lived downstairs from you, a long time ago—"

"That was Hasler," I said. "That's the guy I told you about who got—"

"Hey, you gonna suck me?" Crazy Joey stood in the living-room doorway, leaning back on the jamb. His grubby feet were wide apart, his knees bent. At his crotch, his fist sped on his spiring flesh. "Come on, lemme see some fuckin' tongue, cocksucker, while I shoot my fuckin' load—you scumbag cocksucker, come on over here—yeah, watch my fuckin' dick. You wanna suck it, don't ya'? That's right—"

Leaky let me go, and I slid to the wooden floor.

"You gonna crawl over here, scumbag, and lick my fuckin' nuts?" One hand blurred up and down, while the other jerked and snapped like a sail blown wild at his waist. Joey grimaced, grinding his teeth, face falling forward till I couldn't see it—then back, banging (hard, I heard it) into the wood. "You fuckin scumbag cocksucker, man, you wanna suck my dick so bad, you're leakin' in your fuckin' pants! You gonna pee all over yourself in a minute, nigger—ain't you? You wanna suck my fuckin' cheesy dick so fuckin' bad—" On the stretched cloth of his too-big pants, his balls rolled, side to side, as *he* moved side to side.

I crawled.

Behind me, Leaky whispered, "Yeah!"

I stuck out my tongue and wobbled it.

Ahead, voice shaking with his fist, Joey whispered: "*Fuck*, man!"

The hallway floorboards were old. A loose one gave a little under my hand's heel; my forefinger slipped off the board beside it—and stung.

On the boards, Crazy's Joey's toes spread, knuckles depressing in wrinkles, crowns widening around and before his dirt-outlined toenails. I glanced into the living room, where his other cracked and grubby heel lifted from the rug, lifted again. Above me he beat. His voice quivered to his fist's oscillation: "Get 'em, cocksucker—come on, get my balls—"

I looked up. When his free arm swung out, I grasped it. As I held his forearm, his own fingers locked mine. Across our doubled grip, his shaking shook in me, as if I'd tapped what, within him, was that shaking's source, core, and delivering vortex. Pulling myself forward, I licked his right nut. Within his sack, it turned under my tongue. His fist's bottom beat against my forehead like a mad feather. I lapped his loose, salty nuts and, lifting my face, received the battering of his fist's falling, full now; it hit me like relief. "Oh, yeah, 'sucker—lick 'em...!"

I licked his big balls, up and down—he gasped.

And shot. I felt it through our joined arms. I saw it in his shaking thigh, within his pants' grease-blackened blue. I looked up: another gout splattered his cheek, pearled down across his gasping mouth, to drip from upper lip to lower—and, as he lowered his head, to fall, slowly, from his lower...and, the strand breaking, hit the side of my nose. There was cum on his chin, on his chest, a loose, large web of it, as the small muscles heaved within it, strung from right pectoral to belly, from left flank to sternum. Still holding his arm, as he heaved, I raised to lick his soiled and salted skin free of its mucus. "Yeah, nigger..."

He panted three more times, bending over me—leaning on my head, actually—so that I couldn't reach with my tongue the rivulet running his ribs.

But he grasped my face, one hand scummy, one dry. Below, I saw his cock flop forward, felt its wet head hot and blunt on my collarbone. He wrestled me around. "Hey, man—what are you..."

"What the fuck..." which was my protest.

But he grunted, "Look, scumbag—you see what Tony's doin'? You gotta watch that, man! You'll miss it..."

Held in Joey's gasping grip, I blinked and saw, from beneath his low-bent shoulder, Tony, naked, clothing strewn behind him, crouched on the living-room rug. His knees were drawn under him, his butt in the air. His back was a red rug, grizzled gray at the shoulders. His tattooed arms curved out wide. His face was practically on the floor. At the center of the curve his arms made lay a dark mound. It looked like two small logs, one end half on the other, and a pile of something next to them—the Mad Man's shit.

Dragging his beard back under his chin, Tony's head jerked forward; he tore at a turd with his teeth. His stained mouth came away, chewing, and I could look over his shoulders to see the teeth marks scoring shit, till he lunged for another bite.

I heard the falsetto initiation that, a moment later, took the Mad Man's laughter into its basso plunge. He was sitting on the couch, perched on the back, his combat boots—the laces were opened now—wide on the cushions. He cradled his cock in his fist, leaning forward and stroking it up against his belly, the way you'd imagine a dog with hands masturbating. "Hey, come over here, cocksucker—get off 'em, Joey, and let the cocksucker come over here and suck my dick...!" He spoke the last three words with heavy and equal accent.

"Yeah...!" Joey said, his grip loosening on my head. "The Mad Man, he likes to get his balls licked, too. Him and me, we both like it pretty much the same way—"

"Get off his fuckin' head," the Mad Man said, "and let him get the fuck over here—"

"Sure, Mad Man..." The hands that had been holding me were now pushing. "Go on, you lick his balls, like you done me. He likes that—"

I lurched to my feet and staggered across the rug, barefoot, half-stepping on Tony's hand—I looked down, as he snatched it back an inch: the one with S-H-I-T on the knuckles.

His tattooed fingers arched on the rug. His face jerked forward, with bared teeth, to rip away more shit.

As I reached the Mad Man, he gestured toward my pants. (His other hand moved slowly, like a giant engine, rising and falling on his cock.) "What, I...huh...?"

Behind me—I hadn't realized he'd followed me in, but his hand was on my shoulder again, the fingers still sticky, I felt him behind me (and smelled him over my shoulder): "Come on, get 'em off, cocksucker. So we can see your black ass and watch you pull on your dick."

I pulled open my jeans and began to push them down my legs. "I just need to ask...what? Huh...I wanted—"

The Mad Man's hand came up and went around my neck, pulling my head forward and down.

Behind me, Joey had me by the shoulders: "Go on, lick his balls, I told you! He likes that, just like I do—"

As I went forward, into that shadowed dark, I realized the Mad Man's smell wasn't pleasant. But, after a few moments, it gave me a kind of charge. I licked his big, wrinkled sack. Beneath the salt was a sourness close to the smell. I hooked one hand under his thigh, and, holding on, licked harder. Above, he rumbled a pleased, "*Yeah*, cocksucker...!" So I caught his other leg with my other hand, and licked even harder. "Yeah...!"

Joey was on the couch now—I guess he got one leg around the Mad Man's boot, still pulling on himself, still watching Tony. "How you like the way that nigger licks your balls? He'll do anything for dick—fuckin' cocksucker...!" He let out a near-deranged cackle.

And as much alike as they were, I couldn't imagine time ever changing that into the Mad Man's three-octave black guffaw. The Mad Man grabbed my arm—once his hand slipped over my hair. "You gotta grow you some wool, nigger, so I can hold you by your head!" Then he grabbed my head, fingers locking it the way he'd palm a basketball (his hands were easily big enough to hold one, one-handed, upside down) and pulled me up. "Get your fuckin' pants off, I told you—"

So Joey and I both got them off for me.

In the living-room doorway, Leaky, barefoot now, fingertips hooked overhead on the lintel below the transom, kind of hung, kind of leaned, kind of grinned around. Now he dropped his hands—he was holding a working beer in one—and came in.

He walked up to Tony and stepped across him. "You fuckin' redheaded shit-eatin' bastard…"

He turned. And planted his foot in the shit on the rug and leaned into it. Like four cliffs, rising in some geologic catastrophe, shit mashed up between his toes. It spread out on either side of the ball. "Come on, you low-down, asshole-lickin', puke-eatin' shit pig, eat that off my foot!"

Tony's big hands converged like two animals on Leaky's ankle. He strained his mouth wide and nearly swallowed three of Leaky's toes at once—and Leaky's toes are fucking big! Tony's head rocked on the rug as he strained to take as much of Leaky's foot into his mouth as he could.

Beside me, Crazy Joey, who was sitting on the couch, straddling Mad Man Mike's left leg, holding it with one hand and working on his cock with the other, whispered, "Oh, fuck, look at that!"

"You lick the fuckin' shit out of Crazy Joey's asshole every day, you can lick the Mad Man's fuckin' shit out from between my toes, scumbag—"

"Hey," Joey said. "Hey, I'm gonna shit on the couch—"

I looked back at him.

He was grinning up at me. He reached up and put his hand on my hip. "Hey, nigger, I'm gonna shit on your couch, okay? And Tony can lick my ass clean. He likes to do that shit. Okay? I'm gonna do it right here…" He let go my hip, and brought his hand back to his sagging cock, to whip on it some more, moving his butt from side to side on the cushions. "You ever take a shit while you're beatin' off? Boy, that feels…" Joey grunted—

And the Mad Man yanked me, so that I lost my footing and slipped against him. "Take it, motherfucker! Here it comes, scumbag. Take it—"

I flailed around, trying to find in the odorous hollow of him, the joining of fist and cock. It was against my face, blinding. Then, with knee and hand, I pushed away enough to see it there, inches from my face—while behind me his hand pulled me forward till I thought my neck would break.

I've never seen anyone cum like the Mad Man.

It wasn't like Joey's grand, slopping geysers. It was as if you took a toothpaste tube in your hand and suddenly squeezed. First of all, it was that thick. It shot up, in a coherent white worm, maybe ten inches, before it flopped back, while it kept erupting out of him, making a gray, lucent pile over the top of his cock, over the rim of his fist—before my neck broke. Or, anyway, my neck muscles gave and, opening my mouth, I fell on his dick. I thought his fist and his cock would go into my mouth both. The Mad Man's cum was lumpy—you think of most guys coming in your mouth: and what you do is drink it.

No. This was food. You had to eat it. For the first few seconds, with that viscid, lumpy stuff in my mouth, I was really scared.

Somewhere behind me, Leaky said, with the hillbilly surety with which he told the most outrageous tales as though they were the most ordinary day-to-day happenings, "Eat the fuckin' shit out between my toes, Tony."

And above me, rasp-rough, the Mad Man's voice said, "Hey, cocksucker, that's fuckin' good." A postorgasmic rhythm began to take over his hips. His shaft slid up through his fist into my mouth; and out, and into it. And out and in again. And out. And in. Though on the wrong side of his load, it reassured me. "Hey, Tony and this cocksucker here is my *boys*...! That's beautiful. Both of you. Eatin' my fuckin' shit, drinkin' my fuckin' piss. Takin' my load. One redheaded honky, one scummy-mouthed nigger. Hey, man, I'm really somethin', huh? Yeah, Leaky, I'm gonna buy this one from you, I think."

"Yeah?" Leaky said somewhere. "Well, I wanna see how the two of 'em fuck around together. Come on, little guy..."

The grip on the back of my neck started like the one you pick up a kitten with.

It ended in something that was all Leaky's: hand on my neck, large enough to lift me without hurting—he pulled me up. And the journey was from the harsh and unfamiliar smell of the Mad Man to Leaky's familiar and comfortable body odor: vinegar, old laundry, spices—with an overlay of beer. Leaky's beard brushed, then pressed, my cheek: he was kneeling on the floor beside me. "Hey, nigger, you got one of the fucker's loads, didn't you—don't the Mad Man *shoot* some fuckin' scum! But look at that, out there—"

As I opened my eyes for the first time in minutes, Leaky pointed at Tony: Tony lay on his back, taking big breaths. One knee was up. One leg stretched out. One hand was at his groin absently tugging at the engorged cock. His big, soft fingers passed over the two warts I could see, like minuscule cauliflowers, smaller than dimes and dark with whatever reddens the genitals of redheads.

"He's still got a mouthful of shit." On my foot, I felt Leaky's big toes cover mine, then slide back till they began to work on mine. "Lemme see you get down there an' stick your tongue in his fuckin' mouth. You're a fuckin' piss-drinkin' scumbag, and he's a shit eater—" He paused, to drink some beer; I could hear it gurgling in his throat, going down. "But without you, he's just *half* a fuckin' scumbag. Get on down there; let's us see you roll around together—"

"Yeah—" which was Crazy Joey, behind me.

But I pulled away from Leaky and fell forward, catching myself on my hands, to gaze into Tony's face. He was chewing. There was a broad brown smear on his right cheek. An acorn of shit stuck to the right of his red mustache. He looked up at me. And his eyes didn't look dazed at all. He reached up and caught me by the back of my head. His face lifted under mine. I thrust my tongue out into the hole in his beard, while his lips drew back and his teeth opened under mine, so that I went deep into what was his mouth, saliva clearing parts of his tongue. Surging under mine, I could feel it, and the sweetish walnut taste lumping other parts, a taste I'd known before from him, while I turned myself around him on the bushing our joined mouths made, not just lips, but teeth grating teeth, tongue wrestling tongue, till, locked, he thrust into mine his spit, his tongue, and whatever—and I thrust them back.

I heard the couch creak and give. Tony's big arms came up to hold me, while I tried to get my hand under his shoulders, rug burning my knuckles. Trying to get them under his other shoulder, there was something soft on which they slid. The fat log of Tony's cock and my cock, near half again as long, ground together. His warts, with their crusts, actually scratched me. He rolled and thrust up under me. The edges of his foot rasped against my calf.

And above:

"Now look at them two fuckers, a fuckin' human cesspool—that's what the pair of them are." The rasp ground away stone within its drum.

And Leaky (I felt a bare foot wedge beneath my shoulder): "He's one beautiful nigger, ain't he, Mad Man."

"I love to watch a white guy get off on my fuckin' shit."

"Man...!" Crazy Joey said, voice shaking again, so that I could picture his fist's motion, as he crowded in with them, gazing down. "That's fuckin' horny, man. That's worth a fuckin' penny. Mad Man, I'd pay fuckin' three cents for that. I'd pay a fuckin' dollar to—"

The sound was a smack. But probably with a cupped hand. Even so—on the ground—I jerked. And opened my eyes.

"You pay a fuckin' penny, man," Mad Man Mike growled. "You hear me, you crazy jerk-off scumbag—you don't never pay no more than a penny for somebody else! Or let nobody pay more'n that for you! What you think this is...?"

"Hey, Mad Man, I was just kidding. You know, I was just talkin'. You know—?"

Gathered above us was a forest of legs. (Tony had rolled on top of me. His hips bucked over me.) Their three faces hung in the distance above, looking down. All three of them were jerking off. With the three cocks in their fists's separate rhythms—Mad Man Mike's slow upswing and fast down catch-up, Crazy's Joey's supersonic blur, and Leaky's regular rhythm, somewhere much closer than their heads—even though there were only three, for moments I couldn't get from the legs to the faces without getting all confused.

So I closed my eyes, and held onto Tony—whose hair was in my face anyway, to lose myself in his mouth's fouled canyon.

"Look at 'em—" the rasp, the drum—"ain't they fuckin' beautiful, man? Makes you wanna piss on 'em, don't it? Hey, you crazy little scumbag, you heard me—piss on the motherfuckers!"

Leaky laughed.

Crazy Joey said, "I don't know if I can take a piss before I shoot another fuckin' load!"

"I can." Which was Leaky. And his water hit my face, warm and heavy, to move off over Tony's back—I felt it cross my hand there.

I heard Crazy Joey grunt. Then, apart from the chattering roar of Leaky's waterfall filling the ravine between Tony's heavy belly and my lean one, and running down between us (we were on our sides now), there was the splat of something hot over my cheek and shoulder. "Yeah!" Joey gasped. "*Now* I can fuckin' piss...."

And his stream broke over my elbow, my flank, vanishing a moment somewhere on Tony's back, returning to my face—"Look at the nigger tryin' to drink it! Oh, *shit!*"—to wash away his just-delivered load.

"Now how you gonna pay more than a penny for each of them," Mad Man Mike intoned. "Look at 'em, I mean. Eatin shit? Drinkin' piss? They're stupider than fuckin' Leaky here. And they're *crazier* than you an' me put together!"

I felt Leaky's toes move under me. I felt his waters wash over me. Tony came. And a minute and a half later, still riding him, when Mad Man Mike kneeled down beside us and stuck two thick, leathery fingers in my mouth, I did, too.

PART
FIVE

THE
MIRRORS
OF NIGHT

But Love has pitched his mansion in
The place of excrement;
For nothing can be sole or whole
That has not been rent.

——William Butler Yeats,
"Crazy Jane Talks with the Bishop"

Rette dich, Tristan!

—*Tristan und Isolde*, II, iii.

"The little guy got some money," Leaky said. "In his pants pocket—"

I said, "I kind of wanted to hold on to some of—"

"Just some fuckin' change." Mad Man Mike was perched on the couch back again. His fist moved faster on his cock. (I looked at the window off beside the couch. But probably with the sunlight falling on the dusty pane, nobody across the street could really see in.) "Just the fuckin' pennies."

"Go on," Tony said. He sat cross-legged on the rug, naked, beside me. "He just wants the pennies you got. You got five pennies? Maybe six, when Big Buck gets here."

"Oh," I said. When I leaned forward and pulled my jeans over, the rug squished loud enough to hear under my thigh. I took out the handful of coins from my side pocket.

"Put the rest of it back," Mad Man Mike said from the couch.

433

His fist kept working on his cock. "You just need—" Then he grimaced a moment, leaned back, and shot—

It was the same welling of thick, gloppy cum, over his fist, he'd delivered before.

Tony shook his head and leaned forward. "He gonna be doin' that, every twenty minutes from now on. I swear, I don't know how the Mad Man manages to drop so much fuckin' scum."

Mad Man raised his hand and took, not a lick, but a bite off the stuff on the back of his hand. "Who wants some…?"

From the doorway, where he leaned against the jamb, Leaky said: "There's gonna be so much of that shit around—" he'd put on his sweatshirt again; and taken off his pants, so that his legs were like two, shaggy jungle trees—"ain't nobody gonna have to *fight* for it—"

"I don't ask twice." Mad Man Mike raised his hand and flung it down. Cum splattered on the couch.

Some hit Crazy Joey's cheek; some splatted his pants. "I cum as much as Mad Man Mike does." Crazy Joey just beamed. He was working on his cock again. He looked over at the cum on his pants leg, and with his free fingers, smeared it up and down his dick.

"You cum a lot," Tony said. "But you don't cum like the Mad Man. He cum twice as much as you, you little bastard!"

"I cum a *whole* lot!" Joey protested.

"Yeah—you cum in buckets," Leaky said from the doorway, pulling on his own cock, with its waggling skin (it looked awfully good to me, right now) and the front of his right foot almost clean for the first time. "But the Mad Man cums in bathtubs!"

"Well, maybe when I get as old as him." Joey's hand slowed along his meat, then speeded up again. "Look, he got a lot of pennies now."

"Just put 'em in the middle of the floor." Mad Man wiped his hand on the front of his pants. The cloth there was stiff and stained, in a big circle around the crotch. The flap fell over some of it. But the stiffened stuff went halfway down to his knees on both legs. "We can all sit around, talk for a while—get to know each other. When anybody wants to buy somebody else for a while, we got the pennies right here."

"That's too fuckin' much," Joey said. "The Mad Man's got all these crazy fuckin' ideas. But he knows a lot of shit. You ever met him before?"

"What?" I said. "Me—no."

"Well, he been here, out in the park—how long you say you been in the park, Mad Man?"

"I been there almost ten fuckin' years, this time—"

"But you said, sixteen years ago—seventeen years ago, you knew—"

"The Mad Man's got his place," Crazy Joey said, leaning, beating, "back up in the trees, where nobody but the people who know him go—and he don't hardly ever come down. You can get down to the tracks, through there, you know? We always up in there together, beatin' off and talkin' crazy shit and—"

Leaky said, "You can't find the Mad Man less he wants you to find him. That's the way he—"

"That's how your friend told me to do." The rasp. The stone.

"My friend?" I really wasn't sure. "Who do you—"

"That guy what lived downstairs from you He said I gotta hide out. And he was right—"

"That's what Mad Man Mike told me," Crazy Joey said. "He said if I wanted to keep out of them fuckers' hands, what come and take you and put you in the crazy hospital, or throw you in jail—"

"Wait," I said. "You mean—well, yes, I figured you had to have known—but...?"

"He was a nice guy," Mad Man Mike said. "He was real good fellow...Chinese—"

"Korean," I said.

"—that's right, Korean. He told me that, that he was Korean."

"But that was sixteen—I mean, it was seventeen years ago."

"Seventeen? Was it that long—?"

"But what do you remember? I mean, what—"

Somebody was knocking at the door. Hard.

Beside me, Tony uncrossed his legs. "Hey, man. You got visitors. Come on—"

"But what—"

"Come on," Tony said. "Come on with me and see who it is."

"But—"

From his perch on the couch back, Mad Man Mike nodded.

My shoe still stuck out from under the end of the couch.

Crazy Joey said from the couch itself, "Ain't he gonna suck me off? I'm about ready to shoot another fuckin' load—"

Leaky said, "You still got the first one drippin' all over you, you little scumbag!"

"Come on," Tony said,

So I got up and followed him to the door as, naked, Tony slipped by Leaky. When I went by, Leaky grabbed me, hard, around the shoulder and, as I looked up, dropped his bearded face on mine and slid his tongue, like a big piece of steak into my mouth. As I tried to kiss him back, his hand dropped—and smacked my butt.

"Go on." He grinned down at me. "That's probably Big Buck."

Surprised, I went out after Tony, who walked, thick set and naked, down the hall before me toward the door.

I hurried after him. "Who do you think—"

The knock came again, slow—and loud.

Behind me, Leaky said: "If that's Big Buck, you cocksuckers do right by him, hear me?"

"Tony," I said. "Maybe I better ask who it is. If it's Jimmy or somebody, it might not look so good if—"

Tony got to the door and opened it. "Hey, Buck, is that you?"

"Is that you, Tony? This is where the Mad Man said I—Oh, man—I'm fuckin' beat—"

Over Tony's shoulder I could see a big, black, shabby and shambling guy, who seemed in the hall's shadow wholly without definition.

"You found the place—Hey, Buck, come on in—"

"I'm one beat nigger, man. Over in the park I woke up and I'd shit all *over* myself. I mean—"

"Hey, Tony," I said. "Maybe we better not bring this guy—"

"Come on in, Buck. We'll set you up—"

"Tony, don't you think—"

"Come on in," Tony said. "The Mad Man's here. We'll get you—"

"Pissed myself up like a motherfucker—"

"Christ, Tony, I mean he smells like—"

"Big Buck's a good guy, man—don't worry. We'll get him set up, won't we, cocksucker—"

"Well, at least close the door. *We* don't have any clothes—Oh, man, he's dripping on the—"

"I shit all over myself, man. Over in the park, you hear what I'm sayin'? An' then I pissed myself—" Tony was behind him now, closing the door. Demonstratively, he took hold of my hand and pressed it into the dark rags of his crotch. They were dripping wet. "See, all over myself, man, but nobody saw me—"

The stench was sour wine and something worse. His face was just darkness and unformed shadow. His hand got hold of my neck and when he pulled me into him, I stumbled, thinking I might fall into him, not like stumbling into a person but falling into a well, a cave, the night itself.

"Nobody saw me comin' in here. That what the Mad Man said, so I waited, until nobody—"

"Lemme get these pants down, Buck—"

It looked as if he was trying to hold them up on him, while Tony was trying to peel the shitty cloth from him—which is when I went down on my knees, my face against the wet crotch of his pants. And I guess it was better than his breath. Above me he was fumbling with my face.

"They said they got a cocksucker over here what likes to drink piss. Jesus, I could use me a fuckin' blowjob, man—that would really—"

"Damn, Buck. Hold still a minute, and let go your fuckin' pants—"

"Tony, what you doin' back there—Jesus, no, wait a minute. Lemme pull 'em apart for you. Yeah, that way you can get to it. Oh, hey, that feels good. Yeah, guys, that's good—"

Unheld by belt, string, or rope, his sopping pants dropped from between my face and the flesh of his velvety black crotch—so that I pushed my cheek against the one as I had been pushing against the other. In a kind of desperation, I got his wrinkled, meaty dick into my face.

"Yeah, that's good—Hey, Tony, you lickin' out my black ass? Just a minute—" From the wet expulsion, I think he shit again. "Yeah, that's better—"

I sucked at him—Tony's hand was on top of mine on his hip, with the wet end of his shirttail under two of my fingers.

Within my mouth, he lengthened, he thickened.

"Yeah, that's—"

And above me, he stood up straighter.

"Yeah—"

His voice filled out, even as I heard him take a breath that, for the first time sounded as though it were complete and full and human.

"Yeah, that feels good you suckin' on it, that way—" And though his voice had been a low one, the last words seemed to end an octave below where they'd started out.

"Hold still, nigger—" Tony said. "Otherwise you gonna be a mess—"

"Suck it, guy—" and from the shattered and broken darkness that both was him and that, as well, he'd dragged with him up my steps and across my threshold, a presence resolved in the hall. His hand found my head. His thigh flexed under my hand. I sucked the salts of his body from a cock grown startling in its new size within my mouth. He pushed again and again into my face, first merely translating the pressure of Tony lapping at his butt, but now taking up his own autonomous rhythm, seeking a pleasure of its own. "How you doin' back there, Tony?"

"Almost got you clean, Buck. Just a—"

Then a rumbling came from within him, even as I felt the conduit along the bottom of his cock fill and harden, and, as he grunted, finally spill into my mouth.

"Oh, *shit*, man! Yeah—!" which was Tony, behind him.

"Good fella..." He patted my head.

"Hey, Big Buck—" which was Leaky now. "How you like my cocksucker, there?"

"This *your* cocksucker, man? He good."

"Come on in where the Mad Man is, and we'll get goin' man. I'll get you a beer. They got you set up?"

"Sure do. They really set me up sumpin' nice—"

I pulled back, and Big Buck stepped away from me. On his knees, Tony reeled back and got to his feet.

Leaky looked down at me. In the hall's darkness, I saw him wink. "Big Buck here is the nigger I used to piss on over in the park—"

"—till we had us a little fight over that," Buck chuckled. "That was before we got to be friends, though."

"Buck was so fuckin' scuzzy all the time—" Leaky laughed—"I didn't think it made no difference who pissed on him—any more than somebody pissin' on me when I was sleepin' in my own pee-puddle."

"I know now," Buck explained, "Leaky didn't mean nothin' by

it. It was just somethin' he liked to do to get off—like me leavin' my dick out when women walk by, or usin' a handful of shit to jerk off in. So you're the nigger what he's pissin' on now, huh? Pleased to meet you." He took my dark hand in a hand so much darker it seemed a bushel of blackness.

"Glad you came," I said, shaking. "Yeah, I drink his piss, suck his dick—lick out his asshole. Leaky's a natural pisser. He's great for somebody like me."

"The little nigger here owns me now." Leaky's grin lit up the whole hall—before the darkness that was Buck. "I belong to him."

"That was real nice how you and Tony done me when I come in." Buck seemed twice as big as he had when I'd first seen him.

"Come on," Leaky said, a hand on Buck's shoulder. "Come on inside. The Mad Man's settin' things up."

As Buck turned away, I tried to smile up at him—and don't know if I did or not.

For as I got to my feet, Big Buck. walking up the hall behind Leaky, looked now like some lumbering linebacker for the Rams—who just happened to be wearing his knockabouts that day.

I turned to Tony—who, with his thumb and forefinger, was pulling stuff off his mustache and pushing it into his mouth. "Hey, Tony, did you see—?"

"What?" Now he sucked on his thumb, now on his forefinger.

"Nothing. I just thought—"

"Huh?"

"No, it wasn't anything—"

I started forward. Tony, who put his other hand on my shoulder (still picking the shit off his mustache and beard and putting it in his mouth), came with me, as, naked, we followed Leaky and Big Buck back into the living room.

As Tony and I stepped into the room, Mad Man, still on the back of the couch, flipped something into the air at me. I caught it—

"Hey, Mad Man, how you doin'—?"

"Hey, nigger, how you been—?"

Big Buck loped across the floor and they high-fived and slapped down—while I looked at what I held. A penny—this one bright and newly minted.

"Sit down, man. Sit down there, we just about to get started—hey, cocksucker, why don't you give that there to Big Buck?"

I walked over to where Buck was settling on the other end of the couch from Crazy Joey, and handed him the penny.

"You gonna let him suck my dick now, Mad Man? I got me a good load for that cocksucker—"

"Hold off, Joey, for a minute, can't you?"

"Yeah, I can hold off. I guess, sure, Mad Man—"

Big Buck was a massive, velvety man; in his fingers, darker than wet earth split open, the coin turned and glittered, a red-gold planet within and against the immense night of him. Looking at it, you didn't see his sneakers, one gone over to the side and the other split completely, or the stain down the front of his torn jeans from where he'd pissed himself or the black blot beneath his hips from where he'd shit. He had too much hair, kind of like the Mad Man's, only it was black and woolly. His beard was the sort black guys who can't really grow beards get when they don't shave for month's. And he said, with the same sureness he'd gained in the hall: "Now I done played me this game before. Got me my penny now—"

"And you take this one—" The one the Mad Man handed me was tarnished to an ashy gray. "Now, Tony…"

"It's a good game. I like it when the Mad Man plays his game. The Mad Man cum again—I ate his load right off his hand. You guys weren't here, you was out in the fuckin' hall. I guess there's some guys what'd think somebody eatin' his old man's cum was kind of funny, huh? But if his dad likes it, I don't think anything's wrong with—"

"Jesus—" Tony took his penny and dropped to a squat on the rug, then rocked back to cross his legs, and scratch at his stubby dick. The penny, I noticed, was the same brown at the shit stain on the rug just beneath his knee—"how come you so crazy for that nigger to be your father? The Mad Man ain't your daddy—"

"He *could* be!" Crazy Joey returned. "And when you gonna shut up and eat out my fuckin' asshole, anyway? I been sittin' in shit here for fifteen fuckin' *minutes*—"

"Anytime you wanna come over here—" with the hand that said P I S S Tony reached down to pull at his stubby, warty cock—"and stick your bony ass in my face, you little scumbag. Come on—"

"Now just wait up a minute," the Mad Man said. "Wait up—" He reached down and rubbed Crazy Joey's head. Beneath the weight of the Mad Man's hand, Joey bent his head. And smiled. "He wants me to be his daddy 'cause I'm the only fuckin' dad he got. He can keep away from the police. He do like I tell 'im, he'll keep out the crazy house, like I done. He can beat off almost as much as he want and get his dick sucked whenever he needs it. He don't, and he gonna get himself fuckin' killed. Now we gonna play a little game that's gonna make *everybody* feel good—see who I'm going to sell my boy here to."

Back in school I took an undergraduate course once where the teacher actually had us read the Marquis de Sade's *Justine, 120 Days of Sodom, Philosophy in the Bedroom, Eugenie de Franval, Dialogue Between a Priest and a Dying Man* and about three hundred pages of *Juliette*.(Of course, I finished it.) But, as I told my professor, the most impressive thing—and at the same time the scariest thing—about Sade was the obsessiveness with which he managed to work through all the combinations and permutations of everyone hooking up with everyone else. If I were writing about sex, I thought, I just don't think I could *do* that. Nor do I think I can do it here. But that's what the Mad Man's game essentially was. We all sat around for another forty minutes, joking, eating the chicken that Leaky had brought in or pulling cans from their plastic loops when he'd bring in another six-pack, and talking about what we liked to do, what we'd done that turned us on.

I'd decided that probably all it was going to be was talk; somebody supposed to get up and bring his penny over to somebody else and say, "Here..." and then could—the way the Mad Man explained it—do whatever he wanted with the guy.

Crazy Joey was the first to get up—the smear of crap he was, indeed, sitting in on my couch, just like it didn't mean anything to him, kind of shocked me. I'd have thought I would have smelled it. He "bought" Tony from the Mad Man, and had him lick his ass clean. ("You want me to sit around in that and wait for tonight?") Kind of old hat after Big Buck. Then Leaky told me to go over and suck Crazy Joey off ("To shut him the fuck up!"), at which point Big Buck said, "Hey, that's lookin' pretty good to me—and I already know how it feels. How about I buy that cocksucker from you, Leaky—" And the funny thing is—really, you should try it—it does make you feel better. Call it structure. Call it whatever. The same thing that seems so abhorrent in Sade, when it actually occurs

among people of good will—and I think that's what we all were—
is as reassuring as a smile or a warm hand on a shoulder or a sharp,
friendly smack on the ass.

What stays with me, of course, were those moments that seemed
in excess of this endless systematic interchange: at one point (and
years later, I decided it was probably significant), Leaky had pretty much everybody's pennies; and the Mad Man, by fiat, simply
redistributed the wealth, as it were, as absolutely and autocratically
as any avatar of Marx might have done. Leaky didn't complain; he
just laughed. Even later, the Mad Man was in the kitchen, one
foot—bare now—on the summer-dead radiator by the window,
looking out and pulling on his cock. (But the kitchen light was
off.) And for the third or the fifth time I tried to ask:

"Were you with—?"

"What—?'

"You were with him when—?"

"Who—?"

"Weren't you with—?"

"Huh—?"

"Who? Hasler! When he was killed? You were with—"

"Yeah. Why? What do you—?"

"What can you tell me about it? Down at the Pit, when he got
stabbed..."

"Man, I got *cut*!" Straightening, he reached up to touch the scar
worming from pectoral to shoulder; and with that indication of
the past, he foreclosed all further converse between us for the
moment. "I don't wanna talk about *that* shit!"

Then he took my head between his hands and forced me down,
again, on what I'm so weary of calling the biggest cock I've ever
sucked; and sucked; and sucked.

I thought I'd ask him once more, as soon as I got him off—
although, true, not only have I never known anyone before or
since to cum, that much, that often, I've never known anyone
who was that blasé *about* coming—in the middle of talking to you,
in the middle of paging over a newspaper lying on the kitchen
table, or while eating a chicken breast with one hand and playing
with himself with the other, all of which I'd seen him do by now—
and I've never seen anyone who was less relieved and relaxed by
shooting a load.

Have I said it? Mad Man Mike was weird.

And just as he got off this time, there was some noise from the living room. Tony and Big Buck had taken a mirror down to do something with it, only Crazy Joey—I guess it was—had stumbled against it and it had broken.

Because I was pretty much pissing for all the guys in the place, I spent a lot of time in the bathroom. Once I came in while Tony was flushing something really dark and repellent down the toilet. As it swirled and roared away, he wiped his mouth with a toilet-paper wad, flung that after it, and grinned. "You see," he said to my puzzled look, "*that's* why you gotta be a stoned shit eater *or* a stoned piss drinker. You can dabble in both, but if you're gonna commit yourself, you gotta choose one." He grinned. "At least if you wanna be a piss drinker who likes to suck a good cock. I mean, a good cocksucker usually has a little trouble bringing things back up again, after a while—which don't hurt with piss, 'cause it just comes out the other end. But a shit eater's got to be able to throw up when he gets too much down there." He spat—brown—into the toilet's clearing water. "That's why guys like Leaky and the Mad Man—and Crazy Joey, too, I guess—need a crack at the two of us."

"Tony," I said, "you're just a font of information."

"You *better* understand stuff like that if you're gonna play with these guys. You know how I met the Mad Man?"

"How?"

We were both standing naked in the john.

"Out in the park, I was goin' into the comfort station, lookin' to get my dick sucked, when I seen this humongous turd on the ground beside the steps. I thought, who could this belong to? It was too big for any dog. It had to be a person's. But it was the fuckin' fattest turd I'd ever seen—it kinda hypnotized me. And I'm standin' there thinkin', somehow I gotta meet the guy what laid this monster—when Joey comes by; I'd been tongue-swabbin' his asshole out every night for a week, already, up where he sleeps by the wall. He sees me starin' down at it and he grins at me and says, 'Nice one, huh? Friend of mine left that there when he come down this mornin'. Wanna meet him...?' And here we are."

"Tony?" I sighed. "I'm glad I know you."

"Glad I know you, too, professor." He gave my arm an elbow nudge. "If I didn't, these motherfuckers would've probably *drowned* me!"

"And thanks for sending Leaky over."

"Yeah?" Tony's look began with questioning but—over seconds—grew more and more pleased. "Well, you're welcome, then! I figured he was more you than me, anyway."

There were some other nice moments in it, too. Like when Crazy Joey, Leaky, and Big Buck all got together and jerked off on my mattress in one really humongous puddle—the bottom sheet had been pulled off for something else a while ago—and I lay down in it on the striped ticking and rubbed my dick in it, while Leaky got up around my head and let me suck on his dick and Tony licked my ass out till I shot. Crazy Joey was sitting beside Leaky, watching me suck him and jerking off—and came all over the hirsute rug of Leaky's thigh. Then Leaky said, while I came off his still-hard dick, "You know what I'm gonna do, Joey? I gonna put your cum inside my skin, and keep it there till it turns into one super crop of cheese."

"Huh?" Joey said. "You mean in that fuckin' yoni thing you got?"

"Yeah," Leaky said.

"How about that," Joey said. "My fuckin' cheese in your fuckin' dick? Hey, *I* should've thought of that! I could have gotten a fuckin' penny off you for that, man."

With his blunt fingers, Leaky picked up globs of scum off his leg hair—

"Just a second," Joey said. "Lemme help you—" And with his own, grubby fingers, he held up Leaky's cock and pulled the skin up to hold it open. "There you go—go on, now. Load it the fuck up!"

Which Leaky did.

At another point, when Tony was sitting on the library floor at the behest of Big Buck, Crazy Joey came running in with a handful of some dark crap or other. "Hey, man, look at that. It sure looks like shit, don't it?" Tugging at Tony's shoulder to get Tony's attention, he lifted his loaded hand to his nose and sniffed. "Smells like shit, don't it, Tony?" He took a bite off the edge of the brown-black stuff. "Damn, Tony—it sure *tastes* like shit! Ain't you glad I didn't—" and here he heaved it at Tony's chest, where it went splat, and stuck a moment—then fell down, leaving a dark smear, past "Fuck You & Your Momma's Jammy," past "I'm Ruff, Tuff, Eat Nigger Shit for Breakfast & Piss Battery Acid" into Tony's lap—"throw it at you?"

"Jesus, Joey," Big Buck said. "What the fuck is that?"

"What the fuck you think it is?" Crazy Joey said. "It's shit—it's shit, that's all. I only ate a little of it. It don't taste like nothing. And Tony scarfs it down all the time."

"But *whose* shit, man? Ah, fuck—" Tony said. "You don't wanna waste it—" With his hairy arms out, he looked down where it had fallen in his lap. Panther and dragon coiled and stalked the red jungle.

"Hey, come on, guys," I said. "Come on. Watch it, now—"

"Piss on you, nigger—" Joey said, turning toward me. And lifted up his cock. And did.

Which started both Buck and Tony laughing.

"Come on," I said. "Get out of here, with this mess—"

I don't remember going to sleep—or why we all ended up in the bedroom, me wedged between Leaky and Big Buck. I just remember Big Buck starting to snore—and his hand opening, and the sound of half a dozen pennies falling out.

Someone was snoring on the bed: Big Buck, I figured. Someone else was snoring on the floor: the Mad Man. "Leaky, you awake?"

"Yeah. I thought you was sleepin', though."

Across the curtains' top and down one side, against the black, the light made a steel-colored strip. Under my hip and down to my knee, the bed was soggy and cold, which was why I'd moved up.

"It's funny." Leaky shifted against me; one hand under my shoulder pulled me nearer. "I done heard women all the time sayin' how men just want them for their bodies, and how that's insultin' to them, or something. And I always thought: It'd be great it somebody wanted me for *my* body. I mean, even though I ain't stupid, sure as shit nobody's ever gonna want me for my mind!"

I laughed.

"No, seriously. I been thinkin', I wouldn't mind havin' me a lover—you know what I mean? If we was compatible. Like you and me, I mean."

"Really?" I asked.

"Well, as far as bodies go, mine ain't too much to rave about. It's big and hairy, and my feet stink—'course you're one of them guys what likes that. My dick's a fuckin' cheese factory—thanks to them yoni rings I used to wear. And I really love gettin' it sucked on. And you sure come on like a nigger what loves to suck." He sighed. "But there ain't too much else to recommend it. I don't got no nails, half my teeth are rotted out, and I been a bed wetter all my life—keepin' me around for a friend is like keepin' fuckin' Niagara Falls."

"It'd be fun to try it, anyway," I said. The bed rocked a moment when Big Buck turned over, then back.

"You think so?" Leaky asked. I thought how large the Mad Man's voice was. Big as Leaky was, his voice could be incredibly quiet. I don't think Tony or Joey, sleeping over in the corner, could have heard him. "You know, since I been twenty-five or so, I been on the fuckin' bum—at least half of that time. Sometimes I get me a little room somewhere, get me a job—but I can't never have no friends over, 'cause after a couple of weeks it usually smells so bad. That's if the landlord don't have me put out because of it. Most of the time, you know, I don't mind bein' on the bum—sometimes it's okay. But just before I come here, I was talking to Mad Man Mike and Tony about it, out in the park, and—man, I must have been goin' through that mid-life crisis thing they talk about, you know—'cause suddenly it hit me: if I spent half of the *last* ten years on the bum, I was probably gonna spend *all* of the next ten that way! And suddenly I thought, shit, man, I don't want that. I really don't. I want to get off the streets. I wanna get with a person, you know—somebody what likes havin' me around.

" 'What sort of person?' Mad Man Mike asked me.

"And I said, 'You know, man. Like you an' me like—but a nigger though,' I told him. 'For me.' And Mad Man Mike, I've known him for eight, nine years now—and he was always real smart about a lot of shit—finally, he said, 'Leaky, you sound pretty bummed out.'

"And I said, 'I am. I mean, I'm really wondering if it isn't all over for me. I mean, if I'd decided this, two, three, maybe four years ago, I maybe could've of done something about it. But now, I just don't know. I just don't have it up here no more to do nothin' about it...'

"So Mad Man Mike, he says, 'Well, suppose somebody did something about it for you.' Then he said, 'Tony, what was the name of that black guy you was tellin' me about?'

"And when Tony tells him, he says, 'Okay, Tony give Leaky a penny for himself. Leaky, once he buys you, man, you know, you gotta do whatever he tells you to. You don't have to think about it no more—it ain't your responsibility. You just do what the little red-headed fucker tells you to. So I give Tony his penny—when I was panhandling before, some fucker gives me about twenty-eight pennies: they think that's real funny. I just threw half of 'em away—anyway, Tony told me to come over here, and sit around and wait for you. So I done it. When Tony sent me over, he said he thought you'd like me. I really didn't think it was gonna work—save that it was Mad Man Mike's idea. But since I sold myself to Tony, it didn't matter none. I just did what I was told."

"That's when he told you if I took you upstairs and we got along, I owed it to him?"

"Yeah." Leaky's breath hit my ear, and I turned to face it, beautifully beery, and thick with recently exited sleep.

I chuckled.

"But now that you done bought me back from Tony, it don't seem like keepin' your face full would be too hard a job. You think maybe you'd like me around?"

"Well, you know," I said, "actually, I was kind of wondering if you *were* interested in anything permanent."

"You was?" Then he said, "How permanent you mean by permanent?"

"You know"—I shrugged, wondering if he could hear, or possibly feel, it—"hanging out together, me and you. You'd have some place to sleep, somebody to contribute to your beer fund, to do some cooking for you—pop the tops on your beer cans."

Softly, Leaky chuckled. "Yeah—sure, that'd be nice. You'd really take me in off the street? Let me stop all this fuckin' bummin' around?"

"If—" I said—"it was what you wanted. I got you a collar, didn't I?"

"Yeah." He chuckled again. "But we gotta talk it out, too. And, you know, even if that stuff don't smell after the first three or four times, after six or seven, even beer piss stinks up pretty powerful. A lot of people've told me to get the fuck out in my time, man."

"Well, then, one more won't kill you. And I think I can probably stand it—or do something about it. Or get some rubber sheets. Or something."

"I'm a thirty-six year old drunken hillbilly creep what can't read and write and hold his water—and, the truth is, that ain't fuckin' much."

"I don't think you're a creep. I think you're fuckin' stupid. You're a dumb-shit asshole. But you're not a creep—at least to me."

He grinned at me.

In the dark, I reached between his legs. His dick was half off his belly, a crane thrusting up over us.

"Now, the question is, are you stupid enough to hang out with a nigger who likes to get pissed on?"

"That'd be kind of neat, you know what I mean? Havin' a nigger what was a real professor—"

"Not quite a professor," I said. "Maybe someday, if we're both very, very lucky."

"—havin' a nigger what read all these fuckin' books and know's about philosophy and stuff, that I could piss on anytime I wanted to. That'd be fuckin' somethin', huh?"

"You want to give it a try?"

"That ain't up to me, nigger. That's up to you."

"Well, if it's up to me," I said, "let's try it. What do you say?"

"Okay." I felt him move beside me. "You know, I was just thinkin', before: the first time I told Dad and Big Nigg I was gonna leave home and take off to see what was out in the world, Blacky told me something. You see, when he been in the crazy hospital, he'd run away and got as far as Philadelphia. He'd done some bummin' around himself. I mean, that nigger was pretty smart. He'd been further than Daddy and Big Nigg put together. He runned away and stayed away almost two years before they caught him and took him back to the hospital. And they'd told him he'd have to go back to his family when he got out, which is when Big Nigg come along and took him down to our place. But, I mean, Daddy and Big Nigg, they thought it was a pretty good idea that I should get out and see somethin' too. Anyway, Blacky, he come up to me, and he says, 'Leaky, come on and sit down with me and let's you and me talk.'

"And I grinned at him, and said, 'Nigger, *suck* my dick!' 'Cause that's what I said to that black sonofabitch, mostly, anyway. 'Cause that was mostly what he wanted to hear.

"And he said, 'Sure, you dumb sonofabitch!' I mean, Blacky

picked up on what I liked almost as fast as you did, but this time he went on: 'You know—' he says, with me sittin' on an overturned bushel basket beside the pickup, and him cross-legged on the grass—'nobody loves to suck yo' big ol' cheesy white dick better'n this here nigger!' And he grins up at me, with that toothless grin of his that always got me hard, and I let myself loose a spurt in my pants, 'cause he I always liked that and he liked it, too. And he says, 'Leaky, you gotta know somethin'. You're a fuckin' scumbag.' I really didn't know what the fuck he meant, so I just hefted my meat around between my legs, grinnin' down at him. And he says to me, 'It's cause that's how you was raised. You can't read an' write. You dirty—you pee in your pants. Your feet stink. You play with yourself all day long—when you don't have it out, beatin' on it. You bite yo' nails, and pick yo' nose an eat you own snot'—you didn't know I did that, too, did you?"

"That's all right," I said, "as long as you share it with me."

"Then here. I just had some," and, in the dark, his hand came down over my face again. "You want this?"

"Sure."

Hand over my face, he thrust his second finger into my mouth and let me eat off the salty crust.

"Anyway, Blacky told me, 'Once you get out on your own, most people is just gonna think you're some kind of big, hairy, fuckin' creep. You get out these woods and into some city out there you'll probably be sleepin' in parks and doorways—like I did. You'll be another big, hairy guy, hoboin' and homeless, with hard hands and stinky feet. But the one thing you can do—' and Blacky takes my hand now—'is make a stoned pig cocksucker happier than a stoat in a shitpile. 'Specially if he's a black cocksucker. You gonna find 'em all over the place, too, Leaky. Some of 'em'll be homeless like you gonna be, and some of 'em gonna be professors in the University, and some gonna be church organists an' some gonna be waiters in the restaurants and some gonna be truck drivers, and there may even be another humpback nigger just run away out the crazy house in among 'em too. But you find the right nigger an' treat 'em like you treat me, boy, an' he gonna love you and do anything he can for you.'

"And I told Blacky, 'You know me: I'd do anything to have a nigger suckin' on my dick.'

"And Blacky says, 'An you got the kind of big, nasty white dick a whole lot of niggers is just dreamin' about suckin'.'

"So I says, 'Then I better get out there and find 'em!'

"And Blacky, he says, 'That's good, Leaky. 'Cause that's about the only thing God put you on this earth for that I can figure out.'

"Then I frowned down at him, and I says, 'Nigger, how come you always sayin' you like watchin' me play with my pecker, an' you like how my feet smell, and when you get in bed with me, you always down suckin' my toes, or when I say I gotta go take a leak, you put a lip-lock on my wanger and tell me to let it run?'

" 'That's what I mean,' Blacky tells me. 'That's what gonna make a stoned cocksucker happy. You see, Big Nigg and yo' daddy raised you to do natural all the things a top stud usually got to learn how to do—and don't ever get right, anyway, 'cause he wasn't raised to it. But your daddy and Big Nigg brought you up to do right by a cocksucker. And that's what you do best. That what you do natural.'

"So I thought about that, and looked down at my pants, where the lap was all stiff and streaked with dried-up cum, like Daddy's and Big Nigg's. And I felt my dick, which was about half-hard in my pants. And meanwhile Blacky lifts up one of my big old work boots, that used to belong to Daddy, only the sole was comin' away from the upper on the side and my big toe was stickin' out, and Blacky stuck his tongue in there, ticklin' my toes with it, and I grinned at the black sonofabitch and played with his tongue with my toes and played with my dick through the wet part of my pants. And I wondered what I was gonna find in the line of cocksuckers once I got out in the real world, you know? Just about then, Big Nigg comes along, and he stops and says, 'Nigger, don't you ever leave that boy alone? Rest of us can't get a fuckin' blowjob no more to save ourselves, you always goin' after this horny white bastard.' An' Blacky is sort of working up from my old split boot and is nuzzling between my legs, which I kind of like, 'cause I know what it's gonna turn into soon, and sometimes waitin' for it is almost as good as gettin' it, but Nigg lifts up his hand, and it's all covered with cum, and I realized he probably been sittin' on the end of the porch, watchin' us and beatin' off, 'cause he like to do that a lot. I'm just haulin' out my dick, see, when Nigg grabs my big ol' pecker with his scummy hand, and start rubbin' it and twistin' it up and down—shit, do that feel good!—and he says, 'About the only way I'm gonna get my load in that nigger's mouth is to wipe it all over your dick. I love you, boy, like you was my own, but I'm gonna be glad to be shut of you, so this nigger'll start treatin' my dick and yo' daddy's dick like he should again.' And Blacky says, 'Hey, Nigg, you know I like to suck yo' dick—'

"And Nigg, he scratches Blacky on his hump and he says, 'Nigger, you *love* to suck my big black dick. Only you just can't find the time, with *this* horny bastard around.' At which point Blacky goes home on my cock, all sloppied up with Nigg's half-dried nigger cum. An Big Nigg, he squats down to watch, and starts chucklin' and reachin' in his own pants to play with himself some more. Then he puts his arm around me, and he says, 'Now, Blacky, I can't begrudge you swingin' on Leaky's meat here, since he gonna be goin' away soon. But I sure will be glad once he gets the fuck out of here, and I can get to fuckin' and pissin' into my own brother's scummy ole suck-hole again!' And I held onto Big Nigg's knee, till I shot my load in Blacky's face. Then Blacky, when he comes off me, he said, again, 'What you gotta remember now, like I said, Leaky, is that to most people, you just gonna be a fuckin' pervert. But, you ain't no creep. You somethin' special— you basically a real good boy. And that's what's important. And you know how to make the right pig cocksucker real happy. Don't never forget that, boy.'

"And Nigg says, 'Yeah, Leaky—that's the truth.'

"So I figured they must be right. I knew it was time to leave there. But I was wondering if I was ever gonna find me a nigger outside what was as good as Blacky. I guess I been wonderin' ever since."

In the dark, we were both quiet a while.

Finally I said, "Leaky, you are full of shit."

He chuckled. "It's a good story, though—don't it get you hard?"

"With everything you've been saying, I'm actually startin' to understand about you and…well, me. But what I don't understand is how you get off on people calling you ignorant, dumb, and stupid."

"That? Now that's a funny one. I told you about them tests and all I had to take when I was a kid, but the truth is, I don't really know how that happened. I mean, it had already happened by then." In the bed beside me, he turned over. His arm hooked around me, and he pulled me into his great, hard, hairy body. "But it sure do get me off—like tellin' Tony how low he is. With me it's stupid. With you it's callin' you a piss-drinkin' nigger scumbag cocksucker. Maybe it teaches you how to handle it. With me, I think, it has somethin' to do with my never learnin' how to read and write. But I sure know I like it. Especially when somebody real smart does it, like you. Then it *really* gets me off." I felt him shrug. "Probably, though, it's just some kind of perversion."

"You know," I said, "most very smart people don't go around calling everybody they meet who says 'ain't' stupid and dumb and stuff like that. I may have to work on that a little bit for you."

"Well, you just get your jigaboo ass to work then, nigger. I mean," Leaky said, "most hillbillies don't go around callin' every black fella they meet 'nigger, this' and 'nigger, that' either. If we did, we'd get our fuckin' heads handed to us. I had to put me a little work into figurin' out who to do that with and who not to, too, you know."

"I guess you did."

"Where I come from—" in the dark he moved his hairy thigh against my face—"it maybe come more natural to me than to some others. Man, it sure feels good havin' you down there between my legs. Makes me feel like I'm doin' what God put me here for, you know what I mean?"

"Yeah, you stupid old ignorant ass hillbilly fuck!"

At which point, something hot spurted in my face. "I'm sure glad I can piss with a hard-on," Leaky said. "I wonder how long I'll be able to do that. Somebody told me once he could do it till he was about forty, then he couldn't do it no more."

"What the fuck you doin'," which was Big Buck. "Pissin' in the bed? Cut that out!" Then his head collapsed back down on the mattress.

After a few moments, I said, "You stick around, Leaky, and the two of us can find out. But somehow, I don't think you'll have much of a problem."

"If I took me to the doctor to find out if there was somethin' they could do about me pissin' in the fuckin' bed *every* goddamn night, I mean—how would you feel?"

"Fine," I said. "How would you feel if they told you to wear a diaper? Because that's probably what they'd suggest."

"Really? *That'd* be kinda strange…!"

"Shut up, stupid—stick your dumb-ass dick in my face!"

It came into me hard and, under its loose hood, full of cheese. (Joey's, I guess.) His hands came down to catch my head. And he hugged me with his legs, humping hard and long, but before either of us came, we both fell asleep.

What woke me the second time was some whispered altercation between Crazy Joey and Tony, who'd been sleeping on the laundry pile in the bedroom corner. Tony was saying, "…Well, stick it in his mouth, then!"

Crazy Joey: "But he's asleep!"

Tony: "Then leave him the fuck alone, huh?"

Crazy Joey: "But I'm horny, man! I wanna get my dick sucked!"

Tony: "Then, like I say, stick it in his face."

Crazy Joey, I realized that was crawling around on the bed with us, over Big Buck and Leaky, both of whom slept the oblivious sleep of the very big and very tired: "If I piss in his face a little, you think that'll wake him up?" Something shoved down by my nose, prodded at my mouth. "He likes that—"

"Hey, you fucking scumbag—" I said pushing up—"get over here and let me suck your dick."

"Oh, hey—that's *right*, man!"

Across the room, I heard Tony laugh, then turn over.

Mad Man Mike was sleeping on the floor, curled up like a giant tiger. We managed to step over him, and not wake him. On the laundry pile, first I sucked off Crazy Joey—then Tony, who said it would put him to sleep, once he shot. His warts surprised me all over, again slipping into my mouth. But they made me remember the third one, inside his skin, and what to do with it. Once he came, he started snoring sooner than some drunk wino in the Grotto.

I pulled my head from between Tony's hands—he stretched and rolled away. Joey was on his side, hands thrust down between his legs. Standing, I stepped for the door—tripped over something that *wasn't* Mad Man Mike's out-thrust arm. At least he didn't wake up.

My jeans were hanging over the doorknob, though I didn't remember putting them there. I got one leg into them, but when I pulled on the second, it was cold and sopping. I pulled them up anyway and buttoned them, but I didn't zip them.

In the hall, I went first to the john and sat on the commode in the dark for five or ten minutes. Just kind of breathing. I didn't pull my pants down or anything. I just sat there for a while. Then I walked up the hall again and turned into the living room. My bare foot squished on the rug—at the same time something moved by the wall. But it was the reflection of my feet passing in the broken mirror leaning there. I went into the library, and turned on the corner lamp.

Looking at the various papers and books strewn over the round oak table, I pulled out the chair, sat down, and picked up the pile of index cards in their rubber bands.

The Mad Man...

Both the old yellow ones broke as I took them off. I read over the first card again: *Proposed epigraph for Part One of* The Mad Man...

I looked through three more cards, putting them on top of one another on the table. Then I saw I was leaving brownish fingerprints on the cards's edges. For a moment I wondered whether I should get up, go back to the bathroom and wash my hands before I came in and read more. But I didn't.

The cards were numbered in the upper-right-hand corners, the numbers circled. The handwriting was fairly legible. But it was also clear that it was pretty much Hasler's first draft for whatever it was. The cards read quickly, though. After reading through the first twenty, the best way I can think of to describe them (at least now) was that they read the way you might imagine the first draft of, well, this book.

I mean that the first twenty-odd cards could easily have been the first draft of my meeting with the Piece o' Shit, how many years ago, only with different names and slightly different people: in Hasler's case, he told how a five o'clock in the morning stroll in Riverside Park resulted in his meeting with a young, barefoot bum, sitting on the concrete top of a sewer outlet, up among the trees, masturbating. I quote from some of the less—rather than the more—explicit transition material:

> "...[card 17] the funniest thing about it, I suppose, was that he seemed to be equally pleased, that morning of our meeting, if I sucked his toes or sucked his dick—though I'm not sure whether that means he liked both equally or was equal-

ly indifferent to both. He *said* he liked it. (He came: but—with him—I'm beginning to wonder if that's such a big deal.) Still, that may be because he just likes my conversation. His cum is of the strangest consistency…[card 22] name seems to be Michael Kerns and he says he's from Connecticut. But then, that also is where he was hospitalized for most of the last three years: so I may have it wrong. At twenty-three, he's a good-looking Negro fellow, with yellow hair, an extraordinary build, and granite-colored eyes. A couple of times now he's spoken to me about incidents in southern New Jersey, little towns around Camden, which he knows fairly [on to card 23] well. Like most, I've always thought of chronic masturbators—that's what you'd have to call him (since I first met him, over in the park, I've never seen him with his hand off his cock, at least in his pocket, playing with himself)—as puny, sickly, weak-minded fellows. But Mike's sharp, has a sense of humor, and is built like the proverbial brick shithouse. In the hospital he says he lifted weights—and liked to jerk off, as he will [to card 24] tell you in a minute, more than anything in the world. He says I should call him Mad Man Mike because that's what the other bums in the park have pretty much named him…on that slope on the south [to card 98] part of the park, back up in the trees, there's a break through into the old train tracks. Mike says he's been hanging out down in there, sleeping, doing push-ups, and (presumably) masturbating himself into insensibility. Finally, he took me up to see it—I doubt I'd ever have stumbled onto it by myself. There he told [card 99] me, he has two or three friends, one another gay guy from the neighborhood, who apparently stumbled onto him pretty much as I did when he was out roaming in the park, who comes by to see him and sometimes brings him beer—his capacity for beer is almost as great as his capacity for sex—or sometimes food. He gets fed at the church up on Eighty-sixth Street and sometimes at a place on Seventy-second Street [card 100] between Broadway and West End (typically he doesn't know its name, though he goes there every other morning or so), where they give you (he says) either a ticket to go inside and get a meal or a bag of food to take with you. The problem, he explained to me, is that he can't go for more than half an hour without masturbating—and even that's [card 101] a real chore—so that at the food place he has to get up and go into the men's room and beat off once or twice a visit. One morning last winter, he told me, when it was occupied or out of order, he wasn't sure, he got caught jerking off in the hallway and put out, rather violently. He was astonished and hurt both that the other destitute men were ready to help the security guards give him the toss...[card 142] Al has said, no, I *can't* bring him along out to Breakers' Point, even if I pay his fare. But then, even though she's never met him, and knows nothing about him, the fact is: she's right. What in the world would he *do* there—no, I can't imagine him at one of her literary cocktail gatherings or dinner parties. (Though it's an interesting thought. If I ever write a novel...) But that [card 143] means I'm going to come back after two weeks—rather than the month or six weeks I'd planned. I'm just not going to leave him out in the park again any longer than that. And we can drive back to school, I suppose, with one of those rent-a-cars. No, I'm not sure what I've saddled myself with. But he makes me feel incredibly good. At peace. And that's too important to give up, unless he doesn't want to stay around. And he says he does...[card 237] he says owning somebody isn't bad. He wishes somebody owned him. I pointed out to him in a country as historically entailed with slavery as the United States, that was a rather dangerous position for a Negro to maintain. He says, rather insightfully, that his whole life he had been treated like one form of pervert or another. And (to use his own [card 238] words), "There ain't a whole lot of difference for most people between a pervert like me and a nigger pervert like me." Then he went on to explain, rather fancifully, that nobody should ever pay more than a penny for another human being. He said that knowing somebody wanted you enough even to pay a penny for you meant you were not in the unenviable position that most of the people he knew [card 239] living in the parks and the streets were in: i.e., no one wanted them at all and to most people they were worth *nothing!* I told him there were places that people went to buy sex with men. "How much you think somebody would pay to have sex with me?" he wanted to know. (With a bath, a shave, and clean clothes, I suspect, quite a lot.) But he insisted he wouldn't charge more than a penny. He seems to be somewhat fixated on that one....[card 249] He says he really likes beef liver, of all things; that it's his favorite food. So I've cooked it for the past three days. He says he doesn't understand how people could *not* like liver. When I told him that liver was traditionally a food that most kids hated, he didn't believe me. He even said I couldn't know anything like that because I was "Chinese." He can't seem to get it through his head I'm not. With most people, I suppose I'd find that hopelessly insulting. But, with the Mad Man, really, I think, it's because he just doesn't find such distinctions important. Maybe, being hopelessly in lust with him (and really rather liking him), I [card 250] romanticize his short comings: but I think he finds the distinction between Oriental and Caucasian precisely as unimportant as he finds the distinction between Korean and Chinese or Chinese and Japanese. (Now if Koreans, Chinese, and Japanese just felt the same way...!) But, finally, I must find that admirable. Also, for a liver lover, he puts up well enough with my own passion for fresh vegetables. The fact is, there doesn't seem to be *any* food that he doesn't eat—won't, indeed, devour. Although with practically every one he claims he's never eaten it before in his life: turnips, bok choy, [card 251] mushrooms, strawberries (strawberries!), collards, avocados, nectarines, asparagus, yams. Nevertheless, he still claims beef liver is his favorite. It reminds me of the lack of distinction he shows in his preference among the various sexual acts. He *says* that getting his toes sucked and his dick sucked are his favorite, but I still find myself wondering if that isn't just to please me. A couple of days ago, I discovered that he had gone and shit in the corner of the living room. When I asked him why, [card 252] he said it was because it stimulated him—of all things! I cleaned it up with paper towels. Later, he got out of bed in the middle of the night and I woke to find him urinating out the bedroom window. "Nobody gives a fuck, man—" No, he'd never make it out at Breakers' Point...

But other cards in the stack read like—really—the first draft of my encounter with Crazy Joey out in the park, or with Leaky down at the Grotto. Many of them read like Barthes's *Fragments d'un discours amoureux*. ("…The sensation is as if [card 9] another language—a metalanguage I cannot speak—alone might be adequate to describe the ebullient feelings I have when I am around him, a metalanguage I am always yearning to understand when he is near: the madness of infatuation, of sex, of love.") Many read like rank pornography. "God, he's (card 12) got the biggest cock!")

What made me look up was the sound of water—I turned, to see lamplight over Crazy Joey's pimpled back, its hard little muscles defined under them. In just his pants, he was urinating against the lower bookshelf. "What the fuck do you think you're—!"

"Takin' a piss. what does it—!"

"Cut it *out*, man! Those are my fuckin' *books—!*"

"Hey, I'm sorry! I was just—" not stopping, Joey turned from the bookshelf, mule dick still hosing from his fist its glittering yellow—"takin' a leak, man."

"Well, do it in the *bathroom!* Or in my fucking mouth, or…something! *Jesus*, Joey!"

"I don't piss in the bathroom," Joey said. "Mad Man Mike and me, we don't do that."

I got up suddenly from the chair, sucked my teeth, then took a deep breath. "Yeah, sure—"

"And you were busy readin'. So I just…" His sentence and his pee both failed about the same time.

"Well, man—look!" I was really angry. "Joey—please *don't* piss on my fucking *books*, huh? Do it out the window. Or—" I stepped over to him. He turned now himself, to look at the shelf he'd wet. (Actually, they were a bunch of paperback mysteries wedged up against some of my high-school textbooks, neither group of which I would ever look at again. But they were soaked.) Nervously, he'd begun to pull on his cock. I sucked my teeth again.

"I thought—" His weasely face looked scared and confused and hopeful that someone would approve of him—"it turned you on, people comin' in your house and doin' shit like that.…"

"Well…" I reached over and roughed his hair. "It does, kind of. But not on the books. Or papers—or, really, on anything in this room!"

"Oh," Joey said. "The Mad Man didn't tell me about that. I didn't understand that."

"Joey—you have to have some limits when you're doing stuff like this."

"Yeah?" Joey said. "Oh. I didn't understand. I'm sorry—about the books. You read those, don't you?"

I took another breath and looked around me, then shook my head. "Look. It's okay...." An arch the size of a double doorway connected the library and the living room. "Didn't Mad Man Mike tell you about that—limits I mean?"

Joey's eyes had a unhappy, questioning look. "No," he said.

Which is when the telephone rang.

The only person I could imagine it being was Pheldon. I turned around and started across to pick it up, where it sat on the top of the little cabinet under the window. This time I knew exactly what I was going to say: *Phel, I want to ask you a favor. A big one. As somebody who used to go to the Mineshaft Wet Nights, do you think you, or maybe even you and Lewey, could come over here tomorrow afternoon and give me a hand with some major clean-up work? I mean, really major—*

When I picked up the receiver, though, what I heard was lots of people laughing, as though someone had called me from a party. I said, "Phel? Hello...?"

"Is this John? John Marr?"

"Yes?"

"It's Apple Blossom Time!" Then somewhere someone laughed sharply, as if holding a hand inefficiently over the speaker.

I said: "What? Who is this?"

"John Marr?"

"Yes," I said. "This is John Marr."

"You wanted me to call you when Ronnie Apple came in. Well, he's here now. He said he's got to go somewhere for about forty minutes. But he's planning to be back in—" Then, in that muffled tone: *You said you'd be back in forty minutes.* And someone else said: *Forty minutes. Fifty minutes. But I'd be happy to talk to him.* "Ronnie says he'd be glad to talk to you. Do you want to come down and see him?"

"Excuse me," I said. "Who is this?"

"I'm calling from the Pit. You said—"

"Oh, yes!" I said. "Of course. I'm sorry. My mind was on something else."

"You said you wanted to talk to Ronnie Apple—about the Hasler stabbing, back in '73?"

"Yes. Really, thank you. I—"

At which point somebody else took the phone and said, "He says you're a college student and you're cute. I'd be delighted to talk to you—"

"I'm a graduate student. In philosophy. Mr. Blossom—?"

"Mr. Apple. Hasler was a philosopher, wasn't he? I remember that. But you can call me Ronnie."

"What? Oh, yes. I'm sorry. Look, I'll be—I guess it'll take me a little bit to get down there." I looked around the room.

Crazy Joey stood at the other side of the table, listening with bemused interest.

"I have to leave the bar here for about forty minutes. But I'm coming back. Do you want to meet me here in about forty minutes? Forty or fifty minutes?"

"What time is it?"

"Well, it's—I guess it's about eleven-twenty." Then off the phone: *Is that bar time?* "It's ten minutes after eleven. Do you want to meet me here at midnight? I mean, maybe you can't get down—"

"No," I said. "I'm coming. That's awfully nice of you, Mr. Apple."

"Ronnie."

"Look, Ronnie, I've got to—I'll be down and meet you. At midnight." On the other end of the phone laughter surged. "At the Pit—it's Friday night?"

"It's Saturday night, John. Going on Sunday."

"Okay. I'll see you there."

"If *I'm* not here at midnight, give me fifteen minutes."

"Sure."

At the other end, the phone clicked. The laughter cut.

I hung up. Suppose, I thought, I went out of here to the Pit. I talked with Ronnie Apple, who'd been there just like the Mad Man himself, seventeen years ago—and I came back, two hours later, and my house was stripped...

Of what, I thought. My coffeemaker? My ancient mechanical typewriter? Crazy Joey might try that, maybe. Big Buck, perhaps.

But neither Leaky nor Tony would let something like that happen. Nor, I suddenly found myself thinking, and with a certainty that surprised me, would the Mad Man. In the seconds I stood there, I actually figured it out: If I knew what had happened back on that night, I could get some coherent information out of Mad Man Mike about it. But without a pretty firm structure on which to pin the fragments I heard from him, I probably would have a fair amount of difficulty just interpreting whatever he said.

"Joey," I said. "I've got to run downstairs and go someplace—for a couple of hours. Maybe two or three. Basically, it's to do something for your friend."

"Huh?" he said. "Who?"

"For the Mad Man."

"Oh, yeah?" Suddenly Joey looked interested. "What is it? Where you gotta go?"

I laughed, starting for the door. "I have to go down to a den of iniquity on Fiftieth Street called the Pit, where men sell their bodies to other men for sex."

"Hey," Joey said. "That sounds neat. Can I come, too?"

"Why don't you stay here and watch out for things for me? You and all the guys can hang around and sleep some more. I'll be back."

"The Mad Man told me about those places," Joey said, following me into the hall. "But they charge too much money. I bet I could sell more than any of 'em. 'Cause I would only charge like the Mad Man told me to."

"Yeah, the way you cum, you probably could."

I went into the bathroom and gave my hands and face a good washing, with soap. The big blue Ikea bath towel was still clean; nobody had touched it.

"What you gonna do down there?" Joey lingered in the bathroom door.

"I've got to get some information. I need to find out about some stuff Mad Man Mike probably might like to know about too. It would probably just be easier for him to talk to me if I already knew something about it."

"He knows a whole lot of shit already," Joey said, thoughtfully.

"He knows a lot," I said. "Did he ever tell you about an Oriental guy who got killed down there, with him?"

"Shit!" Joey said. "He never said nothin' about that!"

"Well, I don't think the Mad Man is a guy who likes to tell stories about what happened to him, very much. But he's a good guy. He's a real good guy. And you probably should do what he tells you."

"I do," Crazy Joey said. "I do. He keeps me from gettin' in trouble. Like gettin' caught and put back in the crazy hospital."

In the closet just inside my bedroom door, I took out my suit, which was hung up on a large wooden hanger with clips for the pants.

"You wearin' that?" Joey asked, in the dim hall light.

"Yeah, well," I said. "My regular clothes are pretty messed up, right now."

"Oh," Joey said.

I started to take them in the living room and lay them over the couch; then I thought again and went back in the library, and spread them out over the table there.

"You gonna put your shoes on?" Joey asked, as I finished buttoning my dress shirt and slid my legs into my pants.

"Yep."

"You gonna go down there and suck some more dick?"

"What—?"

"You gonna go down there and get some sex?"

"Me—? No." I laughed. "Just some information."

"That seems pretty stupid, to have a place like that where they're sellin' sex to everybody like that, when most people just like to do it for nothin'."

"Yeah, Joey. It probably is."

I put on my jacket. I went into the bathroom, where one of my shoes was under the tub. Then I went into the living room and, without turning on the light, remembered where the other one was, sticking out from under the side of the couch.

When I was at the door, Joey said: "I could sure use another blowjob. What'll I tell 'em if they wake up?"

"Tell them I've gone out. I'll be back in a couple of hours."

"You were the last person who bought me, weren't you; you wanna suck my dick again?" Joey asked. "Before you go. Me and Mad Man Mike, sometimes we have to have it three or four times, you know?"

"Joey—" I laughed— "I don't have the energy. Or the time, right now. Look, why don't you jerk off a couple more times, go to sleep, and I'll suck your dick when I come back."

I went out the door and pulled it carefully to behind me.

Outside, the Amsterdam Avenue night was warm. Even though I'd left off my tie, in the very first minutes I decided I'd overdressed. College kids prowled singly and eagerly, or strolled in loud, laughing groups, between the bars that had opened up in the last year— spillage from the gentrification over on Columbus Avenue that, a decade before, had been the big thing in the city. I walked down past the Korean vegetable emporium where we got our beer. It was ironic: when Hasler had lived here, when Hasler had walked the avenue on a summer night, there'd been none of this summer revelry, nor would anyone then have imagined his countrymen would dominate this aspect of the city's commerce the way, once, it was assumed Greeks ran coffee shops. Between my corner and Seventy-ninth Street, five different guys—all but one black—held out a hand or shook a cup for change, trying to keep their pleas, their banter, up to the level of the July night's jollity around them that their own rags and dirt belied.

At Seventy-ninth, I stopped and, for a moment, thought about going over to Broadway to get the subway. But it was no more than a half-hour's walk to Fiftieth Street. And Apple had said he would be a while. I decided to walk down. And the fact was, it felt good, however briefly, to be out in the air.

The city was rich with its own summer stenches: black plastic garbage sacks piled outside a small grocery store, or, as I crossed over the avenue, the smell of piss in the doorways to the back of the Beacon Theater, where three homeless guys sat on the concrete, passing a pint of Gypsy Rose.

"A goddamn behavioral sink…" I muttered, but I was wholly unclear, as I said it, whether I referred to the sexual chaos of my own apartment, or the social energy that had received me into the neighborhood, on my emergence from it.

"Pot? Pills? What you want—?" was once whispered and twice asked openly, as I walked by the benches against the fence at Needle Park. At Seventy-second, the city broke open and spilled out upon itself, under the neon enticements of HMV on the right and, to the left, the yellow lights of Gray's Papaya King, while before us, as cyclists passed, in shorts, sleeveless undershirts, and silver plastic crash helmets, by the brightly lit newsstand the kiosk erupted its crowds, this midnight as heavy as at noon, into the intersection thick with turning buses.

At least five guys stood around in front of the Pit. The door was propped wide open. Inside it was crowded. People seemed to be regularly coming in, regularly going out. The younger ones, when they came out by themselves, always seemed in a hurry, always had something quick and heated to say to the loiterers. (But I'm sure another visit would show up as many exceptions to that as to any other systemic observation.) General curiosity, plus something the bartender had said to me about the air conditioning, made me go to the side of the building. Between the diamond-wired gate, glares and flares slid over the green roofs and red fenders filling the weekend-crowded parking lot, as, beyond the cars and out on the avenue, trucks and busses passed each other and the streetlights, to shift the illumination here, moment by moment.

After thirty feet of fence, only a chain hung across the gateway. I stepped over it and walked in among the cars—to glance back at the yellow window of the wooden booth, with the silhouetted head of the security guard (I could tell by his police-style cap), who, I gathered, hadn't even seen me.

The space at the building's back was clear. The back door was open. Heads were dark against faint orange light. Two guys pushed out as I stood there, then one, followed by the other, changed his mind and pushed in again.

I crossed the ripped and raddled tarmac, and beside a window caged with bars—cinder-blocked up, I realized; and the cinder blocks painted black—I stepped inside. I was just curious to see what it was like, coming through the back door.

Crowded—but not as crowded as it had looked. With three or four steps, I edged into a clear space where two guys, angling with cues, circled a pool table under a conical light, one a lean Hispanic in a black tank top, whose helmet of tight-curled hair glittered with the wet look, the other a Nautilus-pumped black guy in no shirt at all, a pair of maroon hefty-pants made out of some greenish plastic-like material, low enough on his hips to reveal three or four inches of red-and-white-patterned boxer shorts—had he been wearing any.

A white ball smashed into colored ones, so that, knocking one another, balls zagged and zigged across green baize to the table's rim. Up on a corner video monitor, geometric squares and circles of peach, violet, and lime collided with one another. Beat timed to their collisions and barely audible under the voices, some very loud music played. Moving now one way, now another, I zagged by a portly black man with snow white hair and silver-framed glasses who, with a blond college kid in a black polo shirt and blue baseball cap turned backward, intently discussed the overthrow of the West. I edged past a heavy white man about my father's age, wearing a colorful scarf that hung down at least four feet, busily talking with four beer-drinking youngsters, the three darker ones in T-shirts and plaid Bermudas, the forth in jeans and a leather vest, his white shoulders a riot of Japanese tattoos, his hair long, no color, and stringy. All of them wedged between the jukebox and an elbow-high serving counter, the quartet regarded the older man with exquisite blankness—unless he directed some loud and gesticulating remark directly at one, whereupon the wannest smile answered. As I pushed by the other side of the jukebox—it took me half a minute to get from one side of it to the other—a really handsome, solid little kid who looked like he could have been Malaysian or Filipino, lingering in the shadow of the machine with the glittering facade, reached for the crotch of his tight white jeans, smiled at me, and said, "Hi. You having a good time tonight?" and gave it a leisurely, meaningful squeeze; I looked down at him, at which point he boldly pulled down his zipper and asked, "Can you buy me a drink?" Feeling silly, I shook my head and managed to get beyond him.

In the crowd between the bar chairs and the wall stools, I tried to see over heads to where the bartenders were. Neither of those working that night were Donny or the talkative one who, I assumed, had just called me at home. Without air conditioning, it *was* hot. Someone reached over my shoulder with a glass to call to a well-dressed man at the bar, who turned with open arms to receive the smiling, curly-headed fellow, angling by me now, with an embrace as volcanic and impassioned—faces buried in each other's neck—as that of elderly father reunited after millennia with prodigal son.

Then the man sitting next to him turned on his chair and held out his hand. "Well, you *are* looking smart this evening. I probably missed you the first time you came by."

The pale blue sweater, the blue beret—off duty now, he was sitting near the corner of the bar, with a drink.

"Hello!" I said. And shook.

Then the man beside him turned and said, "You're right—he *is* cute!" His age was as indeterminate as Aline's: between a frail fifty and a fit seventy-five. His fine-featured face was covered with the palest skin that made you think of parchment, crushed into the smallest ball, then smoothed again, but stretched so tightly it was only a moment from tearing. Made even fainter by the dim bar lights, the wrinkles were not so much *in* his face as they were the lightest overlay across it.

"And Mr. Blossom? I hope you haven't been waiting too—"

"Ronnie Apple. Not more than five minutes. And you're John." He held out an ivory hand. I moved my hand from the bartender's and took this new one in my dark one. And shook it. He returned the shake you'd expect from a bank officer or a university dean—that wouldn't have seemed effeminate anywhere else *but* here.

"Here, now. You've found each other. I'm going to leave you two together to talk. Take my seat here—I'll be back." The bartender got down from his seat, waiting for me to sit.

"Mr. Apple—I'm sorry. Did you get to the place you wanted to get, see the person—Oh, thank you—!" I called after the retreating bartender. "Did you get to see the person you wanted to see?" One foot on the ground, I pulled the seat under me up to the counter.

"Ronnie—*please*. He wasn't there." He spoke very carefully. His summer suit was a light bisque. Blue cuffs just showed at the rims of his tan jacket. "After I waited fifteen minutes, I realized he wasn't coming. So I came back here—no big surprise. You sounded like a much more interesting evening. We cling to these fantasies for various reasons. But so often it turns out just a waste of time. Now, what was it you wanted to know?"

"I'm trying to find out who killed Timothy Hasler—the philosopher who was stabbed to death here in '73. I want to know as much as I can about how it happened, why—whatever I can."

"You want to know who did it?"

"Yes—but even if I don't learn the actual name, at least I want the best description I can get of what happened by somebody who was here—"

"You just want to know who did it? I'm surprised Sheena of the Jungle didn't tell you that when you first came in."

"Sheena of the—?"

Apple nodded into the crowd in the direction the off-duty bartender had gone.

"Oh. You mean—well, did he know—?"

"Who did it? Maybe he forgot. It *was* a long time ago. Perhaps he didn't remember. Dave Franitz."

"Who?"

"Dave Franitz. A perfectly psychotic young man—he must have been about twenty-two or twenty-three, back then. German and Dutch, as I recall. I think he once told me his father was an alcoholic roofer out in Queens. Dave had been eighty-sixed from this place at least half a dozen times in the previous year. I just knew he was going to get into serious trouble if Aline kept letting him back in. He was one of those young men who was very beautiful, didn't do anything to speak of once you got him home, and wanted quite a bit of money for not doing it. It's a type; and there's a type that goes for them. But he could be very belligerent about forcing himself on you. You understand, I never went with him. Still, at least twice, when I came in and found him here, I just turned around and left. He made the place uncomfortable for me. Probably I wasn't the only john who felt that way. But that night, it was almost as crowded as it is now. I was in the back, and I thought there were enough people to…how should I put it: to soak up his bad vibes. So even though I saw him sulking around and looking menacing—for him, that involved a rather tart smile—I stayed."

"He was never caught, though. How come nobody—?"

"No, not for the stabbing. There's sort of a brotherhood down here—it's remarkably effective when it's a case of one of our own against an outsider. Even with someone like Dave. Or maybe *especially* with someone like Dave. But he was a very sad young man, really. The rumor was, he had—" here Apple leaned closer to me— "no meat on him at *all*, if you know what I mean. But he had that immediate surface charm complete psychotics so often do. I saw him two or three years later, right outside on the corner. By then, of course, no place would let him in. He was in terrible shape—filthy, sallow, had lost most of his teeth. If you saw someone like that today, you'd immediately think he'd gotten AIDS. But, of course, there *wasn't* any AIDS back then. He tried to hit me up for a couple of bucks, as he did with everyone that came by that night—it was a freezing cold February, and he just had on this sweater. With holes. You could see his ribs." Apple gave a little shudder. "But I don't believe he even recognized me. He died, not even a month later, somewhere a few blocks over to the west around Ninth or Tenth Avenue—the story was that he was staying in some abandoned building by then, and simply froze to death. Or possibly he had a heart attack. Both versions went around. But I'm sure Sheena could have told you all that, unless she just forgot. But then she—we all—hear so many stories about so many youngsters, who can be expected to remember them—though I'll certainly always remember the night he killed your Korean friend. As far as Sheena of the Jungle is concerned, I supposed once Dave was dead and gone, there really wasn't any *reason* to remember him anymore."

"Was he on drugs?"

"I think we're talking about the wreckage of somebody who was once on drugs, then couldn't get them any more—though Franitz was probably, at one time or another, on just about everything you could *be* on. No, Franitz was not a happy camper. You know, most of the kids who work out of this place are very nice. But there're always half a dozen or so who are really crazy; and somehow, as soon as one of them goes, like Franitz, there's always another one there to step into his place."

"And Franitz—Dave Franitz stabbed Tim Hasler...?"

"It happened maybe four feet away from where I was standing, there in the back. I believe the pool table they had back then was turned the other way. And their jukebox was on the back wall, by the door into the lot—not over there where it is now. No videos then, of course—"

"What was it about? Can you remember what the whole incident was over?"

"Oh, yes. Hasler getting stabbed was actually an accident: he was trying to kill the other one."

"The other—you mean the Mad Man?"

"Pardon me...?"

"He was trying to kill someone else, you said. Go on—please, explain it to me."

"Well, there was another boy in here with the Chinese fellow that night—Korean. No, I know that."

"A black fellow—"

"Well, certainly not *very* black. He was quite striking looking. Tall, muscular, with yellow hair."

"But a black fellow—kind of rusty-haired..."

"Yellow-haired. But, yes, very curly. Nappy, as my southern relatives would say."

"Black though—"

"Now that you mention it, he probably was."

"His name was Michael Kerns. I know that, at least."

"Was it? Now I never knew *that*. I don't think either one of them had been here before—certainly not with any frequency, or I would have known then. I never knew the other one's name. But they were joking around, I guess—and that can be difficult here. People tend to be very serious—here—about what they're buying, what they're selling. This kid, you say his name was Michael—" here Apple leaned toward me and dropped a hand over the gray sleeve of my suit jacket—"had an absolutely immense cock. And he was taking it out in the back and flashing it around—you know, as though it was a big joke! But I think to some of these older queens, it wasn't a joke at all. But you have to understand, we don't really *do* that at a place like this. Basically, what happened is that Franitz got furious. The kid was chatting up some old guy—possibly one of Frantiz's johns, although it didn't have to be. Suddenly Franitz comes at the kid from the other side of the pool table, knife drawn and roaring like a crazy man. The Korean fellow, the other kid's friend, throws himself in the way, tried to grab the blade. And gets the knife—three times—in his chest. (I told you, this Franitz was just a madman!) I think, after the first blow, Hasler got the others just because Dave was so angry at him for getting in the way. But that, of course, is speculation that's rather beyond what you could really take for gospel. Certainly, though, that's what it looked like. By this time, the other boy—you said his name was Kerns—had turned around and run up to catch the Korean fellow, there right beside the pool table—really, I can run the whole thing through my mind, even tonight, as if it were a slow-motion movie. There was blood all over everything. Franitz got a stab in at Kerns, holding the Korean, once he fell—cut his shoulder—for a moment, I thought Kerns had had it too. But Kerns—Lord, he was such a big fellow—dropped the Korean, turned, and barreled out the back door of the bar, into the lot. But from the way he ran, though he was probably cut badly, you could tell it wasn't fatal. Franitz ran up front now, knocking people left and right, and disappeared out the front door. By this time, of course, people were screaming and pushing and pushing back—and the next thing you know they're lugging the Korean fellow out the back door into the lot—"

"People just let Franitz get away? Did somebody try to stop him—?"

"A crazy kid running through a bar with knife? Actually, three or four of the kids had a little sense and jumped on him when he was digging his blade into that poor Korean's chest—that's probably why the other kid, the one he'd originally gone for, got away with only a cut—"

"But why in the world did it get him so angry that he—?"

"The kid, like I said, was flashing this incredible piece of meat in and out of his pants, and joking about the fact that he wasn't going to cost anybody anything—and the Korean was egging him on—really, he thought it was all very funny—that anyone who wanted it could have it for nothing; or, at any rate, for only a—"

"Excuse me…?" someone said, behind me.

I turned on the chair.

Very Jewish looking, with thick glasses, and wearing a suit the same gray as mine, a small, round guy said, "In the back, someone said, if I wanted to go with him, I was supposed to come up here and give you this…?" In his very pale fingers, he held a penny.

I frowned.

"He said that was all he was going to charge me. And that I should give it to you—not him—because he said he couldn't take any money for what we were going to do. The kid is a little strange—" the man nodded at me with a considered frown— "but, Christ, does he have a dick on him—"

"What?" I said. "Where did…" Suddenly I pushed back from the bar and got out of the seat. "*Where* did you say he—?"

"He came in the back—he's been moving around here a while

now. He's kind of on the grubby side, but I don't mind that." He smiled sheepishly through his glasses, looking like a librarian or an accountant. "He said to give you the penny, and that you were his owner—?"

"Is everything all—?" Probably because I was standing, Apple stood up. "Is there something—?"

I pushed away, trying to get between the people filling the bar. Half a dozen were just then trying to leave for the front. I swam through them—rammed through them—probably I tried to move too fast. I bumped into one guy, a kid, and made him spill beer, and he hit me on the shoulder with the back of his fist: "Yo, man! *Watch* it!" I tried to get by some people talking loudly and excitedly over each other's heads, and kept getting pushed toward the jukebox. Then somebody else suddenly shoved into me. Someone else shouted out, "Hey—!" Then, "Hey—!" again. Then there was a high-pitched "Oh, God...! Oh, my *God*...!" and a surge of people suddenly came out of the back. My first thought was that my own bumptiousness had started repercussions. I started to say, "Hey—I'm sorry...I'm—!" Only about three or four people away from me, now, fists were moving over people's heads, and guys were shouting, the way it happens when a fight starts in some ridiculously enclosed space. And people who can't move have turned and are trying violently to get away. Somebody called out, "*Ohhhh...*!" again; really, though, it was a scream. People surged in the opposite direction from which I was going.

Somebody pushed into me. His fist or opened hand went by my face, hard enough for me to take it for a punch. But I ducked and shoved around him, using the space he made to get through—

—and came out by the pool table, practically to stumble into the naked back of the shirtless black pool player crouched in front of me.

A dark smear soaked the pool-table's edge—really, that was all I could see.

Then, over something else—was it a foot?—I *did* stumble— and fell into the black shirtless kid who'd been at the pool table, just as he rose; and, as though I were some insect or weightless creature, he shrugged me aside—and dashed forward.

Lying on the floor—what the pool player had been crouching over—was, yes, Crazy Joey. I went down on one knee—really, I fell. And caught myself on my hand on the sopping boards.

The blood—!

Joey's eyes were closed and his lips were twisted back from his teeth in an impossible grimace. Somehow I'd almost forgotten his broken tooth, but now it looked perfectly grotesque. I grabbed his shoulders—which were as loose and floppy as some beanbag creature's. The black kid with no shirt leaped across the floor, slammed into the crowd, which tried to part before him (though one kid in Bermudas actually fell on the floor, cried out, and scrambled up again), did another leap and, among the parted bodies, dashed out the back door.

I looked back at Joey—who, I realized, with some weirdly detached part of me, was wearing my dirty blue T-shirt, though the blood was so thick on the left side of it, from the too-big collar to the waist of his pants (the pants were soaked with blood on the left side down to the knee), you couldn't see the red circle. Under the orange light, it was all kind of blue-black. "Joey?" I said. "Joey, are you okay...?" knowing I sounded inane. Even when some guy put his hand on my shoulder and said, "I don't think you should be moving him like that," I kept on trying to think of something say, to call, to shout, and all I could think of was, *Help...!* even as I looked up at the circle (young faces, old faces, black, white, Hispanic) of staring men.

Then the black guy rushed back in through the doorway, pants legs aflap—

He stopped, three feet from Joey's head, which lay to the side now, lips all twisted. I jerked back; slimy, Joey's left shoulder slipped out of my hand. The shirtless black pool player gasped out: "The fucker got *away!* He got out through the back door! Jesus, he got away, through the cars in the parking lot! I *knew* he was gonna fuck with somebody tonight! That crazy fucker, he got away...!" Blood splotched his flapping pants legs, spotted his naked chest.

When I kneeled back from Joey, somebody else—it was the other pool player, the Hispanic one in the tank-top—put his hand on my shoulder and said, "Hey, man? Are *you* okay—" and then: "The kid's pretty messed up, ain't he?"

And somebody else said, "That kid's dead, man—!"

"Oh, no," I said. "Oh, *no*—Joey..." Then I reeled upright, into somebody who was saying, right at my shoulder:

"And he said he'd let me blow him outside in the parking lot, if I gave that guy a penny. For just a penny, he said—"

I turned around to the pudgy guy in the gray suit and the glasses, who looked around at me. Eyes decreased in size and sharpened by his lenses, his look was one I first thought recognition, then some sort of accusation, and finally disgust. "Hey, look." I reached out to take his shoulder. "Look, I'm *sorry*—"

He pulled sharply back from my hand—which swiped blood across his suit lapel. I jerked my own hand back. And turned.

"Hey, man, are you—?"

I stepped around the body, toward the door. The black pool player looked at me, then frowned. First, of course, I thought he'd been the one who had done the stabbing. And now, although I realized he'd just tried to go after whoever'd done it, I kept on thinking: No, he's *really* just putting on an act. *He* did it. He's the one who did it, and he's just *pretending* to—

Maybe that's the way I looked at him when I walked past; because his frown, as he regarded me, suddenly got intense. "Hey—" he said. "What the matter with *you*, man?"

"Nothing. I'm sorry— Look, thank you. Really, thank you for—"

"He a friend of yours?" he asked suspiciously.

"Yes—no," I said. "No…I mean, yes…." At the same time, I was trying to figure out what was the best thing to say in a situation like this. Were you supposed to pretend you didn't know anything? Or were you supposed to pretend you knew everything? Because, I realized, either stance with me, now, would *be* pretense.

Suddenly I pushed through toward the open door. Two people stepped back for me real quick. I shoved past two more. Outside, as soon as the cooler air hit, I realized I was gasping. I put one hand over my face, and the other hand over my heart. It was going like a little toy gun: pop-pop-pop-pop-pop.

For a moment, I got dizzy, wondering if I were going to stumble or even pass out. I took half a dozen steps across the tarmac toward the cars. At least a dozen people were out here, milling, talking ("Yeah, man—he run right off through the cars there. I saw him throw the knife over—"), some now and again moving off purposefully, some gathering to decide if they should go back in. I just walked, but not, I think, in a terribly straight line. I turned up one of the aisles between the cars, trying to hold my breathing down.

At which point, this shadow emerged from between the fenders to confront me—really, I didn't recognize him until he said, "Jesus, little guy, what the hell just *happened* in there? And what the hell happened to *you*—what is that? Is that *blood* on you—?"

"Leaky...? Oh, Jesus, Leaky...What are you doing down here? Do you know what—?"

But now Mad Man Mike, Tony, and Big Buck all had stepped up beside or behind him—a convocation of ragged animals, crowding together in the summer night's heat.

"What are you guys *doing* here...?" was all I could ask.

"We were followin' Crazy Joey—"

"—who, I guess," Tony said, "was followin' you." He was stepping about excitedly; I glanced down to see he was barefoot. "Joey woke me up and told me he was going after you. That you were coming down to this place. The little fucker borrowed my shoes, too. He still inside? What the fuck's happenin' in there—"

"The Mad Man," Leakey said, "he told us we had to go and get him. But then, he told us to wait out here, till you and Joey come out. He said we ain't supposed to go in no place like that. What happened? You all right? He said it would be crazy for us to go inside. How you get cut up like that—?"

"I'm all right," I said. "It wasn't me. I didn't get cut. It was—"

Then that voice like a rasp, like stone, like metal: "Is the kid okay...?"

I heard my own voice break: "No, he's *not*—"

Something was happening behind me. The voices in the space behind the building and the movement of the people milling had all changed—hearing it, or feeling it, I turned to see.

Some five people came from the bar door, all bunched together—carrying something. It didn't look all *that* heavy. They moved with it across the clearing, while people stepped back for them and others stepped up to see. On the other side of the black tarmac, by the cars, they squatted to lower it to the ground.

The cortege rose, turned, and—two of them running, three walking quickly—they crossed back to the door. (One fellow—a white kid—tried to stop one of the men, a black with glasses, but the black shrugged his arm away and kept going.) One after the other, they crowded inside. Then—when it happened, it made me jump: a metallic bong—the door slammed.

The white kid who had tried to stop his friend went up to it and pushed. "Yo!" he called. "Open the damned door, huh? You gonna let us back in? God damn"—he looked back at everyone— "how do you like that?" He kicked. "Open the damned door!"

Almost everyone else, though—I started, too; Leaky came beside me, Mad Man Mike was already ahead—converged, some slow, some quickly, about the body on the ground. With maybe fourteen or eighteen people from the bar, we gathered around him. The lips were still drawn back from the teeth in this pained rictus, so that I thought: They're not going to recognize him! But big, bearded Leaky pushed up beside me on my right, and said, "Aw, shit... That's Joey..." It wasn't surprised. It was just sad, and gentle, and what I guess I'd call despairing. Looking kind of shambling again, Big Buck lowered over the head of a short, squat, bald fellow in a yellow and black flannel shirt with a red bandanna twisted in a rope from his back pocket. And taller than all of them was the Mad Man.

Looking down, nobody said anything.

I'd always been struck by how big, how broad, Crazy Joey's hands were. In death, however, both had folded, the way after sunset hollyhocks will fold into thin trumpets. (Along with the right side of the T-shirt, his whole right hand and arm were wet with blood, as though he wore some scarlet evening glove that, once the vamp began, he'd strip off and fling to the crowd.) Even with his fingers like inch-and-a-quarter dowels, his hands—one red and shiny, one pale and grubby—lay by him on the tarmac, like things once his that had been placed beside him, long and uncharacteristically narrow.

By now the blood covered more than three quarters of the T-shirt. Some newspaper still stuck to the shoulder. Two immense rips crossed it that, somehow, I hadn't noticed when I'd been kneeling over him in the bar. With the ridiculous conclusion-jumping that had made me think the black pool player had been the killer, I wondered now if the rips hadn't been put there since I'd left—to make it look like...but look like what? The stabbing it obviously was?

No, I just hadn't seen them. (Maybe they'd been twisted around under him, when he'd first fallen. Or was the shirt particularly twisted now to the front?) There was so much blood on him, you couldn't tell *where* he'd been stabbed!

I looked up at the Mad Man. He stood, quiet, looking with everybody else.

Pushing past me on my left, Tony said, "See—I told you. He got on my shoes!" Tony moved around to the feet, dropped to a squat, and began to pull at the laces to the running shoes Joey wore. "Joey's used to runnin' around barefoot all the time. But I don't know about all this pavement shit." A moment later, he pulled one shoe free. In the light from the lamps around the parking lot, you could see the dirt across Joey's instep and on the sides of his foot.

"Hey!" a belligerent-looking Puerto Rican guy about eighteen or nineteen in a blue-net tank top said, "leave the guy the fuck alone, huh?"

Tony indicated his own bare feet. "Look, I'm not kidding. He took my fuckin' shoes. Didn't he?" He looked up, appealing to the Mad Man. "These were the ones *I* was wearin', right?"

The Mad Man said, "They were his...yeah."

Tony moved to the other foot, picked at the laces, pulled off the other shoe, then dodged back between the crowd to lean back on the low fender of a green Honda, pulling on first one, then the other.

Another guy said, "Shit, won't even leave the guy his shoes! That's *cold*, man!"

Gesturing down at Joey, Leaky said: "You don't want your T-shirt, do you...?"

"Huh?" I said. "No—what am I gonna do with that?"

"I didn't think so," Leaky said.

Then someone said, "Hey—!"

We all looked off to the right. Half a dozen people stepped back.

Because of the cap, because of the uniform, at first I thought he was a policeman: a thick-set black man, standing a little off. He was only a parking-lot security guard, though he still looked pretty official. "Somebody got messed up here, out in the lot—right? The door's been locked to the back of the bar all night. That's the way they always keep it. So somebody must have rumbled with him out here."

Nobody said anything. I'm not even sure if anybody realized what was being said.

"If there're some bloodstains down to the door there, that's because he staggered over there before he fell out over here. Now, look: do any of you folks have any connection with this bastard?"

Still nobody said anything.

"Because if you don't," the guard said, "myself, *I'd* get the fuck out of here—'cause the police are on their way. And they're going to be real interested in asking questions of anyone who's standing around."

People broke up from around Joey as if what had been of interest in him had been switched off inside him like a light. Because everybody else was moving away, I moved, too. Then I heard Mad Man Mike declare like the voice of some thunder god, "Now we got to get out of here—fast! This is disappearin' time! Go on, you stupid motherfuckers." People I didn't know started to run as if he'd commanded them. "We lost the fuckin' kid. We got to move unless you want to lose the rest of you, too—"

Along with Mike, Buck and Tony started across the lot—me coming behind. More people stood outside the fence, though, who had just left the bar. As I neared the diamond wires, I saw Ronnie Apple staring through.

I stopped hurrying.

Ahead of me, Leaky turned back and called: "Hey, little guy, come *on!*"

Ahead of him, the Mad Man may have said something that was all rumble and reverberation; but because a car horn honked at the same time off on the avenue, I didn't catch the words.

Ronnie Apple said through the wires: "Are you all right? Where did you go...? They said someone was hurt—they put him outside. That doesn't seem very wise to me...."

"I think—" I walked over to the fence— "he's been a lot more than hurt. It doesn't matter where they put him now."

"Oh, *dear!*"

I looked along the fence.

The four men who had come down from my apartment were gone.

"Why, oh, *why* will they come in here!" Behind the woven wires, Apple's exhortation seemed neither literary nor affected, only deeply, deeply pained. "*We* come to places like this, to pursue our clean and costly pleasures, looking for the simplest suggestion of some pink-and-gold schoolboy we might have seen or even been, some lean brown athlete we once admired or longed to be or loved—and *they* come to soil it all, pollute it with pain and rage and lust—" And, for just a moment, I wasn't clear who in the world he meant. At which point, behind him, someone said: "Hey, Ronnie— where *were* you? I waited for you over at Hombre's, like we said. But you never showed—so I came over. Jesus? What happened *here?*" It was a young man—need I describe him further, saying if he were white, black, or Asian, eighteen or twenty-eight, grubby or scrubbed, in khaki or denim, leather or Lacoste?

"Funny," Ronnie said, recovering himself. "That's precisely what happened to me—what happened *here?* Well, actually, I didn't see it this time, but apparently *some*one—"

I turned and started toward the gate. A siren and some lights swung around the far corner—as I stepped over the chain.

New York is a city in which, on a summer's Saturday night, a black man in a bloodstained suit, looking perfectly deranged, has a fifty-fifty chance of walking from the Battery to the Bronx without getting picked up. (No chance of getting a taxi. But getting arrested?) It's only a mile and a half to my house.

And—though at the time I thought it was a miracle—nobody stopped me.

At Seventy-second, I angled up Broadway.

When, across from Holy Trinity, I passed I AM THE DOOR, I mumbled, "I hope to hell you *are…*" but didn't stop.

Pushing through the vestibule door, I was numb. I came up the stairs, unlocked my apartment—and went into the dark hall. I didn't close the door behind me.

But they weren't there—any of them.

In the living room, I stood in the dark awhile.

Then I went and turned on the living room light. "Oh, *Jesus…*!" After thirty seconds, I turned it off again. Then I sat down on the floor—and jumped back up.…

But it was only my own movement in the piece of mirror by the wall. So I sat down again.

In the dark, I did some funny things that night. I crawled over to the couch and felt along the edge till I found the place Crazy Joey had taken a shit and sat in it that afternoon. It was half-dry now—much of it. But I scraped some off with my fingers and ate it. Then, I crawled—I don't know why I didn't stand up—crawled, on all fours, into the library and over to the bookshelf. I took out one of the paperback mysteries Crazy Joey had peed on. I could feel the book's edge, almost dry now, had already raddled. I sucked on the corner of one, then another, of the soiled books. They were only vaguely salty. Beer piss. Then I went back into the living room—this time I walked. Pulling loose my shirt from my pants, I found the biggest smear of blood and sucked on that. Besides the salt—stronger than on the urinated-over paperbacks—it was also sweet. (Could the kid have been diabetic?) Then I sat on the rug again, in the dark, and felt around until I found the dampest stretch. I lay my face on it. I wished I could eat some of the guy's come. (What a tremendous and beautiful dick! What a gentle and eager-to-please young man had carried it! What times and places he'd carried it through!) If I could have found some, even dried, and eaten it, I'd have felt I'd gotten near enough to him that I'd said good-bye. That I could let him go. Only I couldn't remember any specific spot he'd spilled himself. So I closed my eyes.

I thought about presents. From inside the body. Timothy Hasler had, by throwing himself in the way of Dave Franitz, saved the Mad Man's life—though it cost his own. But I had not been able to save Crazy Joey. And neither had Mad Man Mike. Once again, I thought, perfectly lucid: Hasler has proved to be not only a remarkable philosopher but a remarkable man—certainly more remarkable than I. If anything, it was my own curiosity—so absurdly and easily satisfied by Ronnie Apple—that had lured Crazy Joey down there to the place everyone but he knew he should never have gone. How in the world was I supposed to convey any of this (and what of this world *was* I supposed to convey) to the Old Poet?

Dear Al, no, you did not kill Timothy Hasler. But I have just inadvertently murdered a...

No, I did not begin to cry. But I felt numb.

I opened my eyes, sat up, went back to the couch, scraped up some more of Joey's shit, crawled back across the floor and, sitting in front of the mirror fragment leaning there, with my finger I wrote in large letters in the dark:

EKPYROSIS

That's what Hasler had written just before he and the Mad Man had gone down to the Pit. Written it, indeed, three times. Had that remarkable philosopher been explaining the meaning of that all-consuming, all-cleansing Heraclitean fire to Mad Man Mike sometime earlier that day—that fire which is itself the Heraclitean notion of change and flux raised to such a level beyond love or rage that nothing can escape it, that no man's or woman's flow can quench it?

There was nothing of peace in me. Every muscle in my body verged on cramp. My stomach was knotted, and once I burped something sour into my mouth. And swallowed. I figured it would probably turn into heartburn in minutes. (Blessedly, it didn't.) The fact that the body can actually fall asleep when it and the mind are in such a state—call it fear and trembling; call it angst—is a natural miracle.

After an hour in the dark, I put my head back down on the rug. And slept.

I'd left my apartment door open, not because I was crazy—though, in New York, that's what most people would assume—but in hopes that Leaky, at least, might come in. (He'd earlier unlocked the downstairs door to let the other guys get in without being seen. If Jimmy or a tenant hadn't noticed it yet, it was still open.) What woke me, with only the light coming from the street through the two living-room windows, was a crash—

I pushed myself up, disoriented.

Somewhere, something overturned, thunderously: lots of things fell off it to the floor—in the library, through the arch, something awful was happening in the dark! My round oak table lay on its side—light from the corner window struck its slanted grain!

Then books flapped and ran over wood.

Someday, take your arm and run it behind a shelf full of books, sweeping them all at once to the floor. You may never have heard the sound before. But if you do it, you'll realize that almost anyone hearing it—even for the first time—will know immediately what it is. More books fell. And more. "Hey—what are...are you *doing* in there—!?" And the dark giant lumbered and loomed into the archway. He twisted one way, twisted back. Then an arm swung by his head—my living-room window smithereened, as a volume smashed through!

"Oh, look—What is it... please—huh? Oh, come *on*—"

The answering voice, torn by gasps and cracking with its own intensity (somewhere, the rasp splintered, the stone shattered) filled the room, the apartment, my head: "It's not your fault—*I* know that!" The breath tearing into him sounded as though it would split his chest. "It's not your fault—it's not mine! But I'm *mad!* I'm mad the kid is dead!" It sounded as if the air animating him would rip muscles from the bone. In the dark, he reeled. "The little bastard don't *have* to be dead! He could be alive. *I'm* alive! I could have taught him how to stay alive—if he would'a' done what I told him! I could'a' taught him how to stay warm in the winter—where to get blankets and stuff. Him and me"—and here it became only a man crying—"we were...were a lot a...alike. I could'a' taught him—" then, again, a man was raging—"taught him how to stay dry—when *I* met him, he didn't even know enough to come in out of the goddamn *rain!* He shouldn't have to be dead—"

"Mike!" I said. "Mike, he...yeah, Joey should be alive! And it's awful that he's not—!"

The Mad Man suddenly strode across the room. I scurried out of his way to the wall (and bumped the broken mirror; it broke again—and cut my hand) as, in the night light from the remaining window, my couch reared up forward and overturned. While I scuttled back from it, it thumped and thudded to the floor.

"Mike!" I said, still on the rug. "Mike, please—don't make so much *noise!* Please! Because people will *hear* you—then they'll send the police or somebody to *get* you! They'll take *you* away! And they'll do awful things to you!" No, I didn't say it. I shouted it.

And the monster within my darkened home turned and raged and cried.

He raped me before he left.

In the mouth.

There's no point in my describing it with any detail that might suggest even the vaguest eroticization; because there was nothing vaguely sexual in it—not for me. Really, I suspect, not for him either. His stony fingers left bruises on my face and neck afterwards. The seam on my suit jacket between my arm and shoulder got a five-inch rip. But if that overquick and overthick eruption (that, by his own hand, he indulged a dozen times a day) meant, for him, even the slightest inward relief, then I'm glad he did it. I cooperated.

And not because I didn't want to get more hurt than I actually did. (Which, finally, wasn't that much—but it was enough.) I didn't want to do it. I didn't like it while he was doing it. I was never even vaguely aroused. There was nothing pleasant about it from the time he grabbed me up to the time he flung me down. Nor, by any gesture, motion, or sound, did he show the least concern for me in any way while we did it. (It really *was* a rape!) But I hold nothing against him for it. Because I also knew that if he ever came to me in the same state, I'd service him again. (Or let him service himself on me—and I'm only lucky that he did it orally and not anally. Because I would have let *that* happen too. And that's just madness.) No, Joey's death was not my fault or his, any more than it was Al's for saying Tim couldn't bring Mike with him out to Breakers' Point that year—or Leaky's for bringing them all over here in the first place, or Tony's for lending Joey his shoes and thinking about it for five minutes before he woke up the others rather than immediately hog-tying the kid and waking Mike to ask his opinion on the kid's going to the Pit on Saturday night. It was all of that operating together—as a system. The individual elements only made the system manifest. But the only reason that I can give you for why I went along with the Mad Man's sexual violence toward me—certainly his act was entirely beyond my own moral boundaries and even any sense of my own safety—is that the world owed it to him, owed it to him for the death of Hasler, for his own life since, and for Crazy Joey. I happened to be there.

The systems of the…what?

But, yes, I am part of the world.

When Mad Man Mike was finished with me, he wandered to the middle of the floor and, again, urinated on the door jamb and the rug. Light through the broken window hit his naked arm, the hip under his torn pants, his glittering stream.

(That I call it rape, Pheldon says, shows I haven't a shred of feminist consciousness, since [one] Mike didn't use a weapon, [two] he didn't hit me—more than once very hard—and [three] he probably wouldn't have killed me if I had really fought back, bit him, or whatever—though, while it was happening, it never occurred to *me* there was any way to stop him. "Extreme sexual rudeness, perhaps," Pheldon says. "Assault with a pronounced sexual element. But if you went into it because you 'owed it to him' for whatever reason, it wasn't rape." To which my response is: "Fuck you! *I* didn't go into it *any* way! It *was* a rape! Jesus *Christ!*")

On the floor, leaning against the overturned couch, I breathed hard and, in the dark, watched him, listened to him—and massaged my arm, which he'd twisted till it really hurt. I swallowed: my throat, especially the right side of it, was sore.

As his water died, he did ask, actually: "You okay...?" Though for all its reverberation, it sounded like something he just said, rather than anything he was interested at all in knowing.

The pain in my arm made me grunt. "It's all right, Mike." I tried to sit forward, pull myself away from sofa back and, just then, couldn't.

Mike turned and walked abruptly into the hall—from his boots on the squeaking boards, I figured he was *still* mad. Even so, when the apartment door slammed behind him, I jumped.

I sat, looking at the jagged glass in the window. Again I thought about Almira Adler. Timothy Hasler was killed by a psychotic hustler named Dave Franitz—who froze to death in an abandoned building a couple of years later. Tim died saving the life of his friend, Mike Kerns, otherwise known as the Mad Man, a homeless quadroon ex-mental patient and sexual deviant he'd picked up in...whom he'd met and had sex with in Riverside Park. The conflict in the bar that night was over Kerns's sexual prowess, or perhaps more accurately over his economic availability—it was, after all, a hustling bar. But even as I spoke the words under my breath, they sounded inane. (That I did not once accuse the Mad Man with the thought: "Hasler gave his life for *this*...?" is my single claim to being a moral entity. What, I thought instead [and maybe this is what love is]: "What would the world have to inflict on Leaky to transform him into such an out-of-touch, hurtful, and outraged sexual creature?" Picturing the specificities of the answer actually gave me chills!) Finally I sat there wondering: How could you explain to someone like Almira Adler what happened when—for certainly this was closer to the problem—one entire system of the world turned on another and tried to obliterate it?

Perhaps because I was more exhausted now, or because I felt I'd paid the Mad Man back my penny's worth, this time I fell asleep—and much more easily.

Light. And voices—

"—John? John…John Marr?" It wasn't Phel. It wasn't Lewey.

"What's that that stinks in there? Somethin's *wrong* in there—I'm not going in that place!" *That* was Jimmy, my super. "You goin' in there, maybe we should get somebody—"

"I think I'd better go in." It wasn't Leaky. "You can wait here—"

"I ain't gonna wait with that stink! That turns my *stomach!* I'm goin' downstairs—you *sure* you wanna go in there? You know the window's broken—you can see it from down on the street. I can get the cops—it smells like somebody's *dead* in there!"

"No, I'd better go in—"

"All right, but *I'm* goin' downstairs!" Outside, footsteps descended.

"No, can't you wait for— I mean, I may need you to…" Then, after a few more moments: "John…? Is anyone in there? John Marr…?"

Careful steps came hesitantly down the hall's loose floorboards—so different from the angry steps that had last rushed up them.

"Is someone *there…?*"

I raised my head, then pushed up on the rug with one arm. "Who is…?" The other arm really hurt.

Then, in the doorway, in a blue denim shirt with a dark teal tie in a four-in-hand at his neck, in summer slacks and cordovan shoes (he held his arms a little from his sides, as though he walked a floor that might any moment give way under him) and his glasses—above them his hair shockingly gray (but I hadn't actually seen him in over half a dozen years)—Irving Mossman said: "Oh, my *God,* John—that's you? John…you're hurt? Someone broke in here…and did this? To you? But how in the…you'd better not move! You've been *cut!* Let me call a hospital! No, you take it easy—"

"Irving," I said. "I'm all right—really. Irving—"

"When did they break in here—what in the world were they trying to get? No—is there a phone? Do you have a doctor? I've got my car—this is incredible. I mean, this is really in—"

"Irving—" Sitting up, I glanced at the broken mirror on the floor. You couldn't read most of the letters smeared on either of the pieces. But I could see my face—and the blood over my shirt and suit jacket. Had I really walked home like that, through the street? But, then, of course, the swollen lip and the bruises had happened *after* I'd come home. "Irving—" it all came out in a torrent, as if to distract him from what I couldn't imagine him *not* thinking: "I *know* who killed Timothy Hasler! He was stabbed death in the Pit by a psychotic hustler named Dave Franitz, back in '73—" It sounded as pointless and inane as I'd thought it would last night in the dark—"Nobody caught him because people are tight-mouthed down there. But a couple of years later, Franitz froze to death in some burned-out building or other, where he was sleeping. Irving," I said, "Tim died saving the life of his friend, a man who I guess was sort of his lover, back then, named Mike Kerns. But *I* couldn't save—"

Then, of course, *I* began to cry.

Irving turned out to be pretty much a true brick. I mean, he did everything you could and should do in such a situation. He was all upset about the blood. But finally when I got it back together and explained the only thing cut was on my hand, he looked at it—it was an inch-long gash along the heel of my thumb. I can't imagine anyone *believing* all the blood *I* had on me had come from such a little slice. But he stopped questioning me about it—and he stopped saying I *had* to go to the hospital. He made maybe three comments about the smell, then dropped it. A couple of times, I caught him just looking at me. Was he, I wondered, remembering Adler's description of *Tim's* apartment? (But how could he have been thinking of anything else?) He stood outside the bathroom door while I took a shower—"Now if you need anything, just call. I'm right out here. If you feel dizzy or anything, just shout"— then put on my jeans. In the hamper I found a shirt that was still wearable.

In the bathroom, though, I'd been thinking. So when I came outside, I explained, "These three guys, Irving—they broke in here last night. Three black guys—they were Haitian. I could tell because they spoke French most of the time. Though one of them *looked* more like he might have been Hispanic—maybe Dominican. One of them knocked on the door and said he was delivering something—and, like a fool, I opened it for him. Then they barged in, roughed me up, wrecked the place! No, *believe* me...I wouldn't have *any* trouble recognizing them! Not at all! They were here for about—well, an hour. I was terrified. They locked me in the bathroom and talked about killing me if I came out or screamed or anything." May the spirit of Toussaint L'Ouverture have mercy on my soul.

"What in the world were they trying to *do?*"

"I don't know! They were *madmen!*"

(Later I asked myself: was I going through all this because I was scared—hidden deep in some closet smelling of old socks, dried piss, and shitty underwear? Or was it because I just didn't want to upset Irving further than he clearly was? One of the ways that the systems of the world work is that the same prevarication may accomplish both.)

Irving helped me turn the couch up—and frowned at the stains on it. He helped me upright the table. Then, while I was picking up papers, he stopped to look down at something on the floor. I went over to see what he was looking at.

He said: "You still have this thing...?"

I said: "You never did send me that replacement photograph of you, did you?"

"No," he said. "I guess I forgot."

I picked up the frame and put it back on the table. "That's all right."

"I will, soon."

"It's all right."

"I don't even know where that photograph is now...actually. I took it out for Sam—"

"It's all right," I said. "Really."

Irving made piles of the books. I stacked up some of the file boxes that had been knocked over.

Finally Irving said, "Come on, John. Would you let me get you the hell out of all this—for a while? We'll get some...breakfast, how about it? I mean, that's what I was planning to suggest when I first came by." The smell couldn't be too conducive to his appetite.

Still, after you'd been in it for even ten or fifteen minutes, you stopped noticing it so much.

We locked up and went downstairs. Outside on the street,

Jimmy was gnawing on his cigar stump. "Mr. Marr's all right...?" he asked suspiciously.

"Yes, I think so." Irving told Jimmy that three Puerto Ricans had broken in and—

"Haitians," I explained. And did not raise my eyes to heaven. "Two of them, anyway. Last night."

But everything, Irving said, was under control.

"Then why does it smell like that?" Jimmy wanted to know.

"They *really* messed up the place," Irving said. "Mr. Marr's had a rough time. I'm taking him to get something to eat. Maybe, when he gets back, you can give him a hand up there—?"

"No!" I said. "That's all right. I can take care of it."

"Hell," Jimmy said, "I ain't goin' in no place smellin' like *that!*"

"I'll take care of it, Irving," I said. "Really—"

We went to a breakfast place called EJ's, a block and a half down the avenue. "Should we take the car?" Irving wanted to know. His red Acura was parked six cars down from the house. "Not with *that* parking place, you don't. Besides, it just isn't that far."

Over Belgian waffles and sausage, Irving explained that he was in the city for a summer conference on Rousseau and Questions of Eighteenth-Century Autobiography at the City College Graduate Center; Mossman's doctorate had been on Rousseau; these last years had seen those early interests start to reawaken. He'd called me this morning, but gotten no answer. (Later, back upstairs, I discovered that, in his rampage, Mike had kicked the phone plug from its jack.) On the chance I was just out for a few minutes, he had decided to drive by anyway and knock. (Yes, he'd wanted to see the building Timothy Hasler had once lived in, whether I was in or not.) The front door had been open. He'd wandered in, knowing I was on the top floor. Coming upstairs, he'd met Jimmy coming down from the Espedrosas' apartment. "Who did you want to see, suh?" So Jimmy had gone up with him to my floor—where they'd found my door swinging wide.

(Of course when Mike had slammed it, it hadn't caught.)

They'd knocked anyway. No answer. Then they'd called...

"But you," he said, "have gone and solved the secret of Timothy Hasler's death!"

"It was just a matter of asking the right people the right questions.

To a lot of people, it wasn't a secret at all. Only to the official forces—the police, people like that. It's a matter of getting yourself in the right system."

"You and your systems," Irving grinned. "I remember those—back from when you first got to graduate school. That's going to be quite an article."

We talked about my reporting the break-in of my three Haitians to the police. I'd do it right away, once I got back, I assured him—the precinct was at the other end of the block.

We talked about my getting some help. "After all, this has got to be incredibly upsetting. You were crying, there, when I first came in!"

When the check came, graciously and generously Irving paid it. "The least I can do. After all—" As we left the cashier and pushed out through the glass doors, Irving gave me one of those smiles under the lowered rim of his glasses that's not supposed to be a real smile, but is. "I'm a professor now—full."

As we walked back to my corner, he said: "The other thing I came by to do, really, was to say thank you."

"For what?"

"For that letter you wrote."

I frowned—wondering how he'd gotten hold of what I'd written Sam; or what he'd made of it!

"The letter you wrote me about Hasler," he prompted, when I looked baffled, "and how much my work on him had…well, influenced yours."

And it came back—the letter I'd written him at Sam's prompting, after my first half-dozen articles had appeared.

"I submitted that along with my promotion case—as an example of my students' response to my more recent work. You know, you're probably my best-known student, at this point."

"You're certainly welcome," I told him. Now I was the one who felt I was walking over an imminently collapsible surface. Summer's Saturday-morning West Siders strolled around us, heading here and there for brunch. "And I meant what I wrote in it."

"Are you sure now you can handle all this, John? I mean, do you want me to go to the police station with you? There're no conference sessions until noon. What a wonderful way to plan a conference Sunday. Really, they're *so* civilized in this city—"

At the corner, just beyond the blue mailbox bolted to the cement before the barber shop, someone leaned over the wire trash basket, digging around inside. His green pants were, if anything, too large. They'd pulled down his flat, hairy buttocks, so you could see the top three inches of the cleft, clamping all that fur. Now he stood up, all six-feet-four of him—the sweatshirt was the same blue one, too small and unzipped. The shoes were the same, one more or less whole, one with the top torn—now—completely off. In the basket, he'd found half a sandwich of whole wheat bread, some waxed paper still around it. Shoving about half of it into his beard with his giant hand, he turned.

"Leaky!" I said. "Hey, Leaky—!"

He regarded me, over the sandwich, chewing.

I said, "Leaky, come on! You don't have to eat that. I'll give you something to eat, upstairs."

"It ain't too dirty," he said, curtly. And, the bottom of his butt (or the top of his thighs) leaning back on the chipped orange rim, he *kept* chewing. With neither belt nor rope, he'd taken some wire and run it through two belt loops, pulling them together, twisting the wire up. The waist button pulled tightly across his gut's fur—but until it broke, it would keep the pants on.

"Irving," I said. "This is my friend, Leaky. Leaky Sowps. Leaky, this is my friend, Professor Irving Mossman."

Slowly, Leaky began to smile. He held out one huge, rough-skinned, grime-gloved hand.

And Irving, his smile only slightly bemused, did the thing one loves Americans for. He reached out for Leaky's huge, hard hand and shook it.

"You a real professor, huh?" Leaky's smile grew around the chewing, ruffling his beard below his gray-shot hair. "That's what some of us call the little guy here, sometimes." With the second bite, the last bread disappeared in his mouth. "'Cause he knows an awful lot—and reads all them goddamn books. He knows a lot more than a goddamn dummy like me." The smile had become an open grin.

I enjoy that grin so much!

In the green cloth, off-center and low on his lap, however, a blotch started darkening to a ripe olive's hue: the stain, the size of a coffee cup bottom, moment's later was the size of the cup's rim, then of a saucer's (I could see the edge expanding), growing into a dinner plate's.

Irving was still smiling up at him. "Maybe John *will* be one someday—if he keeps up doing the kind of work he's been doing. And gets to that thesis!"

"Right," I said. "Irving—look, why don't you go on. I've got a lot to do. I'm going to have to get some serious cleaning done—"

Standing up from the basket, Leaky said, "I'll give you a hand with that, little guy—"

"Hey, Leaky!" I said. "Thanks—"

I turned to walk with Irving to his car. We walked around to his door, and Irving bent down to unlock it, sunlight through the plant of paradise leaves throwing enough mottling on the reflective red to delight Gerard Manley Hopkins. Irving glanced to where Leaky waited at the corner. "The homeless situation in your city, John—" the door came open—"is astonishing. Not only are they all over. But everyone I've met who lives here knows three or four of them by name, personally. That's amazing!" He took a breath. "But I like your friend there."

"Leaky's great," I said. "I love 'im. Say hello to Sam for me, when you talk to her."

"Oh, I will. And if you need anything, now, you can get me at the Graduate Center for the rest of the day, anytime after one—" he gave me an office extension—"they'll know where I am."

"Thanks a lot, Irving. Really, thanks for everything."

The car pulled out into the street—and I turned to hurry back to the corner. "Leaky," I said, "*why* are you peeing in your pants?"

"I didn't know I was till just now." The stain had stopped at dinner plate size. "So you want some help cleanin' up the place? You got some ammonia? You got some Spic and Span? You got some Top Job?"

"We can get those around at the supermarket on Columbus," I told him. "They're open on Sunday. Come on, though—what do you think you're doing, standing here peeing all over yourself in the street?

"Probably," he said, "it's 'cause I'm so happy to see you, little guy. And 'cause you ain't mad at me and tellin' me to get the fuck out of your face. And 'cause you said I could help you with the cleanin'. I know a whole lot about that kind of cleanin'. I done a lot of it in my time."

"Yeah—" I grinned— "I bet you have!" We started down the block—towards Columbus Avenue. I still had a twenty, I knew, in my wallet. "Hey, when we get upstairs, I want to roll around with you some more. I wanna suck you—and drink the rest of that piss outta you." I laughed. "I just didn't want you to waste it down here—"

"You're gonna like it, too," Leaky said, " 'cause I got a good crop of cheese in there today, nigger—"

"And maybe we'll even finish up the rest of the beer in the ice-box. Then I'll make you some real food. God, I don't want to see you eating out any more garbage cans!"

"Okay." He seemed a little surprised.

"I mean, is it okay if I keep you around awhile? To fuck with you? Fucking around with you makes me feel pretty good."

We walked another quarter of a block.

Then Leaky said, "Can I ask you a favor, professor?"

"Anything you want, Dummy."

He was silent another few steps. Then he said: "When you want sex, you don't ever got to ask me for it. I don't care where we are. You want somethin' from me, you just take it. Don't ask me, man. Really. And I promise you, I won't never say no. Not never. That's kind of a pride thing with me, you know?"

"Yeah, sure, I suppose—"

"Don't suppose me. What do they say? Just *do* it. With me, it's like the Mad Man never pissin' or shittin' in the toilet. If we're on the fuckin' Fifth Avenue bus, and you wanna suck on my dick, just take it out and suck it—"

"You probably don't have to worry about that one, Leaky."

"I'm sound asleep, you wanna suck some dick, don't wake me up and ask if it's okay. Just get down there and start sucking."

"You may have put up with some of that—"

"You wanna shove it up my fuckin' asshole, man, you just shove it up my fuckin' asshole—"

"Now, wait a minute there." I laughed. "That's another one you won't have to deal with. You know it as well as I do, that's the way you end up with AIDS. I don't want this to be a life-and-death sort of thing."

"Well, then, you just got to be responsible whether I get AIDS or not. Whether I live or die."

"Leaky, I don't like that."

"I mean, I got your dog collar on my neck. I got some new pants this morning up at the church—but still got my old collar! Is it gonna be hard for you?"

"Not to fuck you up the ass?"

"Well, ain't nobody else gonna do it *except* you. I can promise you that. *You* take it up the ass?"

"Only three times in my life—and all of them before 1979. And I didn't particularly like it, any of them."

"Well, there—if *you* fucked me up the ass, I wouldn't *get* no damn AIDS, anyway."

"That's not something that's *known*, Leaky—or..." I paused, because what I'd really thought what he'd said was something else, where I was the fuckee.

"I'll piss on any nigger what looks at me funny." Leaky reached over, grabbed my head—and shook it, as somebody might reach over a stack of dried squashes and gourds and jostle the pumpkin to hear the seeds rattle. "I like to get my dick sucked. I like to get my ass licked out. I like to get my feet rubbed, my beer cans opened for me, my tonsils swabbed so I can taste my own piss, and I need to feel some woolly-headed bastard scourin' under my balls while he snores—and maybe about a belly-button-full-o'-cum a day in order to feel happy. The nigger what does all that, man, owns me." He flung his head forward, bending from the waist, to speak within the forest of his hair. "See—up at the church when I was waitin' to get my pants, I already took a nail and scratched your name on the copper plate there. See it? 'Property of John Marr'!" I looked at the leather, curled over top and bottom with his neck hair; but between the angle and the fur, I didn't have time to read it before his head swung up again. "I got it off your mailbox. Now, you add onto that that the black bastard calls me a stupid fuck and even kind of *likes* it when I piss in the fuckin' bed when I'm sleepin' holdin' on to him—what you expect me to do? I mean, what's the matter with you? You fuckin' *crazy*, nigger?"

I do not have AIDS. (It's now 1994, going on '95; we're getting on toward the first thousand days of what, for all the media's sniping at the man and his wife, seems the first sane presidential administration in years.) Though whether the sexual acts Leaky and I do, or did, *can* transmit the HIV virus or not, I don't know. Monitored tests for them still have not been done—

But let's get you quickly from then to now:

"Phel," I said, once I'd plugged the phone back in. "I seem to have developed a live-in lover."

"Really? Congratulations!"

"I need some advice, though. I think there're may be a couple of problems with the relationship."

"Already? Believe me, he *can't* be any more of a problem than Lewey. Have you ever *lived* with a New York City sanitation worker? A *white* New York City sanitation worker? We're having another picnic next week, by the way. Lewey's taking the van. You guys want to come?"

The police caught somebody named Allen Simmons for Joey's stabbing, I learned from La Veuve one evening when Pheldon and I dropped in to Cats for a drink. The stabbing at the Pit was gossip in all the gay bars for a month: Simmons had been heavily into crack and apparently quite strung out that Saturday night. Two other working men—among them the black pool player, whose name was Lonnie—had walked the police to his door in a rooming house over on Tenth Avenue. So much for brotherhood. Or maybe that's just another way the world's changed—

"Dear Irving, I reported the break-in to the police later the morning I saw you. They even came over and took notes. But they still haven't caught anyone." Among people who do things like that, I guess, there's a sort of brotherhood. But I never sent the postcard. Rather I wrote up what I now knew of Timothy Hasler's death in a twenty-six-typed-page personal article—the way I would describe it to you, or to you and Sam, if you came over for dinner with us one night. Which is to say the article spoke of my own sexual attractions to this world, told of Joey's inadvertent murder on that night, and quoted from a couple of the more explicit index cards of *The Mad Man*. It seemed reasonable to let Hasler, since he *was* the subject of the essay, speak for us both. As to Mike's more recent history, yes, I was reticent. But much of it was there for (as they say) those who could read. Five days after I sent it off, it was accepted by a Canadian magazine of radical sexual politics out of Toronto called *Umbilicus*.

Later, I wrote it up in a brief and rather stripped letter, with pret-

ty much nothing personal in it at all as to incident, urges, or emotions—almost as I'd explained it to Irving that morning. Only I put
it in an envelope and sent it to Almira Adler at Breakers' Point.

Two weeks after that, an envelope stuffed with my contribu-
tor's copies of *Umbilicus* arrived. (They work fast, up there north
of the border!) I read through the article again—fourteen printed
pages—and corrected four typographical errors. (Of *course* they'd
printed a "now" as a "not" in a crucial sentence!) Then, on a whim,
without even a note and just a paper clip so that it would open to
the start of my piece, I put a copy, with corrections, into an envelope and sent that to Adler, too.

(And, then, one to Irving.)

Five days later, I got an answer from Adler that's probably the
thing that's made me feel better about anything I've written,
whether on Hasler or whatever, than anything else. It began: "Dear
John Marr, Thank you for sending me your extraordinary article…" (She called it "extraordinary"!) It went on to say, over three
and a half pages, how much she'd learned from it, how hard it
must have been to write, how much it had revealed to her, of Tim
in particular and the unsettling work of the heart in general, and
how grateful she was to me for sharing it with her. Her answer, really, used some pretty flattering language.

And that woman has won the Pulitzer Prize—

And it didn't mention my letter—at all.

A year later, when I got Leaky to take *his* first HIV test, I confirmed what I'd been pretty sure from what he'd told me of his
sexual history: HIV-negative, Leaky does not have AIDS either—

"Well, then, if you think I probably don't got it, *why* do I got to
take the goddamn test?"

"Because I'm writing about this stuff now, in articles. I have to
know these things."

"Well, you dumb-ass nigger bastard, *I* ain't writin' the fuckin'
articles!"

"Come *on*, Leaky—"

"Don't look at me like that, you goddamned sonofabitch, black-
bastard, piss-drinkin', scum-suckin' nigger scumbag!" But when he's
really mad, he stops talking—and pees all over himself. We went
to the city testing office and he got the blood test, though, the
next day.

Nor *has* he ever said no to me sexually.

Tony is also HIV negative—though the reason we know is that about a month after Joey's murder, he was hospitalized for ten days (after loosing about twenty pounds) because of what turned out to be a serious case of intestinal parasites. Leaky and I went to see him down at Beth Israel. Apparently, Tony said, the parasite business had happened to him at least twice before. From now on, he explained to us as though it were the most ordinary of seasonal resolutions, no more dog shit—

"When are you guys gonna come over to the park again and see Mad Man Mike? We sure had fun that last time—and down there in the train tracks, you don't have to scrub out your fuckin' apartment with ammonia and Lysol afterwards...."

When the first piece falls into place, I guess the others follow it naturally: a letter arrived, forwarded by *Umbilicus*, from a man in Chicago, Dennis Chung, who explained:

> ...I met Tim when he worked in the Chicago Shoe Emporium. We lived together for nine months, in New York City and Ann Arbor. For the first six months of that, we were lovers—for the last three, we were going through a painful and protracted breakup. Why the breakup? Tim was too much into his work—really, about that, *he* was a madman. And—five years younger than he—I wasn't too much into anything; though today I'm a CPA, here in the Big Windy. (Also, I'm Chinese-American; and my parents, if not Tim's, would have murdered us both if they'd found out we were friends, much less lovers—only secondarily because we were gay!) A year later, with a couple of phone calls, however, we got to be friends again. Your *Umbilicus* article impelled me to write because I was visiting New York in autumn of '73 and came to see Tim, in his apartment, the September he was killed. I don't know the exact date, but I believe it was less than a week before his murder. I'm sure it was that close, because I read about his death in the paper within days of my dropping by to see him. When I came in, he'd just gotten back from tutoring someone, I recall. (Once Tim's Rosenwald fellowship ran out in '67, a good deal of his income when not at Stilford came from tutoring German, French, and Greek, in all of

which he was proficient. I mention this, because, in the three articles of yours on Tim I've read, you haven't. It was a large part of Tim's life—four to six hours a day, six days a week, in the months we lived together. Were you aware of it? If you'd like, I'll put together a list of the names of the private students of his I remember...) Two to four days before his death, Tim's apartment was *not* a wreck—and certainly not befouled. (Except for the water damage to the hall ceiling—which was just his cheap landlord.) While I was there, Mad Man Mike came in (he had the key)—the immense blond Negro you describe—and Tim introduced him to me. Tim was clearly quite taken with him. At the time, Mike's clothes were not those of a homeless man (I assumed even then that Tim had bought him some things), though I remember his shoes came off immediately and he sat with his feet in Tim's lap, while Tim rubbed them and we all talked. About what I couldn't tell you—though I remember thinking Mike's conversation, though friendly, funny, and unbelievably vulgar, most of it, was also *very* strange, if not a little crazy. Also, every once in a while, he'd get up and stride off into another room. Then, five minutes later, he'd be back. Perhaps the third time, I asked, "Where's he *going*...?" Tim answered, fliply: "To masturbate." *I* thought he was joking! Four or five days later, when I read about Tim's stabbing, of course I wondered whether this deranged giant wasn't responsible. I mean, I thought he might be the killer! I'm glad he wasn't—because he *was* engaging, in his way. And the one thing I'm certain was, they liked each other. Once I read about the murder, I was also (back then) quite convinced the police would be contacting me any day—which, as I was living with my parents again in Chicago, I was not looking forward to. But I guess Tim and I had managed to keep our relationship a better secret than I thought! They never did. And I have never said anything about it, really, till now....

As soon as Tony got out, I had him take me over to see the Mad Man in his leafed-over space leading into the abandoned tracks. With Leaky and Tony, the four of us visited about an hour. During which hour Mike jerked off twice—although we had no sex. (At least not *really*.) I told him they'd caught the guy who'd killed Joey, Allen Simmons. I told Mike the name of the fellow who killed Hasler and sliced up his shoulder seventeen years ago, Dave Franitz. But talking with the Mad Man is a little strange, unless you're talking about exactly what he's interested in right then. My visit netted one hard-edged fact, though. At least, I think it did. While we were sitting around on the overturned stones, under the black, arching walls of the track tunnel (Mike's voice made me feel he carried the whole tunnel around with him, making his words reverberate—enough to shame James Earl), I said: "Years ago, Mike, with your friend Hasler, before you went down to the Pit that night, you'd been fooling around in Tim's apartment. Maybe you'd even turned him out, with some other guys, the way you guys did me. You liked to do that. So did Joey."

"Yeah…" Mike said. But it might have been a question.

"It was pretty messy by the time you finished. Right? Maybe that's why you and Hasler decided to leave for a while and go someplace else—to try out the Pit. But after Tim took the knife in the chest that Franitz was trying to stick into you, and you were cut, you came back to the apartment—the one downstairs from my place. Was the door left open? Tim had given you a key. But after Tim was killed, you did pretty much the same downstairs at Tim's place that you did upstairs at mine—all except jamming your dick in my face. You finished wrecking it. You did it because you were mad, right? Because you were angry your friend had been killed."

Mike nodded. He looked puzzled. Then he said, "There wasn't nobody to come with no more.…"

Shortly after that, we left.

Now the nod may have signified just that Mike had heard what I'd said. The look may have meant only that he didn't understand it. And the comment may have had something to do with Joey that I simply didn't follow. But I choose to read from the three together that my supposition was right: he'd questioned the past and told me his reason.

But with madmen such readings are always questionable. And the truth was, the Mad Man remembered Hasler. But he remembered Joey much better.

Let me say it right out: though I love him, Leaky and I disagree about the way the systems of the world work as much as two people possibly can. But you have to tell *me*, then, why we only do anything you could *call* arguing *maybe* twice a year; and when we do, it usually ends with my getting pissed on—in the bathtub (yawn!); then, when I tell him he's a stupid, brainless, retarded, moronic pea-brained idiot imbecile, Leaky lies down on the hall floor, beats off, and says okay, we'll do it my way. It's just not what I think of as the usual fight-then-fuck syndrome.

("Sam, I'm so glad you and—it's Goneril?—came by to see us this evening while you were in the city. Thank you, but—really—it was just a pork shoulder.... No, I just did the roast. Leaky did the string beans.... Yes, that's our bedroom. But it's kind of off-limits to guests.... The stuff around the door? That's stripping, yes— *No!* It's *not* a dungeon! Really, the room's just got a kind of smell that gets to some people. That's all.")

I didn't go back to the temp agency, either. I got—in the following order—a permanent job as a paralegal secretary trainee three very broke weeks later, then my degree (eight months on into '91), and finally (in '92) a job teaching out of the City Graduate Center, which reduced the paralegal secretary job to the most partial of part time. There's a charming novella of manners to be written by someone more skilled than I about the first three academic parties I brought Leaky to. The hero would be Golda P—, sixty-two year old wife of Professor P—. The villain is another graduate student named George. Leaky's assessment, when we returned home, triumphant, from the last of them (Golda: "The point is, George, Leaky's right—and you're wrong!"), to crawl into bed and into each other's warmth and smell—I still love that man's smell, after more than four years—and arms: "I thought real smart people would call each other dumb and stupid a lot more—just joking around, like ordinary people. I mean, I thought it was gonna be a lot more horny. Still, it was interesting. Some of them is borin'— but some of them was nice, though."

Oh, yes: someone at a publishing company with the preposterous name Rhino*ceros* Books read my *Umbilicus* article and wants to bring out the full Hasler's memoir/meditation *The Mad Man*— which I'm supposed to edit! About this, Adler wrote me two letters within the space of a week. The first said, as much as she appreciated everything I'd done, she just couldn't see how it could be a good idea at all. The second said: a conversation with some friends had changed her mind. Go ahead—with her blessing.

"What do you think *that's* going to do to Hasler's reputation?" Phel asked one evening, after I read out loud some sixty consecutive index cards.

Leaky said: "What do you think it's going to do to *your* reputation?"

"I think," I said, "both results might be interesting—or at least an adventure."

Sitting cross-legged on the living floor at Phel's feet, Lewey said: "What'll Mad Man Mike think about it?"

"I don't think it'll mean anything to him at all," Leaky said, "one way *or* the other."

I'm afraid I agree.

In leaf-lavish October of '94, Leaky and I took a bus down to Hagarstown, Maryland. A half-great aunt by marriage or something drove us out to that mountainside farm neither in Fair Play, Lydia, or Speilman. Big Nigg, Leaky had found out on a fugitive phone call to another relative in the area, had had a stroke and died the previous week. We missed the burial by three days. Humpbacked Blacky was shyer, and friendlier—but also a little more of a twitch—than I'd expected. But he was about toothless. And, yes, he had an old dog collar around his neck—that nobody mentioned while we were there any more than they did the one Leaky wore. And Billy (nobody called him "Ol' Fuck" while *I* was there, including Leaky) was a lot quieter—though, of course, (one of) his life companion(s) had just died.

I have no doubt now that what Leaky told me, about him and his father sharing one mother, is true: his father looks like Leaky's twin brother. Not his older brother. His *twin*—though there's a fourteen year difference in their ages—say Leaky, Blacky, *and* Billy.

But Leaky says life on the bum ages you—while life in the country keeps you young....?

Blacky and I went fishing one afternoon while Leaky and his old man tore off somewhere in the pick-up. Blacky and I had a pleasant and informative time, during which Blacky told me a lot of interesting things about our respective big guys, father and son, and we caught a few big ones but tossed back numerous sunnies into the rocky rush. Billy and Leaky got back so drunk they busted the fender coming up the drive, and, after hanging all over Blacky and me, Billy said how we was all family now, 'cause he was a fuckin' nigger-lover and was proud of it—every white-man on this mountainside had cussed him out for a nigger-lover (Leaky stretched out on his back on the porch and said it was the truth, a dribble already making its way from under his hip across the boards)—but Billy didn't give a shit, he'd been a nigger-lover all his life, the only *white* man he'd ever cared shit about was his boy, Leaky ("I miss your big brother somethin' terrible, Blacky. You're good to stay on with me." "Where the fuck I'm gonna go, y'ol' drunk?"), and he'd always hoped his boy would hook up with a nigger what had some brains like he done, and my comin' down here like this had made him feel real good, it had touched his heart, both for him and for his son. Then Billy and Leaky both fell out on the porch—to wake up three hours on, me and Blacky still sitting there, listening to the crickets, drinking beer, and yawing.

Then we fried up the fish.

From nothing else but the smell upstairs (as well as couple of things Billy let drop in the first few evening's conversations), I figure now *maybe* a third the bull-shit stories Leaky told me about his upbringing are based on something *close* to the truth. But I've given up trying to unravel what and which. And though Billy told us to sleep on a single mattress together in the attic, Leaky surprised me by saying, "Don't do anything to make my pop think we're faggots, now!" When I looked at him oddly, he said: "Well, act like you done that time we went out and saw *your* parents! That's all I mean." (I don't know why, but I suspect this is a relationship doomed through family tradition to last.) The next day, after ogling the pomegranate, rust, and mustard foliage scorching the mountainside throughout the Columbus Day weekend, we took the bus from Hagarstown back to the city.

Though Lewey has been talking almost a year now about setting him up with a job as a loader for a private carting company, no, Leaky still doesn't have any regular work. But daily he pisses on his hands to keep them hard and goes down to Forty-seventh Street and Sixth Avenue about every third day to panhandle. He says he likes to pay for his own beer; he drinks enough of it.

I say, "I get about as much out of it as you do."

He says, as well, since that's the diamond sellers' neighborhood, panhandling there he keeps a hard, monstrous, nail-gnawed thumb on a certain pulse and rhythm to the city's glittering dream.

—New York & Canaan
June 1993—March 1994

RISK FACTORS FOR SEROCONVERSION TO HUMAN IMMUNODEFICIENCY VIRUS AMONG MALE HOMOSEXUALS

Results from the Multicenter AIDS Cohort Study*

LAWRENCE A. KINGSLEY   ROGER DETELS
RICHARD KASLOW   B. FRANK POLK
CHARLES R. RINALDO, JR   JOAN CHMIEL
KATHERINE DETRE   SHERYL F. KELSEY
NANCY ODAKA   DAVID OSTROW
MARK VANRADEN   BARBARA VISSCHER

Summary   2507 homosexual men who were seronegative for human immunodeficiency virus (HIV) at enrolment were followed for six months to elucidate risk factors for seroconversion to HIV. 95 (3·8%) seroconverted. Of men who did not engage in receptive anal intercourse within six months before baseline and in the six-month follow-up period, only 0·5% (3/646) seroconverted to HIV. By contrast, of men who engaged in receptive anal intercourse with two or more partners during each of these successive six-month intervals, 10·6% (58/548) seroconverted. No HIV seroconversions occurred in 220 homosexual men who did not practise receptive or insertive anal intercourse within twelve months before the follow-up visit. On multivariate analysis receptive anal intercourse was the only significant risk factor for seroconversion to HIV, the risk ratio increasing from 3-fold for one partner to 18-fold for five or more partners. Furthermore, data for the two successive six-month periods show that men who reduced or stopped the practice of receptive anal intercourse significantly lowered their risk of seroconversion to 3·2% and 1·8%, respectively. Receptive anal intercourse accounted for nearly all new HIV infections among the homosexual men enrolled in this study, and the hazards of this practice need to be emphasised in community educational projects.

*Investigators:

Baltimore.—B. Frank Polk, Robin Fox, and Ronald Brookmeyer, Johns Hopkins University School of Hygiene and Public Health; Richard D. Leavitt, University of Maryland Cancer Center.

Chicago.—John P. Phair, Joan S. Chmiel, and David G. Ostrow, Howard Brown Memorial Clinic, Northwestern University Medical School.

Los Angeles.—Roger Detels, Barbara R. Visscher, John L. Fahey, Janis V. Giorgi and Jan Dudley, University of California.

Pittsburgh.—Charles R. Rinaldo, Monto Ho, Lawrence A. Kingsley, David W. Lyter, Ronald O. Valdiserri, and Alan Winkelstein, University of Pittsburgh Graduate School of Public Health and School of Medicine.

National Institutes of Health.—Richard A. Kaslow, Alfred J. Saah, Mark J. VanRaden, and Rachel E. Solomon, National Institutes of Allergy and Infectious Disease; Andrew A. Monjan and A. R. Patel, National Cancer Institute.

Introduction

EPIDEMIOLOGICAL data on transmission of human immunodeficiency virus (HIV) within the major risk group, homosexual men, have been limited primarily to inferences drawn from cross-sectional studies. Several investigations have shown that receptive anal intercourse, receptive "fisting", and large numbers of male sexual partners are major risk factors for both the acquired immunodeficiency syndrome (AIDS) and seropositivity to HIV.[1-4] Other reports have suggested a low risk of infection due to oral-genital exposure.[5-7] However, direct estimates of the attributable risk for acquisition of HIV infection can be made only from longitudinal (cohort) studies. This paper focuses on risk factors for seroconversion to HIV among 2507 initially seronegative homosexual men enrolled in the Multicenter AIDS Cohort Study (MACS).

Methods

The MACS is a collaborative cohort study of homosexual and bisexual men. Four institutions (the University of California, Los Angeles; Johns Hopkins University, Baltimore; Howard Brown Memorial Clinic and Northwestern University, Chicago; and the University of Pittsburgh, Pittsburgh) are conducting investigations according to a standardised protocol that includes at serial visits an interviewer-administered questionnaire, physical examination, laboratory tests, and collection of specimens. Baseline measurements were obtained on 4955 men between April, 1984, and March, 1985. Follow-up examinations for the first six-month period were completed on 90% of the cohort (n = 4452) by November, 1985. This report will deal with the 2507 men who were seronegative for HIV at entry into the study, completed their first follow-up visit, and were therefore at risk of seroconversion to HIV

Sexual activity data reported here are based on respondents' answers to questions eliciting the number of partners with whom various sexual practices were performed six months before baseline and during the six-month follow-up. In these two time-frames the questions were identical, and elicited information on active masturbation of sexual partners, oral-genital intercourse, oral-genital intercourse to ejaculation, anal intercourse, anal intercourse to ejaculation, anilingus ("rimming"), digital-anal insertion, hand-anal insertion ("fisting"), dildo use, and enema/douche use. For oral intercourse, anal intercourse, digital-anal insertion, "rimming", and "fisting", data were collected for both receptive and insertive numbers of partners. With dildo and enema/douche use, only recipients were considered.

Antibody to HIV (HTLV-III) was determined by two methods. Pairs of sera taken from each participant at entry and follow-up visits were tested by an enzyme-linked immunosorbent assay licensed by the FDA (DuPont HTLV-III ELISA, DuPont Company).[8] All specimens for which ELISA results suggested seroconversion (ie, increase from <0·5 to ≥0·5) were examined by

TABLE I—CHARACTERISTICS OF MACS PARTICIPANTS AT
ENROLMENT: SEROCONVERTERS COMPARED WITH THOSE WHO
REMAINED SERONEGATIVE

	Seroconverters n = 95		Seronegatives n = 2412	
	Median	(range)	Median	(range)
Age at enrolment	31	(19–55)	33	(18–72)
Age at first sex with another male	16	(5–31)	18	(2–55)
Age began regular sex with males	20	(5–31)	21	(2–58)
Years of regular homosexual activity	9	(1–37)	11	(1–52)
No of male partners during previous 6 mo	10*	(1–500)	5	(1–365)
No of male partners during previous 2 yr	36*	(3–1000+)	20	(1–1000+)
No of male partners during lifetime	200*	(4–1000+)	100	(1–1000+)
	% Reporting		% Reporting	
Lifetime history of any gonorrhoea	64%†		50%	
Lifetime history of rectal gonorrhoea	28%†		16%	
History of perianal bleeding (≥1 time) during previous 6 mo	31%†		18%	

For comparison between seroconverters and non-seroconverters: *p<0·001
by chi-square test for median difference; †p<0·009 by chi-square test for
proportional difference.

immunoblot techniques (Biotech Laboratories, Inc). A score of 0
was assigned for a negative band, 1 for a weakly reactive band, 2 for a
moderately reactive band, and 3 for a strongly reactive band to p15,
p24, p31, p41, p45, p53, p55, p64, or p120. The scores of all bands
were summed and a value of ≥3 was defined as positive, 2 as
equivocal, and ≤1 as negative. The validity of this method has been
evaluated by prospective assessment in this cohort.[9]

Statistical analyses used to support inferences were based on the
chi-square test for 2 × 2 contingency tables (for median or
proportions), chi-square test for trend, 95% binomial confidence
limits, and multiple logistic regression.

Results

Table I shows baseline demographic characteristics of the
2507 MACS participants who were seronegative for HIV at
the initial examination and completed the six-month
follow-up examination.

Men who seroconverted to HIV were slightly younger
than those who remained seronegative. Despite similar
durations of regular homosexual activity, the reported
numbers of male sexual partners for lifetime, two years, and
six months before baseline examination were about two-fold

higher among those who subsequently seroconverted. The
lifetime history of gonorrhoea (any site) and rectal
gonorrhoea were also significantly higher in the
seroconverter group, as was a six-month history of at least
one episode of perianal bleeding noticed after sexual activity.

The overall six-month HIV seroconversion rate was
3·8% (95/2507). Six-month HIV seroconversion rates, by
centre, were: Pittsburgh, 2·5% (13/519); Baltimore/
Washington, 3·5% (26/749); Chicago, 4·5% (25/554); and
Los Angeles, 4·5% (31/685). These seroconversion rates did
not differ significantly.

Table II shows the gradient in seroconversion rates to
HIV when MACS participants were stratified according to
levels of receptive and insertive anal intercourse reported for
the six months before documented seroconversion. HIV
seroconversion was rare in those who did not participate in
receptive anal intercourse in the previous six months (0·9%;
9/984), but increased steadily to 13·6% (30/221) among
those who practised receptive anal intercourse with at least

TABLE III—SEROCONVERSION TO HIV ACCORDING TO
PARTICIPATION IN RECEPTIVE ANAL INTERCOURSE DURING THE
TWELVE MONTHS BEFORE DOCUMENTED SEROCONVERSION

Receptive anal intercourse status	Partners with whom receptive anal intercourse reported		Sero-conversion rate (n)†	95% confidence limits
	6 mo before enrolment visit 1	6 mo before visit 2		
None	0	0	0·5% (3)	0·1–1·4%
Stopped anal receptive	≥1	0	1·8% (6)	0·7–3·8%
Continued anal receptive	1	1	2·3% (8)	1·0–4·5%
Reduced anal receptive	≥2	1	3·2% (9)	1·5–6·0%
Began anal receptive*	0	≥1	1·7% (3)	0·4–5·0%
Increased anal receptive	1	≥2	5·4% (7)	2·2–10·8%
Continued anal receptive	≥2	≥2	10·6% (58)	8·1–13·5%

*Refers only to responses for the two six-month periods; lifetime history of
receptive anal intercourse was not obtained.
†n = 2463 because data were missing in 44 participants, 1 of them a
seroconverter.

five partners. Of the 9 seroconverters who had not practised
receptive anal intercourse during the six months before
seroconversion, 6 had done so within the six months before
enrolment. Thus, only 3 men reported no receptive anal
intercourse in the year before documentation of their
seroconversion. This cross-classification also shows that,

TABLE II—SEROCONVERSION TO HIV BY NUMBER OF PARTNERS WITH WHOM RECEPTIVE AND INSERTIVE ANAL INTERCOURSE PERFORMED
DURING THE SIX-MONTH FOLLOW-UP

	Insertive								Row summary		95% confidence limits
	0		1		2–4		5+				
Receptive	n	%	n	%	n	%	n	%	n	%	
0	4/471	0·8	2/234	0·9	2/168	1·2	1/111	0·9	9/984	0·9	0·4–1·7
1	1/142	0·7	9/388	2·3	6/168	3·6	3/56	5·4	19/754	2·5	1·5–3·9
2–4	3/60	5·0	7/105	6·7	19/263	7·2	8/82	9·8	37/510	7·3	5·2–9·9
5+	3/26	11·5	4/20	20·0	7/50	14·0	16/125	12·8	30/221	13·6	9·3–18·7
Column summary	11/699	1·6	22/747	2·9	34/649	5·2	28/374	7·5	95/2469*	3·8	

*n = 2469 because data on 38 participants were missing.

TABLE IV—SEROCONVERSION RATES TO HIV BY MUTUALLY
EXCLUSIVE SEXUAL PRACTICES REPORTED DURING SIX-MONTH
FOLLOW-UP FOR MEN NOT REPORTING RECEPTIVE ANAL
INTERCOURSE DURING SIX MONTHS BEFORE INITIAL VISIT AND
DURING SIX-MONTH FOLLOW-UP

Sexual practice	n	Seroconversion rate (n)	95% confidence limits
Oral receptive intercourse ≥ 1 partner (no receptive anal or insertive)	147	0·0% (0)	0·0–2·5%
Insertive anal intercourse ≥ 1 partner (no receptive anal)	344	0·9% (3)	0·2–2·5%

when each level of insertive anal intercourse is controlled for, a strong trend (p <0·001 by chi-square test for trend) is observed for increasing seroconversion rates with increasing number of partners with whom receptive anal intercourse was practised. No such consistent trend is observed for insertive anal intercourse. Among the 513 men who reported just insertive anal intercourse during the six-month follow-up period, only 5 (1·0%) seroconverted to HIV compared with 7 of 228 (3·1%) for those men who reported just receptive anal intercourse. 2 of the 5 seroconverters who practised only insertive anal intercourse during the six-month follow-up did report receptive anal intercourse before the initial examination.

Table III stratifies the MACS participants by the reported number of partners with whom they engaged in receptive anal intercourse during the two six-month periods before recording of seroconversion. Those who continued receptive intercourse with two or more partners showed the highest six-month seroconversion rate—10·6%. Significantly lower seroconversion rates were observed in those who reduced (3·2%) or stopped (1·8%) receptive anal intercourse. These rates were similar to those in men who continued with only 1 partner (2·3%), "began" (1·7%), or increased the number of partners (5·4%) with whom receptive anal intercourse was reported during the subsequent six-month follow-up period.

Table IV details the HIV seroconversion rates for two mutually exclusive sexual-practice subgroups of the 646 men reporting no receptive anal intercourse within twelve months of measured seroconversion. Of the 147 men who engaged in oral receptive intercourse with at least one partner during the six-month follow-up but reported no receptive or insertive anal intercourse within twelve months,

TABLE V—OTHER SEXUAL PRACTICES AMONG THE 220 MEN NOT
REPORTING RECEPTIVE OR INSERTIVE ANAL INTERCOURSE
DURING SIX MONTHS BEFORE INITIAL VISIT AND
DURING SIX-MONTH FOLLOW-UP

Sexual practice*	n	%	No of partners Median	(range)
Masturbation of partners (≥ 1)	150	68%	2	(1–60)
Oral intercourse				
Receptive (≥ 1)	147	67%	2	(1–60)
Insertive (≥ 1)	160	73%	2	(1–50)
Anilingus ("rimming")				
Receptive (≥ 1)	33	15%	1	(1–5)
Insertive (≥ 1)	23	10%	1	(1–60)
Digital-anal				
Receptive (≥ 1)	27	12%	1	(1–5)
Insertive (≥ 1)	39	18%	1	(1–60)

*Not mutually exclusive.

no seroconversions to HIV were observed. The only 3 men to seroconvert without reported receptive anal intercourse within twelve months were among those 344 men who reported anal intercourse as the insertive partner only—a seroconversion rate of 0·9%. Since no seroconversions to HIV were detected among those not reporting anal intercourse, the distribution of sexual practices in these 220 men is shown separately in table V.

Potential parenteral exposure was quite rare among those who seroconverted. Only 1 of 95 seroconverters (1%) gave a history in the six-month follow-up of shared needle use and none of them gave a history of shared needle use with an individual in whom AIDS developed.

Multiple logistic regression was used to investigate the independence and strength of association between each exposure variable and seroconversion. Stepwise entry methods always indicated that receptive anal intercourse during the six-month follow-up was the most significant sexual-exposure variable. The adjusted odds ratio increased from 3·2 (1 receptive anal partner) to 9·5 (2–4 partners), to 18·0 (5 or more partners). When receptive anal intercourse was controlled for, only enema/douche use entered the model (odds ratio 1·5), despite liberal entry limits (p < 0·10). Thus, although not significant at the 5% level, there was a trend toward an association between enema/douche use before sex with at least 1 partner and seroconversion. The variables used in the stepwise procedure were: insertive anal intercourse at 2 levels (1 and 2 + partners), receptive dildo use (1 + partners), enema/douche use before sex (1 + partners), insertive and receptive anilingus (1 + partners), insertive and receptive digital-anal contact (1 + partners), reported sexual contact with an AIDS case (1 + partners), episodes of perianal bleeding (1 + partners), age (≤ 32 or ≥ 33), and the total number of reported sexual partners in the follow-up period at 4 levels (0, 1, 2–4, and 5 + partners).

The independence and strength of association between receptive anal intercourse and HIV seroconversion provides further support for the inferences drawn from tables II–V.

Discussion

Data obtained from initially seronegative MACS participants clearly demonstrate that receptive anal intercourse is the major mode for acquisition of HIV infection and that discontinuation of this practice sharply reduces the likelihood of seroconversion in the next six to twelve months. Receptive anal intercourse was the only sexual practice shown to be independently associated with an increased risk of seroconversion to HIV in this study, and could account for nearly all new infections. The gradient of risk for seroconversion accelerated in proportion to the number of receptive anal partners, from about 3-fold for one partner to 18-fold for those with 5 or more partners during the observation period. Further, these risk calculations are conservative because they are based only on reported receptive anal intercourse in the six-month longitudinal follow-up period. In fact, 6 of the 9 seroconverters who denied receptive anal intercourse during the six-month follow-up did report having practised this activity within six months before the initial evaluation. Seroconversion in these 6 men may have resulted from exposure via receptive anal intercourse that had occurred before baseline.

Of the remaining 3 seroconverters who did not participate in receptive anal intercourse, all did participate in insertive anal intercourse, during both the pre-enrolment period and the six-month follow-up period. These data suggest a low (less than 1%) six-month risk of seroconversion due only to the practice of insertive anal intercourse. Alternatively, this may reflect misclassification of men who actually did participate in receptive anal intercourse.

The most important finding of this study comes from a comparison of HIV seroconversion rates based on receptive anal intercourse before the initial assessment and during the six-month follow-up (table III). Significantly lower seroconversion rates were noted in the men who reduced (3·2%) or stopped (1·8%) receptive anal intercourse than in men who continued the practice with at least 2 partners (10·6%). As previously noted, the fact that the seroconversion rate was not zero for those who stopped receptive anal intercourse very likely reflects exposure via receptive intercourse before study enrolment. The public health message from these findings is clear. Reduction of this high-risk practice by homosexual men dramatically reduces risk of HIV infection. Furthermore, it is clear that the degree of modification of this high-risk behaviour necessary to make a substantial impact can actually be achieved.

The absence of detectable risk for seroconversion due to receptive oral-genital intercourse is striking. That there were no seroconversions detected among 147 men engaging in receptive oral intercourse with at least 1 partner, but not receptive or insertive anal intercourse, accords with other data suggesting a low risk of infection from oral-genital (receptive semen) exposure.[5-7] It must be mentioned that we were unable to determine the infection status of the sexual partners to whom these men were exposed. Perhaps these 147 men who practised receptive oral intercourse were never or rarely exposed to HIV seropositive men. However, this explanation seems improbable. As noted, the 220 participants who did not engage in receptive or insertive anal intercourse within twelve months before the follow-up visit had ample opportunity to be exposed to HIV-infected men since 67% had engaged in receptive oral intercourse with at least 1 partner (median 2, range 1-60).

From a public health point of view, we can affirm to homosexual men that receptive anal intercourse is the principal route by which they may become infected with HIV. We must also communicate that a small but real risk from other exposures may have been undetectable, even in this large study. Receptive fisting, enema/douche use before sex, and perianal bleeding, as markers for rectal trauma, have all been strongly associated with prevalent HIV infection in the cross-sectional Multicenter AIDS Cohort Study of nearly 5000 men (38% HIV seropositive).[10] That none of these trauma indicators was significantly associated with seroconversion in the present study may indicate only that the smaller sample size (95 seroconverters) precluded their detection. Enema or douche use before sex did, however, show a trend toward association with seroconversion (odds ratio 1·5, p < 0·10). Although the prospective nature of this analysis makes it a more compelling assessment of risk factors, the potential importance of the traumatic practices in promoting HIV infection should not be overlooked.

The relative "safety" of the sexual practices not detected as risk factors for seroconversion in this report deserves comment. Oral intercourse with ejaculate introduced in the oral cavity, anilingus, "fisting", enema/douche use, and dildo use are all potentially unsafe. HIV infection apart, many of these practices have already been associated with

other sexually transmitted diseases that present a public health threat to male homosexuals.[11] These sexual practices should be considered in the light of all the infections transmissible by these means—eg, hepatitis B, cytomegalovirus, herpes simplex virus, amoebiasis, syphilis, and gonorrhoea. "Safe sex" guidelines should not apply only to prevention of HIV infection.

Among homosexual men avoidance of anal intercourse may be the only existing means of limiting future morbidity and mortality from HIV infection. A prudent course would be to stop anal intercourse entirely. This study demonstrates a 3-fold greater risk of seroconversion for the MACS men who engaged in receptive anal intercourse with only 1 partner in six months. Even if exclusively monogamous men know their serological status, the risk of exposure to HIV remains a concern, in view of the reports of virus-positive, antibody-negative homosexual men.[12,13] We cannot comment on whether the consistent and proper use of condoms (with or without spermicides) reduces or eliminates the risk of HIV infection. Although latex and natural condoms do not permit passage of HIV under laboratory conditions[14] and spermicidal nonoxynol-9 preparations are viricidal for HIV,[15] more data are needed to examine the efficacy of both condoms and spermicides in preventing infection.

Avoidance of anal intercourse must be the principal focus of efforts to reduce risk in the male homosexual community.[16] This educational message must be given the highest public health priority.

We thank C. Perfetti, W. Amoroso, and S. Jones for assistance in data analysis and D. Laurie for preparation of the script. This study was supported by NIAID research contracts A1-32511, A1-32513, A1-32520, and A1-32535.

Correspondence should be addressed to L. A. Kingsley, Departments of Infectious Diseases and Microbiology/Epidemiology, Graduate School of Public Health, University of Pittsburgh, PO Box 7319, Pittsburgh, PA 15213, USA.

Requests for reprints should be addressed to AIDS Program Office, National Institute of Allergy and Infectious Diseases, Westwood Bldg, Rm 753, 5333 Westbard Avenue, Bethesda, MD 20892, USA.

REFERENCES

1. Jaffe HW, Choi K, Thomas PA, et al. National case-control study of Kaposi's sarcoma and Pneumocystis carinii pneumonia in homosexual men: Part 1, epidemiologic results. Ann Intern Med 1984; 99: 145–51.
2. Goedert JJ, Samgadharan MG, Biggar RJ, et al. Determinants of retrovirus (HTLV-III) antibody and immunodeficiency conditions in homosexual men. Lancet 1984; ii: 711–16.
3. Marmor M, Friedman-Kien AE, Zolla-Pazner S, et al. Kaposi's sarcoma in homosexual men: a seroepidemiologic case-control study. Ann Intern Med 1984; 100: 809–15.
4. Melbye M, Biggar RJ, Ebbessen P, et al. Seroepidemiology of HTLV-III antibodies in Danish homosexual men: prevalence, transmission, and disease outcome. Br Med J 1984; 289: 573–75.
5. Jeffries E, Willoughby B, Boyko WJ, et al. The Vancouver lymphadenopathy-AIDS study-II: seroepidemiology of HTLV-III antibody. Can Med Assoc J 1985; 132: 1373–77.
6. Scheuter MT, Boyko WJ, Douglas B, et al. Can HTLV-III be transmitted orally? Lancet 1986; i: 379.
7. Lyman D, Winkelstein W, Ascher M, Levy JA. Minimal risk of transmission of AIDS-associated retrovirus infection by oral-genital contact. JAMA 1986; 255: 1703.
8. Samgadharan MG, Popovic M, Bruch L, Schuphach J, Gallo RC. Antibodies reactive with human T-lymphotropic retrovirus (HTLV-III) in the serum of patients with AIDS. Science 1984; 224: 506–08.
9. Saah A, Farzadegan H, Fox R, et al. Sensitivity of the ELISA for human immunodeficiency virus antibodies during early stages of infection. Unpublished.
10. Multicenter AIDS Cohort Study (MACS). Prevalence and correlates of HTLV-III antibodies among 5000 gay men in 4 cities. Interscience Conference on Antimicrobial Agents and Chemotherapy (ICAAC) October, 1985 (abstr).

References continued at foot of next column

11. Ostrow DG, Altman NL. Sexually transmitted diseases and homosexuality. *Sex Transm Dis* 1983; 10: 208–15.

12. Mayer K, Stoddar AM, McCusker J, et al. Human T-lymphotropic virus type III in high-risk, antibody negative homosexual men. *Ann Intern Med* 1986; 104: 194–96.

13. Groopman JE, Hartzband PI, Shulman L, et al. Antibody seronegative human T-lymphotropic virus type III (HTLV-III)-infected patients with acquired immunodeficiency syndrome or related disorders. *Blood* 1985; 66: 742–44.

14. Conant M, Hardy D, Sernatinger J, et al. Condoms prevent transmission of AIDS-associated retrovirus. *JAMA* 1986; 255: 1706.

15. Hicks DR, Martin LS, Getchell JP, et al. Inactivation of HTLV-III/LAV-infected cultures of normal human lymphocytes by nonoxynol-9 in vitro. *Lancet* 1985; ii: 1422–23.

16. McKusick L, Conant M, Coates TJ. The AIDS epidemic: a model for developing intervention strategies for reducing high risk behaviour in gay men. *Sex Transm Dis* 1985; 12: 229–34.